Mary E. Pearce, a Londoner by birth, now lives in the relative peace of Gloucestershire. She tackled various jobs – shop assistant, filing clerk, waitress, usherette – before settling down to write seriously in the 1960s. Her career began with the appearance of short stories in magazines and has led to the publication of nine highly successful novels which have been translated into Dutch, French, German, Italian, Japanese, Norwegian and Portuguese, as well as being bestsellers in America.

Also by Mary E. Pearce

The Apple Tree Saga:
APPLE TREE LEANDOWN
JACK MERCYBRIGHT
THE SORROWING WIND
THE LAND ENDURES
SEEDTIME AND HARVEST

THE OLD HOUSE AT RAILES

MARY E. PEARCE OMNIBUS

Cast a Long Shadow
The Two Farms
Polsinney Harbour

WARNER BOOKS

A *Warner* Book

This omnibus edition published by Warner Books in 2000

Omnibus edition © Mary E. Pearce 2000

Cast a Long Shadow first published in Great Britain in 1977
by Macdonald and Jane's Publishers.
First published in paperback by Warner Books in 1994.
The Two Farms first published in Great Britain in 1985
by Macdonald & Co (Publishers) Ltd.
First published in paperback by Warner Books in 1992.
Polsinney Harbour first published in Great Britain in 1994
by Macdonald & Co.
First published in paperback by Warner Books in 1994.

Cast a Long Shadow copyright © Mary E. Pearce 1977
The Two Farms copyright © Mary E. Pearce 1985
Polsinney Harbour copyright © Mary E. Pearce 1994

A CIP catalogue record for this book
is available from the British Library.

ISBN 0 7515 3131 6

Printed and bound in Great Britain by
Mackays of Chatham plc, Chatham, Kent

Warner Books
A Division of
Little, Brown and Company (UK)
Brettenham House
Lancaster Place
London WC2E 7EN

I've travelled the world twice over,
Met the famous: saints and sinners,
Poets and artists, kings and queens,
Old stars and hopeful beginners,
I've been where no-one's been before,
Learned secrets from writers and cooks
All with one library ticket
To the wonderful world of books.

CAST A LONG SHADOW

Chapter 1

When Ellen Wainwright was married to Richard Lancy in July, 1873, the day was so hot that the church doors were left wide open, and towards the end of the ceremony, a stray dog ran in and stood howling in the central aisle.

The incident caused some amusement among the small congregation but the vicar, Mr. Eustead, was seriously displeased and waited, tight-lipped, while Dyson the verger drove the dog out. He then turned back to the bride and groom and angrily pronounced them man and wife.

'It warnt hardly our fault the dog got in,' Richard said to Ellen later, 'but the way Mr. Eustead bellowed the blessing at us, you'd think it was.'

'Never mind,' Ellen said. 'We *are* married, that's the main thing. – I thought he was going to leave it half done!'

Nothing could mar her contentment that day: neither the terrible sultry heat; nor the disturbance caused by the dog; nor the vicar's burst of temper. She and Richard were now one. The day was theirs and nothing could spoil it.

The dog itself was something of a mystery. It had never been seen in Dingham before, nor was it ever seen again, and the only explanation was that it must have strayed off a barge passing through the lock on the river. The matter was talked of for some days. A few people thought it rather a joke. Others thought it a minor scandal and the vicar was censured for having allowed the church doors to remain open. But it was only a good deal later, when Ellen and Richard had been married five years and things were not quite the same

1

between them, that people remembered the dog in church and spoke of it as some sort of omen.

'The moment I saw it,' Mrs. Dancox used to say, 'I felt a shiver go down my spine, and I warnt the only one, I don't suppose.' And Mrs. Dyson always said: 'A dog in church is bad enough but a dog at a wedding – anything could happen after that! And nobody never did know how it got there, neither, did they?'

'It came off a barge,' Dyson said. 'Nothing very strange in that.'

'We don't know for sure, though, do we?'

'If you had such premonitions, woman, how come you never said so at the time?'

'On the wedding day?' Mrs. Dyson said. 'And cast such a blight on everything? That's not my way, Bob, and never was. Such a fine handsome couple they made that day! And everything seemingly set so fair! It warnt for me to cast a shadow. There's some dark things we must keep to ourselves.'

Dyson gave a little grunt. He had never known his wife to keep anything to herself, dark or otherwise, in twenty-six years of marriage. He had only taken the post of verger to secure some measure of peace and quiet.

One good thing at least had come of the business of the dog in the church, for the Stavertons of Dinnis Hall, on hearing about it, had given a pair of wire-gauze doors, and now the church could be kept aired without the incursion of stray animals and nesting birds. The summers were hot in the mid 1870s.

Ellen was twenty when she married, and Richard was almost twenty-five. Their courtship had been a happy one, and as they were well-suited to each other, their marriage got off to a good start. Everyone in Dingham agreed that they deserved their good luck, for Ellen's life hitherto, with a jealous-natured mother and invalid uncle, had brought little joy; and Richard, too, left alone at eighteen, with a half-ruined mill

2

on his hands, and his father's creditors at the door, had had a hard struggle to make his way.

Within a month of his father's death, Richard had repaired the old machinery, re-dressed the millstones, and cleared the weeds out of the millstream. Soon the old mill was working again: noisily, perhaps, with many a screech that set Richard's teeth on edge and sent him hurrying round with the oilcan; but working, certainly, and coming slowly to life again after two years of idleness. And when the first grinding of barley-meal came squeezing down the narrow chute, into the open sack below, a few Dingham folk were there to see it, ready to try it between their fingers and offer advice on its quality.

'You'll come to it, young fella,' said George Danks, whose barley it was that was being ground. 'It takes years to make a good miller – ten or twelve at least, I'd say – but you'll come to it surely in the end.'

'I shall come to it sooner than that!' Richard said, rather sharply, and his listeners believed him.

True to his word, Richard was master of his trade by the time he was twenty, and Pex Mill had a good name. But the business itself, having been allowed to run down, was not won back again all at once: often there was only work enough for three days' milling in the week; and Richard made money on the side by dealing in various second-hand goods. He travelled about with two donkeys, collecting anything he could find that lay rusting or rotting in farmyards or workshop sheds. Sometimes he paid a copper or two, but mostly he was 'doing a favour', clearing away unwanted rubbish.

'It's a funny thing!' Michael Bullock said once: 'It's a funny thing that if I buy a hen-coop offa you it's a valuable article worth five shillun, but if you take a seed-drill offa me it's only old junk needing clearing away!'

Richard was certainly sharp in his dealings, but most people admired him for that. He was a man who meant to get on and, the way he worked, he well deserved to.

'You want a cage for your canary?' people would say. 'Or maybe a medal to stick on your chest? Go to Dick Lancy. He'll have one for sure. And if he hasn't, well, you can bet your life he'll know where to find one!'

Although he dealt in all manner of things, there was never any rubbish left lying about the mill, to mar its tidiness and neatness. Everything Richard brought home was carefully mended and made good, given a coat of paint, perhaps, and placed in the shed behind the millhouse. No one was ever taken inside. If a man came asking for elm planking or an old barrel for a water-butt Richard would say: 'I dunno – I shall have to see.' And in a day or two the required item would be delivered. But only Richard himself ever entered the shed.

When Ellen Wainwright came into his life, he worked all the harder. His father's debts had been squared by then and he was beginning to pay his way. Gradually, he made improvements. The walls of the mill and the millhouse were repointed, the roofs were re-tiled, and the worm-eaten weatherboarding over the luccomb was replaced by new. The old mill was itself again and, reflected in the millpond, where the water now ran pure and clear, looked just as it did in the old picture, painted by Richard's great-grandfather, that hung above the mantelpiece in the kitchen.

Downriver from the mill, the banks in summer were crowded with tansy and comfrey and flags and the tall spires of purple loosestrife, and it was among these bright flowers that he first saw Ellen Wainwright. She was sixteen then and had come to Dingham with her widowed mother to live with her uncle, a retired seaman, at Victory Cottage, in Water Lane. Old Captain Wainwright was almost a cripple. He suffered much pain and was dying of cancer. He cared little for this sister-in-law of his who had condescended to keep house for him, but he and Ellen became great friends. She was at the river that day looking for the nest of a coot, so that she could report to him on the progress of the young brood. Richard went down to speak to her.

4

'If the keeper'd known that nest was there, I reckon he'd have smashed the eggs.'

'Why would he?' Ellen cried.

'Because of the fish, I suppose,' he said.

'Surely there are enough for everybody?'

'I shan't say nothing, anyway. I like to see the coot here, larking about.'

And, crouching beside her, he showed her how cleverly the nest was loose-tied to two or three upright reeds so that, when the river rose, the nest rose with it and escaped flooding.

'You tell your uncle there's six in the brood, all of 'em swimming and doing well. He'll be glad to hear that. It'll cheer him up. He was always down here, before he got sick, watching them birds and making notes. You tell him the kingfisher's here as well. I seen it a day or two, like a streak.'

'Yes, I'll tell him,' Ellen said.

She was often at the river after that, and Richard soon got into the way of looking out for her. Both were lonely and both were older than their years. There was soon an understanding between them. Once Ellen was caught in a storm and took shelter with him in the mill, and while they leant together over the hatch-door, looking out at the white rain, he talked of marriage.

'I can't afford a wife just yet. I'm only just getting on my feet. There's a lot to do before I can think of such a step. I daresay it might be two or three years.'

'I couldn't leave Uncle John, either. I promised I'd stay with him till the end. I hope that won't be for ages yet, though he's in such terrible pain sometimes—'

'You must certainly stop with him, no doubt of that. It'd break his heart if you left him alone with that mother of yours. She'd have him in the grave in no time at all.'

'Hush!' Ellen said. 'You mustn't say such things. She's not that bad.'

'Ent she indeed! She's bad enough! And if it warnt for

5

your poor old uncle, I'd up and marry you tomorrow morning, just to get you away from her. But as it is, we must just be patient, and make our plans accordingly.'

'Yes,' she said, 'we must be patient.'

They had known each other for five weeks, but it was taken for granted between them, quietly, without surprise, that their lives were linked and always would be.

Ellen's mother did not approve of Richard Lancy. Meeting him, she was barely civil, and behind his back she was often contemptuous.

'A miller!' she said. 'Why not throw yourself away on a road-mender and be done with it? I will certainly not receive him here!'

But Ellen's uncle took Richard's part.

'This is my house, remember, Adelaide, and Dick Lancy will always be welcome in it, at least so long as I am alive.'

He and Richard got on well together. The old man trusted the younger one and towards the end, when he grew more frail, it was Richard who carried him to bed at night and who came every morning to put him into his chair by the window.

'You've been like a son to me, my boy, and Ellen has been like a darling daughter. Take care of her, after I'm gone, and don't let Adelaide bully her.'

Uncle John died in June, 1873, and Ellen married Richard in July. Mrs. Wainwright was disgusted. There should have been a year's mourning at least, but to have the wedding within a month—! She washed her hands of the whole affair. Victory Cottage was now hers and no wedding-breakfast should take place *there*. Nor would she be present in church.

So the wedding-breakfast took place at Pex Mill and the little parlour was so crowded with well-wishers that they overflowed into the garden, and young Simon Shaw, playing the fool out on the footbridge, fell with a splash into the mill-race and had to be rescued by Will Gale, the smith, no less tipsy than himself.

6

'Drink up by all means,' Richard said. 'There'll be little drinking done in this house after today, cos Ellen and me is both teetotal.'

Indeed, it was noticed that he himself touched not a drop, and his wedding-guests could guess the reason. It was drink that had hastened his father's ruin.

'You can't be teetotal and live in Dingham,' said George Danks of Cockhanger Farm. 'Not when it's got two inns to support.'

'Teetotal or not, I wish you good health and prosperity,' said Bob Dyson, raising his glass, 'and may your waterwheel never stop turning.'

'He'll prosper all right,' said Michael Bullock. 'Did you ever know of a *poor* miller?'

'I knew a poor miller's daughter once . . .'

'Any man will prosper,' said Joe Dancox, 'so long as he has a good wife behind him.'

'Wedlock's a padlock,' said Simon Shaw. 'It's a brave man that turns the key.'

Just after sunset, when a pink moon hung in the sky, the noisy revellers at last went home. The mill and the millhouse became silent, and Ellen, at the kitchen window, stood listening to the quiet sounds of the river: the plopping of fish in the millpond; the fluttering of water-fowl among the reeds; and, in the distance, the rush of the weir. These sounds were now her life. They would fill all her wandering thoughts by day and her dreams by night, heard and yet not heard, like her own heartbeats or the drumming of blood between her ears.

'Quiet, ent it, now they're gone?' Richard said, coming into the room.

'Yes, quiet,' Ellen said. 'I can hear the Abbey clock striking.'

'Can you? Golly? That's all of three miles. Did it strike the quarter? Then our clock is slow.'

He went to the tall grandfather clock and put it right. Then he turned and stood watching her as she leant at the

7

window, a dark outline against the violet-coloured sky.

'I reckon there's going to be a storm. The wind is as hot as a drunkard's breath and I'm damn near melting in this suit.'

'Perhaps a storm will clear the air.'

Ellen came away from the window and they looked at each other in the fading light.

'Shall I light a candle?' Richard said.

'No need for candles,' Ellen said, 'it isn't really dark yet.'

The moon, now whitening, lit them to bed.

Soon after the wedding, Ellen's mother sold Victory Cottage and bought a house in Lyme Regis, as far away from Worcestershire as she could well manage. The day she left Dingham, she called at the mill in a hired carriage, and handed down a bundle of clothes. Ellen never saw or heard of her again.

Old Captain Wainwright had left Ellen sixty pounds and as soon as the money was in her hands she went to Sutton Crabtree on a secret errand. Three weeks later, as arranged, a brand new waggon drew up at the mill, with a strong grey horse between the shafts, driven by Gleddow, the Sutton wheelwright. Ellen went to the mill-door and called Richard.

'I can't come now – I'm busy!' he said, shouting above the noise of the mill.

'You *must* come!' Ellen said. 'You'll be sorry if you don't!'

Richard followed her out to the road, wiping his hands on his apron. His scowl deepened when he saw the waggon, – he thought it was somebody asking the way – but as he drew close and saw its newness, he began to perceive what was afoot. The waggon was painted dark green, its chamfered panels picked out in yellow, the rims of its wheels fine-lined with black. And along its shafts, dark green on yellow, Richard read his own name: Richard Lancy; Miller and General Dealer: Pex Mill, Dingham, nr. Rainborough, Worcs.

8

'Would you believe it!' he kept saying, walking round the horse and waggon. 'Would you ever in God's name ... Oh, I shall be somebody, driving this!' And, after Gleddow had gone, he said: 'Seems I was onto a good thing, Nell, when I married you!'

'It's only right that a miller should have a horse and waggon. How can you carry on your trade with only a couple of old donkeys?'

'I'm not just a miller,' Richard said. 'I'm a miller *and* a General Dealer. That's what you got them to put on them shafts, and very well it looks, too.'

His pride in the horse and waggon was boundless. He kept them always in perfect condition. And the fact that Ellen should have spent her legacy in such a way moved him deeply. But there was one matter arising out of the gift that was less pleasing. She made him give the two donkeys away.

'You don't need them now. You'll never have to use them again. So why not give them to someone in need?'

'Dammit, woman, I can always sell them! The money would pay for that new hursting. I ent so rich that I can afford to give things away.'

'Just this once you can,' she said. 'Just this once, to please me.'

So the two donkeys were given away: one to Old Trussler, the fishmonger, whose pony had only recently died; the other to Mr. and Mrs. Grey, to pull their little home-made cart, so that they could take their invalid daughter for drives.

'Don't thank *me*!' Richard said, parting with the donkeys. 'It was my wife's idea, not mine.'

The matter rankled for a long time, though he managed to turn it into a joke.

'I seen one of my neddies in Sturton this morning. He don't look too happy, delivering fish. I hardly knew how to meet his eye. I reckon he liked it a lot better when he worked for a miller and general dealer!'

In September, 1874, their son was born, and they called him

9

John after Ellen's uncle. Richard was a proud and boastful father. There was nobody like this baby son. No one so forward, so clever, so strong. And his customers often felt the urge to take him down a peg or two.

'Is he talking yet, Dick, that boy of yours?'

'Talking? Dammit! He ent hardly more'n eight weeks old!'

'Oh, he's only an ordinary baby after all, then. From what you'd said, I thought he'd be keeping your books for you by now!'

In November that year, something unusual happened to Richard. He spent an evening in The Old Tap and got very drunk. The landlord, Archie Shaw, had wanted an old cattle-trough for his stableyard, and Richard as always had known where to find one. The night he delivered it, the weather was cold and wet, and when the trough had been unloaded, Shaw invited him inside and together they shared a bottle of brandy.

Richard, unused to strong drink, was soon helpless, and Will Gale, the blacksmith, a regular customer at The Old Tap, volunteered to take him home. Ellen, waiting anxiously, heard the horse and waggon coming, and the two men's voices upraised in song. She also heard the commotion they made as they bedded down the horse in his stall. Then Richard stumbled into the kitchen, looked at her with rolling eyes, and fell insensible at her feet. Will Gale stood grinning in the open doorway.

'One handsome husband delivered safe and sound to his wife,' he said. 'There's nothing to pay, though I wouldn't say no to a little nightcap.'

'Safe and sound?' Ellen said, stooping to loosen Richard's collar. 'Do you call this safe and sound?'

'He's all in one piece, surely? No broken bones? Nothing wrong that a night's sleep won't cure?'

'What *use* is he? You tell me that!'

'It all depends what you had in mind.'

'If there's one thing I detest,' Ellen said, 'it's the sight of a man in a drunken stupor.'

10

'Me too,' Will said. 'I'll help you to get him up to bed.'

'Thank you, no! Just leave him be.'

'Maybe you're right. He's better lying as he is. He won't be much company for you tonight, though he'll need your sympathy in the morning.'

'He won't get it!' Ellen said. 'And I'll say goodnight to you now, Mr. Gale, while I've still got patience enough to be polite.'

'Don't I get no nightcap, then?'

'No,' she said, 'you've had enough.'

She moved to the door and pushed it against him. Will fell back a few paces, still with a foolish grin on his face, and, finding himself shut out in the rain, hammered three or four times on the door.

'Mrs. Lancy, ma'am, you're a damned shrew! Thank God I'm a single bachelor chap and can come and go as I damn well please! I never knowed a woman yet that hadn't got rennet in her veins!'

Will went off singing and his heavy footsteps pounded the bridge. Ellen lit a storm-lantern and went out to see that all was well with the horse in his stall. She returned to the kitchen, where Richard, except that he snored loudly, lay on his back as though dead. She covered him over with a blanket and went up to bed. Baby John lay asleep in his cot.

In the morning, Richard was surly and sick-faced. He went to his work without any breakfast. At twelve o'clock, when he came in to dinner, he fidgeted with his knife and fork and eyed Ellen, who ate in silence.

'Well, woman?' he said at last. 'Has the cat got your tongue?'

'What is it you want me to say?'

'Hells bells! It's the first time it's ever happened!'

'I hope it's the last,' Ellen said. 'I hadn't bargained for a drunken husband.'

'You can be sure it's the last,' he said. 'There's no pleasure in drinking for me. My head is boiling like a kettle.' A sudden thought came to him as he thumped the table.

11

'Archie Shaw is a fly devil! He never paid me for that trough. I shall have to see him about that.'

But although he went to The Old Tap again, to collect his money, he could not be persuaded to take a drink.

Chapter 2

Their second child was stillborn, a sad disappointment to both of them, and to little John, too, who had hoped for a brother. But at least this one son was strong and healthy and full of spirit, growing straight and tall and clever; able to count at the age of three; able to read before he was four; always eager to ride with his father in the waggon and especially when he went to the market in Runston or Sturton or Rainborough.

'One of these days,' Richard said, 'you'll be a miller the same as me and then that name on the shafts there will have to be changed to something else.'

'Why will it?'

'It'll have to be changed to "Richard Lancy and Son" instead, cos you and me will be partners together, both of us millers and general dealers.'

'When will we?'

'Why, when you're a man like me, of course. And the way you're growing, that won't be all that long, neither.'

One day, when they were delivering meal at Brooks, the farmer, Mr. Rissington, seeing this little boy, not yet four, sitting erect with the reins in his hands, came right up to the side of the waggon.

'Lord almighty! What have we here?'

'Richard Lancy and Son,' said John, 'delivering bean-meal from Pex Mill.'

And the old man was so amused that he asked John into the dairy and gave him a cup of buttermilk, a rare honour,

13

Richard said, for the Rissingtons were very close.

When John, soon after his fourth birthday, began going to the village school, Richard insisted that he should have the best of everything. Best boots, best clothes, and a smart leather satchel with his name on it. But Ellen set her face against this. She refused to obey Richard's orders.

'Do you want our son to be disliked? They are ordinary folk in this village, with ordinary children, mostly poor. If we set John above the rest, how is he ever to make friends?'

'I hadn't thought of it like that. Seems I'd better leave it to you. But I want my son to be tidy, mind! No great patches on his seat. No knots in his laces nor nothing like that. He ent going scruffy, as I had to do when I was a boy.'

Richard, if he could have had his way, would have seen wife and son clad always in the finest clothes, and once, when Ellen was turning up the hem of a dress, he snatched it from her and threatened to throw it into the fire.

'There's no need for you to do all that mending. I ent so poor as all that!'

'Don't be ridiculous,' Ellen said. 'Everybody renews frayed hems. This dress is my favourite. I've only had it six months.' And she took it, crumpled, from his hands. 'We've had so many new things lately. China. Curtains. That new Indian rug. Folk will be taking advantage of you if they think you're growing so well off.'

'They'll have to get up pretty early in the morning, Nell, before they can take advantage of *me*.'

But although he wanted everything to be of the best for his wife and son, in other matters he was cautious to a degree, and would never buy anything if instead he could make it or mend it or persuade someone else to lend it to him.

'Always look after the pennies,' he said, 'and the pounds will surely look after theirselves.'

Once he travelled all the way up to Derbyshire because he had heard of an old millstone quarry having closed there and he hoped for a bargain. He was gone four days and returned in high triumph with two good stones.

'Were they a bargain?' Ellen asked.

'A bargain, yes. I got them for nothing. And if it hadn't been for considering the horse, I'd have brought another couple more, cos they was just lying there, scattered about.'

'You mean you just took them?' Ellen said.

'That's right. I helped myself.'

'But surely the stones belong to someone? Didn't you try to find out?'

'No, not me. I was there at night.'

'Then many people would call it stealing.'

'Stealing? Rubbish! I ent having that! The quarry is closed and out of business, and the stones is just lying there, going to waste. They're no use to no one, except men like me.'

Ellen was silent and Richard, meeting her steady gaze, became annoyed. He did not care to be called a thief.

'Dammit, woman, they're only roughhewn! Think of the work I've got to do, dressing them and setting them up. They was just lying there, out in the weather, so much rubbish throwed aside. I'm damned if I'll let you call me a thief!'

'How did you load them onto the waggon?'

'I managed all right: No trouble there. There's nothing much a man can't do, given a horse and the right tackle.'

'You shouldn't have done it all alone – you might have killed yourself,' Ellen said.

'I've got too much nous for that,' he said. 'It'd take a mighty clever stone to catch me napping, be sure of that.' He became very busy, making notes in a little book, and then he said, without looking up, 'You'd have minded about it a bit, then, if your thieving husband had got hisself killed?'

'Don't be silly,' Ellen said.

The mill was half a mile from the end of Dingham, and because of this Ellen lived a life apart, meeting other women only when she went to the shops.

'I reckon that's lonely for you,' Richard said, 'with no neighbours nearby to pop in and out like they do in the village.'

15

'No, I'm not lonely,' Ellen said. 'I like it down here beside the river. I see enough people to satisfy me, what with the barges when they pass, and the coming and going at the mill.'

'But that's all menfolk,' Richard said, 'and business at that.'

'I enjoy the business,' Ellen said, and she always knew who had been to the mill that day, what grain they had brought for Richard to grind, or how much flour they had taken away. 'I wouldn't change places with anyone.'

But for little John, an only child, it was a very different matter, and that was why she sent him to school as soon as Miss Robinson would agree to take him. From that moment she had no more fears. John made friends easily and every Saturday and Sunday there would be a group of children playing all day on the river bank or fishing from the footbridge over the stream.

Once, when Richard was going on an errand to Runston and had promised that John should go for the ride, he found a group of seven boys sitting waiting in the waggon.

'What the deuce is all this?'

'These are my friends. They're coming with us into Runston.'

'Oh no they're not!' Richard said, and made them all get out at once. 'Either you come along by yourself or else you stop at home with your friends. You can't have it both ways. You've got to choose.'

On that occasion, out of loyalty to his friends, John decided to stay behind. His father went to Runston alone and afterwards, when he returned, he spoke to John in a serious manner.

'Them boys is all very well, but I don't want everyone knowing my business, and that's what'd happen if they came along. So just mind your p's and q's and don't be so free with your invitations.'

On every other occasion, of course, John chose to go with his father, for this was the greatest excitement of all. To visit

16

so many outlying farms; to drive down the narrow streets of towns; to see the barges tied up at the wharves in Rainborough, and to watch their cargoes unloaded into the warehouses there: the sacks of grain or wool or hops hoisted so high on the chain and pulley: John would not miss it for the world. The whole of Worcestershire, it seemed to him, was full of the most exciting things, and over the border, not far away, was the unknown county of Herefordshire.

Not far from the mill, in Water Lane, which ran with the river for a mile or so, an old rough grey stone stood out of the grass at the side of the road and marked the boundary for all to see. On one side there was an H; on the other a W; and the children of Dingham liked to straddle this stone, for then they stood in two counties at the same time. But they always took care to stand so that Worcestershire was 'on the right' and Herefordshire was 'in the wrong'. It was said that the people living over the boundary were all left-handed and had four thumbs, and John sometimes wondered if this was true.

'Why don't we never go driving into Herefordshire?' he asked his father in the mill one day.

'I dunno. I just don't happen to have no business there, that's all. Not that I try for it. No, not me. Why, if you go into Herefordshire, you're very nearly in Wales!'

'Do they speak English in Herefordshire?'

'Not as good as you and me. But they manage to make theirselves understood.'

'Are they left-handed and got four thumbs?'

'I shouldn't be surprised,' Richard said. 'They're funny folk, sure enough. And then of course Old Rag-Face is said to ride over there.'

'Who's Old Rag-Face?' John asked.

'Old Rag-Face on his flying horse. He swoops down on travellers out of the dark and carries them off to his lair in the hills.'

'What does he do to them?'

'I dunno. Nobody knows. The travellers is never seen again. But they say there's a cave under Willer's Knob that's full of human skulls and bones.'

Richard turned to look at the boy and saw that his face was very white.

'It's only an old tale,' he said. 'You've got no call to look like that. Here, come and help me tie this sack, and let me see how you manage a knot. You ent scared of an old tale? A big boy like you, past his fourth birthday? Surely not? I don't believe it!'

John shook his head. He would never admit to being afraid. Not to his father, anyway.

But he had bad dreams for several nights after that, and once when Ellen went in to him he flung his arms around her neck, crying and sobbing against her breast. It took a long time to comfort him and get him to go to sleep again and Ellen, returning to her own room, shook Richard roughly and woke him up.

'Frightening the child with such horrible talk! I should have thought you'd have more sense! Old Rag-Face indeed! Skulls and bones in a cave! He was in such a sweat, the poor mite, that I had to give him a clean nightshirt.'

In the morning, at breakfast-time, Richard looked at his small son across the table.

'You got me into trouble, you know, crying out in the night like that. Your mother says it's all my fault on account of my talking about Old Rag-Face, but I told you it was only a tale, didn't I? I said there warnt really nothing in it.'

John hung his head, unable to meet his father's eye.

'Laws!' Richard said. 'You ent scared of Goldilocks or Jack the Giant Killer or Simple Simon, are you, boy? And that Old Rag-Face is just such another. Nothing more than an old tale.'

'Don't he live over the border, then, and carry folk off on his flying horse?'

'No. He don't. Cos there's no such man. Herefordshire is pretty much the same as Worcestershire. I'll take you one day and you'll see for yourself. So promise you won't have no more bad dreams?'

'Yes, I promise,' John said.

'Good! That's the spirit. You're a sensible lad.'

And Richard sought his wife's eye, as much as to say, There! You see? That's soon settled that! A lot of fuss about nothing at all.

Not long afterwards, on a wet windy day in the new year, Richard announced that he was going into Herefordshire, to the old watermill at Cutlowell Park. The mill had recently had a fire and there was to be a sale of tackle. It was a Saturday afternoon and Richard suggested that John should go along for the ride.

'I promised I'd take you there one day so's you could see what it was like. You ent too scared to go, I suppose? You ent still thinking about them bad dreams?'

'No,' John said, 'I ent scared.'

But his face was very white indeed as they set out in the waggon that day, and he sat very close at his father's side, looking about him with wide-stretched eyes. The day was cheerless, for big black clouds moved low in the sky, and rain blew down on the northwest wind. Still, the lanes they travelled along were commonplace enough; the fields on either side were peaceful; and the three villages they had to pass through were not much different from Dingham itself. The people, if anything, were more friendly. Some of them even nodded and waved. Richard spoke of it to John.

'Does it seem the folk is all left-handed?'

'No, I don't think so,' John said.

'Seen anyone with four thumbs?'

'No.'

'There! You see! The people here ent no different from us. Nor we ent seen no sign of Old Rag-Face neither.'

'You said he mostly rode out at night.'

'Well, he don't!' Richard said, impatiently. 'I told you before, it's a fairy-tale, so let's not hear no more about it. Just look around you and see what you see.'

'That old woman was smoking a pipe.'

'Ah. I saw her. She'd got a black nose.'

'We're getting near the river again. The cattle is going down to drink. I can see two men fishing. I wonder if there's salmon here?'

The boy's fears were soon forgotten. Herefordshire, as his father said, was not so different after all. He saw nothing frightening. Nothing strange. Nothing to bring back those horrible dreams. But the places were new and therefore exciting, and when they arrived at Cutlowell Park, he was the first down from the waggon, eager to join the knot of men gathered at the door of the burnt-out mill.

The fire had occurred eight days before, and the mill was in ruins. The roof and both floors had gone; even part of one gable wall; and the other walls, where the bricks themselves had been on fire, had cracks in them more than three inches wide. Above the doorway was a notice saying: DANGER: BEWARE OF FALLING MASONRY.

Most of the mill machinery had been rendered useless, but some smaller tackle, though badly damaged, was being offered for sale as spare parts, and this was laid out on the stone-flagged floor, in a space cleared among the rubble.

Everywhere, all around, the floors were covered with burnt corn and blackened brick-dust and timbers reduced to bits of charcoal, and in a far corner stood a few sacks of flour that had kept their shape, though charred and blackened all the way through. And all this, soaked by the rain, gave off a strong sharp choking smell that burnt the lungs and turned the stomach.

The mill belonged to Sir Godfrey Sayer, and his agent was there to conduct the sale. Sir Godfrey would not be rebuilding the mill, and the hired miller had been dismissed, for it was his carelessness that had caused the fire.

'Take a good look, boy,' Richard said to his little son who stared, appalled, at the burnt-out shell, 'and let it be a lesson to you that a miller must always be on his guard against getting up heat between stone and stone.'

There were four other men there beside Richard, all

millers like himself, looking out for a bargain. The sale had been set for three o'clock but already, when Richard arrived, the best bits and pieces had been knocked down and the men were loading them into their carts. The agent, Mr. Jones, was unashamed. He did not seem to think he was in the wrong.

'What was you wanting, Mr. Lancy? Anything in particular?'

'I wanted some four-pound weights,' Richard said. 'And some pitwheel parts if they was still sound.'

'Too late, I'm afraid. These gentlemen here have cleared the decks. There's only a few odds and bobs still left, but you're welcome to look around, of course.'

'Three o'clock was the time of the sale. I was here at quarter to. How come I'm late when I was early?'

'Mr. Hilliard was keen to begin. He's got another appointment elsewhere. We didn't expect no one else to come.'

'You mean Mr. Hilliard greased your palm? Is that how you always do business in these parts? If it is, I'll be sure to remember.'

'Now look here, young man!' the agent said. 'The sooner you take a quick look round, the sooner I can call it a day. It's not the weather for standing about in.'

'Dirty weather for dirty work,' Richard said, as he passed the millers loading their carts. But they were silent, avoiding his glance.

Inside the mill, he kicked at the worthless items of junk laid out in rows among the ashes, turning them over with the toe of his boot. Three bundles of sacks, badly burnt, and a coil of belting, about the same. A wallower wheel, badly buckled. Two hoppers; two bins; a rigger chain: all these things were beyond repair and he walked among them in growing anger. Little John followed behind, coughing because of the acrid fumes.

'Well?' said the agent, from the door. 'Do you see anything there you want?'

'I ent finished looking yet,' Richard said.

'Then how much longer are you going to be?'

'If you're in such a tarnal hurry, man, you get off by all means and leave me to look round in peace.'

'So that you can help yourself? I'm not such a fool! My men are waiting to clear this stuff up. They're taking it down to the smith at Lodding.'

'Your men can wait,' Richard said. 'I ent leaving till I've looked my fill.'

The agent, swearing, turned and went out. Richard, in an obstinate mood, went through the mill and into the house, inspecting the shoddy items for sale as though he had all the time in the world. John trailed after him, gazing at the cracked walls, bulging out high overhead as though they would topple at any moment.

'I don't like this place,' he said. 'I don't like the *smell*.'

'We shan't be long,' Richard said. 'Just mind you don't touch nothing, that's all, or you'll get yourself as black as pitch.'

He was in the millhouse kitchen now: a sad place, all blackened with soot, empty save for the mess of ashes covering the floor. All the furniture had been burnt and lay, mere sticks, among the rubble. The glass had burst from the casement window and a ragged fringe, like burnt cobwebs, hung from the curtain-rod above.

Richard was about to leave when he kicked something heavy in the ashes. He knelt down and uncovered a bag full of millwrighting tools, all in good order, unharmed by the fire. A proof-staff in its wooden case. A couple of dozen mill-bills of the finest steel, with three beechwood hafts. Two millpecks, a brush, and a pair of gloves. How they came to be in the house and how they could have escaped the fire was altogether rather strange, but the only thing that mattered to Richard was that he had found something worth buying, and he laughed very softly to himself, because his persistence had brought some reward.

Outside the mill, the agent was shouting to him again, demanding to know how long he would be. Richard stood up with the bag in his hands and carried it with him to the door. But then, suddenly, irritated by the agent's shouts, he hesitated and looked around.

In the middle of the kitchen floor, amongst the big square flagstones, he saw that there was a wood trapdoor with an iron ring in it. He went to it quickly and kicked away the ash and rubble. He raised the trap about eighteen inches, dropped the bag of tools into the cellar, and let the trap down again, carefully, without a sound. Then he kicked the ashes over it, wiped his hands on the seat of his trousers, and turned away feeling pleased.

John, who had come to look for him, stood in the doorway, watching intently, but Richard put a finger to his lips, and the little boy remained silent. They walked out together, hand in hand.

'Well?' said the agent. 'Did you find anything you wanted?'

'No, nothing,' Richard said. 'He done a pretty thorough job, burning the place down, that miller of yours. There's nothing left worth having here, so I'll bid you good day.'

He passed between the agent's men and lifted John onto the waggon. He climbed up beside him and took the reins, and as they drove slowly past the agent, he spoke a last word over his shoulder.

'You should take care how you waste a man's time, holding a sale that's no sale at all, cos time is money to a man like me and I can't afford to throw it away on fools' errands like today.'

He pulled a little on the nearside ribbon and turned the waggon towards home. It was raining coldly, steadily now, and John sat huddled close beside him.

'Now you know what it's like in Herefordshire. Folk are the same wherever you go. No more honest than they are at home.'

That evening, as she gave him his supper, Ellen asked how he had got on.

'There warnt nothing there worth having,' he said. 'The

23

crows had been down and picked the place clean. All I done was waste my time.'

He glanced at John, who sat in a chair beside the fire, intending to warn him against mentioning the tools, but John, half dozing as he sipped his milk, had not even heard what his father was saying. And in the morning, after a long night's sleep, the matter had faded from his mind.

Richard allowed three weeks to pass and then, after dark on a Friday evening, he set out again for Cutlowell Park.

'Don't wait up,' he said to Ellen, 'cos the chances are that I shall be late.'

'Why, where are you going?' Ellen asked.

'Nowhere much,' he said, shrugging. 'Just a bit of business to attend to, that's all.'

He went to Cutlowell Park on foot, following the course of the river, keeping to the towpaths all the way. The night was a rough one, with a gale blowing from the northwest, threatening a heavy downpour of rain. The trees along the river bank were loud with the noise of the wild wind, and the river itself was very high, sloshing over in many places, whipped up choppily in white-edged waves.

The whole of the month so far had been wet, and the waning moon, showing now and then through the tattered clouds, had its worst quarter still to go through. When the wind dropped and the rain fell, coming together with the spring-tide, there would be floods along this valley, as there had been in many a winter past. And as he approached Cutlowell, a few drops were already falling, cold and stinging in his face.

The burnt-out mill was a skeleton, black and jagged against the sky, its gable walls broken off in rough steps. Some of the brickwork had crumbled and fallen in the three weeks since he had last been there, and he had to clear away a heap of rubble before he could find the trap in the floor. He swung it up, both hands in the ring, and propped it open on a stout stick of wood.

When he lowered himself into the cellar, there was water lying at the bottom, and he hung for a moment, wondering about the probable depth. Then he let himself go, dropping down with a mighty splash, and when the water had stopped surging, it reached about half way up his thighs.

Very slowly he waded about in it, feeling with his feet for the bag of tools, but although he moved in widening circles, until in the end he had covered every inch of the floor, he encountered nothing but a small empty cask. Plainly, the agent's men had searched the cellar, and the bag of tools had been discovered. Richard, once again, had wasted a journey, but this time, as he told himself, he had nobody but himself to blame. He waded back to the open trapdoor and reached up to haul himself out.

The opening, when he raised his arms, was almost a yard away from his hands. He had to jump to get a grip. But his hands were wet and coated with slime, and when he tried to haul himself up, his fingers slithered on the ledge and he fell back clumsily into the cellar, knocking away the piece of wood that was keeping the trapdoor propped open. As the water surged about his body and he staggered, trying to keep his feet, the trapdoor fell shut with a heavy thud, and the shock that ran through the ruined millhouse brought one of the gables crumpling down, so that timbers and masonry fell with a terrible rumbling crash, covering the trapdoor above his head.

He groped his way about the cellar until he found the empty cask. He climbed on it to reach the trapdoor. His strength had always been a source of pride. Often when loading his waggon at a farm he had run to and fro perhaps twenty times, with a hundredweight bag of grain under each arm, and scarcely even sweated at it. But in this moment, when he needed it most, his strength was nothing. Although he pushed with all his might, the trapdoor never budged an inch, for three tons of rubble were weighting it down.

Standing quite still in the utter darkness, he told himself he would have to die. He was five miles away from his own home and nobody in the world would know where to find him. Cutlowell Mill was a lonely place, a mile and a half from the nearest village, half a mile from the nearest road, and, it being nothing but a ruin, no one now had reason to come there. No barges plied this stretch of the Ail, for the canal did not join it until Sutton Crabtree, and no pleasure craft would be out in winter.

The cellar was small. It was twelve or thirteen feet high and perhaps about fifteen by fifteen across, with only a slight amount of air finding its way through cracks in the walls. But worst of all was the river water surrounding him, for if the gale brought heavy rain to coincide with the month's springtide, the river might easily fill the cellar and he would be drowned like a rat in a trap.

He took his watch from his waistcoat pocket and wound it carefully to the end. He could see nothing of its face, but its ticking brought him a measure of comfort, and he put it into his breast pocket, so that it should be safe from the wet. He got down from the little cask and began feeling his way round the cellar. The floodwater washed about his thighs.

Chapter 3

In the days following Richard's disappearance, Ellen became more closely acquainted with the people of Dingham than she had ever been in all the nine years she had lived there, and she learnt that, in times of trouble at least, they were good neighbours. Many were ready to set aside their own affairs and go searching the countryside around. Others came to the millhouse with words of comfort and stayed talking by the hour, feeling that she should not be left alone to brood. Among these was the vicar, Mr. Eustead, and on the next Sunday, at each of the day's services, he offered up prayers for Richard Lancy, asking that his wife should not be left long in such terrible doubt as to the fate that had befallen him.

But although they were kind and sympathetic, Ellen was far from comforted, for nobody offered her any hope. Will Gale and Archie Shaw, with all the helpers they could muster, were dragging the river below the mill. Bob Dyson and his son had searched the railway line from Runston to Milby, a distance of nearly eleven miles. And the constable from Sutton Crabtree, calling on Ellen at the millhouse, seemed to think that Richard could have been attacked and robbed by a man from Sturton, already wanted for several crimes.

'Everyone's looking for a dead body!' Ellen burst out to Jerry Trussler, when he and some others returned from searching Skyte Quarry. 'Why does no one believe he's alive?'

'As to that, we all hope so, of course. But if he's alive, then where's he got to? Why's he missing all this long time?'

'Perhaps he's been taken ill,' Ellen said, 'or hurt himself and can't move.'

'Then we shall find him, never fear. Though in this bad weather we been having—'

'You sure he never said where he was going, Mrs. Lancy?' asked Bob Dyson. 'No hint nor nothing of what he was doing nor who he was going to see that night?'

'No, nothing,' Ellen said. She had been through the matter a hundred times. There was nothing new she could tell the men. 'He said he was going out on business. No why or where or what about. But he did say he'd be late coming home.'

'It's a blooming mystery, that's what it is!' said George Danks of Cockhanger Farm. 'I don't know what to make of it nohow.'

'You don't think it's some sort of joke on his part, do you, George?' asked Joe Dancox.

'No, no. Not him. Richard liked a laugh well enough but he warnt what you'd call a *joking* man. And what sort of joke would it be, anyway, doing a thing like that to his wife? No, it's no joke, be sure of that. Something's befell him. You mark my words. And what with the floods and the bad weather—'

George broke off and looked at Ellen, who stood erect, staring before her. The five men were silent, sitting awkwardly, hands on their knees, wishing themselves elsewhere yet unwilling to leave her all alone. But at last Joe Dancox rose to his feet.

'Mrs. Lancy, ma'am, you shouldn't ought to be by yourself. Just say the word and I'll get my missus to come along and sleep in the house till it's all over.'

'No, Mr. Dancox,' Ellen said. 'It's kind of you but it won't do. If I'm to be left without a husband, I must get used to it as best I can. Thank you all for your kind help, and thank you for coming to tell me the news.'

'We shan't give up!' said Jerry Trussler, and the others,

following him out of the kitchen, echoed his words: 'No lections of that! Oh dear me no! We shan't give up till we've tarnal well found him and brung him home!'

Ellen closed the door on them and stood for a moment listening to their footsteps thudding across the wooden bridge. Then she went upstairs to the back bedroom, where little John lay fast asleep. So far, although he knew of his father's absence, he took it for granted that all would be well, and she had done everything to encourage him in this belief. But soon the holidays would be over and he would be going back to school, and there he would hear the worst rumours. In the morning, therefore, she would have to tell him the truth of the matter: that his father was lost and might be dead; for by now it was the seventh day.

Now that the mill was no longer working, the little millhouse seemed dreadfully quiet. The gales had blown themselves out at last; the rain was no longer sluicing down; and sometimes, in the course of the day, the silence was so encompassing, it seemed to her that the whole world outside had gone dead. She had to go to the door and open it, so that she should be reassured by the sound of the weir pouring into the stream, and the sight of the sparrows squabbling for crumbs on the garden path.

Sometimes, alone in the kitchen, she would sit and concentrate her mind, thinking of all the places where Richard might be, and of all the possible accidents that could have befallen him. Surely, surely, so close as they were, her mind should be able to reach out to his? She had to *concentrate* with her whole being. And at these times, her small son, coming in from school, would find her sitting in a trance. He would come to her and touch her hand.

'He ent gone for good, has he, mother? He ent gone and left us all by ourselves?'

'I hope not, John. I hope not indeed.'

'I wish he'd come back this very minute. I wish he'd come walking in at the door. I don't like it without my dad. I'm

29

scared Old Rag-Face will come and get us and carry us off on his flying horse.'

'You mustn't be scared,' Ellen said. 'Nothing will happen to you while I'm here. I won't let it. And you mustn't start thinking about Old Rag-Face or you'll have bad dreams like you did before.'

'Maybe my dad has gone on a journey to Derbyshire. Maybe he'll bring back another stone.'

'I'm sure he hasn't gone on a journey. He would have told us all about it. He would have taken the horse and waggon.' Ellen got up and began moving about the room. She struck one hand against the other. 'We ought to be able to *think*!' she said. 'We ought to be able to work it out!'

The boy looked up with wrinkled forehead. He watched her walking to and fro. The fire in the stove had burnt low, the lamp was unlit, and the kitchen was growing very dark. He thought of his father out at night, stumbling into the swollen river.

'Don't let him be dead!' he said, trembling. 'Don't let him be dead, mother! – Not my dad!'

Ellen turned to him with a little cry. She knelt and took him into her arms.

'Of course he's not dead, John! He can't be! He *can't*! I won't believe it and neither must you. We must both be brave and strong about it and keep on praying for his return.'

But there were times when even the worst news would almost have been welcome, if only to end the uncertainty. She pictured someone coming to tell her that Richard's body had been taken from the river or the railway line, and the feeling that came over her was one of relief, like the melting away of a heavy burden. For at least such a thing could be understood: death was straightforward, however dreadful: it struck at people in broad daylight and those who were left did at least know what had happened and why; whereas, with her, there was only blankness; a tormenting bewilderment that left her a prey to every fancy and superstition. So that once or twice, in her innermost mind, she almost wished she

30

could see Richard's body brought to the door. But immediately she would feel ashamed; would feel herself guilty of betrayal; and then it seemed to her, somehow, that Richard's safety depended on the strength of her faith.

'We *must* go on searching!' she said every day to Jerry Trussler. 'We must! We must!'

But, as Jerry said to Joe Dancox, there were not many places left to be searched, even outside the parish boundary, and he for one was losing hope. Twelve days had now gone by and Richard Lancy's disappearance looked like remaining a mystery for ever more.

'I'll tell you what, Mrs. Lancy, ma'am. I reckon you ought to see Grannie Franklin. You never know. It might be worth trying, as a last chance, and it can't do no harm one way or the other. Of course, some people say it's a lot of nonsense, and maybe you're against such things—'

'What would Grannie Franklin do?'

'Well, she'd need something belonging to Richard, and she'd need a map of the district too. That's easy enough, it seems to me, so why not try it and see what happens?'

'I'll try anything,' Ellen said.

So, that afternoon, in the tiny cottage next to the churchyard, old Mrs. Franklin took the penknife Ellen had brought her and, dangling it on the end of a string, allowed it to swing slowly to and fro, above the map laid out on the table. Ellen watched, willing to believe in any magic, and Jerry Trussler held his breath, following every move of the penknife as it swung like a pendulum back and forth.

'D'you get any feelings, Grannie?' he asked.

'No, not much,' the old woman said. 'A slight pull northwards, that's all, and you generally nearly always get that.'

'Then what use is it?' Ellen asked.

'Sometimes it shows a will of its own. I feel it twirling in a certain direction.'

'But you get no such feeling now?'

'No, not a thing, I'm sorry to say. You sure this knife belonged to your husband?'

'He was using it the night he disappeared.'

'Then I reckon I'll give it another chance.'

The old woman closed her eyes. The penknife swung slowly to and fro, northward to southward, above the map.

'No, nothing,' she said again. 'Just the slight pull northwards and that's nothing.' She opened her eyes suddenly and looked at Ellen. 'But one thing I feel and the feeling is throbbing right up my arm. – Richard Lancy is still alive!'

Ellen's heart moved painfully. She found it impossible to speak. Jerry Trussler spoke for her.

'Is he hurted, Grannie? Can you say?'

'Hurted? Maybe. I dunno for sure. But he's alive, I'm sure of that. I can feel the throbbing of his blood. Now it's up to you to find him.'

'Can't you say *nothing* of where he is? Not even the *sort* of place to look?'

'No, no more,' Grannie said, and began folding Jerry's map. 'I've told you all there is to tell. I'm not a magician, you know, nor a witch neither. It's a special power in my hands and the power ent so good today.'

Ellen gave the old woman a florin and left the cottage with Jerry Trussler.

'The trouble is,' he said to her, 'she says what she knows folk want to hear, and we ent much the wiser for that, I'm afraid.'

'We *must* go on looking all the same.'

'Ah, but where?' Jerry said.

Ellen herself was out every day with the horse and waggon, driving to every neighbouring village. She travelled a great many weary miles, calling at the remotest farms, questioning everyone she met on the road, but no one could help her to find her husband. The people of Dingham, seeing her driving through the village, treated her with a solemn respect, because of the nature of her errand.

'There she goes again, poor woman, wearing herself to a tarnal shravel. She don't never give up, does she, poor soul, but what good can she ever do, toiling about like that, day in, day out? Better if she was to face the facts.'

Some felt ashamed at seeing her pass, because they themselves had abandoned the search, and her perseverance was like a reproach. And now that so much time had passed without Richard's body being found, the gossip began to blossom out. There was speculation on all sides.

'You don't think,' said Jem Williams in The Feathers one evening, 'that Dick Lancy's gone off with another woman?'

'And left a good business behind like that? Not him, by golly! He's a sight too smart. Besides, he ent never favoured no other woman, apart from his missus. He ent that sort.'

'All things is possible, however, I reckon. Nobody knows another man's mind.'

'Oh, anything's possible!' Jerry Trussler said with scorn. 'He could've gone off and jumped in the sea or took a ship to foreign parts. Or maybe his missus upped and killed him and fed him to the little fishes. Or maybe he got catched up in the moon for grinding corn on a Sunday! Anything's possible in this world – so long as there's big enough fools to believe it!'

'All right, all right!' said Jem, nettled. 'And what do *you* think has happened to him?'

'I dunno,' Jerry said. 'We've just about turned over every stick and stone between Sturton and Runston. That's a rajus of eignteen miles, southwards and eastwards and mostly downriver. Dick didn't hardly ever go upriver. He always said it was like foreign parts.'

'He was upriver, though, not long ago. He went to that sale at Cutlowell Park.'

'Ah, I know. And some pretty hard things he had to say about it too. He never thought much of folk in them parts and I'm inclined to feel the same. Herefordshire is a queer country.'

Jerry drank the last of his beer and watched the froth sliding back in his tankard.

'It's his missus I feel so sorry for. It's enough to turn a

33

woman's mind. And them such a well-suited couple together! It's a blooming mystery, that's what it is, and I'd give a fortune to fathom it out.'

'How long is it since he went missing?'

'A fortnight tomorrow,' Jerry said. 'Too long, I reckon, for any hope of his being alive.'

Richard was trapped in the cellar for sixteen days and during that time, at the height of the gales, the floodwater rose to such a level that even when he stood on the cask, it reached to his waist. Then, after a day and a night, it fell again slowly, little by little, till only ten or twelve inches remained, a thick sludge on the cellar floor.

On the seventeenth day, in the early morning, two young gipsies, picking over the ruins of the burnt-out mill, heard a knocking from below and a faint voice calling. They set to work to remove the rubble and discovered the trapdoor with its ring. They opened it and Richard was free.

The day was a dull one, the sky close-packed with low grey cloud, yet its light to Richard was a blinding glare, and he pulled his cap down over his eyes, cowering a while with his head in his arms before allowing them to haul him out.

The gipsies took him to their camp nearby and he sat at their fire with a horse-blanket round him. The womenfolk gave him hot soup and bread and afterwards, when he had eaten, an old man proffered a bottle of brandy. Richard took it and drank many times, gulping the brandy with a kind of lust and making little grunting sounds as it ran hotly down his throat. The old gipsy leant across and took the bottle away again. He had to use force to loosen Richard's tight-clasped fingers. By then, only a cupful of brandy was left, and he emptied it into Richard's boots.

'Did somebody put you into that hole?'

'No,' Richard said, in a hoarse whisper. 'Accident. Nothing more.'

'How long was you there?'

'I dunno,' Richard said, and sat quite still, looking into

34

the fire. His strength was almost at an end. His eyes kept rolling in their sockets. 'A long time,' he said, and his voice broke in utter weakness.

They put him up into one of their waggons and drove him to Dingham, wrapped as he was in the horse-blanket, and wearing his cap down over his eyes. They were seen as soon as they entered the village, and as they drove down the long main street, people gathered to watch them pass. Richard saw them, but only dimly, like faces and figures seen in a dream. And they in turn stared in silence, for his face showed how close he had come to death.

'Leave him be,' the old gipsy said, as one or two people moved forward. 'Leave him be. He wants his home.'

When they set him down at the millhouse door and took the blanket from his shoulders, he stood for a moment as though puzzled, as though asking, What is this place you've brought me to? — What am I supposed to do? And he half looked round, with a little gesture of appeal, as the gipsy waggon began moving off, leaving him standing all alone.

Ellen, hearing the sound of wheels, went to the window to see who was there. The gipsies were already driving away. She saw Richard with his hand on the door and she hurried to open it, reaching out to him, saying his name, and weeping to see him so changed, so gaunt. Supporting him, she led him indoors, and there he stood like a hollow man, looking at her with burning eyes, unable to speak a word to her, unable even to move his lips. Ellen put her arms around him, giving him her warmth and strength, and he clung to her as the giver of life.

Nursed by Ellen, and with Dr. Reed in attendance on him, he soon recovered. He had always been a strong healthy man, and possessed an iron will besides. His strength and his will had saved his life.

In less than two weeks he was up and about again, eager to get the mill working, determined to make up for lost time. But his ordeal in the cellar had left its mark: his brown hair was streaked with grey, and his face was deep-lined, the nerves pulsing visibly under the skin of jaw and temple; and sometimes, when something upset him, the sweat would come out on his upper lip, and his eyes would take on a blind-staring blankness.

'My dad's gone old,' John said once, alone with his mother.

'No, he's not old,' Ellen said. 'He's still sick, that's all, but he's getting better all the time.'

'He never laughs nor nothing now. He wears a long face like old Mr. Groom.'

'He'll soon be better, you'll see. It's up to us to try and be helpful and not make his head ache with too much noise.'

Ellen watched over Richard anxiously and always, if he left the house, tried to find out where he was going.

'Don't worry!' he said. 'I shan't get into a scrape like that again. I ent going nowhere near Cutlowell Park.'

When Ellen asked what had taken him to the ruined mill, he was inclined to be evasive, but the story came out eventually.

'I was looking for something, that's all.'

'Something that wasn't really yours?'

'A bag of millwrighting tools, that's all. They owed me something, them upriver folk, for wasting my time at the sale that day. But the tools had gone when I went back, and now you'll say it served me right.'

Ellen, however, said nothing. She was too thankful to have him back. But the villagers, calling at the mill, anxious to welcome him back to life, eager to hear the whole story, might have been less indulgent towards him, and for them he had a different answer.

'I thought I'd lost my watch and chain there. I went back to look for it and got buried alive.'

'And did you find it, your watch and chain?'

'Yes, I found it,' Richard said, producing it and showing it round, 'and I reckon it just about saved my life.'

'How do'you make that out?' asked Fred Byers.

36

'I dunno. It was just an idea I got into my head. I felt, somehow, that so long as my old watch kept going, well, *I* could damn well keep going too!'

'Then I reckon you took good care to wind it?'

'I did,' Richard said, 'and I took good care not to let it get wet.'

'It was company, like, I suppose?'

'It was all the company I had!'

'I dunno how you could've stood it, being shut up so long like that, in the cold and the dark, with not a bite of nothing to eat, and only that dirty water to drink. I'd say it's a marvel you're alive.'

'Was there rats in that cellar?' asked Joe Dancox.

'Rats and all sorts!' Richard said. 'Dead uns, mostly, drowned in the floods, and they floated around on the top of the water. But here! Lumme! Look at the time! I got work to do today. I can't stand gossiping hours on end – not like some folk I could mention.'

He talked very little of his sixteen days trapped in the cellar. It irked him if they pressed him too hard. He would say just so much and no more, and afterwards would turn to his work, being brisk and busy and preoccupied until his questioners went away. But one day, suddenly, alone with George Danks in the mealroom, he said: 'I had to eat *slugs*, George, to keep alive! Slugs and snails and dead worms. I had to *eat* them to keep alive.' And then, avoiding George's pitying gaze, he said: 'Don't tell no one else about that. It's something I generally try to forget.'

Every day now, after school, John hurried home and went straight to the mill, hauling himself up on the half-door until he could see over the top and call to his father, busy inside. He followed Richard everywhere, watching everything he did, wanting to help at every turn.

'Glory, boy!' Richard said at teatime one day. 'You look at me as though you could eat me. Don't you believe it's really me?'

'He missed you dreadfully,' Ellen said. 'He used to pray for you every night.'

'If he used his headpiece,' Richard said, 'he'd maybe have known where I could be found.'

'How on earth could he?' Ellen exclaimed. 'When nobody knew where you had gone?'

'Seems to me he didn't think. If he had done, he'd have figured it out.' Richard was eating a piece of cake. He removed a cherry and gave it to John. 'Well, boy, where was your wits? You remember going to the sale at the mill?'

John nodded, eating the cherry.

'Of course you do,' Richard said. 'And what happened when we got there?'

'It warnt no good,' John said. 'There warnt nothing left worth buying.'

'And what about that bag of tools? You saw me put it in the cellar? You was watching me, warnt you, when I closed the trap?'

'Yes.'

'Then if you'd used your headpiece,' Richard said, 'you'd have known I meant to go back and get it.'

John sat quite still and said nothing. He looked at his father with dark frowning eyes. Ellen was indignant on his behalf. She rounded on Richard and spoke sharply.

'You seem to forget he's only a child. He's four years old, not a grown man. How could he know what you meant to do? Did you ever say you were going back?'

'I would've thought it was plain enough.'

'Were you so clever when you were his age?'

'Ah, that's going back a bit, ent it, Nell?'

'You expect too much of him,' Ellen said. 'You even expect him to read your thoughts.'

'Maybe you're right,' Richard said, and leant across to ruffle John's hair. 'You're only a tiddler, ent you, boy? You're only tailings and a bit of bran? We've got to wait a good long while before you're grown up and using your brains. Still, I hope you won't be too slow a-learning, boy, cos you don't get anywhere in this world unless you got a bit of nous.'

Richard's recovery of his physical strength was something of a miracle to Ellen, and she never ceased to marvel at it. Within a month of rising from his bed, according to his own boast, his weight was back to normal again, and when Ellen doubted his word, he took her into the mill and weighed himself in her presence.

Within two months, he was working harder than ever, on the go at all hours, for he still travelled about the district, dealing in all manner of things, as well as running the watermill and grinding, most days, for a good seven or eight hours. And in the mealroom, as of old, he would demonstrate his strength by raising a full sack of flour from the ground until he held it above his head. Sometimes he did this special trick with John sitting astride the sack, and the little boy, having no fear of heights, would hang his cap on a nail in the beam, shouting with laughter all the while.

'My dad,' he would say to the customers, 'is the strongest man in the whole world.'

But Richard's recovery in other respects was much slower. He showed signs of strain and weakness. One wet Saturday afternoon, when he was in the woodshed, splitting logs, John crept up to the door and shut it, twisting the hasp and locking him in. It was a favourite trick of John's; it had happened often in the past; and the joke had been for Richard to bargain with his son, offering a penny or a shoulder-ride in exchange for his release. But this time, as soon as the door slammed shut and the place became dark and close about him, Richard felt himself trapped again. There was not enough air for him to breathe. The roof was pressing lower and lower, and unseen water swirled about him, waiting for him to topple and fall. And suddenly, with a loud cry, he sprang at the door in a kind of frenzy and hacked it open with his axe.

Outside, in the yard, John stood and stared in fascination as the axe came splintering through the door.

His grin of expectancy faded away, yielding to the chill whiteness of fear as his father burst out and lunged towards him. Too late, he tried to run. Richard caught him and swung him round.

'D'you think it's funny to shut me up in there like that? Would you like it yourself if I done it to you? Maybe you don't think I had enough of being shut up the way I was, day and night for sixteen days? Maybe you'd like me gone for good?'

Richard was holding the boy by the arms and was shaking him savagely to and fro. With every word another shake, and his fingers pressed harder all the time. John was crying, hurt and frightened, when Ellen ran out from the back kitchen.

'Richard! Please! Whatever are you doing? Control yourself! The boy is choking.'

'Ent it likely I've had enough, without his shutting me in that shed? I've a mind to do the same to him – shut him up in the dark with the rats and see if he thinks it's funny then! What d'you say, boy? Will you go in?'

'Control yourself, Richard, for pity's sake! It's only a little childish prank. He's done it often enough before.'

'I'll damn well make sure he don't do it again after today! By the time I've finished with him—'

Ellen thrust herself between them and tried to unfasten Richard's fingers, pressing hard into John's arms. Richard's rage was slow to die down, but gradually he loosened his hold, and the little boy turned to his mother, hiding himself against her skirts.

'Poor boy! Poor boy!' she said, holding him close. 'It's all over now. There's no need to cry. Your daddy didn't mean to hurt you. It's just that he doesn't know his own strength.'

And, over his head as he sobbed against her, she challenged Richard with anxious gaze. His face was wet with perspiration. Anger was still a film on his eyes. But gradually, little by little, his breathing became steady again, and his voice when he spoke was more like his own.

'He shouldn't ought to've shut that door. He knows what I've been through. If he don't, he ought.'

'He's only a child. He can't imagine your sufferings. He's just glad to have you back.'

'He ent got enough to do on Saturdays and Sundays, seems to me. Where are them kids he plays with sometimes? Why don't he go off with them?'

'He was hoping you'd take him to Rainborough today, when you go to Henden's with that flour.'

'Oh, he's always ready to go gadding about! He's bright enough when it comes to that. But I ent going to Rainborough today. I've put it off till Monday or Tuesday. I've got too much to do at home.'

Richard went back to his work in the woodshed. Ellen took the boy indoors. And at bedtime that night, after he had said his prayers, she tried to explain his father's bad temper.

'He's not really well yet. He gets upset. We've got to be careful not to annoy him, and if he flies out at us now and then, well, we must try not to take it to heart.'

'Does he fly out at *you*, mother?'

'He's very touchy with me sometimes. He gets bad headaches that makes him cross. He was very ill, you see, after being in that cellar. You remember how ill he was, lying in bed? You remember the doctor coming in? Well, he's not really strong yet, and we've got to help him to get better.'

'He *is* strong,' the little boy said, and showed her his arms, which were badly bruised from the elbows upwards.

'I know, I know. But he didn't mean to hurt you, John. You must try and forgive him and be very good. He'll soon get well if we don't vex him. Promise me you'll do your best?'

John's face was still stubborn. He looked at her with rebellious eyes.

'Won't you promise,' she said again, 'even if only to please me?'

This time he gave her the briefest of nods, and, knowing it was the most she could hope for, Ellen kissed him and said goodnight.

All through Sunday and during the week, John kept out of his father's way. He no longer went to the mill after school but marched straight past, into the house, and stayed with his mother in the kitchen. At mealtimes he sat like a little image, speaking only when spoken to, and when Saturday came round again, he took himself off to play by the river.

'Is he sulking, that boy?' Richard asked, coming into the house from the mealroom. 'Is he paying me out cos I went for him?'

'I don't think he means to sulk,' Ellen said. 'I told him he must be good and quiet, and it seems to me he's doing his best.'

'That don't mean he's got to be dumb, however, and sit like a malkin on a stick. Why, he looks at me with such eyes sometimes, you'd think I was some kind of wild fierce bear.'

'You frightened him badly in the yard that day. You hurt him, too, inside himself. You made him feel you didn't love him.'

'That's rubbish, that is. I've no time for that. He's supposed to be a boy, not a whey-faced Mary Ellen. There's no call for him to be so soft.'

Richard walked about the kitchen, fidgeting with the backs of the chairs. He went to the window and looked out and could see John, on the river bank, poking with a stick into the deep holes where the martins had nested in the summer.

'He ent got enough to do, that boy. I reckon I'd better take him fishing. Would he like that, Nell? D'you think he'd come?'

'You've only got to ask him,' Ellen said. 'Just open that window a few inches and see what happens when you put your question.'

And, a quarter of an hour later, watching the two of them setting off, the one a small counterpart of the other, she saw that the sun was shining again, after several days of darkness.

Chapter 4

Richard had quite a few new customers at the mill that spring, some of them strangers from as far away as Aston Charmer, for the story of his amazing survival after sixteen days underground had gone round the county, and many people were curious to see him.

'I know why they come,' he said to Ellen. 'It's to see the man that rose from the dead. You'd think I was something out of a raree show, the way they go on, but it's all right by me! – It's good for trade! I ent been so busy in all my born days. I shall make the most of it while it lasts.'

The mill was certainly doing well, and Ellen was glad to see him happy. But often she worried about him, too, for he still did everything himself and sometimes worked throughout the night, re-dressing the stones by candlelight, so that no precious milling time should be lost next day. She wished he would take on a millboy to help, or employ one of the travelling millwrights who called occasionally, asking for work. But Richard scoffed at the idea. He would not pay outsiders for doing what he could do himself.

'I ent made of money, Nell. Besides, I can't trust them to do a good job.'

'You'll wear yourself out,' Ellen said. 'The doctor warned you against too much strain.'

'Work never hurt us. It's *lack* of work that wears a man down. A man with business coming in is thankful for it and finds the strength of two or three.'

True, he never seemed tired, physically, but there was

strain of a kind, all the same: a certain excitement of the mind as though, having defied death, he felt he had nothing more to fear and could drive himself as hard as he pleased. His energy was unnatural. It overflowed the normal bounds.

One night in April, Ellen awoke in the small hours to find that Richard had gone from her side. His clothes, too, had gone from the chair. She pulled a shawl over her shoulders and went downstairs, drawn by noises in the mealroom. And there, by the moonlight entering the south window, she found him moving sacks of meal.

For a little while she stood and watched him, half in amusement, half in worried exasperation, with some teasing remark beginning to form, ready on the tip of her tongue. But as he crossed the white path of moonlight, dragging a heavy sack by its 'ears', she became aware of some strangeness in him and sensed that he was still asleep.

Her teasing remark almost hung in the air, so near had it come to being uttered, and the quietness thrummed like a drawn string. At the back of her neck, a coldness crept upwards into her scalp, sending a tremor through her nerves, and she stood undecided, half inclined not to interfere. But Richard, sleepwalking in the mill, could easily do himself an injury, so she went and put a hand on his arm.

'Come along, Richard,' she said in an ordinary, quiet voice. 'This way. We're going to bed.'

A touch was enough. He turned towards her silently, eyes wide open, seeing nothing, and meekly allowed her to lead him away. She kept her hand upon his arm, and they went together like two grey ghosts, through the kitchen, into the passage, and up the narrow wooden stairs. His feet found their way without hesitation, and the lightness and quietness of his walk, although he wore his heavy boots, made him an unreal presence beside her, not a living man at all. Yet his arm was warm and solid enough, under her own icy fingers.

Once in the bedroom, he undressed and lay down without prompting, and drew the bedclothes up to his shoulders. He was soon breathing heavily, and did not stir

44

again that night, but Ellen lay on her back beside him and watched the moonlight on the ceiling giving way to the light of dawn. The night, for her, was an anxious vigil.

When she mentioned the matter the next day, Richard threw back his head and laughed.

'Sleepwalking? Me? You're having me on. I never walked in my sleep in my life.'

'You did last night. I had to bring you back to bed.'

'Without my knowing naught about it? Get away! I ent having that!'

'I'm sure it's because you've been working too hard instead of trying to take it easy. It's got on your mind. It's a worry to you. Your health is not so good as it was before you were trapped in that cellar.'

'That's rubbish, that is. I'm as fit as a flea. Sleepwalking? Get away! You must've dreamt it and thought it was real.'

'Have you been in the mealroom yet? Is everything there as it was yesterday?'

'I've had enough of this!' Richard said. 'I don't want to hear no more about it. I've got enough to occupy me, without you adding your woman's fancies.'

A week later, it happened again. Ellen followed him downstairs and all the way through into the mill. She saw him remove three bricks from the wall and take something from the space behind. It was a bottle of some sort, and she saw him put it to his lips. Afterwards, he hid it again, putting the three bricks back in their place. Then he walked into the mealroom, passing quite close to where she stood. Deliberately, she moved forward, almost directly into his path, and waved a hand in a circular movement in front of those seemingly wide-awake eyes. He passed, however, without a sign, merely stepping aside to avoid her, and there was the same strangeness about him, the same remoteness as before. He was walking in his sleep. Now, if she woke him, he would have to believe it. But such a course was said to be dangerous, and she hesitated to take the risk.

But the thing that disturbed her most of all was the smell

of brandy he left behind him. She thought of the bottle in the wall and wondered how many were stowed elsewhere. Was it possible for a man to be a drinker in his sleep and not know it? No. It was not. For he had known what he was doing when buying the brandy, and had gone to a good deal of trouble to keep the matter to himself. The secrecy of it cut her off. He seemed a stranger, suddenly. The distance between them was cold and dark.

Shivering, she pulled her shawl close about her, and followed him into the mealroom. He was moving among the sacks, apparently counting them, touching each one. She went to him and took his arm and led him back upstairs to bed.

Now that she knew of his secret drinking, the signs of it were plain enough. The slight slurring of his speech sometimes and the uncertainty of his gaze; the bursts of temper arising out of nothing at all; the habit he had of chewing a mouthful of wheat-meal several times in the course of the day. These things spoke for themselves and she wondered that she had not noticed before.

It was easy to understand how the habit had come to him. Working so late into the night, alone in the mill, doing tedious, exhausting work such as dressing the stones or making new cogs for the spurwheel, surely he could comfort himself in whatever way he chose? But much of his work could be dangerous if his judgment were ever impaired by drink, and Ellen, being afraid for him, decided that she must speak her mind.

'Don't you think it's unwise to drink so much, when you're working all alone in the mill? If the stone were to slip when you're turning it up, or if you should knock the candle over—'

'What're you on about?' he said, and his eyes slid away, as they so often did nowadays, till he seemed to be looking, not at her, but at something shadowy moving behind her. 'What're you on about, drinking indeed? How many times have I been

46

to the inn? Once! That's all. Just once! No more.'

'I'm talking about what you do in the mill. You've always said how easy it is to start a fire in such a dry, dusty place and if you were to have an accident—'

'What do you take me for? A fool?'

'Drink can make any man foolish, even you.'

'Drink is nothing to do with me. I dunno what the hell you mean.'

'Oh, Richard!' she said reproachfully. 'I've seen you, myself, with my own eyes. I've seen where you hide the brandy bottle. I've even seen you drinking from it, so why deny it all the time—'

'Seen it?' he said, with a quick glance, and began moving about the kitchen, fidgeting with the chairs at the table. 'What've you seen, I'd like to know? You take me and show me what you've seen! Let's go this minute into the mill and get it settled once and for all!'

'No, I don't want to. Where's the point? I know what I mean and so do you. You've got a hiding-place in the wall.'

'All I know is, you've been snooping around. That's the truth of it, right enough, and I don't like it, I'll tell you straight. When a man's wife starts spying on him—'

'I never meant to spy on you. I followed you down when you walked in your sleep.'

'Here we go! Them fancies of yours! Are you saying it's happened again?'

'Yes, it happened on Monday night. You went down to the mill and I followed you. I had to bring you back to bed.'

'Get away!' he exclaimed. 'I shan't swallow that!'

'How else would I know?' Ellen asked, watching him as he flung about. 'How else would I know of your hiding-place if I hadn't seen you go to it? You haven't been out of the mill since Monday. You were there all day yesterday and today and I never came in for a single moment.'

'That's nothing. You could've been in there before.'

'And what would I have seen then, any different from what I've said?'

47

Ellen stepped in front of him and tried to make him meet her eye, but he merely flung away from her and went towards the mealroom door.

'You won't have seen nothing! Not a stitch! Cos there's nothing there for you to see! As for my walking in my sleep, if I hear that old tale again—'

'Richard! Please! If only we could talk this out!'

Richard, however, would not stay and talk. He went back to the mill and worked on into the night, and when he came in, after midnight, he went to bed without a word.

But, strangely enough, although he denied it had ever happened, the sleepwalking stopped after that, and Ellen's nights, in part at least, were free of anxiety on his behalf. She noticed, too, on going into the mill one day to ask for a new bag of flour, that the three loose bricks in the far wall had been cemented into place.

The drinking went on as before. Ellen was beginning to know the signs. And although Richard took such care in his attempts to keep it secret, it was soon suspected in the village. Ellen was at Whitty's shop one morning, buying the week's groceries, and one of the items on her list was a bottle of sarsparilla. Mr. Whitty fetched it for her and put it into her shopping-basket.

'So long as it's nothing stronger, eh?' he said with a laugh, and Ellen, taking money from her purse, pretended that she was busy counting.

That same morning, returning home, she heard voices inside the mill, raised so loud that they could be heard above the noise of machinery. An old cart stood in the roadway, loaded with sacks of meal and bran. It belonged to George Danks of Cockhanger Farm. And after a moment, as she stood, George came stumping out of the mill, red in the face and scowling fiercely, slamming the half-door shut behind him. He went to his horse and removed its nosebag with trembling fingers. He threw it into the back of the cart.

'George! What is it?' Ellen said. 'Whatever's the matter?'

'Ask *him*!' said George, jerking his head towards the mill.
That husband of yours! The miller hisself! Ask him what's
wrong with his weights and measures!'

'Do you mean he's made some mistake?'

'Twelve years I've been coming to this mill. I was one of
the first, when Dick was a lad, and I did my bit in starting him
off. But I shan't be coming after today. I shall trade with Holt
n Runston in future, where I can get an honest deal.'

'Whatever it is that's happened today surely it can be put
right?'

'Nobody likes to be cheated, ma'am, and I've had more'n
I can take. That husband of yours is too sharp by half.'

'Isn't there anything I can do?'

'No, no, there's nothing to do. It's past mending and I'm
away off.' George climbed onto the box and took the ribbons
from the cleat. He looked at Ellen, standing below. 'There's
only one way to help your Dick – keep him away from the
damned bottle!'

Ellen watched him drive away. She put down her shopping and went into the mill. Richard had a sack on the
handbarrow and was wheeling it towards the hoist. His
handsome face was dark with anger. A pulse was beating in
his cheek.

'What happened?' she asked, above the rumble of the
mill. 'How come you've quarrelled with George Danks?'

But although he heard her and glanced round, he made
no attempt to answer her, and she saw by the tightening of his
mouth that to question him now would make matters worse.

At midday, when he came in for dinner, he was chewing
a mouthful of wheat-meal. The dust of it was on his lips. He
washed himself in the back kitchen and splashed cold water
over his head. He came to the table with wet hair.

'Well?' Ellen said, bringing his dinner. 'Are you going to
tell me what happened?'

'If you mean George Danks, and I daresay you do, I damn
well threw him out of my mill.'

'That's no answer. I want to know what it's all about.'

49

'He accused me of giving him short measure. Now you know as much as me. God! But the fool has got a nerve! He's lucky I didn't break his neck. Him and his tuppenny tinpot farm! Accusing *me* of giving short measure!'

'And did you?' she asked, quietly.

'God!' Richard said, striking the table. 'That's your loyalty, I suppose? That's your idea of being a wife! Supposing you think of the day we got married, how you promised to honour and obey! Is this how you keep that sacred promise, accusing me the same as Danks?'

'I notice you don't really answer my question.'

'No, nor shan't, if you ask for ever! It's not a wife's place to ask questions. Not *them* sort of questions, anyway, concerning a man and his private business.'

'Since you don't deny it,' Ellen said, 'I suppose that's an answer in itself.'

'Is it? Is it!' he exclaimed. 'And what in hell's name do you mean by that?'

Hands flat on the table, he leant towards her, jaw out thrust, the blood rising in his face and burning darkly in his cheeks. His anger leapt out at her like heat, causing a prickling in her skin, but before either could speak again, John came running in from school with a wren's nest he had found in the lane, and while Ellen inspected the nest, Richard took up his knife and fork and began eating.

Throughout the meal, as they ate together, Richard scarcely spoke at all, but stared at his wife across the table and followed every move she made. John's bright prattle gradually ceased. He saw that his father was in a mood. He looked at his mother questioningly and she gave him a reassuring smile. She asked him about his school lessons. Then suddenly, in a pause, Richard put down his knife and fork and pushed his empty plate aside.

'I might've known you'd side with Danks! It's not the first time you've called me a thief! You done it that time when I fetched the stones. Don't think I've forgotten cos I ent!'

'I'm not taking sides,' Ellen said. 'But why quarrel with

50

George Danks, who's been so good to you all these years, helping to set you on your feet?'

'Why does he up and quarrel with *me*?'

'You've lost his custom. I suppose you know that. He's going to Runston in future, he said, and he's a man who means what he says.'

'Let him go, by all means! What loss will it be if he gets his pigfood ground elsewhere?'

'I don't understand you,' Ellen said. 'George has always been your friend. When you were missing all that time, he was out with the other men, searching everywhere day after day.'

'Don't tell me he lost any sleep!'

'Does it mean nothing at all to you that so many people were worried about you, doing their best to find where you'd gone?'

'People?' he said contemptuously. 'Danks and Bullock and Rissington? I doubt if they was concerned for *me*. They just wondered who'd grind their corn!'

Ellen was silent, looking at him, and under her unwavering gaze his own fell away, uneasily, trying to focus elsewhere. He gave a shrug and tried to laugh, as though it was nothing but a joke and she was at fault for taking it all so seriously.

'Anyway! What use was it? They never looked in the right place, did they? I could be there still, just bones in a cellar, for all the good they done searching around.'

'How could they know where to look for you? How could anyone know, even me, your own wife, when you chose to be so mysterious, poking about where you'd no right to be and telling no one what you were doing? How *could* we have known where you had gone?'

In the silence that followed Ellen took herself to task, ashamed of her outburst in front of her child. John sat quite still, his shoulders drooping, making himself very small in his chair. His dinner, half eaten, lay before him, the food growing cold upon the plate. And in his hands, hidden down in his lap, he held the tiny wren's nest, made of sheepswool and moss and bits of dried grass. Looking at it, he shut himself off. Harsh words between his mother and father were becoming common nowadays. He crouched beneath them and made himself small.

Richard got up and rattled his chair in under the table. He looked at Ellen and at his son.

'You should have asked the boy where I was. He could've told you, Cutlowell Park. He could've told you about that cellar.'

'That's ridiculous!' Ellen said. 'We've been through all this once before. John couldn't know you were going back.'

Richard took his cap from the peg and opened the door. He stood for a moment with his hand on the latch, looking back over his shoulder.

'*He* knew,' he muttered, half to himself, and went out, shutting the door.

Soon the waterwheel was turning again, swish and clack, swish and clack, and the house became filled with the muffled rumbling of the mill. John slid from his chair and came to lean in Ellen's lap, still holding the wren's nest in his hands.

'What's the matter with my dad?'

'I think he's not feeling so well today.'

'Is it his elbow?' John asked.

'Elbow?' she said. 'What do you mean?'

'Jacky Williams said he reckoned my dad had been tipping his elbow. Did he hit it in the mill?'

Briskly, Ellen rose to her feet. She began clearing away the dishes.

'Just look at the time!' she said, laughing. 'You'll soon be running back to school, and you haven't finished telling me how you came to find that nest.'

One Saturday afternoon in June, Richard loaded the waggon with flour, and drove towards Sutton Crabtree. He always locked the mill door these days and he alone kept the key. No one was ever allowed in except when he himself was there.

John was on the footbridge, fishing in the stream with two other boys, Ernie Horn and Lukey Strudwick. They watched Richard driving away.

'I've never been in the mill,' Lukey said. 'Is it spooky like they say?'

'No! It's not!' John said. 'Who says it's spooky, I'd like to know?'

'Can we go in and look around?'

'How can we?' said Ern. 'You saw his father lock it up.'

'Can't we get in through the house instead?'

'No,' John said, 'that door's locked too.'

'Glory be!' Lukey said. 'Ent you allowed in your own dad's mill?'

John withdrew his line from the stream and examined the cube of cheese on the hook. It was sodden and beginning to crumble. He squeezed it into a lump again and dropped it back into the water.

'*I* can always get in,' he said, 'if you really want to see the mill.'

'Ent you afraid?' Lukey asked.

'No,' John said, 'I ent afraid.'

A little while later he led the way to the side of the mill, to the small slatted doors that covered the cog-hole. He opened them and crept inside, and the others followed his example, clambering over the pit-wheel and sidling along the greasy axle. John led them through the wooden shutters, and they were in the mill itself, with the sun coming in through the three windows, making three separate shafts of light, each one showing the dust in the air.

'Lumme!' said Lukey. 'Ent it big?'

'I don't like it in here,' said Ern. 'It feels the same as it does in church.'

'Is that why you're whispering?' Lukey asked. He was older than John and Ern. He was almost ten and a half. 'Are you going to say your prayers?'

A sudden sound startled them, and the mill cat leapt down from a rafter above. Lukey's face was as shocked as

Ern's. He gave a little nervous laugh.

'What's up that ladder?' he asked John.

'The stones is up there,' John said.

'Come along, then, let's have a look.'

From the stone-floor they climbed yet another ladder and mounted to the top floor of all and from there, peeping through the cracks of the luccomb door, they looked down on the open yard, thirty or forty feet below.

'Makes me feel giddy,' Lukey said. 'I shouldn't like to go down on that chain.'

They returned again to the stone-floor and looked at the tools laid out on the bench. Lukey picked them up in turn and asked John what they were for. He picked up the little haresfoot brush and tickled Ernie under the chin.

While they were playing like this together, John heard the sound of the horse and waggon. He whispered urgently to the others and they all lay on their stomachs on the floor, peering down between the cracks into the sunlit millroom below.

Richard walked in carrying a sack over his shoulder. He set it carefully down on the kist, untied the string about its neck, and took out a roll of paper money. The boys could see him counting the notes. They even heard the crisp rustle. And Lukey, lying next to John, gave him a sharp nudge in the ribs.

Richard walked across the mill, unscrewed a tie-plate in the wall, and hid the roll of money behind it. He screwed the plate back very hard. He returned to the sack, took out three big round black bottles, and put them into the wooden kist. He covered them over with a bundle of sacks and let down the lid.

When he had gone, driving away in the waggon again, the three boys hurried down the ladder and crept through the cog-hole, out of the mill.

'Whew! That was close!' Lukey said. 'If your dad had come and found us up there—'

'He wouldn't have done nothing,' John said.

'I dunno so much. I dunno. I reckon he'd have skinned us alive.'

They returned to the upper bank of the stream and took their fishing-rods from under the bushes. John sat down to re-tie the hook on the end of the string.

'Your dad's a miser,' Ernie said, 'hiding his money away like that.'

'Oh no he ent!' John exclaimed. 'Miser your own-self! You mind your tongue!'

He *is* a miser,' Lukey said. 'Ask any one. Ask my dad. *And* he's a tippler, on the quiet. Anyone'll tell you that.'

'What's a tippler when it's at home?'

'You saw them bottles, didn't you?'

'Bottles is nothing,' John said. 'It's none of your business, anyway!'

'Seems to me you're green as grass.'

'My dad's not a tippler!' John said. 'Nor he ent a miser neither!' And, wriggling forward a little way, he kicked hard at Lukey's foot.

'What is he, then? You tell us that!'

'He's nothing,' John said, twisting the ravelled ends of the string and tying them to the tiny hook. 'He's my dad, that's all.'

'Are you coming to fish at the weir?'

'No! I'm not. I'm stopping here.'

'Suit yourself,' Lukey said. 'Suit yourself – miser's boy!'

They left him sitting on the bank.

Richard came home at four o'clock but left the horse and waggon outside because he had business elsewhere at five. He ate a very hurried tea and rose immediately from the table. He was on his way out when John came in, and as the boy walked past, Richard took hold of him and dragged him back. He had seen a red smudge on the boy's jacket.

'How come you got ruddle on yourself? You been getting into the mill? Answer me, boy, and be quick about it! I ent got time to waste on lies. You been larking about in there the

55

moment my back was turned today?'

'No!' John said, white-faced. 'Not larking, no!'

'What, then? You was in there for sure. That smudge of ruddle tells the tale. So what was you up to while I was out?'

'Nothing, honest. Just looking round.'

'Touching things and interfering? Poking your nose into my affairs?'

'We was just looking at things, that's all. We never touched nothing. Cross my heart!'

'We? Who's we? What others was there?'

'Lukey Strudwich and Ernie Horn. Lukey wanted to see the mill.'

'You been playing about with my tools? Taking the edge off? Doing them in? How many times have I told you—'

'Richard!' said Ellen, stepping forward. 'Is it such a terrible matter? The boy always *used* to go into the mill. Why should it be so different now?'

'You keep out of this, Nell. It's a matter between the boy and me.'

'He's my son as well as yours.'

'Then you should learn him he's got to obey!'

'Leave go of him and let him sit down. He'll answer you if you give him a chance. He's not a dog, to be shaken so!'

'Get out of my way!' Richard said. 'The mill is my business, not yours, and I'll deal with things as I think fit.' With his fist twisted in John's collar, pressing hard against his neck, he shook him and lifted him off his feet. 'The mill is my business!' he said again. 'And what I want to know is, how the hell did you get in?'

'Through the cog-hole!' John said, gasping.

'You and two others? Kids like yourself? Poking about everywhere, letting them know about my affairs, getting it spread about the place! If you've interfered with anything—'

'I haven't! I haven't!' John cried. 'Leave me alone! You're hurting me! What do I care about the mill? I hate it! I hate it! I hope it falls down!'

Squirming, he managed to wrestle free, and when his

father lunged towards him, Ellen quickly stepped in the way. The boy escaped and ran headlong from the house. Ellen clutched at Richard's arm.

'By God!' he said, and his face, close to hers, was ugly with temper. 'You dare to take his part against me? You let him defy me and treat me as though I was nothing at all? No wonder he thinks he can do as he likes!'

'So much anger?' Ellen said. 'And all for such a little thing! Is it the drink that makes you like this?'

'I can't stop to argue with you! I've got to go to Whitestone Farm. But I shall be home in due course and young Master John had better watch out!'

He left the house and drove away, and Ellen went out to look for John, walking along the bank of the stream to where it flowed into the river. The boy, as she guessed, was up in his place in the old pollard willow, sitting in the crutch of it, hidden among the grey-green leaves.

'You can come out now. Your father's gone.'

Reluctantly, he climbed down. She helped him and lowered him to the ground. His face was cold and white and stiff, his gaze fixed, defying the tears. The feeling she had, of wanting to take him into her arms, had to be set firmly aside, for, young as he was, he had his pride, and softness from her would have meant his undoing. They walked together hand in hand.

'I don't like my dad,' he said. 'I wish he'd never come back that time. I wish he'd stopped away for good.'

'You mustn't say that. It's very wrong. You shouldn't have taken your friends into the mill. You saw the lock was on the door. You knew that meant you were not to go in.'

'What'll he do to me when he gets home? Will he whip me?'

'No, of course not,' Ellen said. 'He won't do anything. I won't let him.'

She put him to bed early that night and sat up late waiting for Richard. She steeled herself for the sound of wheels. But when at last he returned home he was steady-

57

eyed, quiet-voiced, in great good humour with himself, having spent the evening with the new tenant at Whitestone Farm.

'Mr. Temple farms six hundred acres. He's promised he'll let me grind his corn. That more'n makes up for George Danks and his paltry bits of peas and beans. I reckon I've done a fair evening's work.'

'Yes, that's good,' Ellen said. 'Very good. It is indeed.'

'I reckon I must've kept you up. You're about dropping with sleep, I can see. Still, at least it's Sunday tomorrow, eh?'

Of the trouble with John he said not a word. Nor did he mention it the next morning. The whole of Sunday passed in peace. Ellen was relieved but also puzzled. Richard was not a forgetful man yet the matter it seemed had been forgotten, and even John's white, fearful face did not remind him.

The next time she went into the mill, however, she saw that the shutters over the cog-hole were now fastened with a padlock and chain. No one would enter that way in future. The mill was as safe as a fortress these days, and Richard's pocket was full of keys.

'What are you afraid of,' she asked, 'that you always keep the place locked up?'

'I don't want people snooping around. They got light fingers, some of them, and I can't afford to lose my stock. I reckon they done pretty well for theirselves when I was missing all that time but they'll never get the chance again.'

'That's not true!' Ellen said. 'How can you say such a wicked thing?'

'You don't know. You wasn't here all the time. You was out looking for me. Or so you told me, anyway.'

'Don't you even believe that?'

'Of course I believe it. People saw you driving out. I've heard them say so often enough. And that's what made it easy for them to help theirselves out of my mill.'

Chapter 5

It was a wet summer that year, and harvests everywhere were spoilt. Richard knew this as well as anyone. He had seen the corn laid low in the fields, the soaked grain sprouting in the ear. Yet when autumn came, and farmers like Bullock and Rissington had only a few bushels of grey peas to grind, Richard accused them of holding back. He had already lost three customers, and he blamed George Danks.

'It's him that's turning folk against me, you know. Him and his lies about short measure. I reckon he means to ruin me. He'd like to see me go down the drain.'

'No one's against you,' Ellen said. 'You know the crops have been bad this year. It's the same for everyone, everywhere. But you *will* turn them against you, certainly, if you keep accusing honest men.'

'Oh, I knew it'd all be my own fault! I expect no sympathy at home. My wife is as bad as all the rest.'

All through that summer, the change in him had grown more marked. He was not the Richard she had married. His attitude to everyone, friends and strangers alike, was hard and suspicious. He trusted no one. And often some petty hinderment would put him into a sweat of rage.

The millstream had always attracted children, especially boys, and whenever they had a holiday they would come very early in the morning, bringing a satchel full of food, and play along the banks all day. It had always been so, years without number, and sometimes if rain had fallen hard they had taken shelter in the mill. But now, if a boy so much as set foot

59

on the footbridge, Richard would lean out over the hatch and shout to him to be off at once.

'Ent there enough river for you, without you got to come just there? How'd it be if I chopped that bridge down? I reckon you'd look pretty silly then!'

But the boys still came to the bridge just the same, and the more he shouted to them to be off, the more inclined they were to stay, drumming on the boards with their hobnailed boots and doing their best to provoke him further.

'Mr. Lancy! Yoo-hoo! We're on your bridge! Aren't you coming to chop it down?'

Sometimes they went even further than that and closed the upper sluice-gate, so that the waterflow was reduced and the waterwheel gradually slowed to a halt. Then Richard would rush out and pursue them as much as half a mile, trying to trip them up with his broom as they ran along the narrow towpath.

'Why don't you leave them alone?' Ellen asked. 'Boys have always come to the bridge. You used to be friendly and make them welcome.'

'And see where it's got me!' Richard said. 'Great big boys of eleven and twelve, they ought to be going out to work. And what're they *doing* on my bridge? Not fishing! Oh, no! They're looking for ways to get me riled. Well, they'll go too far one of these days and then they'll be sorry, you mark my words!' And, turning to John, he would say: 'Friends of yours? Is that what you said? Then tell them to keep away from my mill or they'll regret it sure as fate!'

Sure enough, the next time the boys interfered with the sluices, Richard was ready with his shotgun and fired both barrels over their heads. Ellen was in the back garden. She and John were picking peas. When she ran round to the mill door, Richard was leaning over the hatch, the twinbarrel smoking dirtily, and a small powder-burn on the side of his face. Three or four boys, with frightened faces, were running like hares towards the village.

'For God's sake, Richard, what are you doing? Surely you didn't use real shot?'

'A full charge! Both barrels! And I reckon they must've felt the draught!'

'But they're only children!' Ellen said. 'You might so easily have done them harm!'

'I ent a fool. It's not the first time I've used this gun. It was only to scare them, that's all, and learn them a lesson to keep away.'

'You've got no right to do such a thing! That old gun is dangerous. You've got no right to take such risks.'

'Ent I, though! We'll see about that! I've got a right to protect my mill!'

He was perfectly matter-of-fact. Nothing she said affected him. He went to see to the sluice-gate and returned to his unfinished work in the mill, and that afternoon, in the kitchen, he sat down with powder-flask and bag of shot and carefully reloaded the gun. He put it into the long-case clock and locked the door.

'If they come meddling with the water again, I'm ready for them and so's my gun!'

John, sitting quietly whittling a stick, looked up and sought his mother's gaze. Ellen, sighing, turned away.

But that was not the end of the matter, for later that day, Dave Jukes and Alfred Meadows came knocking at the millhouse door, threatening Richard with the law if he ever shot at their boys again.

'I suppose you'd been drinking,' Meadows said. 'It's the nearest thing to an excuse I can find for you. But if you ever harm them boys of ours, that'll go hard with you, miller, so don't say you was never warned!'

Richard said nothing in answer to this. He merely shrugged and spread his hands as though it was nothing but a joke. Still, their threat seemed to carry weight with him, and he was more circumspect after that. And the boys, too, less bold than before, kept away from the sluice-gates and contented themselves with hurling stones into the millstream. Richard by now had a bad reputation with the people of Dingham, and although there were some who felt sorry for him, knowing what had caused the change, many gave him a wide berth. He became known as the Mad Miller.

People felt even more sorry for Richard's wife and little son, shut away with a man of such uncertain temper, down at the millhouse beside the river, without the solace of near neighbours. And it was at this time that people remembered the stray dog that had run through the church on the day of the wedding. Plainly, it must have been an omen, they said, and the marriage that had seemed so promising had in fact been ill-fated from the start.

Ellen, whenever she shopped in the village, was aware of receiving pitying glances. She tried to ignore them. She tried to preserve a cheerful manner. But it was not easy and sometimes, when the pity overstepped certain bounds, it became irksome.

'Good morning, Mrs. Lancy, and how are you, my dear, today? How's *Mister* Lancy, the poor man? It's your little boy I think of most, and the three of you down at the mill like that, cut off from the rest of us, all by yourselves. Why, if that was me—'

'We're perfectly well, Mrs. Whitty, thank you. Now if you will kindly look at my list ... I *am* in rather a hurry this morning.'

Ellen's rebuffs were not well received. She soon had an enemy here and there. The habit she formed, of walking quickly through the village, gaze fixed upon the ground, soon called forth a few spiteful remarks.

'She's like her mother, after all, and what with never speaking nor nothing, I'd say her and Lancy is all too well matched. The two of them is best left alone.'

Custom was falling off at the mill because of Richard's strange behaviour, and although he scoffed at the loss of trade, he took such good care of his few remaining customers that they often called him Smarmy Dick. He was always offering to do them favours, and gave them presents of fish he had caught in the river.

Yet he trusted no one. He thought the villagers spied on him, and he put a gate across the footbridge, with an odd assortment of cowbells and sheepbells tied, trailing, along the bottom, so that no villager could approach that way without a loud warning clangour. The Dingham children delighted in this. They would open and close the little gate and, having set the bells jangling, would retreat to the shelter of the blackthorn bushes, where they watched for Richard's suspicious face to appear at the hatch. And often they teased little John about it.

'Why've you got bells on your gate, John? Does your father like the tune? Your dad's a bit touched, ent he, John? He ent quite right in the upper storey?'

'Touched your own-self!' John would say. 'Shut your rattle and get off my tail!'

Throughout that wet and dismal summer he played less and less with the other children, for he could not bear the way they talked about his father and it led to quarrels. He therefore withdrew and when the long holidays came he took to wandering off alone to be rid of them; to find his own refuge in some secret place where he could lie among the reeds and watch the fish in the quiet water.

He was turning in on himself, growing more silent day by day, and Ellen, seeing the change in him, seeing how rarely he smiled or laughed, would leave her housework and follow him, to keep him company on his walks. One day in September, she took a basket and a stick, and they went together to Sanditch Common to pick blackberries.

The day was dull and rather cold. The blackberries were poor withered things for lack of sun to ripen them. But John went from one bramble clump to another, peering into every thicket, hoping to see a stonechat's nest or a whitethroat's, perhaps, and collecting every fallen feather until he had a little bunch to stick in the band of Ellen's hat. And she, seeing some light come into his eyes, gladly gave herself up to him, allowing the day to spin itself out, until he was prattling as of old. Until, for a little while at least, he was a child like any other, fully enjoying childish things.

Then the coming home again, with Richard sitting, tightlipped, drumming with his fingers on the table, waiting for her to give him his tea.

'Where've you been to all this time?'

'We've been to Sanditch, blackberrying. We know how you like a blackberry pie.'

'I've been waiting nearly an hour but that don't mean nothing, I don't suppose, when you and your lambkin go off together?'

'You could at least have laid the table. You knew I'd be back by and by.'

'It's women's work, getting a man his tea,' he said, 'and I don't care to be kept waiting.'

'I'm sorry, Richard, but I never know when you'll finish work.'

Ellen put her basket aside and began laying the table for tea. She motioned John to help her with it and obediently he went to and fro, setting out bread and cheese and pickles, honey and jam and black treacle.

'Seems to me these holidays of yours don't never finish nowadays,' Richard said, taking the tin of treacle from him and planking it down on the table. 'You spend more time at home than you do at school.'

'They had an extension because of the late harvest,' Ellen said, 'but he'll be going back next week.'

'Can't he answer for hisself?'

'I don't think he realized you were asking him a question.'

'He ent very bright, then, that's for sure! Though he's bright enough when it damn well suits him!'

'Richard, please! Not again today! Can't we have just one mealtime in peace, without you swearing and picking a quarrel? Must you spoil a pleasant day?'

'*You* may have had a pleasant day but *I've* been working for twelve hours, breathing mill-dust all day long and slaving my guts out for small thanks!'

Ellen was silent, tilting the kettle on the hob, filling the teapot with scalding water.

'Didn't you hear me?' Richard asked.

'Yes, I heard you, Richard,' she said. 'I'm sorry you've had a bad day.'

She often made herself humble before him. Only thus could she keep the peace. His mood that day was sneering and sullen. The meal was eaten in total silence.

But sullenness was the least of evils. Worse, much worse, were the quick and ungovernable rages that nothing, even her utter humility, could avert or appease. For Richard, worried by poor trade, seemed to find relief only when his feelings had overflowed in some act of violence in the home.

One day at dinner, John left a piece of fat bacon on his plate, and Richard ordered him to eat it up.

'That's good food. I won't have waste in my house. Eat it up or there'll be trouble.'

'It's nasty gristle,' John said. 'I don't like it.'

'Like it or not, you don't leave this table to go to school until I've seen you eat that bacon, so you might as well get on with it.'

'No. I shan't. I don't like it.'

'God in heaven! I've stood enough! I'll teach you to sniff at good clean food that's cost me money I can't afford! You're getting a lesson you won't forget!'

Richard got up and hurried out into the garden and Ellen, watching from the window, saw him stooping among the plants. He returned with three big yellow slugs and flipped them onto John's plate where they uncurled, wet and pudgy, showing their wrinkled underbodies. John recoiled, looking sick. His lips were tightly pressed together. Ellen went forward in disgust and tried to take the plate away but Richard pushed her roughly aside.

65

'Well?' he said, nudging John. 'How would you like to eat *them*?'

John looked away, his face a sickly greenish-white. He leant back, shrinking, in his chair.

'Well?' Richard said, with another nudge. 'I asked you how you'd like to eat *them*!'

'I *wouldn't* like it!' John exclaimed. 'Nobody would! I shan't neither!'

'Well, *I* had to eat em!' Richard said. 'All that time I was in that cellar, *I* had to eat them to stay alive!'

'For pity's sake!' Ellen said. 'Will you stop this or are you completely out of your mind?' She pulled at his arm with all her strength, but again he merely thrust her aside.

'Keep out of this. No son of mine is turning his nose up at good wholesome food. After today, he'll know better!'

He put his hand on the boy's neck and pushed him forward against the table. The three slugs were moving on the plate, leaving glistening trails of slime.

'Are you going to eat what I've brought you, boy?'

'No! I'm not!' John cried shrilly. 'Nor you can't make me, neither, so there!'

And he pressed his lips together again, stubbornly enduring pain as his father's fingers, squeezing his neck, forced him forwards towards the plate.

'Can't make you, by God? We'll see about that! We'll see who's strongest, you or me!'

Richard was enclosed in his own anger. It gave him a look of blind dogged calm. He picked up a slug between his fingers and held it against the boy's mouth.

Ellen went quickly round the table and leant across from the other side. She struck sharply at Richard's hand and the slug fell onto the plate. She snatched up the plate before he could stop her and took it to the open stove. She brushed the slugs off into the fire.

'Richard, you've gone too far today! Do you really expect me to stand by and see my child subjected to this? Take your hands off him at once and try to behave like a normal father!'

66

'*Your* child, did you say? Is he any more yours than he is mine? Yes, come to think of it, maybe he is, seeing you set him against me so much!'

But he loosened his hold on the little boy and watched as he went to stand by his mother, hiding his face against her body and pulling the folds of her skirts about him.

'Ah, that's right! That's touching, that is! Put your arms around him, Nell! Whisper to him how clever he is, defying his father and answering back! Kiss him and make it up to him and tell him he can do as he likes!'

'Do you want him to hate you?' she asked. 'You're going the right way about it if you do.'

'I want him to have a bit of respect and do as he's told once in a while. He's got no right to leave good food.'

'It's no good demanding his respect when your drinking makes you behave like this.'

'Oh, you'll turn it round in the end, I know, and make out that I'm the one to blame! But what about him and the way he provokes me? What about all I went through that time? Have you any idea what it was like?'

'I know how terrible it was. I can see what it's done to you clearly enough. But must you take it out on us?'

'Sixteen days I was in that cellar and every day I said to myself, "My boy John will know where I am. – *He'll* soon tell them where to look." That was the thing that kept me going. I thought of it over and over again. I even used to call to him—'

'Richard, if only you'd see the doctor!' she said. 'He could help you and give you advice.'

'Yes, it suits you to try and make out I'm sick, instead of listening to what I say. But I'm paying no doctor to fuss over me. No doctor can take away the truth and the truth is what I had to live with all the time I was trapped underground.'

'What truth?' Ellen asked.

'That nobody cared if I lived or died!'

'You are indeed sick,' Ellen said. 'The sickness is in your mind, Richard, and it gives you bad thoughts.'

'What'll the doctor do for that? Will a bottle of medicine cure bad thoughts?'

'No, perhaps not, but the brandy bottle only makes them worse.'

'I ent listening to you no more, twisting everything I say. I've got to go out and look for business. I've got to make a living somehow to pay for the food *he* throws away!'

When Richard had gone Ellen spoke to the little boy and unclasped his fingers from her skirts. She knelt before him and dried his tears; straightened his tie and his torn collar; and tried not to notice the marks on his neck. He looked at her and his lip trembled.

'I hate my dad! He's horrible! I wish he was dead!'

'Hush, now. You mustn't say that. It's a very wicked thing to say.'

'It's him that's wicked, not me! When I'm bigger I'll run away!'

'And leave me behind?' Ellen said.

'No,' he said in a small voice, and his face puckered uncertainly.

'I should hope not indeed!' she said briskly. 'What should I do without my son? Who'd stone the raisins for me when I bake a cake?'

'You could come too. We'd go together. We could go to the lock and get on a barge. We could live on the barge like the bargemen do and nobody wouldn't know where we was.'

The little boy reached out to her and put his hands against her breast.

'Shall we, mother? Shall we go? Shall we run away on a barge?'

Ellen, with an effort, managed to laugh. She touched his face with her fingertips.

'We'll have to see!' she said lightly. 'But now it's time you went to school, otherwise you'll get a bad mark. What are the lessons this afternoon? Reading? Counting? Doing sums? Miss Robinson says you're good at sums. Are you learning tables yet? Well; you will be soon, I daresay. Come along, then, and I'll walk with you as far as the gate.'

Alone in the millhouse that afternoon she made herself busy, bottling the last of the apple jelly and drying the last of the garden herbs. Outside, a cold grey mist rose from the river and pressed up close against the windows, squirming as though to gain admittance. Ellen felt herself confined. The mist was a presence, shutting out the light of day. She lit the lamp and turned the living flame up high. She stood arrested, stilled by thought.

A wife's duty was to her husband, for better or for worse, according to her vows, and Richard had need of her, now more than ever. But what of her duty to her son whose bright little spirit, day by day, was being dimmed while she looked on? He was only five years old. He had no defence, no strength but hers. What was her duty to her child?

She asked the question in her prayers, but received no guidance.

Chapter 6

Richard would never admit that he had been drinking, even when the smell of it was strong on his breath. Even when he stumbled, crossing the threshold. Even when it made him sick.

'I don't feel so good today. It's a touch of something on my stomach. I reckon maybe I've got a chill.'

'You know what it is that makes you like this.'

'Do I? Do I?' he exclaimed.

'Yes,' she said, 'we both know.'

He never bought his drink in the village. He dealt with a man in a back street in Runston, and he could say with perfect truth that he never set foot in a public house. Yet although he took care in smuggling his bottles so secretly into the mill, once they were empty he made no further attempt to hide them, but let them accumulate in corners here and there, till Ellen quietly took them away.

Sometimes he stayed in the mill quite late, 'doing the accounts' as he always said, and Ellen, as she lay in bed, listening to the slamming of the mealroom door and his clumsy footsteps on the stairs, could tell at once how bad he was and what his behaviour was likely to be. She would lie very still, her face averted, and try to pretend that she was asleep.

'Funny the way you're always asleep! Always lapped up tight like that, set on keeping yourself to yourself. But you needn't worry! It's no odds to me! I don't want where I know I ent wanted!'

But at other times he would strip the blankets away from her and force her round until she faced him.

'You ent much of a wife lately. Not like you ought to be, loving and kind. D'you think I'm going to beg for you? Why should I beg when you're my wife?'

His strong hands punished her flesh. There was no tenderness in him as there had been in the early days. He used his strength and humbled her. She prayed she would not have another child.

Often, during that autumn and winter, he drove about the countryside, buying and selling all manner of goods. He bought eggs and butter at different farms and sold them in the market at Runston. He bought a few bullocks and fattened them up in the mill yard, feeding them on cheap 'misky' corn which he ground, black and smutty though it was, and mixed with molasses to hide the bad taste. As always, he worked hard. Bad times or not, he would make his way. And as Michael Bullock said to his son, 'Dick Lancy may tip the elbow but he's never so far gone in drink that he can't sniff out a fourpenny piece and damn soon turn it into five pence!'

But one good thing was said of him: he paid every tradesman on the nail. He always grumbled, certainly, and wanted something knocked off 'for cash'; but that was business and why not?

'You may not be doing well these days,' Rissington said, selling him butter, 'but at least you never ask for credit and that makes you one all on your own.'

'Who says I ent doing well?'

'I meant the mill,' Rissington said. 'How much do you grind? One day a month? Maybe two? It surely ent more, from what I hear.'

'You shouldn't believe the tales folk tell. A good miller has always got trade. I'm miller first and general dealer afterwards, and don't you make any mistake about it!'

That the mill should so often be standing idle was a thing that hurt Richard through and through, and Henry Rissington's remark weighed heavily on his mind.

'I know what they're likely saying, Nell. They're saying it's gone back to what it was, that I've done no better than my dad who muddled all his business away and let the mill go down and down. But it ent true, you know. I ent like my dad. It's just their spite.'

'It's been a bad year,' Ellen said. 'Things will improve, given time.'

They were together in the mill. She was helping to mend torn sacks. They sat on two big bags of bran where the light was best, at the south window, each of them busy with bodkin and twine. Richard for once was talking to her in the old way, quietly, in a friendly tone, and his sadness as he looked round the mill, swept and garnered but oh! so bare, brought them together in sympathy for the first time in almost a year.

'Just look at it!' he said. 'I built up such trade in this here mill. Now it's all gone down again. But it ent my fault, is it, Nell? It ent my fault it's all gone down?'

'No, Richard, it's not your fault. And next summer, God willing, the harvest will be a better one and you'll be as busy as you were before.'

She leant across and took his hand, and he looked at her for a long while, with something of the old warmth and with a gleam of cheerfulness too.

'You're right,' he said. 'I ent finished yet and they needn't think it. Rissington shall eat his words. Just cos *he's* got no corn for me to grind he seems to think I'm out of business. But I'll soon make him change his tune, and all the other gossips too!'

Early next morning, the waterwheel began to turn, swish and clack, swish and clack, splashing water in an arc. Ellen, astonished, went into the mill. No corn had come as far as she knew. She asked Richard what he was doing.

'Never you mind!' he said gruffly. 'You attend to your own work and leave me to attend to mine.'

He had put the two pairs of stones out of gear and was letting the waterwheel run by itself. He would not have it said that he was a miller without any trade, and anybody passing by would soon know better and spread the word.

Two or three times a week after that he opened the sluices and worked the wheel, and if anyone passed the open hatch he would make sure that he was seen, wheeling the sack-barrow, fully laden, or working the chain-hoist to the loft.

'You seem pretty busy this morning, Dick?'

'Busy enough!' Richard would say.

And if somebody, putting his head inside, listened for the rumbling of the stones and remarked on its absence, Richard had his answer ready.

'I'm just about finished for today. I'm on my way out to see to the sluices.'

It was not believed for long. Soon it became a village joke. 'The miller's milling air again. He'll soon have enough to fill a sack!'

Early in November John was ill with whooping cough and Ellen wanted to fetch Dr. Reed. Richard said she was making a fuss. She had only to keep the boy in bed and let the fever take its course.

'All children get whooping cough. It's one of them things that go through the school. It's up to you to nurse him through it.'

But Ellen was worried. The boy's face and body burnt with a terrible throbbing heat, and yet he complained of feeling cold. His throat was so sore he could hardly speak. The soreness brought the tears to his eyes, and sometimes he whimpered wearily, mouth open, in distress. Ellen kept him as warm as she could with plenty of blankets and a stone hot water bottle wrapped in flannel. She fed him on gruel and chicken broth. On the third day, seeing that he was just the same, she fetched the doctor.

The old man examined John and even managed to make him smile by the way he twitched his bushy eyebrows when listening with his stethoscope. He left a bottle of medicine to bring down the fever and some 'drops' that would help the boy to sleep.

'Go on nursing him as before and give him warm milk with honey in it. Try to get him to eat if you can. Custards, you know, and things of that sort. I'll call again in a couple of days.'

Richard was out when the doctor came, but returned in time to see him drive off.

'So you went against me as usual? You called him in behind my back!'

'Yes,' Ellen said, 'and any mother would do the same.'

'You'll be sorry for doing that.'

'No, I don't think so, Richard,' she said.

'Yes, you'll be sorry,' he said again. 'You mark my words.'

His behaviour daily grew more strange. He never went up to see his son. He never even asked how he was. And the sight of Ellen preparing egg custard or arrowroot produced such irritation in him that he would stride about the room, flinging open cupboards and drawers until she was forced to take notice and ask what he was looking for.

'It won't interest you, will it?' he would say. 'You're much to full of your lambkin up there, waiting on him hand and foot! He's making a fool out of you, you know, and you'll never be able to do nothing with him after all this cosseting. You'll have spoilt him rotten and *I'm* the one that'll have to put it right!'

At the end of a week the worst of John's fever was over, and on the ninth day he was allowed up for a while, to sit in a chair beside the fire. Dr. Reed came in to see him and brought him a monkey-on-a-stick. He advised Ellen to take care of him and keep him away from school for a month.

'Keep him occupied,' he said, 'but gently so, for it's pulled him down.'

Richard, coming in from the mill later, stood on the hearth with his back to the fire and looked at his son.

'So you're up, then, I see! I thought you was stopping in bed for good. Have you had your curds and whey? Has your mother made you comfy? Sweets to suck and liquorice to chew? I shouldn't like you to go without!'

John, still weak and shivery, sat, very small, and said nothing. His father's tall presence beside him made him cower in his chair. His fingers plucked at the fringe on his rug.

'Why do you flinch like that?' Richard said. 'Have I ever raised my hand to you? Have I ever cuffed you or tanned your hide?' And to Ellen he said irritably: 'What's the matter with the boy? Why don't he never speak to me?'

'It hurts him to talk. It makes him tired.'

'He talks to you, though, right enough. I heard him at it when I came in. But he's never got nothing to say to me. It's like as though I wasn't there.'

The attention she gave the little boy was maddening to Richard. He jeered and scoffed repeatedly and said she was making a fool of herself, allowing the child to run her around. And although she tried to be unobtrusive, performing most of her ministrations in his absence, he always noticed everything. If John had been given a change of clothes; if his chair had been moved close to the window; or if he was sucking a cough lozenge; Richard was sure to have something to say. And the more sarcastic he became, the more the boy shrank into himself as though deaf and dumb. Richard found fault with everything. The dumbness, he said, was insolence, and the boy's coughing got on his nerves.

'Cough-cough-cough! God in heaven! How much more? He only does it to see me vexed!'

Often, Ellen's own temper was in danger of breaking out, so extreme was the provocation, but when she looked into Richard's face and remembered him as he had once been, she found new patience and remained calm. She thought of his sufferings, trapped underground for sixteen days, drinking foul water, breathing foul air, unable to sleep because of the cold and for fear of drowning.

The effort of will that had kept him alive had cost him dear. He was a man who had lost his soul, as though he had given it in exchange for his life. There were dark places in his mind and dark fancies had taken root there. He sought escape in the brandy bottle and made matters worse, and his eyes at these times had the shifting shadows of madness in them.

Ellen felt she could have helped him, but any tenderness made him suspicious, and whenever she tried to talk things out he almost always flew into a rage. Once he overturned the table and hurled her work-basket into the fire. Once he took the dress she was mending and tore the bodice from the skirt. 'Now you've really got something to mend, ent you?' he said, and walked out, slamming the door.

She hated this stranger that she and her son were obliged to live with. But always she remembered the man he had been and prayed that some miracle would restore him to her.

John recovered eventually and went back to school, but two weeks later he was at home again for the Christmas holiday.

'Seems it's all holidays for you!' Richard said. 'I shall have to find you something to do.'

When the doctor sent his bill, Richard dropped it in Ellen's lap.

'You can pay that.'

'How can I?'

'I dunno how. That's up to you. I said you'd be sorry for calling him in.'

'Very well,' Ellen said.

She went to Rainborough the next day and sold the cameo brooch that her Uncle John had given her on her eighteenth birthday. When she had paid the doctor's bill she still had fourteen shillings left, and she put the money into a jug on the top shelf of the dresser.

'Well?' Richard said at suppertime. 'Did you pay the doctor's bill?'

'Yes, I called at his house.'

'Where did you get the money from? Out of the week's housekeeping?'

'That goes nowhere. You should know that. I had to sell my cameo brooch.'

'You'll have had a bit left over, then.'

'Yes. I thought it would buy some extras for Christmas.'

But when she went to the jug again her money was gone, and when she spoke to Richard about it he merely shrugged.

'It came in handy, that fourteen shillings. Say I borrowed it as a loan. I'll pay it back when business gets better, though when that'll be it's hard to say.'

Whereas in the past he had wanted the best for his wife and son, now he grudged every penny she spent. John's clothes had to be turned, and his boots had to be bought second-hand. Even food was difficult, for Richard grumbled at the amount of flour she used and doled it out to her, so much a week, never allowing her into the mealroom. He gave her no extra money for Christmas and if Jerry Trussler had not called as always, bringing a twelve-pound goose, they would have had no Christmas dinner.

'I've got no money for extras,' Richard said. 'This has been a bad old year. You must manage as best you can.'

'You've got money to spend on brandy,' she said, 'but none to buy your son a present.'

'The boy is spoilt enough already. He's getting too full of hisself by half.'

Christmas that year was the saddest Ellen had ever known. There was no softening in Richard's manner; no show of cheerfulness for the child's sake, nothing to set the day apart except what she herself could contrive. Richard went to the mill as usual and spent the morning tarring the luccomb. He was up at the top of a ladder when a few people from Water Lane passed on their way to the church in Dingham.

'Don't you know what day it is, Mr. Lancy?'

'Yes, it's Thursday!' Richard said.

Ellen, in the kitchen, cooking dinner, gave John little tasks to do and tried to create a festive feeling. She got him to climb on a high stool and hang sprigs of holly on the beams. She gave him the apples to peel for sauce. She allowed him to baste the roasting goose, growing brown and crisp-skinned in the oven of the range. He was happy enough in his quiet way, until his father came in to dinner.

Richard as usual had little to say. When he did speak, it was only to grumble at the church bells, ringing in Dingham and Sutton Crabtree and three miles away in the abbey at Rainborough.

'They've been at it all the morning and that's a noise I can't abide. Dothering, dothering, in my head, all the time I was up that ladder. The ringers must want something to do!'

'It *is* Christmas, after all.'

'D'you think I don't know?'

Ellen, talking cheerfully, remarked on the tenderness of the goose.

'Aren't we lucky,' she said to John, 'that Mr. Trussler should be so kind, giving us a goose at Christmas time?'

'Kind? Why kind?' Richard said. 'I reckon he owes me something, don't he, seeing I gave him one of my donkeys to carry on his smelly trade?'

That afternoon, when Richard had shut himself in the mill, Ellen and John sat in the kitchen and roasted chestnuts at the fire. The nuts were small. She had picked them up in the woods at Spinnam. When they popped open and flew out into the hearth, John laughed and clapped his hands. But then, suddenly, even as he laughed, his small face crumpled and he was in tears. Sobs shook him. He bowed his head. Ellen took him in her arms.

'Don't cry, don't cry,' she said to him. 'Why, I was going to sing some carols! Favourites of yours, like "The First Nowell", and I shall need you to tell me the words. What about "I Saw Two Ships"? You know how I get in a muddle with that. How can I sing it without your help?'

'*Three* ships,' he said, drawing back to frown at her.

'Three? Are you sure?' And she wiped his eyes. 'I do believe you're right,' she said. 'But where were they sailing to, those three ships?'

'Everybody knows that!'

'I suppose they were sailing to Sutton Crabtree.'

'Silly!' he said. 'It was Bethlehem.'

'There! I told you I always got in a muddle. What a good thing it is that you know the words.'

But although she could comfort him in the end, and even bring back the laughter again, secretly she was afraid. What of next Christmas? she asked herself. What would their lives be like by then?

After Christmas, the weather worsened. 1880 came in cold. There were several days of hard frost. One morning, when Richard had some beans to grind, the waterwheel was frozen up. He laid a plank from the footbridge to the wheel, resting it on the edge of a paddle, and went across with a big kettle of boiling water, to thaw the ice surrounding the axle. But the axle, frozen, had warped a little, and the waterwheel, after less than a quarter turn, caught against the mill wall. Richard, swearing angrily, put the plank across again and set to work with hammer and chisel.

It was not easy for him to reach from the plank, and he was about to climb up the wheel when he saw John watching him from the garden.

'Ent you got nothing better to do than stand there gawping at me?' he said. But when the boy would have turned away, Richard called him back again. 'Come round here. You can give me a hand. You're a lot smaller and lighter than me. This here job is just right for you.'

Half an hour later, Ellen, going in search of John, found him crouched on the waterwheel, struggling with hammer and cold chisel, chipping at the brickwork of the wall where the rim of the wheel had caught against it. Richard, on the plank, was peering between the wheel and the wall, shouting instructions, but the little boy, his hands blue with cold, could scarcely lift the heavy tools and more often than not the blows of the hammer went astray.

'Lord Almighty!' Richard said. 'Can't you do no better than that? Get the chisel against that brick and keep tapping until it chips.'

'I can't!' John said, with a little sob. 'I can't do it! It's too hard. I shall drop the hammer in a minute.'

'You do, that's all, and see what happens!'

Ellen ran forward onto the bridge and cried out to Richard to bring the boy down. He glanced at her over his shoulder and muttered something under his breath. Then he turned to the boy again and put up his arms.

'You may as well come down, I suppose, for all the use you are up there! Come on, come on, I ent got all day. You'll have to come down further'n that or I can't reach you.'

Inch by inch, the boy moved towards him. Crouched as he was on the ice-covered paddles, he was terrified that the wheel would move and that he would be borne down into the stream, where the swift white water ran full pelt. He was paralysed with cold. His fingers were stiffened, twisted like claws, clutching the heavy hammer and chisel.

Richard took hold of him, under the armpits, and carried him back along the plank. He swung him over the rail of the bridge, into Ellen's waiting arms.

'Here, take your chilver, he's no use to me! I'll have to do the job myself.' He snatched the tools from John's hands and turned towards the waterwheel. 'He don't even try to help me, that boy. All he does is snivel and cry.'

'He might have been drowned!' Ellen exclaimed, pressing the child against her body. 'Supposing the wheel had begun to turn? Have you got no sense at all?'

'The wheel wouldn't shift as fast as that. If it had I'd have tumbled in myself.'

'That boy is frozen through to the bone. Have you no feeling left for him? Can't you see him suffering?'

'Then get him into the house, woman, instead of standing there ranting at me! And take that empty kettle with you. I've finished with it for today.'

Ellen left him and went indoors. She put John to sit in a chair by the stove and wrapped her shawl around his shoulders. Now and then a shiver shook him, but he was quite silent and sat in a trance, staring into the heart of the fire. When she spoke he seemed not to hear her. His face was shuttered, unreadable, the eyelids drooping, hiding the eyes, the lashes shadowing the pallid cheeks. He was shut up inside himself. Even she could not reach him.

Richard got the waterwheel turning at last and all that afternoon he was grinding bean-meal. But the day was full of accidents and his mood grew blacker with each delay. He was using a runner stone that was very old, worn to a mere two inches, and during the day it split across with a loud crack. He lost two hours putting on a new stone. Then the pulley in the loft became jammed, putting the sack-hoist out of use, and when he went up to see to it he found that the rafter had given way, eaten by worm, which meant another hour's work.

He did not come in for his midday dinner, nor for his supper at five o'clock, and Ellen, worrying about him, went into the mill with a plate of bread and cheese and pickle.

'You ought to eat. You'll make yourself ill, working so hard in this cold weather without proper food inside you. You can surely find time for bread and cheese.'

'No, I don't want it. Take it away.' He was weighing sacks of meal. He spoke to her without looking up. 'And don't come pestering me again.'

'Perhaps if I were to leave it here—'

'Damn you!' he said, swinging round. 'Didn't you hear what I said to you?' And he struck the plate out of her hand, so it fell to the floor and smashed. 'Get out of my mill and leave me in peace! I'll *tell* you when I want to eat!'

'Very well,' Ellen said, stooping to pick up the scattered food. 'I only hope you won't drink tonight, that's all. In your present mood, and not eating, God knows what it will do to you.'

Richard picked up a ten-pound weight and raised it in his hand as high as his shoulder. He took a sudden step towards her.

'Are you going or not?' he said.

'Yes, I'm going,' she said quietly, and looked at him with

81

steady eyes. 'But I won't be threatened, Richard, even by you. Let it be understood between us.'

'Won't?' he said, not meeting her gaze. 'That's your favourite word, seems to me! I get it twenty times a day!' But he turned back to the weighing-machine and lowered the weight onto the ledge. 'Just get out, that's all,' he said. 'Just get out and leave me be.'

Ellen went back into the house. She had not been afraid of him, rounding on her with the upraised weight. She had never for an instant felt herself to be in danger because something of the past remained between them and in facing him she had made him ashamed. Yet now she was trembling. Now she was very close to tears. For the violence was there, in his mind. She had seen it, ugly, in his eyes, and had sensed how destructive it could be.

She put John to bed early that night and sat with him until he slept. She herself stayed up till ten. Richard was still shut in the mill when she went to bed. She left his supper on the table.

She was wakened by the slamming of the back kitchen door, and as she lay, listening, she heard him being sick in the yard. Then the door slammed again, shaking the house, and after a while he came stumbling up the stairs and into the bedroom. He set his candle on the chest by the bed. Ellen lay with her face to the wall.

'Are you awake?' he said, touching her.

'I couldn't be anything else but awake, after the noise you've been making downstairs. Did you eat the supper I left for you?'

'I hadn't the stomach for it, Nell. It's too late for eating. It's past one o'clock.' He sat on the bed with his face in his hands. 'Nell, I feel wretched. I reckon I'm ill.'

'I'm sorry to hear it,' Ellen said.

'Ah, I know, you *sound* sorry.'

'You know what it is that makes you ill. The cure is easy. It's in your own hands.'

'I dunno what you're on about. I've been doing my accounts.'

He took off his boots and threw them into a far corner. He stood up and undressed and slung his clothes over the bedpost. He blew out the candle and got into bed.

His breath on her face was hot and sour, smelling of vomit, and she moved away from him even further, seeking the coolness of her pillow. His hands thrust their way to the front of her body and worked at her breasts with ungentle fingers until, in some pain, she fought against him.

'Richard, please, I beg of you! Leave me alone. I'm very tired.'

'You're always tired! It's just an excuse. What about thinking of me for a change? You never want me nowadays.'

'How can I want you when you come to me in this condition? Have you no pride in yourself any more? Can't you see what's happening to you?'

'*Will* you turn round to me?' he said. 'Or must I make you?'

He clutched at her nightdress and dragged it up over her stomach. His hands went roughly down to her thighs, thrusting against the tender flesh, into the secret parts of her body.

'No!' she said, and struggled against him. 'No, I will not, and you shall not make me!'

'Won't? Won't? That's all I hear! You go against me the whole time! But who's the strongest of us two? Who's in the right of it, you or me?'

'You're drunk and disgusting,' Ellen said, 'and you make me hate you, behaving like this.'

'Drunk, am I? Is that your excuse?'

'Yes! You are! Your breath is loathsome!'

'Then get out!' he said, and began pushing her out of the bed. 'If I'm so disgusting to you, woman, you can damn well get out and sleep elsewhere! Why should I let you share my bed? What do you do to earn the right to be called my wife? Nothing whatever, so just get out!'

His knees were in the small of her back. His hands were pressing against her shoulders, pushing her over the edge of the bed.

'Are you getting out of here? – Are you?' he said. 'You'll be sorry if you don't!' He brought up his feet and kicked at her spine. 'Are you getting out, then?'

'Yes,' Ellen said, 'I'm getting out.'

She slid from the bed and stood for a moment shivering. In the dark, she could not find her slippers. The floorboards were cold under her feet. She went to the door and took her knitted shawl from the hook. She drew it over her head and shoulders. Her hand was on the sneck of the door when Richard lumbered out of bed. He snatched at the shawl and pulled it off her and as she moved to go out of the door he took hold of her nightdress at the throat and tore it down from top to bottom. Ellen stumbled and the door swung open against the wash-stand. The pitcher and basin fell with a crash, and water flooded over the floor, wetting her feet.

The noise woke John in the room next door. He came out onto the landing, peering fearfully round the rail. Ellen went to him at once. She felt him trembling, close against her, as she led him back towards his room. Richard moved suddenly and blocked the way. His face, seen dimly in the starlight, had an ugly intentness. He was breathing heavily through his nose.

'Where d'you think you're going?'

'I'm taking John back to bed. I shall sleep the rest of the night with him.'

'Oh no you won't!' Richard said. 'I shall decide where you sleep tonight!' He was pushing her towards the stairs.

'Don't you dare hurt my mother!' John cried in a shrill voice. 'Let go of her! Just leave her be!'

'Down you go, you and him both!' Richard shouted. 'I've had as much as I can take!' And he pushed them in front of him, down the stairs. 'Go on, get a move on, I've had enough! I'll show you who's master in this house!'

On reaching the kitchen, he unbolted the outer door

and flung it open. Outside, beyond the porch, the night was still cold, the sky splintered with frost-bright stars above an earth steeped in silence and darkness.

'What are you doing?' Ellen asked. 'Would you put us out?'

'I said you'd be sorry, going against me all the time! Now you'll see that I meant every word!'

'Are you insane?' she exclaimed. 'On a winter's night? Do you mean to kill us?'

'It was you that chose to leave my bed! You can damn well leave my house altogether!'

'You can't do such a thing to us!'

'We'll see about that! Oh, yes, we shall see!'

Roughly, he pushed them towards the door, where the frosty night awaited them, reaching for them with cold embrace. Ellen resisted and little John, throwing himself against his father, struck at him with both fists.

'Surely you'll let us put on some clothes?'

'Clothes I paid for? No, I will not! You can think yourself lucky you ent stripped bare!'

'For God's sake, Richard, listen to me! Doesn't it mean *anything* that you and I are man and wife? It's only since you had that bad time—'

'You're no wife to me!' Richard said. 'Setting yourself and the boy above me! Going against me at every turn! I've had more than I can stand and we'll damn well see how you get on without me! Go on, get out, I've had enough!'

He was indeed mad, Ellen thought, and she knew she ought to pity him. But as he thrust them out of the house and she heard him bolting the door against them, she felt only hatred and bitterness and knew she would never be able to forgive him. Her hands went up, two puny fists, knocking helplessly at the door, and she shouted to him through her angry tears.

'We shall never come back to you after this! Richard, do you hear what I say? We shall never come back to you! Never! I swear!'

There was no answer. The millhouse was silent as the grave. She stooped and lifted John to her naked breast, settling him there, inside her nightdress, wrapping the two torn halves around him. She sheltered him as best she could, her arms completely encircling his shoulders, and he in turn, with his arms round her neck and his legs gripping tightly round her waist, gave his warmth to the front of her body.

Underneath her naked feet the frost was sticky, so that with every step she took, each foot was released with stinging reluctance. The cold struck upwards into her legs, tightening the muscles and twisting them, till the pain of cramp was almost more than she could bear. Her body, too, was clenched tight, the flesh cringing upon the bones, and as she walked she moved the upper part of herself from side to side, with a swaying motion, inside her nightdress, thus creating a rub of warmth as the coarse flannel moved on her skin. But the cold was killing. Her face and skull were splitting with it. She began to feel light-headed.

Inside her nightdress, her child was a close-clinging burden upon her, taking warmth from her breast and giving it back as he stirred against her.

'Mother?' he said, murmuring. 'Where are we going?'

'We're going to the village. Another few yards and we shall be in the main street.'

'What'll we do there? Where shall we go?'

'I'm hoping we'll find a place to shelter.'

'In somebody's house? Will they take us in?'

'Hush, now,' she whispered to him. 'Hush, now, there's a good boy. I'm trying to think.'

But the truth was that she knew no better than he what would become of them that night. She was drawn to the village because it was her only hope; because she and her child would surely perish unless they found shelter from the cold. Yet now that she was here, among the houses, their silence and darkness terrified her, for what would the people sleeping behind those doors and windows say to her if she roused them up? What claim had she on their goodwill? What had she ever said or done to win their friendship?

Had there but been a single light burning in one of those cottages, it might have been easy. A light would have been a sign to her that God, through some wakeful villager, was stretching out a merciful hand. But the houses slept, hunched up black against the stars, silent as death in the bitter cold, their doors and windows sealed in darkness. And she walked on, with the unthinking obstinacy of despair, tightening her arms about her child.

'Mother?' he said, against her throat. 'Shall we get there soon? Somewhere indoors? I don't like it out in the cold.'

'Just a little way on,' she said to him. 'Not much further. We'll soon find a place.'

'What place? What place? It's a long way.'

'Try to be brave,' she said, pressing her face into his hair. 'Try to be brave, for my sake.'

The road was now running steeply downhill, turning a little towards the left, and in another hundred yards or so she came out onto the green, where stood a curving row of cottages, the church, the smithy, the shop, the inn. This was the last of Dingham village. Beyond the green lay open country. Ellen knew she could go no further.

Chapter 7

Will Gale, the blacksmith, had been drinking with friends in Sutton Crabtree. It was no new thing for him to be coming home in the small hours. Nor was it strange that he should loiter on the green. For he was a man who, much as he loved company, especially when the drink was flowing, could still enjoy these late hushed moments of the night, when he and the shadowy gliding owl had the darkness to themselves.

His little cottage, adjoining the smithy, was merely a place where he ate and slept. No one but he had crossed its threshold since his parents had died in 1870, and the place was nothing but a shell. The smithy, of course, was a different matter. He brought it to life at six o'clock every morning when he lit his fire in the forge, and all day long it rang and resounded with the noise of work and the comings and goings of horses and men. But the cottage was nothing. He could never bring that to life. And he always delayed going in, for out of doors on a fine night there was at least the company of stars.

Looking across the open green he smiled to himself, because fancy tonight was playing him tricks.

'Dammit!' he said. 'I surely can't be as drunk as that! What did Lovell put in my ale?'

There was a movement. A pale figure. A woman, white-clad, crossing the green, vanishing into Draycott's cartshed.

'Lumme!' he said. 'I must look into this! There's something funny happening here.'

The cartshed was open along the front, its roof

supported on four pillars. At the back of the shed, behind the carts, lay a tumbled litter of hay and straw, and Ellen was on her knees among it, trying to pile it up in a bed that would give some protection to herself and her child. When she heard heavy footsteps crunching the frosty track outside, she swung around with a little cry, covering herself with her torn nightdress and pressing John closer still. Will, a dark shape against the sky, stood with one arm about a pillar, peering in between the carts. He could see her kneeling among the straw. He gave a little tipsy laugh.

'What the devil! It *is* a woman. My luck has changed and no mistake! No need to be frightened, whoever you are! It's only Will Gale from the smithy there. I daresay you know me well enough?'

Yes, Ellen thought, she knew him all right. Fate had sent her another drunkard.

'Why don't you speak?' Will demanded. 'Who the hell are you, poking about in there, and what are you up to at this time of night?'

Swaying a little he stepped inside. He struck a match and held it before her and in its brief yellow flare he recognized her and saw her plight.

'Why, it's Mrs. Lancy and her boy! Whatever's happened to you, my dear, to bring you out in such a fashion? What're you doing scrabbling in there?'

'There was an upset,' Ellen said, but it was some time before she was able to speak again. She was in the grip of a terrible rigor. Only by keeping her teeth tight-clenched could she still the spasms that shuddered through her. 'There was an upset. With my husband.'

'You mean you're running away from him?'

'Yes. No. He turned us out.'

'Turned you out? In this bitter weather? Without no proper clothes on nor nothing? Why, bless my soul. That's murder, that is! It's the wickedest thing I ever heard. You can't stop here. You must come home with me.'

He took off his jacket and put it on her, drawing it round

till it wrapped both her and the child in her arms. He turned up the collar behind her neck and fastened the buttons down the front, and the warmth of it, after the flaying cold, made her shrink as though she would swoon.

'Steady a minute,' Will said, and his voice seemed to come from a great distance. 'Steady a minute, I'll give you a hand. You can't move. The cold has got you. Just leave it to me, I'll soon get you home.'

It was true, she could not move. Her legs were paralysed with the cold. She could not have raised herself from the straw. But Will bent over her and the child and lifted them into his strong arms. The night's events had sobered him. He managed a perfectly steady course across the green to the smithy cottage. And there, in the kitchen, he wrapped them in a cocoon of blankets and sat them in a chair by the hearth. He then lit a fire in the old iron range and gradually, as the light spread, she saw that John was watching darkly, his eyes just visible above the enveloping folds of the blankets.

'It's all right,' she whispered. 'It's Will Gale, the smith. He's taken us in, out of the cold. We shall be safe enough here for the night. We'll be all right, John. We'll be all right.'

Whispering thus to the child at her breast, she felt hot tears begin to fall, and, being too weak to brush them away, she bent her face to the rough blankets. Will saw, but said nothing. He made himself busy at the stove. Soon he had milk growing hot in a pan. He poured it into two mugs and gave it to them, and all the time, while they drank, he kept heaping wood onto the fire, till it filled the stove and roared up the chimney. He took the empty mugs away and sat in the chair opposite. He began talking.

'I thought you must be a ghost at first, when I saw you out there on the green. And you would've been, too, if you'd been left in the freeezing cold! – You'd both've been ghosts by morning for sure! What does Lancy think he's up to, turning you out on such a night? You may have quarrelled, you and him, but there's *nothing* excuses his doing that. Why, you and your boy there, you would've died!'

He leant forward across the hearth and lifted her feet, wrapped in the blankets, onto the step of the brass-topped fender. He threw a lump of coal on the fire and sat back again, wiping his hand on his corduroys.

'Mind you,' he said, 'you don't have to tell me about it if you don't want to.' Looking at her, he scratched his jaw. 'What happens between a man and his wife is a private matter, certainly, and it's nothing to do with the likes of me. But a man who can do a thing like that—! Why, if you and your boy had died of cold, he'd have found hisself on the end of a rope. But you don't have to tell me about it if you don't want to. I shan't press you. I'll hold my tongue.'

'There was a quarrel,' Ellen said. 'I can't really say more than that.' With the heat of the fire bringing her body to life again, she was full of pain. The waves of warmth ebbed and flowed in her blood and every so often, drowningly, she felt her senses slipping away. She looked at Will with eyes that ached. 'There was a quarrel. That's all.'

'Is it likely to mend itself?'

'No, no. It's past mending.'

'I should damn well think so too! A man that can do a thing like that—! Is he all right, the little boy? He ent said a word since he came in. Seems he don't think much of me. I reckon he's wondering who I am.'

'He's all right. He knows who you are.'

'Not surprising he's quiet, is it, after what he's been through tonight? Of course, I know Dick Lancy ent quite right, since his accident that time, but for him to do a thing like that—'

'Perhaps, if you'll let us, we can sleep by the fire here, and tomorrow I'll think what I must do next.'

'Stop by the fire? What, sleep in that chair? You'd be a lot better sharing my bed.'

'I'd rather stay here,' Ellen said.

'Lumme!' he said. 'I didn't mean share in that sort of way. I meant you and him. You two together can have my bed and I'll have the room above the smithy.' Pausing, he gave a little laugh, then passed a hand across his face as though to wipe the laugh away. 'Share!' he exclaimed. 'What a thing to say! As though my luck would change like that—' He broke off again, scowling fiercely, and stooped to throw more coal on the fire. 'You don't want to take no notice of me. It's just the way I talk, that's all. It don't mean a thing. Just close your ears.'

For a while he was silent, his big broad face, black-jawed, black-browed, resting on the knuckles of his fist. Then he leant forward across the hearth and laid his hand on Ellen's knee.

'I shan't take advantage. You needn't think that. I'm a rough sort of chap, the way I talk, but I wouldn't harm you or try nothing on.'

'If you did I should kill you,' Ellen said, and her voice, though quiet, was so full of angry vehemence that Will recoiled, withdrawing his hand. 'If you did I should kill you,' she said again.

'Ah!' he said, staring at her. 'Then I can't say I haven't been warned, can I?' And after a little while he said: 'Well, if you're going to stop here by the fire, I must stop with you, that's all!'

'I'd sooner you left us by ourselves.'

'I'm stopping here, to keep up the fire. It wouldn't do for you and your boy to get yourselves chilled again, twice in one night. Are you comfy, you and him? Warm enough in them there rugs? Then just you lie back and go to sleep and don't worry about nothing else. I shall look after you. Bible oath!'

So Ellen lay back in the Windsor chair, her head against the hanging cushion. John, on her lap, was almost asleep, lying perfectly still at her breast, wrapped with her in the warm blankets. And after a while, with the heat of the fire stinging her eyelids, she also slept, slipping into a midway world where, although exhaustion sucked her down into a whirling pool of darkness, she was at the same time always aware of the leaping, living fire in the stove and of Will Gale reaching out now and then, moving quietly, feeding the flames.

Something happened to Will that night, watching over the woman and child. Something touched him and changed his life. For these two, through their sleeping faces, became so intimately known to him that they took possession of his mind. He was only a young man, but he had no wife or family, no relations in the world. This cottage of his was nothing to him. Just a place where he ate and slept. He was rather a lonely man, once he closed the door. But by the end of his vigil that night, guarding the sleep of this mother and child, he felt the place belonged to them. He couldn't imagine it empty again. Everything he had was theirs, and they in turn belonged to him. Their two lives were in his keeping.

They, of course, having been asleep, did not share his feeling of intimacy, and in the morning when they awoke he was still a stranger to them, or at least a man they hardly knew. When he made hot porridge for them, they took it shyly, as though in his debt. They did not know, as he knew, that their lives and his were already linked.

Having given them breakfast and eaten his own, he brought a big stoneware bowl to the table and filled it with steaming hot water for them to wash. He put out a scrubbing brush and soap and hung a towel to warm at the fire. He also brought a great pile of clothes – corduroys, waistcoats, stockings, shirts – and a workbasket full of needles and threads.

'I ent got no women's clothes. Nor no clothes for boys neither. But if you're handy with your needle, you can maybe cobble up the things you need, just to make do for the time being.'

'Yes. Thank you. You're very kind.'

'What do you aim to do, after?'

'I think I must go to Cheltenham. I'm hoping I might find work there and some sort of lodging for John and me.'

'It's twenty miles to Cheltenham. You can't walk there without good shoes. You'd better stop here a day or two and then maybe I can get you fixed up.'

93

'I've got no money to buy shoes.'

'Then I shall have to lend you some.'

'I don't want my husband to find me here.'

'Then it's up to you to lie low. Keep as quiet as you can and if anyone knocks don't answer to them. The front door is bolted so you're perfectly safe. There's the back door into the smithy, of course, and I shall come in and out that way, but nobody else ent likely to and they can't anyhow without they pass me.'

Will put his hand on John's head and ruffled his hair in a teasing way.

'How about you, young fella?' he said. 'Can you keep quiet as a mouse so's nobody knows you're here at all? Of course you can! I'd no need to ask. You're the quietest chap I've ever seen.'

'John will be quiet enough,' Ellen said, 'but what if something is said in the smithy?'

'I shan't let on. No lections of that. But now I must go and open up. I'm late already. Just look at that clock.'

Before leaving he showed her the larder, telling her she must help herself.

'I take my dinner at The Old Tap. Archie Shaw gives me bread and cheese. I'd better go on as usual, otherwise it'll cause a stir, so you stay snug and warm in here and see that you eat to keep up your strength.'

Will went through into the smithy and opened up the outer door. His helper, Jim Pacey, was on the step.

'You're slow off the mark this morning, Will. You been making a night of it, drinking with Lovell at Sutton Crabtree?'

'Been sleeping it off,' Will agreed. 'It's a good house, The Post Horses. They don't sling you out till you've had enough.'

All through the greater part of that day, although many people came to the smithy, nothing was said about Ellen Lancy. Nor was she mentioned at The Old Tap. But towards the evening, about half past six, Ted Gore the carrier drew up outside, delivering a load of iron, and when Will went out with Jim Pacey, Ted had a small knot of people around him.

'The Mad Miller's been after me, asking me if I've seen his missus. Seems she's gone off with their boy in the night and nobody knows where she might've got to.'

'Gone off?' said Will. 'What, Mrs. Lancy? Good gracious me!' He began unloading the bars of iron, flinging them down on the frosty ground. 'Why should she have done that?'

'According to Lancy, she ent only left him high and dry, but she's took all his money and left him broke.'

'She won't get far, then,' said Billy Jukes, 'if she's carrying all the miller's money!'

'Supposing there's somebody with her, though? Some other chap that she's gone off with?'

'Why, is somebody else missing from Dingham?'

'Not that I know of, but it might be a chap from some other district.'

'On the other hand,' Will said, 'he might not exist.'

'She surely wouldn't go off alone?'

'I can't see her with another man. Not Mrs. Lancy. She ent the sort.'

'They're often the worst, them quiet ones. They're often the ones that give us a shock.'

'Are they, Ted?' said Simon Shaw. 'You seem to know a lot about it. How many shocks've you had that way?'

'I don't know nothing about the woman, save what Lancy hisself was saying, down at Pex Bridge a while ago.'

'Then if I was you,' said Alfred Meadows, 'I'd take it with a pinch of salt.'

When Gore had gone and all the iron was stowed away, Will began clearing up in the smithy. Pacey watched him cleaning his tools.

'You're stopping early today, ent you? What about old Temple's drill?'

'He can't sow seed in this weather. Any time will do for that drill. You get off while the going's good.'

Pacey left and Will bolted the door behind him. He hung his apron on its hook and went through into the kitchen. For the first time in almost ten years, firelight and lamplight welcomed him there, and the kettle was steaming on the hob. It was not much of a cottage, he thought, but it *had* been once in his mother's time. Now this woman and her child, by their presence there, had made it into a home again.

Ellen had spent the whole day sewing. She had cut up the clothes Will had given her and had made breeches, jacket, and shirt for John. She had made a corduroy skirt for herself, from an old pair of trousers, and a long-sleeved blouse from an old flannel shirt. Undergarments she made from a sheet and boots for them both from an old leather jerkin. And for most of the day, while she worked, John sat with her at the kitchen table, going quietly through the needlework basket, sorting out the old loose buttons, the tangled wools, the reels of cotton, and laying them out in tidy rows.

Sometimes he sat, perfectly silent, his hands together in his lap, content to watch her as she cut and measured and pinned and stitched. And when she tried some garment on him, he stood quite still in front of her, obediently raising an arm when told, or holding a fold of cloth in place while she made some adjustment. The two of them shared a sort of exhaustion and were quiet together, drawn extra close in an understanding that needed no words, passing between them as it did in each warm touch and each slow, comforting glance.

Once, when wandering round the untidy kitchen, he drew a finger along the dresser and showed it to her, black with dust.

'It's rather a dirty cottage, ent it, mother?'

'Men are not fussy when they live alone. And it seems the smoke gets in from the smithy too. Can you smell it? I can.'

There was a scullery and passage between the kitchen and the smithy, but the smell of the smoke got in all the same, and so did the noise: the cling-cling-clink of iron on iron, the rampling of horses now and then, and sometimes the voices of men upraised. The smithy yard was a busy place. John wanted to peep from the kitchen window. He raised a hand to the drawn curtain.

'No!' Ellen said. 'You mustn't look out! Nobody must see you here. D'you want your father to come for us?'

The boy's face became deathly white. He returned to his place at the kitchen table, and sat very still again, as before. Sometimes, when Ellen looked at him, his stillness and quietness hurt her heart. It was all wrong that a child should be so mute and grave. And she had added to his fear.

When Will came in, there was a change. John was amused at himself in his new clothes, and he walked about for Will to see them, showing off his square-toed boots and worsted stockings, his knee-length breeches and fawn flannel shirt, and, best of all, the shiny brass buttons on his jacket.

'I remember them buttons,' Will said. 'They come off a weskit I had years ago. You look pretty smart in em, don't you, eh? Have you seen yourself in that old mirror? You ent? Laws! Then I'll have to show you!'

Will took the mirror down from the wall, dusted it with a sweep of his arm, and held it for the boy to see.

'You're smart enough for two or three! Just look at them boots! I never did!' Will put the mirror back on the wall and looked at Ellen, who stood at the table, winding up the cotton reels and putting them back into the basket. He surveyed her newly made skirt and blouse. 'Your mother looks smart, too, don't she? She must be a clever needle-woman to get you both dressed up like that, out of them cast-offs I brung down this morning. I'll have to get her to sew for *me*!'

He went to the fire-place and took a big frying-pan from a hook. He set it on the trivet on the stove and went to the cupboard for a bowl of dripping.

'You been all right in here today, lying low and keeping mum?'

'Yes,' Ellen said, 'we've been all right.'

'Seems your husband's been out looking round a bit for you. I reckon he's wondering where you've got to. He's putting it about that you've upped and left him, and he says you've took his money, too.'

Pausing a while, the bowl in his hand, he saw that they were watching him.

'Ah! I knew that'd make you stare!' he said, and dropped a lump of dripping into the pan. 'That riled me no end to hear the story he's putting about, knowing he turned you out of doors without a stitch of clothes nor nothing, on a freezing cold night like it was last night. Why, you could be dead in a ditch some place, for all he knew any different about it.'

Ellen, making the table tidy, said nothing. She brushed threads and remnants into her hand and threw them into the ash-can.

'It was Ted Gore who told it to me. Me and one or two others, that is. I never said hardly nothing at all but if that'd been Lancy hisself standing there, telling such a lying tale, I'd have had to throw it back in his face.'

Busy with a knife at the kitchen range, he soon had sausages frying in the pan, with onions, potatoes, parsnips and turnips, all cut up and jumbled together, filling the place with their savoury smell.

'You hungry, John? So am I! I'm just about ready to eat the chair! How d'you like your sausages? D'you like em laughing and splitting their sides?'

So boisterous were Will's ministrations with his knife that one fat sausage flew out of the pan and rolled across the rusty stove. He snatched it up quickly and hurled it back, and, licking his greasy finger and thumb, looked at John with a nod and a wink. The little boy watched, a faint smile touching his lips, and a faint gleam coming into his eyes.

'That's not the proper way to cook.'

'Ent it? Why not? What's wrong with it?'

'It's not the way my mother does it.'

'Well, tomorrow maybe she'll cook for us, and we shall have something worth eating, eh? Like meat pie with gravy?

Or maybe a stew? I'll have to mind my p's and q's and then perhaps she'll agree to do it.'

Ellen set out the knives and forks and placed three plates to warm on the stove. She warmed the teapot and made the tea. Will took a huge crusty loaf from a crock and hacked it into two-inch slices. He sent them skidding aross the table. In the same rough fashion he dished the supper onto their plates, one sausage for John, two for Ellen, and three for himself, together with the sliced vegetables, fried crisp and brown.

'Eat up, young tucker,' he said to John, 'and one day you'll be as big as me.'

'Can I come into the smithy tomorrow and see you bending the hot iron?'

'Not in the daytime,' Will said. 'That'd be all round Dingham in two shakes of a ram's tail. But tomorrow night, when I've shut up shop, I'll take you in and show you what's what.'

'We must be gone by then,' Ellen said. 'We ought to leave first thing in the morning and slip away before it's light.'

'You can't walk to Cheltenham without proper boots.'

'You did say you'd lend me a sum of money.'

'So I will! And gladly too! But—'

'If we can get as far as Runston, I can buy boots for both of us there, and we'll be all right the rest of the way. I'll pay you back as soon as I can.'

'You can't make a little boy like John walk all that way, Mrs. Lancy, ma'am. You can't. It's unheard of. It is, that's a fact. And what if you don't find a lodging there? Supposing you're stranded in the town?'

'I know, I know!' Ellen said. 'But that's a chance I've got to take!' She would not show her fear in front of John. 'I must hope for the best, that's all.'

Will shovelled food into his mouth and munched it loudly. He washed it down with a draught of tea.

'I'll tell you what!' he said, passing his mug for her to fill. 'I reckon you're better stopping her!'

'No, no! We can't do that.'

'Why can't we, mother?' John asked. 'Why can't we stop here along with Will?'

'It's out of the question,' Ellen said. 'We must get away as far as we can.'

'Away from Dick Lancy, you mean?' Will said. 'But I should look after you, you know. If he was to come buzzing round after you, I'd soon send him packing, never fear.'

'No. It won't do. I must get away.'

'Well, wait until Friday at least,' Will said. 'I go into Runston myself on Fridays, to do a bit of this and that, and no one'd think more'n twice about it. I could borrow Draycott's horse and cart and take you to Cheltenham myself. We could leave before light so's nobody sees you, and buy what you need on the way, like you said. So how's that for a proposition? Better than walking, I'll be bound!'

'You're very kind to us,' Ellen said.

'Right, then, it's settled! Friday, first thing. And then if you don't find a lodging there, you can come back with me in the cart again.'

'I *must* find a lodging. And I *must* find work.'

'Yes. All right. It's up to you. We'll see what happens, anyway. Friday ent very long to wait. It's only three days, it'll soon go by. I know it's hard on you and the boy, having to skulk in here all day, but if you can stick it out for three days—'

'Yes, we can stick it,' Ellen said. 'We're very grateful, my son an I.'

'I know the place is none too clean. It's a pigsty in here, I grant you that. Worse, in fact, cos pigs get mucked out a sight more often than I get mucked out in this here cottage. And that goes hard on a woman like you, having to stick in such a place.'

'A woman like me. What sort is that?'

'House-proud,' he said, cleaning his plate with a piece of bread. 'I remember that time I came to the mill and brought Dick Lancy home to you, the place was as clean as a new pin.

It was a palace and you was the queen. You warnt too pleased at having your husband brought home drunk. The way you spoke to me that time and the way you showed me out of the door—'

'Yes, I remember,' Ellen said. 'You called me a shrew.'

'Did I?' he said. 'Oh glory be!' And, looking at John, he made a face. 'That was the ale talking,' he said. 'It does that, you know, when I've had enough. It takes over and talks with tongues. I can't get a word in, myself, oftentimes, on account of the ale got to have its say.'

'Then why drink it?' Ellen asked, and was at once ashamed of herself for presuming on his good nature. 'Take no notice of me,' she said. 'I had no right to say that.'

'You're right all the same, I shouldn't ought to do it,' he said. 'But it's thirsty work, being a blacksmith, and where else should a man go to be with his friends if it ent to the inn? Still, I shan't be going tonight, however. I'm going to be busy airing the bed in the spare bedroom and finding some linen for you to sleep in.'

'We can perfectly well sleep in the chair.'

'Whose house is it, I'd like to know? You'll sleep upstairs and no nonsense about it. You can both of you help me to get it ready.'

Will pushed his empty plate aside and cut himself a slice of bread. He spread it with honey and bit into it with strong white teeth. He looked across the table at John who watched him, wide-eyed, astonished to see a slice of bread vanish so quickly, in three or four bites.

'You got to be firm with womenfolk, John, otherwise they do as they like. You got to show em you mean what you say.'

So Ellen and John slept that night in a warm featherbed, between twilled sheets and woollen blankets, with a stone hot water bottle at their feet, and if everything was not as clean as Ellen in the past would have expected, such was her gratitude that she hardly noticed.

The following morning, with John's help, she swept and

cleaned the kitchen. It was not easy, confined as they were, unable to open the doors or windows, but Will, coming in to see how they were, marvelled at the change in the brick-nogged floor, scrubbed and ruddled; looked into the larder, where clean pots and pipkins were ranged neatly along the shelves; and stooped over the kitchen stove, pretending to look at himself in the dark-gleaming slab, now blackleaded to perfection.

'The place ent looked so spick and span since my old mother was alive and ruled the place like a proper tartar. She took a pride in it, just like you, and woe betide my dad and me if we walked in here with dirty bootses. I reckon that'd warm her heart, if she could see it nice again, after the mess I let it get into. I reckon she'd shake you by the hand!'

That day in the smithy, always a favourite gathering-place, especially in winter, Will's customers talked about Ellen Lancy.

'She still ent been found. Nor the boy neither. The miller's been asking everywhere but it seems like they've vanished without a trace.

'Funny, ent it?' said Jonah Middling, one of the grooms from Dinnis Hall. 'Just a year ago, pretty exactly, Lancy hisself was gone missing, with nobody knowing where or why, and now it's his missus and boy the same. Seems queer to me. Seems like there's something fishy in it.'

'Fishy's the word,' said Ben Tozer, the carter from Neyes. 'There's one or two folk think Lancy hisself has got them locked up in the millhouse down there. Well, he's queer enough for anything, ent he, these days? D'you know what he said to me last harvest-time? He said I warnt to water my horses no more when crossing the ford at Biddy's Dip cos it took the water and slowed down his wheel. He did! Mortal fact! And he meant it too!'

'Touched,' said Middling. 'Dangerous too. You never know which way he'll jump. If his wife *has* left him and took the boy, I dunno that I blame her, nohow. I reckon he's brought it on hisself.'

102

Over supper that night, when his day's work was finished. Will repeated the gossip to Ellen and saw how she blenched at her husband's name.

'Looking for us? Are you sure? Is he going from house to house?'

'Well, he's asking questions everywhere, and knocking at one or two places, it seems. And somebody saw him out at Skyte, poking about in the hedges there. He knows you can't have got very far, well-nigh naked as you was, and he knows there's only two things could've happened to you. – Either you asked for shelter some place or else you're lying out dead of the cold. I reckon it's got him rattled a bit, and serves him right, too, after what he done to you.'

'You mustn't blame him too much. It's not his fault that he does these things. It's something that happened to his mind when he was trapped underground all that time. He was a good man up till then, and you must make allowances.'

'If you say so, of course. But he knows what he's doing, right enough, and it's no good your asking me to think kindly thoughts about him or remember him in my prayers, cos I shan't and that's flat. It's too soon since I saw you and John out there, scrabbling about in Draycott's cartshed, trying to make yourself a bed in the straw.'

For a little while he ate in silence. Then he spoke again.

'You ent changed your mind by any chance? You ent thinking of going back to him?'

'No, no. I shall never do that. Not now the break has come. I couldn't bear to go back now. We must get away, John and I, and start a new life by ourselves.'

'Friday ent long to wait,' he said. 'All you got to do is lie low here and build up your strength against the future. Strikes me you'll need it, come what may, for that's a hard old world out there, you know, for a woman struggling all alone.'

But although she remained close in the cottage, and took good care that John should be quiet, their presence there was soon suspected. Will's neighbours around the green observed that his chimney smoked all day, and Mrs. Beard, in the next cottage, whose bit of garden ran with his, swore she heard a child coughing. The door, when Mrs. Jennet tried the sneck, proved to be locked, and that was a strange thing indeed, for nobody living on the green ever locked their doors during the daytime. There was also a smell of good home baking which no door or window, however tightly closed, could prevent from escaping, and Will Gale, surely, said Mrs. Beard, had never been known to make pastry?

'You got company, Will?' asked Tommy Breton, coming into the smithy to light his pipe.

'Company? What makes you ask?'

'Something my missus said to me, that she heard from your neighbour, Mrs. Beard.'

'You listen too much to that missus of yours. You should get her a nosebag and strap it on.'

'You *are* still single, I suppose? You ent took a wife on the quiet, like, just now lately, these past few days?'

'Not unless it was while I was drunk.'

'Nor another man's wife by any chance?'

'No, Tommy, not even yours!'

There was some laughter among the men gathered round the forge, and a few ripe jokes accompanied the departing Tommy, but Will was aware, as he worked on, that his customers eyed him with sharpened interest.

'Was there anything in what Tommy said?' Bert Franklin asked in a casual way.

'Don't talk to me now,' Will said. 'I got to concentrate on this here plough.'

They took the hint and left without asking further questions. Will and Jim Pacey, for a few minutes, had the smithy to themselves. Jim was a man of fifty odd. He had worked with Will for sixteen years. They had a good understanding together.

'You muzzled their snouts in here, right enough, but they'll soon make up for it outside.'

'I know. My ears are burning like them coals.'

'Seems you've got yourself into a pickle of some sort. What're you going to do about it?'

'I dunno. I got to think.'

When Will went out at dinnertime, crossing the green to The Old Tap, a small group of neighbours, men and women, stood gathered under the oak tree, gazing at the smithy cottage.

'All right, Will?' asked Ralph Jennet.

'Why shouldn't it be?' Will said.

'I been racking my brains,' Ralph said, 'but I can't for the life of me think why your curtains is drawn across the window all day.'

'It's to stop the sun from fading the carpet.'

'Hah! Since when've you ever had a carpet?'

'Since when've you ever had a brain?' Will said.

In The Old Tap, when he walked in, the customers there became silent, and Archie Shaw, as he filled Will's tankard at the barrel, spoke loudly enough for them to hear.

'Do you want your bread and cheese today, Will?'

'Why shouldn't I want it? Are you short?'

'I just got it into my head that somebody – I dunno who – might be getting your dinner for you at home.'

'A good chunk of Cheddar, that's what I'd like, and the crustiest part of a loaf,' Will said. 'If not I'll settle for Double Gloster.'

For once he ate in a corner, alone, and left as soon as his meal was finished. He returned to the smithy and went through into the cottage. Ellen and John were at the table, drinking the last of their mutton broth. He pulled out a chair and sat down with them.

'Our secret's out, all over the village. They know I've got somebody here with me and they're pretty sure they know who it is. It's only a question of time before one of em goes and tells Dick Lancy.'

Wearily, Ellen put down her spoon. She half glanced away, as if he were to blame. John looked at them each in turn, his eyes darkly questioning, full of thought.

'I should've known better,' Will said. 'You can't keep secrets on this green.'

Ellen turned and looked at him.

'What am I to do?' she asked.

'This evening I'm going up to Neyes to pick up Draycott's horse and cart. He said I could have it at six o'clock. You get yourselves ready by that time and I'll take you to Cheltenham straight away instead of tomorrow like we planned. I don't see there's nothing else we can do, unless—'

'Unless what?'

'Unless you stay on and face him out.'

'No,' she said, 'I must go.'

'Right you are. It's up to you. I'll root out some coats to keep you warm. It's going to be nippy, travelling this evening after dark, but I'll get you there, safe and sound, and help you to find some place to live. You leave it to me. I'll sort it out. If you get a move on at six o'clock, you should be safe in Cheltenham by the time the gossip's got around.'

But in fact it was already too late. The gossip had gone right through the village and had reached Richard Lancy at Pex Mill. At half past two that afternoon the smithy was filled with villagers. Will looked around and counted fifteen. Some were there on genuine business. The carters from Whitestone had come for their drill. But most were there on some pretext or other, such as wanting a poker straightened out or begging a shovelful of fire from the forge. Outside the smithy, other loiterers stood in groups, and all round the green, although the day was bitterly cold, elderly cottagers stood at their doors.

'By the deuce!' Jim Pacey muttered. 'You'd think the circus was coming through.'

'I reckon it may be,' Will replied.

'Shall I chase this lot out and lock the door? Shall I put this hot rivet on Sue Breton's bum?'

'What, and waste good metal?' Will said. 'I'd sooner get on with the job in hand.'

A little after three o'clock, young Barney Roberts came running in to say Dick Lancy was on his way.

'I seen him coming up past Tanner's. He's got a shotgun under his arm. He's coming here as sure as fate. My mother asked and he said yes. He said he'd got business with Will Gale.'

'Did you hear that, Will?' asked Billy Jukes. 'The miller's coming and he's got a gun.'

'Yes, I heard,' Will said, and, straightening up from the seed drill, turned towards Barney Roberts. 'Is the miller's shotgun loaded, boy?'

'Laws, I dunno!' Barney said. 'How should I know a thing like that?'

'Trust that mother of yours,' Will said, 'to send you here with half a tale.'

'It's no laughing matter,' Ralph Jennet said. 'I don't like the sound of it, not one little bit. He's after you, Will, be sure of that.'

'You came to see some fun, didn't you? You and all these others here?'

'Not a shotgun, no,' said Tommy Breton, looking round in search of his wife. 'Somebody ought to go and stop him. Reason with him. Take it away.'

'Tommy, lad, the job is yours!'

'Ent you afraid, Will?' asked Fred Byers. 'The miller is mad as a March hare. He's used that shotgun once before. Supposing he was to use it again?'

'You'd better all clear out of the way.'

'Ent you afraid, Will? Not even a bit?'

'I'm too busy trembling to be afraid.'

'Know what he's coming for, do you, Will? Know what business he's got in mind?'

'He certainly ent coming to bring me a bag of flour.'

'Then what're you going to do about it?'

'I reckon I'm going to let him come!'

Will bent over the seed-drill again and went on working as before, hammering out the red-hot rivets that Jim Pacey

107

pushed through the holes in the flange. But although his back was towards the door, he knew when Lancy appeared there by the sudden quietness of the crowd and the way they parted, giving way, leaving a space around the anvil. He flattened out the last rivet and plunged the drill-section into the trough, where the water sizzled and boiled up white. He put the section on one side and turned with his hammer in his hand.

Richard came forward, steady-paced, and confronted Will across the anvil. His long, handsome face, with its fine bones, had the slackened look of the man who drinks, the features blurred by thickening flesh, the skin inflamed with an angry redness. And although he stood face to face with Will, his gaze slid away repeatedly, as though he disliked the glare from the forge. His shotgun lay in the crook of his arm. He allowed the muzzle to rest on the anvil. Will saw that both hammers were cocked.

'Is it true, what I hear, that you've got my wife and son?'

'Supposing it is?' Will said. 'They're safer with me than they are with you.'

'Oh, I daresay she's told you some tale about me, making me out to be this and that! But I don't call it safe for her to be living in with you here, a man that's enticed her away from her home, along with my son only five years old.'

'You're a liar!' Will said. 'You was the one that turned them out and these listeners may as well hear about it. *You* turned them out in the small hours on Monday night with next to nothing hardly on. No shoes on their feet, nor coats to wear, only their nightclothes and nothing else! *You* locked them out of their own home on a night that meant death, so cold it was, and for all you knowed or cared about it, they might both be dead and in their graves.'

'If she told you that, it was just a tale!'

'I ought to know – I was the one that found them!' Will said. 'They was both near naked and just about froze to the very marrow, so don't talk to me about tales, man! *I* saw them. *I* took them in. If it wasn't for my doing that, you would be up for murder by now, and you'd find yourself on the end of a rope!'

'You're as big a liar as my wife. It's you that's enticed them away from me. No one will believe what you say.'

'The folk here today will make up their own minds who's telling the truth. They know you and they know me. It's up to them to decide for theirselves.'

'Are you going to let me see my wife?'

'I dunno that she wants to see *you*.'

'I'm her husband. I've got my rights.'

'You gave up your rights when you turned her out.'

'Damn you!' Richard shouted, and took a step or two past the anvil, towards the door leading into the cottage. He was breathing heavily, through his nose, and in the smoky-red glare of the forge it was easy to see that he was sweating. 'If you don't let me past—'

'You're all in a sweat,' Will said. 'I shouldn't go too near that fire if I was you. You're that full of brandy, you'll go up in flames.'

'That's rich, that is, coming from you! – The biggest soak for miles around!'

'At least I drink where folk can see me. I don't soak in secret and then take it out on my wife and child. And I stick to good clean honest ale, not spirits and such, that rot your guts.'

'I've had enough of wrangling with you!'

'Then all you got to do is get out of my smithy.'

'I ent leaving,' Richard said, 'without I take my wife and son.'

'They'll never come with you,' Will said. 'You're wasting your time and mine too.'

'Then fetch them out for me to see, and let her tell me so herself.'

'Do you think I'll do that,' Will asked, 'when you're standing waiting with a gun?'

'What, this?' Richard said, and, raising the shotgun gradually, he pointed it at Will's stomach. 'I brought this for you, not for them. You're the one that's enticed them away. You've got them in there, my wife and son, and won't even let me speak to them. There's many a man been killed for less and folk would say you'd asked for it. A wife-stealer's no loss to the world. A wife-stealer's dirt and deserves all he gets. Any husband would say the same.'

Slowly, as though enjoying himself, he raised the shotgun higher still, till the muzzle was pointing at Will's chest. The people watching became very still. Only Jim Pacey twitched a little and muttered something under his breath. He was standing close and could see Richard's finger on the trigger. He sensed the excitement in Richard's mind. Will sensed it too. He was trying to think of something to say.

'Well?' Richard said. 'Who's sweating now?'

'I am!' said Will. 'I'm sweating pints. Is it loaded, that gun of yours?'

'Both barrels. A full charge.'

'Then hand it over to Pacey here and I'll fetch your missus out to you.'

'So you're ready to bargain after all?'

'I said I'd fetch her. I didn't say you could take her away.'

'That ent for you to decide,' Richard said. 'She's my wife, not yours. Her proper place is with me. But fetch her out by all means and let us hear what she's got to say.'

He surrendered the gun to Jim Pacey, who carefully lowered both the hammers. Will cast a glance around the smithy and saw that the crowd inside had grown. He went to the door leading into the cottage.

'Richard? Here?' Ellen said. She turned to John and drew him close. 'In the smithy, do you mean?'

'Turns out we're too late. Somebody told him where you was. So he wants to see you and take you home. He won't take no for an answer from me. He wants to hear you say it yourself.'

'Can't you get him to go away?'

'I reckon it's better to face him out.'

'That's what you wanted, isn't it? Are you satisfied now you've got your way?'

'I reckon it's better to clear the air. He's been spreading lies about you. Now's your chance to answer him back, and there's witnesses to hear the truth.'

'Witnesses?' Ellen exclaimed. 'Am I appearing before the Bench? Would you play magistrate over me?'

But gradually her anger died. She composed herself and thought deeply. After a while she nodded assent. She and John followed him into the smithy. The crowd by now had almost doubled, and people were pressing in at the door. She was a public spectacle, but it was too late to turn back now. She felt John's hand tighten on hers and saw that Richard was coming towards them.

'Well, Ellen?' he said to her, and his tone was so gentle that it came as a shock. 'Ent it time you came back home?'

Ellen stared, unable to speak. This, if she let herself be deceived, was the old Richard revived from the past, a tender, loving husband to her, a devoted father to their son. But, looking into his shadowy eyes, she saw beyond the gentle smile to the dark, unloving hardness behind.

'Ellen, come home,' he said again. 'This ent very well done in you, dragging our son about like this, living under another man's roof. You bring him home where he belongs.'

He put out a hand towards his son, as though to touch him on the head, but John shrank away, behind his mother, and Richard's hand fell to his side.

'There, now,' he said reproachfully, 'you've even turned my boy against me.'

'We're not coming back to you,' Ellen said. 'Nothing on earth will change my mind.'

'I'm willing to try and make amends. I know I've done wrong, I grant you that. But a man and his wife must stick together. Neither one has got a right to go running off with somebody else.'

'Don't try and twist the truth, Richard. You turned us out on a winter's night, with only our nightshirts on our backs,

111

and we should have perished in the cold if it hadn't been for Will here, finding us and taking us in.'

'So you better prefer to stop with him? You set him above your own husband?'

'Will and I are nothing to each other. I hardly knew him before Monday night. He gave us shelter, that's all, and tomorrow we shall be moving on.'

'You don't expect me to swallow that!'

'It's the truth, every word, and you know it as well as I do.'

'Are you coming back with me or not?'

'No, Richard, I am not.'

'Well, you've had your chance!' Richard said. 'If that's the way you answer me, I wash my hands of you, good and all. But my boy John is a different matter. You've got no right to take him away. He's coming back to the mill with me.'

'Never! Never!' Ellen exclaimed, and little John, looking out at his father from the safety of his mother's skirts, cried shrilly: 'Go away and leave us alone! We're not coming back to you! No, we are *not*!'

'Aren't you, by God?' Richard said.

'You've had your answer,' Will said, 'so now maybe you'll take yourself off and leave me a chance to get on with some work.'

'I'll tell you this much!' Richard said. 'You'll never get work from *me* again! Any ironwork I've got, I'll go to Lovell at Sutton Crabtree.'

'I daresay I'll manage,' Will said.

'You ent heard the last of it!' Richard said. 'Do you think any good will come of you, stealing my wife and son from me? I reckon you'd better think again!'

Will spoke to Jim Pacey.

'Give the miller his shotgun,' he said, 'and let him take hisself back to the mill.'

'All right. Just as you say. But I reckon I'd better empty it first, just to be on the safe side.'

Jim, with the shotgun under his arm, pushed his way to

112

the door of the smithy. He drew the hammers and fired both barrels into the air, and the two shots echoed around the green. He turned to Richard, who had followed him, and handed over the empty gun.

'You want to take care with that old piece of junk,' he said. 'It kicks worse than Joe Hooper's mare.

Richard stood in the open doorway, looking at Will, who was seeing him off.

'It's as well your helper's emptied this gun or I might've been tempted to shoot you yet. But one thing, blacksmith, I promise you! – I'll pay you back, somehow, one of these days, for coming between my family and me! I'll pay you back if it takes twenty years!'

Shouldering the gun, he strode away, up the track that ran round the green. Will and Jim Pacey went back to the forge, and Jim at once began working the bellows, blowing up the dying fire. Ellen and John had gone back into the cottage. Will addressed the crowd in the smithy.

'All those who've got work for me are welcome to stay. The rest of you can clear off home. The raree show is over for today. If you stop much longer, I'll pass round the hat! Come along, neighbours, get moving, please! How can I work if I can't swing my arm?'

Reluctantly, the crowd moved out. They stood about, talking, on the green. Only a few now remained in the smithy, among them the carters from Whitestone Farm, and one of these, who was new to the district, spoke to the other in a low voice.

'Is there always such goings on in this here village?'

'Laws, no!' said the other man. 'It's mostly no more than once a week!'

When Will went in to speak to Ellen, he found her sitting all alone, her hands lying idle in her lap. The shabby curtains had been drawn back from the windows, and for the first time in three days, daylight came into the cottage kitchen: dull grey daylight, for it was nearly half past three, and the winter dusk was coming on. Ellen sat straight-backed in her chair, staring into the fire in the stove. She was thinking of Richard and the change that had come to spoil their lives.

'Where's the little un?' Will asked.

'He's out in the garden, talking to your neighbours over the fence. It's the first time he's been out of doors for three days. Now that it's known we're here with you, it doesn't matter any more.'

'I've been thinking about that.' He sat in the chair opposite and studied her face in the light of the fire. He saw that her eyes were full of sadness. 'Now the secret's out like you say, there ent so much hurry for you to move on. Any old day will do for that. You may as well take time to think.'

'I don't seem able to think,' she said. 'I seem to have lost the power completely.'

'Then why not let me decide for you? There's no need for you to move on at all. Strikes me you're better stopping here.'

'For good, do you mean? I don't think I can.'

'It's only common sense to me. Seems as though it was meant that way, as though we was throwed together on purpose, like. You and young John without no home. Me with a home and no one in it. Seems to me it's common sense.'

'Live here with you, in this cottage, when Richard is only a mile away, out at the other end of the village? Have you thought what people will say?'

'They'll think the worst. They always do. And that'll be harder on you than me cos it's always harder on the woman. I've got a tough hide and it's no odds to me what people say, but if you can't take it, we'll think again.'

'Richard threatened to shoot you. I heard him say he'd pay you out.'

'He can't do nothing. What can he do? I can look after myself all right. I'm big enough. I ent a dwarf.'

'Why should you have to bear his threats? And all the gossip there's bound to be? It's hardly a fair return for you, after being so good to us.'

'That's my decision, ent it?' he said. 'If I don't mind, that's up to me.'

'I don't know. I just don't know...'

'You stop here. That's the best thing to do. Cheltenham ent the place for you. Think of having to look for work, going among a lot of strangers, you with the little un to support. Does it seem better than stopping here?'

'No, it's not that,' Ellen said. In truth, the world seemed a frightening place, beyond the boundary of the village. 'It's just a question of right and wrong.'

'I'll tell you what, just give it a try! A month or two, say, and see how it goes. Seems you can't say no to that. Seems to me it's common sense.'

'All right,' she said. 'We'll give it a trial as you suggest and see how we all get on together. It's a bargain between us. We'll see how it goes.'

There was immense relief for her in having come to this decision, even though she still had doubts, and when she looked across at him, it was with a brighter, clearer glance.

'Right so!' he said, slapping his thigh. 'It's a bargain between us, like you say, and we'll work it out to suit both sides. You don't need to be afraid no more. I'll look after you from now on. You and young John, you're all right with me, and the first thing I aim to do for you is to get you fixed up with some proper clothes.'

'You're very good and generous. I don't know why you should be so good. I shall never be able to pay you back.'

'I dunno about that,' he said. 'A bargain's a thing that works two ways. There's more than one party involved in it. It's all a question of give and take.' Leaning forward across the hearth, he put out a hand and patted her knee. 'You'll pay me back all right – in your own way.'

Ellen stiffened and drew away.

'I'm not sure that I know what you mean.'

'Why, getting the house to rights, of course! Mollying for me and getting my meals! I've let this cottage go to the bad, but that ent to say I like it that way, and I shall expect to see a change now that you're stopping here with me.'

Will rose from his chair and stood for a while with his hands in the waist of his leather apron. The expression on his big broad face was half offended, half amused.

'What did you think I meant?' he said. 'Did you think I'd got thoughts of a different kind? That I'd take advantage and try it on? I reckon you've got a suspicious mind.'

Before she could answer, the back door burst open and John came in, red-faced from the cold and with a dewdrop on his nose.

'Well, young fella?' Will said. 'Your mother and me have been having a chat. I've been saying she ought to stop here, at least for the time, to see how it suits. So what's your opinion on the matter? Do you say go or do you say stay?'

'I want to stay,' John said, 'and be a blacksmith the same as you.'

The boy's face was eager, expectant, full of trust and he looked up at Will with bright-shining eyes. Ellen might still have her doubts, but her son had none.

Chapter 8

A few days later the Christmas holiday came to an end, and John began going to school again. The children plied him with endless questions. The older ones were rather sly.

'Who does your mother like the best? Will Gale the smith or the Mad Miller?'

'What does she call herself nowadays, Mrs. Lancy or Mrs. Gale?'

'How many wedding-rings has she got? Does she wear them on either hand?'

John, in his innocence, merely stared. He thought them silly to ask such things. But other questions made more sense.

'D'you think Will Gale would mend my skates?' Lukey Strudwick asked one day.

'He would if I asked him, I daresay.'

'*Will* you ask him, then, for me?'

'I might,' John said carelessly, 'so long as you lend me a loan of them.'

There were many advantages, he found, in having the blacksmith as his friend.

Will, in the smithy, also had to endure questions. He answered them all with a smile and a shrug.

'Mrs. Lancy's still with you, I see, Will. I thought you said she was moving on?'

'We came to a sort of agreement together. She's stopping

here to keep house for me. As long as it suits her, anyway.'

'Has she any idea what she's taking on?'

'What about Will?' said Billy Jukes. 'Has he any idea what *he's* taking on, seeing she's another man's wife?'

'First the miller, now the smith,' said Tommy Breton, thoughtfully. 'I wonder why she always chooses a man in an apron.'

'I can soon tell you that,' said Ralph Jennet. 'It's so's she can wear the breeches herself. You can see she's that sort by the way she carries herself and all. I'd sooner Will than me, by God! I should think she's a tartar and no mistake.'

'Now see here,' said Will, straightening from his work at the anvil and admonishing Ralph with his long-handled hammer, 'Mrs. Lancy is keeping house for me, and so long as she goes on doing that, I shall ask you to speak of her with respect.'

'Why, surely, surely,' Ralph agreed. 'That's only reasonable, ent it, Tommy?' And then, in a sly way, he said: 'Is she a woman that deserves respect?'

'*I* think she is,' Will said.

'Well, you know her better than we do,' said Ralph, 'so we'll just have to let you have the last word.'

Afterwards, alone with Jim Pacey for a while, Will laughed ruefully.

'You can't get the better of that lot. I should've known better than waste my breath.'

'You can't stop people talking, Will, especially when they got a talent for it. You just got to let it drip, that's all, like it was a shower of rain.'

Once, when Will was alone in the smithy, the vicar, Mr. Eustead, called on him.

'It's wrong of you, Gale, to have Mrs. Lancy living with you. It's scandalous. You should send her away.'

'Mrs. Lancy is my housekeeper. There's nothing wrong between her and me.'

'All the same, you are playing with fire.'

'I'm used to that, being a smith.'

'This is *hell* fire,' the vicar said.

'Then maybe I'll save a bit on coal.'

The vicar, tight-lipped, stalked out of the smithy. He hardly spoke to Will after that. And Will, who had until then been a bellringer, received a curt note under his door, saying that he was no longer needed, for his place had been taken by Albert Jukes.

More and more, as the spring weather came, Ellen was turning out the cottage, scrubbing the rooms from top to bottom, taking down the dirty curtains and hanging them up again, washed, ironed, and crisply starched. Will hung a clothesline between the two fruit-trees in the garden, and for days on end, wet blankets thumped in the boisterous wind, and clean white sheets bellied out like sails. The cottage was soon as clean as a pin. Gleaming windows let in the light. And Will, whenever he had a moment to spare, was busy with a paintbrush, outside and in.

'She's certainly stirring you up, ent she, your Mrs. Lancy?' said Charlie Beard, from next door. 'Your mice is all coming in to us, to get a bit of peace and quiet.'

'Then mind and be sure to treat them right. They've had nothing but kindness all these years.'

'It doesn't seem hardly fair on you, a bachelor chap like you are, to have a woman running you round.'

'I ent complaining,' Will said.

'Well, I daresay you get something out of it, to make it all worth-while,' Charlie said, 'but it strikes me you're a bit of a fool, saddling yourself with another man's wife, not to mention the shaver there.'

Will was painting his window-frames, and John, on a ladder against the wall, was watching ready to hand him a rag if the paint went over onto the glass.

'This young shaver,' Will said, 'is coming into the smithy with me, or so he reckons, anyway, as soon as he's old enough, of course.'

'He should be a miller by rights,' Charlie said, 'seeing that's his father's trade.'

'No!' said John, his chin jutting. 'I *won't* be a miller! I shall be a smith!'

Whenever Ellen went shopping now, she was served with a cold courtesy by the grocer, Whitty, and the butcher, Styles; and only Jerry Trussler, delivering fish at the door, treated her with the same old friendliness as before.

'Herrings, Mrs. Lancy, ma'am? They're the best you can buy and every one is full of roe. You'd better take a good half dozen. Will likes his herrings. You take my word.'

The villagers rarely spoke to her. Most of them went to a lot of trouble to step aside and avoid a meeting. One or two would merely nod. And those who did speak, during the first few weeks at least, did so only to express disapproval, as on a day in early March, when she was walking along Dip Lane, taking Will's boots to the cobbler, Mustow. A group of women followed her, calling out again and again: 'Get back to your husband, where you belong! It's Lancy you're married to, not Will Gale!'

Ellen walked on with burning face and did her best to close her ears, and although the scene was twice repeated in the week following, she went on her errands just the same and held her head defiantly erect. She never turned towards the women or answered them by a single word.

'She thinks herself somebody, don't she, by God? Living with Will Gale the smith like that, yet giving herself such mighty airs! And her poor crazy husband at the mill, going downhill all the time for want of someone to care for him. It's a disgrace and that's a fact.'

It was certainly true that the change in Richard was more marked than ever nowadays. He crossed the green once, on his way to Rillets Farm, and Ellen, who happened to be at the window, saw how shabby he had become and how badly he slouched as he walked up the track. From behind he looked an old man and his hair, which had only been streaked before, was now as grey as a panful of ashes.

There were many stories told about him and his strange

behaviour. Every week brought something new. He had been quarrelling with the bargemen when they passed through the lock upstream from the mill. He accused them of stealing his chickens and eggs. He had slung a rope across the river, tied to a tree on either side, and when a barge had come along after dusk, a man had been swept clean off the deck. His mates had rescued him just in time. They had threatened Richard with a hiding but he had locked himself in the mill, and they in the end had gone on their way, cutting the rope and taking it with them.

He never let anyone into the mill now. His customers, such few as there were, had to leave their grain outside the door, and their meal, when ready, was put out at once to await collection. Michael Bullock of Rillets Farm complained that his bean-flour was spoilt by rain, and he took the matter to a court of law. Richard was ordered to make good the loss and pay a fine of two pounds. He paid the fine in penny pieces, poured out onto the table in the courtroom, but he never reimbursed the farmer, and the mill lost another customer.

'The man's off his hinges, no doubt of that,' Fred Byers said to Bob Dyson. 'I can't really blame that missus of his for leaving him the way she did.'

'According to some, she didn't leave him. It was Lancy himself that turned her out. But the strange thing is, to my mind, that she should take up with Will Gale the smith. She was always a superior sort of woman. I can't get over her doing that.'

'She's only his housekeeper, so they say.'

'He's a man and she's a woman. It's not like a couple of old maids that've set up together to share their grub. Something'll come of it, no doubt at all, and that'll end badly, it always does.'

Bob Dyson was sorry about it. He had always admired Ellen Lancy.

One day when John was returning home from school with

121

three other boys who lived on the green, his father came out of Ainsley's malthouse, and they met face to face in the narrow lane. John stared, going white with shock. He edged away and prepared for flight.

'Don't you know me?' Richard asked. 'Ent you got nothing to say to me? I'm your father. You know that.'

'No!' John said, in his shrill voice. 'You're not my father any more! Will Gale's my father and I'm his son!'

And, putting his head down like a bull, he charged past Richard and ran down the lane, followed closely by his friends. He thought his father would chase after him, and he ran home as fast as he could, there to shut and bolt the door.

'What's the matter?' Ellen asked.

'My father!' he said. 'He's after me!'

Ellen went to the window to see, but although she kept watch for an hour or more, Richard did not come to the cottage that day.

He was not often seen about the green, but once, when Will was shoeing a horse, he came to the open door of the smithy and stood for a few minutes looking in.

'Seems he's keeping an eye on you,' Jim Pacey remarked.

'He'd be better keeping an eye on his mill, instead of letting it go to rack and ruin,' Will said. 'Go to the door, will you, Jim, and see what he's up to out there.'

'Just going round, that's all. I reckon he's calling at the shop.'

Once Richard came very late at night, in the small hours, about three o'clock. He came to the cottage itself this time and hammered loudly on the door until Will leant out of the window above.

'You got my wife in here with you? Keeping her close, are you, warming your bed?'

'Your wife is in a bed of her own. Now shut your row and get back home. D'you know what time it is, standing there, waking the whole damned village?'

'If I can't sleep, why should *you*? I want to know what you've done with my wife!'

'She's safe enough. You leave her be. She ent coming back to you if that's what you think.'

'I don't want her! Oh, no, not me! Not if she came to me on her knees. But I ent forgot what you've done to me, enticing my wife and son away, and one of these days I'll pay you out!'

He knocked several times at the cottage door, and the noise he made echoed all round the green, bringing one or two people to their windows. Eventually he went away. The next day was Sunday and in the morning, when Will stood 'airing his lungs' on the green, his neighbour, Mrs. Beard, setting out for church, stopped and waited for Mrs. Jennet.

'Good morning, Margaret. How are *you*? I hope you slept – when you had the chance? No, I couldn't get off again, not after that. And this little bit of a green of ours was always such a *quiet* place.'

'It will be again,' Will said, 'when you two women have done yaffling.'

Over breakfast, when he went in, Ellen was quiet and preoccupied. The night's disturbance worried her. After a while she said so to Will.

'I ought to go away from here. Away from Richard, as far as I can. It's all wrong that you should have to put up with this. The unpleasantness of it. The threats. The talk. Why should you bear it? It's all wrong!'

'I ent complaining,' Will said.

'I ought not to stay here, month after month. I really should be moving on. It's time I stood on my own two feet.'

'You stop as you are. You're all right with me. We get on all right, the three of us? You're comfy, ent you, you and John? There you are, then! Where's the sense? Why, John's got ideas about being a smith. I reckon you ought to think of him.'

'No, we can't stay!' Ellen said. 'Not if Richard is going to do this, coming knocking at your door, disturbing you and making threats. We must think of going. Yes, we must!'

123

But some time went by and Richard did not come knocking at the door again, and Ellen and John stayed on in the cottage.

Every moment, whenever John could slip away, he was sure to be in the smithy, watching Will and Jim at work. The iron heating in the fire, changing shape under the hammer, hardening again in the cooling-trough, had a fascination that never failed. Whenever horses were being shod, he would stand watching tirelessly, and, although he was only five years old, he seemed to divine the significance of every single thing he saw.

Once, when Jim Pacey had gone on an errand to Cockhanger Farm, Will was shoeing a mare alone, and John, standing by, was watching him. Will, with the mare's first forefoot on the stand, was about to remove the old shoe, and when he reached out for chisel and buffer, John handed them to him out of the box. Will said nothing at the time, but secretly he was impressed, and afterwards mentioned the matter to Ellen.

'He's quick on the uptake, your boy John. If he does take up smithing, later on, he's going to be good at it, no doubt of that.'

Will was very good with horses. He knew all there was to know about them and rarely, if ever, caused them pain. One day, shoeing a docile gelding from Neyes, he allowed John to come quite close and showed him the parts of the upturned hoof.

'This here in the middle we call the frog. It's spongy, you see, like a leather pad. Then all around here's what we call the horn. The outside layer is pretty tough and that's where we always put the nails.'

John, leaning over the gelding's hoof, made a face and wrinkled his nose.

'Hoo! Ent it smelly?' he exclaimed.

'Most people's feet is smelly,' said Will.

'Mine ent smelly,' John said.

'Well, they would be,' said Will, 'if you was a horse.'

'Can I feel the hoof and see what it's like?'

'Certainly. You go ahead.'

Will let the boy feel the gelding's hoof and then gave orders to stand away.

'I'm going to try seating the hot shoe, so you get back and stand by your mark.'

'But I want to see!'

'You can see as well from there. It ent safe for you to come too close. And the burning will make your eyes smart. Now do as I say and stand back or I shan't let you into the smithy at all.'

Will could be very firm when he chose, and at these times his word was law. But his nature was always so easy-going that the boy, for the most part, twisted him round his little finger. When John wanted a metal hoop to trundle around with a little stick, Will had to make him one in the smithy, and when Davy Bullock's trolley broke, Will had to put a new axle on it and hammer out the wobbly wheel. It was a great convenience to John, having the blacksmith as his friend, and he revelled in the importance it gave him. 'Don't worry, I'll take it to Will. He'll fix it all right – if I ask him to.' So Will melted lead for fishing sinkers; cut up pellets for catapults; and supplied old horseshoes for playing quoits; and Ellen, seeing how her son took advantage of him, sometimes put in a word of protest.

'You shouldn't do everything he wants you to do. He's a lot too free in the way he asks for this and that.'

'I was just the same when I was a boy and my father was in the smithy,' Will said. 'I'll soon let him know when I've had enough.'

'I don't want him spoilt,' Ellen said. 'He's rather full of himself just now.'

John at this time paid little attention to his mother. Her restrictions irked him; he thought himself above such things; and often, as the days grew long, he stayed out playing till after dark. What the older boys did, he thought he could do, and when his mother scolded him, he tried out a few of the new words learnt in the farmyard at Rillets or Neyes.

'Buggle the time! What do I care? Why should I go to bed at seven? Let me see the flaming clock!'

Sometimes when she was busy baking he would swagger into the little kitchen, kicking at the floor with his new boots because he liked the noise of his 'hobs', and would snatch the wooden spoon from its bowl to lick the cake-mixture, under her nose. Often, at bed-time, he hid himself up in a tree in the garden or climbed on the roof of Charlie Beard's shed, and when she went to call him in, would answer cheekily, defying her.

'Nell! Nell!
You must not yell!
If you do
I'll tell on you!'

Will soon became aware of the way John defied his mother, and one Sunday morning, when they were out on Roan Hill, sitting not far from Tinker's Pond, he took the little boy to task.

'You shouldn't ought to cheek your mother like you been doing so much lately. It grieves me a lot. Why do you cheek her and play her up?'

John was ashamed and hung his head. He hated Will to think badly of him. But there was a sense of grievance in him and it came out in an angry burst.

'She treats me like a little boy!'

'*Does* she?' said Will, in great amazement, and his eyes became very blue indeed. 'Laws!' he said, solemn-faced. 'And you getting on for six years old!'

'She tries to make me say my prayers!'

'It's not only little boys that say their prayers. I say them myself when I get the time.'

'Do you?' said John, much struck. 'D'you say "Our Father" right through to the end?'

'I always *used* to say it through. I should never have grown so big and tall if I hadn't always said my prayers.'

There was a little silence between them. John plucked a grass and chewed its end. He spat out the fragments between his teeth.

'What else must you do,' he asked, off-hand, 'to make yourself grow up tall?'

'For one thing, you got to eat your greens. Greens is good for you. Carrots, too. They help to make good strong muscle. But you shouldn't suck no lumps of sugar . . .'

'I didn't! I didn't!' John exclaimed.

'. . . nor you shouldn't tell no lies . . .'

'It was only one or two lumps, that's all, that fell on the floor and got all dirty.'

'. . . but the worst thing of all a boy can do is when he don't respect his mother . . .'

'I *do* respect her,' John said. 'I do. Honest. Cross my heart.'

'I daresay you do, but how is she to know that, when you're always saucy and don't obey? How can *anyone* know it, hearing the way you talk to her? It's only *small* boys that cheek their mothers and small boys grow up to be *small men*.'

John's head drooped again, and there was a brightness in his eyes, which Will pretended not to see.

'Well, now, young fella, I reckon we've sat here long enough. Shall we go on to the top of the hill or round the pond and home by Neyes?' Will got up from the mossy stone and dusted the seat of his Sunday trousers. His little lecture was at an end. 'If we go round by the pond,' he said, 'we must keep an eye open for the treasure.'

'What treasure?' John said.

'The tinker's treasure,' Will said. 'They say the tinker hid it here, somewhere close by the old pond, and nobody's never found it yet.'

'Is it golden sovereigns?'

'I dunno. Nobody knows. But I shouldn't think it was gold, somehow, cos tinkers ent so rich as that. Tin, perhaps, or copper, maybe, but I wouldn't reckon on finding gold.

127

Still, we'll keep a look-out, you and me, and maybe we'll find something, who can tell?'

They walked together down the track.

There was a definite improvement in John's behaviour after that and Ellen knew it was due to Will. He and the boy were good friends and often on a Sunday afternoon they rambled about on Roan Hill, 'keeping an eye out for the tinker's treasure' or stalking the fallow deer in the woods.

'You ought to come with us sometimes,' Will said to Ellen. 'It'd do you good to get out a bit.'

But Ellen was reluctant. She shook her head.

'Why not?' he said. 'You never go nowhere, only the shops.' Then he thought he understood. 'You think we'd look too much like a proper family, going out, the three of us? But does it matter how it looks? The villagers talk whatever we do. You may as well please yourself.'

'I'd sooner not ask for trouble,' she said. 'They're beginning to accept it now, I think, and I would like to keep it that way.'

'All right,' he said, 'it's up to you.'

Once every four or five weeks or so, Will went to Runston to see the ironmonger there, to order his stock and meet other blacksmiths for a gossip. He made a day of it, looking round the market shops, and drinking afterwards at The Swan, and always, when he returned home, he had some 'surprise' for Ellen or John. Once he brought her a beautiful shawl of dark red silk with a fringe around it, quite the richest, costliest thing she had ever seen.

'What's up?' he asked, as she opened the parcel and took out the shawl. 'Don't you like it?'

'It's lovely,' she said. 'But I can't wear it. You must take it back.'

'Maybe the colour ent right for you? I could always change it for another. There was plenty of different colours there.'

'It's too extravagant,' she said. 'You're much too generous and I can't accept it.'

128

'I know you need a shawl,' he said. 'I seen you unpicking that old knitted rug. I heard you say you'd be making it up—'

'I know what I said. I have only to mention this or that and out you go to get it for me. I shall never say anything, ever again! I shall button my mouth and bite off my tongue.'

'You say it!' he urged. 'You just say whatever you need. I ent short of a shilling or two and as for this shawl—'

'Who have you ever seen in Dingham wearing a shawl such as this?' she said.

'You think folk'll talk and make too much of it the way they do? You're right, of course. I should've thought. But it's only this once. Won't you try it on?'

'No, I'm wrapping it up again, straight away.'

'All right. I'll take it back. But I'm sorry about it all the same. That red would've suited you just about fine.' Sadly, he watched her wrap up the shawl. He saw that she was not to be tempted. 'What'll I get for you instead?'

'Just ask for your money and pocket it.'

'That'll only go on drink.'

'I don't mind where it goes, so long as you don't spend it on me.'

'You'd sooner see me catching stars!'

'If it makes you happy, by all means.'

'I'm happy sober and I'm happy drunk.'

'Yes,' she said, and smiled a little. 'You're the happiest man I've ever known.'

When she had first agreed to stay with Will, she had worried about his drinking habits, and, for John's sake, she had been afraid. What madness possessed her, she asked herself, that, having escaped from one drunkard, she should deliver herself and her son straight into the hands of another? But Will, however much he drank, was always good-humoured, always kind, and after a while she no longer worried. Foolish he might be, and noisy at times, but he had never quarrelled seriously with anyone, nor did he ever neglect his work. However late his revels lasted, the smithy would open the following morning as usual, and any piece of work that had been promised for such-and-such a time would be completed on the dot.

The worst sin ever laid at his door was that, when he had drink inside him, he was apt to say outrageous things. Once, encountering the respectable Mrs. Batty, big in the body with her seventh child, he called out in the village street: 'Been at it again, Mrs. Batty, my dear? Some people never learn! You should try putting salts in the old man's tea!' Another time, coming out of The Old Tap, he espied the vicar across the green. 'If Jesus Christ was a Jew,' he bawled, 'how come they gave him a Christian name?' And there was the night when he and Frank Coe, another bachelor like himself, drank a whole cask of home-brewed ale in Frank's cottage and made such a noise, singing and playing the concertina, that Mrs. Thurrop got out of bed and knocked on the wall with her candlestick. Will went out and called through the keyhole of her door. 'Shut up your knocking, you silly old flowerpot, you, or I'll come in there and give you something worth knocking for!'

And always, afterwards, meeting these same people when he was sober, he would give a slow sheepish smile, then pass his hand across his face as though to wipe the smile away.

'It was the ale,' he would say to them. 'You've got to blame it on the ale.'

But although he often said things to make the girls and women blush, no mother feared for her daughter with him, or ever had cause, one way or the other. He was all talk, as they said, and it meant nothing. The brown jug had always been wife and mistress to Will Gale.

'Ah, but what about him and Mrs. Lancy?' people were asking nowadays, and, 'What indeed!' others answered.

There were some fine hot days in July and August that year, and in the evening, when Will had extra work in the smithy, he would stroll up the green every half hour or so to get his tankard filled at The Old Tap. And those neighbours of his who sat on the bench surrounding the oak tree would be sure to call out some teasing remark.

'Why don't you have a hogshead in the smithy, Will, and save your bootleather, to-ing and fro-ing?'

'That'd get warm in the smithy, Fred, and besides I like to air my lungs.'

'Where's your Mrs. Lancy, then? She ent indoors on a pretty evening like this, is she?'

'She's sitting out in the back garden.'

'Don't she like our company?'

'The question is, do you like hers?'

'I dunno. I never spoke to her in all my life.'

'Exactly so,' Will said, 'and I call that unfriendly, I do, that's a fact.'

But a few were speaking to Ellen now. Bob Dyson had come to the door one day and given her a dozen eggs, and Sue Breton had sent her little boy to ask for the loan of a cupful of sugar.

'Soon you'll have Mrs. Beard stopping by to tell you about her bunions,' Will said, 'and then you'll have really been let in!'

In the garden behind the smithy cottage, Will had cut down the breast-high grass, clearing a space about ten yards square, and here in the evenings Ellen brought a chair and her needlework and sat in the golden evening sun, between the overgrown currant bushes and the sweet-scented roses gone half wild.

'Sewing? Sewing? You're always sewing!' Will exclaimed, going out to her, pint-pot in hand. 'And when you're not sewing you're knitting, crocheting, or making rugs!'

'It occupies my mind,' she said.

'It don't stop you thinking, I don't suppose?'

'Not altogether.'

'Do you think about *him*?' Will asked. 'That husband of yours, down at the mill?'

'Yes. I think of him as he was before, in the early days, when we were first married and everything was happy between us.'

131

'I dunno that it's very wise, dwelling on the past like that.'

'Would you have me think of him only as he is now, behaving so strangely, so—'

'You may as well say it! – The man is mad and we both know it. There's no point in beating about the bush.'

For once he seemed brutal, almost as though he wanted to hurt. He stood for a moment watching her, then emptied his tankard and wiped his mouth.

'It's no good looking back on the past. You've got your life to live, same as anyone else. It's no good whiling it away like that, looking back on days gone by, cos there's no kind of miracle can bring them back.'

'Do you think I don't accept that?' she said. 'Do you think me such a fool?'

Will gave a shrug and went back to the smithy.

One evening in late September, Will went out to the back garden and found Ellen at work with a spade, trying to dig the tussocky ground.

'Here, what're you up to, for goodness' sake? You'll kill yourself, digging there. That ground ent been touched for ten years or more. Breaking it up ent no job for you.'

'Mr. Dyson has given me some cabbage plants and Mrs. Jennet has promised some seeds. Peas and beans, I think she said, and they ought to go in fairly soon if we're to have them next spring and summer.'

'So they shall!' Will said. 'But I'll do the digging, if you please. I ent much of a gardener. My dad and mother looked after that and I've let it go since they died. But I'll soon get it digged for you, and you can do the sowing and planting.'

He took the spade and started at once, slicing at the tussocks of couch grass and sending them flying to one side. Ellen gathered them up with a fork and carried them to her bonfire nearby, and all the time as they worked together, he was watching her with a sidelong glance.

'Spring and summer! That's what you said. Sounds like

you think you'll still be here. Settling down, like, feeling at home.'

'Perhaps I'm feeling too much at home, taking things too much for granted,' she said.

'That's the way it ought to be. You can take things for granted as much as you like.'

'If ever you change your mind,' she said, 'you must tell me at once and no nonsense.'

'Right you are, it's a bargain,' he said. 'I'll send you both packing, you and your boy, and turn you out of doors in the cold—'

Stricken, he came to a sudden stop.

'Laws! What a thing to say!' he said. 'I need grubbing out. I do, that's a fact. And I ent even tipsy so there's no excuse.'

But Ellen merely smiled at him and her face in the shade of her straw hat was perfectly happy and serene. His joke had not hurt her. The past was beginning to bury the past.

'It ent very likely I'll want you to go – you feed me too well for one thing,' he said. 'You see that there's buttons on my shirts.'

'You may want to marry, one day.'

'Me? Never! No lections of that!'

'Why not?' Ellen said. 'You're a young man. You can't be much over thirty.'

'I'm thirty-three. But that's nothing to do with it. Marriage is a lottery, so they say, and I reckoned the day my number was called, I must've been sleeping it off some place, or else making too much noise to hear. Besides, I'm happy as I am!'

Leaning forward on his spade, his hands clasped one over the other, covering the handle, he looked at her with a straight steady stare, and his eyes, reflecting the evening sky, were a clear and vivid shade of blue.

'You and me and young John,' he said, 'we get along pretty well together, and that's the way it's going to stay, spring and summer, rain or shine, peas and beans and spring cabbage!'

133

Within a few days, the whole garden plot was dark brown, double-dug, trodden and raked, the surface soil a tilth of fine crumbs, ready for Ellen to sow her seed. Will was at hand, watching her, nodding approval at everything she did, ready to offer help if needed.

'I can see them beans in flower in my mind already. *And* I can smell the scent of them! There's no scent so sweet in all the world. As for the cabbages, well, you can't accuse them of smelling sweet. But the thought of them, sappy and green and fresh, why, my mouth is watering for them already!'

He strolled among the currant-bushes, now pruned down to the very bone, and with dung from the smithy around their roots, and returned to the edge of the seedbed.

'Spring and summer!' he said again, watching her as she put in the seed. 'I like the sound of that.'

Chapter 9

However hard Ellen worked, keeping the cottage cleaned and scrubbed, she could never quite get rid of the smell of the smithy, even when the two doors between were kept firmly closed. There was always a hint of it in the air, a faint smokiness hanging over everything, and Ellen knew without fail when a hot shoe was laid on a hoof.

One morning when Will had been into the cottage in a hurry, he left both doors ajar behind him, and Ellen, coming in from shopping, found the kitchen full of smoke. Newly laundered clothes, hanging on the airer, were all covered in black smuts, and so were pastries cooling on the table. She went through to the smithy and called out to Will.

'I *wish* you'd remember to close these doors! The whole house is full of blacks!'

She closed both doors on that side and opened the others to let out the fumes. The smeech, she knew, would hang for hours.

Will, in the smithy, had to endure the inevitable teasing. Ben Tozer was there and so were the grooms from Dinnis Hall,

'Seems as if housekeepers is pretty much the same as wives, the way you get it in the neck, Will. The next thing you know, she'll be stopping you going to The Old Tap.'

'Not with a thirst like mine,' Will said.

'You ent there so much as you used to be, however,'

'Maybe he's got something better to do,' Tozer said thoughtfully, 'or maybe he's thinking of signing the Pledge.'

'Maybe I'm tired of the folk there,' Will said, 'with their everlasting nodding and winking.'

But his tone and his glance were just as good-humoured as usual. No one ever got a rise out of Will, even when they worked at it.

It was certainly true that he spent less time at the inn these days. A couple of pints and a game of skittles were just about his limit now and sometimes indeed, as winter came in and the days shortened, he stayed at home the whole evening, chatting to John after supper, telling him stories about the smithy, and perhaps seeing him up to bed. Afterwards he would sit by the fire, occupied with some small task, such as scraping the soot from the old kettle or mending the leg of a kitchen chair. Ellen noticed the change in his habits and one evening she mentioned it.

'I hope you don't keep away from the inn just because of me,' she said.

'I was there on Monday,' Will said. 'I go when I want to, never fear.'

'You used to go every night, either here or Sutton Crabtree. You used to stay till they closed the doors.'

'It's a fine thing, I must say, when a man gets nagged for *not* drinking!'

'So long as you're not denying yourself.'

'I don't need to go to the inn now I got someone to chat to at home. Besides, I'm too busy nowadays.' And he held up the new potato-masher that he was making out of wood. 'There's no end to the jobs a man has to do when there's a woman in the house.'

'I hope I *don't* nag you,' Ellen said.

'A man likes a woman about the place, to keep him in order and say what's law. I should live like a pig if it warnt for you. You saw this place when you first came. A man needs nagging and that's a fact.' He paused in his work of smoothing the masher and looked at her with a little smile. 'Not too much of it, of course! Just a pinch now and then, like salt with meat.'

*

Winter set in early that year and was bitterly cold. One day in November, Mrs. Beard slipped and fell on the ice outside her door, and Ellen went out to help her up. She took her into the smithy cottage and gave her a cup of hot sweet tea. She washed her grazed hands and face, and, before taking her home again, threw ashes over the slippery ice. She went to the shop for Mrs. Beard's 'arrants' that day and the old woman became her friend.

'To think I ent spoke to you all this time!' she kept saying, again and again, and Will, on hearing the story from Ellen, said: 'She'll soon make up for it now, I'll be bound.'

Most of the people living nearby were speaking to Ellen by Christmas time, and once, when little John had a cold, Mrs. Jukes called in with a bottle of home-made cough-syrup and a ha'penny bag of boiled sweets. Not that she approved of Ellen even now. She thought she ought to make that clear.

'Poor little boy,' she said sadly. 'It's not his fault. We can't blame *him.*'

On Christmas Eve, at four o'clock, work stopped for an hour or two in the smithy, and many of the neighbours from around the green, not to mention a few from elsewhere, came in to sing carols around the forge, led by Will's cheerful baritone. It was something of a custom, and mulled ale was served to all who came, and this year, as a surprise, Ellen took in a huge dish piled up high with hot mince-pies, a sight that was greeted with a loud cheer.

Will was delighted at the way she contributed to his festive party, and when she had set the dish down on the anvil, he took hold of her and whirled her round in a little dance. The watchers sent up another cheer, and little John, clapping his hands, shrieked with over-excited laughter to see his mother swung off her feet.

Ellen herself was not best pleased. She was too well aware of the glances cast in her direction. But she stayed and joined in the merry-making and helped to pass round the mulled ale, heating in an enormous pan at the forge. She was rather shy in this gathering. She had never been used to a lot of people. And they were equally shy with her. But towards the end Billy Jukes, who was rather drunk, came up to her and bowed low.

'Mrs. Lancy, ma'am, when you've got a mind to swap husbands again, you might be kind and consider me! Will ent such a fool after all and it strikes me he knows what he's about!'

'Billy, be quiet!' his wife said, and edged him away, angrily.

Ellen said nothing, but, looking up, saw that Will was watching her, over the rim of his steaming tankard.

Later that night, in the cottage, he helped her to fill John's stocking.

'It wasn't very wise,' she said, 'to dance me round as you did in there, with all those people watching you.'

'You don't want to mind about Billy Jukes. He don't mean no harm, not really, you know.'

'He only says what the rest are thinking.'

'We knew it was going to be like that. We made up our minds we'd ride it out.'

'It makes me angry all the same, when there isn't a shred of truth in it.'

'You mean if there *was* some truth in it, you wouldn't mind so much?' he said.

Ellen glanced at him sharply, but he was intent on what he was doing, packing an orange and some nuts into the foot of John's stocking. It seemed he did not expect an answer.

'It's you I mind about most,' she said. 'After all, I have chosen to live apart from my husband, and that's a sin in the eyes of the world. But you've done nothing wrong at all and for your sake I mind what they say.'

'Then don't!' he said bluntly. 'I can fight my own battles.'

Ellen looked at the toys he had laid out on the table. A tiny clasp-knife. A catapult. A packet of chalks. A rubber ball. And a tin pea-shooter, with a bag of peas.

'I'm not sure that I like these things.'

'You don't have to like em. They're meant for John.'

Christmas Day was very cold, with a grey wind blowing out of the north. In the morning, after breakfast, while Ellen was busy cooking the dinner, Will took John for a walk on the hill, to look for a good stout Christmas log.

'But we've got a whole heap of logs in the house! And a whole heap of coal as well.'

'We must have a proper Christmas log, it's a sort of tradition,' Will said. 'My dad and me, in the old days, we always came out on Christmas morning, to look for a proper Christmas log. So you keep your eyes skinned, sharp as sharp, and if you see a likely log—'

'There's one!' said John, going forward into the wind. 'Over there, under that tree.'

'So there is! And just the job! Nice and old and daddocky, so's it'll burn up nice and bright. I reckon I'd better carry that. It's a bit big for a chap like you.'

As they went down the track again, snow began falling thick and fast, a cold white blindness enveloping them. Will took hold of John's hand and the two of them stumbled down the hill, across the pasture at Neyes Farm and out onto the green again. They ran the last fifty yards or so, arriving breathless at the cottage, and bursting in with a great deal of noise, laughing and puffing and flinging about, shedding wet snowflakes everywhere as they hung their coats in the backplace to dry, bustling to the fire with outstretched hands and asking when dinner was going to be ready.

The kitchen smelt of roasting goose, savoury sage-and-onion stuffing, and potatoes sizzling in the fat. And Ellen, in the act of setting the table, paused to give them warm spiced wine.

'You two!' she said, as they quietened down. 'You'd think there were six of you, racketing in.'

'We're hungry enough for six,' Will said. 'We're hungry enough for umpteen!'

After dinner, when everything had been cleared away and the table had been pushed back, they drew up their chairs around the hearth, and, wearing the paper hats from their crackers, sat toasting themselves at the big fire. Will took up the Christmas log and made to heave it into the stove, but in doing so he appeared to drop it. It fell with a heavy thud in the hearth; the old rotten wood split open wide; and there, among the soft splinters, was something that glinted in the light.

'There's something in it!' John exclaimed.

'Is there?' said Will. 'Fancy that!'

'Whatever is it?'

'I dunno. You'd better look.'

John got down in front of the fender and put his fingers into the log. The two halves of it came apart and lo, fallen out upon the hearthstone, were six brand new pennies, shining bright, winking and twinkling in the glow of the fire. John's eyes opened wide. He picked up the pennies one by one, and, sitting back on his heels, looked first at his mother, then at Will.

'It's the tinker's treasure,' he said, in a hushed voice.

'Why, so it is!' Will agreed. 'Would you believe it? In that old log!'

'How did it get there?' John asked.

'Ah, now, I wonder! I do indeed!'

'*You* put it there! I can see by your eyes!'

'Me? Why, lumme! What makes you think that?'

'Did he, mother?' John demanded. 'Did he put them in the log?'

'Yes,' Ellen said, 'I'm sure he did.'

'And supposing I did?' Will said. 'What d'you think of your treasure, then? Have you looked and seen the date? They're next year's pennies, new as new, that've never been spent yet, not even once, and can't be neither till New Year's Day. See the date on them? What's it say?'

'1881,' John said, turning each penny in his hand.

'Right so. Next year, like I say. And the queen on em, smart as smart!'

'Where did you get them?' Ellen asked.

'I've got a friend in the bank at Runston. He let me have them, special favour. And come next Saturday, New Year's Day, I'll take John into the town and he can spend them at the fair. How'd that be, young fella, then? Would you like to spend them at the fair?'

John nodded, bright-faced and bright-eyed. He sat with the pennies clasped in his hand and leant against his mother's knees.

'I like Christmas,' he whispered to her. 'I wish it was Christmas every day.'

Ellen, putting her hand on his head, looked at Will sitting opposite.

'You spoil this boy of mine,' she said. 'Yes. You do. You spoil us both.'

Will, with his blue paper crown over one eye, stooped and put the log on the fire. It burnt up like tinder and lit their three faces in its glow. Outside, the wind was blowing hard, and snow was beginning to fall again.

Sometimes, during the winter evenings, when she and Will sat together, he would fold his paper and put it aside and sit scarcely moving in his chair, watching her as she knitted or sewed.

'What are you thinking,' she asked once, 'when you sit so silent by the hour?'

'I dunno. You got me there. About the smithy, I suppose, and the job I'm doing for Mr. Lord. I'm mending a backboiler for him and I was remembering how my dad and me first made it for him twenty years ago.'

'You still miss your parents very much.'

'We was good friends, the three of us. They warnt all that old when they died and the way it happened, so sudden, like—'

'Tell me about it,' Ellen said.

'I was over at Brooks on a job. My father was in the smithy alone, working as always, clink-clink, and all of a sudden he

141

collapsed. My mother found him lying there. Nobody knew his heart was bad. She tried to lift him and strained herself, and what with the shock and everything, she followed him in less than three weeks. They was all I had in the world. When they were gone, there was nobody. Only the smithy, that's all, and this here cottage, left to me.'

'You're a very solitary man.'

'Not now,' he said, looking at her. 'I've got you and John to think about now, and one day, perhaps, if all goes well, the smithy and cottage will go to him.'

Ellen, who was making a rug, allowed it to fall into her lap.

'You can't look as far ahead as that. John is only six years old. Anything could happen by then.'

'I hope not, by golly! What sort of thing?'

'You might get married and have a few children of your own.'

'That old song of yours again? Seems you're determined to find me a wife! Have you got anyone in mind! It ent Nolly Byers by any chance?'

'Who's Nolly Byers?'

'Fred's sister. She's fifty odd. A nice enough girl in her way—'

'I wish you'd be serious for a change.'

'I ent getting married. I'm serious enough about that.'

'Very well. I'll say nothing more. But I don't know why you should set your face against it so.'

'Don't you?' he said, looking at her. 'You ought to know. It's simple enough.'

For a moment he seemed to be challenging her. There was something different in his mood. But it was his gaze that fell away first.

'What I mean is, you're a pretty good manager. The way you do things suits me fine. I should be pretty hard to please if I was to start looking round for a wife.'

Abruptly he rose and walked to and fro about the kitchen. He returned to the hearth and looked at the clock.

'Will, what's the matter?' Ellen asked.

'Nothing at all. Why should it be? I was thinking of going for a drink, that's all. Would you like me to bring you anything back?'

'No, thank you,' she said, and resumed her work with ragstrips and hook.

A few minutes later, looking across at his empty chair, she felt that she had driven him away.

The next year came in and brought hard frosts. The horse-pond at Rillets Farm was frozen across from rim to rim, and one afternoon, the carter's boy, dared by two or three of his friends, drove his horse and cart onto the ice. When he was roughly half way across, the ice broke with a loud crack, and horse and cart were in the water, badly stuck in the deep mud. Michael Bullock sent for Will, and he spent half an hour in the pond, with the icy water up to his armpits, half lifting, half coaxing the horse from the mud, while other men hauled on a rope round its neck.

No sooner were horse and cart delivered safely from the pond than someone came running to fetch Will because Mr. Rissington's bull had got out and was trampling all over the vicarage garden. Will got home at six o'clock and stood streaming in front of the fire.

'Aren't you going to change your clothes?'

'No, I've got work in the smithy,' he said.

'Why is it always you,' Ellen said, 'that gets called out at times like these?'

'I'm a big strong chap, that's why,' he said. 'I know that bull of Rissington's. It was me that put the ring in his nose. Why shouldn't they come to me about it?'

'They take advantage,' Ellen said. 'Because you're always so willing to help, they take advantage, all of them.'

'You may be right. But if one takes advantage, like you say, then why not another and all the rest?'

'You mean I do the same myself?'

'I never said that. I never did.'

'You thought it, however. I saw you smile.'

'You don't know what I was thinking. That was private, in my head. A man's mind is his own affair. It's the one place in all the world where he can be safe from nosey parkers.'

He took the bread and cheese she brought him and ate it, standing as he was, filling his mouth and chewing quickly.

'You women!' he said. 'You'd like to know us through and through, but that'd never do at all. My thoughts are my own, such as they are, and you shan't know them except when I choose.'

'It's perfectly true, anyway. I do take advantage. I know that. You've been so good to me, and you ask so little in return.'

'You keep house here and look after me. I don't see that I could ask much more.'

'You know what I mean.'

'Do I? Perhaps!'

'Will,' she said, touching his arm. 'I've seen the way you look at me—'

'Have you?' he said in a harsh voice. 'Then I must stop it, mustn't I?'

'Why are you in such a difficult mood?'

'We're different sorts of people, you and me,' he said, and, having finished his bread and cheese, he wiped his hand across his mouth. 'You're only got to hear us talk. The way we say things. I ent your sort.'

'You mustn't belittle yourself,' she said.

'That's what I tell myself sometimes. After all, you married Dick Lancy, didn't you, and I reckon I show up better than him?'

'Don't say things like that, Will. Richard was always a good man, until that accident turned his mind.'

'And you still love him, I know that. The man he was, anyway. You're still a faithful wife to him, and I've got no right to look at you.'

'That's what the world would say to us. But why should you do so much for me and get so little in return? I know I

144

can never pay you back but at least—'

'No! That's right! You can't!' he said, and moved away suddenly, so that her hand fell from his arm. 'I wouldn't want you to try, neither!' He went to the door and opened it. He spoke to her over his shoulder. 'I shall be working late tonight. Don't sit up and wait for me. I'll get what I want when I come in.'

At eleven o'clock he was still working. Ellen went through into the smithy and stood beside the glowing forge. The smeech of it made her eyes smart, and she stepped back a little, watching him work. He was making two new ploughs, identical in every respect, and was beating out the two new coulters, laid out together on the anvil. He did not look up when she came close. His sweat-moistened face was closed against her.

'Will,' she said, 'what is the matter?'

'Nothing,' he said, and went on working without pause.

'I've never seen you in this mood.'

There was no answer, only the noise of his hammer-strokes, with the chink-chink between as he turned each coulter with his tongs. She drew her shawl across her breast.

'Why are you treating me like this?'

'It's what you said to me, that's all! About your owing me this and that, and about your wanting to pay me back. As though I was someone who'd sent in a bill!'

'I didn't mean it like that. I put it badly. You misunderstood.'

'I don't want paying for what I've done! I'd have done it for anyone, not just you!'

'Yes,' she said, 'I know that.'

'Being so kind!' he said, scoffing. 'Offering yourself to pay a debt! What sort of man do you think I am?'

'It seems I can't talk to you in this mood. I shall leave you to take it out on the anvil. Your supper is ready whenever you want it. I'm going to bed and I'll say goodnight.'

He gave no answer, and she left him working.

*

It was sad and strange and almost unbelievable that two people could live so close, coming and going under one roof, and yet be such a distance apart. There was so much they knew about each other: the face of each, the man's, the woman's, was so familiar to the other, betraying feelings, thoughts, fears; yet still they were strangers, a barrier between them, and even while they talked together, as they had to whenever John was there, each took refuge in an inner silence.

'We've been here a year now, in your cottage. John and I were discussing it. A year tomorrow, to the very day.'

'A year? Is that so? Ah, it would be, you're right. The calendar says so if nothing else . . .'

Meaningless words, tossed between them for the sake of the child, who looked from one to the other with a worried, suspicious frown.

That winter was very severe, snow and frost coming by turns, and in the blizzard that blew all night on January the twenty-fourth, sheep at Neyes Farm and at Eddydrop were buried in snowdrifts fifteen feet deep. Will, in demand as usual, worked all day on the twenty-fifth, helping young David Rissington to dig out his flock. He then worked on throughout the night, repairing two snowploughs for the haywarden, and early next morning, when a message came from Mr. Draycott, he went immediately after breakfast to help with the buried flock at Neyes.

'Must you go?' Ellen said. 'Surely the Draycotts can manage together?'

'They're three men short, absent sick. They need all the help they can get. Don't keep dinner for me. I daresay I'll get a bite at Neyes.'

He was gone all day and returned home at nine that evening. He had been on his feet for forty hours, and, strong as he was, the weariness of it showed in the slow, sluggish way he removed his coat, in his heavy stillness as he sat in his chair beside the fire. He drank the tea Ellen gave him and passed his cup to be refilled. He looked at her through half-closed eyes.

'You ent going to scold me again, I hope, just cos I've been helping a neighbour?'

'No,' she said, quietly. 'I learnt my lesson the last time. Did you get the sheep out safe and sound?'

'Every last one,' he said, 'and that was a hundred and thirty-five.'

'What would you like for your supper?'

'Nothing, thanks. Old Draycott fed me like a king.'

His mood of the past few days was gone. He had driven himself to the point of exhaustion, and his bitterness had been purged away.

'I ought to go and shave by rights, instead of sitting taking my ease. I must be as black as that there hob.'

'Sit and be peaceful. You've earnt your rest. You're not indestructible, you know, and you've worn yourself out these last few days.'

'It ent very easy to wear me out. I'm a bit lapsadaisical, that's all, but I ent worn out. Oh dear me no!'

But as the warmth of the fire worked over him, gradually he began to nod. Soon his chin was on his chest and he was asleep, snoring gently. Ellen, in the chair opposite, sat quite still and studied him. She felt she knew him through and through.

He was a man who would answer any call for help. Nothing she said would alter him, and she smiled to think that she had tried. His face, with its broad cheekbones and blunt chin, had stubbornness in every line, and his straight black eyebrows told the same tale. His mouth, for all its readiness in smiling, could close as tight as a mussel-shell, and to anyone who read the signs it meant he was set on his own course and woe betide those who tried to turn him aside. He was a good man, Ellen thought, and he was obstinate in his goodness.

He awoke with a start and sat up straight in his chair.

'I wasn't sleeping if that's what you think!'

'Yes, you were. I've been watching you.'

'Well, dozing a bit, I grant you that.'

147

'You really ought to go to bed. You haven't slept for I don't know how long.'

'That's too good a fire to leave,' he said. 'I was always one for a good fire. Just to be sitting here like this is all the rest I want or need.'

But as he leant back in his chair again, his head against the hanging cushion, she could sense the aching tiredness in him as though it throbbed in her own bones, and, getting down on her knees beside him, she began untying his bootlaces.

'Here, what're you doing?' he exclaimed, and leant forward, trying to stop her. 'You ent a skivvy, to wait on me!'

But she merely pushed his hands aside and went on picking at the leather laces. They were tightly tied and still damp. She had some trouble, untying the knots.

'I'm something worse than a skivvy, I think, from what you said the other night.'

'Don't remind me what I said! I reckon I was in a mood.'

'You've got a right to say what you think.'

'I was just hitting out at you. Don't ask me why. It was a mood.'

'You thought I was offering myself to you without any tenderness or love, as payment for your kindness to me. You scorned being paid in such cheap coin.'

She had got the laces undone at last and now she drew off the heavy boots. She placed them beside the hearth to dry. She put his slippers on his feet, and remained where she was, sitting back on her heels, her dark green skirts spread out around her, her hands together in her lap.

'I don't blame you for hitting out, but I'm not really as bad as that.'

'Don't rub it in to me, what I said.'

'We should be able to understand each other by now. We know each other pretty well, if only we are honest about it.'

'I dunno so much!' he said. 'Know each other? I ent so sure!'

'Is it so hard to understand?'

148

Her face, reflecting the glow of the fire, had a delicate warmth in it and was tilted towards him, the shape of nose and chin outlined, the hollows in her cheeks very softly shadowed. Her dark brown hair, drawn so smoothly over her ears, had flecks of golden light upon it, and the same fireflecked light was in her eyes.

'Well?' she said. 'What are you thinking?'

'I'm thinking about the night you came, when Lancy turned you out of the mill. You warnt too happy, taking shelter here with me, and you said if I ever touched you—'

'Yes, I remember what I said.'

'You said you'd kill me, didn't you? And you looked at me in such a way, I reckon you would've, given the cause. "Glory be!" I said to myself. "I wonder what she thinks I am!" But that was a whole twelve months ago. I ent so pert about it now. And I've come pretty close to getting myself killed, once or twice, since that night a year ago. So don't be too sure about knowing me. You've got no idea what goes on in my mind. I'm only flesh and blood, you know. I'm only a man like any other.'

'And I'm only a woman,' she said. 'You don't make allowances for that.'

'I made a vow from the very start that I'd always treat you with respect—'

'Perhaps you treat me with too much respect.'

'Ah, no, you mustn't say that! I don't like to hear you say such things.'

Will leant forward a little way and put out his hands. They were big, scarred, work-hardened hands with square knuckle joints and square-tipped fingers, and, looking at them, he shook his head as though to say, 'What hands! What hands!' But the touch of his fingertips on her face was gentle, loving, rather shy, and she looked at him with fearless eyes.

'What've you been saying to me?' he asked in a voice she could barely hear. 'Ellen? Have you really thought?'

For answer, she turned and kissed his hands.

Chapter 10

Their son, Peter William, was born in December, 1881, a black-haired baby, the image of Will. At his baptism, after Christmas, the vicar stood as far away as he could from Will and Ellen, refusing to look them in the eye, and as soon as the ceremony was over, he hurried out without a word. There was no congregation in the church. He had told the village to keep away. Only the godparents, Bob Dyson, Jim Pacey, and Mrs. Beard, were there with Will, Ellen, and little John.

'Don't take no notice of *him*,' said Bob, jerking his thumb after the vicar, and Jim Pacey, sour-faced as ever, said: 'Just wait till the next time Rissington's bull gets into the vicarage garden again!'

Little John, now seven years old, was delighted at having a baby brother, and every day, coming in from school, he went at once to the cot in the corner to see if Peter was awake. One day, however, he seemed perplexed and turned to his mother with a frown.

'Why is he always sleeping, sleeping? Is there something wrong with him?'

'No, of course not,' Ellen said. 'Babies always sleep a lot.'

'You sure there's nothing wrong with him?'

'Quite sure. Why do you ask?'

'I only wondered, that's all. On account of his being ... oh, I dunno ...'

'Have they been saying things at school?'

'They're always saying things,' he said, and then, in a sudden angry burst: 'Somebody called him a little bastard!

150

Bobby Tozer it was said that. Why should people call him names? It's a bad thing, ent it, what they said?'

'It's because Will and I are not married. Some people will say things like that. But there's nothing wrong with your baby brother. Not in any way at all. And the best thing is to take no notice of what people say. They'll soon get tired of it if you ignore them.'

'I'm not going to let them call our Peter bad names!'

'Well, don't go getting into fights, or you will have to answer to me.'

'I shan't fight with Bobby Tozer. He's bigger than me. He's nearly ten. I'll have to wait a bit for that.'

'Good!' Ellen said, cheerfully. 'I'm glad to hear it. You've got good sense.'

But often she felt deeply ashamed of what the boy had to bear for her sake. She spoke about it to Will, alone.

'They are the ones that will suffer,' she said, nursing her baby at her breast. 'John now and Peter later – they'll have to bear the brunt of it all, because of what I've done with my life.'

'You ent done nothing. What've you done? It's just the way things've gone for you.'

'I've chosen to live with you like this. I've brought this baby into the world. I must take the blame for what I've done.'

'Not by yourself,' Will said. 'We've both done wrong, you and me, in the eyes of the village, anyway. I know how you feel. I feel the same. But I wouldn't change it, even so.'

Sitting on the edge of his chair, he leant forward across the hearth and touched the baby in her arms, poking at one tiny hand till it closed in a fist about his finger.

'We can't very well send him back, can we? Not now he's made hisself at home?'

'No, nor I wouldn't want to,' she said, and held the baby closer still, till it suckled sleepily at her breast. 'He's the best of babies. He is indeed.'

'No regrets, then?' Will said.

'Not on that score. None at all.'

'Me neither. Not a jot.'

In the smithy, sometimes, his customers tried to get a rise.

'How does it, feel, Will, being a father?' Billy Jukes asked one day.

'You should know. You got enough kids of your own.'

'Ah, but I'm a lawfully married man. My boys ent bastards. They're just little sods. Having them warnt no fun at all. It was just like pinching a pot of jam out of your own larder, like.'

Fred Byers, watching Will as he shaped a shoe on the beak of the anvil, shook his head regretfully.

'I knew you'd land in a peck of trouble when you gave up going to the inn and took to stopping at home in the evenings. There's many a good drinking man that's gone to the bad along that road. You should've stuck to your pint-pot of ale. It's a lot less costly in the end.'

'Costly? Rubbish!' Will said. 'Peter will come in the smithy with me. Him and John, the two of them, they'll be a support in my old age.'

Will was proud of his baby son. He would bring him into the crowded forge and show him off to his customers, and he was determined from the start that the boy should be accepted there. At the same time he took great care that John should never feel left out. He saw to it that the older boy got as much attention as the younger one. There would be no cause for jealousy if *he* had anything to do with it.

One day, when John was in the smithy, Mr. Preedy of Town End came in. He rapped Will with his riding-crop and said in his loud hallooing voice: 'How's this famous boy of yours that I'm always hearing so much about?' And Will, with his hand on John's shoulder, said: 'Both my boys is doing fine.'

One day in the summer of 1882, someone knocked at the smithy cottage, and Ellen went to the door with her baby in

152

her arms. The man who stood there was thin-faced and hollow-eyed, with a shock of grey hair and an untidy beard, and it needed an effort on Ellen's part to realize that this was her husband, Richard Lancy.

'Don't you know me, Nell?' he said. 'No, maybe you don't. It suits you better to forget I'm still alive, don't it?'

'What do you want?' Ellen asked.

'I came to wish you well,' he said, looking at the baby in her arms, 'and bestow my blessing on you both.'

'You don't expect me to believe that?'

'The way I see it is this,' he said. 'Now that Will Gale has given you a bastard son, you can spare me my own son back again, seeing he's all I've got in the world.'

'No! Never!' Ellen said.

'Then you'll be sorry, I promise you! One of these days, sure as fate, you and Gale will get paid out!'

'Richard, can't you leave us alone?'

'Why should I?' he said. 'I've got a score to settle with you and him and I shan't rest till I've settled it!'

He slouched away across the green and turned into the main road. Ellen watched till he went out of sight. At the smithy door, Will also watched. He came to Ellen and touched her arm.

'What did he want?'

'He was asking for John.'

'You look a bit peeky,' Will said. 'You'd better go in and sit down.'

'It gave me a shock, to see him again. He looks even wilder than before. It frightens me, Will, the way he's always threatening us.'

'He just likes to stir us up. He can't do nothing. It's just his talk.'

'I don't know. I wish I were sure.'

'He's made threats before and it's never come to nothing yet. You go indoors and take it easy. There's nothing for you to worry about. He just likes to stir us up.'

'Yes,' she said, 'I daresay you're right.'

153

But she worried about it all the same and sometimes, in dreams, she saw Richard's face as she had seen it long ago when he had walked in his sleep at the mill: blank, expressionless, blind-eyed, but with a queer intentness in it. She saw him walking, a grey ghost, moved by whatever it was that had taken the place of his own soul, stealing quietly into the room where she and Will slept side by side.

'What is it? What is it?' Will would say. 'You been having that dream again? There's nobody there, I promise you. Richard ent coming to do us no harm. You've been dreaming again, that's all.'

Will's strength and gentleness kept her safe and comforted her. He never for an instant shared her fears.

'I shall look after you,' he would say. 'And look after myself as well. Lancy can't hurt us, I promise you that.'

Often her fears were for little John, lest his father waylay him after school, but as time and its seasons passed by, these fears were pushed to the back of her mind. If John saw his father in the distance, as he did now and then in summertime, he would turn and run off in the other direction, and always, whatever temptation there might be from the other boys, he kept well away from the old mill.

'I ent going *there*! Oh, no, not me! I'd sooner fish upstream at Chack's.'

John, in his bedroom over the smithy, awoke every morning to the noise of iron striking iron, and went to sleep every night with the tune of it chinking in his dreams. The sounds of the smithy were music to him. The smell of horses and their dung, of hot iron and coalfire smoke, were the very breath of life itself. He longed for the day when he could take his place with Will.

'When can I start work in the forge?'

'The moment you've done with your lessons at school.'

'Mother says I must stop till I'm twelve.'

'That'll soon go,' Will said. 'You'll turn yourself round one of these days and find the years've gone like a flash. Why, look at young Peter, the way he grows. It's only five minutes since he was a baby cutting his first tooth. Now he's talking and walking about and weighs a hundred-weight on my scales.'

'D'you call that *talking*?' John said.

But Will was right about time passing. It went on wheels, there was no doubt of that, and every six months or so, when he put the two boys to stand at the wall, the marks would show how much they had grown.

'Peter will never catch up with me! Not if he grows and grows and grows!'

'He might do,' Will said, 'when you're both men.'

'Well, he'll never be as old as me, anyway.'

'No, that's true, he never will. There's seven years and three months between you and nothing will ever alter that.'

John, looking down on his little brother, was nevertheless protective towards him, helping him to cut up his food, fastening his buttons and bootlaces, and speaking up in his defence when Ellen scolded him for some misdeed. He could never bear to see Peter crying and once, when the little boy was ill with chicken-pox, John drank his nasty medicine for him, morning and evening for three days, before Ellen found out about it.

Peter, developing fast, was soon aware of the power his tears had over John. Whenever he wanted a pick-a-back ride, or a share of John's liquorice strings, or a story read to him at bedtime, he had only to cry to get his way. John once relinquished his best blood alley and six white commoneys to stop Peter's tears, only to find afterwards that Peter had dropped them down the drain.

'You shouldn't give in to him,' Ellen said. 'I don't spoil him. Neither does Will. You must be firm and say no.'

John did his best, but Peter's tears made him miserable, and always in the end he gave in. Until a day in September, 1885, when he said no and meant no. John had a small spyglass that Will had given him for his birthday. It was a miracle to John and he prized it above all other things, for

155

with it, as he rambled about, he could watch the birds of the air in their antics as though they were only a few yards away.

'No, you can't have it, you're much too young. You'd only break it. The answer is no.'

Peter cried and howled in vain. John for once was adamant and kept the glass in a secret place. But he felt uncomfortable all the same, especially as Peter, in his rage, ran blindly against the table and hurt his head.

'I hate you, John! I think you're mean! I hate you and hate you! I think you stink!'

'Hate away,' John said, with a great show of indifference, but he felt uncomfortable all the same.

Watching the flight of wild birds was a thing he never tired of, and as he grew older it occupied more and more of his time.

'Come along, John,' Will would say, when he took the two boys out on Roan Hill, 'Peter and me is wanting our dinner.'

But John would be watching a hovering kestrel as it hung without moving on the air. Through his spyglass he saw how very still it was. He would count the seconds while it hung.

'I dunno how they do it,' he said. 'I dunno how they manage it, stopping so still in the air like that, with scarcely a bivver in their wings.'

'I daresay they've practised a bit,' Will said.

He himself knew nothing of birds, although he was full of sayings about them.

'When you see a rook by itself, it's a crow!' he would say, and, whenever he saw a woodpecker: 'There goes the mean old baker's wife!' Geese going over meant a storm and the Seven Whistlers or Curlywhoos might just mean the end of the world. 'There's six of them flying about, you see, all on the look-out for one more, and when they find him, the old folk say, this world of ours will come to an end.'

'Will it really?' John asked.

'I shouldn't worry if I was you. The world will last long enough for you to come into the smithy with me!'

'And me? And me?' Peter said.

'That's right, the pair of you!' Will said. 'And shan't we see the sparks fly then!'

When Peter, aged four, began going to the village school, in the room above the butcher's shop, John held his hand all the way there and kept an eye on him during lessons. That same spring, in 1886, a new school was built at the north end of Dingham, with two separate classrooms in it, a playground with drinking-fountains, and a handsome gate with a stone arch above, on which were engraved some words.

'What's it say, John?' Peter asked.

'As-the-twig-is-bent-shall-the-tree-grow,' John said, reading slowly.

'What twig?' Peter asked. 'Is it Mrs. Tanner's stick that she canes us with when we're naughty?'

'Don't be silly. Of course it's not. It's only us older ones that get the cane.'

'Then what's it mean, about the twig?'

'I expect it's something out of the Scriptures, that's all.'

John was worried because in this big school Peter would be in a different room and he would not be there to protect him. He called all the younger children together and showed them his fist.

'If anyone calls my brother names, they'll get what-for, so just watch out!'

But Peter, from the first, was very well able to fight his own battles, and often it was the other children who came to John asking for help.

'Your Peter's a bully. He punched my nose. Just cos I wouldn't let him share my oneses.'

'Then it's up to you to hit him back. I ent got time to worry over you little uns. You run along and buck yourself up.'

John, during his last year at school, was something of a leader with the other boys of his own age, and was always up to some sort of mischief. Once, when Mr. Rissington left his horse and cart on the green, John and his followers sneaked up and loosened the traces, so that when Mr. Rissington returned and gave the ribbons a little twitch, the horse moved forward without the cart and he was pulled clean out of his seat. On another occasion, after dark, the boys put soap down the well on the green, and when the pump was used in the morning, bubbles issued from the spout and Mrs. Naylor's bucket was soon full of suds. Often the whole village was up in arms at once, because John and his band of desperadoes had been busy and had left a trail of havoc behind them. They removed knockers from cottage doors, released frogs in church on Sunday, and changed Mrs. Parker's line full of washing for that of her neighbour, Mrs. Pie.

'That'll be a good thing when John Lancy starts work in the forge,' people were always saying to Will. 'Sooner the better. He wants wearing down.'

On the day he left school John, with three other boys, raided old Mr. Draycott's orchard and carried away as many apples as each could tuck inside his shirt. The apples were green and John, having eaten one and found it sharp, took the rest home to his mother so that she could make a tart.

'Where did they come from?' Ellen asked.

'The orchard at Neyes,' John said.

'Then they must go back there, straight away. You must see Mr. Draycott and give them back.'

'I can't do that! He'd very likely tan my hide.'

'It may well be what you deserve.'

'Just a few apples? Glory be! What a tarnal fuss for a few apples!' And he watched her putting them into a basket. 'They ent even worth eating!' he said. 'Besides, I warnt the only one. There was three others along with me. I bet *they* ent got to take them back!'

'I'm not their mother. But I am yours. And you're taking these apples back at once.' Ellen, facing her angry son, saw rebellion in his eyes. 'I don't want my son to be a thief.'

'I ent a thief! No, I am *not*! Scrumping ent thieving. It's just a lark. You've got no right to say such a thing!'

'It seems you don't care to be called a thief?'

'No! I don't! And I won't have it!'

'Then you shouldn't be one,' Ellen said.

'All this fuss!' John exclaimed. 'What if I say I ent going?'

'You *are* going,' Ellen said, 'and don't think to deceive me for I shall see Mr. Draycott afterwards and make sure you've done as you're told.'

John snatched the basket out of her hand and stamped angrily to the door. He knew this unyielding mood of hers. His life would not be worth living until she had seen her order obeyed. But that he should have to face Mr. Draycott, that stern old man with the fierce white brows!

'The sooner you go,' Ellen said, 'the sooner it will be all over.'

So John went out across the green, up the track leading past the cartshed, and round to the back door of the farmhouse. As it happened, old Mr. Draycott was just coming out of the big barn, and behind him came Hannah, his granddaughter, a girl of about John's age, hugging a puppy in her arms. That John should have to face Mr. Draycott was bad enough, but that Hannah should be a looker-on was too unfortunate for words, and under her steady, critical gaze he felt himself growing as red as the turkeycock in the yard. She thought herself somebody, this girl, because she had left school at ten to keep house for her father and grandfather, and old Mr. Draycott encouraged her, saying she kept them both in hand.

'Well, boy, and what's this?' The old man looked at the basket of apples. 'You selling something?'

'I've been in your orchard. I took these.'

'Speak up, boy, speak up! Let's heart it plainly, whatever it is.'

'I took your apples,' John said, 'and my mother told me to bring them back.'

'Did she, by God! And who is she, this mother of yours, who means you to be an honest man?'

'Mrs. Lancy,' John said.

'Ah, yes, I know you now. John Lancy. Yes, of course. And what've you got to say for yourself, John Lancy, apple thief?'

'I reckon I'm sorry,' John said.

'So you should be! So you should!'

The old man took the basket of apples and emptied them into a barrel nearby. His face, although it seemed severe, with its white whiskers and flaring brows, had a certain humour in it, and his eyes especially seemed to laugh. He spoke to his granddaughter, standing by.

'What shall we do with him, eh, Hannah? Are we to let him off scot free?'

'If I had my way, he'd get a whipping,' Hannah said.

'What, after he's brought the apples back?'

'He's always in trouble of some sort. It was him that rode Mr. Grey's pony and got him all muddy that time.'

'At least he obeys his mother, though. I reckon he ought to have some reward.'

'H'mph!' Hannah said, and looked away, fondling the puppy in her arms.

'What about you?' the old man said to John. 'What do you reckon you deserve?'

'I dunno,' John said, and gave a slight shrug. The old man, he felt, was having him on.

'Well, I shan't whip you as Hannah suggests, but I'll let you do me a favour instead. She's just going to take the goats to the green. You can go with her and give her a hand. How's that? Does it seem fair?'

'I dunno. I suppose so.'

The old man took Hannah on one side, and something passed from his hand to hers. John pretended not to see. He stood with the basket on his arm and stared at a wagtail on the roof. The old man took charge of the tiny puppy, and Hannah walked across the yard.

'Come on, you,' she said to John, and he followed her round the end of the barn, into a field that was part oat-stubble and part beans. 'Leave the gate,' she said, tossing the words over her shoulder.

160

'So you'd have me whipped, would you?' he said.

'Yes, I should. It's what you deserve.'

'Your grandfather don't agree with you.'

'My grandfather is much too easy-going.'

'I can see that,' John said, 'by the way he lets you speak to him.'

The two nanny goats, one white, one brown, were tethered on the oat-stubble. Hannah pulled one tethering-rod out of the ground, wound the rope in a loose coil, and held it like a halter, close to where it encircled the goat's neck. She stood waiting while John did the same with the other, then she led the way down the stretch of stubble, taking the shortest route to the green.

But John's goat refused to move. It dug its feet into the ground, pulled hard on the rope, and, putting its muzzle into the air, knuckered at him, showing its teeth.

'I thought you were supposed to be strong!' Hannah said, waiting for him.

'I don't want to choke her, do I?' he said.

'No fear of that. Try pulling harder. She's playing you up.'

But although John pulled with all his strength, the goat merely yielded a step or two and once again came to a halt.

'It's because she don't know you,' Hannah said.

'She *will* know me in a minute!' He held up his fist.

'Don't you hit her! Don't you dare!'

'Glory be! As though I would!'

'I'll hurry on with Rosalee, then perhaps Belinda will follow.'

Sure enough, when Hannah walked on with the white goat, the brown goat followed with a burst of speed, and John, completely taken by surprise, was pulled stumbling along behind it. The tethering-iron fell on his toe, the coil of rope slid from his arm, and his feet got caught in its many tangles. He fell headlong, onto his face, and the empty basket, round-bottomed, went bowling merrily down the slope. So that by the time he reached the green he was breathless, bruised, covered

161

in mud, and very thoroughly out of temper.

When they led the two goats onto the green, several children gathered round, and the rumpus they made brought a few neighbours out to watch. Little Peter came out of the cottage, and Will came out of The Old Tap.

'If it ent our John there, acting the goat! And him so thick with Hannah Draycott! Would you believe it? I never did!'

'Don't speak to *me*!' John muttered, still struggling with the tangled rope.

'Don't speak to *him*!' Will said. 'He's doing his knitting and he's dropped a stitch.'

John was looking round for a stone, and when he bent to pick one up, the brown goat, Belinda, butted him hard against the rump, pitching him forward head over heels in a neat little somersault on the grass. The people watching laughed in delight. Will's laughter was loudest of all and Peter, beside him, almost choked.

But John, as he stood, was chiefly aware of Hannah Draycott's superior stare, and rage for a moment blinded him. He felt he could strike her in the face. Then suddenly he was calm. He brushed himself down with a certain jaunty deliberation, retrieved the lost stone, and hammered the tethering-iron into the ground, keeping an eye on the goat and assuming a comical nervousness.

Hannah had already dealt with her goat and now, as John finished, she came to him and held out sixpence.

'My grandfather told me to give you this.'

'I don't want it, thanks all the same.'

'It's yours for helping with the goats.'

'I don't need to be paid for that. I reckon you'd better keep it yourself. – Buy yourself a string of beads.'

John was rather pleased with this. It put Hannah Draycott in her place. But then, as he was turning away, the glittering sixpence fell at his feet.

'*I* don't want it!' Hannah said. 'Why should I want it, for heaven's sake?'

She turned and walked across the green.

'In that case,' said John, to those who watched, 'it'll just have to damn well stay where it is!'

Peter ran forward and snatched up the coin.

'If you don't want it, can I have it?'

'If you like,' John said. 'It's no odds to me.'

He picked up the empty apple-basket and sauntered homewards across the green.

Soon after that, John's indentures were drawn up, and he was formally bound apprentice to Will Gale, blacksmith, of Dingham Green. On the following Monday, he was at work in the smithy, starting at six o'clock in the morning and going on till eight at night. He considered himself a man now and he was determined to do a man's work. When Will suggested an hour's rest, John only drove himself harder still. He worked the bellows till every muscle quivered and ached; he brought in the coals and got rid of the ashes; he drew and carried supplies of water; and he ran to and fro, fetching new iron from the shed at the back. At the end of that first day, when he sat down to supper, he had barely enough strength left to eat, and Ellen, packing him off to bed, looked reproachfully at Will.

'Must you work him so hard? He's only twelve.'

'There's no stopping him,' Will said.

During his early days in the smithy, John was forever getting grit in his eye, or burning his hands, or dropping iron on his toes. But there came a time when he was so hardened to these misfortunes that he scarcely noticed them any more. And there came a time, too, when the accidents happened less and less. He had been in the smithy about six weeks. He came to a standstill one afternoon and looked at his hands.

'Just look at that,' he said to Jim. 'Hardly a scratch anywhere.'

'Ah, you're finding your feet, sure enough. You're a lot more nimble than you was.'

'He gets the practice,' Will said, 'keeping out of the way of them goats.'

The two Draycott goats remained on the green till the end of September, and every two or three days or so, Hannah came to take up the rods and move them to a fresh place.

'There's young Hannah,' Will would say. 'Ent you going to give her a hand?'

'Not me!' John said. 'Oh dear me no!'

But one morning when Hannah came, the ground was hard for lack of rain, and she had trouble driving the rods into the turf. John stood at the smithy door and watched her at it. She was using a tiddly bit of stone that anyone with half an eye could see would break in a few seconds. So he went and fetched a sledge hammer and walked briskly across the green. He ordered Hannah to stand back, and, with two clean, swinging blows, drove the rod into the ground. When he stood erect again, Hannah bobbed him a little curtsey.

'Thank you kindly, sir, I'm sure.'

But there was no gratitude in her glance. There was only a bored, superior amusement, as though she thought he was showing off.

'It's nothing,' he muttered. 'You'd have been all day, patting at it with that stone. Let's get on and do the other.'

'All right, but mind you keep out of Belinda's way.'

'D'you think I'm afraid of a damned goat?'

'Tut,' she said, moving on, 'he's swearing like a grown man.'

When the second rod had been driven in, John shouldered his sledge hammer and would have turned away at once, but Hannah was looking at his leather apron, which, with its raged untidy fringe, reached almost to the ground, and he saw that she was hiding a smile.

'Something amusing you?' he said.

'That apron of yours is so long, you'll trip over it if you're not careful.'

'I shan't trip over it, don't you worry.'

'The rats've been at it, too,' she said. 'They've made it all ragged at the end.'

John looked her straight in the eye.

'A blacksmith's apron,' he said with scorn, 'is always ragged at the bottom.'

'Tut-tut, he's a blacksmith now,' Hannah said, turning away, 'and there was I, thinking he was only an apprentice!'

John went back into the smithy and met Will's enquiring glance.

'I thought I'd give her a hand,' he said. 'She warnt getting nowhere, fooling about with that bit of stone.'

But it would be many a long day, he added grimly to himself, before he helped Hannah Draycott again.

Chapter 11

His work in the smithy was a passion with him and the day he made his first horseshoe he became certain in his bones that he had it in him to be a good smith.

Until then he had had his doubts. There was such a tremendous amount to learn: about the iron in the fire; about the iron under the hammer; about the unity there had to be between eye and brain and hand and tool. It seemed he would never learn these things, and often he railed at his own slowness and clumsiness. But, from the day when he made his first horseshoe, the doubts fell away. He would do it, given time. The fire and the iron would yield their secrets up to him and he would fashion forth those things, from the blades of scythes and reaping-hooks to the shafting and drums of the traction engine, by which men got a living from the land.

That first horseshoe was made for stock. It hung upside down on a nail on the wall. And John, in passing, would give it a tap, setting it swinging to and fro. Sometimes he stopped and took it down, trying the weight of it in his hands, feeling the crimp of its inside edge, squinting at the nailholes, four and three. And Jim Pacey, catching him at it, would say in his dry old sourpuss way: 'It's a masterpiece. That's what it is. You ought to wear it round your neck.'

But the horseshoe in fact was not very good and John knew it. He had to do better, and better again. He watched Will Gale with hungry eyes and schooled himself to a man's patience.

166

'If I could only be half like Will . . .' he said to his mother one day, and Ellen, watching his eager face, smiled at her own innermost thoughts.

For John, after years of imitation, was so like Will in many ways that he might have been his own son. Everything he did, in the smithy and elsewhere, was done with Will's little tricks and manner. The way he rolled his shirtsleeves up and the way he handled a pair of tongs; the way he sauntered out to the green and said he was going to air his lungs; the way he splashed and gurgled and gasped when washing himself in the scullery; even his voice, deepening when he was four-teen, became exactly Will's in tone, and he had the same teasing, easy-going humour.

He and Will worked well as a team. There was a special understanding between them. Even while John was still quite young, not yet fully skilled, Will would ask for his opinion.

'Two heads is better than one, even if it's only two sheep's heads, so come and have a look at this here cart-brake, will you, John?'

And although at first he did it chiefly to encourage John in thinking things out for himself, there soon came a time when the boy's opinion had some value of its own.

'John can *see* things,' he would say. 'He'll be a better smith than me by the time he's through, and when I get to fifty or so, I'll take a little farm some place and let him get on with it in the forge.'

'What about me?' Peter demanded. 'I shall be in the forge too!'

'Why, yes, of course,' Will said. 'You and John'll work together, ding-dong, while your mother and me sit back a bit and raise a few chickens on our farm.'

Peter, as a boy, like John before him, was always hanging about the smithy. Often he had to be driven out forcibly to go to school and on one occasion John had to drag him all the way to the gate. Peter was so enraged by this that he wouldn't speak to John for a week. He was, as his father said sometimes, a powerful and determined sulker. But it was not

167

that he disliked school. It was merely that he liked the smithy better.

'When can I have some iron to work on? When can I have a go with the hammer?' And John, teasing his half-brother, would say: 'When you're tall enough to see over the top of the anvil!' Peter would fly into a passion at this. 'I ent that small! You! I am not! I'll be a better smith than you!' And often as he grew older, repeating what he heard on the green, he would say: 'I'm Will Gale's son. I shall take after him. You ent his son. *You* ent got smithing in your bones.'

John had no answer to make to this. He could not take refuge in pretence, as he had done in earlier times. His brother had him cornered here and made the most of it time and again.

'*Your* father,' he would say, 'is the Mad Miller of Pex Mill!'

John would turn away with a shrug but it was a good many years before he could hear Peter's jibe without a sinking of the heart. And even then – even when he was a grown man – it still cost him a pang that he could not boast, as Peter did, of being Will Gale's son.

Sometimes he saw his own father here or there about the village. A scarecrow figure of a man whose face, although gaunt, was somehow fleshy and looselipped, always dewy with drops of sweat. Whose dulled eyes were never still but seemed always, even when he stopped to talk, to be seeing something that crept or crawled just behind you.

'The way Lancy looks at you,' Jim Pacey said once, 'it makes you feel as if you'd got a lot of snakes coming out of the back of your collar.'

John never met his father if he could help it. Seeing the waggon in the distance, he would contrive to slip away. But a meeting could not be avoided for ever, and one day in the summer of 1891, father and son came face to face, unexpectedly, in Gow's Lane. John by then was nearly seventeen. He was tall, well-made, square-shouldered, strong, and he carried himself with something of Ellen's graceful ease. Richard stood in front of him and looked him over with hungry eyes.

'My God!' he said, and his voice had the strained huskiness of the man whose throat has been roughened by drink. 'It's my son John, grown a man. You ent denying you're my son? Cos you did do, once, when you was a boy, and it hurt me worse than you'll ever know.'

He put out a hand and touched John's arm. His fingers moved up to the shoulder, feeling muscle, flesh, and bone. Briefly, he even touched John's face, and John endured it, surprised to find that fear had gone. The revulsion he felt as he looked into the hot-fleshed face and tried to meet the slithering eyes was because he saw his father's sickness. Felt it, smelt it, like a disease. But now he no longer felt afraid. He was a man and had a man's strength and courage. His father, once, had been very strong. Now John could have felled him with a blow. Somehow it made him pity him.

'You ent denying you're my son?'

'No.'

'You're working in Gale's smithy, ent you? I can see by your skin. That ent no proper work for you. It's not healthy. It's not right.'

'I like it,' John said. 'It's what I want.'

'You should ought to come to me. I need your help in running the mill.'

'I better prefer to be a smith.'

'You running off again?' Richard said.

'I've got an errand out at Brooks.'

'Running off! Turning your back! Can't you even stop and talk?' And, following John along the lane, he called out in his husky voice: 'Tell Will Gale I'll be even one day! I ent forgot what he done to me! I'll serve him out and make him pay!'

When John repeated this in the smithy, Will merely shrugged.

'He's been saying that for years. It ent come to much, I'm glad to say. But you'd better not mention it to your mother. It'll only start her worrying again.'

'I reckon he's going downhill.'

'I reckon he is,' Will agreed.

There were still plenty of stories told about Richard's strange and violent behaviour. Only a few weeks before, he had attacked old Jerry Trussler, delivering fish in Water Lane, and had tried to steal old Jerry's donkey.

'I gave you that donkey as a loan. I reckon it's time I had him back!'

There had been an exchange of blows. The parish constable had come and Richard had received a summons. Nothing much had been heard since, but some people said that Richard ought to be put away, and Jerry Trussler was one of them.

'I had to have stitches in my head! Fred'll tell you, he was there. And that ent the same donkey Lancy gave me years ago. This here donkey is only three!'

'Mad as a hatter,' Fred Byers said. 'He really ought to be put away.'

'But he ent never done no one any serious harm, has he, Fred?' said Joe Dancox. 'Apart from Jerry's stitches, that is?'

'Have we got to wait till he kills someone, then, before they ups and puts him away?'

One day in 1893, as John walked through Dingham on his way to Cockhanger Farm, he came on his father a second time, being teased by a crowd of children.

Richard's waggon stood in the road, and a sack of meal had fallen off. The sack was rotten and had burst open. Three or four boys were kicking it along the road. And while Richard lunged at them, others were at the back of the waggon, rocking it from side to side in the hope of dislodging another sack.

John descended on them in wrath, and, being quicker than his father, made himself felt with a few stinging slaps. Within a minute, the children had retreated to a safe distance, and John was helping his father to rope the sacks onto the waggon.

170

'You're a good boy, John. I knew you was. You're a good son to me, in spite of it all, and I shan't forget what you've done today. I shan't forget. You mark my words.'

Having secured his end of the rope, he got down on his haunches and began gathering up the loose bean-meal that had spilt in the road, scraping it up between his hands and throwing it into the burst sack. John watched him, ashamed to see him scuffling about, gathering meal and dirt together, and yet unwilling to leave him alone while the children watched from nearby. And after a while he too got down in the road and helped to scrape up the scattered meal, aware that two or three women had come to their doors, to join their jeering, sneering children.

'There, we've done our best,' he said, rising. 'I should move on if I was you.' He wiped his hands on his corduroys.

'Where are you heading for?' Richard asked. 'Maybe I can give you a lift.'

'No, I'm cutting across to Cockhanger Farm.'

'Suit yourself. Suit yourself. But you're a good son to me after all and I shan't forget what you done today.'

Richard drove off along the road and John, with his toolbag slung over his shoulder, took the pathway up to Skyte. He was gone until late in the afternoon, and when he returned to the smithy at five, the story of his meeting with his father had got there before him. Jim Pacey mentioned it.

'Seems you and your dad is getting pretty matey these days, from what Tommy Breton was telling us.'

'The kids was teasing him,' John said, and sought Will's gaze. 'A sack'd fallen off the waggon. I gave him a hand fixing the rope.'

'You don't have to explain yourself to me, John. There's plenty of people, I daresay, who will find it funny to watch how you act when you meet your dad. But you don't want to mind them. They ent worth the paper they're printed on.'

'I couldn't very well pass him by.'

'Of course you couldn't,' Will said. 'You got to do what you think is right.'

Some weeks later, on a rainy morning in July, Richard, with his waggon, drew up outside the smithy door. His mare had cast a shoe, he said, and he wanted John to see to it. He completely ignored Will, who had come out in case of trouble, and addressed himself only to John. He would wait, he said, while the job was done.

It was the first time Richard had come to the smithy on business for twelve years. John was rather at a loss, but, receiving a little nod from Will, he went ahead and did the work. Richard remained where he was, sitting up on the waggon in the rain, his coat-collar up and his hat-brim down. He made no move to get down and help when John took the mare out of the shafts, nor when he brought her back again, but sat hunched, perfectly still, a bundle of rags, apparently lifeless. But when John came round to the side to be paid, he sprang to life perkily and looked down in great surprise.

'Pay?' he said in a loud voice. 'What, pay my own son for a fiddling little job like that, just putting one shoe on and nothing else? You're having me on, boy. You're pulling my leg!'

John went prickly hot all over. He felt the blood rush into his face. Behind him, in the smithy, all noise of work had stopped abruptly, and as he stood, trying hard to find his tongue, he knew that Will and his customers had come to the door. Richard, having achieved his object, pretended not to see them. As before, he spoke only to John.

'A son don't charge his father, boy. It's one of the perkses between two trades. I wouldn't charge *you* if you came to me with some corn to grind. Nor I don't expect to pay for a trifle of shoeing, neither, not when the smith is my own son.'

'I ent the master here,' said John, 'I'm only the apprentice.'

'You do a good job, though, I daresay?'

'I hope so, yes.'

'As good as your master would have done?'

'I dunno about that, I'm sure.'

'You did the work, not your master, boy. And you surely

172

wouldn't charge your own dad?'

'Look here!' said John. 'Seems I'd better pay it myself.'

But Will stepped forward and stood at his side.

'No need for that, John. Let it go. Like your father said, it's only a trifle, nothing more. If he means to bring his trade here again, well, that'll be another matter. He can settle up at the end of the year.'

Richard looked directly at Will.

'I've got a long score to settle with you already and you needn't think that I've forgot. You stole my wife and son from me and turned them against me all these years, but now my boy is a grown man and I reckon he can think for himself. We ent enemies, him and me. We're the same flesh and blood. We belong together. And I shall get him back again if it takes me a lifetime, I promise you that!'

He flicked at the ribbons and drove slowly down the road, round the bottom of the green, and back again up the far side, into the main road of the village. John and Will stood watching him go.

'I'm sorry about that,' John said. 'It's all my fault for helping him the other day.'

'Don't worry about it,' Will said. 'He's bound to feel sore, the way things are, and this is his way of getting back at me. It's only a fleabite, that's all. We must just bear it as best we can.'

Ellen, however, on hearing about the incident, was gravely troubled.

'Sometimes I wish we could go away from here,' she said. 'Right away, where Richard can't reach us.'

'Laws!' said Will. 'I shouldn't like that. I've lived in Dingham all my life.'

And young Peter, now eleven, looked at them all with his black-browed scowl.

'Why should we go away from here, just because of Dick Lancy? Who cares a damn for the Mad Miller?' And he turned to John. 'If Lancy wants you so bad,' he said, 'why not go and live with him and help him with running his old mill?'

'Because I don't want to,' John said.

'The mill'd be yours when your dad was dead. Seems to me you haven't thought.'

'That'd just about suit you, wouldn't it, eh?' And John, with a laugh, punched Peter's chest. 'I know how it is with you, my lad! – You want to take my place in the smithy!'

'Not me,' Peter said, with a shrug. 'My own place is waiting for me and I shall be in it come August time.'

'I pity that anvil!' John said, winking at Will. 'We shall see something soon, eh, Will, when our Peter starts work in the smithy?'

'By golly, yes!' Will agreed. 'The sparks'll be flying then, I'll be bound!'

And afterwards, alone with Ellen, he spoke to her about her fears.

'You don't really want to leave Dingham, do you, Nell?'

'It's Richard coming and pestering John. I'm always afraid of what he'll do.'

'He won't do nothing. What can he do? I know he stirs us up a bit, but it's only a fleabite, that's all. I reckon it's something we've got to bear and it's little enough, all told, compared with how happy and comfortable we all are most of the time, ent it, now?'

Ellen, smiling, agreed with him. She put the matter out of her mind.

At the end of that summer, Peter started work in the smithy. He scorned staying at school until twelve and Will, for the sake of peace and quiet, gave in and let him have his way. His indentures were drawn up by the lawyer in Runston, and were locked away in Will's iron document-box which was kept, safe from thieves, on a ledge inside the kitchen chimney. And just as Peter's apprenticeship began, John's was drawing to a close.

It was a Saturday in September; a beautiful day, sunny and warm; and at four o'clock in the afternoon, Will called a halt to all work in the smithy. Followed by John, Peter, and

Jim Pacey, he led the way out, up the green, to the open door of The Old Tap. There he called for the landlord, Shaw, who, knowing what was expected of him, came out with a gallon jug of beer and fistful of tankards. The customers also came out and stood around watching as Will, with a certain dignity, took a rolled document from his shirt and gave it into John's hands.

'There's your indentures back again, that was drawn up and signatured seven years ago, all sealed and witnessed in the proper way by the lawyer chap in Runston town. You've served your time in the smithy with me and that there paper's a proof of it. You can go wherever you like with that and any smith will give you work, and I'll say in front of these witnesses that any smith will be lucky to have you.'

John, somewhat flushed, shook Will's hand. It took him a moment to clear his throat.

'I'd a lot rather stop on here.'

'That's what I hoped you'd say, my boy, and that's what we'll drink to, all of us. Now ale all round for everyone so's they can drink to my boy John.'

'Your very good health, John!' the onlookers said, raising their mugs.

'And yours!' said John. 'I'm much obliged.'

As he took his first draught, Peter put a hand under the mug and tilted it against John's mouth, so that the ale sloshed over his face and trickled down his throat and neck.

'Your very good health, John! Mind you don't choke!'

John untied his sweat-rag and wiped the ale from his face and throat.

'I'll give you choke in a minute!' he said. 'I'll put you under that there pump.'

'Oh, he's somebody now!' Peter said. 'Now he's got his indentures and all. It's tuppence to speak to him today!'

'Never mind, Peter,' said Fred Byers. 'You'll have your day, all in due course, and your dad will do the same for you.'

'I know that!' Peter said. 'Tell me something I don't know!'

Standing well away from the group for fear of John's retaliation, Peter drank from his pint tankard, and the older men watched, much amused, as his throat-muscles worked manfully and the tankard was drained to the very bottom.

'Be careful you don't fall in, my lad!'

'You're doing mightily, that you are, for a little tucker twelve years to be!'

Peter set his tankard down and wiped his mouth with the back of his hand.

'Time we was getting back to work.'

'I reckon it is,' Will agreed, but to John he said very casually: 'No need for you to hurry, boy. Have another drink on me and enjoy yourself while you got the chance.'

So John, it being his special day, lingered outside The Old Tap, talking to the Shaws and Billy Jukes and old Byers and Joe Dancox, and making his second mug of beer last. And as he stood there in the sun, one hand in the breast of his shirt, where the rolled indentures lay half-hid, Hannah Draycott came out of the cottage next to the church and walked past on her way to the shop. She carried a basket in one hand and a leather purse in the other.

'Nice day!' said John, nodding politely. 'Makes you feel glad to be alive.'

Something had happened to him today. He felt he could talk to anyone, even Hannah. And she perceived the difference in him. She eyed him warily as she passed.

'Nice day for drinking, seemingly.'

'A man must drink if he's got a thirst.'

'A man?' she said, and walked on.

'I shouldn't stand for that!' said Jukes. 'It's saucy, that is. You should answer her.'

'You're right and I shall,' John said, and, seeing that Hannah had stopped to read a poster on the wall outside the shop, he strolled along and tackled her. 'If I'm not a man, what am I?' he said. 'I surely ent a woman, I hope!'

Hannah turned and looked at him. Her eyes were a clear light shade of brown.

'A pint-pot in your hand doesn't make a man.'

'What does, however? You tell me that.'

'I've got errands to do for my aunt. I've got no time for gossiping.'

'Come along, now, I want to know. I'm turned nineteen and I'm fully growed and I've been shaving for donkey's years. If that don't make me a man, I should like to know what does.'

Hannah was cornered. He had her now. She was wishing she'd never made that remark, and it served her right, he told himself. But she was as cool as ever she was and her voice when she answered was quite unflurried.

'Perhaps a little common sense.'

'You think common sense would make me a man?'

'It would help,' she said, 'certainly.'

'Maybe you're right,' John said. He was enjoying himself today. He had suffered enough from her in the past, but now he was in command of himself and could match her coolness word for word. And he knew, furthermore, that the few men listening were on his side, willing him to win if only because this was his special day. 'The trouble is,' he said, 'how can us men have common sense when plainly you women've got it all?'

He then sauntered back to the grinning group at the inn door, taking his place there, a man among men.

'Now what was we talking about?' he said. 'Ah, yes, the cricket match—'

Behind him, the grocer's doorbell rang, and he knew Hannah Draycott had gone inside. He finished his drink and went back to the forge.

'Seven years!' Peter said. 'Seven years learning the trade. I shall be an old man like John by then! When am I really going to *start*?'

'I hope you're learning something already,' Will said indulgently.

'Oh, yes!' Peter said. 'I'm learning how to sweep the floor!'

'All in good time,' Will said, handing him the watering-can. 'Rome wasn't built in a day, you know, nor a blacksmith can't be made over-night.'

Peter, at the age of twelve, was exactly the image of his father, and the likeness grew stronger all the time. But although he had Will's face and features, the same straight black hair, the same square build, he had little of Will's easy-going temper, and little of Will's extreme patience.

'Why does it always have to be me that sweeps up the horse-muck and empties the ashes? Why always me and never John? I've already brought in the water, ent I? Why does it always have to be me?'

'The apprentice always does them jobs,' said Will. 'John done his share, by golly, yes, right up to the very day you came. Ah, and he made a lot less fuss about it than you, boy, I tell you straight.'

'Oh, John is a masterpiece, no doubt of that! The sun can't rise in that there sky without he gets the credit for it!'

'I knew he'd be in a mood,' said John. 'He tried my new cap on this morning, first thing, and no one could find him for half an hour!'

'I didn't try your rotten cap! I picked it up by mistake for my own.'

'Here, I'll give you a hand,' John said, and, turning the ashbin on its side, began to shovel out the ash, into the waiting wheelbarrow.

'That's Peter's job,' Will said, 'and you should leave him get on with it.'

'Just this once,' John said. 'He wants to watch you weld them bars.'

'I don't just want to watch,' Peter said. 'I want to help with making them tyres.'

'Well, you can't, and that's flat!' Will said. 'You'll do as you're told and watch, that's all, and see that you don't get in our way.'

Peter, scowling, went to the forge. He took up a pair of long-handled tongs and turned an iron bar in the fire. The red-hot coals were a-tremble with heat, and the iron itself was almost white, pulsing as though with a life of its own. *That* was where a smith's work lay; where he made his mark and showed his skill; and Peter felt the pulse of the iron, the same way he felt the pulse of his heart. The craft of it was in his bones. The knowledge of it was in his blood. It was all wrong that he should be held back like this, day after day, week in, week out. He could show them something, given the chance. Now if *he* was going to weld two bars—.

'Get away from that fire and leave that tarnal iron alone!' Jim Pacey roared, working the bellows. 'How many times've you got to be told?'

'Don't you shout at me!' Peter said. 'I ent going to stand for it! By God, I'm not!'

And, shedding his apron as he went, he dashed out of the smithy door. It was not the first time he had stormed out and left his work. They knew he would not be home until after dark, when his family were all in bed, and in the morning, sidling late into the smithy he would take up the empty water-pails and go without a word to the pump.

'That boy!' Will would say, shaking his head. 'He'll learn, I suppose, but don't ask me when!'

Time for Peter seemed not to move. His first year at work in the smithy seemed the longest in his life. Even the second was not much better, for he was given only the simplest tasks, such as cutting old horseshoes up for tuckers, or cleaning old implements of their rust, or mending the neighbours' pots and pans. These tasks were hateful to him and one day when Pacey gave him a pair of sheep-clipping shears to grind he hurled them into a far corner.

'I'm sick to death of these fiddly oddlies! When am I going to do something worth doing?'

'The trouble with you is, you want to run before you can walk,' Jim Pacey said to him. 'You want to be a frog without serving your time as tadpole.'

'You seem to forget I'm Will Gale's son. My dad, my

179

granddad, and right back for five generations, have all been blacksmiths in this place and all been masters of their trade.'

'Ah, and the line'll likely come to an end with you, lad, the way you're going.'

'What d'you mean?'

'Them cart-springs you mended yesterday and that there hinge you made last week – you should be ashamed of such shoddy work.'

'It warnt worth the labour, that's why. It was just to give me something to do!'

'That's how you learn, boy. That's how you learn. Every job's worth doing if you've got somebody paying for it.'

'Hah! Tuppence-ha'penny down the drain! I won't lose no sleep for that.'

'Jim's right,' Will said. 'If you don't buck up your ideas a bit, you'll get no jobs to do at all. You must show yourself to be a smith in the making, and there ent much sign of it so far.'

'A smith in the making!' Peter sneered. 'That makes me laugh!'

But he went and retrieved the sheep-clippers and spent half an hour grinding them until, as he said, a man could have shaved with them, easily. He cared very much what his father thought of him. His work showed improvement for a while.

The trouble was that Peter, proud of being Will Gale's son, expected everything to come easily to him. The blacksmith's skill was his birth-right. It should come as naturally to him as walking and talking and drawing breath. He should not have to strive for it, as did the sons of lesser men, nor should he have to be ordered about by anyone but Will himself. When Will was out, he did as he liked, and he tried giving orders to Pacey and John. Pacey merely turned his back, and John laughed at him, saying: 'Right you are, young un! You show us how!'

Whereas John, from the very first, had approached each task with deep suspicion, sensing the problems, prepared for the worst, Peter would rush at it eagerly, thinking to toss off a piece of work with his father's quickness, his father's apparent lack of thought. Perhaps, had he been the only boy, it might have been different, but rivalry was a sharp spur that goaded him and destroyed his judgment. He was seven years younger than John and yet he expected to catch him up. After all, he was Will Gale's son, and John was not.

This was a favourite taunt of his, repeated often over the years, and on one occasion, Peter being by now sixteen, John rounded on him in a moment of utter exasperation.

'Yes, yes, we all know whose son you are! And we all know that it makes you something different from the rest of us, though what that is I don't like to say!'

Peter looked at him with a smile. He was pleased to have stung his brother for once. He made the most of it while he could.

'I'd rather be Will Gale's bastard,' he said, 'than Richard Lancy's son by marriage, and so would you if the truth was known.'

'Yes, well,' John said. His outburst had not been a serious one, but Peter's answer made him ashamed, and he was aware of Will nearby, watching and listening although hard at work. 'Yes, well, you're right there.'

At supper that evening, Peter referred to the incident. He looked at his mother and told her about it.

'Our John's been throwing it up to me that I'm a bastard. You want to watch out for yourself, mother, or God knows what he'll be calling *you*.'

'I shan't call her nothing,' John said. 'That other was just between you and me. I'll say I'm sorry if that's what you want, cos I never meant to hurt your feelings.'

'It's no odds to me,' Peter said. 'It's my mother's feelings that count, not mine.'

'Mother would never have known about it if you hadn't told her,' John said.

Ellen looked at her two sons and under her gaze they became sheepish. She looked across the table at Will and began speaking, quietly, about other things. No quarrel would last long in that household if she had anything to do with it, and within a few seconds, John and Peter were laughing together at her story of the currant cake that had disappeared.

'Where did you find it in the end, mother?'

'Upstairs, in the bedroom, on the bed. And your father's underwear, only just ironed, was in the cake-tin in the larder.'

'Seems like you're getting absent-minded, don't it, mother?'

'Yes,' Ellen said, with a little smile, 'I'm getting old.'

Again she looked across at Will and in the glance that passed between them, as John had often noticed before, there was a deepening of amusement, as though there were something beyond the particular joke of the moment, and only they had the key to it.

Watching his mother's face now and thinking of what she had just said, about getting old, he said to himself: Yes, well, perhaps it was true. She was a woman of forty-four. There were little lines about her eyes, there were traces of grey in her soft brown hair. But she was beautiful, he thought, and the sudden discovery took his breath. He saw her as though for the first time and he thought it must be some trick of the light or some soft fancy in himself. Then he looked from her to Will, and saw by the warmth in the man's eyes, smiling over the rim of his cup, that Will knew, and had always known, just how beautiful she was.

Chapter 12

John, growing older, had an extra keen sense of the closeness between his mother and Will. It had always been there from the very beginning: as a child he had warmed himself in its glow; depended upon it; drawn strength and assurance from it. But now, growing older, becoming more and more aware of his own manhood, he sensed the closeness in a different way. He understood it in his bones. He was often caught up in the little currents of humour and tenderness passing between them, and would turn away, smiling secretly to himself, with the warmth slowly spreading and growing inside him.

But afterwards he felt cut off. Alone. Restless. Full of unease. He would go for long walks, squaring up to his own aloneness, fighting a feeling of emptiness that he could not quite understand. Or he would work long hours in the forge, getting rid of his mood on the anvil. Work was the one fulfillable passion. The things he made were the one source of pride. He was a man and knew he had other men's respect. Surely that ought to be enough? He had the respect of women too. There were plenty of pleasant, pretty girls willing to stop and talk to him, with plenty of teasing, this way and that, and no commitment on either side. Why not take life as it came?

With Hannah Draycott, of course, it was different. She could not accept teasing, it seemed, but must always be on her dignity, taking a harmless joke amiss and turning it against you, adding a few extra barbs of her own. He and she were like tinder and spark together, though which was tinder and which was spark it would have been difficult to say.

Once, when John stood gossiping on the green with young Billy Jukes and a few others, Hannah came down the track from Neyes, herding the cows out to the pasture behind the church, for the Neyes fields were much scattered. The cows spread out over the green and began grazing, and the young men watched as Hannah, using a short stick, herded them back to the track again.

'Now there's a sight for sore eyes,' said young Billy Jukes, who, like his father, worked as a cowman at Rillets Farm. 'A prize bunch if ever there was one, especially the roan there, coming behind.'

'I'd pin a rosette on her with pleasure,' said his brother, Chris, admiringly.

'Shapely,' said Scowers, a youth of few words. 'Plenty of milk.'

'It's in the breeding,' said Georgie Byers. 'You can tell it a mile off, can't you, eh? It's wrote all over her, every inch.'

'She's got a nice swing to her, certainly. Style, that's the word, you can't mistake it. You can see it in the way she's swishing her tail.'

'I suppose,' said John, in an innocent voice, 'you are all talking about a cow?'

'Lumme, what else, for goodness' sake?'

'I only wondered, that's all, especially when you mentioned the tail.'

Hannah, coming behind the cows, shot John a glance. It was meant to make him feel very small.

'Nice day,' he said, nodding with exaggerated politeness.

'Is it?' she said. 'Seems to me there are too many *insects* about on days like this.'

'You're right there. The muggy weather brings them out.'

'It's idleness that brings them out.'

'You don't mean me by any chance?'

'Flies *will* sting, won't they?' she said. 'It's their nature to be annoying.'

184

'I reckon I'm a bit big for a fly.'

'I've seen bigger,' Hannah said, and tapped a cow on the rump with her stick.

'Eh, well, I'm sorry if I've annoyed you,' he said, 'but don't take it out on that poor cow.'

'It'd be a relief,' Hannah said, 'if flies would stick to their own midden.'

'B'zz, b'zz!' John said.

By now she was some little way ahead. The cows were moving slowly on, into the track that led past the church. She rested her stick on the roan's back.

'Seems she's got it in for you,' Billy Jukes said to John. 'I reckon you'd better watch your step.'

'I shall, never fear. I've got a healthy respect for my own skin.'

'You ent afraid of Hannah Draycott, are you, John?'

'Ent I?' said John. 'Well, I dunno!'

The other young men were much amused. They were still laughing when the group broke up. It was a marvellous joke to them that John, six feet tall, with a frame that was all hard bone and muscle, and a fist that could have felled an ox, should be afraid of Hannah Draycott, and the joke had soon gone round the village, enjoyed by young and old alike. John played up to it, in The Old Tap and out on the green. He had only to give a little solemn shake of the head and everyone would be in fits. And the joke, for him, had one great advantage. It took Hannah Draycott by surprise.

It was a day in the autumn of 1897, and John was out on the green, repairing the old iron seat that encircled the oak tree, watched by three elderly men who were waiting to sit on it to eat their lunch. Hannah passed on her way to the shop and Tommy Breton caught her arm.

'What've you done to our poor John, to frighten him the way you have?'

John straightened up, hammer in hand, and looked into Hannah's light brown eyes. For once, there was some uncertainty there, and the sight of it brought him a jolt of pleasure.

'Tell us, John,' said Tommy Breton, 'what is it about this young woman here that's got you shaking like a leaf?'

'Shaking?' said John. 'I ent shaking. Whatever next?' And he held out a hand, fingers stretched, that trembled as though with a terrible palsy. 'That's blacksmith's ague, that's what that is, and I'll thank you not to poke fun.'

'What's your nonsense today?' Hannah asked. 'Some childish jape again, is it?'

'Excuse me,' John said. 'I got business in the smithy.'

'Laws!' said Fred Byers, pulling him back. 'You ent running away, are you, John? What is it about her that scares you so?'

'I reckon maybe it's mostly her tongue.'

'Sharpish, you mean? Well, they're all like that.'

'Not all,' said John. 'There's one or two that're sweet enough.'

'How do you know? Have you had a taste?'

'I can't answer that,' said John.

'He's a good chap, our John,' Fred Byers said to Hannah. 'There's plenty of other girls in Dingham ready enough to be kind to him.'

'There are some girls,' Hannah said, 'who're silly enough for anything.'

'Oh, she's got it in for you, John! There's no doubt of that!'

'The best thing for me,' John said, 'is just to be sure and keep out of her way.'

'That,' Hannah said, 'is all I ask.'

'There!' John exclaimed, as she walked away. 'And you wonder why I'm scared of her!'

The joke lasted a few days and was good for many another laugh. Will got to hear of it in the smithy.

'What's this about you being scared of Hannah Draycott?'

'Oh, that! It's just a joke.'

'There's many a true word spoken in jest.'

'Dammit!' said John. 'I ent *really* scared of her.'

'I reckon our John is smutten on her,' Peter said, knowingly. 'Either that or she's smutten on him.'

John threw back his head and laughed.

'You know all about such things, of course!'

'I know enough not to waste my time getting tangled with girls.'

'I should think so too. At least until you've begun to shave!'

'I been shaving for two whole years!'

'And it still don't make the whiskers grow!'

'At least I ent scared of Hannah Draycott!'

'You got no reason,' John said. 'She don't hardly notice little boys.'

But the joke about Hannah had had its day. John was sick of it, and of her. It was easy enough to avoid meetings and that he now resolved to do. The smithy was busy that autumn and winter. He worked long and hard, day in, day out.

Peter's work was improving slowly. He no longer let the iron burn, nor did he spoil it on the anvil. He had learnt to think before tackling a task; to consider its needs and guard against problems and sometimes he even accepted advice.

Physically, he seemed to develop in a burst. At fifteen he had been a boy but at sixteen he was a man, and he was determined to be treated as such. He grew no more after that and never attained his father's height, but he was heavier and broader than Will, and somehow, because of this stocky build, he looked a lot older than his years. His face, like Will's, was broad and square-jawed, and his eyebrows were even thicker and blacker, giving him a scowling look. Unlike Will, he rarely smiled, and when he did, as Jim Pacey once remarked, it was nothing more than a show of teeth. Amusement, pleasure, satisfaction, showed as a wicked gleam in his eyes, or was heard as a chuckle deep in his throat. But his smile, as Jim said, meant he was probably hating your guts and thinking of some way to do you down.

In the new year of 1898, Will had an order from Mr.

Staverton of Dinnis Hall for scythe-blades, billhooks, hay-knives and spades, a dozen of each for the two Hall farms, with two new ploughs and two new harrows. Will was going to divide the work between the four of them, but Peter had his own ideas.

'Why not let John and me do this, half and half of all the items, while you and Jim do something else?'

'All right,' Will said. 'Seems me and Jim can soon retire!'

Peter took immense pains in making his scythe-blades, hooks, knives and spades, and put his initials, very small, on the handle-end of every one. Pacey saw him doing this and gave a little scornful grunt.

'You needn't bother putting your mark cos anyone with half an eye can see which is yours and which is John's.'

'What the hell do you mean by that?'

'I mean exactly what I say.'

'What's wrong with these tools, I'd like to know? Just look at them and tell me what's wrong!'

'They're all right,' Pacey said, 'but you've got a long way to falter yet before your work is as good as John's.'

'You can talk!' Peter said. 'Just a journeyman all your life!'

And he walked out, into the store-shed behind the smithy, to vent his feelings in heaving iron bars about. There was no love lost between him and Jim Pacey, for Jim made no bones about showing which of the two boys he preferred.

'It's a funny thing,' he said to John once. 'Peter's the spit of Will in looks but as for everything else, well, you're more Will's son than he'll ever be, even though you ent related.'

When it came to making the ploughs and harrows, Peter refused to have anything to do with it. The task had gone sour on him. He told John he had changed his mind.

'Seems my work ent good enough yet. You can damn well do it by yourself. I'm still a new scholar where smithing's concerned – at least according to old Pacey.'

'Why don't we do them together?' John said.

'No, no. You go ahead. I don't want to spoil your work.

188

You're the one with all the skill.'

'Dammit all!' John said. 'I'm seven years older than you, boy. I've been smithing a lot longer and I damn well *ought* to be better than you.'

'I suppose so. Yes. Maybe you're right.'

'You expect too much of yourself, too soon. You're only sixteen. I'm twenty-three. You'll catch up in skill in time, but you've got to work at it yet a while.'

'Oh, I shall work at it!' Peter said. 'But I ent going to make them ploughs and harrows. Not till I know I can do a good job.' And then, sincerely, without spite: 'I shouldn't want poor work going out of this smithy, specially not to Dinnis Hall.'

Will at this time was a man of fifty. Old for a blacksmith, he would say, and often he talked of giving it up; of taking a farm of a few acres, somewhere not too far away, and leaving the boys to run the smithy. But he hung on because of Peter.

'I'll see you through your time, boy, and then I'll look round for a little holding. That's another couple of years. You'll have taken up your indentures by then. You'll be your own man, along with John, and the two of you will work in the forge while your mother and me retire to our farm.'

'What about Pacey?' Peter asked.

'Why, he'll stop on with you, of course, so long as he wants to, that is.'

'I'd say he was getting past it, myself. He must be ninety in the shade.'

'Jim's all right,' John said. 'We surely ent going to sling him out.'

'You should start looking out for a farm pretty soon,' Peter said to his father, 'so's you got it in mind when the time comes.'

'You're right,' Will said, 'I shall have to ask questions here and there.'

But the months went by, spring and summer, and somehow the questions never got asked. There was plenty of time, Will said, and the day would come soon enough.

'Our John gets about quite a bit these days. He might get to hear of a little place that'll just about suit your mother and me.'

John often travelled about the district to jobs of work on outlying farms. He would sometimes leave at four in the morning and not return till eleven at night. He liked to get out and about like this, and whenever such work was in the offing he was sure to volunteer.

'Seems you like to get out,' Will said. 'I suppose it's because you get the chance of meeting up with Hannah now and then.'

'Oh no it ent! She's nothing to me.'

'Nobody'd blame you,' Will said. 'Hannah's grown up a fine-looking girl. There's no one to match her for miles around.'

'And don't she know it!' John exclaimed. 'The way she walks past us chaps sometimes, you'd think we warnt human, to see her looking down her nose.'

'You young chaps!' Will said. 'You and young Jukes and all that lot, when you stand about in a group out there, have you ever thought how awkward it is for a girl like Hannah going by?'

'There's other girls go by the same. Not all of them give theirselves such airs.'

'In that case,' Will said, casually, 'you'd do better to get yourself tied up in knots over one of them instead.'

'I've told you before – Hannah Draycott is nothing to me. And as for our making it awkward to pass, it'd take more than that to put *her* out!'

But one summer morning, at ten o'clock, when Hannah came round the green as always, delivering the morning milk, John remembered Will's words, and, instead of his usual sarcastic greeting, gave her only a brief nod. He and Peter were out on the green, removing the rusty iron tyres from a set of four waggonwheels, and young Billy Jukes, with his brother, Chris, stood lounging about nearby. They watched as Hannah, with the pony and float, stopping at intervals on the way, made her slow progress round the green, and when she drew up at the Dysons' cottage, and the old lady came out with her jug, Billy Jukes called out to her.

'If I give you a penny, can I have a sup? I've got a throat like a thirsty cat.'

Hannah ignored him. She filled Mrs. Dyson's jug from the churn and drove on to the next cottage.

'She's deaf today,' Billy said.

'Offer her tuppence,' Chris said.

'Leave her alone,' John said. He was watching Hannah's face and remembering what Will had said. 'Leave her alone, both of you.'

'I haven't touched her yet,' Billy said.

'Be careful in case she touches *you*!' said Chris.

'I dunno that I'd mind that.'

'Ask if she'll meet you up at the huts.'

'What's the use if she's stone deaf?'

'You might try asking by making signs.'

'No, it's no use. She's taking no notice of us chaps today. We're just the dust beneath her feet.'

'*I'll* make her take notice!' Chris said, and flipped a pebble at the pony's rump.

Hannah had just stepped onto the float when the pony kicked out with both hind feet. She had no chance of taking the reins. It was all she could do to keep her balance and stop the churn from overturning. The pony pulled off with a violent jerk and would have bolted down the road, but John ran forward and took the bridle and in an instant all was well.

'Are you all right?' he asked, as Hannah, in a temper, groped for the reins.

'It's no thanks to you if I am!' she said. 'You and your stupid childish games!'

'I ent bothered about your thanks but Posy here would've been in Runston High Street by now if it warnt for me upping and stopping her.'

'And whose fault was it she started to bolt in the first place?'

'Not mine for sure,' John said.

'I suppose that pebble fell from the sky?'

'Are you calling me a liar?'

'Leave go of that bridle and let me get on. I've lost enough time because of you.'

'I want to know if you think I'm a liar.'

'What does it matter what I think? It was either you or one of them. There's nothing to choose between none of you!'

'It matters to me,' John said, 'and I'm waiting to hear you say you're wrong.'

'I beg your pardon, humbly, I'm sure!'

'I can see exactly how humble you are. It's very nearly making you spit.'

'I've said I'm sorry and now I'd like to get on with my round.'

'I was going to offer a helping hand.'

'Oh, no! You've done enough!'

'All right. Just as you please. It was only a friendly thought, that's all, to make amends as you might say.'

John let go of the pony's bridle and stepped back a little way. He put his hands in the waist of his apron. The anger still burning in Hannah's face was enough to set light to a bunch of green sticks, but her glance, instead of scorching him, only made him calmer still. This was what happened, he told himself, when a fellow did her a good turn. But he saw the milk that had splashed all over her pinafore and knew that he, in her place, would have felt the same.

'I should simmer down if I was you,' he said, 'or the milk in that churn will be on the boil.'

He watched her move on to the Beards' cottage, then he returned to his work on the wheels. The Jukes brothers grinned at him.

'That was a damn fool thing to do, throwing that pebble,' he said to Chris. 'Supposing the girl'd broke her neck?'

192

'Why should she, indeed, when you was here to save the day?'

'It *was* a damn fool thing,' said Peter. 'We very nearly had no milk.'

In November that year, Will was called out to Eddydrop Farm, where the threshing-machine had broken down, and John went with him to help with repairs. The work was done in a couple of hours, but when the thresher was going again, Will, climbing down from the platform, missed his footing and fell against the revolving fly-wheel. His forearm caught against the shaft and the flesh was laid open from the wrist to the elbow. Dr. Nathan came out to the farm, cleaned the wound with carbolic acid, and stitched it up on the spot. He told Will to go straight home and to put the arm in a sling at once.

'See that you do no work for a while and give that arm a chance to heal.'

'It's lucky for me,' Will said, 'that I got my two boys to carry on while I take a holiday, ent it, eh?'

That evening, at home, he sat in his chair beside the fire and smoked his pipe like a man of leisure. Peter had fetched him a quart jug of ale and John had brought him an ounce of tobacco, and there he sat, like a bishop, he said, living off the fat of the land while his two boys went back to work in the forge. He was rather self-conscious, wearing the big white calico sling: 'Just like a pudding in a cloth!'; and every so often he would take a peek into the folds: 'I'd say that's just about boiled to a turn!'

Ellen watched over him anxiously and brought cushions to put at his back. She could see that the arm was giving him pain.

'I've always hated threshing-machines – you might have been killed,' she said to him.

'I ent so easy to kill as that. But I'm getting clumsy in my old age, missing my footing like that.'

'Are you quite comfortable now? Is there anything you'd like?'

193

'I'd like for you to sit in your chair and for us to talk a little while, just the two of us, all by ourselves. That don't often happen nowadays, not since the boys've grown to be men. We can't pack them off to bed no more and have the hearthplace to ourselves, the way we did when they was small. So you sit down there, where I can see you, and let's make the most of it while it lasts.'

'Very well,' Ellen said, and sat in her chair opposite, looking at him in the light of the fire. 'There, I'm sitting, does that suit?'

'Remember them days when you first came? How we sat of an evening, just like this, with little John asleep upstairs? I used to wonder what'd happened to me, a woman and child all of a sudden, under my roof and in my care. Yet somehow I felt it was all meant to be. I felt I'd been chosen to take you in. And whenever I look at you, like I am now, I think to myself, "She's mine, she's mine".'

'Yes. Well. And so I am.'

'I dunno that I deserve the happiness I've got,' he said. 'All I know is, I'd fight tooth and nail to make sure I keep it.'

'You don't need to fight,' Ellen said.

'Just as well, ent it, seeing I've got a gammy arm?'

John, coming into the kitchen a while later, was struck by the way they sat together, with the lamp not yet lit, although it was after eight o'clock, and only the firelight on their faces. He was struck by the way they smiled at each other; by the fact that for once his mother's tireless hands were lying idly in her lap; and although there was silence in the room, he felt himself an intruder there, a trespasser on private ground.

'Your mother's been making a fuss of me,' Will said. 'I shall get to like being laid up if I ent careful.'

'How're you feeling?' John asked.

'Right as rain, boy, right as rain. You just finished in the smithy?'

'I have, yes, but Peter's still at it and will be for hours. He's doing that stove for Mr. Grey.'

'Well, draw up a chair, John, and sit yourself down. Get a mug and share my ale.'

'No, I ent stopping,' John said. 'I thought I'd take a walk up the hill and give my lungs a bit of an airing.'

The feeling of trespass was very strong. He suddenly saw his mother and Will as two people with a life of their own. The warmth they created in the home, which he and Peter took so much for granted, sprang from the secret tenderness that a man and a woman shared together. Never in his life had John been witness to caresses between them: their warmth had all been outward-given, filling the house and flowing over the two boys, while their own needs had been met in secret; but now, just this once, he felt he had blundered in where he was not wanted, so he made his excuse and went out into the darkness, leaving them alone together, sitting in the firelight.

His walk took him right to the top of the hill, which was blanketed in descending cloud, and where he disturbed the roosting lapwings who cried out, peewee, before settling again on the ground. He came down out of the cloud and took the footpath across Neyes Farm, over fields of plough and stubble, into the pasture near the house. A light shone in a window there and the dogs barked at him from the yard. His footsteps pounded the steep stony track.

Passing the end of the old cartshed, he almost collided with someone turning in from the green. It was Hannah Draycott, wearing a cape, leading two goats on a short rope rein.

'Whoa, there!' John said. 'Did I give you a fright?'

'You frightened the goats more than me.'

'I remember them goats,' he said, grinning. 'I reckon I'd better keep out of their way.'

'They're not the same ones,' Hannah said, and although he could not clearly see her face, he knew by her voice that she was smiling.

'You remember, then? Although it was such an age ago?'

'*You* remember. Why not me?'

'I've got good cause. One of em went and catched me bending.'

'These two are quiet. You're safe with them.'

'How long *is* it, that other time? Donkey's years if you ask me! Twelve at least, maybe longer.'

'Goat's years,' Hannah said, and they both laughed, making a grey fog with their breath.

The two goats were leaning against them, one against John and one against Hannah. He put out a hand and fondled each of them in turn.

'Funny our meeting like this,' he said, and then, realizing the foolishness of his remark, he became quite dumb, hoping that Hannah would not ask why.

'Yes, it is funny, for I wanted to ask about Will's arm.'

'It's not too bad. So he says, anyway. Did you just drop in at the forge?'

'I did look in, but that's as far as I dared go. Your brother Peter looked very busy, and I didn't like to call at the cottage.'

'Lucky we met, then, chancelike and all. I'll tell Will you was asking about him.'

'Yes, do, and wish him well.'

'You know what I think?' John exclaimed. 'I think we've made history today. It's the first time we've met without having words.'

'We'd better make a note of the date.'

'Red letter day!' he said with a laugh. 'Put a circle round it, eh?'

There was a silence, and he wished he could see the girl's face, but the mist and the darkness were too close, and her loose hood cast a deep shadow. He knew she was smiling, certainly, but what sort of smile might it be, he wondered, and was she mocking him even now? The goats were beginning to stamp their feet. He saw the girl's hands as she shortened the rope.

'Well,' he said. 'I'll say goodnight.'

'Yes,' she said. 'I'd better get on.'

'We're late birds tonight, you and me.'

'Yes. Well. I'll say goodnight.'

'I'll give Will your message about his arm.'

'Yes. That's right. Wish him well.'

'Goodnight!' he called, as she led the two goats into the darkness, and her voice came back to him: 'Goodnight!'

On the far side of the green, a dim light still showed in the smithy doorway, shining out on the squirming mist, and the chink of iron striking iron told him that Peter was still at work. John thought he would look in and tease his half-brother; Peter was a demon for work these days; but as he approached the open door, a man stepped out from the shadows nearby and addressed him by name. It was his father, Richard Lancy.

'I heard a rumour Will Gale was hurt.'

'Yes,' John said, 'he hurt his arm.'

'Nothing more? I heard it was worse. He ent nearly dead, then, the way I was told?'

'Far from it, I'm thankful to say.'

'Ah, the devil looks after his own, so they say. But I'm thankful, too, that he ent dead, cos I've got a score to settle with him and I should be sorry if he was to go and get hisself killed before I'd a chance to pay him out.'

'After all this time?' John said. 'Do you still bear your grudge, after all these years?'

'I'm like the man in the old tale. He kept a stone in his pocket for ten years, turned it over once or twice, and kept it another ten years, to throw at the man that done him harm. I reckon I'm the same sort. I don't forget things, no more than him, and I've got a stone in my pocket, too.'

'Can't you forget it and leave Will alone?'

'I might,' Richard said. 'I might at that.' And in the dim smoky light from the smithy doorway, his grey-bearded face was eager and watchful. 'If you was to come back home with me and help me out with running the mill, I'd say no more against Will Gale and I'd throw my stone away for good.'

John impatiently shook his head. He made as though to turn away.

'The mill would be yours,' Richard said. 'Don't that count for nothing with you? You was born to the miller's trade. It's your proper place, where you belong.'

'My work is here, in the smithy,' John said, 'and my home is here, in this cottage.'

'Home!' Richard said, in a hollow voice. 'And what home have I got, down at the mill? No wife! No son! No company! Nothing to take a pride in at all. *He's* took it all, what I ever had. Him in there behind them shutters. It ent enough that your mother gave him a son of his own. He's still got to keep his claws on *you*! And you wonder that I bear a grudge?'

'He don't stop me coming to you. I'm my own man, I decide for myself.'

'Then you should decide to do what's right. What sort of son denies his own father?'

'You seem to forget you turned us out, my mother and me, that winter's night. I was only a little chap then, but I ent forgot what you done to us, and I reckon you've got no further claim.'

'Now who's the one that's bearing a grudge?'

'I'm sorry,' John said. 'but I ent coming whatever you say.'

'Right so!' Richard said. 'Right so! You've had your chance! You won't get another so easily! I ent got time for coaxing you round. Why the hell should I? My own flesh and blood!'

In his anger, as he talked, he turned away many times, and each time turned back, swinging his arms, until at last he put up his fist in front of John's face.

'You can deny me if you like but just you be sure and remember this! – I've still got a stone in my pocket, ready to throw at Will Gale, and when the right moment comes, he shall have it, you mark my words!'

When at last he had trudged away, John turned and went into the smithy. Peter had stopped work now and was sweeping the floor.

'Was that Lancy's voice I heard? What's he want by any chance?'

'Oh, the usual,' John said. 'About the mill and all that. About what he's going to do to Will.'

'You surely ent worried over that!'

'I dunno if I am or not.'

'He's been singing that same old song for years. He's off his hinges. Cuckoo, that's what. You don't want to take no notice of him.'

'No, well, I don't,' John said, 'but I wish he'd shut up about it all the same.'

A few days later, Will was at work in the smithy again, obliged to go carefully with the injured arm but refusing to wear the calico sling.

'This arm's got to learn who's master,' he said. 'It'll only get soft if I molly-coddle it overmuch.'

That afternoon, Hannah Draycott looked in at the smithy door, sent by her menfolk to ask about Will.

'I take that kindly,' Will said, 'but are you sure it was really me you came to see?'

'Why, has anyone else hurt an arm?' she asked, and left without glancing in John's direction.

'Laws!' Will exclaimed. 'Did I say the wrong thing?'

'I dunno, I wasn't listening,' John said.

The following Sunday, after dinner, wearing his suit of dark brown serge and his best shirt with a new white collar, John took his corduroy cap from the peg and brushed it on the sleeve of his jacket.

'Where you off to?' Peter asked.

'I feel like a good long walk on the hill.'

'Shall I spruce up and come along with you?'

'Yes, if you like,' John said.

'No, I don't think so,' Peter said. 'I've got an idea I'd be in the way.'

'If you must be talking rot . . .'

'Strikes me you've forgotten something. You ent got

199

a flower in your coat.'

'Get back to your kennel!' John said, and went out, putting on his cap.

All the way up the steep hill track, along the edge of the earthworks, and down again by the narrow winding sheep-paths, he drew deep breaths of clean air, for that was his purpose in coming there, to rid his lungs of the smithy smoke. The day was a warm one for November, and although he often stopped in his walk, looking down on the village below, all landmarks were hidden under a haze.

'I can't even see Grannie Naylor's bonnet!' he would say if anyone came up the path, and in his mind he heard their laughter. He was full of little jokes today. He could talk to anyone. Anyone at all. He could tell them what was in his mind.

Then, suddenly, down below, Hannah Draycott appeared on the track, coming slowly up the hill. He knew who it was immediately, even though they were some way apart. He knew her by her swinging walk; by the easy way she carried herself; by the dark blue jacket and dress she wore; by the two black sheepdogs at her heels. He knew her by her shining hair.

Any moment now they would meet. He was walking very quickly indeed, the steepness of the hillside lengthening his stride, his boots crunching and slithering on the loose stones of the rough track. He was only a few yards from her and now his feet were refusing to stop. They were bearing him onward all the time; closer and closer; then swiftly past; and he was looking back at her, over his shoulder, a foolish grin on his face, a hand raised in casual greeting.

'I'll be late for tea if I don't watch out! I reckon it must be nearly four!'

If Hannah answered, he failed to hear her, for he was already some way past. But in his mind's eye he could see her face at the moment of meeting: a hint of colour in her cheeks; a shy glance, but perfectly steady; the beginnings of a smile that came to nothing; and surprise when she saw he was not going to stop.

His own face was on fire. He was cursing himself for a damned fool. And the moment he was out of sight, screened by a clump of oaks and beeches, he stopped dead, grinding his teeth. Late for tea! What a thing to say! Like a little boy going home in a hurry from Sunday school! And, going up to a beech tree, he struck at its trunk with both his fists.

There was one thing about it, he told himself. If she thought he had come to the hill just on the chance of meeting her, well, she knew better now! But – late for his tea! Surely he could have hit on something better than that!

The fault was Hannah's, more than his. It was something to do with her proud swinging walk; with the steady way she looked at you, her light brown eyes full of unknown thoughts; it was something in the way she smiled. Yes, the fault was hers, for being a woman. There was a certain strangeness in her, a holding out against such as he, even while she walked on the hill, which nobody surely ever did without a reason.

He turned left through the clump of trees, and left again, back up the hill. Hannah by now should have reached the top. She might be looking down from the fort. But instead she was only a hundred yards off, sitting on a log beside the pond, leaning forward a little way and drawing a stick through the weeds in the water. The two sheepdogs lay nearby.

For a while he stood, just watching her, taking time to gather his wits, for he had to think of something to say. But she raised her head and saw him there, and, in spite of the hundred yards between them, he felt he could see her plain as plain. He could see her eyes and their expression: questioning, yet knowing the answer. He could see that her lips were slightly parted: not in a smile but as though she had taken a hurried breath.

For a moment he even saw himself, a dark figure, as Hannah must see him, standing above her, against the sky, and he felt the silence and stillness between them, across the reeds and feathery grasses, touched by the misty autumn sunlight. Removing his cap, he began walking down towards her, and as he went, it occurred to him that he still hadn't thought of anything to say. But now it no longer seemed to matter. Hannah was sitting waiting for him. Words would come if he gave them a chance. And sure enough, when he sat beside her on the log, and stooped to pat each of the dogs, and Hannah took care not to look too directly into his face, talking was not so difficult after all.

'I came back.'

'Yes. So I see.'

'You don't object to my sitting here?'

'No. Of course not. But what about getting home to your tea?'

'Damn the tea! The tea can wait.'

'If you say so,' Hannah said.

'Yes, I do say so. I mean it, too.'

Their glances met just long enough for each to see that the other was smiling. Then they looked at the water again and he watched as she trailed her stick through the weeds.

'What're you hoping for, fishing like that? An old boot?'

'They say there's treasure on this hill. Maybe it's here, in the tinker's pond.'

'No, it ent there,' John said.

'How do you know?' Hannah asked.

'We found it, that's why, Will and me, when I was a young un, six years old.'

And he told her about the Christmas log, with the six new pennies hidden in it, bright and shining in the cracks.

'You must be very fond of Will.'

'I suppose so. Yes. You could say that. He's a good man, you know, even though—'

'Even though what?'

'Well. You know how it is with him and my mother.'

'I've never heard anyone speak against Will.'

'No. Maybe not. It's my mother they speak against, mostly, I think. It's always the woman that gets the blame.'

'That's true,' Hannah said. 'Us women are not allowed to·

202

breathe. We're supposed to be saintly all the time.'

'Not too saintly.' John said.

'Just saintly enough to please you men?'

'We've got our ideas, I daresay, on how a woman ought to behave.'

'And we've got our ideas about you men.'

'H'm,' he said, and became silent.

But the silence no longer caused him unease, as it would have done in the recent past. He no longer felt he must say something teasing or manly or smart. It was enough to be sitting with Hannah in the sun, an understanding growing between them, and a certain trust.

He was looking at her all the time now. He was willing her to look at him. For if she faced him and met his gaze, he would learn something important to him. He would see it plainly in her eyes.

'Hannah,' he said, in a quiet voice, and she turned towards him, meeting his gaze. The stick she was holding fell from her hands.

Chapter 13

It was a day soon after Christmas. In the smithy, the Eddydrop horses were in for shoeing, and the two carters, Fossett and Spring, stood near the shoeing-stall, watching Will work. The big grey mare, Jessamy, was having her near hind foot trimmed, and two village mongrels, Tiny and Spot, were running about just out of range, waiting for the parings that fell from the hoof.

The mare was docile; her foot rested peacefully in Will's lap; and he, as he worked with his short sharp knife, caught the pairings in his left hand and hurled them towards the open doorway. The two dogs sprang, snapping and snarling, and each went off with a sliver of hoof, to consume it outside on the green. Will called across the smithy to John.

'Close that door, if you please, John. I don't want them rascals back in here till I've got these horses out of the way.'

John, who was emptying a drum of oil into the oil-trough, failed to hear Will's request. It had to be shouted twice more. Then, red-faced, he shut the door.

'He ent rightly with us these days,' said Jim Pacey. 'His mind goes a-wandering. Don't ask me where.'

'It takes some chaps that way,' said Will.

'What does?' asked John.

'Courting,' said Will, working at Jessamy's hoof with a rasp.

'I dunno what you're talking about.'

'No more don't I, boy. No more don't I. It's just these rumours been going about these past few weeks.'

204

'Rumours? Hah! You know what you can do with them!'

'Yes,' said Will, 'I can use 'em to light the fire in the morning.'

The two carters were much amused. They watched John as he went to and fro.

'Is he courting in earnest?' Fossett asked. 'Or is he only trying his wings? And who's the girl or can I guess?'

'Ask him yourself,' Will said.

'I can't do that. He might take offence. Some young chaps is funny like that. They keep so close and secret about it, the first thing you know is, they got three kids.'

'I can tell you who it is,' said Peter, turning a horseshoe in the fire.

'You be quiet!' John said. 'And for pity's sake leave them shoes as they are. You're always so tarnal *busy*, boy!'

'It's somebody with an aitch and a dee,' Peter said, enjoying himself.

'An aitch and a dee?' Fossett said, and made a great show of removing his cap and scratching his head. 'Could be anyone, couldn't it?' he said.

'I was never much good at spelling,' said Spring, 'but I daresay the dee'll be an ell before long, eh, John?'

But John, with a shrug, merely walked away. It was a pity, he told himself, that folk could not mind their own business.

Later that morning, when the carters and their horses had gone, and John was shovelling up the dung, a boy came in and gave him a note. Puzzled, he took it to the door to read, while Peter, Will, and Jim Pacey all hung around, watchfully.

'She's sending him notes now,' Peter remarked. 'It must be pretty serious between them, for her to do a thing like that.'

'It's not from a her. It's from a him.'

'Glory be! Whatever next?'

'It's from my father,' John said, and handed the note to Will to read. 'Seems he's bad with the asthma, he says. He wants me to go and stay with him and give him a hand with running the mill.'

In his note, which was scribbled on the back of a bill, Richard asked John to come at once. His illness had taken his strength, he said, and the mill stood idle for lack of help. 'If you don't come and give me a hand, to tide me over till I'm well, I shall be a ruined man.'

'What d'you think?' John asked, as Will handed back the note.

'Seems pretty genuine, ¹d say. I'd heard he was getting the asthma bad. One or two folk've told me that.'

'Then you think I should go and do as he asks?'

'I dunno what to say to that. If you want to go, that's up to you.'

'I don't want to go. It's the last thing I want. But maybe I ought to. I wish you'd say.'

Unhappily, he stared at Will, but Will was reluctant to give advice.

'You know how things are between me and your dad. I reckon you've got to decide for yourself.'

'Yes. You're right. I reckon I have.'

'I'll tell you what,' Will said. 'Seems to me you should ask your mother.'

So Ellen, during their midday meal, had to give judgment on the matter, and John saw by her clouded face that she was as unhappy about it as he.

'I don't like the thought of your going there, after the threats Richard has made, but he is your father and I suppose he's got some right to ask for your help. But you're a grown man and as Will says, it's up to you to decide for yourself.'

'I think I should go,' John said. 'It's only for a week or two, and he's got no one else to turn to for help. I'd better go up and pack a few things.'

He rose, having eaten little food, and pushed his chair in under the table. The thought of the mill, like a dark prison, and the thought of his father, sick as he was in mind and body, filled him with a kind of dread, and he would have given anything to be rid of the burdensome sense of duty.

'I wish to God he hadn't asked me!' he said, and the words burst out against his will. 'I wish to God he'd leave me alone!'

'Strikes me you're daft,' Peter said, 'going where you don't want to go.'

'No, he's not daft,' Ellen said. 'John is doing what he thinks is right.'

'Oh, he's a great one for doing what's right, our John! But what about us others in the smithy, having to do his work for him, while he plays the miller down at Pex Mill?'

'Peter, be quiet!' Will said. 'What're you talking such rubbish for?'

'I'll go and pack,' John said. 'I may as well get down there at once.'

A little while later he left the cottage and set off across the green. Peter stepped out from behind the oak.

'You're going the wrong way,' he said. 'That's not the way to Pex Mill.'

'I've got a call to make first.'

'Going to say a fond farewell?'

'What're you on about?' John asked.

'I'll tell you what!' Peter said. 'I'll go up to Neyes myself if you like and do what I can to comfort Hannah. I can take over where you've left off. After all, if I've got to do your work in the smithy, I might as well do it elsewhere as well. She's maybe a bit on the old side for me but I daresay we'll get along all right—'

'Look here!' John said. 'I don't much like the way you talk. I ent going to listen to nothing more. If you can't talk about Hannah with some respect, you can damn well keep your mouth shut! Otherwise I'll shut it for you!'

'You *are* in a temper and no mistake.'

'I ent too well pleased, I must admit.'

'You shouldn't take it out on me, just cos you've got to go to the mill. I was only joking. I meant no harm.'

Peter, amused at John's bad temper, was suddenly smiling. He was showing his teeth, as Jim would say. Those beautiful teeth, very white and strong, square and even and all of a size.

'We ent going to part bad friends, I hope?'

'You talk as though I was going for good.'

'You never know!' Peter said. 'You might take a shine to the miller's trade and stop there for good.'

'Oh, no, not me! I shall be back in a week or two, or maybe even sooner than that. You don't get rid of me so easy as that, my lad!'

And John swung off across the green, a few belongings in a bag, slung by its handles over his shoulder.

The day was a dull one, much overcast, but the weather was still unusually mild, and under the trees in Berry Lane, as John and Hannah walked there, the midges were thick on the windless air.

'I don't want to go to the mill, but I couldn't hardly say no, could I?'

'Of course you couldn't,' Hannah said.

'I doubt if I shall see you much, for a week or two at any rate.'

'Surely you won't be working every minute of the day?'

'I dunno. Maybe not. But I'd just as soon stick it out, down there at the damned mill, and get it all over as you might say.'

'All right. It's up to you.'

Hannah felt his unhappiness. She put a hand in the crook of his arm.

'The time will soon go – what's a couple of weeks out of a whole lifetime?' she said.

'I'd give anything in the world to have it over and done with, though, and be back in the smithy where I belong. I'm no miller! I'm a smith. Always will be, come what may!'

'Very well,' Hannah said, teasing him for his vehemence. 'No one's trying to persuade you any different.'

'It was just something Peter said. Oh, I dunno! I'm feeling sore. I don't like my life getting upset like this.'

'You're getting too set in your ways,' she said.

John stopped and turned towards her. They looked at each other for a time. There was a smile in her light brown eyes and it soon awoke a smile in his.

'You've nothing against marrying a blacksmith, I hope?' he said.

'If a blacksmith should ask me,' Hannah said, 'I might perhaps consider it.'

'You mean to say I've never asked?'

'Not in so many words. No.'

'I suppose I was taking it for granted.'

'How like a man.'

'Well, I'm asking you now, right enough.'

'Then, I'd better say yes, straight away, just in case you change your mind.'

'That's settled then. We know how we stand.'

'Yes,' she said. 'But you ought to be getting on to the mill.'

'Ah. You're right. I better had.' The thought of it weighed on him heavily. 'No sense in putting it off.'

A few minutes later they parted company at the stile, and John took the footpath down to the river, where the midges were biting worse than ever.

The mill and the millhouse, to any stranger coming there, would have seemed derelict, dead as the grave, for the buildings were in disrepair and bits of planking were nailed across two broken windows. The place was quiet; both river and stream were running deep; but when he opened the gate on the bridge, there was a loud clanging noise, because of the sheepbells and old tin cans tied along the lower rail. Promptly, in response to the noise, his father's face appeared at one of the broken windows. Then came the noise of rusty bolts being drawn, and the door, scraping the stone-flagged floor, was opened just wide enough to let John in.

'I knew you'd come, boy! I knew you'd come! Blood is thicker than water yet and you're the only kin I've got. Here, light that candle on the table there, so's we can see enough to talk.'

The millhouse kitchen, close shut, smelt of sickness and old sweat. When John lit the candle and held it up, the place was everywhere thick with dirt, and his father's narrow makeshift bed was a tumble of blankets green with mould. Sacks were nailed across the windows, the fireplace was full of soot, and in the space beneath the dresser, a heap of empty brandy bottles glinted darkly through their dust.

'I'm a sick man,' Richard said. 'You can see that, can't you? It ent a lie. I need looking after and that's a fact. If you hadn't come, I'd have likely died. Nobody else would care a damn.'

The truth of his illness was plain indeed, for he breathed with immense difficulty and pressed his hand to his chest in pain, and as he struggled across the room, sweat trickled slowly down from his brow, into the beard that covered his cheeks. His skin was pinched and bruised-looking. He sat down heavily on the bed and stared before him with filmy eyes.

'I ent got the strength I was born with, let alone to do my work. That's why I need you running the mill, otherwise I'm a ruined man.'

'Have you had the doctor?' John asked.

'What use is he? You tell me that! The doctor would come and look at me and he'd say to me, "Lancy, you are a sick man!", and then he'd go home and write out his bill. Why should I pay to be told I'm sick? I know I'm sick. I'm just about done.'

'Have you eaten today?'

'My stomach's against the sight of food.'

'You ought to eat. It'd give you strength. And you ought to have more air in here—'

'Ah, I can see you're looking round. It's a lot different from the old days when your mother was here and kept it so trim. Remember when you was a little lad? You could eat off that floor in them days, and see yourself in them pots and pans, so bright and shining they used to be. We was happy in them days. Do you remember, when you was small?'

'Yes, I remember,' John said. But he also remembered how, in this room, his father had tried to make him eat slugs, and he felt the horror of it even now. 'I remember everything,' he said, and, taking a rag, began cleaning the dust from the table.

'She had no call to go off like that, leaving me to struggle alone. You can see what I've come to, without her.'

'Let's not talk about that,' John said, 'or we shall end by quarrelling.'

'Ah, that's right,' Richard said. 'Let's talk about the mill instead. You'll get it going, first thing, and put me back in business again?'

'Yes, if you tell me what to do.'

'I'll tell you all right. I can at least talk! Except when the coughing gets my guts. I'll get you to put this bed in the mill and then I can watch how you go on. Tomorrow morning, first thing. I'll soon make a miller out of you, boy, and we shall be well away, working together. Lancy and Son! That's the style. Working together the way we ought.'

'Now look here!' John said. 'I'm willing to stop a week or two and give you all the help I can, but as soon as you're on your feet again, I shall be going back to the forge.'

'Supposing I never get on my feet again?'

'Then it's up to you to employ a helper. But you'll get well. I'm sure of that. It's just that you need looking after a bit.'

'You going to nurse me and molly for me?'

'I'm going to do the best I can. And the first thing is to get you to eat.'

'I feel better already, having you here. I do, that's a fact, it's a real tonic. I've been so long alone, you see, and it does me good to see you here.'

'Just so long as it's understood that I shan't be stopping once you're fit.'

'We'll see about that when the time comes. Maybe by then you'll have changed your mind.'

'No,' John said, 'I shan't change my mind.'

'All right, all right, just as you say! Seems like I've got to be in your hands.'

For a while Richard sat in silence, watching as John, unpacking his bag, brought out bread, cheese, tea and sugar, a jar of meat jelly and a cold roast fowl, a boiled ham and an onion pie.

'Your mother send them things to me?'

'Yes.'

'Paid for by that swine Will Gale!'

'You don't have to eat them, if that's how you feel.'

'I'll eat them all right. You see if I don't! He owes me something, the rotten swine, seeing he stole my wife from me!'

John made no answer. He laid out the food on the bare table, and went to fetch water from the pump.

It was a strange experience for him, to be back in the old mill again after nineteen years, and during the first morning's work, when the sluice-gates were opened and the waterwheel began to turn, the sound of it brought his childhood back in a rush that threatened to overwhelm him. Inside the mill, as the runner stones turned and the whole building rumbled and shook, he knew a moment of childish panic, for he was in charge of all this cumbrous machinery that drew such strength from the river flood, and he felt its power like a living presence, as though it had a will of its own and would surely never submit to him.

The fear attacked him again and again as he ran to obey his father's instructions, and often his heart was in his mouth. When the warning-bell tinkled up above, he felt he would never get up the ladder quickly enough to feed the grain into the hopper, and when the water needed adjusting, his hands shook so badly that he could hardly grasp the control lever. He felt sick in his stomach. He was sure he would do the wrong thing. And in his mind's eye he saw the most dreadful catastrophes: the stones heating up and starting a fire, or the millstream flooding through the mill.

His father's instructions, shouted hoarsely from the bed against the wall, were often difficult to understand.

'God almighty! Are you daft? Don't you know what I mean by clewers, boy? Don't you remember nothing at all from the days when you was a little lad?'

Sometimes, enraged by his own helplessness, Richard shouted such abuse that his voice broke altogether and he would be seized with a fit of coughing. Once he struggled up from his bed, took a hammer from the wall, and hurled it straight at John's head, missing only because John was quick to duck. Then he fell back, gasping and coughing, blue in the face, pressing his hand against his chest.

'You want to go easy,' John said. 'You'll kill yourself if you go on like that.' He picked up the hammer and hung it back in its place on the wall. 'You'll very likely kill me too if you don't mind your temper better than that. I don't take kindly to having hammers throwed at me. Nor shall I work any better for being bawled at all day long, so just you tell me in simple words, which is what I'm used to at the forge.'

Richard, recovering, sat propped against a few bags of bran, chewing the ends of his long moustache. He watched John narrowly by the hour, and sometimes swore under his breath, but he made some effort to keep his temper under control, and often sat with his fists stuck muff-like into his sleeves, to keep them out of temptation's way.

'I shan't hurt you,' he said once. 'My own son? Oh, dear me, no! I shan't hurt you, I give you my word.'

By the third day, John no longer feared the mill, but became calm and confident, attuned to each small telltale sound, heard under the rumble and clack, and sensing the need of every straining shaft and cogwheel. He even came to enjoy the work and when, in the millroom, the fine flecked flour ran from the shute into the bag, he felt some pleasure touched with pride. But it was his father, hobbling across now and then to rub the flour between finger and thumb, who pronounced on its quality, good or bad; who knew by its texture and dryness and warmth whether the stones were

213

grinding too close or, perhaps, not close enough.

'I dunno how you do it,' John said. 'It all seems much of a muchness to me. I dunno what you can *feel*.'

'That takes time,' Richard said. 'But you'll come to it in the end, my son, and I'll make a miller out of you if it takes me from now to my dying day.'

'I shan't be stopping as long as that. As soon as you're well enough, I shall be off. That was our bargain, don't forget.'

'Don't you like the work here?'

'I'm a blacksmith,' John said. 'I ent much good, away from the smithy.'

'You got no business being a blacksmith. Gale had no business making you one. Your place is here with me.'

'Why go on about it all the time? You ent going to make me change my mind.'

Sometimes, at the end of the day, when the waterwheel came to a halt and the mill was hushed, John would walk a little way along the towpath, listening to the quiet sounds of the river, coming to him through the thickening dusk. The voice of the water in its shallows and the voices of the feeding waterfowl were a part of his earliest memories, and when he pulled the dead dry seeds from the tall hemlock and crushed them in his hands to get the scent, he was a little boy again, out in the dark, all alone, marvelling at the evening star. The river-world was a world apart and had a feeling all its own. The quietness of it went down deep into the soul. The stillness of the waters soothed the mind.

Inside the mill, there was no such quiet feeling, for Richard, growing gradually stronger, followed John from place to place; questioned every move he made; ran him about without pause. In the house, too, it was the same, and when they sat down to their meals together, he grudged every mouthful of food John took. He himself ate very little. It hurt him to see John eat so well. And he would sit grumbling, clicking his tongue, till a moment came when, unable to control himself any longer, he would rise and·

214

gather the food together, all anyhow, within his arms, and put it away in the corner cupboard.

'Strikes me you've had enough. Food ent got without money, you know. You can't go on eating for evermore.'

'I brought that food,' John said.

'What about when it's all gone? I can't afford to feed you, boy, if that's the way you always eat. I'd be in the poorhouse in no time at all.'

'Then I shall have to buy it for myself.'

'That ent good for any man, eating as much as you do, boy. Just look at *me*. I never eat as much as that.'

'It must be the brandy that keeps you alive.'

'Tales! All tales!' Richard exclaimed. 'When've you seen me drinking, boy?'

'Never once,' John said, 'but I can smell it all the same, and I've seen enough bottles lying about.'

'It's Will Gale that's set you against me like this. Him and your mother, telling you tales. They've brung you up on a pack of lies.'

'I'm not against you,' John said.

'Then why don't you treat me with proper respect? I'm your father. You seem to forget.'

'I came when you asked me, didn't I? I'm here helping to work the mill.'

'You know which side your bread is buttered, that's why. You've got your eye on the future, my lad, when I'm dead and gone and the mill is yours.'

'That's nothing to me cos I don't mean to stop. I made that clear from the very start.'

'I mean you to stop, though!' Richard muttered. 'I mean you to stop, and stop you shall!'

'What's that you said?' John asked sharply.

But his father, instead of repeating his remark, cleared the last of the supper things and firmly closed the cupboard door.

'You've had enough for tonight,' he said. 'You've had enough to sink a barge!'

215

*

The millhouse, so often surrounded by mist, was chilly and damp, but Richard rarely lit a fire. 'Work is the best thing for keeping warm,' he said, 'and you may be sure there's plenty of that.' John, every morning at five o'clock, rose from the mildewed mattress where he slept in a single worsted blanket, washed and shaved in cold water, and ate a cold breakfast in the cold kitchen, lit by a single tallow candle.

His day's work, eighteen hours long, was no harder or heavier than many a day's work in the smithy. He and Will, at busy times, had often been known to work all night. But in the smithy, there was always cheerful companionship, and at the end of the day's work, there was the comfort of the cottage kitchen, the reward of good hot food and drink, the ease of a chair drawn up to the hearth. There was friendly talk and a few jokes, perhaps, about the happenings of the day. The place was home. The people lived in friendliness. The warmth of it was shared by all.

At the millhouse, however, the only time Richard allowed a fire was when he caught a fish or two on the lines which, fixed all day from one of the mill windows, trailed in the water down below. Then he would light a fire in the rusty broken stove, on top of the heap of ash and soot, and would sit crouched in front of it, with the black smoke blowing out in his face, cooking a couple of tiny perch, stuck on the prongs of the toasting-fork and held among the meagre flames. John, receiving his share of the fish, found it more than half raw and pushed it from him in disgust. But his father finished every scrap.

'You've been spoilt by your mother's cooking. It's made you particular and I ent surprised. There's nobody cooks so well as her. I was particular myself once when she was here and cooked for me. But now I've had too many years alone. I can't afford to be fussy now. I must do the best I can.'

In the mill and the millhouse, shut up as they were, the windows covered with old sacks, day and night were almost the same, and the darkness often got on John's nerves.

216

'I wonder you choose to live like this, shut up in the dark, after what you went through that time, getting shut in that there cellar.'

'D'you think I choose to live like this?' Richard asked, shouting at him. 'If I didn't keep the place shut up I'd have the villagers snooping around, spying on me at every turn, poking their noses everywhere—'

'Nobody spies on you,' John said.

But Richard was convinced that they did: the bargemen plying up and down the river; the river-keepers; the wandering boys: he was determined they must be shut out. And if John removed a corner of sacking, to let in a tiny ray of light, Richard would rush to put it back and would hammer two or three nails into it.

The weather was still quite mild and sunny, although it was early January, and sometimes when John went out to see to the sluices he would linger a while on the river bank, watching the ducks swimming about and the dabchicks diving among the reeds. Often their antics made him laugh and one day he lingered there so long that his father came out to call him in.

'What're you up to, mooning about, when you ought to be getting down to work?'

'I was watching them dabchicks, that's all. Seems they're all wound up today, the way they're playing about out there. It's this mild weather. They think it's spring.'

'H'mph! Is that so? Seems there's some truth in what they say, that little things please little minds!'

Richard turned and went into the house. John went back into the mill and was soon busy working the hoist. A few minutes later he heard a shot. When he ran outside again, his father was standing on the bank with his gun in his hands, and smoke was squirming from one barrel. Down below, on the river, feathers floated among the reeds and the two dead dabchicks, stained with blood, were being swept away downstream.

'What did you have to do that for?' John cried, hating

217

the look on his father's face.

'They eat the fish, that's why!'

'Ent there enough blasted fish without your killing harmless birds?'

'You get back to your work!' Richard said. 'It's none of your business what I do.'

John said no more. He knew he was only wasting his breath. But every day after that, if any waterfowl came near the mill, he frightened them off by clapping his hands.

Sometimes, when milling was finished for the day, John had to take the horse and waggon and deliver meal at distant farms or flour to the bakehouse at Sutton Crabtree. Richard had quarrelled with every farmer in Dingham itself, and all his trade was further afield, so that John had to travel a great many miles.

Once, after dark on a cold wet night, he was returning from Upper Mayse, and when he reached the green at Dingham, he stopped the waggon on the round road and sat for a moment, hunched in his jacket, looking across at the old smithy. The upper half of the door was open and a wedge of light shone out on the rain, while another light, ruddier, duller, glowed at the opening in the roof. The sound of iron ringing on iron came, chink-chink, to John's ears, and the smell of the forge, burning coal, caught in his nostrils, acrid and rough.

He felt he had been away for a lifetime, although it was only ten days, and such a longing came over him that he half rose from the box of the waggon, thinking to run across the green and put his head in over the hatch, just for a word or two of gossip. But he sat down again, still holding the reins, for he felt that if he once set foot inside the smithy, it would be all the harder for him to return again to Pex Mill.

'Stick it out,' he said to himself. 'Another week should see the end. Then I'll be back for good and all.'

Sometimes, during the night, John would awake on his comfortless bed and hear his father moving about in the room below. One night the shuffling, unsteady feet came very slowly up the stairs, and John's bedroom door creaked open a little way. But when he spoke there was no reply and after a while he heard the footsteps shuffle away again down the stairs.

Once he awoke to a smashing of glass and in the morning, when he entered the kitchen, the floor was covered with the fragments of five or six brandy bottles. He never once saw his father in the act of drinking, but always in the morning the smell of it was hot on his breath, and a sullen redness burnt darkly in his face.

'What sort of time d'you call this?'

'I reckon it's just about after six.'

'Is that the earliest you can rise?'

'It's early enough,' John said, 'seeing I had a disturbed night.'

'It's a funny thing,' Richard said, 'that although I'm only a sick old man, I should always be up before you.'

'Not so funny,' John said, 'seeing you never go to bed.'

'You'd better go and find a broom and make yourself useful sweeping this rubbish out of the way.'

'I think I'd better open a window, too, and let some fresh air in here. The place is stinking like a drain.'

'Don't you touch them windows, boy! They're all nailed up to keep out the thieves.'

Even when the sun shone, the sacking must never be pulled aside. Richard disliked the light of day, shortlived as it was in wintertime, and his one idea was to keep it out. The mill, too, was kept close and dark.

'No wonder your asthma's bad,' John said, 'cooped up so close with all this dust.'

'Who owns this mill, you or me?'

'Please yourself,' John said, and although he felt stifled, imprisoned there, he comforted himself that he would soon be returning home.

After the rain, there came a spell of cold weather, sunny and dry. Richard's health was improving apace. He was growing stronger; coughing less; and no longer came out in a sweat at the slightest exertion.

'Seems to me you're a lot better,' John said at supper one evening. 'You'll soon be able to manage alone.'

'I ent a hundred per cent yet. Look at my hands, the way they shake.'

'It's not your asthma that causes that. It's the medicine you take for it.'

'I doubt if I shall ever be fit enough to run this mill by myself again. I'm an old man now. I've lost my strength. I need you here like I need to breathe. What'll I do if you go off?'

'You'll have to do what every other miller does – get another man to help.'

'Not while I've got a son of my own. Why the hell should I, in God's name? It's little enough to ask of you, seeing the mill will be yours when I'm gone.'

'I'll stay to the end of the week,' John said. 'Then I'm going and that's final.'

'You're a good son to me,' Richard said. 'You won't let me down. I'm sure of that. You know how I depend on you. You're all I've got in the whole world.'

Chapter 14

One bright afternoon when John was out on the wooden footbridge, looking down into the leats, a voice spoke to him from behind and there was Hannah on the towpath, wearing a brown cloak with a hood and carrying a basket. The hood was pushed back and her hair in the sunlight was golden brown. Her look and her smile gave him a little jolt inside, and he was struck dumb, in a strange shyness. He had kept away from Neyes Farm, denying himself a sight of her as a test of his own strength and endurance. His task at the mill must be got through alone. But now that she had come to him, seeking him out so openly, without any silly girlish pride, his self-denial seemed absurd. A childishness. A waste of time.

'Your mother sent you a basket of food. She thought you might be going short.'

'She's about right. I ent getting half what I get at home.'

'There's one or two things from the farm as well. A piece of bacon and two score eggs. I made you a mutton pasty too.'

'Your arm must be breaking, carrying all that food like that. What am I thinking of? Give it here.'

He opened the rickety wooden gate and there was a clangour from the bells. He took the basket and exclaimed at its weight.

'Glory be! We shall feast like kings!'

'You seem surprised to see me,' she said. 'You're looking at me as though I'm not real.'

'Yes, well,' he said, still shy, 'I hadn't thought of your coming here.'

'It's strange to see you dressed like that, all dusty and white, instead of black.'

'I suppose you're laughing at my apron, like that time when I was a lad, wearing one of Will's old leathers.'

'How've you been getting on?'

'Muddling along, like, just about keeping the wheels turning. But my father's better, I'm glad to say, and I shall be home in a few days more.'

'Where is he?'

'Oh, he's around. He'll have heard the racket of them bells and he's probably watching from a crack somewhere. D'you want to come in?'

'I'd better not,' Hannah said. 'I've got to call at Uncle Bob's. I'm already later than I said.'

'Hang on a jiff, then, and I'll empty this basket,' John said.

At that moment, his father appeared at the open hatch, eyes narrowed against the sunlight, looking Hannah up and down.

'What's all this? Visitors?'

'Hannah's brought us a basket of food.'

'Hannah? Hannah? Hannah who?'

'Hannah Draycott from Neyes Farm.'

'You two getting married, then? Seems you're pretty thick together.'

'Yes, in due course,' John said.

'Then let me warn you, young woman! – You'll have your work cut out to keep him fed!'

'I'm used to that,' Hannah said. 'My menfolk at the farm are just the same.'

'When's the wedding going to be?'

'We haven't decided yet,' John said. 'We've got to find a place to live.'

'Stop here with me,' Richard said, 'and you've got a home all ready made.'

'No, no, I've told you before. At the end of this week I'm going home.'

'What about Hannah? What's she think?'

'John will do what he wants to do,' Hannah said, in her clear voice, 'and that is to go on working in the forge.'

'Then it's up to you to try and talk some sense into him. This mill could be a flourishing business and that'll be his when I'm dead and gone. He's my one and only son and the milling trade is in his blood.'

'Oh no it ent!' John said with a laugh.

'Then it damn well ought to be!' Richard snapped. 'God almighty! Can't you *see*?' Then, with a sudden agreeable smile, he addressed himself to Hannah again. 'You're a sensible-looking girl. You don't want to marry a damned blacksmith when he could be a miller and own his own mill. Oh, I know the house has been neglected! I see what you're thinking right enough! But you and John could put it to rights. Take a pride in it. Make it nice. And John and me, us two men, we could set the mill on its feet, doing good trade and flourishing, just like it was in days gone by.'

'No, Mr. Lancy,' Hannah said. 'John's heart is in the smithy. You'll never get him to give it up.'

For a moment Richard stared at her, his smile dying on his lips, giving way to a tremulous anger. Then he pushed himself away from the hatch and slammed the upper half of it shut, and a moment later, listening, they heard him flinging about the millroom, rattling the chain of the sack-hoist and sending it smashing against the wall. Hannah's eyes opened wide. She looked at John in anxiety.

'Now I've put him in a temper. I hope he won't take it out on you.'

'There's nothing for you to worry about. He threw a hammer at me once and he likes to smash things now and then. But I don't think he'd do me any harm. Not while I'm useful in the mill!'

'It's nothing to laugh at!' Hannah said. 'I've heard strange stories about your father. I'll be glad when you're safe back home again.'

'Ah, well, it won't be long now.'

Her look of anxiety made him feel warm, and the warmth went spreading slowly out inside him, so that he stood and smiled at her, moved by the fearfulness in her eyes. He was filled with a knowledge of his own strength. His youth and manhood. His lack of fear. No harm could come to him, for his life was set on a definite course, and Hannah was part of it, his to keep. He saw it so clearly in his mind that he *knew* no harm could come to him. But her fearfulness moved him all the same.

'I can take care of myself,' he said.

'Then see that you do,' Hannah said.

'Hang on a jiff. I'll take this food. No doubt you'll want the basket back.'

When he returned with the empty basket, his father was calling from the mill. John made a face and gave a shrug. He parted from Hannah cheerfully, breezily, with a smile and a wave, but when he went inside the mill, its darkness and closeness pressed on him, and the days ahead seemed very long.

Over at the workbench, his father, with a lantern in his hand, was searching for a lost chisel. John found it and gave it to him. They both had work to do on the cog-wheels.

'She's a fine-looking girl, that Hannah of yours.'

'Yes, she is.'

'A bit of a madam if I'm any judge. You'll have your hands full, managing her. But she's the sort that gets things done. She'll soon have the house all shipshape again, when you've married her and brung her home. She'll make things hum for us, no doubt, but I shan't mind too much about that, so long as she's a good wife to you and does her duty, caring for us.'

John, who was turning the pitwheel and knocking out the damaged cogs, stopped and stared at his father's face.

'Didn't you hear what Hannah said. We shan't be coming to live here with you. We're getting a cottage of our own.'

'I heard what she said, right enough, but she'll come round to it, given time.' Richard, working with hammer and chisel, was intent on shaping a new cog. His mind was closed to everything but what it suited him to believe. 'She'll come round to it. You mark my words. It's up to you to see that she does.'

Saturday came, and it was the day for John's departure. He had been at the mill for nearly three weeks. His father was fully recovered now, or as nearly as he could hope for, anyway. His breathing was easier; he no longer coughed; and his stamina was astonishing. He could work without tiring from dawn to dusk, though his strength, when it came to lifting weights, was now a thing of the distant past.

'It pleases me to see you so strong. It's like myself all over again. You've done pretty well by me, my son, seeing me through while I've been bad, and if you stop on you shall have your reward.'

'No, father,' John said. 'I must go and today is the day. We'll get this last lot of barley done for Mr. Treeve and then I'm off home.'

Richard looked at him with a sidelong glance.

'That's the first time you've called me father,' he said, 'in all the time you've been here with me.'

'Is it?' John said. But he knew it was. 'It don't come all that easy to me, after nineteen years apart.'

'It means a lot to me, my son, to hear you give me my proper name. I *am* your father. You can't escape that. And blood must count for something, I'm sure, especially between a man and his son. I'm only sorry it don't count for more.'

John had no answer to make to this. He went and busied himself at the shute, putting the wooden stop-board in, while he took away the full sack and put an empty one in its place. There was some change in his father today. A quietness. A softness of speech. His eyes were not so dulled by drink, nor was the smell of it on his breath. His fretful temper was under control. John was puzzled. The change, instead of comforting him, filled him with a vague unease.

By two o'clock, the whole day's milling was done. Mr. Treeve's barley was ground, and the twelve sacks of meal stood tied and labelled near the door, awaiting collection. John went out and closed the sluice-gates. He removed a dead branch of wood from the stream. A strong wind was blowing from the cold northwest and there was a hint of drizzle in it. He stood for a while on the river bank and watched it roughening the dark water. Then he went into the mill again, hung up the sluice-key, and removed his borrowed miller's apron. His father was cleaning the weighing-machine.

'Seems you're just about ready for off.'

'Just about,' John said.

'Won't you stop for a bite of food?'

'No, I shall eat when I get home. I'm just going up to get my things.'

'In such a hurry?' Richard said. 'In such a hurry to be gone?'

John stood, hesitant, at the door.

'If you need me again, I'll always come. So long as I'm able to, that is, and it don't hinder my work at the forge. I'd be quite willing to spare a day or two helping you out.'

'A day or two! What use is that?'

'I reckon that's up to you,' John said.

He went through the mealroom into the house and up the stairs to his bedroom. He threw his belongings into his bag. Outside, the drizzle had turned to rain, and was skittering hard against the window. The sky was heavily overcast.

When he went down to the mill again, the millroom was even darker than usual, for both halves of the door were now closed and the curtain of sacking covered the cracks. When he went to the door he found that the bar had been put across and the padlock inserted into the hasp. He tugged at the padlock and found it secure. Anger got him by the throat and he swung quickly round to where his father, stooping low, was lighting the lantern on the kist. The bearded face was watchful, intent, purposeful. The hand, holding the lighted match, shook and was clumsy with curbed excitement. And as the light of the lantern grew, he turned to John with a little smile.

'You ent leaving here, my son. Oh, dear me, no. You're stopping on. You're going to help me run this here mill. I'm going to set it on its feet and you got a duty to help me out. You ent leaving. I'll see to that.'

'D'you think you can keep me against my will?'

'There'd be no need if only you could see some sense.'

'If you think a locked door can keep me here—'

'It's only until we've had time to talk.'

'We've talked and talked these past three weeks! We've thrashed it out a hundred times! I'm not going through it all again!'

John turned and strode through the mealroom into the house. His father followed, holding the lantern high in his hand, and by its dingy, flickering light, John saw that the house-door too was barred and locked.

'You can't get out of here, my son. The door is padlocked, as you see, and the windows is all nailed up to the frames. You got no choice but to stop with me.'

'I've just about had enough of this! If you don't open up I shall do some damage breaking out!'

'You're my son,' Richard said. 'I've got first claim on you, my boy, and I aim to keep you where you belong.'

'I'm warning you! I mean what I say!'

'And I'm warning *you*!' Richard said. 'I know my rights.'

John looked at his father's face and knew it was useless to reason with him. The old man's eyes, though watchful, intent, were blind to the light of the daylight world. His mind, like his mill, was full of dark places, shuttered and barred, and in the thickening shadows there, his thoughts gnawed like imprisoned rats. Shut up in himself, inward-coiled, he was a man who needed help. A man whose reason had gone astray because of an accident in his youth. A man to be pitied, not reviled. And John did indeed feel pity for him. This man was his father, his own flesh and blood, alone in the world, cut off by his madness. It was John's duty to reason with him.

'Father, give me the key and let me go, and I promise I'll come and give you a hand whenever I can spare the time. One day a week, say. I'll do my best.'

'One little day is no use to me.'

'Then let me find you a man full-time.'

'I don't want strangers in my mill.'

'Then there's nothing I can do to help you.'

'You've got a duty to stop here with me and help me to put this mill to rights.'

'I've got a duty to myself!' John said. 'If you won't open up for me, I must get out as best I can!'

He went to the window and wrenched the sacking from its nails. He picked up the nearest kitchen chair and smashed it with all his strength against the casements, which splintered apart and swung outwards, hanging askew from their broken hinges. Richard gave a cry of rage and lunged forward, swinging the lantern. It struck John on the side of his head and cut his scalp above the ear, and a few drops of paraffin, spilt from the drum, splashed over his face and neck. As the lantern swung again, he yanked it out of his father's hand and hurled it into the fireplace, where its glass broke and its flame was extinguished in ash and soot. He snatched up his bag and dropped it out of the open window. Patience and pity had left him now. His one idea was to get away. He wrenched himself free from his father's grasp and vaulted over the window-sill.

'You'll be sorry for this!' Richard cried. 'You'll be sorry for leaving me all alone! I gave you your chance! I was always willing to do well by you! And this is how you turn me down!'

Sobbing and crying in his rage, he suddenly snatched off his ragged cap, and, leaning out after John, struck him two or three blows with it and eventually hurled it at his head.

'You'll be sorry for this, my son, and so will some others I could name! You and your mother and Will Gale and all, you think I'm nothing, you laugh at me! You think you can trample me underfoot! But I'll make you sorry, the pack of you, and you won't laugh at me for long!'

John shouldered his bag and walked away. He felt rather sick and there was a sourness on his tongue that he longed to be able to wash away. The smell of the mill was in his clothes; the mustiness was in his hair; and the stale bad smell of his father's breath seemed to lodge forever in his nostrils. But he was free of the place now, out in the Godsent wind and rain, and as he walked towards the village he took deep breaths of cold clean air.

Richard, left alone in the millhouse kitchen, pulled the broken casements shut and tied them together with a piece of string. He fetched a hammer and a handful of nails and nailed the sacking back in place. The kitchen was now dark again, so he took the lantern from the hearth, shook off the ash and broken glass, and set it on the table. He struck a match and touched the wick and reluctantly, because of the dirt, there came a circle of dim blue flame. His hands were trembling. He breathed heavily, making a noise in his nose and throat. Now and then he licked his lips.

He went to the cupboard in the corner where, in the leg of an old boot, he kept a bottle and a glass. He brought them to the table and sat down to drink, and the brandy went noiselessly down his throat in a single draught that emptied the glass. For a moment more he sat unmoved; it might have been water flowing down; but the sudden spasm, when it came, shook him as a terrier shakes a rat, and afterwards he sat bent and cowed, the moisture running from his eyes, the sweat standing out on his brow and forehead. But his hands were a lot steadier now. He tilted the bottle and refilled the glass.

After a while he got up and took his shotgun out of the clock-case. He laid it on the table with powder-flask, wads, the bag of shot, and the clay pipe-bowl broken off at the stem which he used as a funnel for the powder charge. He sat down again, placed the gun upright between his knees, and set to work, loading both barrels carefully. His face was clenched in concentration. His lips were tight-pressed and he breathed very heavily through his nose. He was always careful when loading his gun. His wads were cut exactly to size, powder and shot were measured just so, and the charge was always rammed well home. The gun had been his for forty years.

The brandy bottle was empty now. It went on the heap under the dresser. Richard turned down the lantern-flame, wrapped his gun in a piece of sacking, and let himself out of the side door, carefully pocketing the key. The afternoon was already dark, and gusts of rain came down now and then, blowing on the changeable wind. Richard turned up his coat-collar, pulled his hat over his eyes, and set out towards the village. He held the gun very close to his side.

Behind him, the mill stood dark and quiet, doors locked and windows sealed, safe from entry except by marauding rats and mice. But the lantern, although he had turned it down, had not been extinguished. A speck of flame remained on the wick and was drawing oil from a crack in the holder. The oil-drum, too, had been damaged in its fall, and where the joint had opened a fraction, oil was seeping onto the table. Soon the speck of flame would grow, fed by the fumes rising around it. The bits of burning wick would fall and ignite the paraffin on the table. And the trail would lead to the dusting of gunpowder Richard had spilt when filling the pipe-bowl from the flask. The flask itself still lay nearby.

When John arrived at the smithy, work was almost done for the day, and the fire in the forge was burning low. Jim Pacey had gone home and Peter was sweeping the workshop floor. Only Will was still working, in his absent-looking way, cutting shoe-lengths on the anvil, and when he looked up to see who it was who had walked in, his face came alive in a smile that warmed John through to the very marrow of his bones. Stooping over the anvil again, he beat out a tune with his

230

long-handled hammer and cold chisel, lightly, cleverly, drawing a different note from each part and making a joyous message of welcome. Ting-tinker-*tink*-tink! – Ting-*tink*!

'Peter! Peter! Look who's here! Your mother's son as ever was!'

'Lord almighty!' Peter said, sweeping the dust to John's feet. 'You back for good or just for tea?'

'We'd given you up for lost,' Will said. 'We thought you'd done with the smithing trade and turned a miller after all.'

'No lections of that!' John said, and because of the warmth of Will's welcome and his own joy at being back, he was stricken with shyness and awkwardness, looking around at the old place and trying to think of something to say. 'Everything looks pretty much the same, don't it?'

'We done our best,' Peter said, 'to keep it tidy while you was away.'

'I should hope so indeed.'

'We heard your old man was up and about at the mill again. We heard he was running you around.'

'How did he take it, John,' asked Will, 'when you upped sticks and came away?'

'Well might you ask!' John exclaimed. 'He tried to stop me. He locked me in.'

'Is that how you got that cut on your head?'

'Yes, he catched me a clout with a storm-lantern.'

'The man is mad,' Peter said. 'It's high time he was put away. There's proper places for folk like him.'

'Yes, well,' John said.

'You'd better get indoors,' Will said. 'Your mother'll be nearly over the moon. She's been looking out for you enough!'

'Yes, I'll go in,' John said. 'I could do with a clean-up and that's a fact.'

'Anything troubling you, John?' Will asked.

'My dad, that's all. You know how he is. He was saying what he'd do to us and how he was going to pay us out.'

'Don't lose no sleep over that!' Will said. 'He's been

singing that song for nineteen years and it's never come to nothing yet. You get indoors and see your mother. Peter and me will be in pretty soon. We're having an easy day today so tell her to get an early tea and we'll celebrate your coming home.'

'Ah!' Peter said. 'Tell her to kill the fatted calf!'

'Take no notice of Peter,' said Will. 'His nose is out of joint a bit but he'll soon get over that.'

'I'll go on in, then,' John said. 'I'll be glad of the chance of a good wash and shave. The way I smell right at this moment, my mother will put me to eat with the pig.'

As he went to the door leading into the cottage, he was smiling to himself in expectation, picturing the brightness of the kitchen and himself going in, very quietly, to take his mother by surprise. He had his hand on the sneck of the door when he heard someone come into the smithy. He glanced back, over his shoulder, and saw his father among the shadows, outside the central circle of light cast by the fire in the forge and the lantern hanging overhead. Will and Peter also saw him and both became still, peering questioningly into the shadows. Will, who still had his hammer and chisel in his hands, straightened himself to his full height.

'You got business with us, Mr. Lancy?'

'Certainly I have,' Richard said. 'You're a blacksmith, supposed to be! Maybe you can fix this here.'

'What is it?' Will asked.

'It's this!' Richard said, and stepped forward into the light, allowing the sacking to fall from the gun. 'What you should've had long years ago!'

Will, at a range of only three or four yards, received the murderous charge of shot in the abdomen, yet such was his enormous strength that when they reached him he was still on his feet, supporting himself against the anvil. The front of his shirt was a glistening mess, and as they lowered him to the ground, he reached out and pulled at his leather apron, drawing it up to cover himself, to spare them the sight of his terrible wound.

Peter, seeing his father's plight, turned away, his face contorted, and seized the shotgun from Richard's hands. He gave a terrible strangled howl.

'D'you see what you've done to him?' he cried.

'Yes, I see it!' Richard said. 'I always said I'd pay him out!'

'Well, it's *your* turn now!' Peter said. 'And *I* shan't wait for nineteen years! If both these barrels is loaded up, you're getting the other in the guts!'

The gun was pointing at Richard's stomach, but as Peter began squeezing the trigger, John sprang forward and struck at the muzzle and the shot went up into the rafters. Peter, beside himself with rage, struck at John's face with the gunstock, and John, wresting the weapon from his hands, hurled it into the water-trough.

In that instant, Richard quickly left the smithy, vanishing into the winter darkness, and when the brothers turned to Will, their mother was on her knees beside him, cradling him within her arms and weeping, weeping, hopelessly, knowing that he was slipping away. His blood had soaked her pinafore, and her hands were stained with it, so was her face. With such a wound, he could never live.

As her lips kissed his forehead and her fingertips gently touched his cheek, he moved a little, against her arm, trying to look at her, trying to speak.

'All my own fault—' he said weakly, and turned his face towards her breast.

Ellen continued to hold him close and would not be moved for a long time. Her sons could do nothing. The dead man was hers. She would not leave his side so long as some warmth remained in him; so long as his spirit still seemed near; so long as she still had strength enough to hold his body in her arms. All her sons could do for her was to close and bolt the smithy door against the villagers gathered outside. Only when Dr. Nathan came would she consent to leave the body and by that time she was perfectly calm. She watched as the doctor closed Will's eyes and covered him with a clean white sheet.

'Where is the murderer, Richard Lancy?'

'Ask my brother!' Peter said. 'If I'd had my way he'd be lying there dead the same as my father and I should be wiping my feet on him! I got the gun out of his hands. I'd have shot him without a second thought. But my brother had to interfere and the murdering swine just walked away.'

'Better to leave it to the law,' Dr. Nathan said to him. 'The police will be here in due course. They'll probably find him at the mill.'

'If I get to him first,' Peter said, 'I shall save the law a lot of trouble.'

But soon it was known throughout the village that Pex Mill was on fire. The glow of it could be seen in the sky and the smell of it was on the wind. The first men to have raised the alarm were the two river keepers patrolling the bank. They had seen the bright glare in the mill windows and had done what they could with water-buckets. But the fire had already got a hold. The heat of it had driven them back. And one of them swore that the Mad Miller had been inside, trying to rescue his sacks of meal, at the moment when the roof collapsed, bringing with it a part of one wall.

Even when extra help arrived, and a stream of water was piped from the leats, there was no hope of saving the mill. By the time the fire was out, the place was gutted, a black shell, and when at last the ruins were cool enough for men to enter, Richard Lancy's dead body, charred, blackened, unrecognizable, was dug out of the smoking rubble and taken to the mortuary in Runston. Outside the mill, where he had thrown it for safety, lay an iron-bound box with a padlock on it. Somebody took it to the smithy cottage and handed it over to Ellen Lancy. She in turn gave it to John. It contained a few coins and a small roll of banknotes, a total of seven pounds three shillings and sixpence.

All through Sunday, in the smithy cottage, Peter was almost completely silent, even at mealtimes, and whenever John spoke to him, he turned away with a savage gesture. Ellen, who had moved Will's chair from the head of the table because its emptiness gave such pain, looked at these two sons of hers and knew that she must speak her mind. But she knew, too, that although she could often influence the one, she could very rarely influence the other.

'How long is this silence to last between you?'

'Peter must answer that,' said John. 'He's the one that's dumb.'

'Let them that feel like talking, talk by all means,' Peter said. 'For my part, there's little to say.'

'Where's the good in adding hurt to hurt?' she said. 'Isn't it enough that your father is dead?'

'It's more than enough for me,' Peter said.

'Do you think it's any different for John?'

'Oh, John's lost a father, too, I know! The Mad Miller of Pex Mill! Does anybody care for that?'

For the first time that day, Peter looked directly at John, and the effort brought the tears to his eyes. He was only seventeen. His rage and bitterness knew no bounds.

'Well, brother?' he said harshly. 'Your father is dead! Do you grieve for him?'

'No,' John said, 'but I grieve for Will.'

'Do you? Do you? Oh, I daresay!'

'He was as good a father to me as he was to you.'

'And was murdered for it at the end!'

'You don't hold me to blame for that?'

'It was *your* father that murdered him!'

'I'm not to blame for what he did.'

'You're to blame for striking up the gun! I'd have shot the miller, sure as fate, if you hadn't stopped me and let him go. I'd have watched him die in agony, as I had to watch my father die, and sent his stinking soul to hell!'

'Then you'd have been a murderer too.'

'D'you call that murder? I don't!'

'My father was mad. He didn't rightly know what he was doing.'

'Why should a madman be spared, pray, more than a man in his right mind? A man that's mad is better dead.'

'Yes, well, he is dead now,' John said, 'and had a worse death than he would've done if you'd shot him.'

'Yes!' Peter said. 'And I wish I'd been there to see him burn!'

'Don't!' Ellen said, and there was horror in her eyes. 'You don't know what you're saying, my son. Such a thing is too wicked for words. Richard was a man. A human being, like any other. Besides which he was also—'

'Also what?' Peter asked.

'Never mind,' Ellen said.

'He was still your husband, wasn't he? – That's what you was going to say. I suppose it still counts for something with you, does it, even after living with my father all these years and bringing his bastard into the world? Does it, mother? Does it count? Then no doubt we shall be seeing you going into mourning for two husbands at the same time?'

'By God!' John exclaimed, and half rose from his chair. But his mother touched him on the arm and after a moment he sat down again, his clenched fists on the edge of the table. 'Do you think you're the only one with feelings?' he said.

Peter, upright in his chair, sat like an image, hard-faced. But he was ashamed, under his mother's steady gaze, and his glance shifted once or twice, while he made the effort to speak.

'I'm sorry, mother!' he said in a burst. 'I shouldn't have said that. I take it back.'

'You shouldn't be saying these things to John, either.'

'What've I said that ent true?'

'Your father would have hated this. To hear you talk as you have today. To know there was badness between you and John.'

'How long d'you aim to keep it up?' John asked. 'Are you going to be at odds with me even working in the smithy? That's a damn silly thing if you like!'

236

'There'll be no work done in the smithy tomorrow. I'm keeping it closed as a mark of respect.'

'*You're* keeping it closed?'

'That's what I said. I've got business in Runston in the morning. I shan't be home till about twelve o'clock.'

'Then I'll see the vicar,' John said, 'and make arrangements for Will's funeral.'

'No,' Peter said. 'I shall do that when I get home. He was *my* father, not yours. It's my duty to see the vicar.'

John and his mother exchanged a glance. Neither spoke, but their thought was the same. Peter watched them without expression and then, leaning forward over the table, began cutting the loaf of bread. He dropped a slice onto John's plate.

'*You've* got the Mad Miller's funeral to see to. I hope you hadn't forgotten that.'

'No. I hadn't forgotten.'

'That'll come pretty hard on you, but at least he left a few pounds in that box. It'll pay for his burial, I suppose.'

'I shall manage,' John said. 'I've got a bit of money saved. But there's no need for you to worry about it. He was *my* father, not yours.'

Peter glanced at him and smiled.

The next day, in the early morning, John and Hannah walked on the hill in sunshine so warm that steam rose from the wet grass and larks sang in the sky above. The hem of Hannah's skirt was drenched, but she made nothing of the matter, and they continued up hill till they came to the log beside the pond. They sat together and talked about Will.

'My grandfather cried when he heard the news. He said Will had helped him a thousand times. He said the world would not be the same without Will Gale to send it round.'

'It certainly won't be the same for me. Things is already changing a bit. They'll change a lot more in the days to come.'

'What do you mean?'

'Peter's taking it badly,' he said. 'There's going to be trouble between him and me.'

'Are you worried?' Hannah asked.

'I'm preparing myself, that's all. I shan't cross my bridges till I come to them, but I'm getting things sorted out in my mind, and there's one or two things I must talk out with you, about our future, yours and mine.'

'Talk away,' Hannah said.

Later that morning, John went into Runston to see about his father's funeral. He thought it best that the burial should be a quiet affair, and he made arrangements accordingly. He and his mother would be the only mourners.

When he returned home at midday, Peter was there, standing on the hearth in his best suit, his hands behind him. Ellen, pale-faced, sat very still and erect in her chair, and her eyes, seeking John's, gave him some warning of what was to come.

'I've been to town to see the lawyer,' Peter said. 'Not that I had any doubts at all, but I thought I'd like to get things straight, especially seeing I'm bastard-born. The lawyer says, there being no will, the smithy and cottage belong to me.'

'Yes,' John said, 'I daresay they do.'

'I'm his only living kin, so it's all pretty simple, the way things fall out, and you've got no claim on the smithy at all. Nor the cottage nor nothing else. Everything here belongs to me.'

'I reckon I'm following so far, but what happens next, might I ask? D'you want me to touch my cap to you before starting work in the smithy every morning?'

'You won't be working in the smithy no more. Nor living under this roof neither. I've decided it's better if you move on.'

'Ah! I see. So it's come to that!'

'You don't seem all that much surprised.'

'I thought there was something in the wind. I smelt it like you smell bad fish.'

'You've got no claim on my father's property.'

'I don't care tuppence who owns what, but I would've thought we could at least have gone on working together, the same way we have done in the past.'

'Yes,' said Ellen, looking at Peter. 'You know well enough what Will intended. He spoke about it oftentimes. He always said, when the time came for him to retire, you and John would stop on in the smithy and work together on equal terms.'

'He didn't know, when he said that, that John's father would shoot him down!'

'He looked on John as his own son. He'd want him treated more fairly than this.'

'John won't want for nothing much. He's got the old mill if nothing else.'

'The mill?' she said. 'What use is that?'

'It's better than having nothing at all. He might be able to salvage something and get the mill working again. He says he's got some money saved.'

'I'm a blacksmith,' John said. 'What do I want with running a mill?'

Peter gave a little shrug.

'Beggars can't be choosers,' he said. 'But if you don't want to be a miller, you can go as journeyman to some other smith. It should be easy enough to get a job, so long as you don't mind going further afield. You've got your indentures, after all.'

'Which is more than you have!' John exclaimed. 'You've got another couple of years yet before you've properly served your time.'

'Seeing I own my own smithy, I can call myself a master smith.'

'You can call yourself whatever you please! It's what you *are* that really counts!'

Peter was silent. He looked away. His lips were set in a hard line.

'What about me?' Ellen asked. 'I've got no lawful claim

on Will, either. Am I to be turned out along with John?'

'Don't be silly,' Peter said. 'This is your home.'

'Then my word should count for something here!'

'It's no use, mother,' John said. 'I shan't stop where I ent wanted. We could never work as a team, him and me, not with him feeling as he does. The best thing is to do as he says.'

'I am still mistress in this house, whether I have a lawful claim or not, and it's me that says who comes and goes.'

'I'd have to find somewhere to live in the end, when Hannah and me get married,' he said. 'I may as well go soon as late.' And to Peter he said bitterly: 'I know you've always been jealous of me on account of my being a better smith, but I never thought it'd come to this. I'd have been willing to work with you. I'd have helped you every way I could, for Will's sake if nothing else. But seeing you've chosen to sling me out I shall ask you to remember this – the moment I step outside that door, I owe you no duty nor favour nor nothing, and the same goes for you, too.'

'Amen to that,' Peter said.

'I'll go upstairs and pack my things.'

'So soon? So soon?' Ellen said. She was reaching out to take his hands. 'No, I can't bear it to be like this!'

'It's better this way,' John said. 'Too much has been said between him and me. It'll only get worse now, the longer I stay. I'll go along to Grannie Naylor's. She'll give me a lodging, I daresay.'

'Will would have been so distressed by this!'

'I shan't say goodbye to you, mother, cos I shall see you oftentimes. I'll be at Will's funeral for a start. At least Peter can't grudge me that! And if you ever have need of me, be sure to send word without delay.'

'She won't want for nothing with me,' Peter said.

'As to that, I ent so sure!'

'Are you going, did you say?'

'Yes, I'm going,' John said.

Half an hour later he left the house, his belongings

packed into two canvas bags. He went to Mrs. Naylor's cottage and she agreed to take him in. He paid her ten shillings in advance. He sat on the bed in the room she gave him and counted his savings carefully. It came to nearly fifty pounds.

The day was still fine, and as he stood in the burnt-out mill, he could feel the sunshine warm on his head, for the upper floors and roof had gone and the place was open to the sky. Bits of charred rafters stuck out, pointed, from their wall-sockets, and the central beams, although still in place, were burnt to half their original thickness. By a strange chance, the hoist-chain still hung from the main roof-beam, and when he touched its twisted links, he found that they had been welded together by the heat.

The mill machinery lay in ruins, the wooden shafts and cogwheels burnt, the metal twisted, shrunken, deformed, and among the heap, which smoked even now, the broken millstones lay about, their grooves filled with a fine soft black dust that had once been flour.

The smell of the place was foul and loathsome, for such a fire, far from purifying, left behind it blackness and filth, and the evil smeech of it, catching in the throat and nostrils, could turn a man's stomach and make him retch. John had known that smell before, as a small boy, four years old, in the ruined mill at Cutlowell Park, when his father had taken him to the sale. And he thought how very strange it was that his father's misfortunes should have begun and ended with a burnt-out mill.

He had put on his working-clothes to come to Pex Mill this afternoon. Now he took his sweat-rag from his neck and pressed it against his nose and mouth. And as he went from place to place: to the mealroom where his father had died; to the stockroom and sheds and the house itself; he wondered if the smell could ever really be cleansed away. With the smoking refuse gone; the stonework and brickwork scraped clean; with all the timberwork replaced and a roof of

241

new tiles overhead: could the place be made decent and wholesome again, brought to life out of the past, inhabited by a new spirit?

'Well, now, I wonder!' he said to himself.

He stooped and picked up a piece of stone and went around with it, using it as a hammer, testing the condition of the walls. Crunching across the bed of ash, he trod carefully, picking his way, for he felt the heat of it underfoot and saw how, when the wind breathed, the bits of charcoal glowed bright red.

Just after two, Hannah came to the mill door, and he went to meet her.

'Don't come in. You'll dirty your clothes. You might get burnt. It's hot enough.'

'It's all over Dingham that you and your brother have fallen out.'

'It would be,' he said. 'I've taken lodgings with Grannie Naylor.'

'Is it true you've left the smithy for good?'

'Yes, it's true. He's turned me out.'

'Well, for goodness' sake!' Hannah exclaimed. 'Aren't you going to tell me about it?'

'First I want to tell you my plans. Let's go outside, where the air is clean, and I'll tell you what I've got in mind.'

So they went and sat on the lock-gate, and he talked to her in a quiet voice, pointing now and then to the mill. He would lower the mill walls by half and use the spare bricks to build a new chimney and a blacksmith's hearth. A few sheets of corrugated iron would serve as a roof for the time being and then it was just a question of gear and tackle.

'I've wrote a list of things I'll need, and the anvil's about the biggest item, specially if I get it new. Then there's bellows and tools and iron and maybe a couple of tons of breeze but once I've really made a start—'

'So you'd set up as smith against your brother?'

'That's right. Why not? It's my proper trade. He hoped to drive me right away. He thought I'd have to go pretty far

242

afield and give myself to another smith. Well, he's made a mistake, and I'm stopping here. I'm setting up shop in this old mill and if he don't like it that's just too bad.'

'Is there work enough for two smiths?'

'I dunno. We shall have to see. There was four of us working in the smithy. Now there's Peter and Jim Pacey. It's his own fault if he loses trade.'

'He may take on new helpers.'

'He'll never take on a first-rate smith cos he can't bear to be with any man whose work is better than his own. That's half the reason he's pushed me out. He knows I'm a better smith than him, and that's not bragging, it's just plain fact. He's only a lad of seventeen. I've had a start of seven years. I've got the experience. It's in my bones. And there's plenty of people round about who'll come where they know they get good work.'

'So you mean to take half Peter's trade?'

'I shall take it all – if it comes!' John said. 'I owe him nothing. I told him that.'

'It's quiet out this end of Dingham.'

'It won't be, however, when the new bridge is built and the new road links up with the main turnpike.'

'Seems you've got it all worked out.'

'I shall start clearing tomorrow morning, so's I've got somewhere to lay my head, to save paying out for lodgings and that. I'll get a mason to give me a hand, and the moment I've got a fire going in my forge, I shall start smithing straight away. The house'll have to wait a bit. I shall work on that in my spare time.'

'So!' Hannah said, with a faint smile. 'We'll be living next to the smithy, then, with the smoke your mother grumbles about?'

'We may have to wait a bit, before getting married,' John said. 'And I may make a botch of things, when I start, if folk don't come to me with their trade. You don't want to change your mind, do you, now that you know what risks there are?'

'Supposing I was to say yes?'

'Ah, just supposing!' he agreed. 'Women are known for it, so they say.'

Hannah was joking. He knew that. And he answered in kind, with a teasing smile. Yet a certain fear took hold of him now and Hannah, seeing it in his eyes, leant towards him and kissed his mouth. Her arms went round him. She held him close.

'You mustn't look at me like that.'

'I dunno so much. Seems like it pays.'

After a moment she drew away. She became cool and composed again, matter-of-fact and rather grave, though the little flickering smile of warmth was still alive in her hazel eyes.

'Tell me more about your plans.'

Chapter 15

On a boisterous day in March, 1899, when the southwest wind, blowing up the river, hurled spray at the mill walls and thumped around in the new-built chimney, John lit a fire for the first time in his own blacksmith's hearth, and, working the bellows with his foot, watched as the coals began to glow. In front was the cooling-trough, ready filled, and from the rail hung his shovel and slice, bought second-hand at a sale near Gloucester. Nearby stood his anvil, brand-new, on a great block of elm bedded deep in the floor, and beside it stood a strong sturdy table, where his precious tools lay ready to hand.

The first task he had set himself was to stock up with horseshoes, different sizes, for, as old Mr. Draycott had said to him, any blacksmith working alone would need to keep an extra good stock to save time when impatient customers stood at the door. And for a start, to encourage him, the old man had promised that all the horses at Neyes Farm should come to John to be shod by the year.

First he cut up the shoe-lengths, until there were scores of them, on the floor. He then took a bundle in his hands, set them on end upon the anvil, and selected four of them, all of a size. He placed them among the hot coals.

Overhead, as he tended his fire, the wind made music of a whining kind in the roof of galvanised iron sheeting, and outside, on the river, he could hear the calls of the waterfowl nesting among the reeds and rushes. Soon his hammer would ring on the anvil yet again and he would hear nothing else, but all these sounds, worked in a pattern, would be part of his life from now on and he would hear them even in dreams.

Throughout the morning, as he worked, people, mostly in ones and twos, would wander along the river bank or stroll straight down from the village itself to see what was happening at the mill turned forge. Some passed without a word. Others, like Tommy Breton, stopped and looked in at the open door.

'Morning, John! How're you doing? Making the sparks fly already, I see!'

'Morning, Tommy. It's a fine day. Anything I can do for you?'

'I thought I could maybe light my pipe.'

'Help yourself. The tongs is there.'

'You've done a good job, making the place neat and tidy. When're you starting on the house?'

'All in good time,' John said. 'I've got to earn a living first.'

'It's a great thing for Dingham, having a smithy at either end. There ent many places can boast of that, especially places as small as Dingham.'

'No,' John said, 'I reckon that's right.'

'Think you'll get trade, do you, right down here, where nobody comes much nor even knows there's a blacksmith here?'

'Half Dingham's been past this morning. By the time they've had their say, I shan't need to advertise in the papers.'

'What does your brother think of it, your setting up as a smith like this?'

'I dunno. I've never asked him.'

'Well, good luck to you, John. You'll need it for sure. Thanks for the light-up. That saved me a match.'

Later that morning, about eleven, an elderly knife-grinder came to the door, having heard the sound of John's hammer. His name was Bert Toms and he travelled the roads

246

with a treadle grindstone set on a ramshackle pair of wheels.

'Didn't know there was a smith this end. That'll save me a lot of swither. My old axle's packed up on me. Think you can fix it for me, eh?'

'Bring it in and I'll have a look.'

John replaced the broken axle, put new cotter-pins in at the wheels, and put in a rivet to strengthen the brake. Bert was well pleased. He took out a little leather purse.

'How much do I owe you for doing that?'

'I reckon we'll call it sixpence,' John said.

'Then I'll pay cash,' Bert said. 'I reckon you've done a good job. Not everyone would've took such pains. I can just about run to a sixpenny piece. Trade ent good for me these days. Not many folk've got knives and scissors for me to grind, or so they tell me, anyway.' Bert, in disgust, pretended to spit. 'They better prefer to go to the town and get it done dearer!' he exclaimed. 'I hope you do better in *your* chosen trade.'

When the knife-grinder had gone, trundling away towards the village, John went back to his work at the anvil. By noon that day, when he paused to eat his bread and cheese, one beam overhead was hung with foreshoes, six on a nail, ranged along according to size. By the time he had finished that day he was resolved that the second beam would be hung with an equal number of hindshoes.

At about three in the afternoon Hannah arrived, bringing his washing tied up in a cloth. She carried it through into what had once been the old mealroom, where John now slept on a bunk-bed, and gathered up his dirty clothes. She came back into the smithy and stood watching as he worked.

'You've started, then?'

'*And* had a customer, if you please!'

'Whoever was it?' she asked, surprised.

'Bert Toms, the knife-grinder. His trolley-axle had packed up.'

'However much did you earn doing that?'

'I earnt sixpence,' John said.

'Sixpence!' she said, laughing at him. 'I suppose you'll

247

be taking that straight to the bank!'

'It's all very well for you to laugh. Sixpence is sixpence, say what you like.'

He took a shoe-length out of the fire, hammered it round on the anvil-beak, and then, with a movement of his tongs, laid it upon the flat 'table' and proceeded to hammer out the crimp. His movements were easy, unhurried, unfussed. The work seemed to cost him no thought at all. But because the knowledge of it was in his bones, every blow of the hammer told. And Hannah, seeing how it was, took pride in the man because of his craft.

'You're very quick.'

'It was Will who learnt me that quickness,' he said. 'Everything I do I get from him. You could say, and it'd be true, that Will Gale is still working in me, at least so long as I'm at the anvil and got a hammer in my hand.'

'What would he say if he knew you'd set up against his son?'

'The skill he gave me, I've got to use. I couldn't do that half so well if I had to work for some other smith. Will would agree with that, I'm sure. I've got to stand on my own two feet. It's up to Peter to do the same. He's got his name and all his customers ready made. I've got my skill and not much else. Seems to me it's a fair fight.' He glanced briefly at her face. 'Do you think I'm in the wrong?'

'No,' she said, 'but I doubt if it'd make any difference if I did.'

Walking about the new workshop, she looked at the tools hanging up on the walls, the hopper full of pale sand, the shoeing-stalls and halter-rings, the farrier's toolbox, as yet unused.

'The place is as clean as a new pin.'

'It won't be, however, by the time I've worked here a day or two and had a few horses in and out.'

'Not to mention the smoke and smuts.'

'You'll have to get used to that,' he said, 'seeing you're marrying into the trade.'

248

Hannah came from the shoeing-stall and stood again close by the anvil.

'You're very high and mighty today. You seem to think you're on top of the world.'

'Ah. Well. And why not?'

'Just cos you've had a customer? Seems to me it's gone to your head.'

'There'll be others. You'll see. The sound of my hammer will bring them in, just the same as it done with Bert Toms. There's no sound like it in the world.'

'You're very pert and sure of yourself.'

'I've got to be. It's the only way. And I ent done too badly, first day off.'

'A knife-grinder!' Hannah said, and her eyes mocked him, cool and amused. They were still learning about each other, he and she. Their discoveries often brought them close. And there was always a current of humour, running between them, provoking, alive. 'A knife-grinder!' she said again. 'And he paid you sixpence? Oh my stars!'

'Yes, well, it's a start,' John said, and paused long enough in his work to smile at her across the anvil. Then his hammer rang out again, and the iron, answering to the blows, submitted itself to his design.

THE TWO FARMS

For Margaret Peach

Chapter One

The valley ran from north to south and the two farms, Godsakes and Peele, lay on opposite sides of it. The Suttons had been tenants at Peele for four generations, having come there in 1746, but the Riddlers had been at Godsakes only since 1821. The little valley was sheltered and warm and the land was as rich and fertile as any land in Gloucestershire, varying from a light sandy loam in the upper part of the valley to a rich red marl in the lower parts. On the same side of the valley as Godsakes, lying in a hollow beside it, was a third farm known as Granger's, but it was only sixty acres or so and all of it heavy clay.

Peele, on the valley's eastern slopes, was sheltered by the round green hill known locally as Luton Camp, while Godsakes, on the western side, had its back to the twin humps of Hogden Hill and Derritt Hill. On both these farms the fields sloped gently down to the flat green valley floor where the Timmy Brook, with many a twist, made its way through the meadows to join the little River Cran outside the hamlet of Abbot's Lyall.

In summer the Timmy Brook flowed sedately between its banks but every winter without fail it would flood out over the meadows, turning the valley into a lake, sometimes for two or three weeks at a time. This flooding, although it caused problems, was welcomed by the valley farmers, for it left the meadows so enriched that in spring they gave new grass for the cows three weeks before it grew elsewhere. These meadows were common land and, except at haymaking time, stock from all three farms grazed there together, crossing and re-crossing the brook by a number of little bridges set between the steep banks.

7

John Sutton of Peele Farm, with four generations of breeding behind him, was a man of some education and polish. He was also a vigorous, go-ahead man who farmed his land by modern ideas. Isaac Riddler, on the other hand, was a near-illiterate cattle dealer who, after years of scrimping and saving, had taken the tenancy of Godsakes with more courage than capital. His son Morris had succeeded him but farmed in the same haphazard way and was almost always behind with his work. It was inevitable, therefore, that the educated John Sutton, successfully farming three hundred acres, should feel himself superior to the uncouth Morris Riddler, muddling along on his hundred and ten.

Still, they were good enough neighbours until, in 1842, their landlord, James Goodwin of Allern Hall, finding himself in need of money, decided to sell the three valley farms lying so far from the main estate, and offered the tenants first refusal. The estate agent, Mr Maule, called on John Sutton first; he stated the exact terms of the offer and gave him a week to think it over.

'Then I would be much obliged if you would come and see me and let me know your decision.'

Sutton did not need to think. He knew his own mind. And the agent had no sooner gone than he was striding his well-kept fields, already seeing them as his own, already busy making plans. The purchase presented no financial problem because only two years before an elderly uncle, formerly a hop merchant, had died leaving Sutton a tidy fortune. In fact the chance of buying Peele so accorded with his ambitions that it seemed like the answer to a half-formed prayer.

For Riddler, however, it was a different matter. The agent's news came as a shock.

'Buy Godsakes? How much?' he asked.

'Mr Goodwin would accept eighteen pounds per acre for the farm itself and fifty shillings per acre for the hill pastures.'

'But that would be over two thousand pounds! I haven't got it!' Riddler said.

'It would fetch more than that if it went for auction. It really is an excellent farm, with the common rights on the meadows as well, and I'm sure if you were to try the bank they would be only too happy to advance whatever sum you need.'

'Yes, at an interest of four per cent!'

'Does that mean you do not wish to buy?'

'Dammit! Don't I get time to think?'

'Yes, of course,' the agent said. 'You have until a week today. Then I would like you to call on me and let me know your decision.'

'You're in a hurry, aren't you? We're in the middle of haymaking here.'

But although he wanted time to think, Riddler too had made up his mind, for he saw that the chance was too good to miss. And the risk of borrowing from the bank, although it worried him at first, soon came to seem trivial compared with the richness of the reward. He talked about it to his wife, Agnes.

'Well, for one thing, we don't want to leave here, do we, when we've been here twenty-one years and put so much work into the place? We don't want to have to start again in a strange new place, do we, eh?'

He was also thinking of his son, Eddy, at that time nine years old.

'What a wonderful thing it'll be for him – taking over a farm of his very own! We shall never have such a chance again. Not at that price. It's too good to miss.'

'How much will you have to borrow?'

'I reckon about six hundred pounds.'

'You'll see Mr Maule, then?'

'Be sure I shall!'

But the whole week went by and Riddler, behindhand as usual, was still at work down in the meadows, anxious to get his hay carted before a threatened break in the weather. Mr Maule would have to wait. There was no great hurry, he told himself. It would do him no harm to stew for a while.

John Sutton's purchase of his farm was already under way by

this time. An agreement had been signed between the two parties and ten per cent of the purchase price had been deposited with the estate lawyers.

'What about Hessey at Granger's? Have you had his answer yet?'

'Yes, he's decided not to buy. Hardly surprising, really, seeing he's in his seventies and has no sons to come after him.' The agent met John Sutton's gaze. 'Would you be interested?'

'Yes, I would. But that's a clay farm. Sumpy. Bad. It would need a great deal doing to it.'

'Mr Goodwin would accept fifteen pounds the acre.'

'I am willing to pay that.'

'Excellent. I thought you might.'

'What about Riddler at Godsakes? Will he be buying?' Sutton asked.

'He hasn't given his answer yet but it seems very doubtful,' the agent said. 'Not much capital there, I think, and he seems nervous of borrowing. I got the impression he wouldn't buy.'

'Well, if he doesn't, you know where to come – I'll have it off you like a shot.'

'That would give you quite a substantial holding,' the agent said with a little smile.

'It would mean the whole valley was mine,' Sutton said. 'I've been thinking about it a lot and the idea has taken hold of me. Riddler is a good enough chap but he's forty years behind the times. A glance over Godsakes shows you that. I could farm it a lot better than he does, and once I've got Granger's put to rights, every acre in that valley would be farmed right to the top of its bent.'

'Well, I'll give Riddler another few days, then I'll go over and chivvy him up. But I don't think you need worry. I would say Godsakes is as good as yours.'

Sutton nodded as though satisfied but when the agent was seeing him off he brought the subject up again. 'If Godsakes went to auction, how much do you think it would fetch?'

'I would think, perhaps, three thousand pounds.'

'Yes, well,' Sutton said, 'certainly if I were there, I would be willing to bid that high.'

10

The agent smiled understandingly.

'I'll see Riddler as soon as I can.'

'What the hell do you mean, Sutton's made you a better offer? Tenants had first option, you said, and *I'm* the tenant here, don't forget.'

'You seemed doubtful about buying.'

'I wanted time to think, that's all.'

'Quite so,' the agent said. 'But I asked for your answer within a week and it is now eleven days since we talked.'

'I don't sit around on my arse here, you know! I have got my day's work to do –'

'And I have mine.'

'Yesterday I went into town and had a talk with Mr Forester at the bank. I was getting it all fixed up, finding out how I was placed. I told him the price I'd got to pay and he said there was no problem at all. Two thousand, one hundred and eighty pounds. That's the price you set on this farm and you've got no right to welsh on me.'

'If you had come when I asked you to, the matter would have been settled by now, but I have my employer's interest to think of, and in view of Mr Sutton's offer –'

'What *is* his offer?' Riddler asked. 'Thirty pieces of silver, is it?'

'Three thousand pounds,' the agent said.

'And what if I say I'll pay that? Will you stick to the price this time or will you go running over to Peele to see if Sutton will bid higher still?'

'If you're prepared to pay three thousand pounds –'

'I've said so, haven't I?' Riddler snarled.

'Then I shall go back to Mr Goodwin and apprise him of the fact. I can't make any promise, of course, but if I advise him to accept he will most probably do so.'

'Then for God's sake get on with it,' Riddler said, 'and get the lawyers to tie it up.'

In due course the transaction was made and he became the owner of Godsakes Farm. But to do so he had to borrow

11

fourteen hundred pounds from the bank, more than twice what he'd bargained for, and he never forgave John Sutton for that. The old neighbourliness was gone, and a bitter hatred took its place. He always tried to avoid Sutton now but in the Corn Hall one market day they came face to face by accident. The story of their quarrel was well known and the meeting was watched with interest all round and Riddler, being aware of this, stood four-square in front of Sutton and in a loud voice said:

'I would turn my back on this man — except that he'd stick a knife in it!'

John Sutton looked at him with a mixture of tolerance and contempt. 'You don't seem to understand — farming is a business, like any other, and in business there's always competition.'

'Well, in this competition you lost, didn't you?'

'Just for the present, yes, perhaps.'

'What the hell do you mean by that?'

'Farming is not quite the same as it was. Things are progressing. There's change in the air. And you will have to farm a sight more efficiently than you have done till now if you are to keep abreast of the times and pay off the mortgage loan you've been foolish enough to saddle yourself with.'

'I'll pay it off, be sure of that!'

'Well, we shall see,' Sutton said.

In the summer of 1843 the well in the farmyard at Godsakes ran dry. This had never happened before and Riddler knew who was to blame: John Sutton, taking over Granger's Farm in the clay hollow just below, had had the land drained to a depth of six feet or more and this had drawn off the underground springs that had fed the well at Godsakes.

Riddler got on his horse at once and rode into Missenham to seek his solicitor's advice. But it was a question, Mr Nicholson said, of *damnum absque injuria*, or 'damage without wrong'.

'In other words, Mr Riddler, your neighbour has a perfect

12

right to drain his own land if he so wishes, just as you have a right to drain yours, and if it causes damage to some other party, I'm afraid there is no redress for it.'

A piece of legal information which cost Riddler half a guinea.

'Why is it that the blasted law is always on the side of the scoundrels?' he asked his wife when he got home.

The shortage of water was acute. It had to be carried up from the brook. And Riddler had no choice but to sink a deeper well. It was yet another expense he could ill afford; yet another setback to be laid at John Sutton's door; and in its wake, over the years, one misfortune succeeded another until, as Agnes Riddler said, it seemed that the farm had a curse on it. First it was a bout of quarter-ill, which took three of their best cows; then it was the failure of the corn harvest; and then, in 1844, winter gales tore the roof from one of the older cattle-sheds.

None of these misfortunes was ever visited on Peele. There, obviously, everything prospered and Sutton, now that he owned the farm, was making improvements everywhere. Hedges had been grubbed up, throwing two or three fields into one; new farm buildings had been built to house the most modern machinery; and more grassland was being ploughed to grow more corn.

He had also built himself a new house, up on a gentle slope of land just below the beechwoods, set at a slight angle to give a view southwards along the valley. It was a fine square-built house of cream-coloured stucco finish and in front of it lay a gravel drive, a garden laid out with trees and shrubs, and a lawn running down to a small lake. The old farmhouse was occupied by the bailiff now and a row of conifers had been planted to screen it, and the farm buildings, from the windows of the new house.

Riddler would look across the valley and sneer at John Sutton's pretensions.

'He fancies himself as some sort of squire,' he would say to his wife and children, and he called Sutton 'the Marquis of Peele'.

Certainly the new house at Peele was a very handsome residence and drew the attention of anyone travelling along the

13

valley road. The old house at Godsakes, on the other hand, built of locally quarried stone, so merged with its background of fields that had it not been for the pale sandy track climbing the side of the valley towards it, people would scarcely have known it was there.

'What a contrast between the two farms,' visitors to Peele would say, and even those who knew nothing of farming could see that Godsakes was badly run-down.

Riddler, having cut down on labour, was now working harder than ever, hoping to make up for it, but often while he ploughed in one field his two men, Lovell and Smith, would be taking it easy in another. Sometimes he would steal up on them and bawl at them over the gate, but it made little impression on them. They would plod all the way across the field just to ask him what he had said. They had no respect for him nowadays and behind his back they called him 'Mo'. Sometimes, on market days, Riddler was inclined to drink too much and in the morning he would have a thick head.

'Old Mo's been at it again,' Bob Lovell would say to Nahum Smith. 'We shan't get much sense out of him today.'

They argued with him constantly over the work that had to be done and he was too easily overborne.

'No good cutting that hay today, master. There's rain in the offing as sure as fate.'

After four dry days, Riddler, cursing and swearing at them, gave orders that the hay was to be cut. There followed a week of heavy showers and the hay was more than half spoilt.

It was the same with everything. The farm-work was always in arrears. Once they were so late sowing their spring corn that it never ripened properly and Riddler fed it green to the stock. One heifer died of it and a number of ewes slinked their lambs. Stock was down to a minimum now and the lack of manure showed itself in crops of sickly looking kale and mangolds no bigger than a woman's fist. In the autumn of 1844 Riddler found he could not afford to buy seed corn and some of his fields, left unploughed, tumbled down to grass and weeds.

John Sutton, across the valley, could see how bad things were at Godsakes and one afternoon he rode over, coming straight into the field where Riddler was flattening mole-hills.

'It's two years since you bought this farm and if you've got any sense you'll admit that you're just about done for. I don't care to see a good farm going to ruin like this and I am willing to pay you exactly the sum you gave for it. No one else would pay you that. Not in the state it's in today. So why not sell out to me before you're dragged down deeper still?'

Riddler, in shirtsleeves, a heavy mattock in his hands, looked up at Sutton on his horse and gave a deep-throated growl.

'Get off my land,' he said savagely.

Later, at tea with his family, he talked about Sutton's visit.

'My father slaved all his life, scraping enough money together to take this farm for himself and me. He loved this place . . . The valley, the hills, the meadows down there and the Timmy Brook. He slaved his guts out to get this land and I'm damned if I'll ever let it go.'

'We are still slaving,' Agnes said, 'and where will it get us in the end?'

'Things'll get better, you'll see. I've been making a lot of mistakes and that loan is putting a strain on us. We've had bad luck these past two years but things will pick up for us from now on. I promise you that.'

'Why not sell while the price is still good? Sutton means to have this place and he will do sooner or later, I'm sure, being the kind of man he is.'

'Is that all you can say to me? Is that your way of cheering me up?' Riddler's voice, always loud, now rose to an angry shout. 'Christ Almighty!' he exclaimed. 'Things've come to a pretty pass when my own wife wants to do me down. You talk about slaving? Hell's bells! At least you slept in your bed last night! *I* didn't. Oh, no, not me! I was up with a sick cow –'

'Please don't shout at me,' Agnes said. 'I know how hard you have to work.'

Riddler fell silent, staring at her, his anger gradually dying

15

down. Then, as he spooned buttered beans into his mouth, he turned to look at his two children.

'Mother works hard, too,' Kirren said.

'Yes, I know she does,' Riddler said.

'She works just as hard as you ever do. You've got no right to shout at her.'

'All right, all right, that's enough,' Riddler said.

Kirren, although she was only eight always had more to say for herself than her brother, Eddy, who was twelve. And often when she looked at her father, her eyes were darkly hostile.

'Mother isn't well,' she said. 'You ought not to make her work so hard.'

'Not well? Not well? Who says she's not well?'

'Mrs Lovell and Mrs Smith.'

'Kirren, be quiet,' Agnes said.

'What's this about you not being well?'

'Nothing, Morris. Nothing at all. I get a bit tired sometimes, that's all, and I worry about you working so hard. That's why I thought if you gave up the farm – '

'I'm not giving up and that's flat!' Riddler said. 'Neither John Sutton nor anyone else is taking this farm away from me and you'd better make up your mind to it!'

Outside in the foldyard afterwards Riddler talked to his young son.

'Women are different from us, somehow. They don't seem to see things the same way at all. But you understand, don't you, boy? You wouldn't want me to let the farm go any more than I would myself?'

'No, father,' Eddy said, 'especially not to Mr Sutton, after what he did to you.'

Riddler was much moved by this. He gripped Eddy's shoulder and gave it a squeeze.

'Sutton won't have it, I'll see to that. I swear to it by Almighty God. I'm going to make a few changes here, get things back on an even keel. I only need a bit of luck and now that you are leaving school and will be doing a full day's work – '

'I shall work hard, father, cross my heart.'

'I know you will. I know it fine. You're worth two of Lovell

16

and Smith and if we put our backs into it we shall soon pull the place up, shan't we, eh? Oh, we shall show them a thing or two, you and me! We'll make them sit up. We shall, that's a fact!'

Riddler's son was his pride and joy; his hope for the future; his bright star. He saw the boy as a young man – clever, determined, vigorous, strong. Eddy had qualities he himself lacked and in a few years' time he would be making the old place hum. Riddler saw it as plain as glass and the happy vision made him smile.

But this dream, like so many others, was to be most cruelly shattered, for that winter an epidemic of influenza swept through Gloucestershire, and Riddler's family went down with it. His wife and daughter soon recovered but Eddy developed pneumonia and in three weeks he was dead.

Riddler was beside himself with grief. For days he hardly spoke at all but went about his work in an anguished trance. Often he failed to come in for his meals and Agnes would have to go out to him and plead with him to come in and eat. Once she found him in tears in the barn and when she touched him on the shoulder he burst out at her in a terrible howl:

'Why did it have to be the boy that died?'

Agnes turned and left him and outside in the yard came upon her daughter, Kirren, standing like a small statue, an empty bucket in each hand. The child's face was pale and stiff. Agnes saw that she had heard.

'Your father is not himself,' she said. 'He doesn't know what he's saying. We must both try to be patient with him.'

Kirren said not a single word; only stared at her mother with darkened eyes and then, with the ghost of a shrug, turned away towards the pump.

17

Chapter Two

John Sutton was a widower, his wife having died in 1832, giving birth to their only child, a son named Philip. Sometimes Sutton worried about this son of his, brought up in a household run by an elderly housekeeper without other children for company, but in the winter of 1844 this problem unexpectedly solved itself.

The weather was bad in December and one black wet night just after Christmas a drover driving a large flock of sheep through the valley stopped at Peele asking if he could sleep in a barn and leave his flock to graze in the meadows, before moving on in the morning. The bailiff, Warren Oakley, gave permission, but he never learnt the man's name, nor did he see his face clearly, and in the morning, before it grew light, the drover and his flock had gone.

Nothing more was thought of it then; the man had given no trouble whatever; but three days after he had gone a small boy in ragged clothes was caught stealing turnips from a field and told the bailiff that his uncle, the drover, had left him behind deliberately, telling him to lie low and not leave the barn for two or three days. Oakley brought the boy to the house and John Sutton questioned him.

'Do you mean to tell me that you've been in the barn since Thursday night?'

The boy gave a nod.

'Weren't you cold?'

Another nod.

'What is your name?'

'Jim,' the boy said, and gave a small, husky cough, partly from fear and partly from cold.

'Jim what?' Sutton asked.

This time the boy shook his head.

'Well, then, what is your uncle's name?'

Yet another shake of the head.

'Do you mean you don't know or have you been told not to tell?'

'Uncle said not to tell. He said he'd put a curse on me and if I told I should fall down dead.'

'What else did your uncle say?'

'He said for me to stop in the barn and keep out of sight for two or three days. Then to go to the nearest workhouse and ask for them to take me in.'

'Have you no parents?'

'No. They're dead.'

'Where was your home before they died?'

'I don't remember. It's too far back.'

The boy was about ten years old, dirty, louse-ridden, dressed in rags, and with red scurfy sores on his face and neck. He also had a large bruise just below his left eye and a smaller bruise on his upper lip.

'Did your uncle do that to you?'

'Yes.'

'Does he often beat you?'

'Yes, when he's drunk. He doesn't like me. He says I smell.'

'And whose fault is that, I'd like to know? Why, if I had that blackguard here now – '

Sutton was fond of children and the boy's condition angered him. He turned towards the farm bailiff.

'All right, Oakley, you can go. I'll keep the boy here for a day or two while I decide what to do with him. Come along with me, Jim, and we'll see if Mrs Abelard can find you something better to eat than a raw turnip out of the field.'

The housekeeper was none too pleased at having a dirty, verminous child presented to her in her clean kitchen and she told Sutton so in vigorous terms.

'The boy is starving,' Sutton said. 'Give him some good hot food to eat, then get him washed and into clean clothes.'

'What clean clothes?' Mrs Abelard asked. 'Has he brought his valise with him?'

'Some old clothes of Philip's, of course, what else?'

'And what shall I do with him after that?'

'Philip will be back by then. He's gone for a ride with Charlie Clements. He can take young Jim under his wing.'

'Do you mean he's to stop in the house? Sleep in one of our nice clean beds?'

'Yes, of course. Why shouldn't he?'

'And how long for?' Mrs Abelard asked, scandalized at the prospect.

'As to that, I have no idea. We shall just have to see,' Sutton said.

By the time Philip came in Jim had been so thoroughly scrubbed that his fair skin glowed as though lit from within, and, dressed in borrowed velveteens, with his fair hair brushed smoothly down, looked presentable enough, though Philip made a face of distaste at sight of the red sores on his skin.

'What's that? Is it leprosy?'

'Of course it isn't,' Mrs Abelard said. 'Soap and water will cure that – if he stops in this house long enough.'

'What's his name?'

'Jim, he says.'

'Where has he come from? Why is he here?'

'Don't ask me!' Mrs Abelard said. 'Ask your father, standing there.'

John Sutton told Jim's story to his son. 'He's going to stay with us at present, while I make certain enquiries and see if his uncle can be traced. But unless young Jim agrees to tell us his name I don't hold out much hope. At present he refuses to say.'

'Refuses to tell us his name?' Philip said. 'Hah! *I'll* soon get it out of him!'

'Yes, well, maybe you will. Take him out with you, anyway, and show him the farm. Take him to see that new pony of yours. He'll like that, won't you, Jim?'

The two boys went out together and were gone until darkness fell. They then returned to the house and had tea with Mrs Abelard and the maid, Alice, at the kitchen table in front of the fire.

'Well, then, Master Philip, did you get him to tell you his name?'

'No, not yet, but I will!' Philip said.

During the next three weeks the boys were together a great deal, mostly out and about in the fields, for the farm stock, especially the sheep, drew Jim like a magnet. And Philip, during this time, would question him repeatedly, trying to make him reveal his name.

'Is it Smith? Is it Brown? Is it Murgatroyd?'

Jim only shook his head but the name Murgatroyd made him smile.

'That's it! That's it!' Philip cried. 'His name is Murgatroyd! I know it is!'

'No, it isn't.'

'What is it, then?'

'My uncle told me not to tell.'

'Well, you're not going to be called Sutton, so there, and you needn't think it!' Philip said.

One day when Jim was out with the flock, talking to the shepherd, George Abelard, Philip came running up the field in a state of great excitement.

'Jim! You're wanted up at the house. It seems your uncle has come back for you.'

Jim's face went dreadfully white and he stood as though turned to stone. Then, suddenly, Philip laughed.

'I was only teasing you! Lord, if you could've seen your face! I gave you a rare old fright, didn't I? You looked about as sick as a dog!'

The old shepherd, George Abelard, looked at Philip reprovingly. 'You shouldn't do things like that, Master Philip. You ought to be ashamed of yourself.'

'It was only a joke,' Philip said. 'He shouldn't have let himself be taken in.'

And, seizing hold of Jim's arm, he was soon urging him to

leave Abelard and the flock to go ratting with the groom and the dogs.

After three weeks at Peele Jim was scarcely the same boy that Oakley had collared in the turnip field. The bruises and sores had vanished completely, leaving his skin a clear healthy pink, and his straight, fair, almost colourless hair, washed every day by Mrs Abelard, was now as smooth and fine as silk. He was also filling out; the pinched look had gone from his face and flesh was beginning to cover his bones. His eyes, too, these days, were a brighter blue and often twinkled with merriment.

'All thanks to you, Mrs Abelard, and the trouble you've taken with him,' Sutton said. 'But what are we going to do with him when Philip starts going to his lessons again?'

'You said you were going to make enquiries and see about finding that uncle of his.'

'What enquiries am I to make? Where should I start? You just tell me that! We neither know what the man is called, nor what he looks like, nor where he's from. Jim's accent is a mystery. It tells us just about nothing. And even if we found the man, would *you* hand the boy over to him, knowing what a brute he is and how Jim has suffered at his hands?'

'No, I would not,' Mrs Abelard said. 'The bruises he had when he came here – '

'Exactly so, Mrs Abelard, and therefore it seems to me that Jim had better stay with us and go with Philip to the vicarage for the parson to teach him to read and write. How would you like that, young man? Would it suit you, do you think?'

Jim gave a nod.

'He nods to everything, this boy, except when he shakes his head,' Sutton said. He turned to his son. 'What do you think of my idea, that we should keep Jim with us?'

'I thought we were going to, anyway.'

'Glad to have a brother, eh?'

'No, not a brother,' Philip said.

'What, then?' Sutton asked.

Philip gave a little shrug. 'Jim can be my servant,' he said.

22

Sutton, laughing, turned back to Jim.

'Did you hear that?'

'Yes, I did.'

'And do you agree to it?'

'No, I don't.' Jim's eyes were very blue and the jut of his chin as he looked up at Sutton showed that he had a will of his own. 'I want to work on the farm,' he said.

'Well, and so you shall, my boy. When you are old enough, that is. But first a little schooling, I think, to give you a good start in life. I'll see Parson Bannister in the morning on my way into town.'

So every day Jim went with Philip in the dog-cart to the vicarage at Lyall St Mary's where Mr Bannister, primed by Sutton, took his education in hand.

'What am I to teach the boy?' the vicar had asked, somewhat wearily.

'The three R's,' Sutton had said, 'and whatever else he wants to learn.'

Jim was very happy at Peele and his only anxiety was that his uncle might come back for him.

'Now why should he do that,' Mrs Abelard asked him, 'when you say he wanted to be rid of you?'

'He could change his mind, couldn't he?'

'But he doesn't know you're here with us. He'll think you're in the workhouse by now. And if by chance the brute did come here, why, he'd get my rolling-pin over his head!'

Jim was able to laugh at this; indeed he was laughing quite often now; and as the happy months went by, bringing a sense of security, his fears gradually died away until they became a thing of the past. And with the passing of his fears, he at last revealed his name.

'Jim Lundy?' Philip laughed. 'No wonder you kept it secret so long. It's almost as bad as Murgatroyd.'

'Oh no it isn't!'

'It is!'

'It's not!'

'And where did you come from?' Sutton asked. 'What part of the country were you raised?'

'I don't know. All over the place.'

'Don't you remember your parents, boy?'

'No, they died when I was small.'

'And then your uncle took charge of you?'

'No, it was my grannie at first. We lived in a place near the sea – my grannie called it Derry Coomb. Then my grannie got ill and died. Uncle Albert came for me – he was the drover. We moved about. He didn't like to stay in one place. We came up here from Salisbury Plain. Before that we were on the downs. And before that . . .' Jim spread his hands. 'Before that we were everywhere.'

'So! You're Jim Lundy from everywhere, or nowhere, whichever you please.'

Sutton eyed the boy searchingly, wondering if the story was true, but so far during his six months at Peele, Jim had never once told a lie, even to get himself out of trouble, and Sutton was inclined to believe him now.

'Anyway, true or not, it doesn't much matter, does it?' he said, speaking to the housekeeper afterwards. 'It's all worked out pretty well on the whole and Jim is adapting admirably. It's good for Philip to have another boy to play with and he seems to like Jim well enough, allowing for boyish squabbles, of course.'

'What young Master Philip likes is having someone to boss about and lead into mischief at every turn. *That's* what Master Philip likes.'

'Ah, well,' Sutton said, 'you're only young once, Mrs Abelard.'

Certainly the boys got into mischief, what with bringing hedgehogs into the house and putting a number of tiny elvers into Alice's chamber-pot; and certainly, more often than not, it was Jim who owned up to these pranks while Philip denied all knowledge of them. They got up to mischief on the farm, too, and once they wedged a sack full of sheep-raddle over the half-open door of a shed, so that when the door was opened wide the raddle fell on the person below. This happened to be Warren

Oakley and he, always lacking in humour, especially where boys were concerned, complained angrily to John Sutton.

'Dammit, man,' Sutton said, 'weren't you ever a boy yourself?' And when the bailiff continued to grumble, showing his skin still stained by the raddle, Sutton said pleasantly: 'Maybe you're feeling your age these days and think it's time you retired?'

Oakley was silenced by this covert threat, for Sutton paid better wages than any other farmer in the district, and Oakley, in his early sixties, had no wish to retire yet.

When he was not at the vicarage, having lessons with the vicar, Jim spent all his time on the farm, watching the work going on in the fields and, if allowed, joining in. But Philip's favourite activities were those of the young gentleman: shooting, fishing and riding to hounds. He soon became bored with talking to the 'yawnies' on the farm and would try to coax or challenge Jim into some more adventurous exploit. The two boys were much indulged and were given plenty of money to spend; they had the best rods and guns and two good ponies of their own to ride; and, for the most part, they enjoyed a great deal of freedom.

In winter Philip lived for the hunting. He could think and talk of nothing else. And one morning at the end of the season, when the last meet should have taken place, the boy, on being woken by Alice and told that there was a hard ground frost, burst into a storm of tears. Alice stood laughing at him, teasing him for being a cry-baby, and Philip, flying into a rage, seized the pitcher of hot water she had brought into his room and emptied most of it over her. His father threatened to thrash him for this but Alice, who was not much hurt, pleaded so gently on his behalf that he escaped with a telling-off.

Later that same day there was a partial thaw and Philip, still in a state of disappointment, persuaded the groom, Charlie Clements, to let him and Jim take their ponies out for an afternoon ride around the valley.

'All right, Master Philip, but no trotting or cantering, mind.

25

Just a gentle walk, that's all. The frost is only thawing on top, and the ground's still stone-hard down below.'

'I know that, I'm not a fool,' Philip said peevishly.

By an odd stroke of fate, however, as the two boys rode slowly through the beechwoods, a fox emerged from the undergrowth and moved off in front of them and Philip instinctively gave chase. Just as instinctively Jim went after him and when the fox broke from the wood, making across open pasture, the two boys followed at a trot that soon became a canter.

At the lower end of the pasture there was a deep dry ditch and the fox went down into this ditch, ran along it a little way, then leapt out at the other side and began crossing the ploughland beyond. Philip was highly excited by now and leapt his pony straight over the ditch. It was a very easy jump but the ploughland on the other side, lying as it did in the shade, was still iron-hard with frost, and the pony, jarring his forefeet on it, stumbled, checked, stumbled again, and finally fell onto his knees, with Philip sprawling over his neck. Jim, leaping the ditch behind him, was barely able to avoid a collision, and such was the check to his own pony that he was thrown right over its head. The pony then ran off but soon slowed down to a walk which, to Jim's great distress, showed him lame in the near foreleg. Philip's pony was lame in both legs and it was a sad, silent procession that made its way back to the stables.

So Philip got a thrashing after all and so did Jim, and as their offence this time had been a serious one, Sutton had little mercy on them.

'Lord, he fairly lammed into me!' Philip said, in great misery. 'And he said if Beau's legs are not better in a week I shall get another leathering then.'

'Yes, he said the same to me.'

The boys could not sit down all day and even walking was difficult; but worse than this, for Jim at least, was the terrible feeling of guilt and shame. His pony, Sandboy, was suffering and *he* had caused it, needlessly. Worse, too, than Sutton's anger was Charlie Clements's quiet distress and the patient, restrained, perplexed manner in which he reproached the two boys.

'I dunno how you could do such a thing, after what I said to you. Those two ponies, they're such trusting brutes — they'd go through hell and high water for you. And that's just what's happening now — they're going through hell, the pair of them, and all on account of your selfishness.'

'They will get better, though, won't they?' Jim said, in a voice he could only just control. 'They won't be in pain much longer, will they, now that we're looking after them?'

' "We?" ' Charlie said sardonically.

'Yes, I want to help,' Jim said.

'I reckon you've done enough,' Charlie said, but at the sight of Jim's face he relented. 'All right. You can help. So long as you do just what I say.'

'Much better leave it to Charlie,' said Philip. 'He's a marvel at doctoring horses, aren't you, Charlie, old man?'

Philip was never much troubled with guilt. He blamed his misfortunes on bad luck. If only there hadn't been a frost that day . . . Or if only that fox hadn't come along . . . Anyway, if he had done wrong, he had been thrashed, hadn't he, so surely that was the end of it?

'It doesn't help Beau and Sandboy,' Jim said.

'Neither does your long face,' said Philip.

When Jim was not in the stables, helping to change the coldwater bandages on Sandboy's sprained foot and Beau's sprained knees, he was out searching the hedgerows, picking the fresh, succulent greenstuff just beginning to grow there. Both ponies were fond of coltsfoot and cow parsley and with these, in a day or two, Jim was able to tempt them to eat. In a week they were much improved; in two weeks they were themselves again.

'Thank goodness for that!' Philip said. 'The stable's been like a morgue lately.'

For him the incident was over and the only question that troubled his mind was how long would it be before Beau could be ridden again. For Jim, however, it was different; what had happened to the two ponies still weighed heavily on him, and when, not long afterwards, Philip suggested some prank that had a flavour of mischief in it, Jim refused to take part.

'What's the matter with you,' Philip asked, 'acting so pi' all of a sudden?'

'I don't like getting into trouble.'

'You mean you don't like getting thrashed.'

'It's not only the thrashing itself. We did wrong, laming Sandboy and Beau like that, and we deserved every stroke we got. But I don't like doing wrong. It makes me feel bad inside. And I intend to make sure that I don't get into trouble again.'

Philip jeered at him over this.

'Jim's a goody-two-shoes these days,' he said to Mrs Abelard. 'He never wants to do anything in case it gets him into trouble. It's only because he got thrashed that time. It's made a coward out of him.'

'That's not cowardly. That's common sense. It's all very well for you, Master Philip, you're the master's own son. But Jim's only a poor boy who's got to make his way in the world. That means watching his p's and q's, and keeping on the right side of people, especially his elders and betters. So you just leave him be, Master Philip, and don't go calling him nasty names.'

'Oh, I might have guessed that you'd stick up for him!' Philip said. 'Housekeeper's pet, isn't he? But he'd better watch his p's and q's keeping on the right side of *me* as well, because I shall be master here one day and that's something he seems to forget!'

Jim was inclined to laugh at this.

'What will you do? Turn me out?'

'I could do if I wanted! I could get you turned out this very minute if I went to my father and asked him to do it. You wouldn't care for that, would you, going back to being a drover?'

'No. But there are worse things.'

'Such as what?' Philip asked.

'Well,' Jim said, deliberately, and although he was still amused at the turn the conversation had taken, his answer was

28

made in all earnestness, 'I'd rather be a drover any day than stop in a place where I wasn't wanted.'

'There, Master Philip!' Mrs Abelard said. 'I hope you're satisfied with that, because I reckon we've had enough talk about turning people out of the house. And all of it blowing up like a storm just because Jim won't go out with you.'

'I never said I wouldn't go out with him, Abby. I said I wouldn't do anything that landed us in trouble again.'

'Shooting rabbits won't land us in trouble!' Philip said scornfully.

'Well, so long as it's only rabbits,' Jim said.

'It wouldn't be anything else, would it? Not now the breeding season's begun?'

With this assurance from Philip, Jim went willingly enough to shoot rabbits in the plantation just behind the old farm-house. But again they were dogged by the 'bad luck' that always seemed to put temptation in Philip's way and as they were returning home, each with a brace of rabbits in his satchel, they came upon a hen pheasant sitting on her nest in the undergrowth. For a moment the two boys stood looking at her and although they were only some twelve feet away, she continued to sit, quite motionless, her red eyes fixed in a bright, hard stare. Jim could sense that Philip, beside him, was itching to get a shot at her, and he moved to take hold of Philip's arm.

'No, you can't! You mustn't!' he said, speaking with quiet vehemence. 'Can't you see she's on her nest?'

Philip, with an excited laugh, pulled himself free of Jim's grasp and went on his way. As he went he stumbled, however, – on purpose, it seemed to Jim – and the noise frightened the pheasant into flight. She rose explosively, with a loud cry, and went whirring off between the trees. In the same instant Philip swung round, unbreaking his gun, which was already loaded, and bringing it swiftly to his shoulder. He was a very good shot and brought the pheasant down at once. There was a thump as it hit the ground; a flutter of feathers in the air; and Philip, with a satisfied grunt, went forward to pick up his prize.

But the pheasant, shot at such close range, was badly damaged. Philip held it up by the legs, turning it this way and that, his flushed face expressing triumph equally mixed with disgust. Then, as Jim came up, he said: 'Look at her! She's all shot to bits! I should've counted up to five.'

'What does it matter?' Jim said coldly. 'You couldn't have taken it home, anyway, or you would have got a leathering.'

'I know that! D'you think me a fool? I'd have sold it to Manders at the inn. He's paid me a florin for a pheasant before, but he won't look at a bird full of lead.'

'And just for the chance of a florin,' Jim said, 'you shot a bird sitting on her nest!'

'She wasn't sitting. She got up.'

'You put her up on purpose,' Jim said.

'So what if I did? It's no business of yours! And if you hadn't kept so close to me I should've taken more careful aim and got her without damaging her. As it is, she's no use at all. Food for magpies! That's all she is!'

They were near the edge of the wood and Philip, going to the fence, hurled the dead pheasant over into the pasture beyond. He wiped his bloodstained hand on his jacket and turned back towards the woodland path. Jim, in silence, followed him.

The incident did not end there, however, for the pheasant was picked up by one of the farm boys, Peter Gray, when he was sent to bring in the cows. Peter hid the bird inside his jacket, but the bailiff, noticing the bulge, asked to see what was causing it and, on discovering the pheasant, accused Peter of having shot it. The taking of game by the farm-hands was a serious matter at any time and almost certainly meant dismissal; but this offence, in the breeding season, so incensed John Sutton that he threatened to send for the parish constable with a view to bringing a charge. Peter Gray, very upset, protested that it was all a mistake and his story was convincing enough to give Sutton pause. He left Peter in his office and went in search of Philip and Jim.

'Have you been out shooting today?'

'Yes, father,' Philip said.

'Did you shoot a hen pheasant in the plantation or the pasture nearby?'

'No, father. Just rabbits, that's all. Abby will tell you. I gave them to her.'

Sutton now questioned Jim.

'Did *you* shoot a pheasant by any chance?'

'Jim wasn't there!' Philip said. 'He didn't go with me, did you, Jim?'

'I'd sooner Jim spoke for himself,' Sutton said, in forbidding tones, and his gaze remained fixed on Jim's face. 'Well, I am waiting for your answer, boy.'

'I *was* in the wood,' Jim said.

'And were you with Philip or were you not?'

'Well,' Jim said evasively.

'Peter Gray has just been found with a dead hen pheasant in his possession. I was going to send for the constable but Peter says he found the pheasant lying in the woodside pasture. Now, Jim, I ask you again – did you shoot a pheasant today?'

'No. I did not.'

'Did Philip shoot one?'

'Yes,' Jim said.

'What became of it?' Sutton asked.

'He threw it over into the pasture.'

'All right, Jim, you may go. Philip, come with me to the office. You can hear what I say to Peter Gray and afterwards, when he's gone back to work, you can bring me the cane.'

After this second thrashing, Philip came storming into the kitchen to vent his fury on Jim, who was talking to Mrs Abelard.

'Damned dirty, filthy sneak, telling tales on me like that! You got me six lashes! Hard ones too! But that's what you wanted, isn't it?'

'Don't blame me for what you got. If you'd spoken up in the first place instead of telling that stupid lie – '

'Oh, you never tell lies, of course! You never do any wrong at all!'

'Peter Gray could've lost his place on account of that pheasant of yours. He might even have gone to gaol. Some-

31

body had to speak up for him and if only you'd had a bit of sense – '

'That's not why you told on me! You did it to get me a thrashing, that's all! You've always been jealous of me from the start because I am my father's son and you're nothing but a little turd that somebody left on our doorstep!'

Philip went out again, slamming the door, and Mrs Abelard looked at Jim.

'Master Philip's a fine one to talk about your being jealous,' she said, 'when the boot is on the other foot.'

'Is it?' Jim said in surprise. 'But why should Philip be jealous of me? I haven't got anything he wants.'

'Just as well,' Mrs Abelard said, 'or he'd have it off you like a shot.'

'Why would he?'

'Because he's spoilt.'

'I don't think I *am* jealous of Philip,' Jim said, still considering the matter.

'Well, now, and what if you were? It wouldn't hardly be very surprising, seeing Master Philip's got so much and you're a poor boy with nothing at all.'

'Poor?' Jim said, surprised again. 'I wouldn't say I was poor, Abby. I'd say I was very lucky indeed.'

'Yes, so you are, Master Jim, and I'd be the first to tell you so, if you needed telling which you don't. After what you'd been used to, to come and live in this fine new house, with a good, kind man looking after you, giving you everything you want! Oh, yes, you are lucky indeed! But what sort of life will you have later on? That's the question that vexes me.'

'I'm going to work on the farm,' Jim said.

'Yes, I know,' Mrs Abelard said. 'But it seems all wrong to me, somehow, when you're being raised as you are now, and learning to live like a gentleman, that you should later be expected to work like a labourer on the land.'

'But I *want* to work on the land, Abby. I want it more badly than anything else. And I'm not a gentleman, as you know, nor shall I ever be, come what may.'

'No, Master Jim,' Mrs Abelard said. 'You're neither flesh

nor fowl nor good red herring and that's why I feel sorry for you. Still, you'll be all right, I daresay, for you've got a good headpiece on you and you know how to make the most of yourself. But you need to watch out for Master Philip, especially now you're both getting older, because he'll always do you down if he can. It's not that he's a wicked lad but he's got to come first in everything. So mind what I say and watch out for yourself and that way you won't ever come to no harm. Understand me, Master Jim?'

Jim nodded.

'I shall watch out for myself, Abby. You may be quite sure of that.'

Chapter Three

Mrs Abelard was not the only one to worry about Jim's future; the vicar, Mr Bannister, was also concerned; and one day in the summer of 1847 he mentioned the matter to John Sutton.

'Jim's future?' Sutton said. 'What do you mean?'

'Well, he's being brought up with your own son, and yet he is not your own son. May I ask − forgive me − but do you intend to make Jim equal with Philip later on?'

'Good God, no! Certainly not! Jim is going to work on the farm. Work is his portion, he knows that quite well. He'll make a good bailiff one day − better than Oakley, I suspect − and a not-too-distant day at that.'

'Ah, yes. Very suitable.'

'And yet you're still worried. Now why is that? Has he not been behaving himself?'

'Oh, yes. He behaves very well.'

'Does he work at his lessons?'

'Yes, indeed. In fact that is perhaps the problem. He is doing almost too well. Quite remarkable, really, for a boy of his beginnings. He was, as you know, almost completely illiterate when he first came to me, but now he not only reads and writes but has made such good progress with his Latin that he has actually caught up with Philip. Then, again, in mathematics −'

'Are you trying to tell me that Jim is a better scholar than Philip?'

'Well, no, not exactly. It's all a question of application −'

'Then Philip must be made to learn a little application, too, though you've left it rather late in the day to remedy that yourself, seeing that soon he will be going to school.' John

Sutton was somewhat nettled. He thought the vicar a feeble fellow. 'But you said you wanted to discuss Jim and I still haven't got to the bottom of what it is you're trying to say.'

'It's really quite simple,' the vicar said. 'Jim is getting an education better suited to a gentleman than the farm bailiff he is going to be and I think, if we continue with it, it may cause problems later on.'

'Make him discontented, you mean, and give him ideas above his station? Yes, well, you may be right.'

Feeble fellow he might be but, now he had come to the point at last, the vicar was talking good sense.

'What do you advise me to do?'

'I think, when Philip starts going to school, Jim should stop his lessons with me and start work on the farm straight away. After all, he's nearly thirteen, and most boys of his class would have been working long ago. I shall be sorry to lose such a good pupil but I think it's in his own best interests. He's got to find his proper level, and if we leave it too long, that may prove very hard for him.'

'Yes, you're right,' Sutton said. 'He's had a good grounding with you, anyway, and that's about what I had in mind when I sent him to you. I'm glad you mentioned the matter to me. I shall do exactly as you say.'

In the second week in September, therefore, when Philip went off to Surpingham, Jim began work on the farm.

'The boy is to learn everything,' Sutton said to Oakley, the bailiff. 'He'll be treated like any other farm boy and do exactly the same work. Is that understood?'

'Yes, if he hasn't been spoilt for it,' Oakley muttered under his breath; and to Jim, as he led him away, he said, 'Bit of a come-down for you, isn't it, doing some real work for a change?'

But Jim himself had no such feelings. The farm was where he wanted to be. He had never had any doubts about that, and if his lessons with the vicar had absorbed him, his lessons in farmyard and cowshed and field absorbed him even more completely. He was strong, healthy, and energetic, and exulted in his ability to tackle any job on the farm. The work, far from degrading him, brought him satisfaction and joy. He liked nothing better than to take off his coat and roll up his sleeves and 'get pitched in', as old Abelard said. And Philip, home for the holidays, watching Jim heaving and sweating, pitching sheaves to the threshing machine, or loading dung into a cart, would laugh at the vigour and cheerfulness with which he toiled.

'You never seem to mind getting yourself in a muck sweat. I suppose that's the peasant in you.'

'Arr, if thee zay zo, zir,' Jim said with a grin, and tugged at the peak of his corduroy cap.

John Sutton's plan was that Jim should spend two years working with the cowman, two with the carters, and two with the shepherd, George Abelard. This suited Jim very well; he wanted to know everything that cowman and carter could teach him; but his greatest friend on the farm had always been George Abelard and any spare moment he had was spent helping with the flock.

Because of his special interest in sheep he was always allowed 'time off' in the spring so that he could help with the lambing and this was perhaps the happiest of all the year's happy seasons. He would spend a good many days at a stretch up in the lambing field under the hill and would sleep at night with the old shepherd in his hut on wheels, waking to the slightest sound in the pens as quickly as Abelard did himself. Jim had a sort of instinct for sheep; an understanding of their needs; a sympathy with them so acute that by the time he was fourteen he already had the shepherd's gift for sensing in advance that a certain ewe would need help in lambing.

'You're the best helper I ever had,' Abelard said to him once, and this was high praise indeed, for the old shepherd was hard to please.

Jim was not paid with the other farm employees because he already received an allowance, just as Philip did, and this custom was kept up even though he now worked on the farm.

36

Jim's allowance was ten shillings and to him it always seemed a fortune, for even grown men on the farm received no more than this, and they had families to feed and clothe, whereas Jim's ten shillings was his to spend just as he pleased.

In fact he spent very little and in this he was different from Philip who, although he received a whole guinea, was always 'skint' by Wednesday or Thursday and badly in debt by Saturday night. Often Philip would ask Jim to lend him a shilling or two and in the early days Jim would oblige. But there came a time later on when Philip, home for the holidays, borrowed half-a-crown from Jim and returned to school without paying it back. So the next time he was at home and asked Jim for a loan he met with a forthright refusal.

'Lord, you are a mean old stick! You must have stacks of tin put away, always saving the way you do. What are you going to do with it?'

'You'll see one of these days.'

'Do you have to be so mysterious? Can't you answer a chap straight out?'

'All right, I'll tell you,' Jim said. 'I intend to buy some sheep.'

'What on earth for?' Philip asked.

'For one thing, I happen to like them,' Jim said. 'For another, they'll make a good investment.'

'Well, you'll have to ask my father's permission before you start keeping sheep of your own, since you'll be raising them here on our land.'

'Yes, of course, I intend to,' Jim said.

John Sutton gave his permission without any hesitation and at the autumn sheep fair that year Jim bought twenty Cotswold shearling ewes – theaves as old Abelard called them – and a Cotswold ram to go with them. The Peele flock consisted of Downs and Leicesters and Jim chose to keep a different breed so that his twenty-one sheep could be picked out easily from the rest.

His 'investment' cost him thirty-eight pounds, but he had only to walk out into the pasture and see his sheep grazing there, their thick curly fleeces a rich pale gold in the autumn sunlight, to feel that they were worth every penny even of this huge sum. The pride he took in them was immense. There were no sheep like them in the whole world. And because of them he was much chaffed by the men and boys on the farm.

'Here comes the flockmaster,' they would say, and once the head carter, Joe Greening, pinned a bunch of 'daglocks' in Jim's cap, saying, 'There, now you look the part to a tee.'

Jim's flock lambed in April, giving him twenty-six lambs, and of these he lost only two. One of the original ewes proved barren and she was sold off with the twenty-four lambs early in August. Together with the sale of the wool, Jim's profit that year amounted to some forty pounds and the Suttons, who were with him at the sale, watched in amusement as he stowed his money away in a small washleather bag.

'Ah, Jim will end up richer than any of us, you mark my words,' John Sutton said with a laugh. And Philip, with a look of disdain, replied, 'He'll end up a miser if you ask me.'

At the sheep fair in October Jim, again with Sutton's permission, bought twenty-one ewes, so that he now had forty in all. Thus, in the following spring, his flock yielded fifty-three lambs, fifty of which he reared successfully, and that year his total profits amounted to eighty-eight pounds. Once again he planned to buy a new draft of ewes but this time John Sutton was less ready with his permission.

'How many were you thinking of buying?'

'Another twenty.'

'H'm,' Sutton said, doubtfully. 'Well, I think myself it would be better if you were to buy just ten, and keep your flock to a round fifty. That's plenty big enough for you to manage, what with your proper work as well, and we don't want the land getting sheep-sick, do we, eh?'

'No, sir,' Jim said.

But he was puzzled by Sutton's edict, for the main flock at Peele had been reduced in recent years and there was no risk whatever that the two hundred sheep now kept would render the land sheep-sick.

38

'Why does Mr Sutton want me to keep my flock down to fifty?' he asked old Abelard. 'The farm doesn't carry nearly so many sheep as it used to, so why should he say that?'

Old Abelard gave a grunt.

'Mr Sutton's the master here and the master don't have to have any reasons for what he says to us underlings. We've got to be kept in our place, you see, and it seems that goes the same for you as it does for all the rest of us, even though you're a special case and have been brought up with the master's son.'

Jim made a face. He was somewhat cast down.

'It seems I've been overstepping the mark. Getting above myself, as they say. Had I better give up my flock altogether, d'you think? After all, I do graze them on Peele land.'

Old Abelard shook his head. His hand rested briefly on Jim's arm.

'You keep your flock,' he said quietly. 'Keep 'em so long as you're allowed. That's your investment, isn't it? Your stake in the future, as you might say. It gives you a bit of independence and no doubt that goes against the grain in certain quarters, if you follow me, but don't you worry too much about that. Your little flock isn't doing no harm. As for grazing Peele land, why, they manure it at the same time, don't they? And many a flock gets its keep free for doing that.'

So Jim kept his little flock and tended them with earnest care, culling those ewes that were sickly or barren and replacing them with vigorous theaves, but always, conscientiously, keeping their number to the round fifty that John Sutton had stipulated. And every year his profits were such that he added upwards of eighty-five pounds to his savings in one of the Missenham banks.

Philip was always scornfully amused at Jim's interest in sheep. He did not care for them at all. There were 'poor man's stock', he said, and out of place now on a farm like Peele.

'If I had my way, I'd get rid of them all. We only keep them for tradition's sake. We no longer need the Golden Hoof, not with modern farming methods, and God knows there's no real money in them.'

Old Abelard disagreed. 'You're wrong there, Master Philip. There's money in sheep, sure enough, only it's silver, you see, not gold. But silver mounts up in time, you know, if only you've got the patience to let it.'

Philip, with a smile, looked at Jim.

'And is the silver mounting up for you?'

'I'm not complaining,' Jim said.

'How much have you got in the bank so far?'

'I don't see why I should tell you that.'

'God! You are a secretive beggar! I don't know why I talk to you. And what are you going to do with it — all this money you're putting away?'

'I hope one day, if all goes well, to rent a few acres of land of my own.'

'A smallholding?'

'Yes, that's right.'

'But you're going to be our bailiff here and take over from Oakley when he gets old.'

'I can easily do both. Many a bailiff does that.'

'Small farms are a thing of the past. They're uneconomic. They're suicide. You've only got to look at Godsakes, going to ruin over there. That's a hundred and ten acres and yet just look at the state it's in. Fields overgrown with brambles and thorns! Stock reduced to nothing at all. House and buildings falling down!'

'That's nothing to do with the size of the farm. It's a good-sized farm, taken all round, what with the hill pastures and common rights on the meadows and all. It's just that Riddler has had bad luck and isn't very good at managing things.'

'Bad luck my eye! The damned fool bit off more than he could chew when he decided to buy that place. A man's got no business buying land when he hasn't even got the money to pay for it let alone do right by it!'

'No, well, you may be right, but there's more to it than that, isn't there?' The story behind Riddler's misfortunes was as well known to Jim as it was to Philip himself, for it was often discussed at Peele and John Sutton made no bones about the part he had played in it. 'It's not entirely Riddler's fault, is it that he ran into trouble over money when he first bought his farm?'

'He blames my father. We all know that. And to judge by the way you're talking now, it seems as though you take Riddler's side.'

'I don't know about taking sides, but I'm sorry for Riddler, I must admit.'

'Sorry for him!' Philip exclaimed. 'After what he's done to that farm, letting it go to rack and ruin, an eyesore and a damned disgrace? Why, my father says it'll take five years to put that land in order again, when we do get hold of it. Hanging on by the skin of his teeth, year in, year out, the way he does! He only stays there to spite us and stop us getting our hands on it. And yet you say you feel sorry for him!'

Philip turned and marched off and old Abelard said to Jim:

'It doesn't do to stick up for Morris Riddler. Not with the master or his son. The master's been waiting a long time to get his hands on that farm and it's a sore subject with him that he hasn't managed it so far.'

'I suppose he'll have to give up in the end? Riddler, I mean.'

'It's only fair amazing to me that he's hung on as long as he has, but that's how it is in farming, you see. It can take a man twenty years to go to ruin good and proper. And I reckon it's a terrible thing, to see land go back like that, and the people on it brought so low that they're scarcely nothing better than beggars. It's Riddler's wife and young daughter I feel most sorry for, stuck over there, working so hard, scarcely ever leaving the place from one year's end to the next. If Riddler's got any feeling for them he should sell up and get out and give them the chance of a decent life.'

'Yes, I suppose he should,' Jim said. 'But if I were Riddler and had my own farm I reckon I'd feel the same as he does. I'd stick it out to the very end and fight for it to the last breath.'

'Well, that's what he's doing, sure enough,' Abelard said, with a shake of his head.

It happened not long after this that Jim had a meeting with

Morris Riddler. It was a day in early August and he had gone with the other Peele men to begin cutting a field of corn on that part of the farm that had once been Granger's and which lay on the same side of the valley as Godsakes. The men were at work with their scythes, cutting a broad path round the field, to make way for the reaping machine, when the warm west wind, blowing down from Godsakes, brought with it a scent of hay so exceedingly sweet and strong that the men stopped work and sniffed the air.

'Riddler's got a hot stack,' said Joe Greening, and turned to look up at Godsakes, rising in a series of grey-green fields beyond the boundary of Granger's. 'There it is. At the top there, look.' And he pointed to an ungainly haystack standing in a deserted field immediately under Hogden Hill. 'Whew!' he said, sniffing again. 'That'll go up in flames directly if something isn't done about it.'

'Going to tell him about it, are you?' Arthur Slatter asked slyly, for the Peele men, these nine years past, had kept clear of Morris Riddler for fear of offending their employer.

'Somebody ought to,' Greening said.

And Jim, putting away his scythe, volunteered.

Riddler had been milking his cows and was letting them out into the pasture when Jim came up the adjoining field and spoke to him over the farmyard wall.

'You've got a hot stack,' he said, and pointed in its general direction. 'In the field with a hut in it, just under the hill. It'll go up in flames, Joe Greening says, if you don't do something about it soon.'

'Damn and blast!' Riddler said. 'If it isn't one damned thing it's another!' He closed the gate behind the last cow and came across the yard to the wall. 'Did Joe Greening send you to me?'

'He said somebody ought to come.'

'That was good of him. Good of you, too. Your master would never have done that. *He'd* have stood and watched it burn,' Riddler was eyeing Jim curiously. 'You're Jim Lundy, aren't you?' he said. 'The boy Sutton found in his barn that time? I've seen you about these many years, but never close to like this before.' Resting his folded arms on the wall, he looked

42

across the valley at Peele and gave a slight lift of his grey stubbled chin. 'I see the lot of you, over there, coming and going about the place. You look like a lot of puppets from here and no doubt we look the same to you.'

'Yes,' Jim said, and the thought made him smile.

He was just as curious about Riddler, seeing him close for the first time, as Riddler was about him; but, being a boy, barely seventeen, he was rather less open about it and only when the man's queer, crooked face was averted did he steal a few quick glances at him. And after these quick glances he found himself wondering how it was that Morris Riddler, who was not really a big man, should nevertheless give an impression of bull-like solidity and strength.

'Does John Sutton treat you all right?'

'Yes. He treats me very well.'

'Expects you to work, though, doesn't he?'

'Everyone has to work,' Jim said.

'He used to treat *me* pretty well, too, until it suited him not to. But no doubt you know that old tale . . . John Sutton's side of it, anyway.' Riddler's gaze came back to Jim's face. 'Is he still waiting to buy me out?' he asked with harsh jocularity. 'Still waiting like a carrion crow to have my carcass, is he, eh?'

'I must get back to work,' Jim said. He turned away.

'Hang on a minute. I'll walk down with you and look at that stack.'

Riddler, with awkward agility, climbed over the farmyard wall and dropped down beside Jim. Together they walked down the sloping fields, all of which, in one way or another, were in an advanced state of neglect. In one a dozen sheep were grazing and Jim, who had passed them on the way up, now carefully looked away, for the sheep had not yet been shorn, although it was August, and their wool hung from them in tatters, scratched off on the thorn bushes that grew dotted about the field.

'All a bit different from Peele, eh?' Riddler said, as they walked along. 'Those few sheep of mine, now. Different from Sutton's Leicesters, eh? Different from your little flock of Cotswold Lions, aren't they, eh?'

Jim, at a loss, said nothing, and Riddler, perceiving his surprise, laughed deep down in his throat.

'I see what goes on over there, you know, just as you see what goes on over here. And I hear most of the gossip, too, especially on market days. Well, this is where we part. Did I say thanks about the stack? Yes, well, I'm obliged to you – if any man can be obliged when somebody brings him bad news!'

He went off with a wave of his hand and Jim went back to join the mowers in the cornfield.

'What did he say?' Joe Greening asked.

'He said he was obliged to us.'

'And what are things like up there, when you see the place close to?'

'Pretty bad,' Jim said, 'but Riddler seems cheerful enough.'

'Yes, well, from what I hear, there's a reason for that,' Greening said. 'His wife's expecting a little un. But if Morris Riddler is pleased about it, I doubt very much if his wife feels the same. Not at her time of life, poor soul, and with only middling health at that.'

Chapter Four

It was not the first hot stack Riddler had had at Godsakes, and probably wouldn't be the last, for the two men he employed would sooner do a job badly than well. Whenever he grumbled at them they always made the same reply.

'If you only pay us six shillings a week, master, you only get six shillings' worth of work.'

'I'd think myself lucky,' Riddler would snarl, 'if only you did *three* shillings' worth!'

The stack had to be opened out. He sent Smith and Lovell to do it at once.

'And don't build it up again until I damn well tell you to!'

'You told us to build it in the first place,' said Smith, 'and I knew all along that hay wasn't fit.'

'Then why the hell didn't you say so?' Riddler asked angrily.

Lovell and Smith merely walked away, 'trying to see how slow they could go', as Riddler often said of them, and he turned back into the yard, knowing that the job of opening the stack would probably take them all day. 'They'll see to that, sure enough!' he said, muttering under his breath.

His daughter, Kirren, came out of the house with a tub full of washing to hang on the line.

'How's your mother?'

'Just the same.'

'Still in bed, is she?'

'Yes, she's asleep.'

'H'mm,' he said absently, and stood for a while staring into space.

The dairymaid, Florrie Dixon, came out of the dairy with

two empty pails, filled them with water from the trough at the pump, and carried them back again, slop and splash. Riddler went across to the open cartshed and began rummaging about among a collection of old tools that stood in a corner. But all the time he was watching Kirren hanging up the clothes and when she had finished and gone indoors he left the cartshed, empty-handed, and went quietly into the dairy, pushing the door to behind him but not quite closing it.

After a while Kirren emerged from the house again with another tub full of washing. She set it down on the cobbles and began hanging the clothes on the line. Soon, however, she stopped and listened, hearing sounds in the dairy: her father's voice, quiet for once; the rattle of a pail; a muffled laugh. She went across to the dairy door and pushed it open and at the sound of its creaking hinge her father and the dairymaid sprang apart, he to look under the bench, as though searching for something there, she to take up a pan of cream and set it in place over the cooler.

Kirren, without saying a word, returned to her task. Her father came out of the dairy, went into the cartshed again, and this time came out carrying a hoe. For a moment he stood uncertainly, watching Kirren as she hung up the clothes, but her young face was closed against him and he went off with the hoe on his shoulder, swearing softly to himself.

At midday he returned for his dinner and while he was eating he spoke to Kirren about the incident in the dairy.

'You haven't told your mother, I hope, about seeing me with Florrie Dixon?'

Kirren, in silence, flashed him a glance.

'No, well, better not,' he said. 'She might go and get the wrong idea.'

'I've no intention of telling her. She's got quite enough to bear as it is.'

'Yes. You're right. She has, that's a fact.' He put a piece of bread into his mouth and chewed it noisily, clicking his jaws. 'That girl, Florrie! She's full of sauce. She asks for trouble, the way she goes on. But what you saw . . . it was only a lark . . . and it won't ever happen again, not after today, be sure of that.'

'No, it won't, because Florrie is gone.'

'Gone?'

'Yes. I paid her off. She won't be coming here any more.'

'You had no right to do such a thing! How d'you think you're going to manage, doing all the dairywork, and no Florrie to give you a hand? Your mother can't do it. Not just now. And she's going to have her hands pretty full – '

'I shall manage perfectly well. In fact I'd sooner work by myself than have Florrie Dixon about the place. I never did care much for her.'

'Ah, now we come to it, don't we?' he said. 'You only got rid of the girl because you don't care for her!'

'You know why I got rid of her,' Kirren said, quietly, and under her dark, critical gaze Riddler was forced to look away.

'Well, if you think you can manage all right . . . It's a lot to do, for a girl of fifteen.'

'I can manage. I shall see that I do.'

He had finished his meal and now he rose.

'I'm going up to see your mother and have a bit of a chat with her.'

'How are you feeling now, Agnes? Feeling a bit better, are you?'

'Yes, Morris. Not too bad.'

'Then why aren't you up and about, instead of lying in bed like this? Such a beautiful hot summer day it is, and you always did say you liked it hot.'

'I don't seem to have the strength. I come over giddy when I get up. All I want to do is sleep.'

'There's more than three months to go yet,' Riddler said. 'And it's not as though it's your first, neither. You were all right with the other two. You had no trouble with them at all.'

'Didn't I?'

'Of course you didn't.'

'That was a long time ago, Morris, and I've lost three babies since then. I'm older, too.'

'Yes, but not so old as all that. You're forty-five, I don't call

47

that old. If it was, you wouldn't be like you are, now, would you?'

'Oh, I'm young enough to be having a child,' Agnes said, wearily, 'and old enough to be dreading it.'

'Don't say that, Agnes, don't say that. It'll be all right, you mark my words. Now, what about drinking up your milk? It came from old Daisy — I milked her myself — and it's got a drop of something in it that didn't come from any cow! You drink it up. It'll do you good.'

Riddler, helping his wife to sit up, held the glass for her to drink. Then, having set the glass aside, he helped to make her comfortable, plumping the pillows up behind her and straightening the coverlet on the bed. He picked up the glass and stood looking at her.

'There, that'll soon buck you up,' he said. 'It'll put some colour into your cheeks and make you more like yourself again.' And after a pause he said huskily: 'It's lonely downstairs without you, old girl. I'll be glad when you're up and about again. I miss you, Agnes, and that's a fact.'

Riddler could not believe that his wife was ill, right up to the very last, and when she died he was drunk for three days. Hopelessly drunk, in a blind stupor, so that Kirren had to do everything.

On the morning of the funeral she went into the scullery, where her father lay on his back on the floor, and emptied a jug of cold water over him. Then she went back into the kitchen and a few minutes later he lumbered in after her and sat, groaning, in a chair at the table. Kirren put his breakfast in front of him, but he turned away from it, grey-faced and sick.

'Do you expect me to eat that when I've got to go down to Marychurch and see my wife put into the grave?'

'Eat it or not, as you please.'

'First Eddy. Now her. And the parson will talk some cant about God! What sort of God is it that takes away as good a wife as any man ever had?'

'It isn't God you should blame — it's yourself.'

48

'What do you mean?'

'You know what I mean.'

Riddler put his head in his hands but after a while he looked up again. 'We were hoping for a son.'

'*You* were hoping for a son.'

'We loved each other, your mother and me.'

'You may call it love if you like. I do not.'

'You're only a girl, you don't understand. You will do in time, when you've grown up a bit, especially when you're married yourself. You'll understand things better then . . . what a man feels for his wife. There's more to it than you think, and when he finds himself alone . . . Well, you don't understand, that's all. You've no idea what it's like.'

Suddenly Kirren turned on him.

'You seem to think you're the only one that's got any feelings!' she said. 'It was the same when Eddy died! He was mother's son as well as yours but you never gave her a single thought! It was what *you* felt! What *you* couldn't bear! And now we have it all over again! But how do you think *I* feel now that my poor mother is dead and all I've got left in the world is *you*?'

'It seems to me very hard that you should hold it against me for still being alive,' he said.

'I don't see why it should be so hard! You've held it against *me* all these years, because I'm alive and Eddy is not!'

'That's not true. That's rubbish, that is.'

'I heard you say it, out there in the yard. "Why did it have to be the boy that died?" That's what you said. I heard it myself.'

Riddler, sitting slumped in his chair, made a small, helpless gesture with his hands.

'Times like that, people say these things . . . But I didn't mean it, you must know that.'

'How should I know? I'm only a girl! I'm no use to you compared with a boy. You hoped all these years for another son and you killed my poor mother trying to get one. That's all I know.'

'I never said you were no use to me. When did I ever say such a thing? Girls've got their place in the world just exactly

49

the same as boys. They become women, all in good time, and us men need them, there's no doubt of that. Where should I be if I hadn't got you? You're all I've got left to me now, Kirrie. You and the farm – that's all I've got left.'

Clumsily, he put out a hand, taking her arm and squeezing it.

'You're a good-sorted girl, I'll swear to that, and a better daughter than I deserve. There's only the two of us left now and we've both got to make the best of things. I should be lost without you, Kirrie, and I don't mind admitting it

Kirren's glance was sardonic. Firmly, she withdrew her arm. But her anger was gone. She spoke quietly now.

'Eat your breakfast. It's getting cold.'

Kirren had always been old for her years and at fifteen she was almost a woman: tall and slender, yet well-developed, with strong, supple arms and strong wrists, toughened by the work of the dairy: the turning of the heavy butter-churn and the long hours spent at the cheese-tub.

'You're growing into a good strong girl,' Riddler said to her once. 'You're as strong as a man in some respects and you've got a sort of knack, somehow, for doing things quick and sure.'

'It's just as well,' Kirren said, 'or I'd never get through the day's work at all.'

'You shouldn't have got rid of Florrie Dixon. I said you'd find the work too much.'

'Well, we're not having Florrie back, if that's what you are hinting at.'

'I can't see what harm there would be in it.'

'Well, you must decide between Florrie and me, because if you bring her here again, I shall leave home and never come back.'

'Hah! And where d'you think you'd go?'

'I should go into service on some other farm.'

Riddler muttered and grumbled and swore but, knowing

50

that this daughter of his always meant what she said, he had perforce to give in to her and go without the dubious comfort that Florrie Dixon would have given him. For although he might grumble at Kirren, he depended on her in too many ways to run the risk of losing her. Nobody else would work so hard, or manage the house so thriftily, and anyway, as he often said, she was all the kin he had left in the world and he looked forward to the time when she would marry and produce children, who would grow up to work on the farm and take over when he died.

Marriage, however, was a subject that filled Kirren with angry disgust.

'After seeing the life my mother had? One stillborn child after another? All the heartbreak, all the pain! And then to die at the end of it, aged forty-five, worn down to the very bone! Oh, no! That is not for me!'

'You don't know what you're talking about. You're still too young to understand. But somehow I can't see you ending up as an old maid.'

'You *will* see it, though, if you live long enough.'

And the next few years, far from changing her attitude, only seemed to harden it.

Kirren took after her mother in looks but was rather darker than Agnes had been, with hair so brown it was almost black, and skin as dusky as a gipsy's, especially in the summertime when she worked in the fields without a hat. At sixteen, she was growing attractive. At seventeen she was comely indeed. At least she would have been, Riddler thought, if only she were a little less sullen; a little less given to looking at you as though you were something the cat had brought in. Certainly the higgler, Billy Hayzell, who called at the farm once a week to buy Kirren's eggs and butter and cheese, found her attractive enough and was obviously very smitten with her.

Billy was rather a smug young man in his early twenties, deaf in one ear, and he used this as an excuse for coming right up to Kirren and putting his face close to hers.

'I can't properly hear you unless I can see your lips,' he

51

would say, but while standing so close to her he would try to steal an arm round her waist and once, catching her unawares, he succeeded in touching her cheek with a moist, warm, thick-lipped kiss.

Kirren, twisting away from him, let him have the full force of her wrath.

'If you ever try to do that again I'll fetch you such a mighty clout that you'll end up deaf in both your ears!' she said in a voice that rang round the yard.

Billy, calling at outlying farms, was apt to cheat his women customers, paying them prices well below those that their produce would have fetched in the market, knowing only too well that they could not get there easily themselves. Once when Kirren was grumbling to her father about the price Billy paid for her cheese he said he had little patience with her because it was all her own fault.

'If you weren't so hoity-toity with him, you could get good prices enough, I daresay. He's smitten with you, you know that full well. And if only you played your cards right, you could have him eating out of your hand.'

'You mean I should let him maul me about and fumble at me with his hot sticky hands? No, thank you! I'm not having that!'

'No, you'd sooner lose us the farm!' Riddler said with great bitterness. 'God knows we've come desperate close to it for want of some ready cash sometimes.'

'Don't you dare say that to me!' Kirren exclaimed, equally bitter. 'If we are in danger of losing the farm, it's you that's to blame for it, not me! *You* with your drinking on market days and all your foolish goings on!'

'You call that drinking?' Riddler said. 'Just a few glasses of ale once a week? You should see the way some of the chaps there drink! The spirits and suchlike they put away – '

'I don't want to see your chaps! One drunkard is more than enough for me!'

'You're not speaking fair, Kirrie, because I haven't been drunk since you know when. A glass or two, that's all I have, after doing business, perhaps.' Then, eyeing her critically and giving a shake of his head, he said: 'You'll never get a husband, the way you go on. You've no idea how to treat a man, Billy Hayzell or any other.'

'A husband is the last thing I want.'

'Hah, you don't know what you're missing, girl.'

'I know enough about it to make sure I stay as I am.'

'And who's going to take over the farm when I die, if you don't give me a grandson?'

'The farm, in all probability, will have gone under the auctioneer's hammer long before then,' Kirren said, 'and we may as well face up to that fact.'

Riddler, swearing, went off to the fields, and Kirren, studying her account book, tried to work out what profit, if any, she had made from the sale of her produce that day. The conclusion she came to so angered her that when Billy Hayzell called again, she told him in no uncertain terms that she would not deal with him any more, and she sent him away empty-handed.

Thereafter, to her father's disgust, she went in to the market herself, walking the three miles there and back, her two baskets heavy with produce on the journey in, and rather less heavy with provisions on the journey back.

'You must want seeing to,' Riddler said, 'traipsing all that way every week instead of dealing with Billy Hayzell at your own back door.'

'I make nearly half as much again on my produce as I did when I sold it to him. And I pay less for my groceries than when he used to get them for me.'

'Yes, and you're gone very nearly the whole day, when you are badly needed here.'

'Going in to Missenham is the one and only break I get. The one and only day in the week when I see a few fresh faces instead of just yours and Lovell's and Smith's. It's also the one and only day when I don't get shouted at all day long.'

'Yes, well,' Riddler said, suddenly growing rather reflective. 'I suppose it is pretty dull for you, stuck out here, off the beaten track, never meeting anyone much. I reckon you're doing the right thing, getting out and about a bit, going in to the market every week. You meet a good many people there. All sorts of people. Friendly, too.'

Kirren, knowing her father so well, saw the track his thoughts were taking.

'You mean I might find a husband there?'

'Well, you've got to look somewhere, haven't you?' Riddler said, cheerfully.

Chapter Five

In the autumn of 1855, under persuasion from John Sutton, Warren Oakley at last retired and Jim took over his duties as bailiff. The old man was given a pension and allowed to stay in the bailiff's house 'until such time,' Sutton said, 'as Jim should think of marrying and want to live in it himself.'

Jim now earned eighteen shillings a week which, for a young man of twenty-one, was riches indeed.

'You are well worth it,' Sutton said. 'I believe in paying good money to good men.'

Jim was certainly conscientious. Nothing escaped his watchful eye. And in spite of his extreme youth the men on the farm respected him, knowing that whatever job they were doing, he could do it as well as they. But he rarely took his coat off now; it was not expected of him; for the post of bailiff, on a farm such as Peele, carried with it a certain importance; even a certain amount of prestige. He wore a good suit of Cotswold tweed and rode a smart dapple grey horse. He was not expected to sweat now but to organize the work of the farm and see that it was carried out. He took pleasure and pride in his position and he was always acutely aware that, for a boy of such poor beginnings, he had really done very well for himself.

There was plenty of variety in his work and in winter, when there were guests in the house, most of whom came for the shooting, it was his job to make sure that the party got a good day's sport. These guests were all farmers from neighbouring counties; many of them were landowners; and among them were some of the foremost agriculturists of the day, whom John Sutton had got to know through the farming clubs. One of these was Sir Frederick Alton whose estate in Berkshire was said to be the most progressive in England. He was a friendly, affable man who got on well with everyone, whether high or low.

'Remarkable young chap, your bailiff,' he said to Philip Sutton one day. 'Not much he doesn't know about farming, even the latest developments. But he seems pretty well-informed all round and even quoted the Georgics to me this morning. How is it that a farm bailiff is so well-spoken and so well-read?'

'That is my father's doing,' Philip said. 'Jim Lundy was a foundling, left in one of our barns years ago, and my father took him into the house. He and I were brought up together, and my father paid for him to be educated by the local parson, along with me.'

'Yes, I see. That explains a good deal. He's certainly an intelligent young man. I quite thought he must be one of your own family.'

'Oh, no, sir. Indeed not. No relation whatsoever.'

'I thought of inviting him down to Langley, perhaps next year, when you come yourself. But then I had second thoughts and wondered if he could be spared from the farm?'

'To be honest, sir, I don't think he can. We do rather rely on him to keep things running smoothly here.'

'Yes, of course,' Sir Frederick said. 'Just as well I asked you first.'

Those of the Peele visitors who came every year were disgusted to see Godsakes growing more and more run-down, and becoming a terrible eyesore on the other side of the valley.

'There ought to be a law to stop men from occupying good land and letting it go to ruin like that.'

'Just what I feel myself,' Sutton said. 'But I don't think he'll last much longer now, for he owes money all over the place, and no one will give him credit any more. In fact, when you look across at that place, it's a wonder how he survives at all.'

'Then you think your patience will soon be rewarded?'

'I hope so, indeed,' Sutton said, with a smile. 'God knows I've waited long enough.'

Sometimes the Suttons, father and son, went on return visits to these friends, hunting with famous packs, and shooting over great estates of three thousand acres or more. At other times Philip went alone and often in the summer and autumn, when the agricultural shows were held, he had so many invitations that he would be absent for months at a time. John Sutton was not best pleased at this and once he took Philip to task about it.

'I don't want to spoil your fun, my boy, but I think it's time you settled down and found yourself a wife,' he said. 'This house has been without a mistress for more years than I care to remember and it's time you did something about it instead of gadding about all over the country, here, there, and everywhere.'

'You seem to forget,' Philip said, 'that there are three pretty girls at Langley.'

'Ah,' Sutton said, much mollified. 'So that's how the wind blows, is it, eh? And which of the trio do you favour or is it too soon to ask?'

'The youngest, Caroline,' Philip said, 'and when I go on my next visit there, I intend to propose to her.'

'Splendid! Splendid!' Sutton said. 'I couldn't have chosen better myself!'

This conversation took place early in 1858: a year that promised well, Sutton thought; a year that should see Godsakes Farm come into his possession at last; and if before the end of it, Philip should bring home a wife, well, he would ask for nothing more.

'I'm not getting any younger, you know. I'll be fifty-six in a month or so. And I'd like to see you produce an heir in time for me to get to know him.'

'I'll see what I can do,' Philip said.

It was in the spring of that same year that Jim met and fell in love with Jane Reynolds. Her father, who owned a glass manufactory in Birmingham, had recently rented Hide House Farm, near Abbot's Lyall, and John Sutton, as a good neighbour should, had soon called there, taking Jim with him.

57

Alec Reynolds had rented Hide House so that he and his wife and daughter should have all the benefits of living in the country; and the farm, of about a hundred acres, was to be his hobby. He confessed he knew nothing of farming as yet and Sutton immediately suggested that Jim should help and advise him.

'Jim will soon tell you what to do to get the best out of your land. You can't do better than listen to him.'

'That's uncommonly good of you.'

'Not at all,' Sutton said.

And that was how Jim, in the month of April, came to spend so much of his time at Hide House Farm and in doing so met Jane Reynolds. He was now twenty-four; Jane was eighteen; and all through the spring and early summer their friendship grew and blossomed, with Jane's easy-going parents looking on indulgently, and, so it seemed, with approval.

'Jim is such a nice young man and just the friend Jane needs, coming to a new district like this, where we hardly know anyone,' Mrs Reynolds said to John Sutton. And Alec Reynolds, on learning something of Jim's background, said to his wife: 'Well, the boy is not exactly a catch, having no family of his own, but he's certainly made the best of himself, with Sutton's help, and I daresay if he were to marry, Sutton would probably do something for him.'

'Do you think so?'

'I'm sure of it. We can't expect too much, of course, because Sutton's got a son of his own — '

'Oh, quite,' Mrs Reynolds said, 'though for all we see of *that* young man, he might as well not exist.'

' — but he obviously thinks a lot of Jim and I'd say he intends to do well by him.' After further thought Reynolds said: 'There's no doubt about Jim's feelings for Jane but what about Jane herself? Is she in love with him? What do you think?'

'Like you, my dear, I'm not quite sure, and I've thought it wiser not to pry. But Jane is such a sensible girl that whoever her choice may be in the end I'm quite sure it will be for the best.'

58

John Sutton also watched with interest the progress of Jim's courtship and, on the whole, approved of Jane.

'Prettiest thing I've seen for many a long day,' he said. 'Intelligent, too. But will she make a good wife for a working man like yourself?'

This was a difficult question for Jim to answer. Being in love with Jane he naturally assumed that she would make him a perfect wife, but he *was* only a working man and Jane was accustomed to a style of living he could not afford. Still, he had plans and certain ambitions and was by nature an optimist. He had a fair sum of money saved and he had his flock of Cotswold ewes. He earned eighteen shillings a week and there was a good, decent house which, since Oakley had gone to live in the village, was Jim's for the asking, rent free, whenever he chose to claim it. He also had his health and his strength and a good deal of drive and energy, and if Jane was willing to trust herself to him he knew he could do great things for her. But he was reluctant to talk of this to John Sutton until matters had been settled with Jane.

'I haven't actually asked her yet whether she will marry me. We've been pretty busy with haymaking, here and at Hide House, and lately I've only seen her for a short while at a time. But the work will be easing off soon and I hope I'll be able to talk to her then.'

On an evening in late July, therefore, Jim and Jane walked alone together in the hayfields at Peele where the aftermath, now that the hay had been carried, was springing up a bright soft green. Jane had been to Peele many times but never to these outlying fields and Jim pointed out the lonely barn where, thirteen years before, he had been abandoned by his uncle. Jane, who already knew the story, stood staring at the place with intensely blue eyes, her fair brows knitted in a fierce frown.

'That old place, with the fir trees behind? Weren't you frightened, being there by yourself, a little boy only ten years old, sleeping at night with the rats and the owls?'

'I hated the rats but I liked the owls. They were company in the dark. But yes, I was frightened, all the time. I was frightened of the wind in the trees, and frightened of what would become of me.'

'Your uncle was a wicked man.'

'He did me a very good turn, however, quite without intending to, for I have had a better life in Mr Sutton's care than I could ever have had otherwise.'

'I know Mr Sutton's been good to you but he says you have more than repaid him by being such a credit to him and by working so hard for him on the farm.'

They had been walking side by side, but now Jim stopped and looked at her and she met his gaze without any shyness, accepting, without embarrassment, the love he so plainly felt for her.

'Does it make any difference to you, knowing that I am a foundling?' he asked.

'Difference? What do you mean?'

'I think you must know, I'm sure you do, that I love you and want to marry you. But – '

'Oh, I see, there are *buts*!' she said, pretending to be very downcast.

'It's all a question,' he said carefully, 'of whether I am good enough for you.'

'Being a foundling?'

'Well, yes.'

'Silly,' she said, in a soft voice, and reached up to kiss him on the mouth.

His arms went round her, holding her close, and she leant against him with a little sigh, which he felt soft and warm upon his lips. It was the first time they had kissed and Jane's warm response was such that when, in a while, they drew apart, he had to take a deep breath before he was able to speak again.

'Does that mean you love me?' he asked.

'I think it must.'

'Enough to say you'll marry me?'

'Goodness! You *are* in a hurry!' she said.

'No, no, I'm not! That is – Oh, damn!' He paused a moment and began again. 'There are certain things I must tell you first. What money I earn. What my prospects are.'

'Practical things.'

'Yes, that's right.'

'You're a practical man.'

'I try to be.'

'Well, kiss me again,' Jane said, 'and then you can talk about practical things.'

As they walked together over the fields, he did his best to marshal his thoughts, and to tell her all about himself.

'I've got about twelve hundred pounds in the bank and I've got a flock of fifty sheep worth, say, another eighty pounds. I earn eighteen shillings a week – '

'Eighteen shillings! Is that all?'

'Eighteen shillings is very good. Most bailiffs get fifteen.'

'But the work you do, running the farm! You're on the go from morning to night.'

'If my wages seem little to you – and I quite see they must – I want you to know that I've got plans to rent a bit of land of my own. Nothing much to begin with, of course, but about thirty acres or so, where I can raise a few cattle and sheep and maybe fatten a pig or two.'

'Still doing your job as bailiff here? I can see you will work yourself to death if somebody doesn't stop you.'

'Oh, I can work a lot harder than that, without it killing me,' Jim said, amused. 'I'll soon show you how hard I can work, if only you will give me the chance, and one day, if all goes well, and I manage to save enough money, I shall take a really good-sized farm and set up in style as a proper farmer, independent and full-time.'

'And how long do you think that will take?'

'Ten years, perhaps. I'm not quite sure.' He turned his head to look at her. 'Do you think you could put up with being just a bailiff's wife for as long as ten years?' he asked.

'A lot depends,' Jane said gravely, 'on what a bailiff's wife has to do.'

They were now close to the old Peele farmhouse, looking down on it from above, for it lay in a slight declivity and Jim had approached it in such a way as to give Jane the best possible view. The old stonebuilt house, with its casement windows, its

61

porch overgrown with rambler roses, its walled garden and pear-hung espaliers, looked directly towards the west and now, at nine o'clock in the evening, reflected a pink sunset glow.

'That is the house,' Jim said, 'where the bailiff's wife, if she be what she ought, will spend her time looking after the bailiff.'

'Can we go inside?'

'Well, yes, we could, but I think perhaps it's wiser not. For one thing it needs a good cleaning out. For another, it's getting rather late, and if anyone saw us going in — '

'You mean my good name would be gone forever?' Jane said with a merry laugh. 'But yes, you're right, it is rather late, and it's high time I was getting home.'

Hand in hand, they walked on together, down the gently sloping fields.

'If I'm to do things properly, I ought to see your father soon and ask his permission to marry you.'

'I know what he'll say. He'll say I'm too young.'

'But at least he might let us get engaged.'

'I don't know. I'm not so sure. But I think if I spoke to him myself, I might to able to pave the way. Or I might speak to mother first . . . It's all a question of choosing the time.' Jane gave a little sigh. 'You know what parents are,' she said. 'Oh, dear! No, of course you don't, for you never had any, did you, poor boy?'

'What do you think your father will say? I'm afraid he'll think I'm not good enough for you. My prospects, such as they are — '

'Hush!' Jane said, and came to a stop, placing one finger over his lips. 'Hush! Be quiet! I've had enough!'

She leant against him, her face upturned, and he bent to kiss her on the lips. After a while she drew away.

'I really must be getting home. Will you come with me all the way? Yes, very well, but promise me this. No more talk about practical things. I'm more in the mood to be silly and gay.'

At the end of July Philip came home, lured by a letter from his father, mentioning 'interesting developments at Godsakes, concerning our friend Riddler'. And over supper that evening, with Jim also present, Sutton gave Philip the full details.

'Riddler's really done-for this time. He owes money everywhere and at least two of his creditors are threatening him with the County Court. Now, since I wrote to you, he's been served with a distraint for tithes. The collector's men were there yesterday, intending to seize Riddler's cows, – he's only got two left – but he met them at the gate with a loaded shotgun. I daresay he would have used it, too, if the men had not withdrawn. He's mad enough for anything. Anyway, that's how it is. But what is more important to us is that he's fallen behind with his mortgage dues, which should have been paid last April, and the bank has given him notice that unless the arrears are paid off by the end of next month they will be obliged to take the necessary steps. I talked to Forrester at the bank and he assured me that under no circumstances would Riddler be granted any further extension.'

'So the end is in sight, then?' Philip said.

'Yes, my boy, the end is in sight,' Sutton said, with immense satisfaction. 'It's only a matter of weeks now before Godsakes is ours at last.'

Jim, of course, already knew all this, but one detail was new to him and he strongly disapproved of it.

'Surely Forrester speaking to you like that was a breach of professional confidence?'

'He and I are old frinds,' Sutton said, 'and he knows that I have a special interest in this matter.'

'I think it was wrong, even so,' Jim said. 'I'm very glad I don't bank with him.'

Philip, lighting a cigar, was amused.

'Jim is such a moral man. At least where other people's affairs are concerned. And of course he's always been inclined to feel sorry for Morris Riddler, though I can't think why.'

'I could feel sorry for him myself if he weren't such a pig-headed fool,' Sutton said. 'But he's only hung on over there to spite me and when I think what he's done to that farm in the course of the last sixteen years – ' Sutton broke off, looking at

63

Jim. 'Surely you must feel pleased at the prospect of putting the place to rights? We'll be farming more than five hundred acres once we've taken Godsakes in. Surely that's something to be proud of, eh, being bailiff of such a farm?'

'For myself, yes, I can feel well pleased. I just wish that your buying Godsakes didn't involve hurting a man who has struggled so hard for so many years.'

'Well, luckily for us,' Philip said tartly, 'it isn't your business to decide.'

'Quite so,' Jim agreed, and, rising from the table, he excused himself, having work to discuss with old Abelard.

John Sutton, left alone with Philip, pushed the bottle of port towards him and watched him as he filled his glass.

'I haven't yet heard about your latest round of visits,' he said. 'Especially Langley. How is your courtship of Caroline Alton coming along?'

'It's not,' Philip said, with a certain stiffness. 'Caroline was away from home.' Then, somewhat flushed, he said: 'I'm told she is soon to become engaged to one of Colonel Conroy's sons.'

'Oh,' Sutton said, and was silent a while, watching his son with a scrutiny that was at once sympathetic and shrewd. 'Well, there are plenty of other nice girls about, and I think you may be well advised to look for one nearer home. But it seems rather as though Jim is going to pip you to the post when it comes to finding a wife.'

'Does it, though? And who's the girl?'

'Someone you haven't met,' Sutton said, 'because you've been too much away from home.'

'Imagine Jim being in love!' Philip sipped his glass of port. 'You must tell me all about it,' he said.

Out in the pasture where the flocks were grazing, Jim stood in the gathering dusk, discussing with old Abelard the next morning's work, of sorting out lambs to send to market. From across the valley came the sound of a shot and as they stood listening it was followed quite soon by another. There had been similar shots all day.

'That's Riddler loosing off in case the bum-bailies are lurking about,' old Abelard said grimly. 'But they will get him in the end, just as sure as eggs are eggs.'

'Yes, I'm afraid they will,' Jim said, and turned to look across the valley, imagining the feelings of the man who lived almost in a state of siege on that lonely, tumbledown farm where, in the darkness, as Jim looked, a single light came into being and burnt with a kind of stubborn defiance, faintly and dimly, in one of the windows. 'Only some kind of miracle can save Morris Riddler now, I'm afraid.'

Harvest began early in August and from then on Jim was kept fully occupied, for the acreage of corn now grown at Peele was the greatest ever, and both wheat and barley promised an exceptional yield that year. Once he went over to Hide House Farm to see the new reaping machine that Alec Reynolds had bought and while they were watching the engineer demonstrating its use in the field, Jane and her mother came out to join them and invited Jim to stay to lunch. Sadly, he was obliged to refuse, being on his way into town to draw money for the men's wages, but Jane's disappointment at his refusal sent him away almost as happy as he would have been if he could have stayed.

'Jim is a busy man, my dear,' her father said, reproving her. 'I doubt if we shall see much of him until he's finished harvesting.'

'Oh, I shan't be so very busy,' Jim said, 'that I can't walk over and see you sometimes.'

'To see us *all*?' Reynolds asked slyly. 'Or is it only one of us?'

Jim and Jane exchanged a smile.

Philip, at his father's instigation, was at this time often in Missenham, collecting information about Morris Riddler's debts, which Sutton considered might be useful to them when buying Godsakes.

One afternoon at the beginning of August, coming back from one of these errands, Philip turned off at the crossroads just outside Abbot's Lyall and rode up the lane towards Hide House Farm. It was a day of intense heat, with a hot surging wind breathing out of the east, and when he reached the River Cran he walked his mare down to the ford so that she could drink and be cool.

While he sat at ease in the saddle, looking up towards Hide House, a girl in a pale blue muslin frock, with a blue straw hat on her head, came slowly along the river bank, picking meadowsweet and wild tansy. The mare had finished drinking now but Philip, in no hurry to move, sat smiling gently to himself, watching the girl on the bank above. She had almost reached the ford when suddenly a gust of wind carried her straw hat from her head. A quick, clumsy grab; a headlong lunge; and then a small exclamation, with more than a hint of laughter in it, as the hat blew down into the river and began floating downstream.

Philip, having dismounted quickly, was just in time to reach the hat as it was floating across the ford. He fished it out and gave it a shake. The girl had now come to the top of the slip and Philip, with the hat in his hand, stood looking up at her.

'No need to ask who you are,' he said. 'I know you from my father's description.'

'Your father? Now let me see if I can guess who that is!' She studied him with her head on one side. 'No, it's no good, I just don't know. I see no likeness to anyone.'

'Then, of course, I must introduce myself.'

Leading his mare by the bridle he splashed his way across the ford and walked up to the top of the slip where the girl stood waiting for him.

'I'm Philip Sutton of Peele House Farm.' He bowed to her and proffered the hat. 'I'm afraid it's rather wet,' he said.

All through the month of August and during the first week of September, whenever Jim could spare the time from superintending the harvest at Peele, he walked over to Hide

House in the hope of seeing Jane, but each time he was disappointed. She had 'gone in to town to the dressmaker' or 'gone on a picnic with some friends to escape the heat in Lyall Woods'. Once when he called in the evening she was lying down with a sick headache, quite unable to see anyone, but when he called to enquire the next morning she had recovered sufficiently to have gone for an early morning ride by the river, 'with a party from Allern Hall'.

Jim thought it very strange that never once in all these weeks had she strolled over to see him at Peele, as she had done often enough before, but 'really her life is a whirl these days', Mrs Reynolds said to him, 'and she seems to be such a favourite, you know, with all our nice neighbours round about'.

'Yes, it would seem so,' Jim said. 'I'm glad she is better, at any rate.'

As he walked away from the house, thinking of what Mrs Reynolds had said, he became more and more aware that her manner to him had been evasive; had smacked of a certain embarrassment; had even – but maybe this was his fancy – held a hint of pity in it.

The feeling became so strong that instead of going back to Peele he went down to the river and along the bank and there, about a mile downstream, where the willows formed a shady grove, he saw Jane and Philip together, walking along, arm in arm, absorbed in each other, plainly lovers. Their horses were tethered nearby. There was no 'party from Allern Hall'; Philip and Jane were quite alone.

They did not see Jim and he stole away without showing himself. Seeing them together, so intimate, with Jane looking up into Philip's face and laughing in that particular way, although it only confirmed a fear which had been growing for days in his mind, was nevertheless a shock to him and filled him with an anger that weakened him. He felt too hurt, too vulnerable, to face them together at that moment. He needed time to be alone; to absorb the pain and to think things out.

An hour was enough. By then, instead of weakening him, his anger gave him kind a of strength. True, some faint hope lingered in his heart, causing him to ask himself whether there

67

might, after all, be some innocent explanation of what he had seen. But he knew this hope for what it was and derided himself for his childishness. Still, he had to know for sure, and that as soon as possible. So he walked back to the narrow lane leading up to Hide House and stood in the shade of an oak tree there, waiting for Jane to return home.

When he stepped out into the lane she went rather pale and looked, just for an instant, as though she would ride right past him. But as he moved to block her way she had no choice but to stop, and when he took hold of her horse's bridle, she gave a small, nervous laugh.

'Jim! Just imagine seeing you! So early in the morning as well! I thought you were busy harvesting.'

'I've called at the house any number of times. Surely they must have told you that?'

'Oh, yes, of course they did. But I have been out a lot just lately and – '

'Jane, I must tell you,' Jim said, 'that I saw you about an hour ago with Philip Sutton at Dunton Reach.'

'Do you mean you were spying on me?'

'You can call it that if you like. But I wanted to know how I stood with you. Surely I'm entitled to that?'

Jane was suddenly close to tears, quite unable to answer him, and after a while he spoke again, quietly, in a voice well controlled. 'You said you loved me.'

'Yes. Well . . . '

'You also said you would marry me.'

'No, I didn't.' She shook her head. 'I never said any such thing.'

'But when I asked you . . . you didn't say no.'

'That's not the same as saying yes.'

'You were going to speak to your parents about it.'

'Yes. I was. But I didn't say when.'

'You mean,' he said, with some irony, 'that you may still speak to them even now?'

'No. Not now.'

'Why not?' he asked.

'You know why not.'

'Yes, I know. Because something better has come along.'

'I suppose it's only natural that you should feel like this about it – '

'I certainly can't imagine anyone feeling any differently.'

'Jim, I'm sorry. Truly I am. I didn't mean to hurt you like this.'

'Are you going to marry him?'

'Yes.'

'In that case there's nothing more to be said – except for one or two things I shall have to say to Philip himself.'

'What things?' Jane asked.

But Jim was already walking away, impatient now to get back to Peele.

Philip stood in the stable doorway, talking to Charlie Clements who was inside, grooming the mare. He turned as Jim came into the yard and sauntered towards him, tapping his boot with his riding-crop.

'My father is out looking for you. Nobody seemed to know where you were.'

'I've just come from seeing Jane.'

'Ah,' Philip said, and his gaze sharpened, becoming wary, inquisitive, amused, and full of bright expectancy. 'Jane. Yes. Exactly so.'

'She tells me she's going to marry you.'

'Then, of course, it must be true.'

'You haven't wasted much time,' Jim said. 'You've only been home a month or so.'

'Five weeks and three days, to be precise.'

'And never once in that time have you even mentioned meeting her.'

'There was a good reason for that.'

'I can well believe it,' Jim said.

'I was trying to spare your feelings, you see, because, right from the very start, I loved the girl and she loved me.'

'Loving people,' Jim said, 'is something she seems to find easy to do.'

'That is not a very gentlemanly remark.'

'I'm not feeling gentlemanly.'

'No, I can see you're not.'

'But then, I am not a gentleman, nor have I ever laid claim to be.'

'No?' Philip said, with a lift of his brows. 'And yet you expected to marry Jane, a girl of good family connections, not to mention superior breeding.' He spread his hands in disbelief. 'You, a farm bailiff,' he continued, 'earning eighteen shillings a week, hoping to lure the poor girl into marriage with your few paltry hundreds in the bank and your talk of renting a little farm – '

Philip, though watching so warily, was nevertheless taken by surprise when Jim suddenly lashed out and caught him a stinging, back-handed blow on the mouth. Until this moment Jim's feelings had been kept under control but now, as he learnt that his cherished ambitions had been discussed between Philip and Jane, and made the subject of ridicule between them, he allowed his anger a free rein and when Philip, with a muttered exclamation, cut at him with his riding-crop, Jim struck out straight and hard with his fist and sent Philip sprawling on his back on the cobbles.

Behind him, in the stable doorway, Charlie Clements now appeared, but before he could intervene John Sutton walked into the yard.

'What the devil's going on?'

Philip got slowly to his feet.

'Jim,' he said, nursing his jaw, 'has just found out that I am going to marry Jane Reynolds.'

'You are going to do what?'

'And, as you see, he's not taking it well. He's no kind of sportsman, I'm afraid. That's one thing we've never drummed into him.'

'All right, Clements, get on with your work! There's no need to stand gaping there!' Sutton, very red in the face, waited until Clements had gone before turning back to Philip. 'When did all this happen with Jane? It's all very sudden, isn't it? You've only been home a few weeks.'

'So everyone keeps telling me. But a few weeks is all it took.'
Philip stood brushing the dust from his clothes. 'You have said
often enough that it was time I married and settled down and
that is what I'm planning to do. It just happens that the girl
in question is one Jim thought he had a lien on and now that
he finds himself mistaken – '

'Well, it can't be settled by fighting like a couple of stable-
boys.' Sutton glanced questioningly at Jim. 'If the girl has
made her choice – '

'Oh, yes, she's made her choice,' Jim said, with great
bitterness, 'but you mustn't be surprised if I'm not very ready
in offering my felicitations.'

'I'm not pretending to be surprised. I'd feel exactly the same
as you do. But this is no place to discuss the matter. We'd all
be better indoors.'

'I'm not in a mood for discussion,' Jim said. 'I think I'd be
better left alone. Anyway, there's work to be done, and I had
better get on with it, doing my duty as your bailiff, earning my
eighteen shillings a week!'

He strode away, out of the yard, and Sutton turned again to
his son. 'Come indoors,' he said tersely. 'I've got a few things
to say to you.'

At about half-past ten that morning, at work in the rickyard,
Jim received word that he was wanted up at the house. He
went somewhat reluctantly and found Sutton alone in his
study.

'This is a bad business, Jim, and I am more sorry than I can
say. I've had it out with Philip and I've told him what I think
of him. But it seems he's perfectly serious about wanting to
marry Jane and there's no changing his mind about it.'

'How could that possibly help anything? You surely don't
think I would want her now, when she's made it plain that she
doesn't want me?'

'No. Of course not. I didn't mean that.'

Sutton, sitting behind his desk, motioned Jim into a chair,
but Jim, refusing, continued to stand, his fists buried deep in
his jacket pockets.

'Philip tells me,' Sutton said, 'that they intend to marry quite soon.'

Jim said nothing, but stood like a stone.

'In fact they talk of an autumn wedding. Early October, perhaps, he says. It all seems very quick to me, but there it is. You will have to consider what to do.'

'Do?' Jim queried. 'Why, what would I do?'

'Well, you can't very well stay here after this, and surely you wouldn't want to? With Philip and Jane living here and such bad blood between you and him . . . it's out of the question, you must surely see that?'

'You mean I would have to move out of the house? Yes, of course, I do see that.'

'Not just out of the house, but away from Peele altogether. Somewhere new. Fresh woods, as they say. I'm sorry about it. Angry, too. You're a good lad and I'm fond of you and your work here as bailiff these past three years – '

'Am I to be turned off, then?' Jim said.

'That's not the way I would put it, myself, but you must certainly leave Peele, and the sooner it can be arranged, the better it will be for everyone. I've given it a good deal of thought and the ideal solution, it seems to me, is for you to go out to Canada and join my cousin Tom on his farm. He badly needs young men like you and if I write to him straight away – '

'Canada!' Jim said hollowly, and, with a wry twist of his mouth, he asked, 'Is that quite far enough away, do you think?'

'It will mean a new life for you, my boy. A whole new adventure. A challenge, that's what! Tom farms five thousand acres out there in Ontario. Five thousand acres, just think of that! Miles and miles of nothing but corn! It will be a splendid chance for you to make a new start and I'm sure you will agree with me that it will be better for everyone if you were gone clean away before Philip's wedding to Jane takes place. In fact, as soon as it can be fixed. It'll spare your own feelings and theirs.'

'Whatever I do,' Jim said, 'it will not be to spare Philip's feelings.'

'I understand how you feel but – he is my son, remember.'

'And I am nobody's son. I've got no family of my own. No money to speak of. No land, no home. Nothing to offer but what I am.'

'And a very good bargain, too,' Sutton said, 'for the right girl in the right place.'

Jim's face remained clenched, his eyes a cold, glittering blue, and Sutton, looking up at him, gave a small, sympathetic sigh. But he was anxious to have Jim's answer; anxious to get his plan under way; and he spoke now with a touch of impatience.

'Well? What do you say to my idea? Canada is a wonderful place, you know, and it's crying out for young chaps like you. You'll make good there in no time at all. So what do you say? Shall I write to Tom?'

Jim suddenly turned to the door.

'I'll think about it and let you know.'

Chapter Six

Once again Jim needed to think and this time, driven by some primitive instinct, he climbed the slopes of Luton Camp; first the gently sweeping slopes, divided roughly into fields; then the higher, steeper slopes, where the turf was worn away in places, revealing the pale stone beneath, which crumbled under his feet as he climbed.

When he got to the top of the hill he sat on a low grassy mound, underneath a hawthorn tree, and looked down on the valley below. He could see almost everything from this height and everything he saw was dear to him, so that the thought of leaving it caused an angry ache in his heart. In the confusion of his mind it was impossible for him to tell which caused him the most pain: his banishment or the reason behind it; because both these things were so twisted together that contemplation of the one only magnified the hurt of the other.

His sense of betrayal filled him completely, for fate had struck him a two-fold blow and the knowledge that he had no rights in the matter only increased his bitterness. Of course, John Sutton was right: he would certainly not want to stay at Peele; but his lack of choice made him squirm all the same, inducing a fierce rebelliousness in him, and it was this aspect of things — the fact that the whole of his future life was being thus decided out of hand — that made him reject Sutton's plan for sending him to Ontario.

This rejection cleared his mind. The feeling that he was a helpless pawn in a game being played by other men was thus removed at a single stroke leaving room for his rebellion to grow. He saw that although his plans had been spoilt, his life was nevertheless his own to direct and govern as he chose. And as he sat looking down on the valley, comparing the rich, productive lands of Peele, so neat and well cared for, just below, with the rough, neglected, tumbledown sprawl of Godsakes over on the other side, he saw that he could use his life in a way that would not only further his own ambitions but defeat the Suttons in one of theirs.

The idea came to him not in a flash but quietly, almost cunningly, as though it had lain in his mind for some time, developing there, secretly, until it had grown to be part of himself and only awaited recognition. For it came to him whole, this idea of his, and brought with it such a sense of purpose that his pain and anger were transmuted at once into strength and energy. The destructive force in him, that wanted to smash and annihilate, was replaced by a creative force that wanted to mend, restore, rebuild. And as he examined this idea, with all its many implications, he was filled with a subtle kind of excitement. Something immense was growing in him and he made it welcome, allowing it to take possession of his heart and his mind.

He had lost something of himself that day, on learning that Jane was playing him false in a way that took no account of his feelings for her, or of his pride. But now he had found another self, harder, tougher than the first, and he felt the stirrings of a fierce impatience, wanting to put this new self to the test and show the world what it could do.

Impatience brought him to his feet and he set off quickly down the hill, slithering over the loose, broken stones and sending them rattling down the slope until, reaching the regular path, he forced himself to a steadier pace. His plan as yet needed much careful thought and there were details to be worked out before he reached Godsakes Farm.

Morris Riddler had been served with an official County Court notice, three days before, informing him that an Order of Possession had been granted against the property known as Godsakes Farm in favour of Messrs Martin and Moore, bankers, of Missenham, in the county of Gloucester, and that

75

the said property would, in default of payment of certain debts and dues, set out in detail below, be put up for sale by Public Auction on Monday 27 September 1858.

On being served the notice, he had first read it, then torn it up, telling the officer who had delivered it that 'anyone who comes here trying to put my farm up for sale will get a skitter of shot in his backside.' There was little or no work to do on the farm at this time because the only remaining stock consisted of two cows, one of them dry, and some two or three dozen hens. The labourers, Lovell and Smith, had been laid off all through the summer, though they still occupied their cottages, and Riddler's whole day was now spent patrolling the farm, on the alert for marauders.

He had seen Jim coming from a long way off and was at the gate, waiting for him, shotgun nestling in the crook of his arm, suspicion written across his face.

'What do you want?' he asked with a growl.

'I've got a proposition to put to you.'

'If the Suttons sent you, you can go to hell.'

'This is nothing to do with the Suttons. This is business of my own. They don't know I've come.'

'Since when have you had business that wasn't connected with the Suttons?'

'Since today,' Jim replied.

Riddler cocked an eyebrow at him, giving him a long, hard look.

'Something wrong between you and them?'

'Yes.'

'Maybe I can guess what it is. I hear the gossip, you know, now and then. And rumour reached me recently that you and Philip Sutton were both after the same girl.'

'In that case you knew before I did myself.'

'Well, since you've fallen out with the Suttons and haven't come on their behalf, I don't mind hearing what you have to say.' Riddler opened the ramshackle gate. 'You'd better come into the house,' he said.

The farmhouse kitchen was very bare. A table, three chairs, and a Welsh dresser were the only furniture in the room, and these were shabby to a degree. But Jim was not surprised at this for it was common knowledge in the district that every saleable thing at Godsakes had been sold to pay Riddler's debts.

Kirren, who was cleaning the stone-flagged floor with a broom dipped into a bucket of water, stopped and looked up in surprise at seeing Riddler enter with Jim. She leant on her broom, frowning at him, and, sharing her father's first suspicions, only barely answered his nod. Riddler stood his gun in a corner, clumped over the wet flags, and sat down in a chair at the table, motioning Jim to do the same.

'You know my daughter, Kirren?' he said, and, over his shoulder, to Kirren herself: 'This is Jim Lundy from Peele.'

'I know perfectly well who it is.'

'You needn't take that tone with him. He hasn't come to turn us out. Or so he assures me, anyway.' Riddler, sitting sideways in his chair, one arm resting on the table, looked at Jim sitting opposite. 'A proposition, I think you said?'

'Yes, that's right.'

'Well, fire away.'

'I'll make no bones about it,' Jim said. 'You're done-for here. We both know that. And it's only a matter of two or three weeks before the farm is sold over your head. Your loan at the bank still stands at a little over six hundred pounds – you can guess how I come by that information – but it is your payments on the loan, and a few other debts elsewhere, that are your most pressing problem, and if you could only settle them you would be in the clear again.'

'Two hundred pounds! That's all I need! And because I can't find it they'll sell me up!' Riddler exclaimed bitterly. But he was narrowly watching Jim and in his small, screwed-up eyes there was already a gleam of hope. 'But maybe you've come along with some miraculous solution such as I've been praying for?'

'I've come to offer to pay your debts.'

'Have you, by God?' Riddler breathed, and turned his head to glance at Kirren, who, still holding her broom, was standing in silence nearby. 'And in return – what do you want?'

'A share in the farm.'

'What sort of a share?'

'A partnership. Half and half.'

'Just for paying off my debts?'

'No, there's more to it than that,' Jim said. 'I've got twelve hundred pounds in the bank, my savings over thirteen years. I've also got my flock, as you know, worth perhaps eighty pounds. I propose using my money to pay off your debts and re-stock the farm, keeping a certain amount back to cover all the running expenses, such as the men's wages and so on. We then work together to build it up, and in return, when that is achieved, a half share of the farm will be mine, plus a half share of the profits, of course.'

Jim, sitting upright in his chair, turned and half looked at Riddler's daughter, not to win any comment from her but because he was irritated by the way she stood just out of sight behind him. He then turned to face Riddler again.

'That's my proposition,' he said. 'Details would have to be worked out, of course, and some kind of legal agreement drawn up. But, in a nutshell, that's about it.'

'You don't expect much, do you, by God, in exchange for your twelve hundred pounds? Have you any idea, I wonder, how much it cost me to buy this place?'

'Yes, it cost you three thousand pounds, plus the interest on your loan. But you wouldn't get half that sum for it now, being so run-down as it is, and if my twelve hundred pounds is enough to put you into production again, it's surely worth more to you than just its value, counted as coin? Anyway, I propose earning the rest of my share by working and putting the farm to rights, and as that will take a good many years – '

'All right, all right, you've made your point! But I don't much fancy sharing a farm that I've had to myself for thirty-six years.'

'In that case you'll lose it altogether,' Jim said. 'You can't fight the law for ever, even with a shotgun, and when the sale takes place, the farm will go to the highest bidder. And that, as you know, will be John Sutton.'

'Yes, you've got me there, haven't you? Because you know

damned well I'd do just about anything rather than see him get my farm. But go on with your proposition. There's one or two things to account for yet. What happens, for instance, when I die? My share of the farm will be Kirren's then. Do you propose being partners with *her*?'

'By that time, all being well, the farm will be on its feet again and I shall be able to buy her out.'

There was a silence in the room; a silence that lasted a long time; and throughout it Riddler's keen, bright gaze remained fixed on Jim's face. At last, however, he stirred in his chair, twisting round to look at Kirren.

'What do *you* think about it?' he asked.

Kirren shrugged. 'It seems a good enough plan,' she said, 'up to the point where I get turned out.'

'*Bought* out, not turned out,' Jim said.

'It means the same thing, doesn't it? I still lose my home.'

Her words surprised him. Gave him pause. Until today, he had never met the girl face to face. He had only seen her in the distance, at haymaking time in the meadows, perhaps, or trudging along the road in to town, taking her produce to the market. But he knew what her life had been like on this farm and he had assumed that she would welcome a plan that offered some chance of escape.

'Does the place mean so much to you, then?'

'I'm not sure what it means to me. I've never thought about it till now. But this is the only home I've ever known and God knows I've worked hard enough for it, helping my father keep hold of it.'

'You'll be repaid for that work in the end because when I buy your share of the farm you'll be able to rent a cottage somewhere and probably have enough money to make you independent for life.'

'On the other hand,' she said, 'if everything goes as well as you think, and the farm begins making money again, I could in the end buy you out instead.'

'Oh, no, I wouldn't want that!' Jim said, emphatically. 'I would want the farm for myself.'

Riddler, having listened intently to this exchange, now

spoke again. 'Why should you want the farm so much? To spite John Sutton and his son? To show that girl at Hide House what a prize she's lost in jilting you?'

'I don't think my reasons matter,' Jim said, 'but certainly I would want the farm.'

'Seems we all want it,' Riddler said. 'We are united in that at least. But there is one problem in your plan. Supposing I was to drop dead before the farm was paying its way? You wouldn't be able to buy Kirren's share then. You'd both have to stick it out here together and that wouldn't do at all. It wouldn't be decent. Folk would talk.'

Jim became silent. He was badly put out. It seemed to him unbelievable that such a foolish, irrelevant problem should threaten the working-out of his plan. But before he could frame any kind of answer, Morris Riddler was speaking again.

'Your plan is fine as far as it goes but you haven't thought it through to the end. I reckon the best way of making it work is for you and Kirren to get married. That way you get hold of the farm without having to turn her out and it does away with any need for complicated legal arrangements. The lawyers have had enough money out of me in the past. I'm damned if I'll let them have any more.'

Jim and Kirren both stared at him.

'You're surely not serious?' Jim said.

'Oh, yes, I am.'

'Then I'm afraid you must think again, because marriage is quite out of the question. It doesn't come into my plans at all.'

'Nor mine,' Kirren said. 'I thought I'd made that plain enough.'

'You be quiet,' Riddler said, 'and listen to what I have to say.'

'I don't care what you've got to say! I've heard it often enough before. I am *not* going to marry anyone – neither this man here nor any other – just to please you and keep the farm.'

'Please me be damned!' Riddler said. 'It's *you* I'm thinking of, not myself.'

'I can't think why,' Kirren said. 'You never have done in the past.'

'I'm talking about the future now – when I'm dead and in my grave and you're left with no one to take care of you.'

'I can take care of myself.'

'I doubt if you'll get another chance of a husband falling into your lap –'

'How many times do I have to tell you that a husband is the last thing I want?' Kirren, with angry impatience, dipped her broom into the bucket and began brushing the flagstones again, sweeping the water towards the door. 'To saddle myself with the kind of life my mother endured with you all those years? Oh dear me no! I'd sooner be dead!'

The violence of Kirren's outburst had a strange effect on Jim. It gave him a stab of perverse pleasure, enhancing, in a peculiar way, his own dark disillusionment. And, looking at her more closely now, he saw her as though for the first time. Riddler, catching this look of his, shrewdly waited a while in silence, guessing the nature of the young man's thoughts. Then, judging his moment, he said:

'Well, I don't know, I'm sure! But seeing you're both so set against marriage it seems to me you're ideally suited. Made for each other! The perfect match! So why not look on it as a business arrangement, purely for the sake of the farm, without any strings on either side? You say you would want the whole farm for yourself but if you bought Kirren out you'd only have to get someone else to cook and clean and keep house for you. Now you may not think it to look at her but Kirren is a very good housekeeper and you couldn't do better than keep her on.'

'High praise indeed!' Kirren said, speaking as though to the broom in her hands.

'And one thing about a wife is, you don't have to pay her a wage,' Riddler said.

'Ah,' Kirren said, with a little nod, 'and there we come to the heart of it!'

But she had stopped sweeping again and was now looking directly at Jim. Their eyes met in a straight, steady stare; with a curious kind of hostile reserve; but this hostility, in a strange way, somehow formed a bond between them, perhaps because its cause lay, not in their two separate selves, but in the person of Morris Riddler. They had known each other by sight for years but they met today for the first time. They were strangers, the pair of them, and while they frankly appraised each other, both understood perfectly that strangers was how they wished to remain.

Quietly, cautiously, Jim spoke to her.

'Purely as a business arrangement, exactly as your father suggests, would you be willing to consider it?'

'I don't know,' Kirren said. 'Would you?'

'A formality only? Just a marriage in name? It does seem to make some sense, I think, and there's no doubt it would simplify matters when it comes to joint ownership of the farm.'

'Oh, it would simplify matters most beautifully,' Kirren said in a dry tone, 'for a wife has almost no rights whatever in matters concerning property.'

'Yes, well, I suppose that's true. But a wife does have rights of a kind, after all. For one thing she is entitled to expect that her husband will always do well by her. And that, even in a marriage of convenience, is a duty I would most certainly fulfil.'

'No strings attached, as my father suggests?'

'None whatever,' Jim said. 'I would make no demands on you as a husband. In fact, where our personal lives are concerned, we should be scarcely more to each other than we are now.'

Kirren, it seemed, still had her doubts.

'How do I know I can trust you?'

'You don't,' he said bluntly, meeting her gaze. 'But it is scarcely the kind of matter on which I can swear an affidavit, is it?'

Riddler, watching Kirren's face, gave a cynical laugh.

'You can always lock your door, girl. That's simple enough, surely?' he said. 'And if Jim is worried on the same score, he can lock his!'

'Your daughter needs time to think,' Jim said, 'and so, for that matter, do I.'

'All right,' Riddler said. 'But that's my condition – no marriage, no deal.'

'You are hardly in a position to make conditions.'

'No, maybe not,' Riddler said. 'But I'm making this one all the same. And if you want this farm as badly as I think you do, then *you're* in no position to turn it down. Now come with me and I'll show you round. You'll see what you will be taking on and Kirren will have time to think.'

It was seven years since Jim had set foot on Godsakes land and in those seven years its ruination had been complete. In every field it was the same: a wilderness of rank grass and weeds, with clumps of thorn and briar here and there, and hedges so badly neglected that the timber in them stood twenty feet high and brambles spread out over the headlands forming thickets twenty feet wide. No land had been ploughed in recent years and Riddler's ploughs, together with other implements, lay under a heap of junk in a corner of the crumbling barn. All the farm buildings were in disrepair and, like the land itself, were infested with every kind of vermin. The pig-pens and sties were choke-full with nettles and more than half the hen-coops were fit for nothing but firewood.

'A sight for sore eyes, eh?' Riddler said. 'And all Sutton's fault, every bit of it. This was a good farm once but when I was given the chance to buy and Sutton ran up the price like that . . . But there, you know the tale well enough, so there's no point in dragging it out again. But I can never forgive him for that and never will so long as I live, because that big loan has dragged me down. It's like as if I were stuck in the mire – the more I struggled, the deeper I sank. Now if only my son Eddy had lived . . . But it's no good thinking of things like that and maybe I'll get a son-in-law instead. Not quite the same as a son of my own, but a whole heap better than nothing at all.'

The two men came to a halt. Their tour had brought them back to the yard and they leant together over the gate, watching the few scrawny hens pecking about in the dust.

'Well, now you've seen all there is to see, what do you think?' Riddler said. 'Think you can make a go of it? Pull it together, like you said? There's still the damned mortgage, remember — six hundred pounds to be paid off yet, plus the interest at four per cent. D'you think, with that millstone round your neck, you can pull the farm back on its feet and get it to pay its way again?'

'Yes, if you let me have a free hand, to run things my way, as I think best.'

'Oh, so you're to have all the say, are you, and I'm to stand by, clapping my hands?'

'We should discuss things together, of course, as any business partners would.'

'Discusss things between us,' Riddler said, 'and then do exactly what you decide.'

'You've made the decisions up to now and as a result the farm has failed.'

'It's not my fault the farm has failed! I've had the devil's own bad luck these past sixteen years and damn well you know it too —'

'Yes, I know it well enough, but as it will be my money we shall be using to start the farm working again —'

'All right, all right, don't rub it in!' Riddler said with an angry scowl. 'Who pays the piper calls the tune. There's no arguing against that. And if you think you can pull it off . . . '

'Don't you believe me?'

'Yes, I do. I've got to believe it, there's no other hope. I know you can work — I've seen it myself. And you've got your head screwed on pretty well — you wouldn't be Sutton's bailiff else. If anyone can pull the place together, I reckon it's you. You'll get your free hand, right enough, and if it means keeping Sutton out . . . Well, I don't need to tell you, but I'd give a great deal to make sure of that.' He turned his head to look at Jim and after a little while he said: 'It seems as though, from the way you're talking, you've made up your mind to accept my condition.'

'Yes, I accept it,' Jim said.

'So,' Riddler said, quietly, and the word came out in a little hiss. 'It all depends on Kirren, then. Let's go and see what she says.'

Kirren was standing in the back porchway. She seemed to be looking out for them.

'Well, miss? Have you made up your mind?'

'Yes,' Kirren said. She looked at Jim. 'If he agrees to it, so do I.'

'Of course he damn well agrees to it! Can't you see by the look on his face? There aren't any flies on this young chap. He sees the good sense of my idea and I'm glad to find, now you're put to it, that you've got the nous to see it, too.'

Riddler was now cock-a-hoop. He could scarcely contain himself. Boisterously, he turned to Jim and clapped one heavy hand on his back, at the same time taking Kirren's arm and giving it a long, hard squeeze.

'Come indoors, the pair of you! We've still got a few things to sort out yet. And if there's anything left in the bottle we'll drink damnation to the Suttons!'

Just after two o'clock Jim returned to Peele House, quietly mounted the stairs to his room, and put his clothes and other belongings into an old canvas satchel. With this slung on his shoulder he went downstairs and was crossing the hall to Sutton's study when Mrs Abelard came out of the dining-room. Her face clouded at sight of him, especially when she noted the satchel, and, taking his arm, she led him aside, speaking to him in an undertone.

'There's been an upset, hasn't there, about your young lady at Hide House Farm?'

'Yes, Abby. It's all gone wrong. She doesn't want me after all.' Jim had thought himself strong and hard but under the old woman's scrutiny he felt himself a boy again and there was a tremor in his voice as he said: 'She's going to marry Philip instead.'

'Mr Philip has stolen her from you. That's how it is, you mark my words. He was always that way inclined, even when you were boys together. But a girl who changes her mind as easy as that isn't worth bothering about and I'd say she's a lot better matched to Mr Philip than she would be to you.'

Jim said nothing and the old housekeeper, seeing his face, clicked her tongue, much vexed with herself.

'Tchah! What a thing for me to say! As though that was any comfort to you!' Once again she took hold of his arm, distressed for him, at a loss for words. 'And are you leaving us, then, for good?'

'Yes, I'm not wanted here any more. Nor, come to that, do I want to stay. But I shan't be going far, Abby. Just across the valley, that's all.'

'Across the valley?' Abby gaped. 'Whatever do you mean by that, Mr Jim?'

Jim's explanation was cut short because, quietly though he and Abby had talked, John Sutton had heard them and now, opening his study door, he looked out into the hall. Discreetly, the old woman withdrew, vanishing into her kitchen, and Jim turned towards Sutton, who came across the hall to him.

'What's this?' he asked with a frown, touching the satchel on Jim's back.

'I thought, since you wanted me to leave, I might as well go straight away. The sooner the better, I think you said, and I am rather inclined to agree. But I'm not going to Ontario. I'm going to Godsakes instead.'

'Godsakes?' Sutton said blankly, and then, with quick-growing suspicion, 'What the devil do you mean?'

'I'm going to pay Riddler's debts. We shall be partners, he and I, and we'll work together to pull up the farm. I've just been over there, bargaining with him, and now I'm going back – for good.'

'My God! You would do that to me?' Sutton was crimson in the face. 'You know I've always wanted that farm! You know I've waited sixteen years!'

'Yes, I know it very well, just as Philip knew I wanted Jane.'

'All this fuss over a girl! A pretty face! A pair of blue eyes! Dammit, Jim, just look at yourself! You're a young man of twenty-four and you've got enough about you, in the way of looks and ability, to take your pick from a dozen girls. In a few months from now you'll have got over this business with Jane and you'll have no trouble, believe me, when it comes to finding another wife.'

'I've already found one,' Jim said. 'I'm going to marry Kirren Riddler.'

'Riddler's daughter?'

'Yes, that's right.'

'But you don't even know the wretched girl!'

'It would seem I didn't know Jane, either, for all I understood of her.'

'My God!' Sutton exclaimed. 'Do you mean you are marrying her just to get hold of Godsakes Farm? A marriage like that won't bring you much joy!'

'No, well, you may be right. But we'll see how much joy Philip's marriage brings him.'

'I never thought to see the day when you would do a thing like this to me.'

'The day,' Jim said, with irony, 'has brought surprises for both of us.'

'After all I've done for you, giving you a home all these years! Bringing you up and caring for you, almost as though you were my son!'

'You've always been very good to me and I thank you for it,' Jim said. 'But now, although I've done nothing wrong, you would like to be rid of me. You would send me away to Canada, a place where I have no wish to be, and no doubt, if you had the power, you would rub me clean off the face of the earth. Well, I am not to be got rid of so easily, simply because, through no fault of my own, I have become an embarrassment to you. Common nobody I may be but I still have the right to run my own life and that is what I intend to do.'

Following these words Jim became silent, looking straight into Sutton's eyes and seeing there a burning reflection of his own anger and bitterness. Then, with some awkwardness, he said: 'I'm sorry it's ending like this. You've been a good friend to me until now. But after what's happened today, well, I can never feel quite the same way again and I know that my going to Godsakes will put paid to our friendship once and for all.'

'You are going, though, in spite of that?'

'Yes.'

'I suppose it's your idea of revenge.'

'Whatever it is,' Jim said, 'Philip is the one who's to blame for it.'

A few minutes later, with his long shepherding stick in his hand and his dog, Jess, close at his heels, he was crossing the stable yard, on his way to the gate leading into the pastures. He had his hand on the sneck of the gate when Sutton came out of the house and stood in the open doorway.

'Where do you think you're going?'

'I'm going up to fetch my flock and say goodbye to old Abelard.'

Jim passed through the gate and set off up the fields and Sutton, still red in the face, stood staring grimly after him.

Philip, who had been at Hide House lunching with Jane and her parents, returned to Peele in time to see Jim driving his flock over one of the little bridges spanning the brook in the valley bottom. Finding his father in the front drive, where a good view could be had of the valley, he asked what was going on and in a few pithy sentences Sutton explained.

'Paying Riddler's debts?' Philip repeated. 'To stop us getting Godsakes Farm?'

'He not only stops us getting it, but he gets it himself, damn his eyes, for he's marrying Riddler's daughter, he says.'

'Marrying – ? Is this a joke?'

'No, it is not!' Sutton snapped. 'He's in deadly earnest, I promise you.'

'But,' Philip said, floundering, 'he can't possibly make it pay. He hasn't got the capital. Oh, I know he's got some money saved, but not a fraction of what he will need to put that farm in order again – '

'Maybe not. But what he's got is quite enough to keep the place from being sold for another sixteen years or so and by that time I may well be dead. As for not making a go of it, I wouldn't even be too sure of that, because Jim is a very determined young man. Clever, too. He uses his head.'

'It would take him half his life – '

'So what if it does? What's that to him? He is only twenty-four. What better thing could he do with his life than spend it in reclaiming that land?'

'You think it's a possibility, then, that he will make a success of it?' Philip's face was now thunderous. 'And yet you stand here quietly, letting him take those sheep off the farm!'

'The sheep are his. He bought them himself.'

'With money you gave him, don't forget.'

'What's given is given,' Sutton said. 'It can't be taken back.'

'I'm not so sure about that. I think we should see old Kelloway. Those sheep were raised on our land and I'm sure if we took it to law – '

'Oh, be quiet, you stupid fool! Even if we did have a claim on those sheep, how would the story sound, do you think, once it got round the neighbourhood? What sort of name should we have after that? What would people think of us?'

'Good God, it's monstrous!' Philip exclaimed. 'To think of his sneaking off like that and doing a deal with the likes of Riddler just to vent his spite on us! After what we've done for him over the past fourteen years – '

' "We"?' Sutton said, in a scathing tone. 'And what have *you* ever done for him, apart from taking his girl away from him?' Then, with a quick gesture, he said, 'Oh, never mind! Let it pass, let it pass! For heaven's sake, don't let us two quarrel as well, otherwise where shall we be? But it is a pity all the same that out of all the girls in the district you had to fix your fancy on Jane. It's lost us Godsakes, there's no doubt of that.' Sutton turned to go into the house, but paused just long enough to lay a hand on Philip's shoulder and to say, with a touch of dryness: 'Let's hope she turns out to be worth it, eh?'

Down in the bottom of the valley Jim's sheep had now crossed the meadows and he was letting them through a gate that led into Godsakes land. From the top of the main farm track Riddler and Kirren stood watching as the neatly bunched flock of fifty ewes came slowly up the sloping fields with the young man and the dog behind.

The sight of these golden-fleeced sheep affected Morris Riddler deeply, for no such first-class stock as this had been seen at Godsakes for many years, and the surge of emotion was so strong in him that when he suddenly turned to Kirren his queer, crooked, shapeless face was lit with a kind of holy joy and, at the same time, wet with tears.

'Look at them, Kirrie! Just look at them! Did you ever see anything so beautiful in all your born days? Why, that old saying, the Golden Hoof, was never truer than it is for us here today, because that little flock of Cotswold Lions means that this farm is in business again!'

Even Kirren herself was affected and although her glance was sardonic, as always, there was nevertheless a smile on her lips and a gleam of living hope in her eyes. For once she and her father were in accord, sharing the same feelings and thoughts, and he, aware of this sympathy between them, suddenly clasped her in his arms, pressing her head against his chest and giving a little sobbing laugh. Just as suddenly he released her and, with his clumsy, lumbering gait, set off down the track to meet Jim.

Usually dinner at Godsakes was eaten at noon but because of events that day it was almost four o'clock when three people instead of two sat down to eat their first meal together.

'You won't find us delicate here,' Riddler said. 'Plain boiled bacon and cabbage and taters, that's what we live on, Kirren and me. You will find it a bit of a change after the way you've lived at Peele.'

'Plain food is good enough for me,' Jim said.

But the boiled bacon was terrible stuff. The smell of it as he sat down to eat told him what to expect and although he tried to harden himself, at the first mouthful of tainted meat, with its thick coating of rancid fat, his gorge rose in such a way that it required an effort of will to chew the mouthful and swallow it. Taking a generous helping of salt before attacking the meat again, he saw that Kirren was watching him.

'You don't have to eat it,' she said. 'It can go back in the pot.'

'If you can eat it, so can I.'

'We're used to it. You're not.'

Riddler ate stolidly, leaning low over his plate, watching Jim with open amusement.

'You may as well get used to it. There's a tidy bit of it left yet.' He pointed up at the rack in the rafters, on which were laid the whole of one flitch and the half of another, each tightly covered in muslin, each with its dark cluster of flies. 'That old pig was the last we raised. I'll tell you how he came to die.'

The story of how the pig had died did not make it any easier for Jim to finish eating his meal and when at last he laid down his knife and fork it was with a sense of relief that did not go unnoticed by Riddler.

'Think you'll live after that?' he asked. 'Think you'll survive it, do you, eh?'

Jim rose and pushed in his chair.

'I'm going for another walk round the farm.'

'Hang on a minute. I'll come with you.'

'Thanks, but I'd sooner be alone. I've got some thinking to do.'

Looking around the farm again, noting things that had to be done, he could scarcely wait for the morning, so impatient was he to begin. But his first task in the morning would be to go in to town with Riddler and arrange for the payment of his debts, beginning with the mortgage dues, and as it would be market day his second most important task would be to buy new stock for the farm.

But all the time, as he laid his plans, other thoughts were troubling him, and the source of these was the girl, Kirren. He was fretted by feelings of guilt, asking himself what he was doing marrying a girl he cared nothing for; a girl who was so much a stranger to him that until today they had never even spoken together.

For himself he had no regrets; only a bitter satisfaction at taking such a cold-blooded step, as though he would demonstrate to himself and the world that *that* was all marriage meant to him now. One wife would do as well as another. What did it matter who she was? He would never now want to marry for love. He would not succumb to *that* weakness again. And although Kirren was a stranger to him, at least he knew where he was with her, for there could be no betrayal where there had been no promise of love.

But Kirren herself – what of her? Was he not doing wrong, taking advantage of her poverty? Hadn't he, at her father's instigation, pushed her into this doubtful transaction merely to further his own ends, without proper consideration for her feelings, as a girl, as a woman? These questions gnawed at his mind and when he returned to the house and found Kirren alone in the kitchen he broached the subject immediately.

She heard him out in silence, looking at him searchingly, her eyes very dark under frowning brows, and when he had finished she asked bluntly:

'Are you having second thoughts?'

'For myself – no. For you – yes, perhaps. I feel I haven't considered you enough. I've been thinking too much about myself. I feel you've been thrust into this thing without having enough time to think.'

'I'm not a fool. I know what I'm doing. You said you didn't want a proper marriage and I said I felt the same, so as long as we both mean what we say – '

'Don't you want children?'

'No. I do not.'

'Most women do.'

'How do you know?'

'Well,' he said, uncertainly, 'it's an understood thing, I would have thought.'

'When women marry, they generally have children whether they like it or not. They're given no choice in the matter. They just have to make the best of it. But I don't intend that to happen to me because I wouldn't want to bring a child into the world. Another life, another soul . . . And to be responsible for raising it . . . That thought is frightening to me.'

'Frightening?' Jim asked. 'But surely if a man and a woman love one another – '

'Yes? What?'

'Nothing,' he said, with a shake of his head. The subject was painful to him; he had stumbled thus far unwittingly. 'Nothing. Never mind.'

'I've heard my father say that he loved my mother, but he had a queer way of showing it, driving her into the grave.'

'That's a very harsh thing to say.'

'It's true all the same.'

'You have a poor opinion of men.'

'They like their own way,' Kirren said, 'and they always make sure that they get it.'

'Aren't women the same?'

'I've never had my own way in my life.'

'Perhaps you haven't gone the right way about it.'

'If you are trying to tell me that I need to be sweet and pretty and soft and admire everything men say or do – '

'I'm saying nothing of the kind.'

'What *are* you saying?' Kirren asked.

'Well, we seem to have strayed from the subject, rather, but in the beginning I was trying to ask you if you had thought deeply enough about this marriage proposition – '

'The marriage, as agreed between us, will suit me very well,' Kirren said. 'My father's been nagging at me for years to find myself a husband and I am sick of hearing it. By marrying you I shall get some peace. But his idea is a good one all round. It means you get the farm in the end, but without taking it away from me, and if you can really make it pay – '

'That I promise and swear to do.'

'Then I shall be well satisfied.'

'You seem very sure.'

'Yes. I am.' She looked at him with unsmiling gaze. 'If you can be sure, why can't I?'

There was no further argument after that; the matter was settled once and for all; and it only remained to see the vicar and arrange for the marriage to take place at the earliest possible date. And Jim, his last lingering doubts removed, felt free to give his mind to the farm.

Chapter Seven

It was a strange thing after living at Peele all these years, looking across the valley at Godsakes, to find himself now living at Godsakes, looking across the valley at Peele. It induced a queer feeling of dislocation in him, of dislocation, as though the sun itself were at fault for rising in the wrong part of the sky. Sometimes, in the fields at Godsakes, he would look up from his work and be stricken with a sense of confusion, because the tilt of the land was wrong and seemed to rear itself up at him, catching him unawares. But this confusion was purely instinctive, induced by sheer physical habit. He never for one single instant forgot where he was or why he was there.

The work at Godsakes was a challenge to him. His whole being rose to it, embracing it as a kind of crusade. His blood raced in response to it and he felt himself filled with the strength of three men. His mind was forever occupied with schemes, plans, calculations, ideas. While performing one task, he would be thinking over the next, so that no time was ever lost for want of knowing where to begin.

But although his mind was so full of schemes, it remained always cold and crystal clear. He knew what needed to be done and the best way of doing it. There was never any uncertainty. For one thing, he already knew the farm; had watched its downhill progress for the past fourteen years of his life; and had listened to John Sutton and Philip discussing what would have to be done to put Godsakes in order again when at last it came into their hands.

And here Jim's heart always gave a leap, because of the way things had fallen out; because Godsakes had come into *his*

95

hands and the Suttons would never have it now – he would make quite certain of that. Philip had taken Jane from him and he in turn had taken Godsakes from them. There was immense satisfaction in this. It was a method of revenge that had a sense of rightness to it: a sense of fitness so complete that it tasted incredibly sweet on the tongue.

Whether it was right morally was, as he readily admitted, a matter of secondary importance to him, for he would have done it anyway without any compunction whatever. But there *was* a moral side to it and this added an extra dimension to the satisfaction he already felt. He had always had some sympathy for Morris Riddler in his struggles. The man had been treated badly by John Sutton, there was no doubt of that, and much of his life had been spoilt by it. Now Jim had given him the weapons with which to fight back and win. The two of them worked to the same end, the satisfaction of one magnified by that of the other.

'There's justice in this,' Riddler would say. 'I could almost believe in the goodness of God for sending you over to us.'

Not that they were always in agreement. Far from it, in fact. There were endless arguments between them, especially in the early days: arguments over the horses Jim bought; the implements, the new machines; and arguments over the new farm stock: the cows, the sheep, the pigs, the fowls.

'Why Shorthorns?' Riddler asked. 'What's wrong with Old Gloucesters, I'd like to know? And what do we want with so many sheep? The place is swarming with them already.'

'This farm needs the sheep,' Jim said. 'Especially on the lighter lands. They'll tread the soil and make it compact and their dung will put new heart into it. As for the cows, well, Shorthorns are more adaptable and milk better than Old Gloucesters do, and their milk makes better butter and cheese.'

'Well, if you say so, of course! It is your money, after all. I suppose you can spend it how you like.'

'Yes,' Jim said, 'and so I shall.'

'Even waste it,' Riddler said, 'paying it all out in wages!'

This was a sore point with him because Jim had engaged an

extra man, thus making three in all, and was paying them eight shillings a week.

'You can't expect good work if you don't pay for it,' Jim said, 'and six shillings is not enough.'

'You won't get good work out of Lovell and Smith. They don't know the meaning of the word.'

'I know well enough how they've played you up. I've seen the way they slack in your fields. But Townsend is a first class man. Abelard recommended him. And as he will get eight shillings a week, Smith and Lovell will get it, too. And if they don't earn it they'll be dismissed.'

'Have you told them that?'

'Yes,' Jim said, 'and they will find I'm a man of my word.'

These were among the first changes Jim made on the farm, for he wanted to get as much land ploughed that autumn as time and the weather would allow. And so it was, on a warm misty morning in mid-September, that there were five teams at work in the fields at Godsakes, three ploughing the fifteen acres of old oat stubble behind the barn, and two ploughing the borecole ground between the barn and the hazel copse.

Jim had not ploughed for three years. It was good to take hold of the stilts again and to walk behind a team of horses that steamed in the early morning air; to feel the ploughshare cutting the ground and to see the furrow-slice heeling over, burying the stubble and weeds and the rough clumps of couch-grass.

Riddler worked in the same field as Jim, grumbling all the while at his plough, blaming his horses and swearing at them when they turned too sharply at the headland, yet ploughing nevertheless with a certain jaunty, swaggering gusto, because of the new life and hope that had suddenly come to the run-down farm.

'Three years since you ploughed, did you say? For me it's more like five or six!' he called across to Jim once when both, on reaching the headland together, paused to give their teams a rest.

'You've still got the knack of it, anyway.' And Jim looked back at Riddler's stetch, its furrows running clean and straight.

Riddler also turned and looked back. Then he spat into his hands.

'I'm glad I'm still good for something!' he said.

The weather that autumn was open and mild and the work of ploughing, rolling, and harrowing went ahead without hindrance until just a few days before Christmas. Riddler grumbled endlessly at the many cultivations Jim considered necessary for the cleaning of the land and he thought it the height of folly that Jim meant to plough up certain 'pastures' only to sow the ground with new grass. The pasture in question was actually a neglected arable field where couch-grass had been allowed to grow, with stubborn weeds such as thistles and docks and even clumps of thorn and briar.

'This may be pasture to you,' Jim said. 'Myself, I would call it something else. Look at those sheep grazing there. They only graze one tenth of the field – the rest of it is unwholesome to them. Even the grass they do eat isn't nearly good enough for them – it will keep them alive but that's about all. I intend to sow proper leys, with the best seed-mixtures I can buy, containing clover and lucerne, and I'll sow forty pounds of seed to the acre to be sure of getting a good, close pile. And then I hope we shall have some pastures that are really worthy of the name.'

'Yes, if we're not both dead by then!'

Grass was just grass to Riddler and he would stare in astonishment when Jim pointed out the various species, giving their scientific names and describing their respective virtues. *Poas* and *festucas* were nothing to him and although he listened to Jim's 'lectures' it was only to pour scorn on them.

'Cocksfoot and cowgrass! That's all I know in the way of names. The rest is all flummery to me!'

It was the same with the artificial fertilizers Jim had bought.

'Guano?' he said, sniffing the sacks. 'All the way from Peru? Seems a bit far-fetched to me! And as for this bone-manure of yours, I don't see what we want with it. I've never used it in my life.'

'Are you holding yourself up as the best of examples?' Jim asked. 'Because if you are I would like to point out — '

'All right, all right, don't rub it in! I know I'm a failure!' Riddler said. 'You're the one that's running things now. I don't have any say any more. My only business these days is to stand with my mouth wide open in wonderment, watching you run my farm for me.'

But although he argued at every turn and was always making sarcastic remarks, Riddler's desire for Jim to succeed overrode everything else, even his jealousy and pride.

'I'd stand on my head if you told me to, if it meant doing good to the farm,' he said, 'and I damn well mean that, every word.'

'I don't want you to stand on your head, I want you to stand on your own two feet.'

'Hah! And what about my corns? Am I to put guano on them?'

'Yes, if you want them to grow,' Jim said.

Riddler went off with a loud guffaw and, passing Kirren in the yard, he said: 'One thing about this husband of yours! — At least we get a few laughs since he came!'

And as the fine autumn progressed and more and more land came under the plough, changing acres of grey scrub grass to the clean brown-ribbed pattern of ridge and furrow, Riddler's spirits expanded and soared.

'I hope John Sutton is watching this!' he said one day, jerking his head towards Peele. 'I hope he can see what's happening here. See what we're doing, you and me.'

Jim, forking field-rubbish onto a fire, paused and looked across the valley at Peele. The big square house, very white in the sunlight, against its dark background of trees, stood without any sign of life, but out on the land there was plenty of activity, especially in the arable fields, where the winter corn was being sown.

'He can see it all right,' he said quietly. 'He has no choice but to see what we do.'

'Well, that's the whole idea, isn't it? To show them what stuff you're made of, eh, and let that wife of Philip Sutton's see that she married the wrong man?'

99

Jim, in silence, turned back to his work, forking up the couch-grass and weeds that had been raked and harrowed out of the ground and placing them on the slow-burning fire.

'Well?' Riddler said, provokingly. 'Can you deny that's what you want?'

'I understand from Abelard that Philip and Jane are still away.'

'On their honeymoon?'

'Yes. What else?'

'Seems they must be enjoying it, staying away so long as this. How long is it? Five weeks or six?'

'I haven't been keeping count,' Jim said.

Riddler, so often forced to give in to Jim over the management of the farm, could always get his own back by taunting him in this way, and he took a malicious delight in it. Philip and Jane had been married on the second Sunday in October, a week after Jim's marriage to Kirren, and the young couple, according to gossip, were spending their honeymoon abroad, travelling in France and Italy.

'France and Italy!' Riddler would say. 'Now you could never have given her that. Not on a farm-bailiff's wages, eh? Not unless you had been prepared to spend all your savings doing so.'

Towards the end of November the young couple returned home and a week or so afterwards three large covered vans were seen driving up to Peele.

'Paintings and statues and sculptures and such,' old Abelard told Jim when they met down at the brook one day, 'and something my sister calls a spinette, that they've brought back with them from Italy.'

Whatever happened at Peele these days was soon known at Godsakes, and if some of the tales were exaggerated, obviously others were not, for the changes being wrought there, now that the house had a new mistress, could be seen and heard plainly enough. There were often parties in the evenings, when fine carriages came to the door and the whole house was a blaze of lights, and sometimes, when the wind was right, the sound of music could be heard across the valley at Godsakes.

'No wonder that girl jilted you,' Riddler would say, shaking his head. 'She wanted a lot more out of life than you could've given her, didn't she, eh?'

'Yes, it would seem so,' Jim said.

In between those times when the fallow lands were being cleaned by repeated cultivations, Jim and Riddler and the other men were busy cutting and laying the hedges, and day after day great fires of brash blazed and crackled in the fields, sending their thick grey smoke rolling out over the valley. The hedges were hawthorn, hazel, and ash, and because they were so badly overgrown, much stout timber was cut from them. This was trimmed, cut into lengths, and tied in bundles of such a size that each of the men employed on the farm could carry one home on his back when he chose. And the rest of the timber, stacked in the yard, was enough to feed the farmhouse fires for at least six months.

Jim also engaged a warrener to trap the rabbits infesting the farm and during the first month or so more than two hundred rabbits were killed. These were the warrener's source of income but often, when his 'bag' was extra big, he would leave a couple of brace at the house, so that rabbit stew and rabbit pie appeared regularly at the table.

'Better than reisty bacon, eh?' Riddler would say, grinning at Jim, and to Kirren, more than once, he said: 'You're getting to be quite a good cook now that you've got a husband to feed. This rabbit pie is something like.'

'Give me good meat to cook,' Kirren said, 'and I will give you decent meals.'

Certainly the reisty bacon had proved too much for Jim and he had soon asked Kirren to bring home a joint of fresh meat every week from the butcher's in town.

'A pretty penny that must have cost!' Riddler said, when the first of these joints, a rib of beef, was brought smoking hot to the table. 'But that's what comes of being genteel — his viands have got to be paid for in cash before they're good enough for him!'

'It's his own money he's spending, remember.'

'As though I'm likely to forget!'

'Are you going to carve?' Kirren asked.

'No, not me!' Riddler said. 'Not at sixpence a pound, I'm not! He paid for it, he can carve.'

Kirren, in exasperation, picked up the great dish of meat and put it down in front of Jim.

'I'm sorry about my father,' she said. 'He's always had this childish side.'

'Childish be damned!' Riddler said. He poured himself a mug of ale.

Jim picked up the carving-knife, sharpened it on the whet-stone, and tested the blade with his thumb. Then he picked up the carving-fork and began carving the joint.

'Nice thick slices for me,' Riddler said, 'and plenty of fat off the outside.'

These joints of meat, as Jim knew, had to be brought home by Kirren, along with all the other provisions, which meant a six-mile walk in all, sometimes in pouring rain. She would go in to the Wednesday market, carrying a heavy load of produce, and return almost as heavily laden with the week's shopping. As this caused him some concern he would, in the early days, walk down to meet her at Abbot's Lyall and carry her baskets the last two miles home.

Kirren was astonished – she had never been helped before – and because she was unused to it, she was inclined to be ungracious.

'You're wasting good working-time, trailing out here like this. I can manage perfectly well. I always have done, up to now.'

Riddler was even more astonished. He was also amused.

'Kirrie, you've married a gentleman! How are you going to live up to that?'

'We shall see if he stays a gentleman when he's lived here with you for a year or two.'

'One thing we may be sure of at least – he won't make a lady out of *you*.'

'Nobody asked him to!' Kirren said.

102

'It's her own fault she has to go to the town,' Riddler said. 'We used to have the higgler here, buying her butter and eggs and such, but she turned against him and stopped him coming. But you don't need to fuss over her. She's a good strong girl. She can manage a couple of baskets all right.'

'Yes, I daresay,' Jim said. 'But I don't intend that she should for much longer. I'm going to buy her a pony and trap.'

'God Almighty!' Riddler said. 'We shall end up at auction after all if you go on spending at this rate.'

'I don't need a pony and trap,' Kirren said, frowning at Jim. 'I'd sooner you hung on to your money in case of unforeseen trouble ahead.'

'What I spend on a pony and trap will not break us, I promise you.'

The trap was bought at a farm sale: rather old and shabby, perhaps, with its dark blue panelwork blistered and crazed, but sound enough in all other respects; and with it a docile Welsh pony called Griff, said to be eight years old but in fact nearer ten, Jim judged.

'Pot-bellied brute, isn't he?' Riddler said critically.

'He won't be, though, when he's properly fed.'

'I hope he understands English,' said Kirren, offering the pony a lump of sugar, 'because I don't speak any Welsh.'

The pony ate the lump of sugar and nuzzled her apron in search of more. She gave him a second lump from her pocket, then stroked his bristly, mottled nose.

'He understands sugar, anyway,' she said, and turned with a little smile towards Jim, who was standing nearby, watching her.

Riddler was also watching her and because it was such a rare thing to see her smiling in this way, with a faint flush of colour in her cheeks, he could not allow it to go unremarked.

'Why, Kirrie, what a difference it makes to see you looking pleased with yourself. It's something I haven't seen for years.'

'No, well,' Kirren said, 'it isn't every day of the week that you get given a pony and trap.'

'Seems you're like all the rest of them, then, if a man's got to dip into his pocket before he can get a smile out of you.'

'I didn't have to dip very deep,' Jim said, 'for the whole turn-out, harness and all, only cost me four pounds.'

'Oh, is that all?' Riddler said, affecting a grandiloquent tone. 'And four pounds, as we all know, is nothing to a man like you!' Then, in his normal voice, he spoke to Kirren again. 'But I must say it's worth every penny to see you smiling like that. You should do it more often. You should, that's a fact.'

'What for?' she said. 'To please you men?'

'There, that's gratitude for you, by damn!'

'And why should I be grateful to you?'

'Because, if I hadn't found you a soft husband, he wouldn't have bought you a pony and trap.' Riddler, pleased with his own logic, turned and walked away from them, saying in a loud voice as he went: 'A pony and trap, by God! – just to take a few paltry eggs and a bit of butter to town every week. Seems the chap's got more money than sense!'

Kirren, blank-faced, watched him go. 'He doesn't seem to realize that oftentimes in the past the money I've earned from my "few paltry eggs" has kept us out of the County Court.'

'I daresay he does realize it, but it wouldn't be an easy thing to admit, for a man with his pride.'

'Pride!' Kirren said scornfully. 'And what has he got to be proud of, pray, when he came within inches of losing this farm and then was only saved by you?'

'Your father's a fighter,' Jim said. 'Not clever, not wise, I grant you that, but a stubborn fighter through and through. It's always been a wonder to me that he managed to hang on as long as he did.'

'It seems you admire him,' Kirren said.

'Is that so strange?' Jim asked.

'To me, yes, it is very strange. But then, I've lived with him all my life. I know him better than you ever can.'

'You so often speak of him like that, and yet you have stuck by him all these years.'

'What else could I have done? Left him here all alone to drink himself into the grave? Turned my back on the place, knowing the Suttons would filch it from him? This farm is my home, such as it is, and I certainly wasn't going to let it go so long as I still had breath in me!'

'All of which goes to show that, whatever you may say about him, you're your father's daughter after all.'

'Am I indeed?'

'I would say so, yes.'

'Well, I can hardly be blamed for that!'

Kirren turned to the pony again and after a moment Jim spoke of the trap.

'Have you ever driven before?'

'No, never.'

'Then you'd better have some practice,' he said.

A little while later Kirren was driving round the farm and Jim, beside her in the trap, was giving such advice as was needed in making the awkward double turn that led past the linhay and down the pitch. As they drove down the steep rutted lane and out onto the open track they were watched from the Middle Field where Lovell and Smith were at work together digging out the lower ditch.

'I reckon they make a handsome couple, don't you, Bob?' said Nahum Smith, leaning on his trenching-spade.

'Handsome enough,' Lovell agreed.

'I must say it came as a winger to me when Miss Kirren upped and got married like that. Somehow I never thought she would. But she's done pretty well for herself, marrying a chap like Jim Lundy, even if she was second choice as they say.'

'It's the farm he's married, not the girl, and if she has done well for herself, so has he, seeing he'll get the whole lot in the end. He's a fly young chap, our new master, for sure, and knows which side his bread is buttered?'

'As long as he goes on paying me eight shillings a week, he can be as fly as he likes,' said Smith, 'and damned good luck to him all the way.'

Kirren, now that she had her trap, could drive in to town in comfort and was glad of it, for the quantity of produce she took with her was growing all the time. There were six cows milking at Godsakes these days and six more were due to calve at intervals between Christmas and May. She had butter and cheese to sell again now and as there was more poultry on the farm – geese and ducks as well as hens – she also had many more eggs, often two baskets full every week.

Riddler scorned using the trap and even in the worst weather rode in to town on his grey pony mare who, as he said to Jim, could be trusted to bring him safely home even when, 'as happened sometimes,' he had had a glass or two more than was wise. But Jim, if he had business in town, often drove in with Kirren, partly because it suited him to and partly because he somehow felt that he and she, being husband and wife, ought to be seen together sometimes.

He never spoke of this to her. For one thing the feeling was much too vague and, as he told himself, rather absurd. Everyone in the district knew that theirs was not a marriage of love; that it was a cold-blooded partnership entered into for practical reasons; and it was nothing to him or to her that people knew this much about them. Why, then, did he have this desire to be seen now and then in public with her? It was, he concluded after a while, because he wished the world to see that, cold-blooded partnership though it was, he and she were well satisfied with it.

One market day when they went in to town and were on the many-gated road between Abbot's Lyall and Marychurch, they had a brief meeting with Philip and Jane Sutton who, driving a smart four-in-hand, came up behind them at Cooper's Bridge. Jim had got down to open the gate so that Kirren could drive through and he was about to close it again when the four-in-hand came bowling along. He saw at once who was in it and held the gate open for them, giving a little formal nod as they slowed down, crossing the bridge, and passed within a few inches of him. Jane, who was closest, smiled at him, somewhat hesitantly at first, then with a sudden radiance, and as she passed she spoke to him.

'Thank you, Jim. That was very kind.'

Philip drove past without a glance, staring ahead, red-faced and tight-lipped, and his angry annoyance was made worse when Jane again turned her head to nod and say good morning to Kirren, who had drawn in onto the verge.

'Damn it, why do you speak to them, Jim Lundy especially? He only opened the gate for us because he wanted to annoy.'

'Then why give him the satisfaction of seeing that he had succeeded?' Jane said.

Jim returned to his place beside Kirren and they drove on along the road, both of them silent for a time, watching the carriage in front as it rapidly drew away from them. Then Kirren spoke.

'So that is the famous Jane Sutton? I've never seen her close-to before.'

'You certainly saw her close-to today. She stared at you hard enough as she passed.'

'She was probably wondering what sort of creature you had married.'

'Yes,' he said curtly, 'I daresay she was.'

His mind was still full of Jane's smile; full of the memories it had evoked; and dwelling on these memories brought a kind of painful pleasure very difficult to renounce. But with an effort he purged himself, bringing his thoughts back to the present; back to the girl sitting beside him; and, turning to look at her, he said:

'Sometimes I wonder that myself.'

'What sort of creature you've married?'

'Yes.'

'Surely you must know that by now, having lived with me these three months or more.'

'I know you as cook and housekeeper, yes. As dairywoman and rearer of hens; as an extra milker when called upon . . .'

'In other words,' Kirren said, 'you know me as an all-round drudge.'

'You certainly work very hard.'

'So do we all. We have no choice. We are slaves to the farm, all three of us, bound to it body and soul.'

'Do you resent that?' he asked.

Kirren, considering, gave a shrug. 'I used to, in the old days, when everything seemed so hopeless,' she said. 'When it seemed as though we should lose the farm however hard we worked to keep it. But that's all changed now, since you came. It isn't hopeless any more and I don't mind hard work so long as I see some reward at the end of it.'

'What reward?' Jim asked.

'To keep the farm, of course,' she said, 'and get it running properly.'

'It that reward enough for you?'

'What more would I want? Do *you* want more?'

'It's different for me,' Jim said. 'Work is a man's whole life but women, from what I know of them, ask for something more than that.'

'What am I supposed to want? A house full of servants to order about? Statues and paintings from Italy? A spinette to play on in the evenings?'

'I hope you don't want those things because I shall never be able to give them to you.'

'You may rest easy,' Kirren said, 'for the sum total of my ambitions, for today at least, is to get a shilling a pound for my butter and eightpence a dozen for my eggs.'

Jim smiled. 'And what about the future?' he asked. 'There must be things you would like to have.'

'Yes, there are, but I look to my poultry to pay for them, and as I've gone without them for so long, I can easily wait a while longer yet.' She gave him a brief sideways glance and said: 'I am not like your Jane Sutton. I'm prepared to work for what I want.'

No, he thought, as they drove on, Kirren was not like Jane. Indeed the contrast between the two young women – the one he had loved and the one he had married – could not have been greater. And as always when he dwelt on this contrast between them it was with the same angry elation that he had felt at snatching Godsakes away from the Suttons. It seemed peculiarly right, somehow, that whereas Jane was fair and blue-eyed, with gentle manners and a bright, easy smile, Kirren should be dark-haired and dark-eyed, with a temper that, more often than not, moved between sullen reserve and a quick, dark, withering scorn.

Kirren's life, from the age of six, had been made up of

hardship in all its forms. It had toughened her and made her strong, physically and mentally, and now at the age of twenty-two she had no softness or gentleness; no charm of manner; no feminine grace.

Jim took grim pleasure in this because Jane possessed these qualities and he had been led astray by them. That would not happen again; not with the girl he called his wife; for he expected nothing from her and therefore could never be disappointed. And although they had made certain vows in church, strictly as a formality, in private the only vow they had made was to work together for the good of the farm. Nothing else mattered to them. Only Godsakes, first and last.

Sometimes when Jim was working down in the meadows he would pause and look up at the farm and note the improvements made so far. They could be seen plainly from there, the three ploughed fields that were still bare showing up a rich red-brown between other fields already sown, where the winter corn was like a green mist creeping softly over the soil, and the new leys, a darker green, were already growing thick and close. Even the old neglected grasslands, grazed in turn by cattle and sheep, looked a healthier colour now, and where the hedges had been cut, the fields looked very trim and neat: larger, more open, more full of light.

'Are you pleased with what you see?' Riddler asked once.

'Yes, I am well pleased,' Jim said.

'So am I,' Riddler said, and for once he spoke simply and quietly, looking up at Godsakes with a bright, steady, satisfied gaze.

But the changes Jim had made so far were only a beginning: the first moves in a programme of improvement worked out to the last rod, pole, or perch; and the implementation of his plans would, he thought, take five or six years. He kept careful notes of everything that was done on the farm and often on cold winter evenings, beside the fire with Riddler and Kirren, he would discuss his plans with them.

'In five or six years, if all goes well, every acre we possess

109

will have been cleaned and put in good heart again, yielding the best quality crops, supporting the best quality stock. I hope to start work on the buildings soon – I've ordered timber and tiles for the roofs – and next year we'll need to extend the byre. I also intend to build new stalls for fattening steers in wintertime, modern stalls built on modern lines, and in time everything on the farm – the house, the buildings, the land itself – will be in tip-top order.'

'In other words,' Kirren said, 'you want to make it a place like Peele.'

'No! Like itself!' he said sharply. 'It must have been a good place once, and it will be again, I shall see to that.'

'We shall all see to it,' Riddler said. 'But go on with what you were saying. I like to hear these ideas of yours.'

'I mean to have every inch of land producing its maximum yield,' Jim said, 'but exactly what that yield may be only time will tell.'

'If you're talking about corn, I can tell you the maximum yield on this farm – twenty bushels of barley to the acre and fifteen or sixteen of wheat. Not very good, I know, but if you were to sow twice as much as you are, that'd make up for the low yield and with corn prices holding up so well we'd make a small fortune next harvest-time.'

'The corn we grow on this land will not fetch the prices you're thinking of. Not till fertility's been restored. And that will only come about if we stock the land to capacity. All of which means growing crops we can feed directly to the stock. Turnips, kale, vetches, rape, carrots and beans. . . kohl-rabi, perhaps. And dredge-corn fed to them in the sheaf.'

'At present you're *buying* feed for them.' 'I don't see any profit in that. There's plenty of grass here, if nothing else, until we get our own arables. And as for this notion of feeding the ewes –'

'Ewes should always be given extra, coming up to tupping time, just as they get extra again shortly before they are due to lamb.'

'Chopped up dainty and fed by hand?'

'Chopped up, certainly,' Jim agreed.

'And what about the tups themselves? Don't they deserve an extra feed? Spinach, perhaps, or asparagus? Something sweet and tasty like that?'

Just as Riddler jeered at Jim on the subject of artificial manures, calling him 'Old Potassium', so too did he jeer when Jim quoted from certain pamphlets published by The Royal Agricultural Society.

'You can't learn farming out of books!'

'I didn't, I learnt it on the land. But books are written by men, remember − men who have tried things out for themselves − and it's only common sense that we should be willing to learn from them.'

Riddler picked up a small book that Jim had left lying about.

'This isn't one of your famous pamphlets?'

'No, that's something different,' Jim said.

'Shall I learn to suck eggs from it?'

'If you can read Latin, yes.'

'Latin! Good God!' Riddler exclaimed, and, opening the little book, he stared at the printed page in disgust. 'Lawyers' language! The language of rogues! *Damnum absque injuria*! Is that what your damned book is about?'

'No, it's a poem about farming, written by a man called Virgil who lived and farmed in Italy about two thousand years ago.'

'Two thousand years? You're codding me!'

'No, I'm not, I promise you.'

'Read us a bit,' Riddler said, tossing the book across to him. 'In English, so's we understand.'

Jim found a suitable passage, studied it for a moment or two, and then rendered it aloud in English:

' "*There comes a time when the corn is blighted; when thistles spring up everywhere; when no crops grow but wild tares and wild oats, beggar-weed and spiky caltrops. You must, therefore, wage war on the weeds unceasingly; cut down the trees that darken your land; shout the birds away from your crops and, in the summer, pray for rain. Otherwise, though your neighbour's granary be full, you will have to shake the acorns from the oak to stay your own hunger.*" '

Jim, as he closed the book and put it away, found that both

Kirren and Riddler had been listening to him as he read, and that both were looking at him intently, Riddler lounging in his chair, Kirren sitting erect in hers, with her needlework idle in her lap. After a moment Riddler spoke.

'You chose well, didn't you, reading that bit to us?' he said. 'It might have been Godsakes he was writing about, except that we never came so low that we had to eat acorns to keep alive.'

'No, just reisty bacon, that's all.'

Riddler threw back his head and laughed. He enjoyed these exchanges he had with Jim. And, although he continued to mock, he was more than a little impressed by Jim's superior learning.

'Kirrie, you've not only married a gentleman but a Latin scholar into the bargain. What do you think of that, eh?'

Kirren, resuming her needlework, snipped off a new length of cotton.

'I must try not to let it go to my head.'

Chapter Eight

During the worst winter frosts, when all work on the land was stopped, Jim worked on the house instead, replacing tiles that had slid from the roof, repairing ill-fitting doors, and repainting the big kitchen, which was also their living-room. He then began work on the outbuildings, putting new roofs on the sheds, laying new cobblestone floors, and whitewashing all the interiors. With help from Riddler and the other men the most urgent work was done in three weeks, and by then the frosts had gone, making field-work possible again.

'The rest of the house will have to wait,' Jim said to Kirren. 'I'm afraid it may be a long time before we get everything put to rights.'

'It doesn't matter,' Kirren said. 'The farm must come first, I'm aware of that.'

At least now the kitchen was fresh and clean, with its ceiling and walls distempered white and its oak timbers stained dark brown, and Kirren, cheered and encouraged by this, was adding improvements of her own. She had made new curtains, for one thing, and these, of a thick baize-like material in a pattern of rusty reds and browns, gave the room a look of warmth. She was often buying new things now that the poultry money was hers to spend as she pleased, and gradually the big room was becoming more homely and comfortable. There was new brown-and-white china on the dresser now, and a new set of earthenware jugs, brown-glazed outside, pale yellow within, eight of them in different sizes, standing on a shelf of their own.

One day, having been in to town alone, she returned wearing a new dress of dark green worsted, ribbed in black,

113

with a double cape of the same stuff, and a black beaver hat with a curled brim. It happened that as she drove into the yard, Riddler and Jim were standing there, and both men stopped talking to stare at her as she drew up. Riddler was deeply impressed by his daughter's new outfit and hurried forward to help her down, a thing he never did as a rule.

'Why, Kirrie, I hardly recognized you, all dressed up to the nines like that! I thought it was some fine lady or other coming to call on us out of the blue.' And as he helped her down from the trap, he looked her over from top to toe. 'Lord, I'm struck all of a heap,' he said. 'I'd no idea you had it in you to look so very handsome.'

Kirren, with a satirical glance, extricated her hand from his and turned to take something from the trap. It was a large rectangular parcel, bulkily wrapped in paper and sacking, and she handled it with great care.

'What've you got there?' Riddler asked.

'You'll see when we get indoors,' she said.

Jim now went to the trap and took out the two heavy baskets of shopping. Riddler touched him on the arm.

'What do you think of your wife's finery?'

'I think pretty much the same as you.'

'Would you say she looked stylish, now?'

'Yes, I would, most certainly. Stylish and elegant, I would say.'

'Do you know,' Riddler said, as they followed Kirren into the house, 'I never noticed until today what a fine handsome figure she'd got on her.'

'Hadn't you?'

'No, I had not, and I reckon it must be the cut of the skirts and the way they flare out from the waist like that.'

'Fine feathers,' Jim said.

'Right so,' Riddler agreed. 'Still, she must've caused quite a stir, going about the town like that, looking so stylish and elegant.'

Kirren, although she had coloured a little, bore their comments with composure, walking before them into the house, the bulky parcel clasped in her arms.

'Whatever stir I caused in the town was nothing to the stir I seem to be causing here at home.'

'Well, open your parcel, girl,' Riddler said, 'and let us see what it is you've bought.'

What Kirren had bought was a pendulum clock, old but in excellent working order, in a case of polished mahogany, and with an engraved brass face bearing the maker's name, John Smith, and the words *Tempus Fugit.*

'That's one bit of Latin I *do* know, and it speaks the truth,' Riddler said.

Jim hung the clock on the wall straight away. He wound up the heavy weights, set the brass pendulum swinging, and cautiously turned the single hand, waiting at every half-turn while the clock struck, then setting it to the correct hour.

'Nice to have a clock in the place again,' Riddler said approvingly. 'This room is beginning to look very nice, with all the bits and pieces you've bought. More cheerful, like. More homely and kind.'

'And not before time,' Kirren said.

'How much did you pay for the clock?'

'Why, what business is that of yours?'

'I was just thinking to myself that if ever we fall on hard times again, at least we'll have something worthwhile to sell when we need some ready cash, eh?'

Kirren's face flushed darkly. 'You will not sell that clock,' she said, speaking with angry emphasis, 'nor any of the other things in this room, because *I* bought them and they are *mine* and you had better remember that!'

'God Almighty!' Riddler said. 'Can't you take a joke, girl?'

'It is no joke to me,' Kirren said, 'that you've stripped the house bare over the years.'

'I couldn't help but sell those things! I needed the money to pay the bills!'

'And how much of it went on drink?'

'Dammit, I've had enough of this! I'll take myself off outside and make myself useful there, looking after *your* pony for you and putting *your* trap away in the shed!'

Riddler went out, slamming the door, and Kirren, her

temper not yet spent, began gathering up the sheets of brown wrapping-paper, smoothing them out and folding them with quick, angry movements of her hands. Jim turned towards the door but paused a moment and looked back at her.

'It was only a joke, after all. Surely you must know that.'

'Oh, I know it well enough,' Kirren said, putting the paper away in a drawer, 'but I've never cared for my father's jokes and I doubt if I shall learn to now.'

Anger was always close to the surface in all Kirren's dealings with her father and it was easy to see why. The man was so rough and insensitive; everything he did was clumsy, ill-judged, often to the point of brutishness.

One morning in early March a polecat got in among the poultry and the noise and commotion were such that Jim and Riddler, who were in the barn, ran out to the yard immediately, followed in a moment by Kirren herself, who came hurrying out of the house. The polecat, laying about him in murderous fashion, took fright when the two men shouted at him and quickly made off, leaving behind him, on the ground, the mangled remains of three pullets, one of which still shuddered and twitched.

Riddler, bawling at the top of his voice, threw a stone at the fleeing polecat and then, still cursing and swearing, picked up the three mangled pullets and ran with them to the pig-run, hurling them over to the pigs who gathered at once to gobble them up. As he came lumbering back again, wiping his hands on his corduroys, Kirren confronted him in a rage.

'Why did you do that?' she cried. 'One of those pullets wasn't properly dead!'

'Well, it will be by now!' Riddler said. 'The old sow has made sure of that.'

Kirren, with a little exclamation, walked quickly away from him. Her face, Jim saw, was stiff with disgust. Riddler stood scowling after her, but when he turned and met Jim's glance, it was with a certain sheepishness.

'Women!' he said defensively, as they walked back to the

116

barn together. 'The damned bird was torn to shreds. Its head was half hanging off! So what was I supposed to do? Get the doctor out to it?'

'You should have wrung its neck,' Jim said, 'quickly, in the proper way.'

'What difference does it make? Either way, it ends up dead!'

'Women are sensitive about such things.'

'Too damned sensitive if you ask me.'

'Would you have them be hard as nails?'

'Oh, Kirrie can be hard enough when she likes.'

'Yes, well, she's had a hard life.'

'And what about me?' Riddler said. 'Haven't I had a hard life, keeping from going under all these years?'

'Yes, but it's different for you,' Jim said. 'You're a man. You can choose what you do. And you chose to stay put and fight for your farm, although you knew it meant hardship and poverty and possible failure at the end. But Kirren's a girl. She had no choice. And there can't have been much joy in her life, slaving away here with you for the past sixteen years or so.'

'You're just talking flannel, boy. Of course us men decide what to do, and if wives and daughters are what they should be, they're grateful to us for doing it. As for the joy in Kirren's life, it's up to you to give her that, and the sooner you get around to it the better because then perhaps she'll have something to do besides making a damned fuss over two or three bloody fowls!'

Riddler strode into the barn, seized the handle of the turnip-cutter, and began turning it vigorously, resuming the work that had been interrupted by the commotion in the yard. Jim followed him into the barn and stood watching him as he worked.

'In answer to what you've just said to me I feel I really must point out – '

'God, what a meal men make of things when they've had a good schooling!' Riddler said.

'You know the terms of my marriage to Kirren. You should do, since it was all your idea. A business arrangement, nothing more. That was what we agreed between us.'

'Yes, yes!' Riddler said, grunting as he turned the machine. 'But that was all of six months ago. I thought you'd have seen some sense by now.'

'You mean you expected things to change?'

'Of course I expected things to change! You're a man, aren't you, not an oddmedod? Flesh and blood like the rest of us? The same needs as other men?' Riddler stopped working and stood erect, breathing loudly and heavily. 'You're not still hankering after that girl who went and married Philip Sutton, are you?'

'No. I am not. But there's still no question of any change in my relationship with Kirren.'

'Oh, you'll come round to it in the end, sooner or later, you mark my words. You wouldn't be human otherwise. A man needs a woman to be a proper wife to him. It's only natural and right. And as for Kirren, well, I know she's got queer ideas about marriage and men, but she'll get over that in time, especially if you manage her right. I'm as sure of that as I am of death. A fine healthy chap like you, and a girl like her, built as she is! You're bound to come to it in the end. But don't take too damned long over it. I want to see a few children running about on this farm before I go to join my own wife under the sod in the churchyard.'

Riddler now took up a shovel and began shovelling the cut turnips into a wheelbarrow. Jim watched him, half vexed, half amused.

'Have you ever spoken to Kirren about these ideas of yours?'

'Why? D'you think I should?'

'No, I do not,' Jim said. 'I think you should put it clean out of your mind, for nothing will ever come of it.'

Riddler, still shovelling, shot him a glance.

'Yes, well, we shall see,' he said.

Under the brisk March winds, which blew hard and cold along the valley, the land was drying out nicely, and Jim, preparing for his first batch of lambs, chose a field known as the Browse, which lay up behind the house and was sheltered from the

118

north by a belt of trees. The fifty ewes now folded here were those he had brought with him from Peele. They were due to start lambing in a few days' time.

Jim had placed shallow troughs in this field and into them the ewes' extra feed, so much oilcake and so much pulped turnip, was carefully measured twice every day. He had set up three hurdle pens and had scattered plenty of straw in them and here and there about the field he had placed a number of straw bundles, each securely tied with twine, so that the ewes, and their lambs when they came, would have warm 'cooches' as Abelard called them, against which to shelter from wind and rain.

Riddler, as was only to be expected, viewed these preparations with amusement.

'What about warming-pans?' he asked.

But this would be the first crop of lambs to be born at Godsakes for many years and now that the time was drawing close he was struck with a kind of anxious excitement, as though he could scarcely believe in these lambs that Jim took so for granted and talked of in such a glib way.

'I was never keen on sheep myself, and I only ever kept a few, even in the old days. They seemed more trouble than they were worth and I never had the patience for fussing and fiddling over them. But you're a different case altogether. You've got the patience of Job himself. And it shows in your flock. They're just about as pretty a bunch as any you'd see in all Gloucestershire. I'm proud to have such sheep on my farm. I am, that's a fact.'

'I'm quite proud of them myself.'

Jim was beginning the work of clatting. He had a ewe between his knees and was trimming away the soiled wool from under the tail and around the udder.

'I'll help you with that if you like,' Riddler said.

'No, there's no need. I can manage all right.'

'Won't let me near your precious ewes, not with a pair of clippers, eh?'

'You admit you lack patience with them.'

'And what about when the lambs start to come? Will you let me help you then?'

'Well, I've got Billy Smith coming to help with the lambing. He's a good boy with sheep. He's got the makings of a good shepherd.'

'And I haven't, you mean to say?'

'I think you've left it a bit late.'

'Cheeky devil!' Riddler said.

This early lambing went well and was all over in three weeks. The fifty ewes produced sixty-four lambs and of these sixty-two were raised. One ewe died giving birth to twins and these were kept in a pen in the barn, where Kirren tended them during the day, giving them milk from a newly calved cow. The twin lambs were sickly and delicate; so small that when she fed them she held them easily under one arm, letting them suck in turn at the bottle, on which she had fixed a washleather teat.

Riddler was very well pleased with the results of this early lambing but he disapproved of Kirren's efforts to rear the two orphaned lambs.

'It's nothing but a waste of time, rearing lambs by hand,' he said. 'Even if they pull through, they never amount to anything much.'

'What would you have me do with them? Throw them to the pigs?' Kirren said.

'Christ Almighty!' Riddler said. 'Am I never going to be let to forget what I did with those damned fowls of yours?'

He went off, muttering, and ten minutes later was mounting his mare out in the yard. It was a Friday and he was going in to the town to draw money from the bank for paying the men's wages next day. As he rode across the yard Kirren came out of the barn and he shouted over his shoulder at her.

'If I bring you back three pullets in place of the three the polecat took, shall I get a bit of peace at last?'

'I don't want your pullets,' Kirren said.

'Well, you'll get them whether you like it or not, and be damned to you for a nagging bitch!'

He was gone all day and when he returned after dark he was very drunk. He rode right up to the back porch and hammered on the door with his fist and when Kirren, who was alone in the house, reluctantly went out to him, he leant forward in the

120

saddle and dropped a closed basket at her feet. As promised, he had brought her three pullets.

In leaning so far forward, however, he lost his balance and pitch-rolled head over heels to the ground, bringing his saddlebags down with him. A faint sound came from his lips, half chuckle, half groan, and he made some effort to scramble up. But the effort proved too much for him; he gave another feeble groan, rolled himself over onto his back, and lay stretched, out insensible.

It was not the first time that Kirren had had to take charge of the mare, removing saddle and bridle, cleaning her and feeding her and bedding her down for the night. Nor was it the first time that Riddler had slept out in the yard, with a folded sack under his head and a horse-blanket thrown over him. Kirren performed these rough ministrations almost without a second thought. She then went to the poultry yard and put the three pullets into a coop, scattering a little grain for them and putting water for them to drink. By the time she returned, Jim had come in from the sheep-fold and was standing over Riddler's body. He had a lantern in his hand.

'He's pretty far gone.'

'Yes,' Kirren said.

'You surely don't mean to leave him like this?'

'Yes, I do. He's used to it.'

'Lying out on these cobblestones, on a fresh night like this, when it may well rain?'

'It's never worried him in the past. If it had he would surely have taken care to see that it didn't happen again.'

'He's not often as drunk as this.'

'Often enough,' Kirren said.

She picked up her father's saddlebags, heavy with the bags of coin he had drawn from the bank that day, and went indoors. She slung the saddlebags into a cupboard. It was past nine o'clock and she began preparing for bed, making up the fire for the night by heaping wood-ashes over it, and filling the kettle on the hook.

While she was doing this, Jim came pushing in at the door, carrying her father's limp body head downwards over his shoulder. 'I'm taking him up to his bed,' he said.

He crossed the kitchen to the opposite door and went out into the hall; she heard his tread on the creaking stairs; then in the bedroom overhead. She reached up to the mantel-piece, took down her candle in its holder, and lit it at the oil-lamp at the table. She stood waiting for Jim to come down, and the moment he entered the room she said:

'Perhaps you think *I* should have carried him up to bed?'

'No, I do not. But I think you could have done something more than leave him lying out in the yard.'

'That was where he chose to fall.'

'You are very hard on him.'

'Yes, I daresay.'

'He is your father,' Jim said. 'Your own flesh and blood. Don't you care anything for him at all?'

'No, why should I?' Kirren said. 'He's never cared anything for me.'

'I don't know how you can say that.'

'I know him better than you do. I've lived with him all my life. He's never been able to forgive me because I pulled through the flu years ago and my brother did not.'

'I'm sure that's not true.'

'I heard him say it,' Kirren said. 'I was out there in the yard and my mother and father were in the barn. "Why did it have to be the boy that died?" That's what he said. I heard it plain.'

'Did he say that?' Jim was shocked. 'That was a terrible thing to say.'

'Terrible? Yes, perhaps. But it's only what I felt myself. That if we had had the power to choose I would far rather my father had died than my brother Eddy who was only twelve and was always so quiet and gentle and kind. But we cannot choose. We have to accept. And that's what my father couldn't do. Oh, I realize it's not his fault that he cares nothing for me, but it's not my fault, either, that I care nothing for him.'

'What you overheard him say – people do say cruel things in moments of stress, things they don't really mean at all. I can understand how you've felt all these years, after hearing him say that, but I think you should try to forgive him now, if only for your own sake. It's wrong to store up bitterness.'

'Yes, well,' Kirren said, 'you should know about that, shouldn't you?'

For a moment Jim was taken aback. He had not expected such a counterstroke.

'That is scarcely the same thing. And I wasn't talking about myself. I was talking about you.'

'Yes, it's always easier dwelling on other people's faults. It helps you to overlook your own. But what was it that brought you here if it wasn't bitterness against the Suttons? Why did you make up your mind to stop them getting their hands on this farm if it wasn't to have your revenge on them?'

Jim was silent, staring at her. What she said was perfectly true and there was no denying it. But it was not the whole truth and, try as he would when he answered her, he could not prevent some sense of pique from betraying itself in his tone.

'You choose to overlook the fact that part of my reason for coming here was to help your father keep the farm.'

'It was part of your reason, perhaps, but not the whole. But you don't have to justify yourself to me because your coming here was the best thing that ever happened to us and the reasons behind it don't matter one jot. What you are doing on this farm profits us all equally.'

'I'm glad you can find it in your heart to give me some credit at least for doing good.'

'Is credit so important to you?'

'I am only human, after all.'

'A moment ago you were lecturing me for my lack of daughterly tenderness towards my father out in the yard. But at least I covered him with a rug. Perhaps you will give me credit for that.'

'If I did lecture you, I have been repaid in full,' Jim said.

'It seems we are quits together then, so I'll take myself off to bed before we begin wrangling again.'

The atmosphere had eased between them. There was humour in the glance they exchanged. But afterwards, when she had gone and he stood for a while alone in the kitchen, he was filled with an irksome restlessness; a sense of something left unresolved.

*

At five o'clock the following morning he was out in the lambing-pen, attending to his ewes and lambs, and as he went to and fro, he found himself brooding more and more on what Kirren had said to him about his bitterness against the Suttons.

Why it should so vex his mind he could not at first understand. The events that had led to his leaving Peele had indeed caused great bitterness in him, and that bitterness had prompted him to avenge himself on the Suttons. Furthermore, as he had to admit, he still felt immense satisfaction at having taken Godsakes from them. It was so right in every way. There was justice in it, as Riddler said. And Jim felt the same fierce elation now that he had felt at the very beginning. So why, when the fruits of his revenge were still sweet and satisfying to him, should he feel irked by what Kirren had said?

Slowly he realized that it was because the element of revenge was no longer of prime importance. He had been at Godsakes more than six months now and during the latter part of that time he had scarcely thought of the Suttons at all. He had been too busy; too absorbed. And he now saw, with great clarity, that what he was doing at Godsakes had become more important to him than his original reason for doing it – important for its own sake; important because it was good in itself.

This realization gave him a jolt of pleasure; a feeling of wholeness; a sense of release. And as he deliberately let his thoughts dwell on the Suttons – on the treatment he had received at their hands; on the way he had vented his spite on them by snatching Godsakes from their grasp – his feelings became clearer still, his pleasure more and more profound. The satisfaction was still there – he knew he would feel that all his life – but the bitterness and spite were gone.

With this discovery fresh in his mind he returned to the house. It was now half past six and Kirren was laying the table ready for breakfast. Jim was glad to find her alone and he came to the point immediately, wanting to get it off his mind before Riddler came in from milking.

'I've been thinking over what you said, about my feeling bitter against the Suttons.'

Kirren stood looking at him in surprise.

'It seems to worry you,' she said.

'Yes, because it's not quite true.'

'You still want to make me believe that you only came here to help us out of pure Christian charity and goodness of heart?'

'No, I've never pretended that. I came here, as I said at the time, because I wanted to spite the Suttons. But what I am saying now is that I no longer feel the bitterness you charged me with last night.'

'You mean you've forgiven them?' Kirren said, with barely perceptible mockery.

'I don't think,' Jim said, 'that I would put it quite like that.'

'But you do perhaps regret what you've done and would now turn us out of the farm so that your old friends the Suttons can have it after all?'

'I can see you're determined to make fun of me instead of listening to what I say.'

'I am listening now. With all my ears.'

'Are you indeed?'

'Indeed, I am.'

There was a pause. She looked at him. But her assumption of earnestness did not deceive him for one moment. He knew it was not intended to.

'It isn't easy, talking to you, when you so plainly think me a hypocrite.'

'Does it matter what I think? I told you last night that you don't have to justify yourself to me, but it seems you are determined to do so.'

'No. I just want you to understand.'

'You want me to think well of you.'

'I didn't say that.'

'It's true all the same.'

'Very well, supposing it is? Am I so different from anyone else? Don't you want to be well thought of yourself?'

'By you, do you mean?'

'By anyone.'

'Being well thought of,' Kirren said, 'is something I've had to do without, whereas you, being a man, take it for granted as your right.'

'You think me conceited, then,' Jim said, 'and altogether too full of myself.'

'You are no worse than other men. You have at least got something to be conceited about. You do at least get things done.'

'I've been a lot luckier than some. Luckier than your father, for instance.'

'You are always defending him. I don't know why that should be, I'm sure, when he talks to you the way he does, jeering at everything you do, even when he knows you're right.'

'I try not to let that worry me because I understand how he feels. I know how I should feel, myself, if I were in his shoes and had a stranger coming in, telling me how to run my farm.'

'You are certainly very patient with him. More patient than he deserves.'

'Your father is rough and careless, I know, and you have suffered at his hands. But he minds about you, in his way. I'm absolutely sure of that.'

'In his way? Yes, perhaps.'

'You are all he's got left in the world – of his own flesh and blood, that is.'

'So he's reminded me many times, and therein lies my importance to him. I'm all there is left of the old stock and he is hoping to breed from me.'

'*What?*'

'Have I shocked you, speaking so plain?' Kirren's dark gaze was amused. There was mockery in her tone again. 'I'm sorry, but I've lived so long with my father, the language of the farmyard comes easy to me.'

'It's not the language,' Jim said. 'It's the fact that you seem to have known all along what was in your father's mind.'

'That is never difficult. His mind is like an open book. When he suggested a business marriage, he thought it would turn into something else. I could see that as clear as glass.'

'And I,' Jim said wryly, 'saw nothing at all.'

'But no doubt he's spoken about it since.'

'Yes, a few weeks ago. How did you know?'

'He was bound to speak of it sooner or later. And, you may as well be warned, he's bound to speak of it again.'

'You don't have to worry about it,' Jim said. 'You have nothing to fear from me.'

'I know that,' she said steadily.

'I told your father, in positive terms, that he was to put it out of his mind.'

'Good advice, so long as he takes it. But he won't, of course.' And after a short pause she said, 'You never really finished saying whatever it was you were trying to say when you first came in.'

'You wouldn't let me,' he said with a smile. 'You thought I was making heavy weather of it and you were probably quite right. But what I was trying to say was this – that what I felt about the Suttons doesn't matter any more. At least, not in the same way. What I am doing on this farm is more worthwhile than anything else I could ever have done with my life and that matters more to me than simply having my revenge. Or, to put it another way, the fact that I no longer hate the Suttons somehow makes my revenge complete.'

He went outside to wash at the pump, and Kirren, as she prepared the breakfast, heard him talking to her father in the yard. After a while Riddler came in. He stood at one side of the hearth, watching her as she swung out the hook and hung the frying-pan over the fire.

'Somebody put me to bed last night.'

'Yes, I know.'

'Seems I've got a better son-in-law than I have daughter,' he said.

'By that same token,' Kirren replied, 'I've got a better husband than I have father.'

'I don't see that that follows at all.'

'At least he doesn't come home drunk.'

'Did you bring my saddlebags in?'

'Yes, they're in the cupboard there.'

'And what about the fowls I brought you? Did you see after them?'

'I shut them up last night and this morning I let them out with the rest.'

'Don't I get any thanks for them?'

'I'll thank you when they begin to lay.'

'And when will that be?' Riddler asked.

'It will never be, I'm afraid.'

'Why, what the devil's wrong with them?'

'They are all cockerels,' Kirren said.

Chapter Nine

Soon the second and larger batch of ewes began lambing and again, because of the dry conditions, all went well. These hundred ewes produced a hundred and thirty lambs and of these a hundred and twenty-six were raised, so that the lamb harvest altogether numbered a hundred and eighty-eight, including the orphans fostered by Kirren.

By early May, too, the six heifers bought in the autumn had all calved successfully, and were milking well, which meant so much more work for Kirren that Willie Townsend's wife Prue came every day to help in the dairy. They were making a good deal of butter and cheese at Godsakes now and much of the surplus buttermilk went to fatten the barrow pigs which, penned on a new piece of land every few days or so, were clearing the ground of rough grass and weeds, as well as enriching it with their dung, ready for ploughing at the end of the year.

The farm was teeming with life these days. The old silent fields had been transformed and on all sides there was movement and noise. In the evenings, especially, the gentle clamour of the ewes and lambs constantly calling to one another was heard from one end of the farm to the other, and, indeed, all over the valley.

'I hope *they* can hear it,' Riddler would say, jerking his head towards Peele. 'I hope it damn well pleases them that that handsome flock of theirs, bleating away over there, has got company here to answer them back.'

The farm was so heavily stocked now that towards the end of May Jim was glad to be able to turn his flock out onto the hills, thus giving the home pastures a rest and a chance to grow a fresh green bite. And all through May and part of June, in those fields that had been ploughed and harrowed and cleaned and rolled, and harrowed again to a fine tilth, the teams went steadily to and fro, drilling in the turnip seed, the rape and the kale, the chickling vetches, the peas and beans and French sainfoin. One half of the old winter pig-ground was sown broadcast with rye and the other with 'seeds' and so soft and moist was the weather just then that both crops were greening the ground within a mere eight or nine days.

On a warm sunny day in late June, Jim brought his flock down from the hill; onto the meadowland by the brook, where the ewes were separated from the lambs and herded into a long pen that led steeply down to the edge of the washpool. The upper sluice had been opened wide, the lower one almost closed, and as soon as the ewes were all penned, Jim and his helper, Billy Smith, lowered themselves into the pool, into water that reached to their very armpits. Riddler, in the pen with the sheep, seized one in his great clumsy hands and swung it over into the pool, where Jim in turn took hold of it, dunking it three or four times in the water before sending it down to Billy, who guided it onto the stone-paved slip that led up through a gap in the bank and out onto the open meadow.

Each ewe, as she struggled up to the top of the slip, stood for an instant dazed and drooping, weighed down by the water in her wool; but then, as the greater part drained from her, she would give herself a double shake that sent a little glistening shower rippling out from each side of her body. Another quick, rippling shake; a rainbow of droplets in the sun; and the ewe would move out over the meadow, giving a querulous, high-pitched cry that soon brought her lamb, or lambs, running to her with an answering cry; butting her with such eagerness that she was lifted off her feet, working away, pump and suck, at her cold, clean, watery udder.

This sheep-washing pool in the Timmy Brook had been dammed and banked many years before – as long ago, some said, as when the Benedictine monks had lived and farmed in this quiet valley – but the sluice-gates had been put in only a few years before by John Sutton, who at that time, was the only

130

farmer using the pool. Neither Jim nor Riddler, therefore, felt any great surprise when they looked up from their work to find that they were being watched from the other side of the brook by two men on horseback. One, Jim saw at a glance, was Philip Sutton, and the other, he could easily guess, was Dick Bowcott, who had taken his place as bailiff at Peele. They sat their horses, talking together, and some way behind them, under an oak tree, Abelard leant on his shepherding stick, his dogs lying peacefully at his feet.

'Aye, you can watch!' Riddler muttered, as he flung a ewe into the pool. 'And think what thoughts you damn well please!'

He and Jim and Billy Smith went on working without pause but after a while the man Bowcott, obviously acting on Philip's orders, rode across the meadow to the pool's edge.

'How long are you going to be? Our shepherd is waiting to use this pool.'

'It's a damned funny thing,' Riddler said, 'that you should want to use the pool just when we are using it.'

'From what I've been told,' Bowcott said, 'you haven't used this pool for years.'

'Well, we're using it now,' Riddler said, 'and your shepherd will just have to wait his turn.'

Bowcott, plainly disliking his errand, could find nothing more to say, and Philip Sutton, perceiving this, now rode to the edge of the pool, there to look down with angry contempt, first at Jim, in the water, then at Riddler, on the opposite bank.

'You Godsakes people have no business to be using this pool at all, seeing that we put these sluice-gates in without a penny piece from you.'

'Sluice-gates or no sluice-gates, it's all as one to me,' Riddler said. 'The rights of washing our sheep in this pool are written into the deeds of my farm, just the same as they are in yours, and if you think you can stop us using it, you're an even bigger fool than I thought.'

'*Your* farm, did I hear you say?' Philip, defeated in argument, hit back at Riddler with a sneer. 'All things considered it seems to me that the farm is more Lundy's than it is yours.'

131

Riddler looked at him evenly.

'At least it'll never be yours,' he said.

'As to that, we shall see!' Philip said. 'There's many a slip between cup and lip and you've got a long way to go yet before you've paid off that mortgage of yours.'

He and Bowcott rode away. Riddler stood looking down at Jim.

'I don't know which I hate most, John Sutton or his son.'

'Take no notice of Philip's threats. He'll never take the farm from us.'

'No, he won't,' Riddler said, 'because if there was any chance of it, I should damn well kill him first.'

The sheep washing was resumed, but after a while they paused again to let the dirty water out and refill the pool with clean. While this was going on old Abelard came and spoke to Jim.

'That there fuss of Mr Philip's — I didn't have no part of it.'

'I didn't think you had,' Jim said.

'That's all right, then,' Abelard said. 'Just thought I'd mention it, that's all.'

As soon as the washing and shearing of the sheep were done with, it was time for haymaking in the meadows, and as soon as the hay had been carted and stacked, it was time for the weaning of the lambs. The ewes were put into poor pasture so that their milk should slowly dry off and the lambs were put into a field as far from them as the farm would allow so that neither ewes nor lambs should be distressed by the other's cries.

At the end of July came the summer sheep sales at Dunton Payne and here Jim's lambs were sold, together with a number of draft ewes, for a total of four hundred pounds. Riddler was up on stilts at this. He could scarcely believe his ears. That sheep from his farm should fetch such a sum! But Jim was already well known at the many local sheep sales, and, as the auctioneer remarked, so was his stock.

'My Lundy's Cotswolds need no introduction here,

gentlemen, and the interesting circumstance that he now farms at Godsakes instead of Peele has not, as you can see for yourselves, occasioned any decline whatever in the quality of his flock.'

'Why the hell should it?' Riddler muttered, but he was pleased nevertheless by the auctioneer's remark, and later that day, as he and Jim rode home together, he said: 'It's a pity the Suttons weren't there today to see your lambs fetch four hundred pounds, because there's not much chance of our losing the farm so long as we can raise stock that fetch prices like that, eh?'

'Are you still frightened of losing the farm?'

Riddler shrugged. 'I was thinking of what Philip Sutton said down at the washpool a few weeks ago, that showed he's still hoping to see us fail.'

'Philip has always believed,' Jim said, 'that he has only to want something and it will surely come to pass.'

'Sometimes it does, doesn't it, as when he took your girl from you?'

'Yes, well, sometimes it does. But Godsakes is another matter. Philip will never take that from me.'

'She can't have been much of a mucher, that girl, judging by the way she treated you.' Riddler glanced at Jim's face. 'Seems to me you're a lot better off married to my Kirrie,' he said.

'In the circumstances, yes, I am.'

'Damn the circumstances,' Riddler said.

'They are of your making, remember.'

'I thought to have seen you unmake them by now.'

'So you said to me once before.'

'Dammit, what've you got in your veins? Beetroot juice instead of blood? Or is Kirrie so unattractive to you that you can't bear the thought of bedding her?'

'I have no intention of discussing Kirren with you in this manner, now or at any time in the future, and you may as well make up your mind to it.'

'Strait-laced devil, aren't you, by God?'

'If you say so, certainly.'

133

'You're a lot different from what I was at your age.'

'That I can easily believe.'

'D'you want to know what I think?'

'No,' Jim said.

'I think you'll come to it in the end.'

'That, too, you have said before. But if by any chance you are right – '

'Yes?' Riddler said, with a keen, bright glance.

' – you may safely leave the matter in the lap of the gods and spare me all further importunings.'

'I suppose that's a gentleman's way of telling me to shut my mouth?'

'On this one subject, yes,' Jim said.

'Be damned to you, then,' Riddler said, and then, after another few minutes' ride, as they came within sight of The Crown at Marsh End: 'You can buy me a pint of ale for that and I'll drink to these precious gods of yours.'

Long before the day came round for paying their half-yearly mortgage dues Riddler wanted to pay off an extra portion of the principal sum.

'If we were to pay in the four hundred pounds we got for our lambs, that'd reduce the loan by more than half, and then it shouldn't be all that long before we can pay off the rest and be rid of it once and for all.'

Jim, however, would not agree.

'That four hundred pounds – and it's not all profit, remember – must go back into the farm, otherwise it will never improve. For one thing, we've got to buy more stock. For another, I want to build special tanks for dipping the sheep against the scab. Then there are the new sheds we need for stall-feeding steers in wintertime. And by the time we've done all that – '

'I know, I know!' Riddler said. 'There'll be precious little left and I shall be just as I have been for years – still with that blasted mortgage tied like a millstone round my neck.'

'So long as the farm is doing well, the mortgage dues needn't

134

worry us. They amount to little more now than the rent you paid in the old days when you were just a tenant here. But if we let the farm go down again – '

'Yes, well, you're right, of course. I can see it all clearly enough. But somehow, so long as that mortgage is there, sucking the blood out of us, I can't really feel that the farm is mine. And sometimes I get the feeling that I shan't live long enough to see the damned thing paid off at last.'

'Oh, yes, you will,' Jim said. 'It's only another four years and four months. Surely you can live that long?'

Riddler glared.

'I'll damn well have to, won't I?' he said.

It was a good summer that year, the soft, moist, misty spring, which had given the crops such a good start, being followed by dry spells in June and July, which enabled the horse-hoe to be used, clearing the weeds from between the rows and keeping the soil well-worked. And the crops, for the most part, were flourishing. Swedish turnips, sown in May, were bulging nicely in the ground by late July and were covered in a good growth of green sappy 'tops'. The rye, which was mown early in August, before it had time to go to seed, was soon growing tall again and would without doubt give another worthwhile crop in late September. The rape and the kale were doing well; so were most of the pulse crops, especially the long-pod beans; and, most beautiful of all, in Riddler's eyes, the eighteen acres of dredge-corn, oats and barley growing together, were ripening splendidly in the sun.

This was the first successful corn crop grown at Godsakes for ten years and Riddler could not keep away from it. He would visit the two adjoining fields two or three times a day, trying to estimate the yield, weighing a handful of grain from one against a handful from the other, his optimistic calculations rising higher every day. No oats ever danced so merrily, no barley ever bowed so low, as the oats and barley at Godsakes that year, and when the day came to begin cutting, Riddler was the first man in the field, wielding his scythe with such

135

strokes that the corn went down in front of him, h'ssh-h'ssh, h'ssh-h'ssh, as though laid low by a fierce rasping wind.

'Can't you keep up with me?' he roared, pausing once and looking back to where Jim and the other men worked together, in echelon, some little way behind.

'The question is, master,' said Willie Townsend, 'can you keep up with yourself?'

But although, indeed, as the morning progressed, Riddler was obliged to slacken his pace, he nevertheless worked in a fever all through that day, and the following days, until the last of the corn was cut.

'I may not be so clever as some, but at least I can use a scythe!' he said.

Behind the men, as they cut the corn, came the women and children, binding the sheaves. There was much chatter and laughter then, especially from Willie Townsend's wife, Prue, for she shared her husband's sense of fun and could make a joke out of anything. When the last sheaf was bound, Prue tied her red and white neckerchief round it, held it up for all to see, and finally placed it in Riddler's arms.

'There you are, master! There's the neck and my neckerchief round it. What'll you give me in return?'

Amidst a burst of applause from the watchers, loudest of all from Prue's own children, Riddler gave her a smacking kiss and pressed a coin into her hand. He then carried the 'neck' aloft and placed it on top of a nearby stook. A warm southeasterly wind was blowing slantways across the valley; the oatseeds dangled and danced in it and the red and white 'kerchief fluttered gaily, and all over the harvest field, the rows of stooks went marching away, in regular columns, up and down whichever way you turned and looked.

'One thing about it,' said Nahum Smith, looking across the valley at Peele, 'we shall get our harvest in before *them*.'

This was a sly joke on Smith's part, made at Riddler's expense, for against the eighteen acres of corn grown at Godsakes the acreage grown at Peele was immense. Field upon field of pale-ripening wheat, field upon field of bronze-ripening barley, glowed on the opposite slopes of the valley, and day after day, from morning to night, the reaping machines chackered and whirred, and swarms of dark figures were seen, moving busily to and fro, bent double, in the wake of the reaper, first in one cornfield, then in another. These swarming figures looked black, like ants, seen against the pallid corn, moving over the pallid stubble, and all day long like ants they toiled, under the fierce, blind-burning sun.

Riddler made no secret of the fact that he was jealous of the harvest at Peele. Corn at that time was the glory of England. It ripened, guinea-gold in the sun, and, on land such as that at Peele, which had been cultivated to a state of perfection, it meant golden guineas for those who grew it. Riddler, looking across the valley, would sometimes stand in a kind of trance, shaking his head now and then, as though not believing what he saw.

'Just look at it!' he would say. 'More and more corn every year! And prices, from what I hear, just as high as they've ever been!' And once, coming to Jim, he said: 'How many acres all in all do you think they're harvesting this year?'

'Counting Granger's,' Jim said, 'I would say a hundred and fifty of wheat and maybe a hundred or so of barley.'

'And what profit will they clear on that?'

'I would say upwards of three thousand pounds.'

'By God!' Riddler said, and made a sucking noise through his teeth. 'And all we've grown over here is a paltry eighteen acres of dredge corn for feeding to the stock!'

'You know as well as I do that we can't grow good quality corn on this farm until we've built up fertility and as fertility depends on stock – '

'Oh, spare me the lecture for once, will you?'

'Anyway, this is a smaller farm, and even in the long term, when fertility's been restored, it will always need to be managed by different methods from those at Peele, if we're to get the best out of it.'

'*Your* methods, needless to say!'

'That was what we agreed from the start.'

'Everlasting bloody sheep! That's your method, such as it is!'

'Sheep will be the making of this farm. They are already playing their part in founding our prosperity.'

'They'll never make us a fortune, though, will they, the way corn is doing for the Suttons?'

'I promised to make Godsakes pay. I didn't promise you miracles.'

'Didn't you?' Riddler said with a scowl. 'I should have thought the odd miracle was nothing to a man like you!'

Contemptible though their own harvest might be, compared with Peele's, Riddler could think of nothing else and when, in a few days' time, the corn was carted to the stackyard and built into two neat round stacks, his pleasure and pride in them knew no bounds. Not usually a tidy man, he fussed over these stacks for hours, and while Smith and Townsend were up above, thatching them, Riddler was busy down below, first patting the sheaf-ends in with a flat piece of wood and then, still not satisfied, trimming them with sheep-clipping shears until the stacks were neat all round.

As soon as the corn was gone from the fields, the sheep and the pigs were put in onto the stubbles, to feed on the fallen ears of grain and to dung the land ready for ploughing. The pigs, rooting about in the ground, cleaned it thoroughly of couch-grass and weeds and turned it over at the same time, and this too was pleasing to Riddler.

'There are nothing like pigs for turning over the land,' he said. 'They work it better than any plough.'

At the sheep sales towards the end of August, Jim bought fifty theaves to make up his flock and four new Cotswold rams, great sturdy beasts, three years old, with a rich golden bloom upon their wool.

'Pure-bred, every inch of them, and don't they know it!' Riddler said.

At the Missenham cattle sale soon afterwards Jim bought a four-year-old Shorthorn bull, a handsome blue roan, costing thirty pounds.

'I never thought to see the day when Godsakes would have its own bull, let alone a bull like him that's got a dash of blue blood in his veins.'

Riddler enjoyed attending the sales: the outing, the gossip, the company; but, more important than this, was the fact that he and Jim were there, not merely as spectators but as buyers bidding along with the best. After the bleak, empty years it was pure balm to him to hear the auctioneer bring down his hammer with the words, 'Sold to Messrs Riddler and Lundy of Godsakes Farm.' And if it happened that the Suttons were there, as they were at Missenham when the bull was bought, then Riddler's joy was complete.

John Sutton and his son, with their bailiff, Dick Bowcott, always ignored Riddler and Jim and carefully took no interest in any item for which Jim was bidding.

'It's a funny thing,' Riddler would say, 'but they don't seem to get the same pleasure from seeing us at the sales as I get from seeing them!'

He was always conscious of the Suttons. They had become an obsession with him. Whatever improvements were made at Godsakes, he knew that the Suttons were bound to see them, and his pleasure was doubled, even trebled, thereby. As more and more land came under the plough; as old crops were harvested, new ones sown; as cartloads of timber and quarried stone were delivered at Godsakes for building new sheds, he would jerk his thumb towards Peele and say: 'I hope the Suttons can see all this! See what we're doing, you and me!'

One morning at breakfast time when he made some remark about the Suttons, Kirren suddenly burst out at him, exasperated by his refrain.

'Can't we forget the Suttons?' she said. 'Can't we get on with living our lives and give their names a rest for a change?'

'It might be easy enough for you to forget the Suttons, my girl, but it's not for me. Oh dear me no! Not after what they did to me.'

'I have just as much reason to hate them as you. What they did to us years ago spoilt my life just as much as yours and helped my mother to an early grave. But we have nothing to

139

fear from them now and it seems to me only common sense — '

'Nothing to fear?' Riddler said. 'There will always be something to fear so long as this land has a mortgage on it and that'll be for a long while yet!'

He finished his breakfast and went out. Kirren was left alone with Jim.

'Is it right, what he says? Must we always live in fear so long as the mortgage hangs over us?'

'No, there's nothing to fear,' Jim said. 'Not so long as we pay our dues, and that will not be any problem, now that the farm is productive again.'

'Ought I to go more carefully, buying things for the house? The money I make on my poultry these days — '

'Whatever you make, that money is yours, and you may spend it as you please. And in case you are worried about the future, I have enough money put by to cover any calamities.'

He rose from the table and pushed in his chair. He stood for a moment looking at her. 'You do believe me?'

'Yes,' she said.

'And trust me?'

'Yes.'

'I hope you do. You've had too much worry over the years. I'd like to feel that I've changed all that. I'd like you to feel safe and secure. Of course there are bound to be hardships enough. We'll have our troubles, our setbacks, no doubt. But we'll keep the farm and we'll make it pay and neither the Suttons nor anyone else shall ever take it away from us.'

'It's a pity my father can't believe that.'

'He will come to believe it, given time.'

In mid September the green rye was mown. It was turned in the swath and 'made' like hay. The weather was very hot at that time and because there were thunderstorms in the offing, all hands were out in the field, setting the rye up into cocks. But the thunderstorms passed them by; the rye was carted and built into stacks; and all the time as the carting proceeded, the weather continued sunny and hot.

Kirren, who rarely wore a hat when working in the fields, had caught the sun. Her skin, always dusky, became deeply tanned, while her dark brown hair took a lighter hue, especially at her forehead and temples, where the loose curling strands were bleached golden fair. Riddler strongly disapproved of women exposing themselves to the sun. He viewed Kirren's tan with some distaste.

'Kirrie, my girl, you're too brown by half. Jim must think he has married a gipsy. You're as brown as a nutmeg. You should wear a hat.' And, turning towards Jim, he said: 'Just look at her, how brown she is! Can't you get her to wear a hat?'

'I'm not going to try,' Jim said. 'Kirren is a grown woman. She's her own mistress. She may do as she likes.'

'Huh!' Riddler muttered, turning away. 'It's a pity she's not *your* mistress!'

Jim had now been at Godsakes a year. Much had been done during that time. Much remained still to be done.

'You'll do it all right,' Riddler said, as they walked together over the farm one Sunday evening. 'You're young and you've got most of your life before you. How old are you now? Twenty-five? Yes, you're lucky, you've got time on your side. Though in certain respects I must say I wish you would show a bit more dispatch.' Receiving no response to this he suddenly burst out in a passion: 'Dammit, man, don't you want a son?'

Jim looked away over the fields. The question had caught him unawares. Yes, he would have liked a son. Every man wanted that. And when he had hoped to marry Jane, he had taken it for granted that he and she, living together in the old farmhouse at Peele, would have raised a healthy young family. But all his plans had gone astray and he had committed himself to a life in which love and the joys of fatherhood would never now have any part.

Riddler, easily guessing his thoughts, broke in on them in his rough, gruff way.

'It's no good dwelling on the past, you know, moping over what might have been. It's the future you've got to think about and you need to face up to it fair and square. Stand still a minute and look at this farm. When I'm dead it will be yours – you and Kirrie will carry it on – but what about when you and she come to die? What will happen to Godsakes then if you've got no sons to come after you? Who will you leave it to? Answer me that!'

'I can't answer it,' Jim said. 'But the future you are talking about is, I hope, a long way off and at present I have enough to do thinking of more immediate things.'

But although he dismissed the future in this way, reluctant to discuss it with Riddler, he found himself thinking about it all the same and often in the following days he was filled with a kind of restlessness. A strange kind of loneliness came over him, bringing back old memories; not only of Jane, who had jilted him, but of his uncle Albert, the drover, who had treated him brutally as a boy and had at last abandoned him, in a strange district, all alone, caring not what became of him. He felt sorry for himself, a feeling he had not known for years, and he took himself sternly to task for it, remembering that many good things had happened to him as well as bad. Still, the same thoughts and feelings persisted, touching him sometimes with melancholy, and he thought how very strange it was that he, who had never known a father, should be fated never to know a son.

Sometimes, as he worked in the fields, he would see Kirren in the distance, shooing hens from the barn, perhaps, or carrying skimmed milk to the pigs, and he would think to himself: 'That girl, that stranger, is my wife.' And the thought, framed in words like this, brought a sense of shock even now. A sense of amazement and disbelief. How, how, he asked himself, had he come to agree to such a marriage? And, for that matter, how had she?

She was not such a stranger now, of course, for he had lived in the same house with her for a whole year. In some respects he knew her well: he knew what her capabilities were; he knew something of her history; and he knew what to expect of her when her patience was tried, her temper roused. But what of her innermost feelings and thoughts? Her hopes and dreams? Her woman's heart? Was she so hard as she chose to appear? So unfeminine, so self-complete? Could she really be so indifferent to all ideas of love as to close her heart and mind against it so utterly?

He himself had experienced love and, disappointed in his hopes, he had turned against it. But Kirren had rejected it altogether. She wanted no part of it. It was something she scorned. But was such a thing possible? It seemed to him quite absurd that a young girl, in her early twenties, should choose celibacy as resolutely as any nun.

And why, asked a quiet voice in his brain, should Kirren's rejection of love be any more absurd than his? There was no answer to this, he thought, but an answer presented itself all the same: Kirren's rejection of love was absurd because she was a woman. Women were made to love and be loved. That was a fundamental truth. Anyone would say the same. And then he laughed, deriding himself, recognizing that he had been guilty of blatant male hypocrisy. Because, of course, it was man who chose woman's rôle for her, and man made the rules to suit himself; and if Kirren, for reasons he could well understand, chose to reject the whole scheme, why should it matter to him? It was none of his business, he told himself. It had, by a series of chance happenings, worked to his profit and advantage.

Still, he could not help wondering about her, and sometimes he wished they could talk together, quietly, just the two of them, without Riddler chipping in with his sly, provoking remarks. There were few opportunities for this but one day when he was up on the hill looking, for a bunch of sheep that had broken out of the upper pasture, he came upon her quite by chance, picking blackberries in a sunny hollow.

At first she was unconscious of him and he stood for a while watching her as she rose on tiptoe, with arms upstretched, trying to reach a high bramble that arched out from the centre of the thicket. It afforded him a certain amusement to watch her thus, all unknown, observing the slender shape of her body stretched to its uttermost, strong and lithe, as she reached up to the arching bramble. But then his two dogs, Jess and Sam, went running down the slope to her, wagging their tails, and she turned to make a fuss of them, giving each a few blackberries from one of her baskets, which was half full. Jim too went down the slope and when he got close to her he reached up with his shepherd's long stick and hooked the high bramble down to her. With a little laugh she picked the fruit and he let the bramble spring back again.

'Why are the best blackberries always out of reach?' she asked.

'What's out of reach always seems the best, whether it is or not,' he said.

He hooked down another high bramble and watched her pick the fruit from it. 'You've come a long way in search of these.'

'Yes. The farm hedges are so well kept since you came that there aren't any blackberries in them now.'

'The farm hedges are not so well kept as they should be, however, otherwise I shouldn't be here looking for five runaway sheep. You haven't seen them by any chance?'

'No, not a sign,' Kirren said.

'Ah, well, never mind. I shall catch up with them in the end.'

Jim laid his stick on the grass and motioned the dogs to lie down beside it. Kirren watched in surprise as he picked up the second of her baskets and began picking blackberries.

'I warn you, if you are seen doing that, it will lead to talk,' she said.

'Why?'

'Because it is women's work, of course.'

'You do men's work often enough, helping us in the fields,' he said.

'That's different. It's expected of us. But men do not help their womenfolk with such trivial tasks as this.'

'Then it seems I am not as other men.'

'No, that's true, you're not,' she said.

'Knowing your opinion of men in general, I suppose I may take that as kindly meant?'

'Yes,' she said, 'I suppose you may.'

It was a perfect September day and the blackberries, warm in the sun, filled the air with the smell of their ripeness. For a while Jim and Kirren picked in silence, moving slowly away from each other, around the thicket of bramble and briar. In a grove of hawthorn trees nearby a flight of goldfinches twittered and whirred and high overhead a skylark sang. The two dogs lay on the grass, alert yet relaxed, moving only to snap at the flies. Jim came to a bramble bush that grew no higher than his chest. Kirren was on the other side.

'I'm glad to have met you up here like this,' he said. 'It gives us the chance of a quiet talk. I was thinking about you as I came up the hill and it suddenly occurred to me that we have now been married a year.'

'Not quite a year, surely?' she said.

'Well, all but a week or two, anyway.'

'All but three weeks, to be precise. But surely, in a marriage like ours, we shall not be keeping anniversaries?'

'No, hardly that,' Jim agreed. 'It's just that it seemed a good time to be taking stock of ourselves as it were.'

'I'm not sure what you mean by that.'

'I suppose,' he said, thinking it out, 'I am looking for some sort of assurance that you do not have any regrets.'

'Then you have that assurance,' Kirren said. 'Our marriage suits me very well.'

'You are quite sure?'

'Yes. Quite sure.'

There was a pause. She looked at him.

'Have you any regrets yourself?'

'No. None.'

'Yet something is troubling you, I think.'

'I wouldn't say I was troubled exactly, but I have been looking back over the past and . . . thinking rather too much, perhaps, about certain aspects of my life.'

'You mean you've been thinking about Jane Sutton?'

'Yes.'

'Do you still love her?'

'No,' he said. He thought for a while before speaking

145

again. 'Love, as I see it, is a two-way thing. It's a kind of bargain that one human being strikes with another – or fails to strike, as the case might be. If love is one-sided, it doesn't last long.'

'Doesn't it?' Kirren said.

'Well, in very rare cases it might, I suppose . . . where the object is exceptionally worthy. But Jane was amusing herself with me, without any regard for my feelings, and that is not a worthy thing. However, I know I'm not the only man to have suffered such a blow to his pride, and I don't intend to let it spoil my life. We can most of us get along perfectly well without love – if we are called upon to do so.'

'It doesn't seem to bring much happiness to those who are afflicted with it.'

'We are better without it, you would say?'

'I thought that was what you were saying.'

'Yes, well, perhaps it was.'

For a while they gave their whole attention to the business of picking the blackberries. Then Jim spoke again.

'Certainly there's a lot to be said in favour of a marriage like ours, based as it is on a practical footing instead of on sentimental ideas. It means we do not ask impossible things of each other, and that, in turn, means that neither of us can fall from grace. The very fact that we have been married a year without any serious disagreement speaks very well for the arrangement, I think. Indeed, the only person who isn't pleased is your father, whose idea it was.'

'Ah, yes, my father,' Kirren said.

'We are a great disappointment to him.'

'He will get over that in time.'

'I'm not sure that he will,' Jim said.

'Then he must just put up with it.'

'Unfortunately for me, your father's disappointment is not something he keeps to himself, as you already know.'

'Yes, and I'm sorry,' Kirren said, 'but what can I do about it?'

'Nothing whatever, I'm afraid.'
'I think you bear it very well.'
'I have no choice,' he said ruefully.

Chapter Ten

The warm sunny weather continued right up to Michaelmas Day and then came a sudden change. The last of the autumn ploughing was done in a searing north-easterly wind and the winter corn was no sooner sown than it was lightly covered with snow. The snow did not lie long because rain came and washed it away and the rest of the autumn was so wet as to stop all further work on the land.

The wet weeks were not wasted, however, for Jim and the men were hard at work building the new cattle stalls that would house the steers for fattening in winter. Jim was keen on this system, not only because of the profit that winter-fed beasts would bring, but because of the saving of manure. The stalls, open along the front and built round three sides of a square yard, were finished by the end of November and twenty-two steers were housed in them. Jim then turned his attention to the farmhouse, doing all those repairs that had been left over from the previous winter.

If anyone entered the front door at Godsakes – which, as in many a similar farmhouse, was in fact a rare event – and stood in the wide passageway, a door on the left led into the kitchen and a door on the right, under the staircase, led into the only other ground-floor room, which Riddler called the house-place and Kirren the parlour. There was no furniture in this room – it had all gone to pay Riddler's debts – and for years the place had only been used for storing sacks of grain and meal and a great variety of lumber. But it was a fine, spacious room, half as long again as the kitchen, with two double casements at the front, overlooking the valley, and two single casements at the back, looking towards Hogden Hill; and, at the far end of the room, a fire-place with a big open hearth.

The lumber and sacks of grain were removed, the dirt and cobwebs were swept away, and the whole room was scrubbed throughout. Jim then got to work; repaired the cracks and holes in the plaster; whitewashed the ceiling, between the beams, and distempered the walls a pale shell-pink. The timberwork was all oak, including the plank-and-batten door, and this he treated with linseed oil. The casements were metal and he painted them white.

Kirren, meantime, had been busy shopping. She had bought three rolls of thick fibre matting which, laid on the stone-flagged floor, felt warm and kindly under the feet; also a dark red Wilton rug which made a cheerful splash of colour in front of the hearth. She had bought some second-hand furniture, too, which Jim fetched home in an open cart: a dining-table of dark oak, with four ladder-back dining-chairs; three Windsor armchairs, with flat cushions on the seats and backs, for sitting in comfort at the fire-side; and a book-case to hold Jim's books and Riddler's collection of almanacs. There was also a large, handsome lamp, which held a quart of oil at a time, and had on it a round shade of rich amber-coloured glass engraved with a pattern of ivy leaves. Lastly there were some heavy curtains, old but with plenty of wear in them, of crimson and gold brocade. Kirren had to alter these to fit the windows at Godsakes and with the material that was left over she covered the cushions on the Windsor chairs.

'Oh, it's a fine handsome room right enough.' Riddler said, 'if only we had time to sit in it.'

But in less than a week it was Christmas, which fell on a Sunday that year, and Riddler, in the middle of the morning, looking in at the door intending to scoff, stood on the threshold and marvelled instead. For the room, with a great log fire in the hearth, with red-berried holly on the beams over-head and sweet-scented pine-branches over the door, with the table arrayed in a white linen cloth on which the silver cutlery and the smoothly polished pewter mugs reflected the red glow of the fire, was a warm and welcoming place indeed to a man coming in from feeding the beasts on a winter morning, cold and raw.

'It does you credit, Kirrie,' he said, 'and I only wish your mother was here to see the place made so homely again.' He was much impressed by the cutlery – 'You must be making a pretty penny out of your poultry and eggs these days' – and by the three white linen napkins which lay, each in its horn ring, on the side-plates of brown-and-white cottage ware. 'I'd no idea you had it in you to be so genteel,' he said. 'I must go and spruce myself up before I'm fit for a room like this.' And later that day, after a dinner of roast goose, followed by a rich dark plum pudding, served with thick cream, he said: 'Kirrie, I reckon you've done us proud! I doubt if they've had a better Christmas dinner at Peele than the one you've given us today. You're as good a cook as your mother was and I can't speak better of you than that.'

He and Jim went to sit by the fire and when Kirren had gone from the room, leaving them to their hot spiced wine, he sat back in his armchair and looked around him appreciatively.

'It's good to see the old place coming back to life again. You and Kirrie between you have made it into a proper home. All it needs now to make it complete is a few children sitting here, gathered round the fire with us, and all of us playing "Robin's Alight".'

Jim remained stubbornly silent, staring into the heart of the fire, his mug of spiced wine between his hands. Riddler, watching him, gave a sigh.

'Ah, well!' he said, sadly. 'You can't stop an old man from dreaming his dreams.'

The parlour was used every Sunday after that. It became a regular thing and Riddler teased Kirren about it.

'You're getting ideas above your station, my girl. It comes of marrying a gentleman.'

The mockery was automatic. He was in fact well pleased with the improvements Kirren had made. And gradually certain changes were taking place in Riddler himself. He was now shaving regularly and was taking more trouble with his clothes. His boots and gaiters were well-polished, his breeches and jacket brushed clean, and he had bought himself a new hat. Jim and Kirren, although they noted the change in him, said nothing to Riddler himself, but Kirren mentioned it to Jim.

'My father's a different man these days. He's not so slovenly in his habits and he goes off to town now looking quite smart. He's easier to live with than he was. All of which is due to you, because of the way you've pulled up this farm. You've given him back his self-respect. He's able to hold up his head again.'

'Your father has always held up his head, even in the bad times, and so have you,' Jim said.

'You can't refuse,' Kirren said, 'to take the credit for saving the farm, because that would be too absurd.'

'There was a time when you seemed to think I was taking too much credit for it.'

'Did I say that?'

'Well, not in so many words, perhaps. But you had a few sharp things to say about my motives for doing it.'

'Your motives are neither here nor there. They've faded away into the past. It's what you've done that matters to us.'

'Yes, it's what matters to me as well.'

The new year came in cold and wet and although there was nothing surprising in this it was, as it turned out, setting the pattern for the rest of the year. Some ploughing was done in the upper fields, where the land was light and well-drained, but by the beginning of February the heavy unrelenting rain had turned the whole farm to mire. Down in the valley the Timmy Brook flooded the meadows for weeks on end. The little bridges were all submerged and when Kirren drove to town, she had to go round by Marychurch and cross the river at Lyall Bridge.

Even in the wet weather, there was always plenty of work to be done, for the dark winter days were all too short. Horses were taken to be reshod by the blacksmith at Angle Green; plough-coulters went for sharpening; traces went to be repaired; and while the horses were out of the way the stables were given an extra good clean and then white-washed. Every bit of harness was oiled; all tackle checked and repaired. Waggons were varnished; axles greased; every tool and implement cleaned and sharpened, as need be, or given a smart new coat of paint.

Still the rain came teeming down, keeping the men off the land, and still Jim found things for them to do. He set them to whitewash the inside of every outbuilding on the farm; all the sheds, both new and old; the pig-sties, the hen-coops, the privvies, the barns; and 'even the damned cart-shed!' Nahum Smith said in disgust.

'What are you complaining about?' Willie Townsend said to him. 'Would you sooner the master laid us off?'

The bad weather saw them into the spring. Even March brought little relief. There were a few dry days towards the middle of the month but then, just as the first batch of lambs were due, the rain descended yet again, cold and heavy, out of the north.

The lambing went badly from the start and although Jim took extra care, providing all the shelter he could and spreading the lambing-pens with straw, conditions were so wet and cold that many ewes, in giving birth, were too enfeebled to play their part.

'That's the trouble with sheep,' Riddler said. 'They give in too easy. They've got no spunk.'

He and Jim and Billy Smith were out at all hours, attending the ewes in their labour, rubbing life into weak, sickly lambs, and doing their best to get them to suck. But in spite of their vigilance and care, a great many lambs were lost to them, and, in time, a number of ewes.

'Ah, what's the use!' Riddler said, as he added yet another corpse to the heap already awaiting disposal. 'That's how it's always been on this farm – just when you think

152

things are picking up, whoosh, and you get slammed down again!'

Kirren, bringing hot food and drink to the men at work in the lambing-field, saw the heap of small dead bodies lying sodden and limp in the rain and turned away, sick at heart.

'How many have you lost?' she asked, as Jim came to take the food-basket from her.

'So far, more than half,' he said.

His expression was bleak, reflecting her own, and he looked at her with tired eyes. But it was not the work that had tired him; it was because so much of the work had been in vain; and Kirren, who knew what his flock meant to him, was stricken anew.

'So many?'

'Yes, it's bad.'

She looked past him, up the field. A number of ewes, who had yet to lamb, were grazing in a desultory way, each with its rump to the rain and the wind. A few others, with their lambs, lay in the shelter of the hurdle pens.'

'What about the live lambs? Will they pull through all right?' she asked.

'I hope so, but it's hard to tell. A lot depends on the weather. If it goes on like this – ' He gave a shrug. ' – we are bound to lose a few more, I'm afraid.'

Riddler came stamping down the field, impatient for his dinner. He had heard Jim's last words and was cocking an eyebrow at the sky.

'It's no good looking for a change,' he said. 'This rain will be with us till Kingdom Come. I can feel it in my chines.'

It was the cold and the wet together that did so much damage in the flock. A ewe could easily stand the cold if only she had a dry resting-place and a lamb, too, could withstand the cold so long as its birth-coat had a chance to dry out. But the rain that spring showed no mercy and ewes that would not lie down on wet ground remained on their feet until exhausted. Thus, many lambs were stillborn, and others, already weak at birth, died within a matter of hours.

Still, miraculously, there were survivors, most of them lambs from older ewes. Some of these, both the lambs and the ewes, needed special care and attention, and every available shelter had been brought into use as a nursery. There were also a few orphan lambs, kept in a separate pen in the barn, and it was Kirren who looked after these, warming cow's milk for them, carefully diluted with water, and giving it to them from a bottle. She also tended two ewes suffering from garget, washing their inflamed udders, rubbing them gently, morning and evening, with the elder ointment Jim gave her, and, when their condition improved, persuading them to accept their lambs.

Kirren was good with animals. Nothing was too much trouble for her. And Jim, noting her gentleness whenever she handled a sickly lamb or patiently coaxed an awkward ewe, was not only grateful for her help but deeply moved by her concern for the dumb creatures in her care. The animals themselves sensed her concern. They responded to her and trusted her.

And with all this, Kirren still managed her other duties. The dairywork was done just the same; the chickens were fed and the eggs collected; the housework, the washing, the weekly baking, were all accomplished as usual. If the men were out at night with the flock, she would come to them with hot food and drink, and every morning, by five o'clock, she was sure to be in the kitchen, with a good fire burning on the hearth, the kettle steaming over it, and breakfast already on the go.

'When do you sleep?' Jim asked her once.

'When do *you*?' Kirren retorted.

One cold dark morning when she was giving her father his breakfast Jim came into the kitchen and, partially opening the front of his jacket, showed her a new-born lamb which he was carrying inside; a lamb so incredibly small that Kirren had to peer close before she could believe it was there and make out its shape in the jacket's folds.

'Oh, how tiny!' she exclaimed, and put out a hand gingerly, to touch its coat of tight, close curls. 'I've never seen such a tiny lamb. It's scarcely so big my two hands.'

154

'He's one of twins,' Jim said. 'The ewe has turned her back on him – she hasn't enough milk for both – and he's only just barely alive. Can you look after him indoors? Keep him warm here by the fire?'

'Yes, of course,' Kirren said.

'Have you got something to put him in? A basket or a box of some kind?'

'Yes, I'll find something suitable. Just leave it to me.'

All her attention was on the lamb; she wanted to take possession of it; and Jim, opening his jacket further, eased it carefully into her hands. It was the merest morsel of life, all head and ears, its frail body nothing at all, its long legs limp and knobbly, like the legs of a rag doll. Kirren folded it into her arms and it nestled against her, wearily, its head lying against her bosom, moving against her, seeking her warmth, until, with a little sudden thrust, it buried its nose under her armpit and rested there, with a little sigh.

'It must be the smallest lamb ever born,' she said. 'I've never seen such a scrap of a thing.'

'He's spoiling your pinafore,' Jim said. 'I haven't properly cleaned him up.'

'Never mind. I'll see to that. The most important thing right now is to get some warm milk into him.'

'I'll leave it to you, then.'

'Yes,' she said.

Riddler, at the table, now put in a word.

'It's nothing but a waste of time raising lambs by hand. A waste of time and energy.'

'He always says that,' Kirren said. 'He said it last year, just the same.'

'He's probably right about this one,' Jim said. 'I doubt very much if it will survive.'

'Then why have you brought him in to me?'

'I wanted him to have his chance.'

'Exactly,' she said. 'And so he shall. His little heart seems strong enough. I can feel it thumping against my hand.'

'Well, we shall see,' Jim said, and touched the lamb's head

where it lay on her breast, still with its muzzle tucked under her arm. 'If you can manage to pull him through the first two or three days or so . . .'

'I can but try.'

'Yes, that's right.'

Jim turned towards the door. Kirren, frowning, called to him:

'Aren't you staying to have your breakfast?'

'No, I've got to get back to the pens. I'll be in again in about half an hour.'

Riddler, sitting longer than usual over his own breakfast, watched with a mixture of interest and scorn as Kirren dealt with the new-born lamb, bedding it down in a shallow box lined with hay, and placing it to one side of the hearth, where it received the warmth of the fire but not its full heat. She then took some diluted warm milk, stirred a little sugar into it, and added two or three drops of brandy. She put the milk into a drinking-bottle and, crouching down beside the lamb, tried to insert the washleather teat between its tightly clamped little jaws.

This proving difficult, she smeared a few drops of the milk on his lips, gently persevering with him until at last he opened his mouth and licked the milk with his small pink tongue. When she had done this a number of times she was able to persuade the lamb to receive the teat into his mouth. There was a faint snuffling noise as he blew through nostrils not quite clean; a gulping sound as his small throat worked; and, in a moment, quietness, meaning that he had learnt to suck. And at the end of the small wrinkled body lying curled in the box, a wispy tail waggled and twitched.

Riddler had finished his breakfast now. He rose from the table and pushed in his chair.

'It's high time you had a lamb of your own,' he said in a deep-throated growl, and pushed past her to get at his coat which was hanging up by the fire-place.

Kirren was silent, feeding the lamb, and he stood looking down at her broodingly.

'Did you hear what I said?'

'Yes, I heard.'

'Then why in God's name don't you answer me?'

'Because I don't know what answer to make.'

'I just don't understand you at all. You're a woman, aren't you? You're not made of stone? And you've been married a good eighteen months – '

'Married at your instigation, remember, as a business arrangement, nothing more. That's what you said to us at the time, and that's what we agreed, Jim and me.'

'But damn it, girl, you must have known that I had something more in mind?'

He humped himself into his coat and fastened the buttons up to the neck. The lamb had had enough for its first drink and Kirren now rose to her feet, the half-empty bottle in her hands.

'Yes, I knew what was in your mind, but it wasn't in my mind, nor in Jim's.'

'More fool you, then!' Riddler said. 'And more fool him too!'

'More fool all three of us, it would seem.'

'I thought I'd done pretty well by you, finding you a husband like Jim, a well-set-up chap, healthy and strong, with something more about him than most.'

Kirren became silent again, turning away from him to the hearth, where she placed the lamb's bottle on a ledge to keep warm. Then she removed her soiled pinafore, laid it over the back of a chair, and went to take a clean one from the drawer of the dresser. She put the loop over her neck and tied the strings behind her back. She smoothed the pinafore down in front.

'Hell and damnation!' Riddler exclaimed. 'Jim is a handsome enough chap, I'd have thought! Not that looks account for much, but you women set some store by them, especially when it's a case of a chap with clean blue eyes and light fairish hair. Of course, he's got his faults, I allow. He's a pig-headed devil for a start – '

157

'Hark who's talking!' Kirren said.

' – and inclined to think he's always right.'

'So he is, more often than not.'

'Seems you think pretty well of him, then?'

'I have good reason to think well of him and so have you. Without him we should have lost the farm.'

'I'm not talking about the farm.'

'I know quite well what you're talking about.'

'He thinks well of you, anyway. That much is obvious, I should have thought. You can tell by the way he talks to you, the way he treats you so civilly, the way he helps you at every turn.'

'Jim treats me the way he does because he happens to be that kind of man.'

'A gentleman?'

'Yes, I suppose.

'I reckon there's more to it than that.'

'Do you indeed?'

'Yes, I do. He feels something for you, Kirrie, I'm sure. Why, the way he looks at you sometimes – '

'And what way is that?' Kirren asked, in a tone crisp-edged with disbelief.

'It's the way any man will look at a girl, so long as she's comely enough and young, with a face and figure worth looking at. And with Jim being the man he is – '

'You are making all this up. I have never seen Jim looking at me in the way you are talking about.

'You wouldn't, would you?' Riddler said. 'He would take good care of that, just in case of offending you and making you think he'd gone back on his word. He knows your views on marriage and men. You made all that pretty clear from the start. And a young man of Jim's sort needs some sign from a girl, first, before he'll come out in the open with her. Remember, he's been hurt once before and he wouldn't want to risk that again, so it's up to you to encourage him and let him know you've changed your mind.'

'I didn't say I'd changed my mind.'

'Then what the hell did you say?' Riddler exclaimed, his patience giving way to wrath.

'Nothing that's worth saying again.'

'I wish I could get you to talk sense sometimes.'

'And I wish *you* would leave me alone!'

Abruptly Kirren moved to the table and began clearing the used breakfast things. Riddler, swearing under his breath, took his hat from the fire-place and jammed it down hard on his head.

'Stupid cat of a girl!' he muttered, and went out, slamming the door.

Within a few hours of being brought indoors the lamb, thoroughly warmed through, had left his bed beside the fire and was exploring the kitchen, tottering over the flagged floor on legs that were apt to crumple beneath him. In a matter of three or four days, although his legs might still let him down, he was able to right himself without help, and would follow Kirren constantly while she went about her chores. Fed every three hours or so, both night and day, he was slowly picking up strength, beginning to take a lively interest in everything that happened around him.

'He's doing nicely,' Jim said. 'You've pulled him through the most difficult time. He's got it in him to thrive from now on.'

'Do you think he will?'

'I'm sure of it.'

The early lambing came to an end, having lasted fifteen days. Of the seventy-six lambs born, only forty-two had survived, and, with the weather still bad, a few more of these might still be lost. Of the sixty ewes that had lambed, five had died, and another eight or nine would be useless for future breeding.

Anyway, it was over now, until the second lambing began. Life for Jim would be less of a strain during the next three or four weeks and he would be able to sleep in his bed instead of snatching an hour at a time in a chair by the kitchen fire.

On the morning that the last two ewes had lambed he came into the kitchen at ten o'clock when Riddler had just ridden off to town and Kirren was about to begin her baking. As she moved between cupboard and table, setting out the things she would need, the hand-reared lamb, now eight days old, followed her faithfully to and fro, still uncertain on his legs but showing a bright, adventurous spirit.

When Jim entered the room the lamb scampered towards him, put up his chin to be fondled and scratched, and then, with a little flouncing movement, went lolloping over to his bed. It was occupied by a tortoiseshell cat expecting kittens who had that morning chosen it as a suitable place for her lying-in. As the playful lamb nuzzled her body she put out a slow, lazy paw, pushing against his woolly face with just a slight suggestion of claws, sharp enough to make him draw back. He veered away from her to the hearth and peered into a shallow basket wherein crouched a bedraggled hen, surrounded by a number of chicks, all of which Kirren had rescued from a flooded ditch in the home pasture.

'It seems there's almost as much livestock indoors as there is out,' Jim remarked. He stood looking down at the lamb. 'I've come to take this chap off your hands. I think I've got a mother for him. It's the ewe I've just left – her lamb was stillborn.'

'Can I come and watch?'

'Yes, of course.'

They went together through the rain, across the yard to the open barn, Kirren with a shawl over her head, the lamb tucked under her arm. Inside the barn, as they crossed the threshold, there was a gentle surge of warmth; a warmth that was all the more grateful because of the greyness of the day and the steadily falling rain outside. The warm barn smelt of the penned sheep and lambs; of the straw trampled under their feet; of the sweet dry hay in the hay-bags that Jim had tied all along the pens.

He led the way across the barn to a pen against the far wall. In it stood the bereaved ewe, she who had lost her lamb that morning, her rump still red from the birth, her attitude listless and dejected. But her tight-stretched udder was full of milk and she would make a good mother to the hand-reared lamb if she could be persuaded to accept it.

Jim opened the front hurdle a few inches and entered the pen. From his pocket he took a bottle containing balsam of aniseed. He got astride the ewe from behind, uncorked the bottle with his teeth, and poured some of the strong-smelling oil into the palm of his left hand. Kirren, still carrying the lamb, stood close by watching him and he gave her the bottle to hold. He then began rubbing the oil under the ewe's chin and jaws and all round the outer rims of her nostrils. Protesting a little, she tried to break free, but Jim had her wedged between his legs, one hand firmly under her chin, and in less than two minutes the job was done. Satisfied, he let her go, and she moved away, shaking herself. He took the lamb from Kirren's arms, rubbed a little of the oil on its hindquarters, and set it down on the floor of the pen.

Although the pen was quite small, the ewe did not see the lamb at first. She was busy moving her head up and down as though trying to escape the smell of the all-pervasive aniseed. But when the lamb began to bleat she turned and stared at it in surprise, in a way that seemed quite clearly to say: 'Where did you come from? You are not mine. Or, are you?' Jim put the lamb closer to her and she leant towards it, suspiciously, sniffing it without touching it.

But her sense of smell was badly impaired by the strong smell of aniseed; the lamb had the same smell, anyway; and in another moment or two, although still plainly mystified, she had stepped forward and was sniffing him close, working her way down his back with a nibbling movement of her lips, as though she meant to eat his wool. The lamb gave a short, rippling shudder and turned towards her, butting her side. Jim guided him to a teat and as soon as he began to suck, so his tail began to twirl. The ewe, looking over her shoulder at him, viewed the movement indulgently, giving a little whickering cry, quietly, deep in her throat. Ewe and lamb, so it seemed, were very well pleased with one another.

Jim emerged from the pen and lifted the hurdle back into place. Kirren gave him the bottle of oil and he put the cork back into it. They stood together watching the lamb as it pumped with increasing confidence at the ewe's swollen milk-bag.

'He'll be all right now,' Jim said. 'They both will. She's a good mother, this one. He'll do well with her, though they'll both need coddling for a while, just like all the others here.'

Kirren nodded, looking around at the many couples housed in the rows of hurdle pens. She turned back to Jim.

'So that's the last of the lambing for now?'

'Yes, praise be.'

'You've lost a great many.'

'Yes, it's been bad. I've never had a lambing like it before. Smith and Townsend are out there now, burying the last of the carcasses. Still, it could have been worse, I suppose . . .'

'Could it?' she said, doubtfully.

'No, you're right, it couldn't,' he said. 'And I hope to God by the time the next batch start coming the weather will have improved a bit.'

'It must, surely,' Kirren said.

'Yes, surely,' Jim agreed.

They turned and walked to the open doorway and stood looking out at the rain. It was falling coldly and heavily; white shafts of it slanting down to splinter and splash on the cobbled ground.

'It doesn't look like improving yet.'

'No, it's setting in for the day. Your father will have had a wet ride to town and he'll have a wetter one coming back. There's a good two feet of water covering the bridges over the brook and Smith says it's rising steadily. If your father's got any sense he'll come straight home when he's finished his business at the bank.'

'But he hasn't got any sense at all. You should know

162

that by now. He'll stay chatting all day to the market folk, taking a glass with this one and that one, and won't be home until after dark. But his mare usually brings him safe home. *She* has some sense, even if he has not.'

'You are hard on him,' Jim said with a smile.

'You think so, I know,' Kirren said.

'He may behave foolishly now and then, but he's not really a fool, you know.'

'Isn't he?'

'No, he is not. He sees certain things clearly enough, and he has his own rough wisdom sometimes, if only you could recognize it.'

'One thing at least I recognize – he has a loyal ally in you.'

'I'd like to think,' Jim said, 'that I am an ally to both of you.'

Kirren glanced at him; then away.

'Yes, and so you are, of course.'

Staring out at the cold white rain, she seemed for a while to be lost in thought. But she knew that Jim was watching her and as the silence lengthened between them he saw that she was not quite composed. There was a frown between her eyes that suggested some disturbance of mind, and in the dark eyes themselves there was a look of uncertainty. He was about to speak to her when suddenly she turned away, going back into the barn to look at the newly fostered ewe and lamb. The lamb had stopped sucking now and was standing in front of the ewe, bracing himself, splay-legged, as she licked his body with vigorous tongue. Kirren returned to Jim at the door.

'I needn't concern myself about *him*, that much is obvious,' she said. 'He's doing very well indeed.'

'You will be glad, I daresay, to have your kitchen to yourself.'

'Yes, and I must get back to it.'

'Back to your baking?'

'Yes, that's right.'

'Not to mention your hen and her chicks.'

'And Tibby, the tortoiseshell cat,' Kirren said, 'who may well have had her kittens by now.'

'Your kitchen is a menagerie.'

'And you said I'd have it to myself!'

She looked out again at the teeming rain and pulled her shawl up over her head.

'I really must go,' she said.

'But it's raining harder than ever,' Jim said. 'I think you ought to wait a while.'

'No, it's all right.' She flashed him a glance. 'I must make a dash for it.'

He watched her run across the yard and vanish in a flurry of rain between the dairy and the byre.

Chapter Eleven

The rain continued all day, growing heavier all the time. By afternoon it was falling in torrents and the whole farm was awash. Special drains had to be dug to carry the water out of the yards. Ditches everywhere were overflowing, flooding the fields, and every track was a running stream. There was no great gale of wind; no thunderstorm; just a solid downpour of rain, hour after hour, all day long.

Jim, coming into the house at two o'clock, ate his food as fast as he could and went out again into the rain. The greater part of his flock, ninety-five ewes in lamb, were standing over their hooves in water in the home pasture and so chilled and dispirited were they that this new onslaught of rain seemed likely to pound them into the ground.

'We're taking them up to the pinewood,' Jim said. 'It's the only place that's not flooded and at least they'll have some shelter there.'

By four o'clock it was almost dark. The men passing the kitchen window on their way to the milking-shed were dim, dark shapes in the gloom, hooded and hunched against the rain. When Kirren went out to the dairy, a distance of only a few yards, her thick cloak was soaked through and her boots filled with water instantly. And before she could attend to her duties there, dealing with the milk as it was brought in, she was obliged to light the lantern hanging from the beam overhead.

Down in the bottom of the valley the Timmy Brook had broken its banks and was spreading out over the meadows in a great sweeping tide. By half past six the meadows were covered and the water was still rising steadily. Jim went down with Townsend and Smith to take a closer look at it and found that the swirling floodwater had covered the lower part of the track. It was completely dark now and Jim carried a lantern. The three men stood at the gate and watched the floodwater rising until it covered the lower bar.

'It's worse than I've ever known it, even in winter,' Smith said, 'and I've been on this farm more than twenty years.'

'What about the master?' Townsend asked. 'Will he come round by Lyall Bridge?'

'I don't know, but I doubt it,' Jim said. 'He doesn't take much account of the floods and he won't know just how much worse it is until he actually gets to the brook.'

'The bridges will all be under three or four feet of water at least,' Smith said, 'and judging by the way it's swirling here I'd say the current is pretty fast.'

'Yes, I think you're right,' Jim said. 'I'm going down to watch for him.'

'Shall we come with you, master?' Smith asked.

'I reckon we ought to,' Townsend said.

Jim looked at the two men, huddled in the pouring rain, their faces only just discernible in the glimmering lantern light. They had been working fourteen hours and for most of that time had been soaked to the skin.

'No, there's no need for you to come. Get off to your homes, both of you, and get yourselves into dry clothes. But there is something you can do – you can call at the house on your way and tell Mrs Lundy where I am. Tell her I've gone down to the brook to wait for the master coming home.'

'We'll tell her, sure enough,' Townsend said. 'But are you sure you should go down alone? I don't much like the look of these floods and what with it being so tarnal dark – '

'Don't worry,' Jim said. 'I shall take care, be sure of that.'

Leaving the main farm track he went splashing across the meadow through water that reached half way up his shins. The rain, although it had slackened a little, was still quite heavy enough to make the night as black as pitch and in the darkness the great meadow, so familiar by day, seemed like a never-ending waste, full of unremembered dips where thick mud sucked at his boots and made progress difficult. His lantern was no help in finding the way; it merely lit a small patch of rain and cast a will o' the wisp reflection on the floodwater swirling about his feet; but a sense of direction was strong in him and he trusted himself to it with confidence. Still, he knew that caution was needed and when he felt the water deepen, he began moving very slowly, testing the ground with each foot before putting his weight on it. At last a willow tree loomed up at him and he knew he had reached the bank of the brook.

For a while he stood perfectly still, listening to the noise of the brook, waiting for instinct to guide him in choosing which direction to take. When he had made up his mind, he reached up to the willow tree and broke off a long, slender branch, and, proceeding with even greater caution, began moving rightwards along the bank, prodding the brook in search of the bridge. The floodwater now reached to his knees, eddying round him with a force that told him how swift the main current must be, and he felt the force of the main current, too, in the way it dragged at the willow branch.

He knew well enough which of the bridges Riddler was in the habit of using but finding it on such a night was a different matter altogether. He feared that his instinct had played him false – that he should after all have gone left on reaching the brook – and he was thinking of turning back when he felt the ground begin to dip and the water to rise above his knees and knew that he had arrived at the place where the bank sloped down to the bridge. And, prodding the bridge with his willow branch, he judged that the water covering it was, as Nahum Smith had predicted, between three and four feet deep.

There was no telling when Riddler would come. It could be any moment now or it could be as late as nine o'clock. Jim had to resign himself to the possibility of a long wait. And what if, after all, Riddler came home the safest way, by the bridge at King's Lyall? 'Then,' Jim said to himself, 'I shall have had my long wait for nothing.' But he felt sure in his bones that Riddler would come by his usual route, and so it proved, for when he had waited perhaps an hour he heard the sound of hoofbeats coming across the flooded meadow on the far side of the brook.

Standing on the bank above the bridge, he raised his lantern shoulder-high, swinging it gently to and fro, at the same time putting one hand to his mouth and calling out in a great voice that would carry above the noise of the rain:

'Morris! Is that you?'

Riddler, approaching the flooded bank, heard Jim's voice calling to him and was able to pick out the light of the lantern glimmering on the other side. He had no need to draw rein, for the mare, who had already slowed to a walk, now stopped of her own accord, gently pawing the flooded ground where it began sloping down to the bridge.

'Of course it's me!' Riddler called back. 'Who else would it be, for God's sake?'

'I don't think you ought to cross here – it's too dangerous,' Jim called. 'I think you should go round by Lyall Bridge.'

'Don't tell me what to do!' Riddler bawled. 'I've crossed this brook in flood before and never got myself drowned yet, so stand aside, out of my way, otherwise you might get hurt!'

This answer was only what Jim had expected and he knew it was no use arguing.

'Very well!' he shouted back. 'But keep a close rein as you come across. The current is running very fast.'

'My mare's not afraid of the water, current or no current, by damn!'

Sure enough, encouraged by Riddler, the mare picked her way through the deepening water and down onto the narrow bridge, and, with the flowing brook now up to her belly, began very gingerly to cross. When she was half way across, however, a floating log, coming down on the floods, struck her a sharp blow in the ribs. The sudden shock and the force of the blow, together with the swift rush of current, caused her to side-step on the bridge. She gave a high-pitched whinny of fear and the next instant was in the water, hindquarters plunging with a great hollow *plump*, forefeet wildly pawing and splashing.

Riddler, half drowned, held her up, first swearing at her and calling her names, then speaking reassuringly to her.

'Come on, old girl, you must swim for it now. That's the idea! You're doing fine. Don't let the current bother you. It's only a yard or two more to the bank.'

Jim, although he could see almost nothing, knew from the noise what had happened and guessed what had caused the mare's plunge. Knowing, too, that the swift current was carrying her downstream, he made his way along the bank, coming, after twenty paces or so, to the place where mare and man struggled together in the brook.

'Morris?' he called. 'Are you all right?' And Riddler shouted in response: 'Damn you! Get out of the way! We're coming up just there!'

The mare had great difficulty in mounting the steep, slippery bank but, urged on by Riddler's shouts, she humped herself up and over at last in three gallant, heart-bursting heaves. But as she made the final heave, bringing her shuddering hindquarters up over the edge of the bank, Riddler was thrown out of the saddle. He fell heavily sideways, head and shoulders striking the ground, while one foot remained in its stirrup, twisted round in such a way that, try as he might, he could not pull it free; and as the mare cantered away, he was dragged along the ground beside her, bump and splash, all through the mud and the floodwater. Once, for a few brief seconds only, he managed to raise his head and shoulders, reaching up with outstretched arms, trying to catch at the flying reins.

'Whoa, you fool, would you kill me?' he roared. Then he fell back again into the mud.

The mare passed close enough to Jim for him to sense what was happening and as she went cantering over the meadow he heard Riddler's desperate shout. He too shouted for her to stop but she ran on, frightened and confused, making instinctively for the gate that led onto the main farm track. And Jim, splashing across the meadow, followed her blindly through the darkness.

The closed gate brought her to a stop and she was waiting, all in a tremble, when he at last caught up with her. Soothing her as best he could, he hung his lantern on the saddlehook, and gathered up the trailing reins. Riddler was unconscious now, but still alive. Jim freed his foot from the twisted stirrup and heaved him up into the saddle, holding him there with one hand while he opened the gate with the other. Still speaking quietly to the mare, he led her up the track to the farm.

Kirren, hearing him in the yard, came out at once to the porch door. She watched him carry her father in.

'What happened?' she asked.

'The mare missed her footing on the bridge. She had to swim across the brook. Your father was thrown out of the saddle but his foot got caught up in the stirrup and he's been dragged right across the meadows.'

'Is he hurt badly?'

'I don't know. But he's unconscious and he's soaked to the skin. We must dry him and get him into bed. Can you put a warmer in?'

'Yes,' and she went to see to it.

Jim laid Riddler down on the mat in front of the fire and stripped off his clothes. He gave him a good hard towelling and rubbed warm brandy into him; into his chest, his stomach, his back; even into his legs and feet. Then he wrapped him round in a warm woollen blanket round him and carried him upstairs to his bed. Kirren had put a hot brick into it, wrapped in a thick flannel cloth, and this he pushed down to Riddler's feet. She had placed a lighted candle nearby and now she was lighting a fire in the grate. The sticks, kept warm in the kitchen hearth, made a good fire immediately, and she put on a number of small dry logs. She rose from her knees and came to the bed.

Riddler lay flat on his back, with the bedclothes drawn up to his chin, his queer, crooked face as pallid as yeast, his damp hair streaked down over his skull, and a slow trickle of watery blood oozing from a cut above one eye. His breathing was so shallow and quiet that he seemed not to breathe at all. Kirren touched his face with her hand. She looked at Jim.

'How bad is he, do you think?'

'I don't know.'

'He feels very cold.'

'Yes, and his pulse is very weak.' Jim turned towards the door. 'I'm going to fetch Dr Hoad,' he said.

Kirren followed him down the stairs and into the kitchen.

'You're not going to cross the brook, I hope?'

170

'Yes, I am.'

'After what's happened to father tonight? Are you out of your mind?'

'It won't happen to me,' Jim said.

'How can you be sure of that?'

'Your father'd been drinking. I have not. I'll come to no harm, I promise you.'

'Why not go round by the main bridge at Lyall?'

'Because, as you well know, it will add an hour or more to the journey.'

'I see no point in saving an hour if you end up drowned,' Kirren said. 'I know what the brook is like in flood. And what about the mare, anyway? Will she cross again after such a fright?'

'I hope she will. Indeed, she must. It wouldn't be any good taking Griff. He's not used to it. She is.'

'I wish you would not go,' Kirren said. 'You may not have been drinking, it's true, but when did you last have a good night's sleep? Oh, I know you've slept in that chair, a couple of hours at a time, perhaps. But when did you last sleep in your bed? You've been out with your flock at all hours this week – ' She broke off, looking at him, and her eyes were suddenly very dark. 'You're just about tired unto death,' she said.

There was a little silence between them, full of feeling, full of thought, and they looked at each other across the room.

'I'm not so tired as all that . . . and I think it's important to get the doctor as soon as I can.'

'Dr Hoad won't cross the brook. He'll come the safe way like a sensible man and if you had half an ounce of his sense – ' Once again she broke off, giving vent to a short, sharp sigh. 'Oh, it's no use talking!' she said. 'I'm wasting my breath, I can see that! Go and get yourself drowned in the brook if that's what you've set your heart on doing!'

She turned away from him, angrily, but he caught her arm in a firm grip and drew her round to face him again.

'I shan't drown,' he said quietly. 'I care too much about my life to run any risk of losing it.' And, stooping, he kissed her on the mouth.

171

A quick glance between them and he was gone and Kirren, left staring at the door, heard him riding out of the yard. For a moment she stood, listening, her thoughts going with him through the night. Then, with a faint flush of warmth in her cheeks, she turned and went out to the hall and up the stairs to her father's room, to sit with him and watch over him until such time as Jim returned.

When the mare, as Jim expected, jibbed at crossing the brook again, he dismounted and led the way, stepping down onto the bridge, into water that reached above his waist, and coaxing her to follow him. She gave a snicker of protest at first, but responded trustingly enough to the firm pull of his hand on her bridle, and they crossed safely to the other side.

It was turned half past eight by the time he reached the doctor's house and rain was still falling steadily.

'Can't it wait until morning?' the doctor asked irritably.

'No, it can't,' Jim said.

'Oh, very well, very well, I'll come! But not with you, mind, across your damned brook. I'm too old for such pranks as that. I shall come round by the bridge at Lyall.'

Jim returned home the way he had come, again without any misadventure, and Kirren, having been listening for him, came to her father's bedroom window, peering down through the rainy darkness and raising a hand to him as he rode past on his way to the stables.

When he went into the kitchen, after attending to the mare, Kirren was busy at the hearth, preparing hot food for him.

'Did you find the doctor at home?'

'Yes, he's on his way,' Jim said. 'He's coming round by Lyall Bridge. Has your father woken at all?'

'No,' Kirren said, 'he hasn't stirred.' Still busy with her preparations, she turned her head and glanced at him. 'By the time you've changed those wet clothes, your supper will be ready,' she said.

He went upstairs to his bedroom, changed into dry clothes, and brought the wet ones down with him to dry by the fire. The kitchen was empty; Kirren had gone up to her father again; but his supper was ready on the table: hot mutton broth, thickened with oatmeal, and a loaf of the bread she had baked that day. He sat down to it, gratefully, watched by the tortoiseshell cat, Tibby, who lay in her box beside the hearth with four kittens nestling against her.

When Jim had finished his meal he put on the driest coat he could find, and a hood made from sacks, and went out on a round of the buildings, making sure that all was well with the ewes and lambs quartered there. By then it was past ten o'clock so he walked down the track to meet Dr Hoad, whose temper, when he came, was somewhat short.

'Trust that fool Morris Riddler,' he said, 'to bring me out on a night like this!'

The doctor, having made his examination, stood in front of the bedroom fire and drank the brandy Jim had brought him.

'No bones broken as far as I can tell but I shan't know for certain until he comes to.'

'When do you think that will be?' Kirren asked.

'Can't tell you that. Just don't know. He's pretty badly concussed, of course, but he's got a thick enough skull, God knows, and I doubt if much harm will come of it. Dragged along by his nag, did you say? Yes, that explains the twisted foot. As for the bruising to the head and trunk, well, he'll be pretty sore when he does come round, but maybe that will teach him some sense.'

'What should I do for him when he comes round?'

'Keep him warm and quiet and still, that's all, and if he starts asking for food, give him something easy and light. Gruel, perhaps, or arrowroot. No stimulants, mind! No alcohol! He's had quite enough of that for today.' The doctor drained his brandy-glass. 'I'll come out again some time tomorrow. Not sure when. All depends.'

Jim, having seen the doctor off, returned to Riddler's bedroom. Kirren sat in a chair by the bed with a piece of needlework in her lap. Jim stood looking down at her.

'I'll sit with him now while you get some sleep.'

'I don't need any sleep,' she said. 'You're the one who needs the sleep.'

173

'Don't argue with me. Just do as I say.'

'No, I will not! Why should I indeed?' Her dark eyes flashed in the candlelight. 'He's *my* father, not yours,' she said.

'I thought you hated him,' Jim said.

'Yes, well, so I do sometimes. Or at least I have done, in the past.' She looked at the grey-faced man in the bed. 'But how can you hate anyone who lies so cold and still and quiet and looks so − so close to death?' she said. 'Oh, he's a selfish, stubborn brute of a man, and I can't pretend I'm fond of him . . . But he's worked so hard all these years, as you know, and for this to happen to him now, when his life has changed for the better at last −'

'He's not going to die,' Jim said.

'Isn't he?'

'No, he is not. What the doctor says is true − your father is as tough as oak. He's a born fighter. You know that.'

'Yes, I know that.'

'Try not to worry. I'm sure there's no need.'

'Very well,' Kirren said. 'But if there's nothing to worry about you may go to your bed and sleep.'

Jim, with a little smile, gave in.

'You'll call me if you need me?' he said.

'Yes, I will, I promise you.'

He touched her arm and left the room.

At five o'clock the following morning, refreshed after more than six hours' sleep, Jim was in the kitchen making tea. During the night the rain had stopped and the outside world seemed strangely still. When he went up to Riddler's room, taking Kirren a cup of tea, she had already drawn the curtains back and there was a cold pale light in the room. His glance went to the man in the bed and he thought he detected some slight change. He turned to Kirren, questioningly, and she gave a nod.

'A short while ago he woke up,' she said. 'It was only for two or three seconds, that's all, and then he closed his eyes again. But he knew me, I'm sure . . .'

'Here, drink this while it's hot,' Jim said, and gave her the tea.

He went to the bed and touched Riddler's face. He put his hand in under the bedclothes, felt Riddler's body, and tested his pulse.

'He's a lot warmer than he was last night and I think his pulse is stronger too.'

'Yes, I thought the same myself.'

'He'll soon pick up now.'

'Yes,' she said.

'Have you slept at all?'

'Yes, off and on.'

Jim went down to the kitchen again and drank his own cup of hot sweet tea. Then he went out to the milking-shed and told the men what had happened to Riddler.

'Poor old master,' said Nahum Smith. 'Is he going to be all right?'

'I think so,' Jim said.

'It's certainly some old flood down there. It's like the Sea of Galilee. And the state of the fields as we came down – I've never seen so much mud in my life!'

The miry state of the fields and the yards made extra work for everybody. Because carts could not go on the land, hay and turnips for the sheep sheltering in the pine wood had to be taken up on the horses' backs. Because a trough had overflowed and water had got into the root house, the mangolds all had to be taken out and spread on straw in the barn to dry. And all through the greater part of that day there were similar trials and calamities.

First it was a young sow that fell into an open drain; she was heavily in pig and it took three men to haul her out without doing her any harm. Next it was Bob Lovell who slipped wheeling a barrowload of muck across the fold-yard so that it ran into one of the pillars supporting the linhay and brought part of the roof sagging down. The sheep in the linhay were unharmed but the roof, in danger of further collapse, had to be shored up immediately. Then it was Kirren's pony, Griff, who had to be treated for colic after Willie Townsend had carelessly allowed him to drink from a pail of water just drawn from the well. While Jim was giving the pony a mild draught of peppermint and laudanum, Prue Townsend came to him with a message from Kirren.

'The master's awake and he's asking for you.'

Riddler, clad in a nightshirt now, still lay flat on his back, but there was some colour reviving in his face and he was breathing more normally. Jim sat down in the chair by the bed and Riddler, turning towards him, groaned.

'I ache in every particle,' he said in a low, hoarse voice.

'I'm not surprised,' Jim said, 'after what happened to you.'

'How's my stupid cow of a mare?'

'In better shape than you by far.'

'She doesn't damn well deserve to be, dragging me over the lots like that. Did you bring my saddlebags in?'

'Yes.'

'Money safe?'

'Yes, quite safe.'

'I reckon I'd better leave it to you to pay the men their wages today.'

'Yes, all right,' Jim said. 'They sent their good wishes to you, by the way. They hope you'll soon be on the mend.'

'I hope it myself,' Riddler said.

Kirren came into the room with a bowl of warm barley gruel. Jim helped Riddler to a sitting position and propped him up against his pillows. Kirren sat on the edge of the bed, spread a napkin on Riddler's chest, and offered him a spoonful of gruel. He looked at it with some distaste.

'If this is all I'm getting to eat, the sooner I mend the better,' he said.

Jim, with a little smile for Kirren, quietly left the room.

It was a day of comings and goings; of jobs interrupted and left half done, returned to, and left again; a day of hurriedly eaten meals and short, snatched conversations.

At three o'clock the doctor came and Jim, again called into

176

the house, was climbing the stairs to Riddler's room when he heard the old man give a bellowing shout. On going in he found Riddler sitting on the edge of the bed, glaring ferociously at the doctor, who stood nearby, quite unmoved.

'He said he couldn't straighten his foot, so I straightened it *for* him,' he explained.

'I reckon the damned fool has just about crippled me for life,' Riddler said.

'Well, we shall see, shan't we?' the doctor said cheerfully, and downstairs, as Kirren and Jim saw him off, he said: 'Keep him in bed for a day or two – if you can get him to stay there. I'll be over again on Tuesday morning.'

Jim went back to the task of cleaning out the root-house, and Kirren, knowing her father was now well enough to be left alone, went to help Prue Townsend in the dairy. It had begun to rain again and by early evening, when Jim paid the men their wages, it was turning to sleet.

'The master's in the best place, tucked up in bed,' said Nahum Smith. 'I shan't be sorry to get there myself and rest my poor old rheumaticky bones.'

When the men had gone Jim went into the barn to look over his ewes and lambs and found Kirren there. She was with her fosterling and was letting him suck her thumb.

'It seems he still remembers me.'

'So he should,' Jim said. 'You were his mother till yesterday.'

'He likes his new mother best.'

They stood for a little while in silence, watching the lamb. Then they both began speaking at once, Kirren to say what a day it had been, and Jim to ask about her father.

'How is he now?'

'Better,' she said. 'But still very quiet – for him.'

'Make the most of it.'

'Yes.' She laughed.

'I told you he would be all right.'

'Yes. You did.'

They left the barn and went into the house and Kirren at once became very busy, first making up the fire and swinging

177

the kettle over it, next moving to and fro, lighting the lamp on the table and setting out the supper things. Jim, having hung up his jacket and hat, stood quietly watching her as she went again and again to the larder, bringing out bread, butter, cheese, and ham, and two or three different kinds of chutney. At last he spoke.

'Kirren, can't you be still for a moment?'

'What?' she said, with a flickering glance. 'Yes, very well, if that's what you want. But I thought you'd be hungry for your supper — .'

'Supper can wait,' Jim said. 'At the moment I want to talk to you and I can't talk sensibly while you keep flitting about like that.'

'Behold me, then — standing still.'

She stood at the opposite side of the table and placed her hands on the back of a chair, folding them there in a gesture of primness. But although she was now facing him, her glance was still evasive, unsure, and, watching her closely in the lamp-light, he saw a faint tinge of colour come stealing slowly into her face.

'Something's been happening to us, hasn't it, during the past few weeks?' he said. And when she failed to answer he said: 'Or perhaps it's only been happening to me?'

'No,' she said, quickly this time, 'it has happened to me as well.'

'Then why won't you look at me, properly?'

'Because — I don't know — it's difficult. And you haven't yet said what it is . . . '

'I love you,' he said, 'and you love me.'

There was a pause. She drew a deep breath.

'You make it all sound so simple,' she said, 'and you're always so — so sure of everything.'

'Kirren, are you afraid of me?'

'No, of course not. Why should I be?'

'I know what you've always felt about men and I'm thinking of what you said to me the day I first came here from Peele — '

'Don't remind me of what I said. That was then. It's different now.'

'How is it different?'

'You know very well.'

She was looking at him directly now, letting him see what she felt for him, and although, when he moved and came towards her, there was a hint of shy alarm in the sudden widening of her eyes, she turned to him and went into his arms and gave herself to him in a kiss that was free of shyness, free of constraint.

In a little while, when Jim spoke again, it was in a voice very quiet and deep, and he looked at her in wonderment, touching her face, her lips, her throat, delicately, with his fingertips.

'When I married you, I was deceived.'

'Who deceived you?'

'You did,' he said. 'You allowed me to think that your past life had roughened you and made you hard, that you had no womanly passion in you, nor any womanly tenderness.'

'And now you know better?' Kirren said.

'Yes,' he said, in the same deep voice, 'now I know you for what you are.'

There came a knock from the room above, loud and peremptory, making them jump. They looked at each other with laughing eyes, drawing apart, reluctantly, with a last lingering touch of the hands.

'That's father,' Kirren said, 'just in case you didn't know.'

'I told you he wouldn't be quiet for long.'

'I'd better go up and see what he wants.'

'I'll come with you.'

'No.'

'Why not?'

'I don't want you with me. Not just yet. He'd know there was something — he'd see too much.'

'No one would ever see anything that you didn't want them to see,' Jim said. 'Not if you had made up your mind to it.'

'You think so, do you? I'm not so sure. And I don't intend to take any chances until I've had time to — to gather my wits.'

Another loud knock and she hurried away. The kitchen seemed suddenly empty and bare. Jim stood, a faint smile on his lips, listening to the sounds overheard, of Kirren and her father talking together. Then, in a moment, she reappeared.

'He's asking for something to eat,' she said, 'and he wants you to take it up to him.'

When Jim entered the bedroom, with a bowl of gruel and milk on a tray, Riddler was sitting up in bed.

'Is this all I get? Pig-slops again?' he said, as he received the tray.

'H'mm,' Jim said, surveying him, 'you are better, obviously.'

'Yes, if you thought to be rid of me, you'll have to wait a while longer yet.' Riddler motioned him to a chair. 'Meanwhile you can sit and talk and watch me feasting myself,' he said.

Later, Jim and Kirren ate their own supper, sitting opposite one another at the kitchen table, in the golden circle of light from the lamp.

With the curtains drawn close over the windows, against the cold wet night outside, and a good fire burning red on the hearth, they were shut in together in comfort and warmth and because they had the kitchen to themselves and sat there together in strange new special intimacy, the room seemed somehow to take something from them, of wonderment and discovery, and to give it back again in waves.

Knowing that Riddler was now asleep, they talked together in quiet voices, and everything they said to each other deepened the intimate feeling between them.

'If we were not already married, would you marry me?'

'Yes, of course.'

'Ours was a strange wedding,' he said. 'Surely no other two people can ever have married in such a way, knowing nothing about one another, caring nothing, as we did then.' And after a little while he said: 'When did you first find it had changed? That you could care for me after all?'

'I don't know,' Kirren said, 'and I don't think I'd tell you if I did.'

'I would tell *you*, if I knew,' he said.

'But you don't know?'

'No, not quite.'

' "During the past few weeks." – That's what you said a while ago.'

'I think, with me, it's been longer than that.'

'And with me,' Kirren said.

'Your father said this would happen to us . . . that nature was bound to play its part . . . that a man and a woman thrown together were bound to feel something for each other sooner or later.'

'I know pretty well what my father said. But oh, Jim, is that all it is?' She looked at him in laughing dismay. 'Something that would have happened to us, quite regardless of who we were? Just any woman? Any man? I can't believe that.'

'No more can I. Because you are not just any woman and I am not just any man. But perhaps in some peculiar way your father sensed something about us, or perhaps it was just pure chance. Anyway, however it was, he was in the right of it.'

There was a silence. He looked at her.

'Kirren,' he said.

'Yes, what?'

'Your father is much better now. I don't think it will be necessary for you to sit up with him tonight.'

'No,' she said. 'I don't think it will.' She looked at him with dark, steady gaze. 'Tonight will be our wedding night.'

In another three days Riddler was up and about again, groaning and swearing at the pain in his joints, but hobbling stubbornly everywhere, refusing all help save that of a walking-stick. First he went to see his mare in her stall, to give her a piece of his mind, he said, and let her see what she'd done to him. Next he went to look at the fields, which were still badly waterlogged, and the valley meadows down below, where the floods still lay like a great shallow lake. And lastly, sighting the doctor riding slowly up the track, he went hobbling down to meet him.

'Tell me, do I look as if I need you?' he asked. 'No, by God, I'm damned if I do!' But almost in the same breath he said: 'Ah, well, having come this far, you'd better come in and have a drink, I suppose.'

The weather continued wet and cold and the valley lots remained flooded for the best part of ten days. Slowly, at last, the floodwater drained away from the meadows and the green springing grass was seen again, but everywhere, both in meadows and fields, the land was kept wet by repeated rains.

'Is there to be no end to it?' Kirren said. 'Are we never to be dry again?'

'You needn't go out in it,' Riddler said. 'Being a woman, you're lucky like that. You can stay snug and warm in your kitchen here and pretend to be busy about your chores.'

'And what about my dairywork? And going to market once a week? I have to go out of doors sometimes, otherwise I should suffocate. But oh, dear, what wouldn't I give to have a few dry days for a change!'

'You seem cheerful enough, anyway, in spite of the weather,' Riddler said.

'Do I?' said Kirren, on her guard.

It was one morning after breakfast, and she and her father were alone. Jim was out tending his flock but Riddler, whose joints were still troubling him, was taking it easy by the fire.

'Not only cheerful, neither,' he said, 'but something else as well besides.'

Kirren, at the table, washing up, glanced at him from under her lashes, but made no reply, and Riddler, in a thoughtful tone, went on:

'I can't quite fathom it out, but there's something different about you these days. I've noticed it once or twice of late, but I don't just know what it is, unless it's something you've done to your hair.'

'My hair is the same as it has been for years.'

'Then maybe you're wearing a new dress,' he said.

'This is the dress I bought last spring.'

182

'Well, it's a mystery, then, that's all, and I shall have to give it up. But there *is* a difference in you all the same and whatever it is it suits you right well.'

'Does it, now? Fancy that.'

Kirren now came to the hearth to fetch a cloth for drying up, plucking it down from the string line that hung in a loop from the mantelpiece. Instead of turning away, however, she stood with the cloth between her hands, and Riddler, leaning back in his chair, slowly raised his face to hers.

For a little while father and daughter eyed each other, glimmeringly, until the amused satisfaction of one and the indulgent mockery of the other kindled a mutual gleam of warmth mixed with a kind of sardonic understanding. Riddler was the first to speak.

'I knew you'd come to it in the end.'

'Then no doubt you're feeling well pleased with yourself.'

'It seems I'm not the only one . . .'

'I suppose you think the credit's all yours?'

'Of course the credit is all mine! Damn it, girl, if it wasn't for me you'd still be the same crabby spinster you were before, sharp-tongued and hard as nails, all back-answers and black looks and temper enough for two or three!'

'No compliments, please,' Kirren said.

'You were made for marriage, Kirrie. I always knew that, all along. And I'll tell you something else as well – you were made to be the mother of sons.'

'All in good time,' she said, 'perhaps.'

'Time!' he said, glaring at her. 'You've already wasted a year and a half! Yes, and that reminds me, while we are speaking of such matters – next time you go in to town, buy yourself a double bed, so that Jim can sleep with you, decently, as a husband should, instead of creeping about at night, robbing a poor old man of his sleep with all this opening and shutting of doors.'

A few days afterwards news came to Godsakes, via one of the carters at Peele, that Philip Sutton's wife Jane had given birth to a baby son.

'Well,' Riddler said to Jim and Kirren, 'I never thought to say such a thing about the Suttons, but let that be an example to you.'

Chapter Twelve

The spring and summer of that year were the coldest and wettest anyone could remember and the bad conditions brought much trouble to farmers everywhere.

In the second lambing at Godsakes, losses were almost as bad as in the first, and all through the summer there was much to do to keep the flock free of foot-rot and sickness. It was the same with the rest of the stock: a constant watch had to be kept on the cattle and at the slightest hint of a cough or a chill Jim was in close attendance, rubbing the beasts down with a brush to invigorate them, and administering soothing drinks. Even so they lost one of their best cows from pleuro-pneumonia; also a heifer fifteen months old.

There was no proper course with the crops that year. Everything happened out of turn. Swedes and mangolds could not be sown until the first week in June, and carrots were sown later still. They made growth quickly enough but so did the weeds, and with the land so sticky and wet, little hoeing could be done. Three acres of Dutch beans were spoilt by mildew; they had to be cut down while green and fed to the pigs; and haymaking, begun in June, was still in progress at the end of August.

But whatever the trials and anxieties of that dismal year it seemed as though some benign spirit was keeping watch over Godsakes Farm and its people. There was a radiance over their lives; a sense of warm unity in everything they did together; an optimism at work in them that neither anxiety nor misfortune could touch.

Jim had the feeling, new every day, that his life was rather astonishing, and that many great and marvellous gifts had been bestowed upon him. He had always been an ambitious man; had always felt that he could do great things; but now this feeling had another dimension, as though he saw his future life laid out before him, as in a vision, with a rich golden light spread over it. Problems were nothing; he welcomed them; for he felt with utter certainty that he could overcome them all; that he had it in him to mould his life pretty much as he chose. And at the heart of this feeling of his, giving him this special faith, was the love that had grown between him and Kirren.

'Sometimes I feel that I don't deserve the good fortune that's come my way,' he said to her once, 'but I mean to deserve it, in the future, by working for it and earning it.'

'When did you not work?' Kirren said. 'You have always worked, all your life.'

'All that is nothing,' he said with a smile, 'to what I shall do in future years.'

At the end of August, when haymaking was finished at last, they cut their few acres of dredge-corn, oats and barley as before. But this year, due to the constant rain, both barley and oats were spoilt by disease, which meant that the whole crop was fit only for the pigs and fowls.

'God! Just look at it!' Riddler said, holding a sodden, discoloured sheaf aloft on the prongs of his hay-fork. 'Did you ever see such stuff? It'll never be dry in a hundred years!' And as September came in, with the weather still wet and cold, he said: 'I've never known such a summer as this and I never want to see another like it again so long as I live.'

The only comfort Riddler could find for the year's disappointments was that things had been much worse at Peele. Abelard's losses at lambing time had been almost half as great again as Jim's and there had been further losses since. Among the pedigree Alderneys that were such a source of pride at Peele there had been an outbreak of rinder-pest, and ten prize-winning cows had been lost, together with a number of calves. And, even worse than this, for a farm that grew so much corn, was the weather's effect on their harvest.

Their spring corn had never been sown, due to the wet and the cold, and except for a growth of green weeds, many fields remained bare all through the summer and into autumn. And their winter corn was a sorry sight: acres and acres of wheat and barley laid low by the wind and the rain, the barley sprouting in the ear, the wheat so infected with the smut that whole fields were darkened by it. There was no golden glow in the harvest fields at Peele that year, but only a sombre, shadowy pall. There was no happy noise of reaping-machines, for the corn was so wet and so badly lodged that it all had to be cut by hand.

'Just look at them all, swarming about!' Riddler said to Kirren and Jim. 'They're having to put their backs into it and do a bit of work for a change! And their masters won't make three thousand pounds from their harvest this year, by God! They'll be lucky if they make three thousand pence! This damned wet season has hit them a sight harder than it's hit us here. It makes me laugh like a spinning-top to see them slaving away over there, knowing they'll get no gain from it.'

'Why, what good does that do us?' Kirren said.

'I don't know what it does for *you* but it does *me* a power of good to see bad luck come to them for a change.'

It was a dull but dry day and they were at work in their own harvest field, opening up the corn-shocks, soaked by previous days of rain, and setting the sheaves out in twos so that they might dry in the wind. Kirren and Jim were working together, separating the wet sheaves, and Riddler, who had finished his row, was standing near them, his hands on his hips, looking across the valley at Peele.

'After what they did to me I reckon I'm about entitled to crow over them for a change,' he said.

'And do you intend,' Kirren asked, 'to carry your grudge right through to the end of your life?'

187

'Yes, why shouldn't I?' Riddler said.

'It seems to me rather childish, that's all.'

'Childish, is it?'

'Yes,' Kirren said. 'It was all a long time ago. It's silly to bear a grudge for so long. Jim doesn't feel like that. He's put his quarrel out of his mind.'

'Has he, now?'

'Yes, he has.'

'And what's so surprising about that?' Riddler said with a curl of his lip. 'What was his quarrel compared with mine? The harm he got at the Suttons' hands was nothing but a fleabite compared with the harm they did me. In fact it was a bit of good luck for him when John Sutton turned him out, for he wouldn't have come to us otherwise and how else, in God's name, would he ever have got a farm of his own? He's fallen on his feet and no mistake, and well he knows it, you may be sure.'

With his chin jutting pugnaciously, Riddler turned and went stumping off, to work by himself on a row of shocks some little way further down the field. Jim and Kirren, having stopped work, looked at each other across the sheaves.

'It's no good trying to change him, you know. His hatred for Sutton goes too deep.'

'Yes, I know, I know,' Kirren said. 'I'd do better to hold my tongue, I know.'

'Nor is it any good holding me up as an example of Christian charity because what your father says is true − I *have* fallen on my feet and I am well aware of it. Indeed, it is a very strange thing, but twice in my life so far, when someone has done me a bad turn, it has worked out to my advantage in the end. First, when my uncle abandoned me and John Sutton took me in, and then, as your father just said, when John Sutton turned me out and I came over here.'

'You consider yourself lucky, it seems.'

'Yes, I do, for I've not only got this farm but I've got you as well.'

'Riches indeed!' Kirren said.

'Oh, you may mock if you like, looking at me with those dark gipsy eyes! But what more could a man want from life?'

'Surely, if you give it some thought, there must be something more you want . . .'

'Kirren, are you telling me something?'

'Yes: I'm going to have a child.'

They stood looking at one another and there was a quietness over them both. A stillness in him. A growing smile.

'Well, that explains it,' he said at last.

'Explains what?'

'Why you are looking so beautiful.'

'Am I beautiful?'

'Yes. You are.'

'I take it you're pleased, then, with my news?'

'You don't need to ask me that.'

'My father is looking over at us. He will be shouting at us in a minute, asking why we are standing idle.'

'In that case, we'd better get on.'

They resumed their work in unison, taking the wet sheaves from the shock, shaking the raindrops out of them, and standing them up, two by two, in the path of the wind.

In another few minutes, however, they stopped work again because overhead in the grey sky the clouds parted and the sun shone out, falling on them with a gentle warmth and filling the valley with a soft bright light. They stood with their faces upturned to the sun, grateful for the light and the warmth they had seen and felt so rarely that summer, and Riddler, just a little way off, stood in exactly the same way, lifting his blunt, crooked face to the sun in a childlike gesture of gratitude.

And away on the far side of the valley the reapers in the fields at Peele, labouring over their blighted harvest, also stopped work and stood, greeting the sun with a little cheer that was heard clearly in the fields at Godsakes. Hearing the sound of this cheer, Kirren and Jim smiled at each other, and Kirren, putting one hand to her eyes, turned to look out over the valley, softly lit by the golden sun shining through the parted clouds.

'I wonder how this valley will look, and these two farms,

189

when our children are growing up, say in ten or twenty years' time.'

'You are looking a long way ahead.'

'Yes, and why not?' Kirren said.

POLSINNEY
HARBOUR

For
Carole, Roger, and Caryn
and
in memory of Delyth

Chapter 1

1869

Strangers were rare in Polsinney and the girl attracted attention at once, from the moment she was first seen, a tall figure, slim but well-made, carrying a bundle slung over her shoulder, coming down the rough track that wound its way over Wheep Moor to join the road leading into the village.

It was an evening in July and up on the moor, close beside the track, three men were cutting turfs. They stopped work and leant on their spades, watching as the girl came over the brow, past the old ruined engine-house of Bal Kerensa, and across the footbridge over the stream. A little way along the stream she paused and got down on her knees on the bank, letting her bundle slip to the ground while she cupped her hands into the water. The men watched her drink and bathe her face.

'What maid is that?'

'She's a stranger to me.'

'Ess, and to me,' the third man said.

The girl rose, shouldering her bundle, and came on down the track, one hand shielding her eyes from the sun as she gazed upon the roofs of the village, huddled together, below the moor, with the glittering blue sea beyond. When she drew level with the men she stopped again and spoke to them.

'What is the name of this place?'

'Why, this is Polsinney,' one man said.

'Is there work to be got there?'

'What sort of work?'

'Anything.'

The turf-cutters stared in astonishment. A stranger was rare enough but when that stranger was a young girl, tramping the roads and asking for work, it was a thing that passed belief. They eyed her with stern disapproval, noting that her skirts were grey with dust from the frayed hem, drooping about her ankles, right up to the very waist. Noting, too, that she wore no hat – not even a kerchief over her head – and that consequently her face and neck were burnt brown by the sun. And she, seeing that they were struck dumb, put another question to them.

'Is there seining in Polsinney?'

'Ess, there's three seines in Polsinney, but seining haven't started yet.'

'Perhaps I could get work on the farms?'

'I dunnaw. Maybe you could.' The man who spoke was scratching his chin. 'You could try Boskillyer, I suppose. Mrs Tallack has girls to help her sometimes. But they don't generally stop there long cos Mrs Tallack is hard to please.'

'Where's Boskillyer?'

'That's it down there.'

The girl looked down at the tiny farms, lying strung out, half a mile below, between the road that skirted the moor and the cliff-edge with its wind-bent trees. The man was pointing to the farm that lay farthest from the village. It had three small fields, enclosed by stone hedges, and the house, which stood with its back to the road, looked down over these fields and out over the curve of the bay.

'Mrs Tallack, did you say? I'll try my luck with her, then.'

The girl began walking away and one of the men called out to her.

'Where are you from, maid? What's your name?'

'My name's Maggie Care,' the girl called back. 'I've come from the other side of Mew Head.'

The man called out another question, but the girl was already well on her way, walking with a long, almost boyish stride that carried her quickly down the track, so that the question went unheard. The men stood watching her for a while and then returned to their turf-cutting.

'She've walked a good many miles,' one said, 'if she've come from the other side of Mew Head.'

'Ess, you, but what's she about, trudging the roads, looking for work, a young well-spoken girl like her? I never heard such a thing in my life.'

'Maybe, there edn no work to be had, downalong, where she've come from, you.'

'And where *have* she come from, I'd like to know? "Other side of Mew Head," she said, but that dunt tell us nothing at all.'

'Maybe she didn want us to know, but Rachel Tallack, down there at Boskillyer, *she'll* get it out of her, you mark my words.'

The turf-cutting was warm work and every so often the men paused, looking down at Boskillyer, wondering how the girl had fared. But although the house was visible to them, its door and yards were completely hidden because of the clustering outbuildings, and so far, whenever they looked, there was nothing to be seen of Rachel Tallack or of the stranger, Maggie Care.

Rachel Tallack had finished milking and was turning the cows into the field. They lumbered past her, taking their time, and when the fourth and last cow began loitering in the gateway, she closed the gate hard on its heels, giving a little snort of impatience.

On her way back across the yard she stopped and looked out over the bay where the fishing fleet, some thirty-odd boats, was putting out on the first of the ebb, brown sails beginning to draw as they moved from the shelter of the harbour into the freshening offshore wind. Although she was in her early fifties, Rachel still had good sight, and she could distinguish her son's boat, the *Emmet*, among the leading clutch of five which, already picking up speed, were standing out on the tack that would carry them past Struan Point. The pilchard season had been good so far. The weather on the whole had been fair and the shoals were moving in the Channel. 'God grant it continue so,' Rachel murmured as she turned away.

She was about to enter the house when she heard footsteps on the road and a girl with a bundle over her shoulder turned into the open yard.

'Mrs Tallack?'

'Yes, that's right.'

'I was told you might want help on the farm.'

'And who was so good as to tell you that?'

'I met some men cutting turf on the moor. I told them I was looking for work and they sent me to you.'

'I'm much obliged to them, I'm sure!'

The girl let her bundle slip to the ground and Rachel looked at it with distaste. She noted the dust on the girl's skirts and saw that her boot-soles were well worn down.

'Wherever have you come from, girl, to get yourself in such a state?'

'Today I've walked up from Mindren. Before that I was at Tardrew. I've been moving about these parts three weeks, working on different farms, helping with the haymaking.'

'That's no life for a young girl, living like a vagrant,' Rachel said. 'What are your family thinking of to let you roam about like that?'

'I've got no family. They're all dead.'

'Surely you must have a home of some sort?'

'I did have, once, but not any more.' For a moment the girl seemed to hesitate. Then, with a wave westwards, she said: 'I've lived all my life in one place, further down the coast from here, and three weeks ago I made up my mind to leave it and try somewhere new.'

'What's your name?'

'Maggie Care.'

'How old are you?'

'Nineteen.'

'Are you used to farm work, besides what you've done these past three weeks?'

'Yes, I've done it all my life. I worked on a farm near my home. I was dairymaid there for six years.'

'And left it to go tramping the roads!'

Rachel frowned suspiciously. The girl's story was incomplete. That much at least was obvious. 'And if I had any sense at all, I'd send her packing straight away.' But Rachel had to admit to herself that help *was* needed on the farm. Only that afternoon, Brice had talked of going to Penolver to ask if one of the Pentecosts could come and help with the haymaking, but Rachel was always reluctant to ask any favour of her neighbours, and she had rejected her son's suggestion. Now this stranger stood before her: a girl she knew nothing about; but a stranger might perhaps, after all, be preferable to a gossiping neighbour.

'I've had girls working here before but they never stay long. As soon as seining starts they're off, to earn more money in the fish-cellars. I've never had a *dependable* girl, nor one who really knew how to work.'

Rachel paused. She hoped that her keen scrutiny would break down the girl's reserve but in this she was disappointed. The clear grey eyes remained steady and although the girl had come asking for work, and looked little better than a beggar, there was no trace of humility in her manner or in her glance. Rachel resumed her questioning.

'Have you got a written character?'

'No.'

'And yet you expect me to give you work!'

'Did your other girls have written characters?'

'They were from local families, known to me by repute.'

'Yet none of them was dependable.'

Rachel's eyebrows rose sharply. A dry smile touched her lips.

'You make your point, girl, I grant you that. And you're not afraid to speak well of yourself, promising to do better than they.'

'At least I'm not afraid of work. Certainly I can promise that. And all I ask in return is my keep.'

'Yes, very well, we shall see!' Rachel said. 'I'll take you on for a month's trial and then if I find we deal well together I'll think about keeping you on for good. Now you'd better come indoors and have a bite of something to eat. You look as though you're in need of it.'

She went into the house and the girl followed. Inside the porch, on a bench at one side, lay a coil of rope and a few cork floats and an old kedge anchor, coated in rust, with one of its flukes broken off.

'Is your husband a fisherman?'

'My husband's been dead six years. My son, Brice, is a fisherman. He's off for the night, pilchard driving, and won't be back till tomorrow morning.' Rachel spread a cloth on the kitchen table. 'Were your own family fisher-folk?'

For a moment it seemed the girl had not heard. She was stroking the big tabby cat who sat in a corner of the settle. Rachel, with a frown, repeated the question, and the answer was given reluctantly.

'Yes, they were all fisher-folk.'

While Rachel was busy in the kitchen, the girl went out to the yard again, to beat some of the dust from her skirts and to wash herself under the pump. Rachel then called her in and the two of them sat down to eat.

'You still haven't told me where you're from.'

'The other side of Mew Head, a few miles further on from St Lar.'

'It must have a name of its own,' Rachel said, 'and I am waiting to hear what it is.'

The girl remained stubbornly silent, spreading her bread with soft cream cheese, and Rachel spoke impatiently.

'Perhaps they've got the cholera there and that's why you don't want to say where it is?'

'No, there's no cholera there. The name of the place is Porthgaran.'

'Well, well, so it's out at last! And why should you make such a mystery of it? Is it such a terrible place?'

'No,' the girl said quietly. 'It's a place pretty much the same as Polsinney. A harbour town, built into the cliff, with most of the folk getting their living from fishing.'

'You don't seem to have gained much, then, by coming in search of somewhere new.'

'No. Perhaps not.'

'You say your family are fisher-folk but you don't sound like a fisherman's daughter. You speak decent English, as good as my own.'

'My mother was a schoolmistress before she married my father and she was strict about such things. But it all depends

12

on the people I'm with. I *can* speak broad when I've a mind to.'

'You needn't bother on my account! I hear more than enough of it from my neighbours in Polsinney.'

Rachel herself had been born and raised in an inland village, two miles from Truro, where her father had been the curate-in-charge, and her tone betrayed the contempt she felt, even now, after twenty-five years, for the place she had come to on her marriage. Even when she spoke the words 'fisher-folk' it was with a faint touch of scorn. True, her own son was a fisherman, but that was because her foolish husband had muddled away what money he had and as the little rented farm brought only a meagre profit, her son sought his living from the sea, going as skipper in a boat owned by his uncle, Gus Tallack.

Perhaps it was this matter of speech that had prompted Rachel, in spite of her doubts, to receive Maggie Care into her home. And now, as they sat at tea together, she noticed other things as well. The girl's table manners were good; she ate with a certain fastidiousness; and although her hands were roughened by work, they were shapely and well cared for, the finger-nails clean and neatly trimmed. All these things won Rachel's approval, and yet at the same time her doubts remained, because of the girl's stubborn reticence.

'Your mother did well by you but I wonder she didn't see to it that you were trained to something better than hiring yourself out as a servant-girl. You're intelligent enough, I would have thought, to have followed in your mother's footsteps.'

'No, I wouldn't have wanted that. I prefer to work out of doors.'

'You mean you prefer to go tramping the roads.'

'Only until I've found a place I like well enough to settle in.'

'And you think Polsinney will suit you? You are easily pleased!' Rachel said.

For a while the two of them ate in silence, but Rachel's thoughts still dwelt on what the girl had told her so far, and something was stirring in her mind.

'Porthgaran, did you say you came from? Wasn't there a fishing boat lost from there, not long ago, a month or so?'

'Yes, the *Luscinia*, lost with all hands. She capsized in a sudden thunderstorm, only a mile off Garan Head. There were six men in the crew and their bodies were washed ashore at St Lar.'

'No doubt the men were known to you?'

'Yes, they were all known to me.'

The girl by now had finished eating and sat, straight-backed, with her hands in her lap. For a while she stared at her empty plate but at last she looked up and met Rachel's gaze.

'The skipper was my father, John Care, and my brother David was one of the crew.' She spoke in a quiet, toneless voice, without any hint of tears in it, but her clear grey eyes had in their depths the coldness and greyness of the sea at dawn. 'They were all the family I had. When they were gone, and I was alone, Porthgaran became a hateful place, especially as—'

'Yes? What?'

'My father was held to blame for what happened. The *Luscinia* was an old boat and he had been warned many times that she was not safe in bad weather. The other four men who were drowned . . . they were all young like my brother David . . . and three of them left widows and children. Their families were very bitter, because of the risks my father took.'

'He paid for it with his own life. Wasn't that enough for them?'

'No, and why should it be?' the girl demanded, and this time she spoke with vehemence; with a sudden angry catch in her voice. 'He paid for it with *David's* life and the lives of four other men besides! I can never forgive him, myself, for throwing away those good young lives?'

'They didn't have to go to sea. They knew the risks and they made their own choice.'

'I can't forgive him all the same.'

'Your father must answer to God, not to you.'

Rachel was not without sympathy, but because she believed in self-restraint, it would not easily find expression. Maggie Care's story, now it was told, was a story only too familiar all

14

along these Cornish coasts. The churchyards were full of fishermen who had forfeited their lives at sea, but still there were many hundreds more prepared to follow the same calling because, as Brice had said once, the sea was there and the fish were in it and that was inducement enough for any man who had his living to win. The girl had suffered a grievous loss, but she was young and had her life before her. She would get over it, given time.

'So you left Porthgaran and took to the roads? I don't know that you were wise, leaving the one place where you were known, to come away among strangers.'

'The place was too full of memories. I made up my mind to start a new life and put the past behind me.'

'Didn't your home mean anything to you?'

'Our cottage was needed for someone else. The landlord was anxious for me to leave and he offered to buy the furniture.'

'At least you have some money, then?'

'No, I put it into the fund, to help the dead men's families.'

'And got small thanks for it, I'll be bound.'

'I didn't wait for thanks. I came away that very day.'

'With nothing but the clothes you are wearing and what you've got in that bundle there! It strikes me that's not very much to start you on this new life of yours.'

Rachel strongly disapproved. She had never met with such foolishness. But the girl appeared healthy and strong and her help would be welcome on the farm. She had not asked for wages; she had asked only for her keep; and so long as she kept her promise to work, Rachel would be well satisfied.

She rose and began clearing the table and the girl followed suit. Together they washed up the tea things and then Rachel led the way out to the hayfield. There was still time to turn a few swaths before it grew properly dark.

The light was just beginning to fade when one of the turf-cutters, on his way home along the road, stopped and looked over the hedge and spoke to Rachel in the field.

'Evening, Mis' Tallack,' he said. 'Weather's holding, edn it, you?'

'So far, so good,' Rachel said.

'I see you've taken her in, then.' The man jerked his head towards the girl who worked, a dim figure in the dusk, some little way across the field. 'Think it was wise of you, midear, taking a stranger into your house, and you all alone when Brice is at sea?'

'Only time will show that, Mr Wearne, but seeing that you sent her to me, if it turns out badly I'll know who to blame.'

'Aw, twadn me, twas Alf Tremearne. I never spoke to her, not one word.' The man leant closer over the hedge. 'Where have she come from? Did she say?'

'She comes from Porthgaran,' Rachel said. 'Her name's Maggie Care and she's nineteen.'

'She's a fine-looking maid, I will say that, but supposing she should turn out a thief? Have you thought of that, Mis' Tallack, midear?'

'Yes, I've thought of it,' Rachel said, 'and I've hidden my jewels in a safe place.'

'Aw, you must have your joke, I suppose, but if anyone was to ask me—'

'Goodnight, Mr Wearne,' Rachel said, dismissing him impatiently, and the man, after a moment's pause, answered with a muttered 'Goodnight, Mis' Tallack' and went on his way along the road.

Rachel, barely able to see, tossed a forkful of hay in the air. By morning, she told herself, all Polsinney would know that Rachel Tallack, up at Boskillyer, had taken a girl in off the road. But that was something that couldn't be helped and if Maggie Care thought to escape attention here in Polsinney, where she was a stranger, she would find that she had made a mistake.

Soon Rachel was obliged to stop work. She called to the girl and they went indoors, and when the two candles had been lit, she moved about the kitchen methodically, filling the kettle ready for the morning, raking the ashes from the stove, and turning the cat out into the yard.

She then led the way upstairs, took a blanket, a pillow, and two sheets from the blanket-box on the landing, and showed the girl into her room: a tiny room with a bunk bed, a cane-

16

seated chair, a chest of drawers, and a row of pegs in a little alcove hidden by a curtain of worn brown plush.

'The last girl who had this room kept her candle burning all night. I hope you won't do the same. Candles cost money and they're dangerous.'

'I shan't keep it burning, I promise you.'

'Then I'll say good night.'

Rachel withdrew, closing the door, and the girl set about making her bed. She then unwrapped her bundle of clothes, laid her nightdress on the chair, and hung the rest away in the alcove. Her room was at the end of the house, over the stable, and while she was getting undressed she could hear the pony shifting about in his stall below. She blew out the candle and got into bed and lay on her back in the pitch-black darkness. The pony was still fidgeting and the sounds he made were companionable. She turned on her side and went to sleep.

In the morning a mist hung over the sea, and the fishing-boats, returning to harbour, came in with it swirling whitely behind them, clinging in shreds about their sails. Rachel, as she went about her tasks in the farmyard, kept a sharp watch on the boats and when the *Emmet* came in, with the white gulls flying and crying behind her, she gave a nod of satisfaction, knowing that Brice had had a good catch.

Maggie helped her to milk the cows and afterwards herded them out of the yard, across the road and onto the moor, where they would graze throughout the day. Rachel then sent her to fetch the pony and together they harnessed him to the milk-float. Two churns of milk were put aboard and Rachel got in and took the reins. Maggie stepped in behind her and they drove slowly out of the yard, along the road skirting the moor, and down one of the turnings leading into Polsinney village.

Their first stop was in front of the church and Rachel's customers, on the alert, emerged from their houses with their jugs and came hurrying down the street, knowing that if they kept her waiting she would whip up the pony and move on.

'Good morning, Mis' Tallack. You're some early this morning. Dunt ee never sleep late at all?'

The women, gathering about the float, stared with frank curiosity at the girl, Maggie Care, as she dipped her measure into the churn and filled the first jug handed up to her.

'I see you've got a new dairymaid. Now where've she come from all of a suddent? I've never clapped eyes cn her, dunt believe.'

'She comes from Porthgaran,' Rachel said, 'and her name's Maggie Care.'

'Porthgaran? My dear life! That's a pure long way from here.' The first customer, receiving her jug, put a coin into Maggie's hand and looked hard into her face. 'And what've brought you to Polsinney, if I may be so bold as to ask?'

'I came looking for work and Mrs Tallack has taken me on.'

'You got relations hereabouts? Or a chap you're sweet on, perhaps?'

'No, there's nobody,' Maggie said.

The woman was about to question her further but Rachel now spoke sharply.

'Make room, Mrs Prideaux, please. Mrs Tambling is waiting her turn. And be so good as to tell your boy not to keep jogging the float.'

Each of the twenty-one customers was at last served with her milk; the coins jingled in Maggie's satchel; and Rachel, with a flip of the reins, drove past the church and into Tubb's Lane. The milk-float made ten stops altogether and at each of them Maggie was questioned. She was asked about her age and her prospects of marriage, about her past life in Porthgaran, and whether she was church or chapel; and all these she answered with polite brevity; but whenever her questioners probed too close, Rachel took it upon herself to answer brusquely on her behalf.

'She's got no family. They're all dead. Her father and brother were drowned last month. Now move aside, Mrs Roberts, please. I haven't got all day to linger here.'

Their last stop was down at the harbour, outside *The Brittany Inn*, and from there they drove to the fish-quay. This was the busiest part of Polsinney, now that the drifters had all come in, and there was a loud babble of voices as the fish-merchants from Porthcoe and the local jowsters, jostling together, called

18

out to the fishermen the prices they were willing to pay for the pilchards glistening in the holds. At the edge of the crowd stood a number of fishermen's wives and daughters, each with a basket on her arm, and as the milk-float came slowly by, they turned to nod to Rachel Tallack and to stare at the stranger accompanying her.

The *Emmet* occupied a berth halfway along the jetty and Brice, together with his crew, stood on a plank across the hold, picking the last few fish from the nets as he bargained with the noisy buyers standing in their carts above. When the milk-float drew up at the back of the crowd, he threw down his section of the net and picked up a basket of pilchards, hoisting it high onto his shoulder. He stepped out onto the jetty, made his way through the crowd, and came to where his mother waited. His sea-boots and short blue smock were covered with glistening fish-scales and his hands were stained with blood and oil. His cap was pushed back from his forehead and his face was smeared with sweat and dirt.

'Who's this you've got riding with you?'

'Her name's Maggie Care,' Rachel said. 'I've taken her on to help on the farm. But never mind about that now. Let's have that basket aboard, quick sharp, so that we can get out of this crowd.'

Brice and the girl exchanged a glance and Brice put a hand to the peak of his cap. He went round to the back of the float and, with a little twist of his body, swung the basket down onto the floor, beside the two empty milk-churns. The girl moved to make room for it, pressing herself against the float's side, and Rachel turned to look down at the fish.

'Better than yesterday, anyway.'

'Yes, they're all prime fish,' Brice said, 'and the biggest catch of the season so far.'

'See that you get the price they deserve.'

The float moved away along the jetty, to a place where there was room to turn, and Brice went back to the boat. The crew had finished clearing the nets and were counting the pilchards into the baskets. Brice stepped into the fish-hold and Ralph Ellis spoke to him.

'I didn't know your mother had got a new dairymaid.'

'I didn't know myself till now.'

Above him the merchants and jowsters were clamouring for his attention. He paused in his counting to look up at them and his blue eyes were suddenly keen.

'Well, gentlemen, and what's the best bid?'

Rachel and Maggie, leaving the quayside, drove along the harbour road, past the shops and the warehouses, the fish-cellars with their dwellings above, the coopers' huts and the customs house and the tiny stonebuilt fishermen's chapel dedicated to St Peter.

At the other end of the harbour, where it completed its horseshoe curve, there was a second quay with a slipway, now fallen into disrepair and used only by smaller craft, punts and dinghies and lobster-boats. Above this old quay stood a small cottage, built on the edge of the sea-wall itself, backing onto the foreshore, but facing inwards across the harbour. Beside it there was a big cobbled yard and on the inner side of the yard stood a sail-loft and some stonebuilt sheds. Outside the cottage, an elderly man in a wheelchair sat with a spyglass to his eye, looking across the curve of the harbour to the fish-quay on the opposite side. As the milk-float drove past the yard the old man swung his spyglass round and watched it until it passed from sight. Rachel was well aware of this but kept her eyes on the road.

'That's my brother-in-law, Gus Tallack. He's an invalid, as you see, and got nothing better to do all day than spy on people with that spyglass of his, minding everyone's business but his own.' Then, in the same acid tone, she said: 'He owns my son's boat, the *Emmet*, and he'll be on tenterhooks till he knows how much money Brice got for his catch.'

She whipped the pony to a trot and turned up the steep winding road that followed the curve of the cliff.

As soon as they had washed out the churns and sluiced the spilt milk from the floor of the float, they set to work on the basket of pilchards, splitting them open and cleaning them, cutting off the heads and tails, and laying the fish down in salt in two big earthenware bussas. Maggie worked with extreme quickness and Rachel noted approvingly that when she topped and tailed the fish she did it precisely, without waste, and that when she laid them in the bussa, each layer was perfectly even, with the salt pressed well down round each fish.

The bussas were put away in the cellar, the offal was given to the pigs, and the empty basket and chopping-board, already attracting flies, were scrubbed clean under the pump. By now the sun was scorching hot, the dew had dried from the hayfield, and Rachel and Maggie, with their big wooden rakes, began drawing the hay into rows, ready for putting up into pooks.

At nine o'clock Brice came home and Rachel went in to prepare breakfast. On his way up from the harbour, he had been stopped by a great many people, enquiring about the girl, Maggie Care; but, as he said to his mother in the kitchen, *they* had told him a lot more than *he* had been able to tell them.

'I hear you took her in off the road and somebody said she'd tramped all the way from Porthgaran. But what brings her here to Polsinney?'

'Her father and brother were both drowned when their boat was lost off Garan Head. It was in the papers a month or so back. Do you remember reading about it?'

'Yes, I remember,' Brice said. 'The boat was unsafe. I remember that.'

'She's got no family left now, she says, and after she'd buried her father and brother she decided to leave Porthgaran for good. It strikes me as very strange that she should leave her own home town to come away among strangers, but it seems that people in Porthgaran had some hard things to say about her father, so she upped one fine day and came away. She's been roaming about these past three weeks, doing casual work on the farms, and last evening she turned up here saying she'd heard I needed help.'

'Well, that's true enough,' Brice said, 'though yesterday, when I mentioned it, you told me you could manage alone.'

'You mentioned asking the Pentecosts. I can certainly manage without *them*.'

'You prefer this Maggie Care?'

'I said I'd give her a month's trial. After that – well, we shall see.'

Rachel now had a good fire going. She pulled the frying-pan onto the hob and dropped six rashers of bacon into it. She then began laying the table. Brice, standing at the kitchen window, could see the girl out in the hayfield: a tall, slim, rather boyish figure, dark hair bare to the sun, strong arms moving rhythmically as she raked the loosely scattered hay and drew it into windrows.

'Judging by what I see, she's no stranger to work,' he said.

'So far, so good,' Rachel agreed. 'But that's often the way with these young girls. They begin well enough but then they get slack. They take advantage. You've seen it yourself.'

'She doesn't look that sort of girl.'

'You can't judge people by their looks.'

'What did *you* judge her by when you decided to take her on?'

'Whatever it was,' Rachel said, 'I could still turn out to be mistaken.'

'Don't you trust her?'

'I don't know. She seems anxious enough to please and she says she's looking for a place where she can settle down for good. She wants to start a new life, she says, and put the past behind her. But I don't begin to understand her. Not yet at least. It seems to me she's a hard nut to crack and she has a way of looking at you sometimes as though she cares not a penny piece for anything you say to her.'

'Not very surprising, perhaps, considering what's happened to her.'

Brice was young. He was twenty-three. And although he favoured his mother in looks, having the same stubborn jaw and the same keen blue eyes, deeply set, his nature, taken as a whole, was more like that of his dead father. The story of the girl's double bereavement therefore touched his sympathy and he was young enough to be stirred by the thought of her courage and resolution in setting out all alone to start a new life for herself. He began to say something of this to his mother but she cut him short.

'You may call it courage if you like but I have a different word for it! What would have become of that girl if I hadn't taken pity on her and given her shelter in my home?'

'I suppose she would have gone elsewhere and you would have lost a good worker.'

Rachel snatched a fork from the table and went to turn the bacon sputtering in the frying-pan.

'Are you going to get yourself washed? Then hurry up or your breakfast will spoil.'

Brice, sitting opposite Maggie at breakfast, was able to study her at his leisure. His first meeting with her on the quay had shown him a girl of striking good looks, but if he had never met her again, all he could have said in describing her was that her eyes were a pure, clear grey. Now, however, as he studied her closely, he saw how shapely her features were and was struck by the way fineness and strength were blended in the structure of her face.

Her cheekbones, perhaps, were almost too strong, but were softened and rendered beautiful by the delicate hollows underneath and by the perfect curve of her chin. Her mouth had forgotten how to smile and in those clear grey eyes lay a shadow that robbed them of expression; but surely, not so long ago, that mouth had expressed tenderness and those eyes had been full of humour and warmth; and one day, in God's good time, Brice thought, those things would surely be restored.

He wanted to know more about her but was shy of asking direct questions. Instead he talked of the night's fishing and described how he had shot his nets three miles west of the Oracle Rocks.

'The night was perfect, dark as dark, and the sea was as docile as a lamb. We got three hours sleep while the nets were out and when it came time for hauling them in everything went like clockwork. But then we decided to shoot again and that wadn smart, as Billy said, for it meant we had our work cut out making harbour in time to get a good berth.'

'How much did you get for your catch?' Rachel asked.

'Ninepence the long hundred.'

'Less than yesterday, then, although they were better quality.'

'There were big catches all round, that's why. The *Speedwell* did better than us and the *Ellereen* ran us close.'

'I know that. I saw for myself. I knew it would bring the prices down.'

'I banked a cheque for twenty-four pounds. That's not bad for one night's work. Uncle Gus won't grumble at that.'

'Tommy Bray must have made twice as much, judging by what I saw of his catch.'

'You don't grudge Tommy his bit of luck? He hasn't had much this season so far.' Brice looked at Maggie Care. 'Do you know my mother's prayer when I go out for a night's fishing? – "Send them in with your blessing, Lord, but only into my son's nets"!'

A glimmer came into the girl's eyes and she gave a faint smile. She had not quite forgotten how, after all, and Brice felt pleased with himself at having won this response from her.

'And what,' Rachel asked, 'is your own prayer, my son?'

'That all the dogfish in the sea should turn and devour one another, and that when only one is left it should sink to the bottom, never to rise.'

One of his nets had been badly holed by dogfish that night. He had brought it home with him and had hung it over the farmyard wall, and as soon as breakfast had been cleared away, Rachel and Maggie went out and began repairing the torn mesh. Brice, on his way to the hayfield, paused and stood watching the girl's quick hands skilfully plying bodkin and twine.

'I can see you've mended nets before.'

'Yes, I've done it all my life.'

'And does the last mesh come out square at the end?'

'Oh, yes. Usually.'

Rachel turned and frowned at her son.

'You are standing in our light,' she said.

The day's heat had become intense. There was thunder in the air. Brice worked in his shirtsleeves, forking the hay from the windrows and building it up into pooks, each as high as his shoulder. At noon his mother and Maggie Care, having

24

finished repairing the net, joined him in the hayfield, and they toiled together in the sun. Such was the heavy heat of the day that they worked in silence, the three of them, but once, when thunder crackled overhead, Rachel paused and looked up at the sky and said in a voice of great vexation:

'Yes, you *would* break now, I suppose, just in time to spoil the hay!'

The storm, however, was passing them by. The clouds were moving away to the west and at half past one, when Rachel went in to prepare dinner, Brice and Maggie, still in the field, could see the dark thunder-shower spending itself out at sea. The storm-clouds hung like a tattered curtain and were lit by flashes of lightning.

'Crockett Lighthouse is getting that. They say if there's any lightning about, Crockett will always bring it down.'

'Can you see the lighthouse from here?'

'Yes, but you have to stand on this hedge.'

Brice climbed onto the stonebuilt hedge and, stooping to give the girl his hand, pulled her up to stand beside him. They could now see as far as Burra Head and its reef of rocks running out into the sea, but Crockett Lighthouse was hidden from them behind the dark curtain of rain. In a moment, however, as they watched, the rain fell further away and the lighthouse suddenly stood revealed, a dazzling white in the glare of the sun, rising, tall and graceful, from its rock at the outermost end of the reef.

'I used to stand here sometimes when I was a boy, watching it being built,' Brice said, 'and later, when it was finished, I was allowed to stay up late to see it lit for the first time.'

'We could see the light from Porthgaran, on clear nights in winter, sometimes,' Maggie said. ' "That's Crockett," my father would say, and it always seemed like another world.'

Brice turned his head and looked at her.

'I'm sorry about your father and brother. My mother told me what happened to them and I know something about it from reading the news in *The Cornishman*. The lifeboat couldn't get out, I believe.'

'The crew were not willing to try. They said it was too dangerous.'

'Do you feel bitter about that?'

'I don't think so. Perhaps. I don't know. There was so much bad feeling afterwards . . . Everyone blaming everyone else . . . My father'd been warned not to go out, so of course he was blamed more than anyone. The whole town was full of bitterness and there was a lot of ugly talk.'

'That's why you came away.'

'Yes.'

Brice got down from the hedge and turned to give Maggie his hand, but she leapt lightly down without his help. She took her rake and went back to work, drawing the last strands of hay from the grass and spreading them over the top of the pook. Brice also took his rake but only to stand leaning on it, watching her as she worked.

'Didn't you have any friends in Porthgaran? And didn't they try to stop you?'

'Nobody could have stopped me. I'd made up my mind. I felt I had to get right away . . . I didn't know where, I left that to chance . . . And as it was haymaking time I knew I was bound to get work.'

'Chance brought you here to us. Do you think you will stay for good?'

'That depends on Mrs Tallack and whether she chooses to keep me on.'

'I hope she will,' Brice said. 'There's always a lot to do on the farm, small though it is, and the nights are very lonely for her, especially in wintertime. It would ease my mind a lot if only she had company at such times.'

The girl was looking at him with a frown. Something seemed to be troubling her and he tried to guess what it was.

'Am I looking too far ahead?'

'Perhaps.'

'But you must have *some* plans for your future. You surely don't want to spend your life wandering from place to place?'

'No, I should want to be settled,' she said, 'but I'm only here on a month's trial and – a lot can happen in a month.'

'Perhaps you have already heard that my mother is a difficult person to please?'

'Yes. She told me so herself.'

26

'Well, it's perfectly true, I suppose, but she could be a good friend to anyone who won her respect.'

'And to those who don't?'

'Then,' Brice said, 'she is quite the reverse.'

The girl turned away from him and he watched her removing the strands of hay that had wound themselves round the teeth of her rake. He was about to speak again; there were many things he wanted to know; but at that moment Rachel appeared, calling to them that dinner was ready, and they put up their rakes and went indoors.

By half past four that afternoon all the hay had been safely pooked and Brice was well pleased with the day's work. Now the thunderstorms could do their worst, but if by good luck they still kept off, that hay could be carted next day, he thought.

At six o'clock he was in the yard, dressed in sea-boots and short canvas smock, getting ready to go down to the boat. He went to collect the pilchard net that was hanging spread out over the wall and began gathering it together, folding it carefully into festoons. While he was doing this Maggie came out of the cowshed and he called her over to give him a hand. He could quite well have managed alone but it was easier with two and it made an excuse for talking to her. She was on her way out to the moor to fetch the cows in for milking but she leant her stick against the wall and began helping to fold the net.

'There are other cows up there besides ours,' Brice said. 'How will you know which to bring?'

'I helped to milk them this morning. I think I know which ones are which.'

'Well, watch out for yourself or they'll lead you a dance. They're often frisky in the evening after grazing out there all day.'

In a few moments more the net was folded and hung from the wall in a neat double truss. He got his shoulder under it, and the girl eased it away from the wall, freeing the mesh where it caught on the stones. He stood upright, taking the weight, and hunched his shoulder two or three times until the net lay comfortably, an equal burden before and behind. His mother came out of the house with the linen bag containing his crowst: pasties, raw onions, apples, cheese, and half a loaf of crusty bread: enough, he said, to last the whole week.

'You say that every night, my son, but the bag's always empty when you bring it home.'

With the heavy net over one shoulder and his bag of crowst over the other, Brice went swinging out of the yard and along the road that led to the village. Before turning down the hill he paused and looked back and saw the girl, Maggie Care, steadily climbing the narrow path up over the edge of the moor. Clumsily, because of his burden, he put up a hand and waved to her, but she was intent on her task, searching the slopes of the moor for the cows, and apparently did not see him. Disappointed, he turned away.

Chapter 2

On her second morning at the farm, and every morning afterwards, Maggie went out on the milk-round alone. It was a chore Rachel detested and she was only too glad to have it taken off her hands. And unlike all her previous girls, who had taken the whole morning over it, Maggie always completed the round as quickly as Rachel did herself.

'I will say this for you, my girl. – You don't waste time gossiping.'

Every morning, at the end of the round, Maggie drove onto the fish-quay and if the night's catch had been a good one, Brice would have a basket of pilchards ready to put into the boat. As his luck was well in at this time, Rachel was soon telling him that no more pilchards were needed at home. She had salted down some twelve hundred fish and that should certainly be enough to see them through the winter months.

'Will it be enough now that Maggie is with us?'

'Winter is a long way off. Maggie may not be here by then. But yes, twelve hundred will be plenty, even for three of us.'

Brice and his mother were alone in the house. Maggie was out feeding the hens.

'You haven't made up your mind, then, whether you will be keeping her on?'

'The girl is here on a month's trial. I shall make up my mind when that month is up.'

Rachel would not commit herself. The habit of caution was too strong. She wanted to know a good deal more about this stranger, Maggie Care, before she finally made up her mind, and this was proving a difficult thing. Most young girls of nineteen revealed themselves in no time at all; their thoughts, their ambitions, their vanities, came out, whether they wished it or not, in their lively prattle as they worked; but Maggie Care never prattled, never gave away her thoughts, and Rachel, at the end of a week, knew no more about her than she had done at the very beginning.

Brice, when his mother said this to him, was inclined to be impatient.

'You always complained that the other girls wasted too much time with their talk. If Maggie doesn't talk so much it's because she's getting on with her work.'

'Something goes on in that head of hers and I should like to know what it is.'

'Only five or six weeks ago her father and brother were drowned at sea. I would have thought it was plain enough that her mind is still full of that.'

'Yes. Well. Perhaps you're right.'

Certainly the girl was willing to work and whatever task she undertook she proved herself very capable. Rachel was a stickler for cleanliness and everything had to be done just so, but even she could find no fault with the way Maggie scrubbed a floor or blackleaded the Cornish slab or beat the mats on the garden wall. Rachel was an excellent cook but Maggie had a hand equally light when making pastry or bread and she had a way with under-roast that Rachel found better than her own. Altogether it seemed, sometimes, as though the girl was too good to be true.

It was the same out in the fields. Whatever she did was done well. The hay had been carted and ricked now and Brice had begun singling the mangolds in the half-acre strip behind the barn. Sometimes Maggie helped him there and he saw with what clean, confident strokes she hoed the weeds out of the rows and how, if she came on a deep-rooted dock, she would stoop and pull it out by hand. Nothing was too much trouble to her. She took more pains than he did himself.

Once when he turned to look at her he saw that she had put down her hoe and was searching for something on the ground; making her way back down the field, bent double, arms outstretched, hands turning over the weeds that she had left scattered between the rows. She had lost the small silver locket that had hung on a ribbon round her neck and there was distress in her face as she searched through the weeds.

Brice went to help her look for it and saw it almost immediately, glinting two or three rows away, half covered in dry-crumbled earth. He picked it up and gave it to her and her hand closed over it gratefully, and such was the look in her eyes that he felt quite ridiculously pleased because, although it was only luck, *he* had been the one to find this thing which plainly was very precious to her. She tied a new knot in the ribbon and hung it round her neck again, tucking the locket inside her dress.

'It used to belong to my mother,' she said. 'I've worn it ever since she died.'

'She was very dear to you?'

'Yes, she was dear to all of us. If only she had been alive when my father was told the boat was unsafe, *she* would have made him give it up. But he wouldn't listen to anyone else. He sailed that boat for another two years and in the end six lives were lost.'

'You find it hard to forgive him for that.'

'Yes, I do.'

'And yet you grieve for him all the same.'

'I grieve for him because he's dead but I can't pretend I was fond of him.'

They turned and walked back along the field. Brice picked up her hoe and gave it to her and she stood for a moment looking at him. For once she seemed inclined to talk.

'My father was rather a hard man and my brother tried to be like him. They had no friends in Porthgaran and nobody ever came to the house . . . except the rest of the crew, of course, and even with them there were arguments. My father was always quarrelsome and after my mother died it got worse. He thought the whole world had a down on him and in a way I suppose he was right.'

Brice was impressed by her honesty. Nothing was as simple as it seemed. At first he had been rather shocked, hearing her deny having loved her father, but he quickly began to understand that this lack of love in her father's lifetime only

31

added another burden to the grief she felt for him now he was dead.

She was only nineteen. There had been little happiness in her life and she faced the future all alone with a terrible tragedy fresh in her mind. He could see by her eyes how it haunted her and he found himself filled with a fervent hope that the future would bring enough happiness to make up to her for the past. He tried, not very lucidly, to say something of this to her, and she took him up on it straight away.

'I don't know about happiness but the future is there, certainly, and something has got to be made of it.' She spoke with a touch of youthful defiance and a certain light came into her eyes which, just for a fleeting instant, drove the shadow right away. 'I intend to make a new life for myself . . . Start again, from the very beginning . . . And whatever the future brings me, be sure I shall make the most of it.'

She and Brice were standing quite close, grey eyes looking straight into blue. Then, abruptly, she turned away and, finding her place in the row, resumed her work of singling the mangolds. Brice went back to his own place and they worked in silence, three rows apart, moving steadily down the field. But secretly, every now and then, he would turn and glance at her, wondering about this new life of hers which, in spite of everything, she looked to with such faith and confidence. God willing, he told himself, he would play some part in that future of hers, though exactly what that part might be he was not yet willing to consider, even in his innermost mind.

The affairs of the *Emmet*, in common with those of most other fishing boats in Polsinney, were organized on a system of shares. Every day, when Brice had sold his catch on the quay, he would bank the cheque with Thomas Kemp, landlord of The Brittany Inn, and Thomas would then send the cash to Brice's uncle, Gus Tallack, who, as owner of the boat, kept a rough and ready 'log' of its profits and losses. On Saturday Gus divided the week's takings into eight equal shares: two for the boat, two for the nets, and four to be split between skipper and crew; and at intervals, during the afternoon, each man would call to collect his share.

There was no fishing on Saturday night because in Polsinney, as elsewhere throughout Cornwall, the sabbath was very strictly observed. On Saturday evening, therefore, after working in the fields, Brice would wash and put on clean clothes and would stroll down to his uncle's cottage, to collect his share of the week's takings and stay for an hour or two gossiping with the old man.

'I'm going down to see uncle Gus,' he said, seeking his mother in the dairy. 'I thought perhaps I could take him some eggs, unless you intend calling on him after church tomorrow morning, in which case you could take them yourself.'

'No, indeed I do not!' Rachel said. 'I called on him last Monday, on my way back from market, and only got shouted at for my pains. He gets more cantankerous every day and the state he's let that cottage get into is too disgraceful for words.'

'He *is* a sick man,' Brice said.

'All the more reason, I would have thought, for him to take heed of good advice.'

'What advice?'

'Oh, never mind! I should have known better than waste my breath on him. But I'm certainly not going again to be shouted at and abused.'

'In that case I'll take the eggs myself.'

Brice stood waiting obstinately and after a moment Rachel gave in. She put a few eggs into a basket and handed it over with an ill grace.

'I hope for your sake that he's in a better temper today than he was last Monday afternoon.'

Gus Tallack was fifty-two: a tall man and solidly built: almost as tall as Brice himself when he stood upright and straightened his back; but this he was rarely able to do because of the obscure wasting disease which, two and a half years before, had struck him down out of the blue, leaving him partially paralysed.

His condition varied mysteriously: on good days, with the

aid of two sticks, he could walk about the house and yard and could even climb the steps to the sail-loft; but on bad days, and they were more frequent now, he had barely enough strength to crawl out of bed and put on his clothes and get himself into the chair on wheels that the Polzeale blacksmith had made for him.

Gus had been a powerful man and indeed his great shoulders and chest gave an impression of strength even now, so that, sitting hunched in his wheelchair, he looked not unlike a latterday Samson held and constrained by invisible bonds. He had a round head of unruly grey curls and a grey curly beard, trimmed short, that encroached high on his thick-fleshed cheeks. But whereas Samson had been blind, Gus had a pair of dark brown eyes that looked out hungrily on the world, missing nothing, and often burnt with the rage he felt at his own weakness and helplessness.

As always in fine weather he sat outside in the yard. From there he could look out to sea and, with the aid of his spyglass, could watch whatever vessels passed. To the right he could watch the big ships that sometimes put in at Polzeale, hidden beyond Struan Point; to the left he could see across the harbour to the sands of Porthvole and Pellow's Reach, completing the eastern curve of the bay, and, above Volley Head, the four little grey-and-white villages of St Inna, St Idric, St Jean and St Owe, with the green slopes of Goonwelter behind.

'My mother sent you some eggs,' Brice said, 'and asked me to say she hoped you were well.'

Gus cocked a bushy eyebrow at him.

'Either you are a damned liar or your mother's a damned hypocrite!'

'Here are the eggs, anyway. At least *they* are honest enough.'

'Be damned to the eggs!' his uncle said. 'And to the rest of the things she sends! She only keeps on the right side of me cos of getting my property when I'm gone. She wishes me dead, the old catfish, and the sooner the better, that's what she thinks.'

'That's not true.'

'Oh yes it is. I know that mother of yours, by God! She was

in here a few days ago and had the cheek to tell me that since I am failing in health and can't run my business properly I ought to hand it over to you and let you run it for me!'

'She had no right to say that. She certainly wasn't speaking for me and I have absolutely no wish—'

'Tes all the same if you have or not! The sail-loft and the barking-house are nothing whatever to do with you, at least not while I'm still alive, and I pretty damn quickly told her so!'

'Then I hope that will be the end of it.'

Brice drew up a wooden box and sat down beside his uncle. The old man took a pinch of snuff.

'So Rachel's got a new dairymaid? Some poor wretch of a girl that she can bully and put through the hoop! She've come from Porthgaran, I hear, and been tramping the roads looking for work. According to the rumours flying about, her father and brother were fishermen and were lost at sea a month or two back.'

'Rumour has told the truth for once.'

'She's all alone in the world, then? Well, that'll soon be changed, I daresay. She looks a fine docy maid from the little I've seen of her, driving past, and if she've come in search of a husband, she'll soon pin one down for herself, no doubt.'

'Why should you think that of her?'

'I never saw a maid yet that wasn't anxious to get married.'

'Maggie is different from most other girls.'

'Then maybe you've got ideas yourself?'

'She's only been with us four or five days.'

'Long enough for you to find out that she's different from other girls.'

Brice smiled but was not to be drawn and after a while his uncle Gus, although plainly curious, began talking of other things: chiefly of the affairs of the boat and the prospects for the rest of the pilchard season, based on the catches so far.

'You've had a good week this week. Shares worked out thirty shillings a man. Your crew have already been for theirs. You'll find your own on the table indoors. Go in and help yourself and while you're there put these damned eggs away and bring out the rum and glasses.'

35

Brice went into the kitchen and picked up the pile of coins his uncle had put ready for him. Among the clutter of odds and ends that covered the bare boards of the table lay the remains of his uncle's supper: half a loaf, already stale, and a piece of dark, greasy cheese; and when he put the eggs into the larder he saw that the shelves were almost bare. The kitchen was dirty and comfortless and looked as though it had not been touched since his visit the previous Saturday. The stove was stuffed full of rubbish and the hearth underneath was so choked with ash that it fell out over the fender onto the stone flags of the floor. He found the rum and two glasses and returned to his uncle in the yard.

'Has Mrs Kiddy been in today?'

'No, she've got a bone in her leg.'

'She promised to cook you a meal every day but that slab can't have been lit for days.'

'Seems you've been having a good look round.'

'She's supposed to come in and keep the place clean—'

'I know what she's *supposed* to do!' the old man exclaimed, flying into a rage. 'The place is a pigsty! I know that! D'you think I don't *know* what the place is like?'

With an effort he tried to control himself but his temper, once roused, was hard to put down.

'Tes just the same in the sail-loft! Dirt and rubbish everywhere and Isaac Kiddy so bone idle he never comes in till half past eight, sometimes nearer nine o' clock. They take advantage, all of them, but what am I supposed to do? I can't *make* the beggars work when I'm stuck in this chair like a sack of beans!'

Brice poured out two glasses of rum and put one into his uncle's hand.

'Would it be a good idea if I had a word with Isaac Kiddy?'

'No, damme, it would not!' This suggestion made matters worse. 'You may be skipper of the boat but you're not skipper here yet, by God! You'll have to wait till I'm dead for that!'

The old man glared at Brice. His lips were parted in a little snarl. He took a deep breath, trembling, and swallowed his rum at a single draught. Gradually he calmed down and after a while, when he spoke again, his voice was quiet and matter-of-fact, although it still had an edge to it.

'You won't have to wait much longer,' he said. 'This damned disease, whatever it is, is beginning to get a hold on me and two or three years should see me out. Dr Sam has made that plain. I asked him and he told me straight.'

Brice knew that this was true. He had spoken to Dr Sam himself. The wasting disease, which began in the spine, attacked the muscles and the nerves, causing progressive atrophy. Almost nothing was known of its cause and there was no hope of a cure. All Dr Sam could say was that the wasting would spread throughout the system and that when in time it reached the lungs it would inevitably bring death.

'Dr Sam could be wrong,' Brice said.

'Don't talk widdle. It makes me tired. At least your mother spares me that. She never makes any bones but that I'm a dying man and Isaac Kiddy is the same. They're all as bad, the whole boiling of 'm, and take as much account of me as if I was dead already!'

The old man refilled his glass and sat staring into it. Then he looked out to sea.

'I *try* to be a good loser,' he said. 'Tes all in the luck of the draw, after all, and if God've singled me out like this, well, he's in the position to have the last word. But I wish he'd chosen something quick. There've been plenty of times in my life when I've had to ride out a gale in the *Emmet*, with great seas coming over her, higher than the top of her mast, when God could've finished me off like that!'

Gus gave a snap of his hard, horny, misshapen fingers.

'But instead he cuts me down from behind . . . Takes all my strength, inch by inch, and leaves me so helpless as a worm . . .' He turned his head and looked at Brice and there was a kind of childlike puzzlement in his eyes as he said: 'Now why should God do a thing like that? I can't make it out at all. He must have some reason for cutting me down and maybe if I knew what it was . . . I'd be better able to say "Amen." '

There was a pause. Gus sat slumped in his chair, the evening sun full in his face and a faint breeze stirring his hair where it curled from under his seaman's cap. On the old quay below the cottage some boys were fishing with a handline and there was a sudden commotion among them as they landed a handsome mackerel. A few gulls gathered, screaming; trod the air for a moment or two; then wheeled away overhead; over the cottage and sail-loft and sheds and down onto the foreshore beyond.

'I don't know,' Brice said. He could not think of anything to say to this stricken man who was trying to wrest some meaning from the cumbered life that was left to him. 'I just don't know.'

'Of course you don't! Nobody does!' Gus, coming out of his mood of abstraction, dismissed the subject with a wave of his hand. 'Take no heed of my ramblings. Let's talk about something else. Did you know that Martin Laycock is building a new boat for George Newpin? He came to see me to order the sails . . .'

When Brice got home to the farm, his mother was busy in the yard, filling her pails and churns at the pump to cool them ready for the evening milking. Brice took over working the pump and when he had finished he said to her:

'I hear you've been telling uncle Gus how to run his own business. That's why you had words when you saw him last.'

'I tried to give him some good advice and he threw it in my face,' Rachel said. 'That business is going to rack and ruin. The barking-house has been closed for months – goodness knows how much money is lost by that – and the sail-loft will soon go the same way if half the tales I hear are true. Your uncle has lost his grip on things and if he had an ounce of sense he'd hand the business over to you. With your good schooling and your good brain you're wasted as a fisherman and I've said so from the very first.'

'I don't want to take over the business. I'm quite happy as I am.'

'You'll *have* to take over when your uncle dies, unless you decide to sell it up, and the way things are going at present there soon won't be anything left to sell. The cottage and sheds will tumble down if something isn't done soon—'

Rachel broke off and became silent, for Maggie had come

38

out of the byre and was crossing the yard to the gate, on her way to the moor to bring in the cows, and Rachel did not want her to hear this private discussion of family affairs. Brice also remained silent, giving the girl a little salute, but when she had gone out of the gate he turned again to his mother and said:

'We have no right, either of us, to interfere in my uncle's affairs. He's always been very good to me and whatever *your* feelings may be *I* have nothing but respect for him. The sail-loft and the barking-sheds are his property – his alone – and what he chooses to do with them is no concern of ours while he lives.'

'I don't agree,' Rachel said. 'You're his only living relation and the property's bound to come to you and although you may take a high moral tone you can't pretend you don't care what is happening to your inheritance.'

'That's as maybe,' Brice said, 'but if you try to interfere you'll only antagonize uncle Gus and no good will come of that.'

The good practical sense of this was plainly indisputable and Brice saw from his mother's face that he had succeeded in silencing her. He turned away feeling satisfied. The discussion had been disagreeable to him and he was glad it was at an end. He could now turn his mind to other things.

'I think I'll go after Maggie and give her a hand with the cows.'

'There's no need for that. She can manage alone.'

'I think I'll go up all the same.'

He strode away out of the yard and Rachel stood frowning after him. The other girls who had worked on the farm had never attracted his interest at all and she had always been thankful for it. But this girl, Maggie Care, had only to walk past him and he could not wait to follow her. Rachel gave an angry sigh. It was a problem she had not foreseen.

During the first week in August Brice cut the three acres of dredge-corn in the field furthest from the house. His mother and Maggie bound up the sheaves and set them up into shocks

39

and the wheat and barley, ripening together, whispered in the warm dry wind. Everywhere, on the neighbouring farms, harvest was well under way and the bustle of it filled the air. Reaping-machines churred all day long and the voices of the reapers could be heard calling from one field to the next.

Down in Polsinney itself there was bustle of another kind, for it was now the time of year when the pilchard shoals, making their way down the Channel, were expected to come close inshore, and this was when the seine-fishers expected to reap their own harvest. The seine-crews had been put into pay and the boats lay out in the bay day and night, each to its own allotted stem, while the huers up on the cliff at Porthvole took it in turns to watch for the shoals which, when they came close enough, would betray their presence to a keen eye by the darkening and thickening of the waters and a turbulence on the sea's surface.

The seine owners, in smart frock coats and stovepipe hats, were up on the cliff day after day, but so far the shoals had proved shy. Brice strolled up one afternoon and lingered for a while with the crowd of people who, in a state of high expectation, kept the huer company, all staring out to sea. John Lanyon, who owned the New Venture Seine, offered Brice a large cigar and spoke to him in a jocular way that only half hid his fretted nerves.

'You drifter chaps are no friends of ours. You break up the shoals and drive them away. I shall be on the rocks myself if the season's as bad as it was last year.'

Brice refused the proffered cigar and stood staring out at the bay.

'The shoals will come in. They always do. And so long as they come in on your stem all you need worry about is your warps.'

This was a sly joke on his part for twice during the previous season a shoal, enclosed by the New Venture Seine, had been lost because the rope had parted while the beachmen were hauling it up the shore.

'It won't happen this time. I've made sure of that.'

Lanyon now began to ask how things were on the farm. He was Brice's landlord and liked to show a friendly concern.

'I hear you've got a new dairymaid. A mystery girl from down the coast that your mother took in off the road. That was a Christian act on her part.'

'It has been amply repaid,' Brice said, 'for Maggie is a good worker.'

'Your mother is pleased, then?'

'Yes, indeed.'

'And what is your own opinion of her? Is she as comely as they say?'

'No doubt you'll meet her one of these days,' Brice said, 'then you'll be able to judge for yourself.'

He turned and walked home along the cliff.

The hot dry weather continued and soon the dredge-corn was carted and ricked. The seine-boats still lay out in the bay and the huers still kept watch on the cliff but so far no shoals had come inshore. Once a shoal was seen in the distance but it veered away off Burra Head and the groan that arose from the disappointed watchers could be heard in the fields at Boskillyer.

But although the seiners were so far unlucky, the drifters were enjoying a good season. Because of the calm, easy weather Brice was able to fish every night and catches were consistently good. His uncle, paying his share one Saturday evening, did so with a teasing remark.

'If you *are* thinking of getting married, at least you needn't plead poverty.'

'You are in a great hurry, suddenly, to get me married off,' Brice said, 'yet you've been a bachelor all your life.'

'Rumour tells me you're keen on the girl.'

'Does it indeed!'

'Why, isn't it true?'

'I think myself,' Brice said, 'that people should mind their own business.'

'The day they begin doing that,' Gus said, 'it will be the end of the world.' He looked thoughtfully at Brice and said: 'Of course, I can quite understand that you've got to mind your

41

p's and q's, courting right under your mother's nose. She won't exactly be over the moon to see you marry her servant-girl.'

'Maggie's no ordinary servant-girl and I'm sure my mother would say so herself.'

'You think she'll give it her blessing, then?'

'I hope she will.'

'And what if she won't?'

Brice considered carefully.

'I shall be very sorry,' he said, 'but my mother doesn't rule my life.'

'I'm glad to hear it!' his uncle said. 'But it's not for want of trying, eh?'

Brice, as he walked home that evening, was full of a young man's irritation at knowing that he and Maggie Care were the subject of gossip in the village. His feeling for her was still new to him, a secret thing, shut away in his heart, and it was an unpleasant shock to find that onlookers with busy tongues had already been at work bringing out into the open something he had thought safe and secure.

And now, in talking to his uncle Gus, he had been led into making an admission before he was properly ready for it, and this caused him some disquiet. Still, however, it couldn't be helped, and he could only hope that his uncle Gus would at least respect his confidence. As for the rest, his uncle was right: such talk was inevitable and he would just have to accept it; but it irritated him all the same and he knew he would have to be on his guard.

Every morning, coming up from the boat, as soon as he reached the top of Cliff Hill and turned onto the level road, he would look for Maggie in the fields. He would call to her over the hedge and she would glance up and give him a wave. Once he brought home an enormous hake and held it up for her to see. 'Did you ever see such a monster?' he said. 'Its father must have been a shark!' And once he brought home a string of whiting because she had said it was her favourite fish.

One day Brice went up to the moor and brought home a cartload of turfs which he had cut early in June. Maggie helped to unload them and stack them up in the back yard, and while they were working thus together, he spoke about the St Glozey sports, to be held the following Saturday.

'St Glozey sports are a great affair. Wrestling, running, sheaf-pitching, and tea afterwards in the marquee. I hear there's to be a German band and the hand-bell ringers are coming from Steeple Lumbtown to compete with the ringers from Polzeale.' Brice took a pile of turfs from the cart and put them into Maggie's hands. 'I wondered if you'd come with me,' he said. 'It's time you had an outing away from the farm.'

She stood quite still, looking at him, and her eyes were full of deep-questing thought. What she was thinking he could not divine but it seemed to cause her uneasiness and after a moment she turned away to place the turfs on the growing rick.

'No, I don't think I should,' she said.

'Why ever not?' Brice asked. He was somewhat taken aback. 'Is it because you think it's too soon after losing your father and brother?'

'I don't know. Yes. Perhaps.'

But her glance had now become evasive and he saw that she had been too quick to grasp the excuse he had offered her.

'No one in Polsinney would expect you to keep such strict mourning.'

'Wouldn't they?'

'No, they would not.'

'I'd sooner not come all the same. It's kind of you to ask me but – I don't really like watching sports.'

'In that case, of course, there's no more to be said.'

Brice was disappointed and piqued but, brooding afterwards on her refusal, he wondered if his mother might have something to do with it. He decided to find out and spoke to her that very evening. They were alone in the kitchen together. Brice was getting ready to go down to the boat and Rachel was preparing his food for the night.

'St Glozey sports?' she said blankly. 'It's nothing to do with

43

me, my son, if the girl has refused to go with you. I've heard nothing about it till now.'

'I realize that,' Brice said, 'but I've seen the way you look sometimes when Maggie and I are talking together and I thought perhaps you had said something to make her feel you disapproved.'

Rachel took a deep breath. His challenge had taken her by surprise. She had been conscious from the beginning of the interest he took in Maggie Care and the problem of it had vexed her sorely. She had decided to bide her time but now that Brice had broached the matter she knew she would have to speak her mind.

'I've said nothing to Maggie Care but I *have* got plenty to say to *you*. I would have thought you'd have had more sense than to fix your attentions on a girl employed as servant in this house. You can do better for yourself than marry the daughter of a fisherman who hasn't a penny piece to her name and I hope you'll take heed of what I say before it's gone too far.'

'As I am a fisherman myself I can see nothing wrong—'

'You needn't be a fisherman all your days and well you know it!' Rachel said. 'When your uncle's property comes to you, it means you'll be able to give up the sea, and once you've built up that business again and got it properly on its feet, you'll be able to live the life you are best fitted for.'

'You don't seem to understand that none of that means anything to me. The sea is my life. It's all I want. But whatever I may do in the future –' Here Brice paused for thought because once again he was being led into making a premature admission. And yet – was it really premature? No, it was not. He knew his mind. 'Whatever I do in the future,' he said, 'I should still want Maggie as my wife.'

'A girl you know nothing about, that I took in off the road?' Rachel said.

'Don't you like her?'

'That's not the point! What I know I like well enough. It's what I *don't* know that worries me. There is something about that girl that's not quite right and I can't quite bring myself to trust her.'

'Maybe you haven't tried hard enough,' Brice said, quietly,

44

'but now that you know what my feelings are, I hope you will try for my sake.'

This was the nearest he had ever come to a serious quarrel with his mother and he hoped, by appealing to her in this way, to ease the friction between them before he left to go down to the boat. He could see he had made her very angry but anger came so readily to her that he was almost inured to it and he had enough faith in her to know that, given a little time, she would take his words to heart and do what she knew was best for him. Watching her as she packed up his food, he could see her struggling with herself, and when, in a while, she turned to him, he could see that she had reached some resolve.

'You haven't mentioned marriage yet?'

'No. Not yet. It's much too soon. Maggie –' He searched for the right words. 'Maggie is like a wandering bird, looking for a place to rest,' he said. 'She needs time to find herself.'

He took the bag containing his food and slung it over his shoulder.

'You won't say anything to her, will you, about St Glozey or anything? I think it's better to leave it alone.'

'Don't worry, my son,' Rachel said dryly. 'I don't intend to do your courting for you. You're a grown man and you know your own mind – even if you *are* a born fool!'

Brice left the house feeling relieved. The quarrel, he thought, had cleared the air. Things would be easier from now on and all that remained for him to do was to woo and win the girl of his choice.

Rachel, during the next few days, was much exercised in her mind. She still felt bitterly angry over her son's foolishness and wished with all her heart and soul that she had turned the girl away instead of receiving her into her home. But it was too late to wish that now. She would just have to make the best of things. The trial period of one month was now drawing to an end and as far as her work was concerned the girl had given complete satisfaction.

Her one and only fault was that she had engaged Brice's affections and this she had done unconsciously. Unlike the

45

previous servant-girls, who had flaunted themselves in front of him, Maggie had gone about her business and had never for a single instant deliberately put herself in his way. And Brice, who had treated the other girls with good-humoured indifference, had been ensnared by Maggie's reserve. Perhaps after all she knew this. Perhaps she had been more subtle than they. But Rachel had to admit to herself that, shrewdly though she watched the girl, she could detect no guile in her.

Maggie was so wrapped up in herself that she seemed unaware of Brice's interest, and that was a curious thing in itself, singular in a girl of nineteen. But it was only a question of time before awareness dawned on her and once that happened she was sure to respond for no girl, Rachel thought, could resist a personable young man with prospects once she knew she had his love.

Rachel, at the kitchen window, stood watching Maggie out in the yard, taking the washing off the line and dropping it into a basket. The girl had good points, there was no doubt of that, and if Brice had set his heart on her, was it such a bad thing after all? 'I wish I knew!' Rachel exclaimed to herself. 'I wish I could see into that girl's mind!'

Maggie now came into the kitchen and tipped the washing onto the table. She filled a bowl with warm water and began damping down the clothes, dipping her fingers into the bowl, flicking water over them, and rolling them up into tight rolls.

'If only you'd picked them in earlier, you'd have been spared that job!' Rachel said.

Try as she would, she could not always entirely suppress the irritation that rose in her, for what did they know about this girl beyond a few bald facts that told them little or nothing of her character? Rachel respected her for her competance and Brice thought he was in love with her but she was as much a stranger to them now as on the day she had first arrived.

'Tomorrow is Tuesday and you will have been here a month,' Rachel said. 'Do you wish to stay on?'

The girl looked up from damping the clothes.

'If you are willing to keep me, yes, I would like to stay,' she said.

'Very well, it's settled, then.' Rachel gave a little sigh.

46

'You're a good worker, I will say that, but mind and see that you keep it up.'

For a moment it seemed as though the girl was about to say something more and Rachel waited expectantly. But the moment passed in silence, the girl went on with her task, and whatever she had intended to say remained unsaid.

The following morning, when Maggie went out on the milk-round, she was gone longer than usual and when she returned at half past eight Rachel was looking out for her.

'What kept you, miss?'

'I don't know. Everything seemed to take a long time.'

'Are you all right?'

'Yes. Oh, yes.'

But the girl, Rachel thought, was looking wisht. There was a cloudiness in her eyes; her forehead and upper lip were moist; and although the two milk-churns were empty, the effort of lifting them from the float left her palpably breathless.

'Are you ill?' Rachel asked.

'No. I'm just feeling the heat.'

This was a piece of arrant nonsense, for the weather had turned cooler now, and the girl's excuse only served to deepen the suspicion quickening in Rachel's mind.

For the moment, however, she said no more; she pretended to be fully occupied with the business of sluicing out the float; but all the time she was keeping watch and when Maggie went to unyoke the pony, reaching up on tiptoe to lift the collar from his neck, she noted what a strain it was to her and saw how, when the task was accomplished, the girl was overcome by giddiness and had to put one hand on the float to steady herself until it had passed.

Rachel went to her, took the collar and harness from her, and carried them into the stable. She then let the pony into the pasture and when that was done she returned to Maggie, who still stood beside the float, pale-faced but recovering.

'Come with me,' she said crisply. 'It's time we had a little talk.'

In the kitchen she motioned the girl to a chair, fetched a cup of water for her, and stood over her while she drank.

'I felt all along there was something left out of the tale you told when you first came and now I know what it is. You are going to have a child?'

'Yes.'

'Don't you think it was deceitful, wheedling your way into my house without telling me the truth?'

'Would you have taken me in if you'd known?'

'No, I would not. But where was the point in deceiving me? You couldn't keep your secret for ever.'

'I thought perhaps, by the time you knew, you would be willing to let me stay. I thought if I worked hard enough—'

'Then you were a fool,' Rachel said. 'How many people, do you think, would be willing to give house-room to a girl with an illegitimate child? Very few, let me tell you, and I am not one of them.'

'Even though I am willing to work without any wages except my keep?'

'No, it's out of the question, and you should know better than to ask.' There was a pause and then Rachel said: 'Who is the father of your child?'

'His name was Jim Kenna,' Maggie said. 'He was one of my father's crew and he was drowned along with the rest. We were to have been married in September.'

'It's a pity you didn't wait. You'd have saved yourself a packet of trouble.'

'No, that's not how I feel,' Maggie said. 'I'm glad I'm having Jim's baby. It's all I have to remember him by.'

'Have you no sense of shame, girl, at bringing a love-child into the world?'

'No, Mrs Tallack, I don't think I have.' Maggie was quite composed now and although her face was still deathly pale, her eyes were steady and clear again and her chin had a certain lift to it. 'It's a bad start for a child, I know, but . . . I shall try to make up for that in every possible way I can.'

'And how are you to do that when you are all alone in the world?'

'I don't know. But I shall, somehow.'

48

'What about your lover's family? Couldn't they have helped you?'

'Jim had no family,' Maggie said. 'He was brought up in an orphanage.'

'Well,' Rachel said, and drew a deep breath. 'This is a pretty problem indeed but you've only yourself to blame for it. If you've got any sense at all you'll go back to Porthgaran where you belong and let your own parish look after you.'

'No. I shall never go back there.'

'If it's the gossip that worries you, you'll find it the same wherever you go, as soon as people know the truth.'

'Gossip doesn't worry me. I know I shall have to face that. But Porthgaran is an unhappy place, full of bitter memories, and I shall never go back to it now. If I can't stay here—'

'And you certainly can't.'

'Then I must move on somewhere else.'

'If you go tramping the roads again, you'll soon be arrested as a vagrant, my girl, and then you'll be packed off back to Porthgaran whether you like it or not.'

'I shan't be arrested. I'll make sure of that.' The girl rose and went to the stairs. 'I'd better go up and pack my things.'

Rachel, exasperated, clicked her tongue.

'You don't need to be so hasty as that. I'm quite willing to let you stay until you've had time to think yourself out. I'll give you until the end of the week.'

Briefly the girl seemed undecided but in a moment she shook her head.

'There's nothing to be gained by putting it off. I think I'd as soon go straight away.'

'And where do you mean to go, may I ask?'

'I don't know. I haven't thought. I shall think about it on the way.'

'Such a mess you've got yourself into! I can't think what's to become of you! You don't seem to have the slightest idea of the dangers you're running tramping the roads!'

Rachel was angry and upset. True, her discovery of the girl's condition had lit a flame of triumph in her, and never once had she doubted her wisdom in sending the girl away from the farm. But Maggie's predicament worried her and the haste with which the girl was departing made her feel uncomfortable.

Still, perhaps it was all for the best. In two or three hours, when Brice came home, she would have to break the news to him, and that would cause him pain enough. But at least if the girl was already gone he would be spared the added pain, not to mention embarrassment, that meeting her was bound to cause once he knew the sorry truth. Yes, indeed, it was all for the best, and this reflection did much to ease the disquiet in Rachel's mind.

Upstairs, in her little bedroom, Maggie collected her few belongings and put them into the old worsted shawl. It was a task soon done and she wasted no time over it. She tied the shawl's corners into knots and, thrusting her arm through the loop, pushed the bundle up high so that it hung, satchel-wise, comfortably over her shoulder. She took a last look round the room, making sure she had left nothing, and went downstairs.

Rachel, seeing her off at the door, tried to press money into her hand, but she pushed it away.

'I don't want charity, Mrs Tallack.'

'Hah! That's all very fine!' Rachel said. 'But what were you looking for when you came here, if it was not charity, pray?'

'I was looking for friendship,' Maggie said.

She turned and walked out of the yard and Rachel, after a brief delay, followed her as far as the gate to see which way she had gone. The girl had turned left along the road but was already crossing it to take the steep winding track that led up over the moor. For a while Rachel remained at the gate, watching the girl's lonely figure making its way up the lonely moor, under a sky that threatened rain. That was the last of Maggie Care, she said to herself as she turned away, but although her chief feeling was satisfaction, it was not entirely unmixed with regret.

The girl was made of good strong stuff; her help would be sorely missed on the farm; and if circumstances had been different she might even, Rachel admitted, have made a suitable wife for Brice. But circumstances could not be changed and Rachel would not allow herself to waste time in vain regrets. She still had to face Brice with the news and that prospect was enough to drive all other thoughts from her mind.

Maggie's objective, as she climbed the steep moorland track, was the old ruined engine-house of Bal Kerensa, standing close beside the stream on the level ground at the top of the slope. The morning's events had tired her; she needed time to rest and reflect; so when she came to the engine-house she left the track and went inside. Against the far wall, as she already knew, there was a heap of dead bracken, cut by some farmer the winter before and stored there for future use, and on it she made herself comfortable, leaning back against the wall and folding her hands over her stomach.

This morning, for the first time, her baby had moved inside her womb. The lurching of it had caused her pain; it had made her feel giddy and sick, bringing a darkness that clouded her senses; but the pain had been welcome to her and her heart had leapt in response to it, because of the life thus asserting itself, making demands upon her body, giving her own life meaning and purpose.

For this child was fruit of the love and the tender overwhelming passion that she and gentle Jim Kenna had known in those few happy weeks before he had been taken from her. She hoped and prayed it would be a boy, who would grow up to be the sort of man Jim had been: strong and gentle, quiet-voiced, full of good humour and kindliness; but whether it should be boy or girl, she would love it and cherish it just the same, for Jim's sake, because it was his. Indeed she loved it fiercely already and was eager for the feel of it moving underneath her hands. But the baby was quite still now and she pictured it curled at rest in her womb; and in her mind she spoke to it, saying: 'Yes, you are there. You've let me know. I don't mind if you bring me pain so long as I know you are there and alive.'

Jim had known about the baby and he had wanted to bring their wedding forward because of those people in Porthgaran who, as he said, could always be relied on to count up to nine and would take delight in doing so. Maggie had merely laughed at that. 'They will still count, whatever we do, but I don't care what they say so long as we're together, you and me.' But with Jim dead it was a different matter. Her father had been disliked all his life and after his death he had been reviled, and because she could not bear the thought that her child would be born and would grow up among people filled with such bitterness, she had turned her back on the place and had set out into the unknown. Had she been foolish? Yes, perhaps. For here she was, friendless and homeless, glad to seek temporary shelter in this old ruined building, without any roof overhead and without even a door to close against marauding cattle and sheep.

Still feeling sick and faint, and knowing a moment of hopelessness, she instinctively sought comfort by drawing out the silver locket she wore on a ribbon round her neck. She took it off and opened it and looked at the two pictures inside. One was of her mother, sad but serene, looking at her with tired eyes. The other was of Jim Kenna and although the picture was small and dim it was enough to bring to her mind his good, plain, honest face with its kindly look and crooked smile. The picture made her ache for him and after she had closed the locket she sat with it clenched tight in her hand, yielding herself to her memories, of his voice and his touch and his tenderness, and allowing herself to be overcome by the hopelessness of her longing for him.

The longing and the hopelessness passed. She hung the locket round her neck and tucked it away inside her dress. The sickness and faintness also passed; she was feeling herself again; and as her youthful strength and courage began to reassert themselves she sat up straight, hugging her knees, and began to think about the future.

Rachel Tallack's warning, that if she was arrested for vagrancy she would be taken back to Porthgaran, weighed heavily on her mind and she recognized the dangers of taking to the road again in search of work on other farms. Farm-work was what she did best; it was what she was used to; but there were other kinds of work available to girls like herself and she didn't mind what she did so long as she earned enough money to rent a lodging and buy food. In her pocket she had two shillings; enough to live on for at least a few days; but after that, if she failed to find work, she would either have to beg or go hungry.

She rose and went to the open doorway and stood looking down at Polsinney, built hugger-mugger, the houses close-packed, tucked into the cliffside and running steeply down to the sea. The harbour itself was hidden from her but she could see where, out in the bay, the seine-boats still lay-to, their patient crews waiting and watching for the pilchard shoals to come inshore. She could also see that part of the cliff where the huer had his look-out place and she could see that a large crowd still kept the huer company. The shoals were late coming in this year but when they did at last come there would be work for scores of people down in the fish-cellars on the wharf.

Maggie now reached a decision. She went to where she had left her bundle, took a square cotton scarf from it, and hid the bundle among the bracken. A light rain was beginning to fall and she tied the scarf over her head. She then left the old engine-house and set out over the brow of the moor to that part, well away from Boskillyer, where a second track ran down to the road. From there she took one of the alleys that led, by many a twist and turn, down to the harbour and the wharf.

Here, too, as on the cliff, scores of people were gathered, all looking eagerly out to sea. Many of these were the women and girls who, when the great moment came, would be rushed off their feet in the cellars, receiving the hundreds of thousands of pilchards brought ashore from the seine: tipping them out on the cellar floor, arranging them neatly, row by row, one layer upon another, each layer spread with salt, until they rose shoulder-high and formed a solid wall of fish. The women would work by shifts, day and night, till every last silver pilchard was safely in cure in the bulk, and for this work they would earn good wages, sometimes as much as fourpence an hour.

As Maggie mingled with the crowd, people turned to look at her, and one old woman, meeting her eye, tut-tut-tutted with toothless gums, pointing her long, bony chin in the direction of the bay.

'They old pilchers!' she exclaimed. 'They dunt seem to realize that we've been waiting a week or more. But they will come in pretty soon, I believe, for the stones've been rumblen these three nights past and there's no surer sign than that.'

'I hope you're right,' Maggie said.

She stood in the rain looking out to sea and the old woman eyed her up and down.

Brice, on getting home to Boskillyer, missed Maggie immediately and asked where she was.

'The girl has gone,' Rachel said.

'Gone? Where? On an errand, d'you mean?'

'No, she's gone for good, my son, and please do not fly out at me until you've heard what I have to say.'

'Do you mean you've sent her away?' Brice asked in a tight voice. 'Because if you have I must warn you—'

'That precious girl of yours,' Rachel said, 'is three or four months gone with child, and I counsel you to think on that before you begin speaking to me in a way you may well regret.'

She made no attempt to mince her words for she fully intended to shock him, and even when she saw from the look on his face that she had succeeded all too well, she gave no sign of the pity she felt, for he had a hard lesson to learn and the sooner he learnt it the better, she thought.

'I knew from the start there was something not quite right about her. I felt it in my very bones. For one thing it isn't natural for a young girl to have so little to say for herself and if you remember I said so to you—'

'How did you find out?' Brice asked.

'I used my eyes,' Rachel said.

'Did she admit it?'

'Of course she did. She could hardly do anything else.'

'I don't understand it,' Brice said. His face was still stiff and numb with shock but he had great powers of self-control and was beginning to use them. 'Who was the man responsible?'

'He was one of her father's crew. He was drowned with the rest. She was to have married him next month, it seems.'

There was a silence in the room. Brice took a deep and difficult breath.

'Poor girl,' he said at last. 'To lose not only her father and brother but the man she was going to marry as well . . .'

'Yes, poor girl indeed,' Rachel said, 'but what I can't quite forget is her slyness in coming here to me, persuading me to take her in, and all the time practising such deceit.'

'You lost no time in turning her out.'

'I gave her until the end of the week. It was she who chose to leave straight away.'

'Where has she gone?'

'I don't know.'

'Didn't she say what she meant to do?'

'No, she did not,' Rachel said. 'All I can tell you is that she went the same way as she came – up the track and over the moor.'

'How long ago?'

'About two hours.'

'Then I'd better go after her.'

'Oh, for pity's sake!' Rachel said. 'Are you such a poor witless fool that you hanker after her even now?'

Brice, with a gesture, turned away, impatiently scorning his mother's suggestion. His feelings were still too tender, too raw, for him to discuss them openly, but no, Maggie was nothing to him now that he knew the truth about her, for he saw with terrible clarity that the girl he had come so close to loving had never really existed at all.

The real Maggie Care was someone quite different; a girl with a past life of her own that he knew nothing about; a girl who, when he had looked at her with a young man's innocent desire, had carried this secret thing in her, this seed of knowledge in her womb, implanted there by another man. He felt no anger against her, – at least he told himself he did not – for never by a single word or glance had she ever encouraged his interest in her, so how could she be held to blame? There was no question of that. Only he himself was to blame, for his blind, simple-minded trustfulness.

55

Yet even while he assured himself that no blame could attach to her, he could not prevent some bitterness from creeping into his thoughts of her. Her secret, now it was out, had altered his feelings utterly. He thought of her clear grey eyes, looking at him so steadily, and he thought of how, unsuspected by him, this knowledge had lain hidden in her; this thing that set her completely apart and made her just a stranger to him; and gradually, as he dwelt on it, his heart began to close against her.

But he could not help pitying her, for she was all alone in the world, victim of a terrible tragedy, and, turning back to his mother, he said:

'The girl is in trouble. She needs help. Something must be done for her.'

'You'll never catch up with her now,' Rachel said. 'There are three roads out at Nawmenvennor. She could have taken any one of them. And what if you did catch up with her? What would you do then?'

'Bring her back here, I suppose.'

'You are talking like a fool. Can't you see what will happen if you bring that girl back here? As soon as people find out about her condition they will say the child is yours.'

'That's ridiculous,' Brice said. 'Maggie has only been here a month and if as you say she's three months with child—'

'People will forget the facts,' Rachel said, 'if the fable has more spice to it.'

Brice stood irresolute. He knew what his mother said was true. And because he was rather a puritan, at least where his own conduct was concerned, the thought that people would point at him, linking him with the girl's trouble, was more than enough to give him pause. And Rachel, seeing she had scored a hit, made haste to drive it home.

'If she's never seen here again, nothing will be known about the child, and no harm will be done,' she said. 'People here will soon forget her and that will be better for all of us.'

'What on earth will become of her?'

'I don't know. I told her she should go back to Porthgaran and let her own parish take care of her. She said she wouldn't but who knows? – Perhaps after all she changed her mind.

Anyway, whatever happens, she will no doubt fall on her feet. That sort of girl always does.'

'That sort of girl? What sort is that?'

'You know what I mean.'

'Whatever you may think of her, Maggie is certainly no slut.'

'No, well, I grant you that. But she was a ship that passed in the night and if you take my advice, my son, you will put her out of your mind. She has no claim on either of us.'

'Not even the claim of humanity?'

But his mother was right after all. Maggie had already gone on her way and the matter was best left as it was. And although he was still troubled by guilt when he thought of her tramping the roads he could not help feeling some relief that he would not have to see her again.

Rachel, reading all this in his face, remained silent, giving him time, and after a while, when he spoke again, she saw by his altered expression that she had nothing more to fear.

'When people ask why Maggie has left us,' he said, 'what do you think we ought to say?'

Rachel shrugged.

'Other girls have come and gone and this one has done the same. There's nothing strange about that.'

'You won't tell them about her trouble?'

'No, now that she's left the district, there's no need for anyone here to know.'

The following morning, however, when Rachel went on her milk-round, she soon heard that Maggie Care was still in Polsinney, for the girl had been seen the previous day, loitering down on the wharf, apparently hoping for work in the cellars. Rachel was furiously angry at this and when her customers, all agog, asked why Maggie had left Boskillyer, she answered at once with the bald truth.

'Maggie Care is with child. She's three or four months gone with it. A girl of that sort can only spell trouble and I was obliged to dismiss her.'

She felt no compunction in spreading this news, since the

girl, by lingering in Polsinney, had only brought it on herself. The truth would emerge soon enough, anyway, and Rachel quickly made up her mind that *her* account of it should be heard first.

Brice, when he berthed at the quay that morning, heard the gossip immediately from the quayside loafer, Dicky Limpet, who came aboard cadging for fish.

'So that girl you had up at the farm have got herself into trouble, then, and your mother have turned her out of the house?'

'Who told you that?' Brice asked sharply.

'Why, tedn no secret, surely, cos Alice Cox told me she had it from Mrs Tallack herself, and Gladdy Jacka told me she'd seen the girl and asked her straight out and the girl said yes, it was true, sure nuff.'

'Seen her?' Brice said. 'You mean she's still here?

'Ess, for sure. Didn't you know?'

'No, I thought she'd gone away.'

'My dear life, no, she'm here bold as brass. Any number of people have seen her walking about the place, and Gladdy Jacka spoke to her only half-hour ago, I believe.'

Brice gave Dicky a string of fish and bundled him out of the boat but the crew had already overheard. Most of them kept a discreet silence but Ralph Ellis came to Brice and clapped a hand on his shoulder.

'Twadn you, by any chance, that got the girl into trouble, was it?'

'No. It was not.'

'I was only asking, that's all.'

'Well, now that you've had your answer,' Brice said, 'perhaps you'll get on with clearing these nets.'

He was not surprised, on going home, to find his mother full of the news and in a thoroughly bad temper about it.

'I thought we'd seen the last of that girl but oh, no, not a bit of it! – She's chosen to stay on in the district to be the bane of both our lives. The whole place is buzzing with gossip from Churchtown down to the quay.'

'And you have been adding to it, I hear.'

'I only added the truth, my son. Surely you don't blame me for that?'

'No, I don't blame you,' Brice said. 'You've spread the truth about Maggie's child to protect me and I'm grateful for it. What you said yesterday, about people twisting things round, has already come to pass. I had my first taste of it from Ralph Ellis this morning and no doubt there will be more before I'm many days older. But at least, thanks to you, people know the truth, and until the gossip has died down we shall just have to bear it as best we can.'

Having thus spoken Brice went to wash and Rachel, brooding over his words, was able to find some comfort in them. It seemed that twenty-four hours of reflection had done Brice a great deal of good. His tone, when speaking of Maggie Care, had had a coldness and hardness in it and although he now knew where she was, he no longer talked of helping her. It seemed he had cut her out of his heart and that at least, Rachel thought, was something to be thankful for.

Chapter 3

The huers had been keeping watch for ten days; so had the crews of the seine-boats lying-to out in the bay; and now at last, on the afternoon of the tenth day, a shoal was sighted off Volley Head: a red-brown shadow darkening the sea, coming on and on and on, over the sandbar and into the bay, closer and closer inshore until the movement of the water could be plainly and unmistakably seen, breaking the surface of the water and chopping it up into sharp-pointed waves.

The huer's great cry rang out, shouted through his long tin trumpet, 'Hevva! Hevva! Hevva! Hevva!', and was at once echoed by the crowd gathered beside him on the cliff. People now appeared from everywhere and came running down the streets of Polsinney, swarming onto the jetties and wharves, climbing onto the coopers' sheds, and spreading over the beach at Porthvole. And the cry went up on all sides, 'Hevva! Hevva!', again and again, until the whole harbour rang with it.

The shoal came into that part of the bay allotted to the Nonesuch Seine and the Nonesuch owners, Mark Hall and his son, stood on the cliff beside the huer who, with a furze bush in either hand, was signalling to the boat in the bay, directing it into position. The seine crew bent to their oars; the boat went cutting through the water and came up close beside the shoal; and the huer gave the signal to stand. Now there was a hush on the watching crowds. A stillness lay over all the bay. Then the huer, using his trumpet, gave the order:

'*Shoot the seine!*'

Again the boat began to move, its steersman watching the huer's signals, and as it moved the net was paid out, splashing down into the sea. Round and round came the seine-boat and when the shoal was almost enclosed the follower moved into position ready to shoot the stop-net that would close up the opening of the seine. While this was being done the lurker-boat stood by and there was a great deal of splashing and noise as the lurker crew, with their long oars, beat at the water again and again to prevent the writhing silver fish from escaping through the opening. At last the shoal was fully enclosed and the team of hauliers on the beach began hauling in the warps, drawing the seine, with its millions of fish alive in it, into the shallower waters inshore. Soon the warps had been secured. The hauliers raised their caps and cheered and the cheer was echoed by the crowd. Mark Hall shook hands with his son and the two of them hurried down to the beach. The seiners were working the tuck-net now and as the fish were raised to the surface the ravening gulls gathered there in a desperate frenzy of movement and noise.

The sky was darkly overcast and there was more rain in the offing. Maggie, with her scarf over her head, moved among the crowd on the wharf, watching the dipper-boats putting out to bring the pilchards in from the seine. Behind her, Mark Hall's cellar was already alive with people bustling about with buckets of salt, making ready to receive the fish as soon as they should be brought ashore. Many of the cellar-girls stood outside, sleeves rolled up, ready for work, laughing and chatting in small groups, excited at the taking of the season's first shoal, and as Maggie moved among them they watched her with inquisitive eyes. It was three days since she had left Boskillyer and by now, as she well knew, her story was common property.

Three of these girls, watching her, were whispering and laughing together, and suddenly one of them, nudged by the others, spoke out in a loud voice.

'Some folk should go back where they belong and have their babies where they were got. Porthgaran, wadn it, or some place like that?'

Maggie stood still and looked at them and with one accord they turned their backs. But another girl, standing nearby, met her gaze and spoke to her.

'You needn't pay heed to Biddy Grose. Her chap've gone off with Nolly Geach and chance'll be a fine thing if she ever find herself another.'

The girl, who was short and stoutly built, stood with her bare arms folded, picking at the skin on her elbows. She had a broad freckled face and hair as thick and red as a fox's and she wore a man's cloth cap. One of her front teeth was missing and she kept sucking the gap with her tongue.

'You're Maggie Care, aren't you? You were dairymaid up at Boskillyer and Mrs Tallack turned you out. I saw you down here yesterday and the day before, I believe.'

'Yes, I'm hoping to get work.'

'Have you worked in the cellars before?'

'Yes, in Porthgaran,' Maggie said, 'but only two or three times, that's all.'

'Mr Hall will take you on. I'll tell him you're a friend of mine.' The girl took hold of Maggie's arm. 'My name is Martha Cledra but everyone d'call me Bussa,' she said.

The dipper-boats had begun to come back and already the first gurries, wooden handbarrows filled with fish, were being carried up to the cellars. There was a lot of laughter and noise. Children ran about everywhere, trying to flip fish from the gurries, and the carriers bawled abuse at them. Up on the cliff there was more excitement. Another shoal had come into the bay. The huer was shouting through his trumpet.

'Seems they're coming in fitty now. That one's on the Regina stem.' The girl turned again to Maggie. 'Got a place to live, have you, since being turned out at the farm?'

'No, I've been sleeping up at the bal.'

'Aw, my dear life, that'll never do! Not in your condition it won't. You'd better come home with me tonight. There are nine of us but we'll squeeze you in somehow.'

'What about your mother? Won't she mind?'

'My sister Kate's in the same boat as you so none of *us'll* cast any stones.' Martha suddenly squeezed Maggie's arm. 'There's old Mark Hall now,' she said. 'Come with me and I'll get you signed on.'

*

Gus Tallack sat alone in his cottage looking out at the heavy rain which had kept him indoors for almost a week. The cottage kitchen was very dark for the windows, on the outside, were so thickly encrusted with salt that even today's downpour did nothing to wash it away. In his lap, as he sat by the window, he held his big brown bible, open at Ecclesiastes. He had been reading for some time and the words of one verse still ran in his mind, and now, as he stared at the white rain sluicing down the window-panes, he spoke them aloud to the empty room:

'Whatsoever thy hand findeth to do, do it with thy might; for there is no work, nor device, nor knowledge, nor wisdom, in the grave, whither thou goest.'

Gus was not a pious man. He rarely attended church service. But he had been a fisherman and he had a fisherman's simple faith, and in the two and a half years since his illness had first struck him down, he had turned more and more to the Scriptures, hoping to find guidance there. Often in the evenings, especially in winter, the bible was his only companion. He would read some favourite passage aloud and argue it over with himself. It did not always bring comfort, however, and once he had been so enraged by the sheer inscrutability of the Word of God that he had flung the bible across the room. But Ecclesiastes contained good cheer. It was full of simple truths. There was charity in it and plain good sense.

'For to him that is joined to all the living there is hope, for a living dog is better than a dead lion. For the living know that they shall die, but the dead know not anything, neither have they any more a reward, for the memory of them is forgotten. Go thy way, eat thy bread with joy and drink thy wine with a merry heart, for God now accepteth thy works.'

Gus leant forward in his chair and laid the bible on the window-sill. He took his watch from his waistcoat pocket and compared it with the clock on the wall. It was nearly half past twelve and he gave a little fretful sigh, for his nephew should have been here by now. For some days Brice had kept away; he had not even paid his Saturday visit and his share of the previous week's takings still awaited collection; but this morning Gus had sent a message asking Brice to call at the cottage on his way home from the quay.

At a quarter to one Brice came, shedding his oilskin and sou'wester and hanging them up in the porch. He was still wearing his sea-boots and as he came into the kitchen he left a wet trail across the flags.

'Isaac said you wanted to see me.'

'I've been waiting to see you for twelve days! What happened to you last Saturday?'

'I went to St Glozey for the sports.'

'Surely you can't have stayed there all day?' Gus looked up at him irritably. 'Aren't you going to sit down?'

'Well,' Brice said. He glanced at the clock. 'I wasn't really intending to stay. I'm already late as it is.'

But he pulled a chair close to the window and sat down opposite Gus. He was not in the best of moods this morning, for the night's work had been arduous, due to the rain and the squally winds. Neither he nor his crew had got any rest and by morning tempers had become badly strained and then, when the catch had been sold and unloaded, he had quarrelled with Ralph Ellis over cleaning out the fish-hold. Brice was particular about this: not a single fish-scale must be left to taint the next night's catch; but Ralph had no time for such womanish ways and it was not the first time that he had refused to do his share. 'I'm going home to sleep!' he had said, and because the other four men had been inclined to take his part, Brice had sent them all home and had cleaned out the fish-hold himself.

Now, tired and out of sorts, he had to face his uncle Gus, and he could quite easily guess why the old man had sent for him.

'So that girl of yours is expecting a child and your mother has turned her out of the house!' Gus's upper lip curled in contempt, showing his strong, white, irregular teeth. 'How exactly like Rachel, by God, to make no allowance for nature!' he said. 'And she a woman who goes to church, calling herself a Christian.'

'You can't expect me,' Brice said, 'to join you in abusing my mother.'

64

'I don't see why not if tes what she deserves!'

'I hear Maggie's got work in Hall's cellar so no harm has come to her.'

'Have you also heard where she's living?'

'Yes, with the Cledras in White Hope Lane.'

'And you say no harm has come to her! From what I know about that girl, the Cledras' is no place for her, and you know it as well as I do myself. Nick Cledra's a drunkard and a thief and his slut of a wife is almost as bad.'

'Nobody made her go to them. She should have done as my mother said and gone back to Porthgaran where she belongs.'

'Is that all you've got to say about her? A girl you had working on your farm? A girl you as good as told me you loved—'

'No! I never told you that!'

'What *did* you tell me, then?'

'Whatever it was—' Brice began.

'Yes? Well? Spit it out!'

'Whatever it was, I made a mistake,' Brice said, coldly. 'I feel sorry for her, of course, as I would for any unfortunate, but – she is nothing to me in *that* way.'

'Not any more, I can see that! You're just about chokeful with it all. Now that you know the girl had a lover and is going to bear his child it's turned you against her properly and you can't even bear to think of her. You'd like to be able to clap your hands and hey presto! – She doesn't exist!'

There was so much truth in this that Brice, for a while, could find nothing to say and sat in silence, feeling ashamed. But he was tired, both in body and mind, and his uncle's contemptuous attack had roused some stubborn resentment in him so that, for the moment at least, whatever pity he felt for Maggie was deadened by the pity he felt for himself.

'And what,' he asked, eventually, 'would you expect me to do for her?'

'Go and find her, of course, and take her back home with you.'

'That is out of the question. Whatever you may say about my mother, she is mistress in her own house, and I am bound to consider her.'

'You told me not so long ago that your mother didn't rule your life.'

'No, she doesn't, but then neither does Maggie Care.'

'If you had an ounce of spunk in you, you'd marry the girl, baby or no. Your mother would have to accept her then. She would just have to make the best of things.'

'You are joking, of course.'

'Am I? Yes, perhaps I am. You're too much of a stick, my boy, to do what's plainly the bestmost thing. Too much tied up in your dignity. Too much afraid of what folk will say!'

'I certainly don't want a second-hand wife, if that's what you mean by my dignity.'

'You loved her once. You could love her again. And she could come to love you in time, if only you were to give her the chance.'

Brice felt he had had enough. He rose and pushed back his chair.

'Maggie has already loved one man—'

'And that man is dead, so I've been told.'

'Yes, he was one of her father's crew, and they were all drowned together.'

'Father, brother, lover!' Gus said. 'All lost to her in a single night.' He looked up at Brice with dark-gleaming eyes. 'And the only thing *you* can think about is that *you* have suffered some hurt to your pride!'

'I would help her if I could but marriage is out of the question,' Brice said. 'And now, if that's all you wanted with me, I'd just as soon be getting home.'

'Oh, get home by all means, back to your mother!' Gus exclaimed. And then, over his shoulder, he said: 'Don't forget to pick up your share. You'll find it on the mantel-shelf.'

Brice collected the heap of coins and went to put on his oilskins. As he let himself out he called, 'I'll see you again on Saturday,' but his uncle did not answer him.

Gus, left alone in the cottage kitchen, had taken up the bible again and it lay in his lap, between his hands. But he was not reading it; he was staring into space; and between his bushy, grizzled brows there was a frown of intense concentration, for something was working in his mind. His bearded lips were pressed close together and his breath came heavily through his nose.

He was used to sitting long hours in his chair but whereas, most days, he shifted about restlessly, easing his body this way and that, now he sat perfectly still, so deeply absorbed in his thoughts that the old ornamental clock on the wall chimed away the quartered hours without once drawing his fretful glance.

When at last he bestirred himself, it was with a sudden alertness and quickness, humping himself round in his chair and gazing, sharp-eyed, about the room as though to catch it unawares in all its squalor and shabbiness. His upper lip curled in disgust. A little growl moved in his throat. And his hands, taking hold of the heavy bible, slammed it shut and held it aloft.

'Whatsoever thy hand findeth to do, do it with thy might,' he declaimed, 'for there is no work, nor device, nor knowledge, nor wisdom, in the grave, whither thou goest.'

He laid the bible down again and wheeled himself towards the door. At the onset of his illness, he had had a double wooden ramp laid down at the threshold, so that he could wheel his chair up and over the doorstep; and outside the porch door he had had an old ship's bell hung up so that he could summon help when needed. He now wheeled himself outside and rang the bell and its clangour echoed round the yard, and when he looked up at the sail-loft windows, he could see two startled faces looking palely down at him. Rain was still falling heavily, so he wheeled himself back indoors and sat waiting impatiently, and after a while Isaac Kiddy came in, half in eager anticipation that perhaps some calamity had occurred, half in reluctance in case it had not.

'I want you to go to Mark Hall's cellar and find that girl, Maggie Care. Tell her, when she's finished her shift, I want her to come and see me here.'

Isaac stared.

'What do ee want with the likes of she?'

'Never mind what I want her for. Just go and give her the message.'

'This is the second time today I've had to go out on messages,' Isaac said, grumbling. 'First I had to go down to the quay and take a message to Brice and now I've got to go to the cellars and find this maid, Maggie Care, though whether tes right to call her a maid—'

'Are you going, then?' Gus roared.

'Ess, surely, I'm just on my way. I've only got to finish the bit crowst I was eating when you rang that bell and then I'll be off with this message of yours, though just what tes you've got in mind, wanting to see a maid of that sort, is just about past my comprehension . . .'

The old sail-maker went at last and his errand took him almost an hour. He returned smelling strongly of drink, having broken his journey at The Brittany for a nip of something to keep out the wet.

'I gave the maid your message, you, and she said she'd come at eight o'clock. She was besting to know what you wanted her for but of course I couldn't tell her that—'

'She'll know soon enough when she gets here,' Gus said. '*You* can get yourself back to your work.'

It was dark by the time Maggie arrived, for the rain, which was still falling steadily, had brought the day to an early close. Gus had already lit the lamp and it stood on the hob of the fireless stove and in its half circle of light he and the girl, sitting one at either side of the hearth, looked at each other appraisingly.

'We've never met, you and me, but we know as much about each other as the folk in Polsinney have to tell, and that's plenty to be going on with, I seem. Have you been told I'm a dying man? Yes, you're sure to have heard that, having been at Boskillyer a month, and what you didn't hear there you'll have heard in the fish-cellars, no doubt.'

'Well,' Maggie said. She was at a loss.

'You don't have to worry about my feelings, cos what they say is only the truth, and the only difference between them and me is that *I* know when it's going to happen, though not to a navvy-gravvy, of course. There are compensations in that. It gives a man the chance to think and see about putting his house in order.'

Gus gave a sardonic laugh and his glance flickered round the room.

'As you can see, it needs it,' he said.

Maggie also glanced round the room. There was a patch of damp on one wall and the wallpaper was black with mould. Neglect was manifest everywhere and after the recent heavy rain a cold clamminess hung on the air so that, as she looked around, her skin came out in gooseflesh and a little shiver ran over her. Her shoes were full of water from the puddles she had walked through and her wet skirts clung coldly over her knees. She turned to look at Gus again and found him watching her intently. So far she had scarcely spoken. She had left it all to him. But now, in a quiet voice, she said:

'Why have you sent for me, Mr Tallack? What do you want to say to me?'

'I wanted to see for myself what sort of girl this Maggie Care was that I've been hearing so much about.'

'And now that you've seen, are you satisfied? Am I what you were led to expect?'

'I suppose, after the treatment you got from my sister-in-law, you're a bit suspicious of us Tallacks, but I mean you no harm, I promise you.'

'Mrs Tallack only did what many another would have done.'

'She put you out in the road,' Gus said. 'Don't you bear her a grudge for that?'

'No, I don't think so,' Maggie said.

'And what about my nephew Brice?'

'I don't quite understand what you mean.'

'He fancied himself in love with you. Surely you must have realized that.'

'I think he'll have changed his mind by now.'

'Maybe you could change it back.'

'I wouldn't want to,' Maggie said. 'There was only ever

69

one man for me and he is dead. I shall never love anyone else.'

'What was the young man's name?'

'Jim Kenna.'

'He brought you a packet of trouble before he went and got himself drowned.'

'No more than I brought on myself.'

'Life, in this Christian country of ours, can be very hard for a young girl with an illegitimate child to bring up. At present you're lodged with the Cledras, I hear, but that's no suitable place for you, or for your child when it comes.'

'No, I know,' Maggie said. 'The Cledras have been good to me but we sleep three in a bed and I certainly can't stay there long.'

'Well, I'll come to the point,' Gus said. 'I'm not a rich man – far from it – but I *have* got a bit of property. This cottage is mine, such as it is, and so are the sail-loft and barking-house. The barking-house is not in use – I sacked the man who worked it for me and I haven't bothered to find another – but the sail-loft brings in a bit of money, and of course there's the boat but you know about that.'

'Yes,' Maggie said, 'I know about that.'

But she could not follow the trend of his thoughts and waited, still puzzled, for him to go on.

'Well, I've got a proposition in mind and I'll put it to you fair and square, without beating about the bush.' For a moment Gus sat looking at her and his dark brown eyes, in their crinkled lids, reflected the glow from the little lamp. 'If you would consent to marry me, it would give you and your baby a home and some security for the future, cos when the time came for me to snuff out, my bit of property would come to you.'

Maggie sat perfectly still. Whatever she might have expected, it was certainly not this, and she was struck dumb. But Gus was in no hurry for her to answer. There were still a number of things he wanted to make clear to her and he was glad to have the chance of doing it in his own way.

'Don't make any mistake about it. This is a business

70

proposition and nothing else. I'm a sick man and I'm soon for the grave. All I want from you is that you should keep house for me and bring some comfort into the place. I shouldn't want to come to your bed – much good it'd do me if I did! – and you and me would have separate rooms. I thought I'd better make that plain so as not to give the wrong idea and frighten you off before I've begun.'

Gus paused and took a deep breath. Talking always taxed his strength.

'Of course, I *could* just ask you to come as my paid housekeeper and still leave my property to you,' he said. 'But it would be better if we married cos that'd make everything right and tight. Oh, I know folk'll talk just the same! They'll wink and nod among themselves and say they know what's behind it all . . . But marriage, even of this sort, is legal and binding in every way and people have great respect for it. You'd have my name and so would your child and when you came into the property there'd be no room for argument about the rights and wrongs of it. No one could interfere with you. No one could ever take it away.'

Once again there was a pause. The clock on the wall could be heard ticking and rain could be heard on the window-panes. Maggie sat, straight-backed, her hands folded in her lap. Her grey eyes were full of thought and Gus could see uncertainty in them.

'I don't expect you to answer at once. You'll need time to brood on it. And if I read your face aright, you've got a few questions you want to ask.'

'Yes,' Maggie said. 'One question at least. Why should you want to do this for me?'

'It's not just for you. It's for both of us. I've got two or three years at the most and Dr Sam Carveth has said that my end will not be an easy one. At present I can still use my legs but it costs me something, I can tell you, to get myself across this room. In a year or so I shall be worse. Helpless. Dependent on *you*. That won't make me an easy man to live with day in, day out, and I reckon by the time you've seen me through, you'll have earnt what you're getting in return. You need to consider

71

that side of it. You'll have your child to think about and you may decide it's too much to take on.'

'Can't the doctor do anything for you?'

'No. Nothing. He've said so straight. Any more questions you want to ask?'

'Yes. I'm wondering about your nephew, Brice, and your sister-in-law, Mrs Tallack. Won't they, being family, expect you to leave your property to them?'

Gus gave a cynical laugh.

'You're right about my sister-in-law. What she expects would fill a book. But don't worry your head about that. My brother Henry, years ago, sold his share of the business to me and put his money into a copper mine over to Goonwelter. It was Rachel who made him do that. She thought it'd make him a rich man. But instead he lost every penny he had. So whatever hopes Rachel has about getting her hands on my property, she've got no rights in the matter at all, and if you accept my proposition, one of the things that'll please me most is giving *her* a smack in the eye.'

Gus broke off and took a rest. He was breathing heavily.

'Well?' he demanded, after a while. 'Does that shock you, Maggie Care?'

'No. Not in the least.'

'Rachel's had me dead and buried a dozen times in the past two years so what do I owe her? – Not a groat! As for boy Brice, well, a few disappointments here and there won't do him a ha'porth of harm. He's a young man, fit and strong, and he can make his own way in the world. But you're a girl and you're all alone, so surely you won't refuse my help just because of some foolish qualm over putting my nephew's nose out of joint?'

'No,' Maggie said. She shook her head. 'I have my baby to think of and that's more important to me than anything else in the world. But—'

'What?'

'It still seems strange that you should want to do this for me, someone you've never met before, a stranger you know nothing about.'

'Damme, why should it seem so strange? It seems simple enough to me.'

Gus sought to brush the matter aside, but Maggie looked at him in such a way that his gaze faltered before hers and he sat for some time in complete silence, frowning at the oil-lamp on the stove.

'There *is* another reason of sorts and I may as well make a clean breast of it. It's an old story, out of the past, and I've kept it to myself till now.'

Gus shifted in his chair. Somehow the lamp was bothering him and he leant forward to turn down the flame. Then he slumped back again.

'I started life as a fisherman. That was when I was twelve years old. When I was twenty my father died and left me the money to buy my own boat. In winter I used to go up to Bigbury Bay for the herring fishing and one winter there I met a girl. We became lovers, her and me, and we planned to get married just as soon as we could get her father's consent. He was one of the Plymouth Brethren. Too sanctimonious by half for me. Anyway, at the end of the season, I came home to Polsinney for the long-lining, and I didn't go back again till June. By then Ellen had gone. I'd got her into trouble, you see, and her father had turned her out of the house.'

Gus stared at the lamp on the hob. His story was bringing old wounds to life and he still felt some of the rage he had felt as a young man of twenty-two.

'Nobody knew where she'd gone. She'd slipped away without a word. But I'd only missed her by four days and I thought I should find her in no time at all. I spent three weeks tramping the roads, asking at turnpikes, villages, towns . . . But by the time I got news of her it was too late and she was dead. It seems she'd set out to walk down into Cornwall to find me here in Polsinney but on the way she'd caught a chill and been taken into the workhouse infirmary at Dunsett. It turned to pneumonia and she died. She was buried as a pauper in the churchyard at Bayle.'

Gus looked up and met Maggie's gaze.

'I was too late to help Ellen and do what I ought to have

done for her but I *can* help you and your child instead. It's the one last useful job I can do before I have to hand over the helm and when I meet up with Ellen again, to give an account of myself to her, I know she'll say I've done the right thing.'

'How old was she?'

'She was eighteen. It happened thirty years ago. But no one in Polsinney knows the tale and I would prefer to keep it that way.'

'I shan't tell anyone,' Maggie said.

Gus gave a nod. He was satisfied.

'There's something about you, somehow, that makes me feel I can trust you,' he said. 'Do you think you can trust me the same?'

Before Maggie could answer, however, he stopped her with a brusque command.

'Don't answer that! I'm asking too soon. You need time to go besting about to find out something of what I'm like. You'll be told some rare tales, I daresay, and when you've heard them you can make up your mind.'

'I don't need to go besting about. I've been in Polsinney long enough to know what people say about you.'

'Hah! Is that so? And what *do* they say?'

'For one thing, they say you're fond of the rum bottle.'

'Damme! And what if I am? Would they grudge a dying man the one bit of comfort left to him? What else do the beggars say about me?'

'They say you don't suffer fools gladly.'

'Nobody does, except he be a fool himself, and even then he's a lot more shrewd with other folk's foolishness than he is with his own. What else do they say?'

'They say you've got a quick temper and that once you've got an idea in your head you can be peggy as a mule.'

'Is that the whole reckoning?' Gus asked.

'Yes,' Maggie said, 'I think it is, and it seems to me, if that's the worst, I haven't got a lot to worry about.'

'Does that mean you're willing to consider my proposition?'

'Yes.'

Maggie now rose to her feet and took her wet cape from

the back of the chair. She drew it round her and tied the cord.

'I'll come in the morning, before work, and let you have my answer,' she said. 'That'll be just before eight.'

'That's not very long to be thinking all round a step that will settle the whole of your future life.'

'It's as long as I shall need,' Maggie said.

At the back of her mind she already felt sure that she would accept his proposal of marriage and the conditions that went with it. Astonishing though the proposal was, her mind had quickly adapted to it, and she had soon begun to feel that everything that had happened to her since her arrival in Polsinney had been bringing her slowly to this point. She had been in Gus Tallack's company for less than an hour but somehow, during that time, because of what had passed between them, a conviction had grown and taken root that their lives were already linked by fate.

But certainly she needed to think; to look coolly and critically at all the possible implications; to weigh the problems against the advantages, especially with regard to her child, and to try, with what honesty she could command, to sort out the rights and wrongs involved in accepting a dying man's proposal.

On reaching the door she paused and looked back, and what she saw was an old man, aged prematurely by disease, his big body, once powerful, now misshapen and made slack by the slow wasting of his muscles and nerves. But there was a look of strength even now in the set of the head on the powerful neck and as he turned his bearded face towards her, she saw how fiercely the flame of life still burnt in him, glowing in the broad, thick-fleshed cheeks and lighting up the dark brown eyes with a kind of angry energy.

'Well, does it give you pause,' he said, 'to see what a wreck of a man I am?'

'I was thinking, if we do marry, I shall want to speak to that doctor of yours, to see what can be done for you.'

'I've already told you, there's nothing to be done. That's how I come to be sitting here, offering to make you wife and widow all in the space of two or three years.'

'Yes, well, we shall see,' Maggie said.

When she had gone, Gus sat for a while without moving, staring fixedly into space. The clock on the wall struck nine. He looked at it and gave a scowl.

'Get a move on, will you?' he said.

During the night the rain stopped and by seven o'clock the next morning Polsinney was steaming dry in a sun that shone, burning hot, from a cloudless sky. Gus had wheeled himself out to the yard and sat watching the drifters unloading their catches onto the quay on the opposite side of the harbour. He had brought his breakfast out with him: two thick slices of bread and a hunk of cold fat bacon; but after two or three bites it lay untouched on the plate in his lap.

Just before eight Maggie came. Gus had set a stool for her, and she sat down on it, facing him. She came to the point without delay.

'I've thought it over and the answer is yes.'

'Are you sure?'

'Yes. Quite sure.'

'You won't change your mind later on and leave me looking a damned fool?'

'No. I promise you faithfully.'

Gus took a long, deep, quivering breath. His face was flushed with satisfaction. He looked as though he would burst with it. But there were lingering doubts.

'I'm not a saint. You know that. And sickness doesn't bring out the best in a man who's only flesh and blood. Have you thought what it'll mean, seeing me through to my end? Have you any idea what you're taking on?'

Maggie tried to answer him honestly.

'I can't see into the future, Mr Tallack, but I promise I shall do my best to fulfil my side of the bargain and so long as you're good to me and my child—'

'You will be my wife,' Gus said, 'and your child will be like my own child, and the day we are married I shall make my will leaving my property to you, so that it's all as watertight as anything on this earth can be.' After further thought he said:

76

'In some ways we know a lot about each other. In other ways we know nothing at all. It may be I'm doing a bad thing, persuading a young girl like you to marry a sick old man like me, but I mean only good to you and your child, and this much I swear by Almighty God.'

Maggie nodded but made no reply. She trusted him absolutely.

'Are you church or chapel?' he asked.

'Church,' she said.

'Then as soon as Isaac Kiddy comes, I'll send him up to fetch the parson, to see about calling the banns. There's no sense in wasting time. Are you agreeable to that?'

'Yes.'

'So be it. I'll see to it.'

'I must go now. I'll be late for work.'

'There are things we shall need to discuss. You'd better come and see me again tonight.'

'Yes. All right. I'll be here at eight.'

When she had gone out of the yard Gus, in a sudden surge of feeling, took his breakfast from the plate in his lap and hurled it piece by piece to the gulls who swooped instantly, screaming and flapping, to snatch it up in mid air.

At half-past-eight Isaac Kiddy arrived and immediately Gus sent him out again.

'I want you to go to the parsonage and ask the parson to step down here. I want to see him straight away.'

'What do ee want with the parson, you?'

'You can tell him I've got a job for him.'

Even before the first banns had been read in church, news had spread throughout Polsinney that Gus was to marry Maggie Care. Hall's cellar was agog with it. The women and girls could not leave it alone. And just as their hands were ceaselessly busy laying out the pilchards and spreading the salt, so their tongues were equally busy with this latest piece of news.

'You must've known a thing or two when you came to Polsinney, Maggie Care. You'll be sitting some pretty when

77

the old man dies and leaves you his bit of property even if tes all tumblen down.'

'If I'd known old Gus was looking out for a wife, I should have made up to him myself. But tedn no good talken like that. I should have had to get into trouble before I stood a chance, I suppose.'

'Aw, just listen to Deborah Larch! If *she* haven't got herself in trouble it can't be for want of running the risk!'

'Maybe Kate Cledra can give her some hints.'

'If at first you don't conceive—'

'The church'll be full on Sunday, you. Even the chapel folk'll be there to hear Gus Tallack's banns shouted out.'

'Any just cause or 'pediment, en?'

'Only a little one, that's all.'

'Dear of'n, too, tedn hardly his fault.'

'Maggie'll have to make the most of this cheeld. She won't get another from old Gus.'

The noisy gossip went on and on and Maggie let it flow over her. The women and girls, for the most part, were friendly and sympathetic to her, now that her story was fully known, for their own menfolk were fishermen and the tragedy that had befallen her was one that touched them very close. Rough their jokes might be, but they were meant in good fellowship, and Maggie knew it. As for the rest, the spiteful few, she was completely indifferent to them. Their barbed remarks left her untouched. She found she was able to shut them out.

The only thing that mattered to her was the child she carried in her womb and she thought about it constantly. All her life's hopes were wrapped up in this child and to safeguard its future she had agreed to marry a man almost three times her age. An ailing man, close to death. A man she knew almost nothing about. Yet none of this seemed strange to her. Instead it seemed like providence. Gus Tallack might be a stranger to her, but he had appeared in her hour of need, and he had her trust and her gratitude. People would say, and it would be true, that she was marrying him for his money; but a bargain had been struck between them and so long as she kept her side of it there need not be any feelings of guilt; and when his property came to her she would keep it and hold it, for her child's sake, whatever the world might think of her.

All these things so filled her mind that the babble of gossip in the fish-cellar made no impression on her at all. She felt perfectly safe and secure, now that her baby's future was settled, and she followed her own trend of thoughts.

'One thing I should dearly love to see,' said Martha Cledra, at her side, 'and that's Rachel Tallack's face when she hears you're going to marry old Gus.'

Chapter 4

Rachel's anger was bitter indeed and Brice had to bear the brunt of it.

'It was a bad day for us when that girl came to the district!' she said. 'She's brought nothing but trouble, right from the start, and to think I took her into my house! If only I had had the sense to send her packing as she deserved! But no, I took Christian pity on her, and this is how I've been repaid!'

'It surely wasn't Christian pity that made you turn her out of the house, and perhaps if you hadn't done that, none of this would ever have happened.'

'So that's the way it's to be, is it? *I* am to take the blame for it all?'

'It's too late now to talk about blame. All we can do is face the facts. The girl was in trouble and uncle Gus felt sorry for her. This is his way of helping her.'

'Don't you believe it!' Rachel scoffed. 'He's doing it to spite you and me!'

'Why should he want to do that?'

'Because it's the kind of man he is! He's always disliked me, merely because I speak my mind, and now it seems he's spiteful enough to take his feelings out on you!'

'You needn't worry on my account. The property is nothing to me. And my uncle has a perfect right to do whatever he likes with it.'

'Don't speak to me about his rights! You are his brother's only son and what he is doing is cheating you. That business of his may be run down but if only you had the running of it, and got good men to work for you, who knows what would have come of it? Why, you could have been as big a man as

John Lanyon or Mark Hall, if only you'd got your proper rights!'

'I have no wish to be like them. I'm just a plain fisherman and quite content to stay that way.'

'Even after your uncle is dead and that girl becomes owner of the boat? Yes, you can stare, you poor innocent fool! You hadn't thought of that, I suppose?'

No. It was true. He had not thought of that. And the realization came as a shock.

'How will you like it then, my son, when you have to go cap-in-hand to *her*, to answer for the boat's affairs?'

Brice looked at his mother with a cold blue gaze. Just for a moment he hated her. Then abruptly he turned away.

'If the worst came to the worst, I could always go as skipper on some other boat, but I'll cross that bridge when I come to it. And, after all, there's always the farm.'

'The farm! The farm! What good is that? Fifteen paltry rented acres and more than one third of it covered in stones! What profit this farm brings in could just about be put in my eye! Your uncle knows that, devil as he is, and yet you're still foolish enough to stand up for him!'

'Fool I may be but at least I can accept the facts. Whether my uncle is right or wrong, there's nothing we can do about it, so where's the sense in wrangling like this? For my part I've had more than enough so please let there be an end to it.'

'There will *never* be any end to it!' Rachel said, in a passion of anger. 'We shall have to live with it all our days, seeing that girl, when your uncle dies, coming into property that should be yours and passing it on to her bastard child. Oh, how she must smile to herself, having wormed her way into such a good berth! And oh, how the folk in Polsinney are looking on and enjoying it all!'

'It will all die down in time. We'll just have to bear it as best we can.'

But for Brice the gossip was in fact the hardest thing of all to bear. At first, when he had heard the news, he had not believed it; he had thought it was one of Dicky Limpet's jokes; and by the time he knew it was true, he had already betrayed the fact that his uncle Gus had not seen fit to take him into his confidence. Four of the five men in his crew had kept a considerate silence, for they were men of fine feeling and were very well disposed towards him, but Ralph Ellis had been qᵘick to make the most of his discomfiture.

'So the old man've done the dirty on you and pinched your girl from under your nose? I'd have thought at least he'd have told you first, instead of springing it on you like this, but maybe you've fallen out with him?'

'No, I haven't fallen out with him, nor do I intend to,' Brice said.

'You don't mean to say you aren't sore at the trick the old devil's played on you?'

'What my uncle chooses to do is no one's business but his own.'

'Will you be going to the wedding, then?'

'That depends on whether I'm asked.'

'Yes, well, of course,' Ralph said, 'you've got to keep in with him, I suppose, if only on account of the boat.'

Ralph was frankly jealous of Brice because, when Gus had first become ill, Brice had taken over as skipper, a job Ralph felt should have been his.

'Seems there edn much profit in being the old man's kin after all. I reckon I'd just as soon be as I am. At least I can call my soul my own.'

All this from Ralph was only a sample of what Brice had to endure on his way up through the village that morning and of what he would have to endure for a good many days and weeks to come. His mother was not much liked in Polsinney and many people relished the thought that she had been taken down a peg. He himself was liked and respected: among men, who knew him to be a good seaman, and among women because he was a fine upstanding young man who treated them with courtesy; and from some he received friendly words that showed he had their sympathy.

'I would never have thought of your uncle Gus doing a thing like that,' old William Nancarrow said to him, 'but you mustn't take it too much to heart, for your uncle Gus is a sick man and seemingly tes affecting his mind.'

But the gossip, whatever form it took, was all equally hard

to bear and Brice was often sick at heart. The sympathy of some; the slyness of others; the jokes, the probing, the lewd remarks: all were equally hateful to him because, whichever way he answered, he was made to feel a fool. Still, he was determined to put a good face on it, if only for the sake of pride, and one of the first things he knew he must do was to call on his uncle Gus.

When he arrived at the cottage he found it the scene of unusual activity. Jimmy Jenkin, the Polsinney builder, was perched high at the top of a ladder, removing the old rusty launders and pipes which, having leaked for six months past, were the cause of the dampness in the walls. Another man was repairing the chimney and a third was repairing a hole in the roof. And down in the cobbled yard below, Gus, in his wheelchair, sat watching them.

For more than two years now the place had been falling about his ears and he had lacked all heart to order the necessary repairs. But in three weeks' time there would be a woman in the house and that would be a different matter entirely. For her sake, and for her child's, when it came, every inch of the cottage was to be made good, inside and out. New launders and drainpipes were to be put up; the stonework was to be washed with lime; and the roof was to have a coat of cement to keep the slates firmly in place when the south west gales came blowing in. No expense was to be spared, and Gus watched with critical eyes, determined that the work should be properly done.

'I suppose you've heard that I'm to be married?' he said, as Brice stood before him.

'Yes, and I've come to wish you well.'

'No hard feelings, then?'

'No. None.'

'You understand what it'll mean? That Maggie will get my property?'

'Yes, of course,' Brice said. Then, with some dryness, he said: 'I could hardly fail to know since any number of kind folk have been busy pointing it out to me. Polsinney can talk of nothing else. The gossip's enough to stop the church clock.'

'Well, it seems you're taking it pretty well, and seeing we've got three witnesses watching from up there on the roof, I think it would be a good idea if you and me were to shake hands.'

Brice had no hesitation whatever; he had always valued his uncle's friendship; and as their hands met and clasped he knew it was more than just a show for the benefit of the onlookers: he knew that the friendship was still intact. His uncle had said some hard things during the course of their previous meeting but Brice was willing to forget them now, and whatever difficulties lay in the future, so long as he had the old man's goodwill, he would do his best to face up to them.

Gus looked up at his nephew with a certain quizzical understanding. He could guess what deliberations had brought the young man here today. Brice had shown what Gus saw as weakness in his behaviour over Maggie but there was little fault to be found in his behaviour today.

'I suppose it's too much to hope that your mother shares your view of things?'

'I'm afraid it is.'

'The wedding is fixed for September the tenth. Will you come?'

'If you wish it, yes, of course.'

'Would you be willing to do more and give Maggie away?' Gus asked.

Brice stared. He was taken aback. It was more than he had bargained for. But Maggie, as he well knew, had nobody of her own.

'Yes. Very well. I'll give her away.'

'I'm thankful to see that you've got more of your father in you than your mother. Sometimes I've wondered about that.'

'My mother will get over this – in time.'

'I don't much care if she does or not. I've never got much joy from her company so tesn't a thing I'm likely to miss.' Gus looked up with a mischievous gleam. 'Still, you can tell her, if you like, that she's welcome to attend the wedding,' he said.

But Rachel, as Brice expected, only found this message provoking.

'I will *not* be present at the wedding, nor will I ever set foot inside your uncle's house again, and as for that sly, scheming slut of a girl, if we should ever chance to meet, I shall have *nothing* to say to her.'

During the next three weeks people in Polsinney said that the dust rising from Gus Tallack's cottage could be seen from the top of Teeterstone Hill. Gus had succeeded in persuading Maggie to give up her work in the fish-cellars and to turn her energies instead towards putting her future home to rights.

'I've got Mrs Kiddy in and I've told her to give the place a good clean but she needs keeping up to the mark and you would be better employed if you were here to see to it.'

So Maggie now spent her days at the cottage and, in Mrs Kiddy's words, was turning the place inside out. The sail-maker's wife was not best pleased at receiving orders from this slip of a girl, and the high standard of cleanliness that Maggie expected her to achieve was, she considered, unreasonable.

'Why, this old house is so black as a shaft, and no amount of rubben-and-scrubben is ever going to make it come clean. And where's the sense of it, anyway, when Jimmy Jenkin and his crew are coming in presently to put new paper on the walls and paint everything spick and span? *They'll* soon cover up the dirt and no one will ever know tes there!'

But this would not do for Maggie and she said so in no uncertain terms. Every room, upstairs and down, had to be thoroughly scrubbed out before she pronounced herself satisfied, and even when this was all done there was still no rest for either of them, for the rugs and mats had to be cleaned, the curtains and bed-linen had to be washed, and constant warfare had to be waged on the mice that infested every cupboard. Mrs Kiddy was run off her feet. She had never worked so hard in her life.

'Such a skimmage there is down there!' she told her neighbours in the backlet. 'I'm sure if old Gus Tallack had known what he was letting himself in for he'd have changed his mind before twas made up!'

In fact Gus was enjoying it all. The bustle and stir pleased him no end. It was the first time in years that this old neglected cottage of his had seen such a spate of activity and he sat all day out in the yard, looking on with undisguised glee as Mrs Kiddy steamed to and fro, carrying pails of water from the pump to fill the copper in the scullery, where Maggie was washing blankets and sheets.

The only thing that troubled him was the fear that Maggie was working too hard.

'You want to take it easy, young woman, and leave Mrs Kiddy do a bit more, instead of rushing and tearing about, wearing yourself down to the cheens.'

'I'm all right. I'm as strong as a horse.'

'And what about your baby?' he said. 'Supposing you was to do him some harm?'

But Maggie knew what she could do. Her unborn baby was too precious for her to take any risks with it, and although she worked throughout the day, she was careful never to strain herself. As for Mrs Isaac Kiddy, complaining of her own aches and pains, Maggie had no scruples in keeping her hard at work, for Gus was paying her a shilling a day and if, as happened all too often, Mrs Kiddy skimped some chore, Maggie would make her do it again.

'I d'feel sorry for this poor old house, getting pulled and pummelled about,' Mrs Kiddy said to Gus. 'Tes just about been scrubbed to the bone and there edn a stick nor stitch inside'n that haven't been rummaged through and through!'

'And not a moment too soon, neither,' Gus said.

He himself was full of admiration for the way Maggie was doing things for he, as an old fisherman, respected order in all things, and always, in the old days, just as his boat had been one of the best-kept craft seen on this south Cornish coast, so had this cottage of his been object of the same pride and care. The boat, under Brice's skippership, had been kept up to the same high standard, but Gus, since the onset of his illness, had allowed his home to fall into decay. Now it was all being put to rights; he had the incentive, the will, the drive; and with Maggie firmly in charge, the place was now being restored to its former brightness and comeliness, with everything ship-shape and Bristol fashion, neat and tidy and spotlessly clean.

Of course, a great many things would be needed yet to make a comfortable home of it, fit for a woman and her child, but there would be plenty of time for Maggie to buy whatever she needed, and meantime the most important thing was to see that the dirt and dampness were banished and that Jimmy Jenkin did a good job with his repairs and renovations. And when at last, two days before the wedding, everything was done that could be done, even Mrs Kiddy had to admit that perhaps after all it had been worthwhile.

'The house d'look a picture,' she said. 'I wouldn mind living in it myself. And to think they old curtains belonged to be red when all these years I've thought they were brown! As for that old slab of yours, Maggie must've used a ton of blacklead, getting it to shine like that, and I reckon if you was minded to, you could see to comb your hair in it. This cottage is just about as fitty as any bride could wish to come into and it strikes me that Maggie Care is doing better than she deserves.'

'*I'll* be the judge of that!' Gus said.

At noon on the day before the wedding, when Maggie called on Gus to make a few last-minute arrangements, he was absent from his usual place in the yard, and when she walked into the kitchen she found him, not in his wheelchair, but standing a short way away from it, supporting himself on two walking-sticks.

'What are you doing?' she asked, alarmed.

'I'm practising how to walk,' he said.

'Is that wise?'

'I don't know. But that's what I'm doing all the same.' Cautiously, without turning his head, he looked at her out of the sides of his eyes. 'I *can* walk just a short way, you know, so long as the groundswell is not too bad. I'm not completely done for yet and tomorrow when I get into church I intend to stand on my own two feet. Tes just a question of trying it out. Finding my sea-legs, as you might say.'

'Is there anything I can do?'

'Yes, you can look the other way!'

But she was too nervous on his behalf to obey this curt

command and she stood close by, watching over him, ready to help if necessary. The effort it cost him to lift one leg and put one foot down in front of the other required all his strength and concentration and he had to lean heavily on the two sticks. With his back slightly bent and his shoulders hunched, he took a few painfully difficult steps and then came to a halt again, breathing stridently through his nose. The exertion was too much for him and the perspiration, pouring from his forehead, dripped down his cheeks and into his beard. His strong teeth were clenched together and his lips were drawn back from them in a little snarl of rage.

'Damn! I'll get as far as that wall even if it takes all day!'

'Don't you think you're being foolish?'

'Tes my two legs that're being foolish, and if they think I'm giving in to them, they can damned well think again!'

With a stubborn effort he moved forward again and Maggie watched him in distress. She hesitated to go to him, for he was still a stranger to her, and she knew not how he would react. But she feared very much that he would fall and do himself an injury and it was a great relief to her when a knock came at the half-open door and Brice walked in.

Gus, turning to look at Brice, swayed and was in danger of losing his balance. His brief burst of strength was almost spent and he was trembling from head to foot. But Brice, seeing at once how it was, went and put his arms round him and held him in a strong, close grip, and when Maggie pushed the wheelchair forward, the old man, with a scowl of defeat, suffered himself to be lowered into it and thrust the two sticks into Brice's hands.

'I'm to be married tomorrow,' he said, 'and I wanted to be married standing up, not stuck in my chair like a Guy Fawkes!'

'Better stuck in your chair,' Brice said, 'than falling down on the floor in church.'

'You mean I might fall dead, I suppose? Yes, well, you're right, I can't risk that. Not until I've made Maggie my wife.'

Exhausted but resigned, Gus sat back, closing his eyes for a little while and taking deep breaths that filled his lungs. Gradually the tremors passed. He took a handkerchief from his pocket and wiped the sweat from his forehead and cheeks.

Then he looked up at Maggie and Brice and a self-mocking grin spread over his face.

'Well, I may not get married standing up, but at least I shall look some smart!' he said. 'I've had the barber in this morning, clicking and fussing over me, and he've left me smelling like a dockside moll! I've got my Sunday suit on, too, to get the smell of mothballs out of it, and if I don't look the part tomorrow it only means folk are hard to please!'

Gus was highly amused at himself and turned his head this way and that to show off his neatly trimmed hair and beard. He also pointed out his boots, for he had polished them himself and was proud of the brilliant shine on them. And over his head, as he rattled on, making boyish fun of himself, Maggie and Brice looked at each other.

It was the first time they had met since Maggie had been at Boskillyer and it meant there was some constraint between them. Although he had known he might meet her today, he was still foolishly unprepared, and he felt a sudden cowardly urge to make some excuse and depart post haste. But Maggie, perhaps understanding this, looked at him in such a way that he found his mind growing quiet and still and in a while, as his uncle's self-banter petered out, he found himself speaking quite normally, as though what lay between him and this girl had no significance whatever.

'I thought I'd better call on you and find out if everything is fixed for tomorrow.'

'I think it is. Yes, I'm sure. And thank you for your kindness in agreeing to give me away.'

'The wedding's at half past eleven,' Gus said. 'I hope you'll be back in harbour in time to get the fish-scales washed off yourself?'

'I shan't be going out tonight. I don't want to risk being late. Ralph will be skipper for tonight and Joe Tambling is going along to make up the crew.'

'Everything's settled, then?'

'Yes,' Brice said. 'I'll be here at eleven o'clock.'

'I've been thinking out how it will be when Maggie becomes my wife,' Gus said. 'She'll be your aunt-by-marriage, of course,

89

but she won't expect you to call her that. As for her child, when he comes, he will be your cousin, I suppose.'

'He?' Brice said, with a little smile.

'Yes, she've set her heart on a son, to be called Jim after his father.'

'Well, I hope that Maggie's son and I will be more than just cousins-by-marriage,' Brice said. 'I hope, perhaps, when the time comes, I'll be asked to be one of his godparents.'

How this idea had come to him and how it had found expression so glibly he could not have explained to anyone; and afterwards, as he walked home, he wondered if he had been guilty of a piece of blatant hypocrisy. But on the whole he was pleased with himself because, by making this gesture of his, he was putting on a face that the world at large would have trouble in reading. People might surmise as much as they liked, but no one would ever really know what his feelings had been for Maggie Care, nor would they know what his feelings were at seeing her marry his uncle Gus.

There was much comfort in this; he commended himself on his cleverness; and then he realized, with wry self-scorn, that these precious feelings of his were a mystery even to himself.

The wedding day was misty and warm, typical of September month, with a smell of dying leaves in the air.

Brice, as he wheeled his uncle Gus up Bryant's Hill and into the church, found him unusually subdued and perceived with a twinge of sympathy that he was nervous and unsure of himself. But he also perceived, on entering the church, that the sight of Maggie, serene, self-possessed, instantly set his uncle at ease and that in the look that passed between them there was complete understanding and trust.

There were very few people at the wedding and this was as Gus and Maggie wished. Mr and Mrs Kiddy were there, with the younger sail-maker, Percy Tremearne, and Martha Cledra was there, as Maggie's friend. And behind them were gathered those villagers, numbering two or three score, who, having nothing better to do that day, the tenth of September, 1869, had come together into the church to see Gus Tallack put his ring on Maggie Care's finger and to hear them pronounced man and wife.

The ceremony was so simple that many people thought it austere. No hymns were sung; no music was played; and when the couple left the church, there was no sound of wedding-bells. Martha Cledra threw some rice, and a small girl, waiting at the lych-gate, put a bunch of poppies into Maggie's hands, but these were the only festivities. There was not to be any wedding breakfast and Brice, pushing his uncle's wheelchair, was the only person to accompany the bride and bridegroom home. Even he did not go inside; he excused himself on the grounds that he had to go down to the quay and see that all was well with the boat; and so, within an hour of being married, Gus and Maggie were alone in their home.

'Well, here we are, then, man and wife.'

'Yes,' Maggie said. She looked at him.

'No regrets?'

'No. None.'

'I hope it will always be like that.'

'I hope so, too. On your side, I mean, as well as my own.'

'We're talking like strangers, aren't we?' he said. 'But time will cure that, I suppose. – Such time as I have left to me.'

'Don't talk like that.'

'No. Very well. But it's something we've got to face all the same.'

'Is it?' she said. 'Well, we shall see.'

That afternoon, at three o'clock, Frank Rogers the solicitor came, and Gus made his will. Maggie, as his wife, was already his heir, but he intended to make quite sure that no doubt could ever exist regarding his intentions. So the will was made and Isaac Kiddy and Percy Tremearne were called down from the sail-loft to witness Gus's signature. They each got a glass of rum for their pains and so did Mr Rogers, and the three of them drank the couple's health. None of it took very long, for the will was simplicity itself, and everything Gus possessed was left to Maggie.

Gus, with his new responsibilities. was anxious that his

91

property should bring in the maximum profit, and soon he was talking of opening up the barking-house and putting it into business again. The problem was to find a man who would run it honestly and efficiently, and as soon as Isaac Kiddy got wind of the plan he wanted the job for his son Eugene.

'If your son is anything like you,' Gus said, 'I don't want him near the place.'

'What are you talking about?' Isaac said.

'I'm talking about that suit of sails you're making for Matt Crowle,' Gus said, 'that should've been ready two weeks ago and aren't finished even now.'

'Twadn *me* that promised those sails would be ready by October fifteenth. Twas *you* that went and promised that. I do my best. I can't do no more. And I've only got one pair of hands, you know.'

'No, you haven't, you've got two! – Your own and Percy Tremearne's!' Gus said. 'And if two grown men who call themselves sail-makers can't get a suit of sails cut and stitched inside a month there must be something wrong with them!'

Isaac began making excuses but Gus cut him short.

'I'll tell you what I'm willing to do. You get those sails finished by the end of this week and your boy Eugene can have the job of running the barking-house for me.'

This promise worked like a charm. The sails were complete within another twenty-four hours and Isaac duly reported to Gus.

'Can I tell boy Eugene he've got the job?'

'I promised you, didn't I?' Gus said. 'But just you let me tell you this. – Things've got to be different from now on. No more kiddling about, coming and going just as you please, but a full day's work every day, and sails got ready on the dot. And another thing I expect to see is that sail-loft kept tidy and clean. If it isn't – just you look out!'

Eugene Kiddy arrived the next day and quietly, without any fuss, took possession of the barking-house. Gus had already got in a load of cutch and soon the acrid smell of it as it boiled and bubbled in the vat, with the *Maid Molly*'s nets steeping in it, was wafting all around the harbour and up into the terraced town, pungent evidence of the fact that Gus Tallack's barking-house was working in full swing again.

There was no lack of customers because fishermen who, in the past eighteen months, had been obliged to take their nets to be barked in St Glozey, now returned to Gus Tallack and put their names on his waiting-list. Soon the barking-house and yard were full of noise and activity, just as they had been in the old days, and Gus, sitting out in his wheelchair, with men of his own kind to talk to and plenty of business to occupy his mind, found himself closely in touch again with the stirring, bustling life of the sea.

All this he felt he owed to Maggie, because she had given him a sense of purpose, and the will to see that this business of his was working to its proper capacity. He was doing it all for her sake, so that she and her child should lack for nothing when he was dead and in the grave, but what he was doing for Maggie's sake brought rewards for himself as well. He had taken on a new lease of life and although he knew that its days were numbered, there was work and device enough in them to make them rich and meaningful.

Maggie also was content, for she and Gus got on well together, and when, early in the morning of the twelfth of January, her baby was safely delivered to her, after a labour lasting ten hours, she felt that God had been good to her and was making amends for what lay in the past. For her baby was a fine healthy boy and when she held him in her arms and smelt the soft warm smell of him she knew that he, more than anything else, would ease and allay the aching void that his father's death had left in her heart.

News that she had given birth to a son reached Brice on the quay that morning and when he was on his way home he met Annie Tambling, the midwife, coming away from his uncle's house.

'Ess, tes a boy, sure nuff, brave and handsome as any I've seen. Weighed eight pounds if he weighed an ounce and was screamen fit to burst his lungs almost before I'd turned him up.'

'Is Mrs Tallack all right?'

'Ess, for sure. No trouble at all. Did what I told her, good as gold, and never so much as yelled wunst. As for your uncle Gus, well, he's about as bucked with it all as though he'd fathered the cheeld himself.' Mrs Tambling squinted at Brice. 'Going in to see them, are you?'

'Not right now,' Brice said. 'I think I'd better wait a while.'

On getting home he found that his mother, too, had heard the news.

'So your uncle's wife has got a son? A bastard child with a borrowed name! And in time he will come into property that should by rights have been yours.'

Brice walked past her into the house.

When he did call at his uncle's cottage, one wet afternoon, on his way to the boat, Maggie was sitting in the kitchen and it happened that she had been suckling her child. Brice would have withdrawn at once but his uncle motioned him into the room.

'Maggie won't mind you stepping in. Women don't fuss about such things. They've got more sense than us men.'

It seemed that this was perfectly true, for Maggie's glance was quite composed and she showed no signs of prudishness. She sat in a low nursing-chair, close beside the kitchen table, and the light of the lamp, in its pink-frosted globe, fell on her baby's warm flushed face as he lay in her arms, almost asleep. The small mouth had become slack; the shadowy eyelids were slowly closing, and one tiny hand, with fingers curled, lay in the opening of her dress, in the soft warm hollow between her breasts.

'So this is Jim?'

'Yes,' Maggie said.

'You wanted a son.'

'Yes. I did.'

Brice, though he stood in front of her, was still awkwardly keeping his distance, and his uncle Gus remarked on it.

'You needn't be afraid of going close. Neither she nor the child will bite you.'

'Well,' Brice said, and looked down at himself. His dark red oilskins were wet with rain and a puddle was forming on the floor. He had taken his sou'wester off and it hung, dripping, from his hand. 'As you see, I'm not really fit.' But he moved forward a pace or two and, leaning down from his great height, looked closely at the sleeping babe and touched it gently on the arm. 'I can't stay long. I'm due at the boat. But I felt it was time I called on you to offer my good wishes and see young Jim Tallack for myself.'

'And what do you think of him?' Gus asked.

Brice stood up straight again.

'Mrs Tambling called him a brave handsome cheeld and it seems to me she was right,' he said.

The baby stirred in Maggie's arms and she bent over him, holding him close, shifting sideways in her chair so that his face was screened from the light. For a moment she was completely absorbed and Brice saw and understood how it was that the bond between a mother and child, forged in such moments of closeness and warmth, came to be the strongest in the world. He saw that Maggie's whole life was centred on her baby son and that nothing else mattered to her; he saw, too, that motherhood had made her more gently beautiful; and by the sudden twist in his heart as he turned away from her and her child he knew he was still in love with her.

'Going already?' Gus said.

'Yes. I must.'

'You've got a wet night's work ahead of you.'

'At least there's a good wind,' Brice said. 'It's been too still the past few nights and the herring haven't been coming to us but maybe tonight our luck will change.'

Outside in the wind and the rain he pulled his sou'wester onto his head and turned his collar up to his ears. The afternoon was as black as pitch and the rain fell like rods of glass, slantways on the north-west wind blowing down from Mump Head. Most of the drifters had already gone but a few were just pulling away and he saw their lights gleaming fuzzily as they made towards the harbour mouth. Only the *Emmet* remained at the quayside and the crew were waiting impatiently, bowed figures in gleaming oilskins, under sails that hung like wet rags.

'God! What a night!' Ralph Ellis said as Brice jumped down into the boat. 'Tes what you get for grumblen all week about it being too damned fine!'

Chapter 5

Gus's prediction proved correct and Maggie, from the day she married him, found herself treated with respect. Tongues still wagged, inevitably, for Maggie's history was such that it would bear telling and re-telling for many a long day to come. But whatever people said behind her back, to her face they were all civility, such was the standing endowed upon her by her marriage to Gus. She was his wife; her child bore his name; and these indisputable facts were enough to make her position secure.

Only Rachel remained hostile and this too worked in Maggie's favour, for whereas Rachel had always looked down on the ordinary people of Polsinney, Maggie was friendly with everyone.

'At least she dunt give herself airs,' the villagers said among themselves. 'And she *could* do if she had a mind that way cos tes *her* husband, edn it, you, that've got his own bit of property and she'll get it all when the old chap dies. Rachel Tallack edn nothing at all for all she d'look down her nose at we and if old Gus've put a slight on her I reckon tes only what she deserve.'

So it fell out that quite soon Maggie came to be liked for herself. The villagers accepted her and looked on her as one of themselves. And in time it also came about that even the more exalted members of the community raised their hats when meeting her, for it was seen that Gus Tallack was a man of growing consequence, and people like the Halls and the Lanyons treated his wife accordingly.

For Gus, up until this time, the sail-loft and barking-house had never been anything more than a second string to his bow; something he had been glad to fall back on when illness had forced him to give up the sea. But now all that was changed; he had acquired a taste for commerce; and in a small way, without taking risks, he was expanding his business interests.

For one thing, when he had money to spare, he bought a share in the Nonesuch Seine, and out of the handsome profits he got when the seining season proved good that year, he bought a shed at Steeple Lumbtown, installed two net-making looms in it, and engaged two women to make nets. All this was done for Maggie's sake, to make her future more secure, and right from the start he encouraged her to take an interest in his affairs because, as he said to her, 'You'll have to run things when I'm gone.'

Rachel, on hearing of Gus's new business ventures, spoke of them bitterly to Brice.

'Oh, that girl has done well for herself, marrying that uncle of yours! There's no fool like an old fool and it seems he can't do enough for her.'

'The gain is not all on Maggie's side. Uncle Gus benefits too. It's given him something to live for and he's more cheerful now than he has been for years. Maggie is a good wife to him and no one can say otherwise.'

'Wife!' Rachel said scornfully. 'And what sort of marriage is it when he is nearly three times her age and everyone knows he's a dying man?'

'Whatever sort of marriage it is, it seems to be working pretty well, and if uncle Gus is a dying man, at least his last years will be happy ones.'

Brice, calling on Gus every week to discuss the boat's business affairs, had plenty of opportunity to observe the improvement Maggie had wrought. The old man now had a comfortable home where everything was cheerful and bright and where, at every hour of the day, he was considered and waited on. He ate proper meals, at regular times, and instead of spending his evenings alone, brooding on his helplessness, he now had Maggie's company and would yarn to her by the hour. It seemed they had plenty to talk about and in spite of the difference in their ages, there was a close understanding between them, based on mutual need and trust. All these things had made their mark; the old man was in good spirits these days; and Brice felt sure that because of this his health had improved accordingly.

At first, when the boat's business was discussed, Maggie took no part in it but kept herself in the background, out of consideration for Brice. That was in the early days and Gus said nothing about it then because all Maggie's thoughts at that time were centred on her unborn child and she was everlastingly busy with some piece of knitting or needlework. But later, some few weeks after baby Jim's birth, Gus firmly insisted that Maggie should join him and Brice at the table and go through the *Emmet*'s accounts with them.

'The boat will be yours one of these days and tes only right you should know what's what. You needn't worry about Brice. He quite understands how things'll be.'

So every Saturday now, when Brice called, Maggie sat in on these discussions and heard Gus go through the weekly 'log'. She heard what each night's catch had been and what it had earnt in hard coin; she heard that so far the herring season had been slow in getting under way; and she heard that the *Emmet*'s pumps would soon need repair. Sometimes she had some comment to make and always Gus would pass her the 'log' so that she could check his figures.

'Maggie's got a better head for reckoning than I ever had in my life,' he said. 'Her mother was a schoolmistress – did you know that – so brains must run in the family.'

'Yes,' Brice said, 'I did know that.'

'Damme! What am I thinking of? I'd forgotten, just for the moment, that Maggie was up at the farm with you. You must've got to know her pretty well in that time and I doubt if I can tell you much that you haven't already found out for yourself.'

'Well, I'm not sure about that, but we're not exactly strangers, it's true.'

Brice gave his answer clumsily; he knew that the taunt was intentional; and later on that same evening the old man followed it up with a few more pointed remarks. The business discussion had been completed; Brice had received his weekly 'share'; and Maggie, as was her custom, brought out the rum and two glasses and set them down in front of Gus.

'I did the right thing when I married this girl. There's nothing suits a man so well as having a woman to wait on him. You ought to try it yourself, my boy. – Take a leaf out of my book and find yourself a decent wife. You shouldn't have to look very hard. Polsinney is full of docy maids keen to snap up a fine chap like you.'

'Is it?' Brice said, evenly. 'Then I must certainly give it some thought.'

'Don't spend too long thinking,' Gus said. 'You can miss a lot of good chances that way.'

Brice, at this point, changed the subject. His uncle's jokes were too close to the bone. And as soon as he had drunk his rum he rose to go.

'What, leaving already?' his uncle said.

'Yes. I have things to do at home. And my mother is too much alone as it is.'

'Dunt she like her own company? Well, I can't blame her!' Gus said.

These visits to his uncle Gus, now that the old man was married to Maggie, were something of a strain to Brice and sometimes he thought of giving them up. But that would only create fresh problems; for one thing he had no valid excuse; and he knew he would have to resign himself to the visits and the torment they caused.

Sometimes he felt the perverse satisfaction that a man feels when he has a wound and exults in hiding it from the world, and with this went a kind of elation because he knew he had the wit to act out the part he had set himself. It was a challenge. A trial of strength. And if his uncle's barbed remarks made it more difficult, all the more triumph when he won.

The old man might suspect that his nephew was still in love with Maggie but at least he would never know for sure. Nor would Maggie herself ever know. Brice was grimly determined on this; it was important; a matter of pride. So the weekly visits continued and gradually, over the months, fell into a sort of pattern.

'Not found a wife yet?' his uncle would say. 'You're letting the grass grow, aren't you, my boy? It seems you must be hard to please!'

Mostly Brice merely laughed and shrugged but once, by way of a change, he said:

'I'm in no hurry. Why should I be? I've got plenty of time yet before I need think about settling down.'

His words brought a frown to the old man's face and a shadow seemed to fall on him.

'Yes, and you're luckier than you know. You've got your life in front of you. What are you now? Twenty-four? The years go slowly for young men like you but for me they go at a rate of knots.'

Time, for Gus, was slipping away; he and Maggie had been married a year; baby Jim was growing fast and the earth was spinning relentlessly on. But there was much to be thankful for and Gus was the first to admit it.

'I'm in better shape now than I have been for years. I have a good appetite for my meat, I get five hours' good sleep every night, and I've still got enough command of my brain to manage my bits of business affairs. Not bad for a dying man, eh?'

'Have you seen Dr Sam lately?'

'No, nor I don't intend to,' Gus said. 'He can come and see me when I'm dead and according to what he've already told me, that'll be in the next eighteen months.'

'Looking at you right now,' Brice said, 'I find that impossible to believe.'

When baby Jim began to crawl he did not go on all fours as most babies do but by sitting with his left leg under him and his right leg thrust out in front and, with little humping movements of his body, aided by movements of the right leg, propelled himself forward comfortably, remaining always in an upright position. People were highly amused at this; they had never seen such a thing before; and Gus said it showed great intelligence, for by this method of locomotion, Jim could always see exactly where he was going.

According to Gus, who doted on him, Jim was forward in every way. No other child was so sturdy, so strong, or so quick in the uptake. And certainly no other child of his age ever showed a more resolute will. Maggie said that this son of hers was in danger of being spoilt because Gus, as he sat in his wheelchair, would let the child climb all over him, doing pretty much as he liked; and what Jim liked best was to rummage through the old man's pockets where, more often than not, he would find a stick of barley-sugar or a couple of hazelnuts.

The old man's wheelchair fascinated Jim and one of the first words he learnt was 'ride'. He would scramble up into Gus's lap, turn himself round to face forwards, and, with his hands on the arms of the chair, would bounce up and down, shouting: 'Ride! Ride! Ride!' And Gus, always willing to oblige, would take the little boy for a ride round the yard, passing so close to the barking-house door that Eugene, if he chanced to step out, was in danger of being run down or having his nose taken off, as he said.

As soon as Jim learnt to walk he became so adventurous that everyone who came into the yard had to be careful to close the gates. When the fishermen brought their nets to be barked, they had to take extra care because while they were wheeling their wheelbarrows in, Jim would dart out from some hiding-place and go rushing past them into the road. They would have to go after him and Jim thought it a huge joke to be brought back into the yard, tucked under some fisherman's arm or sitting astride his broad shoulders, especially if that fisherman happened to be his uncle Brice.

'See what I've found!' Brice would say. 'Has anyone lost a boy called Jim? A little tacker in petticoats with liquorice all over his face? If not I shall have to keep him myself and take him out in the *Emmet* with me—'

'Here, give him to me!' Gus would say, and Brice would deliver the squirming child into the old man's outstretched arms.

At this time, being so small, Jim was not allowed into the

barking-house because of the open furnace fire and the stinging fumes of the boiling cutch, and Gus, taking him into his lap, would keep him there under restraint until the barking-house door had been closed. Jim would squirm and struggle and kick and make such a hullabaloo that Maggie would come running out of the house and Gus, with a laugh, often said to her:

'Just see what a temper he've got in him! He's more my son than he is yours!'

But Jim learnt better behaviour in time because Gus, though indulgent, meant to be obeyed, and if the little boy went too far he would receive a smart slap on his leg. So he learnt discipline early in life and because of it he and Gus were good friends. Each was amused by the other's antics and Maggie, whenever she watched them together, marvelled at the old man's patience and gave thanks for it in her heart. No child in the world, lacking a father of his own, could have had a better substitute.

Sometimes, however, she was anxious for Gus because of the demands Jim made on him.

'Don't let him climb all over you. He's so energetic, he'll tire you out. Hadn't I better take him indoors?'

'Leave him be. He's doing no harm. Just look at me! – I'm as strong as a horse!' And Gus, to demonstrate his strength, lifted Jim high in the air, holding him up at arm's length for perhaps half a minute or so, then setting him down again. 'There!' he said, breathing hard. 'I couldn't have done that two years ago. I wouldn't have dreamt of trying it. But these days I feel I could lift a whale and if only my legs were as strong as my arms—'

He gave a little wistful sigh. His legs were not much use to him. He still could not walk more than a few yards at a time.

'But if they're no better, at least they're no worse, and I must just count my blessings,' he said.

At least he could still put himself to bed, and get up in the morning and dress himself, and he valued these acts of independence, guarding them with fierce obstinacy. What he could do he *would* do and wanted no help from anyone. Maggie understood this and never tried to interfere. She would take hot water into his room; then she would come out and close the door; and only when Gus had emerged fully dressed, wheeling himself out in his chair, did she venture into the room again, to empty the basin and make the bed.

As for the hundred and one things she did for him during the rest of the day, he accepted them without demur, even with a certain complacency. Sometimes he pretended to grumble. 'Maggie sews my buttons on even before they've come off,' he would say, and, 'I have to change my clothes every week now that I'm a married man.' But in fact he enjoyed Maggie's attentions and was often touched by the trouble she took in putting his boots to warm by the fire, in bringing him hot cocoa to drink when he sat out of doors on a cold day, and in cooking those meals she knew he liked best, such as rabbit pasty with turnip and thyme and plenty of pepper in the crust.

He was always praising Maggie's cooking, especially when Brice was there, and he said that Maggie's heavy cake was the best he had tasted in his life. Sometimes when Brice came on Saturday he would stay and have supper with them and on one of these occasions Gus suddenly said to him:

'Did Maggie ever do the cooking when she was up at the farm with you?'

'Yes, she did, quite often,' Brice said.

'Then your mother must've been properly mazed when she turned Maggie out of the house. Still, there tis! Your loss was my gain. And if you and Rachel have any regrets you've only got yourselves to blame.'

Brice said nothing to this. He was inured to these jibes by now. But he noticed that Maggie, clearing the dishes, frowned at Gus reprovingly.

Gus, however, would not be reproved. He was in an ebullient mood. And when Maggie came close to his chair he suddenly caught hold of her and, pulling her roughly down to him, kissed her clumsily on the mouth.

Maggie was taken by surprise. Released, she stood staring at him, her eyes at once puzzled, vexed, amused. A flush of warm colour came into her cheeks and she turned away with a little laugh, glancing quickly towards Brice but without directly meeting his gaze.

'I don't know what's wrong with your uncle tonight. It must've been something I put in the pie.'

'Damme!' Gus said, in a boisterous voice. 'I was just showing my gratitude at having a wife worth her weight in gold.'

'Perhaps it was too much pepper and salt . . .'

' "So ought men to love their wives as their own bodies," ' Gus said, quoting the Scriptures. ' "He that loveth his own wife loveth himself." '

'Indeed,' Maggie said, 'no wife can ask more than that.'

She busied herself, washing the crocks, and the two men went to sit by the fire, Gus now talking soberly of his new business venture at Steeple Lumbtown, and of how many lengths of herring-net the looms were producing every week. After a while Maggie joined them, bringing a pile of mending to do, and the evening passed as usual. But as soon as Brice had left the house she put her needlework into her lap and looked at Gus with challenging eyes.

'Why did you kiss me like that?' she asked.

'My dear soul and body!' Gus exclaimed. 'Can't a man kiss his own wife?'

'You never have done. Not till today.'

'I'm not going to make a habit of it, if that's what is worrying you. Tes just that I've got a devil in me and Brice always seems to bring it out.'

'So is *was* for Brice's benefit? I had a suspicion it might be.'

'I just wanted to stir him up. See the look on his face and maybe find out what he's made of. But Brice doesn't give himself away. He've got too much nous for that. He might be a block of wood sitting there for all you can see what goes on in his mind.'

'It seems you were disappointed, then.'

'Maybe. Maybe not.'

'What I don't understand is, why you should *want* to stir him up.'

'Because it amuses me, that's why, and because it's only what he deserves. He was in love with you – you know that – and yet he let that mother of his turn you out into the road and never lifted a finger to help although he knew what trouble you were in.'

'All that's in the past,' Maggie said. 'There was nothing Brice could have done for me. There was nothing I *wanted* him to do. And whatever he thought he felt for me was all over and finished with when he knew I was going to have a child.'

'If he'd had any gumption in him he would've married you just the same. I told him that myself at the time but he was so full of his own injured pride that he wouldn't hear of such a thing.'

'Of course he wouldn't! What man would? And I could *never* have married him. For one thing I didn't love him—'

'You didn't love me, neither, but you were willing to marry me.'

'That was different,' Maggie said. 'It was a business arrangement between us. You said so yourself. But a marriage like ours wouldn't do for Brice. He wants more from a wife than that and in time when he falls in love with some girl—'

'All right! All right!' Gus exclaimed. 'You don't have to defend him to me. Brice can take care of himself and he knows I don't mean him any great hurt. He *is* my brother's son after all. I'm fond of him, believe it or not, and I think in his way he's fond of me. Tes jus that sometimes when he's sitting there—'

'That's another thing,' Maggie said. 'The fact that Brice is your own kith and kin and that if I hadn't come along—'

'You troubled with conscience, suddenly, because you're getting my property and Brice is getting nothing at all?'

'It's not so much a question of conscience—'

'Damme! I should hope not indeed! You're my wife before God and man and in my will I've made it clear that *everything* is to come to you. The property's yours by entitlement and tes no good getting a conscience now because that's the way I want it and that's the way it's going to be.'

'What I was going to say was, that Brice has been very good about it. There could have been so much ill feeling . . . just as there is on his mother's part . . . but instead he's always been friendly and kind.'

'Oh, yes, that's true enough. Brice has behaved very well.

106

Never a word out of place. Always very proper and correct.' Gus's tone of voice was dry and his glance sardonic. 'Tes one thing you can depend on,' he said. 'Brice will always do the right thing.'

Maggie looked at him sorrowfully. Then she picked up her needlework.

'You make it sound like a fault,' she said.

She herself was grateful to Brice because he had made things so easy for her and one day when they were alone together she tried to express her gratitude. She spoke of it in much the same way that she had spoken of it to Gus but the words did not come so readily and Brice was obliged to help her out.

'You are thinking about the property? But I am not jealous – not in the least – and I hope you won't let it worry you. It's true I was taken aback at first when I heard you were marrying uncle Gus. It was a shock, I don't deny that, and people were very quick to point out how much I was going to lose by it.'

Brice paused, looking at her.

'That was the worst part of it, knowing what a lot of talk there was . . . Knowing that people were watching me, waiting to see how I would behave . . . But as for losing the property, except for the boat it means nothing to me, and I hope you'll believe me when I say that I'm glad things have gone the way they have.'

'That's what I mean,' Maggie said. 'Only a generous man could say that – anyone else would have hated me – and I want you to know I'm grateful to you for – for accepting me as your uncle's wife.'

Brice had called with a gift of fish and it happened that Gus had gone with Isaac to buy canvas in Polzeale. So Maggie and Jim were alone in the house and the little boy, now two and a half, was helping her to shell peas. Brice sat at the table with them and whenever Jim had difficulty in opening a peapod he would push it across to Brice and Brice would split it open for him.

'I could never hate you,' Brice said. 'I don't think I'm a hating man.'

'No,' Maggie said, 'I don't think you are.'

'You've done so much for uncle Gus. You've given him something to live for. And although he and I have our differences I like him enough to be glad of that.' There was a pause and then Brice said: 'He seems so much better nowadays . . . So much stronger in every way . . . I can't help wondering if perhaps . . .'

'Yes,' Maggie said, 'I wonder that, too, and it's what I pray for, constantly.'

'Is he still refusing to see Dr Sam?'

'Yes. He's very obstinate. *I've* been to see Dr Sam myself and I've told him how much better Gus is, but although he listened to all I said, he wouldn't say anything much himself, not without examining Gus. "It's in God's hands." That's all he would say. I told Gus that when I got home and he gave a loud snort and said, "Well, I can only hope that God is a better doctor than Sam Carveth!" '

Brice smiled.

'My uncle Gus will have the last word right to the very end,' he said.

He got up, preparing to leave, and took his cap from the back of the chair. Little Jim snatched it from him and ran out through the open door. Brice and Maggie followed him and stood in the yard watching as he placed the cap upside down on the ground and, bending over unsteadily, tried to put his head into it. Something went wrong with this plan and instead he tumbled head over heels. He sat up with a look of surprise and gave a little bubbling laugh as he saw that his uncle Brice's cap had somehow got caught up on his foot.

'Can I have my cap?' Brice asked.

'No! Can't have it!' Jim said.

He scrambled to his feet and ran off again but Brice in three strides caught up with him, lifted him, chortling, into his arms, and wrested the dusty cap from him. The little boy struggled and squirmed and as soon as Brice set him down again he went running to Gus's empty wheelchair, standing outside the porch, and began pushing it round the yard.

'The only time he's ever still is when he's in bed asleep,' Maggie said.

'You wanted a son.'

'Yes.' She laughed.

'Is he like his father?' Brice asked.

'Yes, he's the image of him,' she said. 'When he laughs . . . When he frowns . . . When he's thinking hard . . . Even the way he holds his head . . . It really is quite absurd that two people should be so alike.'

There was a sudden catch in her throat but in a moment she was calling to Jim, telling him to take more care and not push the wheelchair into the wall. Together she and Brice watched as the child swung the chair round and pushed it in the other direction.

'He's like you, too,' Brice said. 'He's got your eyes.' He dusted his cap and put it on. 'I must be getting home,' he said.

He waved to Maggie and Jim from the gate.

Little Jim, out in all weathers, grew into a strong healthy boy, and by the time he was three years old he was full of boundless curiosity. He wanted to know about everything that went on in the sail-loft and barking-house and was always climbing onto the yard wall to look at the ships standing out to sea.

'What ship is that?'

'A schooner,' Gus said.

'And that one?' Jim asked.

'A barquentine.'

Where was the schooner bound for and what was she carrying, Jim would ask, and Gus, looking through his spyglass, would do his best to answer the boy.

'That's the *Aurelia*, out of Polzeale. She's probably carrying pilchards – hundreds of hogsheads, all salted down – and taking them to Italy. They're great ones for eating pilchards there. They can't seem to get enough of them and they're always crying out for more.'

'Why are they?' Jim asked.

'Because they're all Roman Catholics there and they've got a chap they call the Pope who tells them they've got to eat plenty of fish.'

'Why does he?'

'Because he's the Pope.'

'Does he eat plenty of fish himself?'

'Well, if he doesn't, he should do,' Gus said, 'cos otherwise where would he get his brains?'

Jim asked questions all day long and Gus answered them patiently, but one day he turned the tables on Jim and the boy had to answer him instead.

'See that ship out there in the bay? The one with two masts and her sails half-reefed? I want you to tell me what she is.'

Jim looked at the ship in the bay and a deep frown wrinkled his brow.

'Is she a brigantine?'

'*You* just tell *me*.'

'Yes! She is! I know she is!'

'How do you know?'

'I know by her rig.'

'Bless my soul, but you're some smart! You can go to the top of the class for that!'

And as Maggie came out to the yard, to hang her washing on the line, Gus shouted across to her, saying how clever her son had been to answer his question about the ship. Maggie was inclined to smile. She thought it was just a lucky guess. But Gus would not hear of this and was highly indignant on Jim's account.

'He knows all right! You mark my words! He's smart as paint, this boy of yours, and getting smarter every day. A brigantine, that's what he said, and a brigantine she is, by God!'

But whether it was pure luck or not, the time came soon enough when Jim really did know which ship was which, and could tell you a great deal more besides.

'There's a full-rigger out in the bay. Handsomest ship I've ever seen. Such great masts she've got on her—'

'What flag is she flying?'

'I can't see.'

'Then you'd better look through my spyglass.'

Gus held the old, battered spyglass so that it rested on the wall and Jim, standing on a box, swivelled it round to look at the ship.

'She's putting another anchor down. There's sailors running about everywhere. One of them's stripped bare to the waist.'

'Can you see her flag?' Gus asked.

'Yes, it's the tricolour,' Jim said.

'Ah, French, I thought she was. Can you see what name she's called?'

'Yes, I can see it plain as plain.' Jim had not yet learnt to read but he knew his letters well enough and he spelt out the name on the great ship's bows. 'H.E.L.O.I.S.E. .'

'The *Heloise*? Why, she's an old friend. I went aboard her once, years ago, when she was berthed in Plymouth Sound.' Gus now took the spyglass and had a look at the ship for himself. 'She's out there waiting for the tide so that she can get into Polzeale and unload her cargo at the pier. I wonder who's her skipper now . . . It used to be a chap called Pradell but that was thirty years ago . . .'

'Did you ever sail in her?'

'Only up the Sound, that's all.'

'I would like to sail in a ship when I'm a grown man,' Jim said. 'Will you come with me, uncle Gus?'

'No, I shan't come with you,' Gus said. 'I'll have gone on a voyage all by myself, long before you're a grown man.'

'Why will you?'

'Oh, just because.'

'Do you have to go all alone? Can't I come too?'

'No, you'll be needed here at home, keeping your mother company.' Gus closed the old spyglass and lowered it into his lap. 'And that'll be a comfort to me, knowing she's got you to look after her, when I set out on this voyage of mine.'

'Do you *have* to go, uncle Gus?'

'Yes, when the time comes, I shan't have no choice.'

'When will that be?'

'Not yet, I hope.'

'Where will you go to?'

'I don't know. I'll be under sealed orders, as they say.'

'Will you be going in the boat?'

'What boat?'

'The *Emmet*, of course.'

'Well, now!' Gus said, and gave a laugh, reaching out with

111

one big hand to ruffle the little boy's dark hair. 'That's how I would *choose* to go if I had any say in it. — Sailing out in the old *Emmet*, with a two mizzen breeze and not too much tide, making for Sally Quaile's, perhaps, when the pilchards are running nicely there . . . Yes, that would suit me handsome, that would, 'cos I should like to get my hand on her tiller again and feel her riding over the swell . . .'

'You'll have to ask uncle Brice,' Jim said. 'He'd let you go. I'm sure he would. After all, it *is* your boat.'

'Yes, that's right, the *Emmet* is mine.'

Gus sat looking out to sea, his eyes screwed up against its pale glare, and was lost for a while in his own thoughts. Then he turned towards Jim again and, thrusting out his bearded chin, spoke to him in a great hearty voice.

'And a good boat she've always been, too, right from the day I had her built. Old Tommy Laycock built her for me and he never did a better job in his life. Pure gold she is from stem to stern.'

'She's the best-kept boat in Polsinney,' Jim said. 'Uncle Brice sees to that.'

'H'mm!' Gus said. 'And so he ought!'

Later that same September evening, when Jim was in bed, Gus sat out in the yard watching the sun going down behind Mump Head. The evening was warm, with only the gentlest south-west wind beginning to breathe in from the sea, barely enough to disturb the gnats that hovered in the air above his head. Behind him the cottage had grown quite dark and Maggie had already lit the lamp. He could hear her moving about, closing the casements and drawing the curtains and speaking quietly to the cat, disturbed from its place on the window-sill. Then she came out with the cat in her arms and stood looking at the western sky, now a saffron-coloured glow streaked with bars of purple cloud.

'Isn't it time you came in?'

'Yes, it's high time,' he agreed, and slapped at a gnat that had settled on the back of his neck. 'I'll be eaten alive, else,' he said.

Maggie put the cat on the wall and wheeled Gus into the house. She went back to close the porch door and when she entered the kitchen again, Gus was at the table pouring himself a glass of rum.

'Well, that's another day gone!' he said. 'They seem to get shorter all the time.'

'Don't they always at this time of year?'

'I wasn't thinking of the time of year.'

'No,' she said gently, 'I know you weren't.'

He had been drinking heavily lately and it was a thing that worried her. She watched him empty his glass at one draught and reach out to fill it again.

'Do you think it's wise to drink so much?'

'I don't see what harm it can do me now. I'm already a dying man, or so I've been led to believe, anyway . . . Two or three years Dr Sam gave me and that was over four years ago. So I'm living on borrowed time now and I may as well make the most of it.'

Once again he drained his glass. Maggie drew out a chair and sat down. She looked at him with troubled eyes.

'I don't believe you're a dying man.'

'Come to that, neither do I!'

'Then why not see Dr Sam?'

'Where's the point in seeing him? He said there was nothing he could do, except pronounce sentence on me, and he've already done that, damn his soul!'

'But you've been getting better, not worse.'

'No thanks to him, is it?' Gus said. 'It's all your doing, not Dr Sam's, so where's the point in seeing him?'

'He knows you're better. I told him so. But he wouldn't say what that might mean without seeing you for himself.'

'An examination!' Gus said with a snarl. 'I've had enough of them in the past!'

'Yes. I know. But I thought perhaps, for my sake, you might be willing to face it again.'

'No doubt you're in a hurry to know when you'll be made a widow!' he said. ''Tes only natural, I suppose.'

Contrition followed immediately and he turned from her in self-disgust.

'Don't mind me – or what I say. I hit out at you – I'm a swine for that – but I don't mean the things I say.'

'I know that,' Maggie said. 'I know why it is and I understand.'

'Yes,' Gus said, looking at her, 'you are more understanding than I deserve.' And then, because he was still ashamed, he quietly gave in to her. 'All right, I'll see Dr Sam. No good putting it off, is it? The devil will get me in the end.'

Dr Sam examined Gus in his bedroom on the ground floor and the door of the room was kept bolted to stop little Jim from bursting in. Dr Sam was very thorough; the examination took half an hour; and at the end of that time he frankly admitted that he was astonished.

'The general improvement in your condition, since I last examined you, is nothing short of miraculous. If I hadn't seen it for myself I would never have believed it possible. Heart . . . lungs . . . digestive organs . . . I'd say they're working as well as my own . . . So, considering your disability and the strain it must put on your system as a whole, you are in pretty good health and I'd say you're a very lucky man.'

'Am I going to die or not?'

'Well, of course, we're all going to die—'

'The last time you examined me, you gave me two or three years, so you've already made one mistake.'

'Such things do happen,' the doctor said. 'You pressed me for a verdict then and I gave it to you in all honesty. It was based on your condition at that time and I'm sure that any other doctor's prognosis would have been exactly the same. You were neglecting yourself badly. You hardly ate. You slept in damp sheets. You'd lost heart in every way and were letting yourself go downhill. Now all that is changed—'

'What about the damned disease? You said the palsy would spread to my lungs.'

'That is the course it most commonly takes and it's usually only a matter of a few years from the onset of the disease. But your general health has improved so much that the palsy, rather mysteriously, seems to have been completely checked.

114

I can't explain it. I don't know enough. But if you would like a second opinion—'

'One doctor's enough,' Gus said. 'How long do you give me now?'

'I really wouldn't like to say. Having already been wrong once—'

'I'm willing to overlook that. You've gone over me pretty thoroughly. You've asked enough questions to fill a book. So what's your latest prognosis, based on how I am today?'

'Well, I can only do my best, but I'd say, judging from your condition now, that there's no very serious reason why you shouldn't live your allotted span.'

Gus stared. He drew a deep breath.

'Three score years and ten?' he said. 'That's another fourteen years!'

'You don't look exactly pleased at the news.'

'It takes some getting used to, that's why. Having faced up to death these past few years, then to be told you've got fourteen to go!'

'That was just a figure of speech. You mustn't hold me too firmly to it.'

'Damme! I'll hold you to *something*!' Gus said.

'Can I unlock the door now?'

'God, yes, let's get out of here!'

The door was unlocked and thrown open and Gus wheeled himself out into the kitchen. Maggie came forward expectantly but his face was difficult to read and Jim, clambering into his lap, was loudly demanding his attention. Dr Sam spoke to her, first remarking on Jim's healthy colour, then complimenting her on the appetizing smell of cooking that came from the Cornish slab. On reaching the door he paused, looking back at Gus in his chair.

'There is no doubt about it,' he said. 'Your wife is the one you have to thank for your amazing recovery.'

'Yes,' Gus said, quick as a flash, 'but *you're* the one that'll send in the bill!'

The doctor departed chuckling.

*

Gus now sent Jim out to play in the yard so that he and Maggie could be alone.

'It's good news, then?' she said to him.

'That all depends how you look at it.'

'But from what Dr Sam just said—'

'Damn fool doctors! They're no use at all! First they say you're as good as dead and then they say quite the opposite!' Gus scowled ferociously and in a voice not quite steady he said: 'He tells me I'm in such good shape that I *could* live as long as any other man of my age. Of course he dunt give no guarantee and he might just be talking widdle again but that's what he said, sure nuff, and he've gone over me with a fine tooth-comb.'

'Oh, Gus! You do sound so *angry*!' Maggie said, torn between laughter and tears. 'But surely, however you look at it, that can't be anything *but* good news?'

'Good news for me but not for you. I promised, when I asked you to marry me, that I should be dead within two or three years. That was the bargain we made, you and me, and I haven't kept my side of it. I've cheated you. Gone back on my word. I've got no *right* to be still alive—'

'Yes, you have *every* right!' Maggie cried. 'And I *hate* to hear you talking like this when you've just been told such wonderful news! Do you think I *want* you to die?'

'No, I could never think that,' Gus said. 'The way you've looked after me these past four years—'

'Then why talk about cheating me?'

'Because tes only the honest truth. You're a young woman. No more than a girl. And it's all wrong that you should be tied to an old wreck of a man like me.'

'Have you ever heard me complain?'

'No, never, but that's not the point.'

'I'm happy. That's the point.'

'Are you?' he said, with a keen look.

'Yes,' Maggie said quietly. 'I have everything in the world I want, for myself and boy Jim, and I consider myself very lucky.'

'I'm the one that's lucky,' Gus said. 'You've kept me alive. You've made me well. You heard what Dr Sam said about that. But it's all wrong just the same and if I had known I was going to live I would never have married you.'

'And what would've become of me then?'

'You could've been my housekeeper. I'd still have left my property. But that way you would still have been free to marry some chap of your own age who'd have been a proper husband to you.'

'But I never wanted such a thing.'

'Not at first. I know that. Jim's father was not long dead and the way you felt at that time no one else could have taken his place. But that was more than four years ago. You've had time to get over his death—'

'Have I?' Maggie said tonelessly.

'Well, if you haven't, you will do in time. And then if you weren't married to me—'

'But I *am* married to you!' Maggie said. 'And I only wish I could make you believe that I am content in every way.'

'You may not always be content. You've got your life in front of you and it could happen, one of these days, that you find yourself looking at some young chap . . . and thinking of all the things you've missed . . . You might well turn against me then for standing in the way of your happiness.'

'I shall never turn against you.'

'How can you be so sure of that? You don't know what the future holds.'

'Come to that, neither do you,' Maggie said, with a smile. She came and stood close to his chair and put a hand on his arm. 'It seems to me we must just have faith.'

'I reckon I came off best all round, in that bargain of ours,' Gus said. 'The past four years have been good ones for me, even stuck in this chair, expecting death, and now I've been told I shall live after all! But what've *you* got out of it? I've led you up the garden path!'

'You don't understand what it means to me that Jim and I have a home of our own and are wrapped around in security. Jim is only a little boy and he doesn't know what we owe you. But *I* know it and I don't forget.'

Gus took her hand and gripped it hard. He looked up at her, searching her face.

'Some good've come out of it, then, eh?'

'Yes, and a great deal of happiness.'

'You don't feel I've played a trick on you, making a promise I couldn't keep?'

'It's a promise nobody wanted you to keep.'

'I never thought to see boy Jim grow up . . . but now it seems I may after all . . .'

'Yes, and it's what I've prayed for,' she said. 'A boy needs a man he can turn to, especially as he begins to grow up, and Jim thinks the world of you.'

'That's an honour I share with Brice.'

'Brice has been very good to him, too.'

'Naturally. He's your son.'

'It could have been very hard for Jim, having no father of his own, but he has you and he has Brice, and he's really a lucky little boy.'

'Maggie—' Gus began to say.

'Yes? What?' Maggie said.

'Aren't you afraid of the future at all?'

'I thought we'd already settled it that the future could take care of itself.'

'It's bound to be hard for you, you know, whatever you say about having faith. You're a young girl. I'm an old man. There are bound to be problems, you must surely see that.'

'We shall face them together, as they come.'

'You've certainly got your share of faith! But yes, you are talking sense, of course. The future is hidden from all of us and nothing we say will change it one jot. Tes God who determines these things and if I'm to live another few years—'

'We shall give thanks for it. – Both of us.'

'You really mean that?'

'Yes. I do.'

'So be it, then,' he said, quietly.

Almost as soon as Brice entered the room, on the following Saturday evening, Gus was pouring him a drink.

'This is a drop of Jamaica's best that I bought specially to celebrate with.'

'Celebrate?' Brice said. 'Is it a special occasion, then?'

He caught Maggie's glance and she smiled at him.

'He's been celebrating for days – ever since he saw Dr Sam.'

'Ah,' Brice said. He understood.

'It seems I'm not dying after all,' Gus said in a loud voice, as Brice pulled out a chair and sat down, facing him across the table. 'At least, no more than anyone else . . . I might even live my allotted span . . . That's how the good doctor put it to me . . . And he was man enough to admit that his verdict was all wrong last time.'

'Why, that's wonderful news,' Brice said, 'and makes it a special occasion indeed.'

'Will you drink to it, then?'

'Yes, with all my heart,' Brice said, and touched the old man's glass with his own. 'Long life to you and all happiness – and I know the crew will say the same.'

He drank, half emptying his glass, and set it down on the table. Gus reached out to refill it but Brice covered it with his hand, and Gus, refilling his own glass, eyed him with a humorous, sidelong glance. Maggie now came to the table, bringing the *Emmet*'s account book, and Gus touched her on the arm.

'That's something you'll never see – Brice the worse for drink,' he said. 'I think tes a great pity, myself. It would make him more human. Approachable.'

'I'm human enough, surely?' Brice said.

Gus disagreed. He shook his head.

'Tes the sins of the flesh that make a man human,' he said, 'and what do you know about them?'

'As much as anyone else, I suppose.'

'Oh, is that so?' Gus exclaimed. He looked at Brice with rounded eyes. 'Are you going to tell us about them?' he asked.

'No. I think not.'

'That's just the trouble with you. Always close-reefed. Trimmed by the head. Hatches securely battened down. But you needn't be shy with us, you know. I'm a man of the world myself and Maggie, although she sits there looking so very prim, is only flesh and blood after all. *She's* no stranger to the sins of the flesh—'

119

Gus broke off. He had shocked himself. He stared for a moment into space.

'What in God's name am I saying?' he said, and, looking into his glass, he added: 'Seems I've had more than my full allowance.'

He slammed the glass down on the table and forced himself to meet Maggie's gaze. But she, though her cheeks were warmly flushed, merely looked at him with glimmering amusement.

'Yes, I think perhaps you have. It's the rum talking, not you.'

'The rum has got too much to say for itself!'

'It was only speaking the truth even so.'

'I'm damned if I touch another drop! Tes turning me into a drunken sot!'

But he was sober enough now. He had shocked himself into sobriety. His glance flickered towards Brice but Brice, no less than Maggie, it seemed, was inclined to be tolerant and amused.

'You young people, sitting there, letting an old man make a fool of himself!' Gus turned towards Maggie again. 'Tes all your fault!' he said to her. 'You are old beyond your years, my girl, and you've got no right to sit there so calm, making me feel so small as a worm.'

'You will not pick a quarrel with me,' Maggie said, 'even if you try all night.'

'No, nor with me,' Brice said.

Gus suddenly gave a laugh and, leaning forward across the table, drew the *Emmet*'s account book to him.

'We may as well talk business, then, and see if we can fall out over that!'

Chapter 6

Jim, when he was not with Gus, was sure to be in the sail-loft, watching Isaac and Percy at work. He loved the big spacious room with its many windows and fanlights and he loved to see the way the sun, coming in at all angles, slanted in so many criss-cross shafts and made little pools of light and warmth here and there on the bare-boarded floor. The sail-loft floor seemed to stretch for miles; it was twenty paces from end to end and eighteen from side to side; and those were a man's paces, not a boy's.

Isaac, with a piece of chalk, drew his sail-plans on this floor. He was always full of importance whenever he came from the boat-yard, after measuring-up a new boat, and Jim, sitting crouched on his haunches nearby, would have to keep very quiet and still while Isaac, after consulting his notes, drew the appropriate mast-length on the bare boards of the floor. Isaac used a measure for this but when it came to drawing the sails he did it all by eye alone. He would stand deep in thought for a while, squinting this way and that, and then, bent two-double as he himself said, he would lick his piece of chalk and, moving backwards with short, shuffling steps, would draw the clean, faultless lines of the sail. Jim never ceased to marvel at this. The miracle of it was fresh every time.

'How do you know exactly what size the sails've got to be?' he asked.

'I've seen the boat, of course,' Isaac said. 'I've measured her and I've measured her masts and I'd be a poor sort of sail-maker if I couldn't schemey the shape and size of the sails that John Ellis d'want on her.'

At the end of the sail-loft, on deep wooden shelves, the bolts of new canvas were stored, and when the sail-plan had been drawn out, Percy would fetch one of these bolts and lay it down at Isaac's feet and Isaac, with a little kick, would send it unrolling across the floor. Jim liked to see the canvas brought out, so clean and new, a bluish-white, and to see it go rolling out like this, rippling across the sail-loft floor. He liked the peculiar smell of it and the feel of it, so thick and strong, and best of all he liked to watch as Isaac, with his big sharp scissors, went snip-snip-snip so courageously, cutting out the first 'cloth' of the sail.

'Supposing you was to cut it wrong?'

'Ess, you'd like to see that, I believe.'

'No, I wouldn't.'

'Aw, ess, you would. That's why you're geeking at me so close.'

'Did you ever cut it wrong?'

'No, I never did, not wunst. I'm a sail-maker, not a fool, and I don't *belong* to cut it wrong. But if I *was* to cut it wrong, that'd be your fault for prattling at me.'

Isaac at first did not approve of the little boy's presence in the loft and he grumbled about it to Percy Tremearne. 'Is this a sail-loft?' he would say. 'Or is it a blamed nursery?' And Percy Tremearne said once, 'Maybe the old man d'send him up here to keep an eye on the two of us.'

But one day when Isaac was cutting out a sail it happened that the lower point of his scissors kept catching in a rough bit of floor and Jim, who was crouching nearby, put out a hand and lifted the cloth so that it could be cut more easily. Isaac was impressed by this, for Jim was not quite five at the time, and, turning to Percy Tremearne, he said:

'Did you see that?'

'Ess, I did. He d'knaw like a 'uman, sure nuff.'

'Seemingly this tacker of ours is just about brave and smart enough to be a sail-maker when he grows up.'

Isaac was friendly to Jim after that. 'So long as you're good, you can stay,' he said. And often the little boy made himself useful, rubbing out old sail-plans, perhaps, or crawling under a great stretch of canvas in search of a thimble Isaac had lost.

Even when Jim began going to school, he always found time every day to call in at the sail-loft, and he would always try to be there when he knew that a new suit of sails was ready to be taken down to the barking-house. There was great excitement in this and he would be allowed in to watch. He enjoyed the smell of the boiling cutch, even though the fumes stung his eyes, and he liked to watch as the new white sails were lowered into the dark brown liquor seething and bubbling in the vat. The sails would have to be steeped for hours and Eugene, with his short wooden 'oar', would swirl them round every so often to make sure they were well 'roused'.

'How dunt ee take off your smock, young Jim, and dip it in the cutch?' he would say. 'That'd last you a lifetime, then, *and* it'd keep the weather out.'

This was a favourite joke of Eugene's because Jim wore a short canvas smock exactly like those the fishermen wore and many fishermen did indeed dip their smocks into the cutch at the same time that they dipped their nets. But Jim preferred his smock as it was. His mother had made it and it was blue, just like the one uncle Brice always wore.

'No! Shent do it!' he would say, whenever Eugene made his joke. 'My smock is weatherproof as it is.'

Uncle Brice never barked *his* smock and that was good enough for Jim.

As he grew older his world opened out, for his mother and his uncle Gus, although they imposed certain rules on him, allowed him to come and go as he pleased. They gave him his freedom; they trusted him; and because he felt that their rules were fair, Jim never betrayed that trust.

Released from school in the afternoon he would rush with the other boys to the shore and only when hunger gnawed at him did he think of setting foot indoors. There was always so much to do, always so many things to see, all round the little harbour town, that the days were over all too soon. Even the long midsummer days were never really long enough and always when he went to bed his mind would be seething with those things he had meant to do and had not yet done but would certainly do after school next day.

His world was full of activity. There was always something

going on. The harbour, the fish-quay, the rocky shore, lured him from his own home and kept him away for hours on end. But Maggie never fussed over him. She had seen to it that he could swim; that he knew and understood the tides; and that he could handle whatever small boat he managed to beg the use of from some special 'friend' on the quay. He learnt these things early in life and the water had no terrors for him. He was sturdy and strong and sure of himself and when he went stepping from boat to boat, in the harbour pool at high tide, his feet, whether booted or bare, would move so quickly and confidently that a boat scarcely had time to rock before he was out of it into the next.

Sometimes, if he and his friends could borrow a boat, they would go rowing out of the harbour and make their way along the shore, whiffing for mackerel. Mackerel were very easy to catch; they would even snap at unbaited hooks; but it was a triumph all the same for a small boy of seven or eight to go home at the end of the afternoon with a string of them in either hand.

'Bless my soul!' uncle Gus would say. 'That's a brave lot of mackerel you've got there. We shall all feast like kings at teatime today!'

And for Jim this was perfectly true because no fish was so good to eat as the fish you had actually caught yourself, and mackerel, whether fried in flour or marinated in vinegar with a bay-leaf and a few peppercorns, was indeed a dish for a king.

'There are twelve fish here,' his mother would say. 'We shall never eat them all ourselves.'

And Jim would know the pleasure and pride of calling on old Mrs Emily Newpin or some other solitary neighbour with a gift of two or three fish.

'My mother asked could you do with these?'

'My dear soul and body! I should just think I could! But where've they come from, I'd like to know? You surely never catched them yourself?'

'Yes, I did,' Jim would say, and then he would give a little shrug. 'You know how tis with mackerel. You always catch more than you can eat.'

'Your mother's a good kind neighbour to me and you're my

bestmost boy in the world. And if you just wait there a minute I'll fetch you a slice of my new saffron cake.'

Almost everyone in Polsinney was young Jim's friend; the older people, especially, always had a kind word for him; but there was one exception and that was Mrs Rachel Tallack. She, if he passed her in the village, always pretended not to see him, and her face, so deliberately turned away, was always set in harsh lines.

'Why dunt Mrs Tallack like us?' Jim asked his mother one day. 'Is it something to do with the time when you was her servant up at the farm?'

'Yes, it is partly that,' Maggie said. 'Certainly that's when it all began. And then she didn't like it, you see, because I married your uncle Gus.'

'Why didn't she?'

'Well, because—' Maggie began, but here she was interrupted by Gus.

'Because she's a jealous old crabpot, that's why, and have had her nose pushed out of joint. You needn't fret over her, young Jim. Just leave her to stew in her own sour juice.'

'Uncle Brice doesn't hate us so why should she?'

'You'd better ask him that yourself.'

But Jim never broached the subject with Brice. He sensed that such questions would bring a rebuff. Besides, when he was with uncle Brice, there were better things to talk about.

The sea and all things connected with it were the very breath of life to Jim, as to the other Polsinney boys, and together they talked of nothing else. In late summer, when the seining season came round, they would be out on the cliff at Porthvole, watching for the pilchard shoals which, from early August onwards, came closer and closer inshore. At the sighting of a shoal, when the huer's great trumpeted cry, 'Hevva! Hevva!', rang round the harbour, the whole of Polsinney went mad and the madness could last for days and weeks. The bay would be dotted with seine-boats and when a shoal was successfully netted the beach and the wharves and the fish-cellars swarmed with such activity that the noise of it could be heard for miles.

The work went on all day and all night and Polsinney was gripped as if by a fever. Pilchards were its meed and creed. For these small silver fish could be eaten fresh out of the sea; could be salted down for the winter; could be shipped in their millions to other countries, thus bringing the seine owners rich revenue; and, in addition, would provide the oil that lit the lamps in humble homes. 'Meat, money and light, all in one night,' the old Cornish saying went, and this was why, at this time of year, everyone, whether rich or poor, whether they took an active part or were watching for the fun of it, was infected by the happy madness of this great pilchard jubilee.

The seining season was at its height in August and early September; in the following month it dwindled away and in November came to an end; the seine-boats were laid up again in Scadder Cove and the seine-nets were put into store. But the drift fishermen went to sea all the year round and when the pilchard season was over they would go after the herring; and for Jim, as for most young boys, there was no excitement so great, nor any sight so beautiful as when the luggers pushed away from the quay, in late afternoon or early evening, according to the state of the tide, and, their sails first flapping and rippling, then growing taut as they drew the wind, sailed out through the harbour entrance and went tacking across the bay, making for those fishing grounds that lay far out of sight of land. The harbour would be very quiet then and there would be a sense of loss but in the morning, on the flood tide, the boats would come sailing in again, each with its following of gulls, and this was a sight that never failed to bring a boy's heart into his mouth and set him dancing on his feet.

Jim, if he could manage it, was always out and about first thing, to see the fishing fleet return. However cold and dark the morning, he would not miss it for the world, and would stand with his little bunch of cronies, elbowing them, competing with them, eager to identify each boat as she came stealthily in from the dark and passed under the lamp on the quay-head. The *Speedwell*; the *Ellereen*; the *Rose Allan*; the *Boy Dick*; the *Emmet* and the *Trelawney*: these were always amongst the first, for their skippers were first-rate seamen and could get the best out of their boats; and this was a very important thing, for the first boats got berths at the quay, where the fish merchants were waiting for them, while the latecomers had to come in on the beach and would thus miss the best prices.

You could always tell when a boat had an extra good catch of fish in her by the way she sat low in the water and by the large number of gulls escorting her in, and as soon as Jim sighted the *Emmet* he would be on tenterhooks, reading the signs. Had she a good catch of herring in her? No need to ask. Of course she had! Everyone in Polsinney said that if there were any fish about Brice Tallack was sure to find them. He was a 'lucky' fisherman. Other skippers would follow him. But it was not only a question of luck. There was more to it than that. Brice was shrewd, energetic, alert. He knew the fishing grounds as well as though he carried a chart of them in his head and he had that extra bit of good judgment that told him which were the best grounds to try.

He was a good man with a boat: one of the best, William Nancarrow said; and this reputation Brice had among the older fishermen was a matter of great pride to Jim. He would try to look unconcerned as the *Emmet* slid in beside the quay. He would turn and kick at a stone and pretend it meant nothing at all. For in this, as in everything else, he took his cue from Brice himself. His uncle Brice never showed off, but was always quiet and businesslike, getting on with the work in hand; and although he could give and take a joke as well as any other man, he was never boastful or blustering.

All these things impressed young Jim. There was nobody like his uncle Brice. And he longed impatiently for the day when he himself would be old enough to go as one of the *Emmet*'s crew, learning the hundred and one things that a good seaman needed to know; learning the secrets of the sea; learning that quiet self-reliance he so admired in his uncle Brice. Then, perhaps, when he was a man, he would have a boat of his own: a new one, specially built for him in Martin Laycock's boatyard; and that would be the best thing of all because then he would really be equal with Brice, hailing him at the quayside, one skipper to another, exchanging a few words with him as each made ready to put to sea. They would move out of the harbour together, the two of them leading the rest of the fleet, and would sail away to those distant places where there was nothing to see but the sea. And then – the fish had better look out for themselves!

Isaac Kiddy was full of scorn when he heard that Jim meant to be a fisherman.

'I thought you were going to be a sail-maker.'

'I never said that. Twas you that said that.'

'Well, and what's wrong with it, I'd like to know?'

'Edn nothing wrong with it, I just don't belong to do it, that's all.'

Isaac sniffed. He took an immense pride in his craft and he felt Jim had cast a slight on it.

'A sail-maker, I'll have you know, is somebody special, a man apart. You could meet a hundred men – two or three hundred, come to that – and not one of them would be a sail-maker. That'll tell you how special we are. But a fisherman! Well! My dear soul! They're about as common as scads!'

Isaac's scorn left Jim unmoved. He merely turned away with a shrug. His father had been a fisherman; so had his mother's father, too; and that meant it was in his blood. Besides which, the sea was always there, and Jim had only to look at it to feel its restlessness in his heart; to feel something rising up in him, catching his breath in a little gasp; something that filled all his thoughts by day and got into his dreams at night.

Maggie knew and understood this. She had lived all her days within sight of the sea and she knew what a powerful influence it wielded over the minds of boys and men. She knew the sea would be Jim's life. She saw it like a picture clear in her mind. And she knew it was something she had to accept.

Jim's thoughts often dwelt on his dead father and sometimes, especially at bed-time, he would ask his mother questions about him. No one else in Polsinney had ever known him, for he had been a Porthgaran man and Porthgaran was a long way away, thirty or forty miles down the coast. His mother had a picture of him in a locket she wore round her neck but this picture was so small that Jim, whenever he looked at it, would click his tongue in vexation.

'I wish you had a better picture than this. I can't even tell if he's dark or fair.'

'His hair was dark brown, the same as yours.'

'Was he tall?'

'Tall enough.'

'Strong?' Jim asked.

'Yes. Very strong.'

'Was he as tall as uncle Brice?'

'I think, perhaps, not quite so tall. But very strong and quick and brave . . . and always very clever with his hands.'

'Was he a good seaman too?'

'I think he was,' Maggie said, 'but he was only nineteen when he died.'

'I wish he hadn't been drowned like that.'

'I wish it, too.'

'You must've been lonely, left all alone like you were. Granddad gone . . . Uncle David gone . . . You had nobody left after that.'

'Yes, I did, I had you,' Maggie said.

'But I wadn born then, was I?'

'No, you were just a secret then.'

'You brought me with you, didn't you, when you came to Polsinney?' Jim said. 'You carried me with you all the way, wrapped up in a bundle with your clothes, and nobody even knew I was there.'

'Who told you that?'

'Willie Wearne.'

'Did he indeed!'

'Why, edn it true?'

'Oh, yes, it's true enough. Or as near the truth as makes no odds.'

'Some old surprise you must've got when you opened the bundle and I was born.'

'Oh, no, it was no surprise. I knew you were there all the time.'

'How did you know?' Jim asked.

'Because,' Maggie said hugging him close, 'mothers always know these things.'

*

129

His uncle Gus had been a fisherman, too, before illness had struck him down, and his old white oilskins hung in the cupboard even now, after all these years.

'I know I shan't wear them again,' he would say, 'but I like to see them hanging there, to remind me of the old days.'

On cold dark evenings in wintertime Jim would often sit for hours listening to his uncle Gus yarning about the old days. It seemed there was never any end to the tales his uncle Gus could tell: of the great catches taken sometimes, that had filled the *Emmet*'s holds to the coamings and overflowed onto the deck; of terrible storms ridden out to a sea-anchor made of oars and spars with sails wrapped round them and of how, during one of these storms, the foremast had been snapped off; of how, once, a steamship had passed over the drifting nets and carried them all clean away; of the great whales the old man had seen, breaking the surface of the sea and blowing water up in a spout forty or fifty feet high.

Jim never tired of his uncle's tales. They were so full of marvellous things. And he would sit very quiet and still, pretending not to hear the clock when it struck the hour for his bed-time, but knowing only too well that in another minute or two his mother would draw attention to it.

'I'm not tired. Honestly. Can't I have another half hour?'

He would open his eyes very wide to show how untired he was but although his mother laughed at this she rarely gave in to him.

'Off you go. No arguments. I'll be up in ten minutes to hear your prayers.'

Sometimes when the fierce south westerly gales came blowing in from the sea, the cottage would shudder most dreadfully, for it was built on the very edge of the old sea wall itself and had its back to the foreshore.

'Ho! We're in for it good and proper tonight!' uncle Gus would say at these times. 'Just hark at it thumping against that wall! We'd better put an anchor down!'

That was just a joke, of course; the little house was as strong as a rock; but in the morning, after the gale, coral, seashells and seaweed would be found strewn all over the yard and perhaps even big stones from the shore, evidence of the sea's angry power as it hurled itself over the sea wall. Sometimes, especially in winter, the gales would last many days and nights, keeping the fishermen fretting at home, thus bringing hardship and poverty. And sometimes, worse than this, a gale would blow up very suddenly, while the fishing fleet was at sea.

Jim, from an early age, knew just what the sea could do when it was whipped up into a fury. The knowledge was inescapable and came to him in a great many ways. He saw it in the eyes of the old men when they stood on the quay in the grey dawn, watching for boats that were overdue. He heard it in old Mrs Lewin's voice as she wept for her grandson, Billy Joe, swept overboard from the *Jenefer* on a dark December night in 1877. Even when the sea was flat and calm there could be death and danger in it and once, on a fine September day in 1878, a Polsinney gig, overloaded with mackerel, capsized and sank in St Glozey Bay, drowning all three of her crew.

Jim knew about these things and the knowledge of them got into his bones. You could never turn your back on the sea. You had to watch it all the time. His uncle Brice always said that. 'Rough or calm, lion or lamb, you can never take the sea for granted,' he said, and Jim never forgot those words.

Still, the sea had this fascination, somehow. The *idea* of it got a hold on you. Boys and men felt it the same and the danger was all a part of it. It was something you had to face; any seaman would tell you that; and most of them, in saying it, would give a little careless shrug. There were other sufferings, too, and fishermen's hands and wrists were scarred where saltwater boils had festered and burst and where the cuffs of their oilskins, wet with the sea and razor-sharp, had cut the flesh until it bled. They made nothing of these things. They would show you their scars and laugh at them. They said it was all in the night's work.

The only thing that embittered them was when bad weather kept them at home for days on end. There was no laughter among them then. They were angry and sick at heart because their livelihood was gone and their wives and children went hungry. Brice was all right; he had the farm; and often, when

131

the weather was bad, he would be down on the seashore, loading seaweed into a cart to spread as manure on the fields at Boskillyer.

Sometimes Brice would persuade his crew that a little money could be made by loading seaweed into the *Emmet*'s punt and taking it up the River Shill to sell to farmers on riverside farms. On these occasions Jim went, too, and it was a great adventure for him to row up the silent, sheltered river to these mysterious places inland. But the men got no joy from it. They felt they were demeaning themselves.

'Three shillings!' Ralph Ellis exclaimed, when Brice shared out the money they had earnt from one day's work of this sort. 'My family will get *some* fat on that!'

But poor though the reward might be, it was that or nothing, uncle Brice said, when the weather turned bad and kept them at home.

Every morning, summer or winter, Jim would be on the fish quay to see the drifters coming in, and often, as he grew older, he would go aboard the *Emmet* and make himself useful there, helping to clear the last fish from the nets or counting them into the baskets. He was always reluctant to leave; he loved to be part of the busy scene enacted at the quayside in the early morning; but always there came a moment when uncle Brice took out his watch and held it up for Jim to see.

'Time you went home to breakfast now, otherwise you'll be late for school.'

'Aw, there's plenty of time yet!'

'I shall count up to ten,' Brice would say, 'and if you aren't out of this boat by then—'

'What will you do?'

'Try it and see!'

Jim, with an air of unconcern, would linger to the very last, but always, by the count of ten, he was out of the boat and on the quay. There, he would spin round on his heel, giving a little excited laugh, but he never tried anything with Brice; not with the crew looking on; there was something in Brice's blue eyes that somehow kept you up to the mark.

On Saturdays he was allowed to stay until the fish had all been sold and the boat had been thoroughly cleaned out. One Saturday morning in late summer, at the height of the pilchard season, Rachel Tallack, driving the milk-float, came onto the crowded quay to collect a basket of fish that Brice had put ready for her. It happened that Jim was standing nearby and when Brice beckoned to him, he went forward immediately and helped to lift the basket of fish into the float, beside the churns. Rachel, as always, ignored him, even though he was standing so close that he could have reached out and touched her skirts. She merely glanced down at the fish and made some remark on their quality.

'This is Jim,' Brice said, putting a hand on the boy's shoulder. 'He's been helping us in the boat.'

'I know quite well who he is,' Rachel said, and before Brice could say any more she was already moving away, pulling on the nearside rein to bring the pony sharply round.

Brice and Jim went back to the boat, where the crew were busy with buckets and brooms, cleaning out the fish-hold. Neither the man nor the boy spoke of the incident, for there was an understanding between them that Mrs Tallack should not be discussed, but Brice, on getting home, spoke to his mother reprovingly.

'What's past is past,' he said. 'Jim's only a boy, just eight years old. Surely you could find something to say to him?'

'That boy is his mother's son and for his sake she's robbed you of your rights.'

'Maggie has robbed me of nothing.'

'Well, she will do in time,' Rachel said, 'and the only comfort to me is that *she* thought your uncle was going to die and it must be a sore disappointment to her that the awkward, obstinate old fool is lingering on as long as he is.'

'That's not true and you know it,' Brice said. 'Anyone in Polsinney will tell you that it's Maggie who's kept uncle Gus alive.'

'More fool she, then,' Rachel said.

All seamen were heroes to Jim, and Brice, being skipper of the

Emmet, was the biggest hero of them all. His name was always on Jim's lips and everything he said or did was reported in detail at home.

'Uncle Brice says we're in for a cold snap – the gulls are flying inland,' he would say, or, 'There won't be no mackerel catched for a while – uncle Brice says they go down deep when the weather's as cold as this.'

'That's nothing,' Gus said. 'Any fisherman knows that.'

'The herring season starts next week. Uncle Brice is going to try the Bitts. He says that's always a good place to start. Better than Coggle's Deep, he says.'

'They're all good places – when the fish are there,' Gus said with a little growl, and afterwards, when Jim was in bed, he said to Maggie: 'The way that boy talks sometimes, you'd think my nephew Brice was maker of all heaven and earth.'

'Yes, I know.' Maggie said, with a smile, 'but you surely aren't jealous of him, I hope?'

'Of course I'm blamed well jealous of him!'

'Why?'

'Because he's a young man, healthy and strong, and got two good legs he can walk with, and because he can do a man's work, the kind I'd still be doing myself if I wasn't stuck in this damned chair.'

'Yes, I know,' Maggie said. 'It's natural you should feel like that.'

'Still, there tis, and can't be helped.' Gus turned back to his bible again. He was re-reading the Book of Job. 'I daresay, if the truth were known, Brice is a lot more jealous of me than I am of him, and with very good reason, too,' he said.

For a brief season in spring or summer Brice and two or three of his crew would go crabbing in the *Emmet*'s punt and sometimes Jim was allowed to go too. He would take his turn at sculling, and was glad of a chance to display his skill, but he always took great care that no trace of pride should show in his face. When, one day, without hesitation, he took the punt through the narrow gap between Ennis Rock and Scully Point, he pretended not to notice the smile that passed between Brice and the other two men, or to hear the quiet remark that Jacky Johns made to Clem Pascoe later.

'He's a born seaman, edna, you? I wouldn mind a son like he in exchange for the three maids I've got at home.'

Sometimes, in the school holidays, Jim was even allowed to go out in the *Emmet*, and these were special occasions indeed. A whole night at sea, like a grown man, right out beyond the Oracle Rocks in search of the great pilchard shoals as they came sweeping madly down the Channel.

Jim was turned nine by now. He had good sea legs and was never sick. If there was a swell he exulted in it; his head remained clear; his stomach steadfast. But that was only half of it; the bad part came when you reached home; because, as soon as you stepped ashore, the solid ground would not stay still! The land went lurching from under you and landmarks heaved this way and that, tilting and swaying drunkenly, so that you felt giddy and sick. Your legs went like jelly under you and you had to hold on to something firm to keep yourself from tumbling over.

The feeling passed off after a while but it could return unexpectedly as Jim found when he got home and was washing himself in the scullery. The instant he bent over the sink, it swung away from under him, and there was a terrible sickly blackness reeling and rolling inside his head. He gritted his teeth and clung to the sink, staring at the water in the bowl until it became steady again. Washing himself was no easy task but in time he learnt the trick of it and did it without bending too low and without properly closing his eyes.

It was some comfort to Jim to know that even grown men suffered the same reeling sensation after long hours on a heavy sea and this he discovered quite by chance. One morning he and a few other boys were passing Scrouler Tonkin's cottage when Scrouler, just home from a night's fishing in the *John Cocking*, was about to wash himself, stripped to the waist, at a tub on a stool in the back yard. The yard door stood open wide and Scrouler, bending over the tub, clinging to it with both hands, was bellowing to his wife indoors.

'Emmeline! Come and hold this plaguey tub so's I can get myself washed in it! Tes swingen like the pit of hell!'

The eavesdropping boys were in transports and soon passed the story on at school, which meant that poor Scrouler, for months afterwards, had only to walk down the streets of Polsinney to be followed by a group of children crying:

'Emmeline! Come and hold this tub! Tes swingen like the pit of hell!'

Scrouler never lived it down; the joke became common property, enjoyed by young and old alike; and in Polsinney the chances were that it would follow him to the grave.

'Do you ever feel queer, uncle Brice, when you first step ashore?' Jim asked.

'Everyone does,' Brice said. 'At least, if there's been any kind of sea. But you get used to it in time and then you no longer notice it.'

'Scrouler Tonkin still notices it.'

'Yes,' Brice said, solemnly, 'Scrouler's a bit on the delicate side.'

Jim hugged himself at this because Scrouler was six and a half feet tall and almost as powerful a wrestler as the champion Hitch Penter himself. But, as uncle Brice said, it was not always your big strong man that had the strongest stomach at sea. That was a gift bestowed chancelike and if you were one of the lucky ones, the gift was worth more to you than gold.

'Have I got a good sea-stomach?' Jim asked.

'I would say so, yes,' Brice said.

'Tes nearly six weeks since I last went out.'

'Six weeks? Surely not!'

'Well, a brave long time, anyway.'

It was a day at the end of September, a bright sunny day, very warm, and the *Emmet* was laid up on the beach at Porthvole, supported by the wooden 'legs' that kept her upright on her keel. The pilchard season had been a disappointment that year, both for the seiners and the drifters, and for almost three weeks now the *Emmet* had caught no fish at all. Brice and his crew therefore had decided to call it a day; the pilchard nets had been put into store and the mackerel nets had been overhauled ready for taking aboard; and it seemed to Brice a good opportunity to give the boat an extra 'paying.' The crew, however, were not there; they had gone with their families to the Michaelmas Fair at Polzeale; so Brice and Jim, on the beach, were cleaning and scraping the *Emmet*'s hull in preparation for tarring it.

Brice, on a ladder against the boat's side, was working with scraper and brush while Jim, with a hammer and chisel, was knocking off the barnacles that clung below the waterline. Nearby, on a fire of driftwood burning between four flat stones, stood a large iron pot filled with tar and the smell of it, with the smell of the woodsmoke, was hot and rough and rather pleasant, drifting on the fresh sea breeze. There were ten or twelve other luggers dotted about on the beach but because it was Polzeale Fair Day only a handful of men could be seen working on them.

'Can I come mackerel driving with you?'

'One day, perhaps. I'll have to see.'

'How can I ever learn anything if I never get the chance to go out?'

'You *have* been out.'

'Three times, that's all.'

'You'll have your fill of it soon enough when you leave school and join the crew.'

'That won't be until I'm twelve.'

'And how long is that?'

'Two years and a bit.'

'It will soon pass. You mark my words.'

'Georgie Dunn and Denzil Grose were only ten when they went to sea.'

'They come from poor families, that's why. Georgie's father is laid up sick and Denzil's mother, as you know, is a widow with five other children to raise. So they had to leave school and go to work.'

Jim, with a smart blow of his hammer and chisel, knocked a barnacle from its place on the hull.

'I wish I was poor like Georgie Dunn.'

'Do you indeed?'

'Yes, I do!'

'Well, if you were to ask him,' Brice said, 'perhaps he'd like to change places with you.'

Jim looked up with a sheepish smile that spread over his

fresh-skinned face and then slowly faded again. Georgie Dunn was poor indeed. His family lived on parish help and this meant that the boots he wore were branded on the inside to show they were parish property.

'I shouldn't have said that, should I? About wishing I was poor?'

'Nobody heard it, only me.'

'I didn't mean it.'

'No, I know.'

'Shall I put some more wood on the fire?'

'Yes, if you think it needs it.'

While Jim was thus occupied, poking bits of dry wood into the fire under the tar-pot, his mother came along the wharf and down the slipway onto the beach. She had a piece of paper in her hand and Jim, guessing that he would be sent on an errand, glanced up at her with a mutinous scowl. Couldn't she see that he was busy, helping uncle Brice with the boat?

'Your uncle Gus wants you to go to the boatyard with this note. Wait for Mr Laycock's answer and then bring it home to him.'

The boatyard. That was different. Jim was always pleased to go there and, taking the note from his mother, he paused only long enough to exchange a quick word with Brice.

'You'll wait for me, won't you, before you begin tarring the boat?'

'Yes, all right, I'll wait for you. – So long as you're not gone all day.'

Brice, left alone with Maggie, stepped down from the ladder and picked up the tools Jim had dropped on the sand.

'He's growing up fast, that boy of yours.'

'Much too fast,' Maggie said. 'He's very independent sometimes.'

'Finding his feet.'

'I suppose so.'

'He's quite determined to be a fisherman.'

'Yes, he can talk of nothing else. It's always the fishing, the boat, the sea . . .'

'It must worry you very much, after what happened at Porthgaran, but I notice you never try to discourage him.'

138

'I know it wouldn't be any use. I'd keep him from the sea if I could, but I know I can't. For one thing, it's in his blood and there's no going against that. For another thing—'

'What?' Brice said.

'He models himself on you,' Maggie said.

'Does he?'

'Yes, of course. You are his hero. Didn't you know?'

'In that case you must wish I was anything but a fisherman.'

'No,' Maggie said, absently, 'I don't wish that.'

There was a long silence between them. Maggie was thinking about the past. But she was thinking of Brice, too, and there was something she wanted to say.

'My father took terrible risks. He went to sea time and again in a boat he knew to be unsound and in the end he drowned himself and five other men besides. But you are a different kind of man from my father and you never take any risks except those that can't be helped. That's why I'm glad that when the time comes, Jim will go to sea with you. You're a good seaman. One of the best. I've heard Gus say so oftentimes.'

'Does he say that?' Brice was surprised. 'Well, whatever I know of the sea, I learnt it all from him, and *he* was a seaman if you like. There was no one to touch my uncle Gus in the days when he was fit and strong. Anyone will tell you that.'

'I know what they say about Gus and I know what they say about you. No young boy, going to sea, could be in better hands than yours. Jim is intelligent. Quick to learn. And I know he'll learn nothing but good from you.'

Brice stood looking at her. Not a muscle moved in his strong, lean face. And when in a while he answered her it was with a certain formality that kept his voice toneless and flat.

'I shall do my best, I promise you, to see that it is always so.' And then, because of the way she looked at him, he asked: 'Is there something troubling you?'

'Yes, I'm often troubled,' she said, 'when I think back over the past . . . Of how I first came to the farm and persuaded your mother to take me in . . . I'm not surprised she hates me when I think how I came, a perfect stranger, and caused such an upset in your lives.'

139

'That was ten years ago. You are scarcely a stranger now. And uncle Gus at least has cause to be thankful for you coming. You saved his life.'

'But you have no such cause,' Maggie said.

'Haven't I?'

'You know what I mean.'

'We talked like this once before. Years ago. Do you remember? I said then – and I say the same now – that being cut out of my uncle's will meant less than nothing to me.'

'You said you did mind about losing the boat.'

'Did I say that? Perhaps I did.' Brice looked up at the *Emmet* and with a quick, mechanical movement, scraped at a patch of moss with his scraper. 'But I haven't lost her, have I, not yet? I'm still her skipper – so far at least – and will continue so, probably, until Jim is old enough to take over from me.'

'And then?' Maggie asked.

Brice smiled.

'Jim is not quite ten. We don't need to think about that yet.'

'No, perhaps not,' Maggie said.

But afterwards, as she walked slowly home, she was thinking about it a great deal.

Chapter 7

The year 1879 was a bad one for the Cornish fisheries. The
pilchard fishing had been poor everywhere and in most areas
the mackerel fishing turned out little better. Catches were
slight throughout the season and already, by early December,
many boats were coming back 'clean.'

The *Emmet* was no exception. Night after night she shot her
nets, only to take them up empty, or to draw in a few
rabblefish, which, when divided among the crew, were
'scarcely enough to feed the cat,' as Ralph Ellis said with great
bitterness.

'I hope to God the herring season will turn out better than
this!'

'Tes all we *can* hope for, edn it?' Billy Coit said snappily.

Tempers were often short aboard the *Emmet* at this time, as
they were on all those boats whose crews, having suffered two
bad seasons, faced hardship and poverty.

During the first week in December the mackerel nets were
put into store and the herring nets were taken aboard and
early on a calm Tuesday afternoon the *Emmet*, with the rest of
the fleet, set sail for the herring grounds thirty or forty miles
up the Channel.

The season began well enough. Catches were not big at first
but that was only to be expected, for the weather continued
soft and mild, and it wanted a good steady breeze to set the
herring shoals running. In the new year there was a change;
a cooling and freshening of the air; catches improved accordingly and the drifter crews, with high hopes, talked of it being
a good season. One night the *Emmet* caught ten thousand fish;
on another twelve and a half thousand.

'Seemingly your good luck haven't deserted you after all,'

141

Ralph Ellis said to Brice. 'None of the others have done so well as us so far.'

But luck was something you could never take for granted; not if you were a fisherman; and sometimes it happened that what appeared to be good luck could suddenly turn into bad, all in the space of a couple of hours, as Brice and his crew discovered one night early in February.

They were fishing that stretch of the English Channel which Cornish fishermen called the Dings and which lies some ten to fifteen miles due south of Kibble Head. It was a fine clear night with a brisk wind from the south east and the moon just entering her last quarter. With Brice and Clem Pascoe sharing the watch, the *Emmet* rode to her fleet of nets, rocking rhythmically on a sea that murmured busily to itself and slap-slapped against the boat's hull.

Brice and Clem stood in the bows, looking along the line of floats stretching away into the distance. In the bright moon-light they could see a large number of gulls gathered on the surface of the sea, all along the line of floats, and this was a sure sign that the herring were coming into the nets.

'We've found'm tonight, sure nuff,' Clem said, and put up his nose to sniff the air which was strong with the smell of fish-oil. 'I wonder how the rest are doing, you.'

Astern of the *Emmet*, away to the east, could be seen the lights of the rest of the fleet, like tiny stars in the distant darkness. Brice turned and studied them and saw that a few of the lights were on the move.

'Some of them are giving up. Four or five of them at least. So plainly *they've* got no fish tonight.'

'Poor souls,' Clem said, contentedly.

By six o'clock in the morning, the wind had freshened appreciably and there was a big sea running, causing the *Emmet* to roll badly. The assembled crew were now at work, shifting ballast in the holds and getting the bankboards and roller in place, ready for hauling in the nets. They were all in high spirits, for they had let down a sample net and, having found it full of fish, knew they were in for a record catch.

142

'We've struck it rich tonight for sure. There's a herring in every mesh, very nearly, and all prime maties at that. And if we're the only ones that've found'm we'll be able to ask what price we please! We shall make our fortunes tonight, boys, and not before time, neither.'

Brice, though he shared their jubilation, was cautious in expressing it because, with the wind and sea as they were, he feared they would have a difficult haul.

By half past six, all was made ready; the men took a pause for food and drink, then put on their oilskins and big sea-boots; and, as the first light grew in the sky, prepared for the long task of hauling. Brice went forward into the bows and, lying back on the spring rope, began pulling the lugger close up to the nets. Clem Pascoe and Martin Eddy wound in the warp on the capstan and as the first net came splashing up out of the water, Billy Coit and Jacky Johns reached out with eager hands to ease it in over the roller.

A great many fish fell out of the net and rained down into the sea and the frenzied gulls, flapping and screaming, swooped on them and snatched them up. But the bulk of the catch was firmly enmeshed and at sight of the glittering silver mass the men gave vent to a shout of excitement. This was a splendid catch indeed and although Billy Coit was in his sixties even he had to admit he had never seen anything like it before.

'If this is what the first net is like, how will it be with the rest?' he said, and Jacky Johns answered him, 'Billy, my handsome, tes three shoals in one!'

As the net was pulled in further, however, a change came over these two men, and over the rest of the crew, for, in spite of the heavy bags of ballast carefully stowed on the boat's port side, she was listing badly to starboard, pulled down by the weight of the nets. Billy Coit gave a shout and the capstan men stopped work at once but even so, such was the list, that when a big sea came rolling at them it broke clean over the gunwale, immersing the men for a moment or two and washing some of the fish from the net, sending them spinning and slithering all along the waterways.

Brice, his earlier fears not only confirmed but magnified a hundred times, hurried to join the two net-hands and, looking

143

down at the laden net sloping so steeply into the sea, knew at once there was danger in it. He turned towards Billy Coit.

'Are you thinking what I'm thinking?'

'Yes,' Billy said, in a grim voice, 'we shall never be able to get them in.'

Ralph Ellis now came up with a face as black as a thundercloud.

'What do you think you're talking about? Of course we can damn well get them in!'

'The nets are too heavy. We've got too much fish. You can see what's happening to the boat.'

'Once we've got some fish in the holds, that'll soon steady her,' Ralph said.

'No, it's too dangerous,' Brice said. 'We shall have to cut away the nets.'

Another sea came rolling at them and again they shipped it over the bow. The men bent their heads to it and when it had passed they stood in silence, shaking the water out of their eyes. Each, as he hung on to the nets, was sick to the heart with disappointment.

Every fisherman, being human, dreamt of taking a record catch that would put extra money into his pocket, but this night's catch was so big that instead of gain it meant heart-breaking loss. Their fleet of nets was one mile long and, with hundreds of thousands of fish enmeshed in them, formed such an enormous weight that if they attempted to haul them in the *Emmet* would almost surely capsize. All the men knew this. Ralph Ellis knew it as well as the rest. But the bitterness of the loss they faced made it a difficult thing to accept.

'Tedn just *your* nets you're talking about, tes ours as well!' he said to Brice. 'And two of mine were new this year!'

'Better to lose our nets than our lives,' Brice said.

'Skipper's right,' said Billy Coit, and Ralph Ellis turned away, kicking savagely at a fish that floated in the scummy water frothing along the edge of the deck.

So the *Emmet*'s nets were cut away and quickly sank to the bottom of the Dings and in a while, as the crew watched, large numbers of dead fish floated to the surface of the sea and were swooped upon by the ravening gulls. The men turned their

144

backs on this sad sight and set about cleaning the boat, gathering up the few scattered fish and putting them into a basket. Bankboards and roller were stowed away, ballast was redistributed, and the punt was put back into place. They then heaved up the foremast, made sail and headed for home, and, having a good strong wind behind them, reached Polsinney at half past ten.

On the quay, as usual, the fish merchants and jowsters were waiting, but even before the *Emmet* berthed they could see that she had no fish in her. A few other boats lay at the quayside but they had all been unlucky too.

'They've all of'm come in clean so far,' one old jowster said to Brice, and Ralph Ellis, leaping ashore, said with spluttering anger: 'At least they've still got their nets, haven't they?'

He strode off towards the village, leaving Brice and the rest of the crew to explain the loss of their herring nets to the sympathetic crowd on the quay.

On his way home, an hour later, Brice called at his uncle's cottage, where the old man and Maggie were expecting him.

'I hear you cut away your nets,' Gus said without preamble. 'I've just had Ralph Ellis in here. He was feeling pretty sore.'

'We're none of us over the moon about it but it was something that couldn't be helped.'

'You are quite sure about that, I suppose?'

'I wouldn't have done it otherwise.'

'Ralph seemed to think different from you.'

'Yes,' Brice said tersely, 'he always does.'

'He said, if you'd only given it a chance, you could've got that catch aboard, or part of it at any rate.'

'Since when, might I ask, have you or anyone else taken any notice of Ralph?' Brice was suddenly very angry and, looking down at his uncle, he said: 'I've skippered the *Emmet* for thirteen years but perhaps you feel the time has come when you would like to make a change? If so I would prefer that you said so straight out in plain simple words!'

Gus made a gesture of impatience.

'Now you're talking plumb foolish,' he said. 'I'd back your

145

judgment against Ralph's any day and well you know it. That's why I made you skipper in the first place – not because you're my nephew but because you're a first-class seaman. It just seemed, from what Ralph said, that you'd been a bit over-cautious, perhaps, when you decided to cut away.'

Brice, although mollified, would not for one instant agree with this.

'By the time we had known for sure, it would've been too late,' he said. 'Plenty of boats have gone that way.'

Maggie, who was standing nearby, now spoke for the first time.

'There's no such thing as being over-cautious,' she said. 'Not when men's lives are at stake.'

Gus looked at her for a while in silence. Then he looked at Brice again.

'Yes, well,' he said at last. 'You've made your point, both of you, and there's nothing more to be said. Except to discuss the nets, of course . . . How many are there in the store?'

'Five or six new ones, perhaps,' Brice said, 'and three or four old ones, but they're badly shrunk.'

'Then you'd better take the horse and cart and get what you need from Steeple Lumbtown. The sooner the better. Today if you can. Then Eugene can bark them this afternoon.'

Brice nodded and turned towards the door.

'I'll go straight away after breakfast,' he said.

The new nets were fetched and barked and put aboard the following Monday and that night, though their catch was small, there were few complaints from the crew.

'I shall never pray for big catches again,' Billy Coit said, shaking his head. 'Not after that strike in the Dings. I'm content to take what comes. I leave it in the hands of the Lord.'

Not all the crew were as philosophical as this. The loss of a whole fleet of nets, together with an exceptional catch, still rankled with Ralph Ellis and a few weeks later he left the *Emmet* to go as skipper in a new lugger built by John Lanyon of Penlaw. Brice was not sorry to see him go; there had been

146

friction between them for years; and Ralph, now that he had been lucky enough to get a first-class boat like the *Bright Star*, was even disposed to be friendly, hailing Brice at the quayside and exchanging good-humoured banter with him.

'How're you getting along without me?'

'Oh, we muddle along, somehow.'

'Cut away any nets lately?'

'No, but I hear you lost your jib.'

'Ess, we had some old weather out there, fishing the Cowlings last night. – While you were skulking in the Chawls!'

Ralph's place in the *Emmet* was taken by Clem Pascoe's son Reg. Brice was well pleased with the change and so were his crew. And it happened that from that moment on, until the season ended in March, the herring catches were much improved.

Some weeks after the loss of the nets Maggie decided to speak to Gus about an idea that had lain in her mind for a long time: that he should, by process of law, make the *Emmet* over to Brice; but although she used all possible tact in putting forward her suggestion, Gus's reaction was hostile.

'Your conscience playing you up again, because you'll inherit my property?'

'Yes, I suppose you could say that. We've got so much, you and me . . . Not only of worldly goods, but so many other things besides . . . And over the boat it seems to me that you could afford to be generous.'

'I'm not in the habit of giving things away like that.'

'Not even to please me?'

'Why *should* it please you? That's what I should like to know. Because when I'm dead the boat will be yours and you want to spare Brice's feelings at having a woman employing him?'

'I wasn't looking so far ahead as that.'

'It can't be all that far ahead. I've lived thirteen years with this disease and that in itself is a miracle. But my luck can't hold out for ever and it's only right, I suppose, that you should look ahead a bit and make plans for the future.'

'I'm not thinking about the future. I'm thinking of now. Brice is your own kith and kin and if it hadn't been for me—'

'Brice has said often enough that he doesn't care tuppence for the property. Why don't you take his word for that?'

'But the boat is different, isn't it? The boat really means something to him—'

'Don't you think it means something to *me*?' Gus's anger now came to the boil. 'The *Emmet* is mine! My very own! Tommy Laycock built her for me and I sailed in her for thirty years. That's something you seem to forget!'

'Yes,' Maggie said, in a small voice, and was vexed with herself for her lack of wisdom. 'I shouldn't have tried to interfere. It was wrong of me. I see that now.'

Gus leant forward in his chair and poked the fire in the stove. It burnt up bright immediately and the red glow lit his bearded face. For a moment he sat watching the flames, broodingly, his face creased with thought. Then he dropped the poker into the hearth and leant back in his chair again.

'I don't need to give Brice the boat. He'll get it anyway in the end. *And* everything else as well.'

'What do you mean?'

'I mean, when I'm dead, you'll marry him. He will have everything then. Boat . . . business . . . cottage . . . wife . . . I daresay he've got it all worked out.'

'That's a terrible thing to say. Why do you say such terrible things? Brice isn't that sort of man at all.'

'Oh, it isn't so bad as I've made it sound, bearing in mind the important fact that he's been in love with you all these years.'

Maggie looked down at her hands, at the piece of needlework, so far untouched, that lay meaninglessly in their grasp. Absently, she turned it over; stared at it in a blank way; then allowed it to fall again. Gus watched her closely and shrewdly.

'You're not going to say, as you did once before, that all that was over years ago when he found out you were having a child? Because we both know that isn't true. Oh, he hides it well enough! He certainly never makes a fool of himself. But it's there all the same, no doubt of that, and if *I* can see it, so can you.'

'Even if what you say is true, I don't think we ought to talk about it, if only for Brice's sake.'

'Brice! Brice! Never mind about Brice! I *want* to talk of it!' Gus exclaimed. 'This is something that needs threshing out. We've always been honest with each other, you and me, and we must try and keep it so. That means facing up to facts.'

There was a long, difficult silence and in it he watched her consideringly. But at last, in a dry tone, he said:

'You'll run into some trouble, of course, when it comes to marrying him, owing to affinity. "A man may not marry his father's brother's wife." But you can always get round that. Others have done, often enough. The parson will soon sort it out for you.'

'It seems,' Maggie said, haltingly, 'that you've given the matter a lot of thought.'

'Yes, well, so I have. I want your happiness. You know that, I hope. So of course I've given it a lot of thought. Brice is a good enough chap in his way. He's grown up in the past few years. You'll be in good hands, married to him, and I've got no worries on that score. It will all work out well enough, I'm sure, once I'm dead and out of the way . . . I can see you together, plain as plain . . . and in my more Christian moments, I ask God's blessing on you both.'

Maggie tried to speak but could not, and he saw that there were tears in her eyes.

'No need to get upset,' he said gruffly. 'My Christian moments are all too rare and there *are* times when I'd damn him to hell. I know I've got no right to be jealous, but I *am* jealous all the same, knowing that when I'm out of the way Brice will step straight into my shoes.'

'I wish you wouldn't talk like that.'

'I'm just facing up to facts.'

'But you've got no *cause* to be jealous of Brice, because I never think of him in that way.'

'Don't you?' Gus said, with a keen look. 'Are you certain sure of that?'

'I wouldn't lie to you,' Maggie said.

'Don't talk so foolish! Of course you would! You'd lie to me with your last breath if you thought it would only spare my

149

feelings. And the lies would come easy to you because you believe in them yourself. Not that I have any claim on you – our marriage being what it is.'

'Those vows I made when I married you . . . they were not without meaning for me, you know, whatever sort of marriage it is.'

'You don't have to tell me that,' Gus said. 'You'll be a loyal wife to me, whatever it costs you, I know that. But it's hard on you all the same and I did you a grievous wrong when I married you and tied you down. You're a young woman, not thirty yet. You've got warm blood in your veins – Jim is living proof of that – and with Brice always so close at hand, a handsome young man, devoted to you, you wouldn't hardly be human, else, if you hadn't come to feel something for him with the passing of the years. As for boy Brice himself, well, he's only human, too, and I can't say that I blame him if he wishes me out of the way.'

'You don't really think that, knowing Brice as you do?'

'I only know what I should feel if I was him,' Gus said. 'And that's something I'd like brave and well – a chance to change places with Brice. To be a strong young man again and walk about on my own two legs. *I'd* soon show you a thing or two if I was in boy Brice's shoes, cos I couldn't suffer to stand by and see the one woman I loved tied to a useless old hulk of a man more than twice her own age. *I* should've upped a good while since and carried you off across the sea, to Jersey or Guernsey or some such place.'

'Would you indeed?' Maggie said. 'And supposing I didn't want to go?'

'If *I* was boy Brice, my girl, I'd damn well *see* that you wanted it! But that's Brice all over as he is. – Just enough sin in him to covet another man's wife but not enough to do something about it!'

'Why do you always speak of him in that disparaging way?' Maggie asked. 'Even when you say something good about him, it always comes grudgingly, with a sneer.'

'*You* won't grudge him nothing much, once I'm out of the way, will you?'

'Gus!' Maggie said beseechingly.

'Oh, I know, I know!' he exclaimed. 'I ought not to talk like that. It's hard for a young woman like you to understand an old man's feelings and you mustn't take too much heed of me if I burst out in a temper sometimes.'

'I suppose it's only what I deserve. I had no business trying to tell you what to do with your own property and I can only say I'm sorry.'

'Yes, well, never mind, we'll say no more about it,' he said. 'It's over and done with and wiped off the slate. We've said what we think, both of us, and that's an end to it, once and for all.'

But that was not the end of it and during the next two or three days it became only too obvious that the matter was still very much on his mind.

It happened just then that the weather was bad and he was obliged to keep indoors. This always produced choler in him and now, in his present brooding mood, he would sit in front of the window, often silent for hours at a time, looking out across the harbour and watching the great wind-vexed seas breaking over the far quay-head. At meal-times, when Jim was present, he made some effort to talk, and whenever Maggie spoke to him he answered her readily enough; but his manner and tone were cold and abrupt and Jim soon noticed it.

'What's the matter with uncle Gus? Isn't he feeling too clever just now?'

'He's got something on his mind. I expect he'll get over it quite soon.'

But Gus's mood only got worse and, as always at such times, he was drinking heavily. It was something that worried Maggie and she felt she had to speak of it.

'Why do you drink so much? Dr Sam said it was bad for you and surely you've proved it often enough?'

'I shall drink as much as I choose! And if it kills me, so what of that? – You'll be your own mistress then and all your problems will be solved!'

151

'Oh, dear!' Maggie said, distressed. 'And all this has blown up because of what I said about giving Brice the boat.'

'Damme! That boat is mine! Why in hell's name should I give it away?'

'No reason at all,' Maggie said. 'I wish I'd never mentioned it.'

'Brice is her skipper. What more should he want? I'd change places with him like a shot if it meant I could go to sea again. And *I* wouldn't skulk at home days on end just because of a blow of wind!'

'It isn't only Brice,' Maggie said. 'All the boats have stayed in ever since the gale on Monday night.'

'No, not all of them,' Gus said. 'Two or three have been out since then.'

'Two or three mad ones, that's all.'

It was now early April; the long-lining season had begun; but strong south-westerly winds, coinciding with spring tides, had kept the fleet at home all the week. The skippers and crews could be seen on the wharf, shoulders hunched and caps pulled well down, sheltering from the worst of the wind in the space between the coopers' sheds; chatting together and smoking their pipes; constantly watching the sea and the sky and discussing every subtle change.

Brice was not among them because, however bad the weather, there was always something to do on the farm, and he was particularly busy just now, repairing the damage caused by the gales. So it happened that he did not come for his usual Saturday evening visit but came on Sunday afternoon instead. Maggie and Gus were alone together; Jim had gone to Sunday school; and the moment Brice walked into the kitchen it was plain that Gus had it in for him.

'Where did you get to yesterday?'

'I was mending the barn roof. We lost a lot of slates in last Monday's gale. The cowshed door was damaged too. I only finished repairs this morning.'

'Seems you're more of a farmer than a fisherman these days.'

'I'm afraid that's true,' Brice said. 'Not that I've got much cause to complain. It means I can catch up with all the odd jobs. But it falls hard on the crew when we lose so many nights in a row.'

'Shares worked out two and tuppence a man. None of them was best pleased at that. You'll find yours up on the mantel-shelf there.'

Maggie, who was standing on the hearth, took down the money and gave it to Brice. He looked at her enquiringly, hoping for some guidance as to the cause of his uncle's mood, but there was little she could convey in a glance, beyond her own anxiety, and he turned away with a puzzled frown, slipping the money into his pocket.

'Don't spend it all at once,' Gus said, 'cos dear knows when the next lot'll be coming.'

'That's nothing new in fishing, is it, especially at this time of year? But luckily the weather is on the mend. The glass is rising steadily and now that the spring tides are slackening off I'm hoping with a bit of luck we shall maybe get out tomorrow night.'

'Wonderful! Wonderful!' Gus said. 'If you haven't lost the knack of it!'

Brice, trying hard to keep his temper, looked the old man straight in the eye.

'Would you have had us go out, then, in spite of conditions all this week?'

'Not for me to say, is it? You're the skipper, not me. I'm just the owner, no more than that. But a few boats did go out, didn't they, unless my old eyes were playing me false?'

'Four boats went out,' Brice said, 'out of a fleet of thirty-three.'

'Ralph Ellis was one, I believe, and even managed to get a few fish.'

'Yes, that's right,' Brice said, and this time it was his turn to be sarcastic. 'He got all of two stone of hake, I heard.'

'Better than nothing,' Gus said. 'More than *you're* likely to get, kiddling about up there on the farm.'

Brice, tight-lipped, walked to the door. He felt he had been patient enough. He paused and looked back at Maggie.

'It seems I'm not welcome here today so I may as well take

153

myself off. I'm sorry I couldn't wait to see Jim. Tell him I ran into a squall.'

As soon as the door had closed on him Maggie rounded fiercely on Gus.

'Are you proud of yourself, I wonder, for driving him away like that?'

'You don't need to fight Brice's battles for him. He can stand up for himself. Else, if he can't, tes high time he could!'

'But he doesn't even know what it's all about!'

'Maybe you'd like to tell him?'

'Yes,' Maggie said, 'that's a good idea!'

She took her shawl from the hook on the door and went out into the wind.

Brice, having walked at a furious pace, was well on his way up the steep cliff road when Maggie, calling out to him, at last managed to make him hear. He turned in surprise and stood watching her but then, seeing her toiling up the hill, fighting against the boisterous wind, he began walking down towards her and they met just as an extra strong gust came in over the sea wall, bringing a skitter of spray with it.

For a moment she was unable to speak; wind and hill had defeated her; and she stood before him, quite breathless, giving a little choking laugh as she clumsily rearranged her shawl, pulling it tight over her head and twisting her hands into its folds so that the wind should not whip it away. Brice stood in silence, too. Under the peak of his close-fitting cap, his face was clenched in angry lines and there was still a look in his eyes that made them glint, a cold, hard blue, yet failed to hide the hurt in them. Maggie, seeing this look in his eyes, and the bitter lines about his mouth, felt the hurt in her own heart as though a knife had twisted there. At last she found enough breath to speak.

'You mustn't mind what Gus says to you. He doesn't mean it most of the time. It's just that he's – he's feeling under the weather these days.'

'Yes, the weather's to blame for a lot just now. If it doesn't let up pretty soon—'

'You won't take any risks, will you? You won't let him goad you into it?'

'Is that what he wants by any chance?'

'Oh, Brice!' Maggie exclaimed. 'I don't know which of you is the worst, you or your uncle Gus, for saying things you don't mean.'

'I can guess what things he says about me and I daresay he means them sure enough.'

'No, no, that's where you're wrong! It's only the mood he's in at the moment and I'm the one who's to blame for that.'

'You?'

'Yes. It's something I said.'

In a few words Maggie explained about her suggestion concerning the boat. Brice listened. He understood. But it did nothing to soften his mood.

'You certainly made a mistake there. What made you think that uncle Gus would ever do such a thing? The way he feels about the boat, he'd just as soon give his soul, and most seamen would feel the same.'

'I know! I know!' Maggie said. 'And oh, how I wish I had thought more clearly before speaking about it to him! But anyway, it's my fault, as you see. It isn't anything you've said or done and I wanted you to know that.'

Where they stood, on the narrow road that wound its way steeply up from the harbour and skirted the edge of the rising cliff, they were some half mile out of the town and it lay below them, grey in the wind, an irregular jumble of slate roofs and smoking chimneys, the houses and the narrow streets all sunk in their Sunday afternoon stillness and quiet.

But Polsinney, even on the Sabbath, was never completely deserted and down on the far side of the harbour, overlooking the fish-quay, a number of fishermen leant on the rail, gossiping and smoking their pipes and watching the luggers that curtseyed and bobbed, moored close together in the harbour pool. Outside the shelter of the harbour there was still a big sea running and although it was not yet high tide, the waves already covered the foreshore and reached as far as the undercliff, where they reared themselves up against the

155

revetment, fifteen or twenty feet high, and sought to hurl themselves over the edge.

Brice turned and leant on the parapet and Maggie did the same. The wind was now full in their faces, blowing in from the open sea, and below them, at the foot of the cliff, the green and white water seethed and tossed. Brice glanced sideways at Maggie's face; then he looked straight ahead again, across the bay to Struan Point. A kind of angry detachment was slowly taking possession of him, and, in a spirit of defiance, he yielded himself up to it.

'It isn't just your idea about the boat that has made uncle Gus the way he is. It's because he knows I'm in love with you.'

Maggie remained perfectly still. She too was looking straight ahead.

'Did you *have* to say that?' she asked, and her voice, though quiet, was like a cry. 'Where is the *point* in saying that?'

'Foolish, isn't it?' Brice said. 'After keeping it secret all these years, to go and blurt it out like that! I suppose it's the sort of mood I'm in. – I'm taking my revenge on uncle Gus.'

'You mustn't think of him like that. I know he can be provoking sometimes, and he was specially so today, but surely I've explained why that was?'

'I've loved you all along,' Brice said. 'Right from the start, more than ten years ago, when you first came to us at the farm. I think you must have known that because I didn't try to hide it then.'

'Yes, I knew you felt something for me . . . but I thought it would change when you knew the truth . . . when you found I was having another man's child.'

'I thought so, too, but I was wrong. I soon found I loved you just the same and I could do nothing to alter it. I did my best to hide what I felt but I think uncle Gus has known all along. That's why he's always making these jokes about my finding myself a wife.'

'Yes, he knows,' Maggie said.

'Has he spoken about it to you?'

'Yes. Twice.'

'So you knew I still loved you, if only from him?'

156

'I did my best not to believe it. I hoped you'd find somebody else. But yes, in my heart, I knew all along.'

'No doubt my uncle Gus thinks it's a judgment on me because I did nothing to help you when my mother turned you out of the house. He's always despised me for that and of course he's right. I was a paltering, spineless fool. But God knows I've paid for that, over the past ten years, by loving you and longing for you and not being able to speak of it.'

'You are speaking of it now.'

'Yes, there's no going back on it now. Somehow there's relief in that.'

Still leaning over the parapet, he turned his head to look at her, and, for the first time in his life, allowed his feelings to show in his face, so that Maggie, when she met his gaze, found herself almost overwhelmed. Just for an instant their eyes held but then abruptly she bent her head and stared blindly down at the sea boiling over the rocks below.

'Brice, don't look at me like that. Please.'

'Why not?' he said harshly. 'What have I got to lose – now?'

'People might be watching us.'

'They're too far off to see us plain.'

'If you love me—'

'If! Dear God!'

'Then please don't make things difficult for me.'

'But you've known about it all along, so why should it be difficult now?'

'That's a foolish question to ask. Things are always more difficult once they're – once they're out in the open.'

'You'll put it out of your mind in time. That's what you did before. You'll say to yourself, "Poor Brice," and then you'll put it out of your mind.'

'No, I shan't. Not after today. That will be impossible now.'

'Why? Does it mean something to you, then?'

'That's another foolish question,' Maggie said impatiently. 'I'm a woman, not a stone, and to have a man look at me and speak to me as you're doing now—' Her voice failed her. She took a deep breath. She was careful not to look at him. 'Of course it means something to me but it happens that I'm married to Gus.'

'You don't have to remind me of that.'

'No, I know I don't,' she said, 'but perhaps I have to remind myself.'

Her words, spoken so quietly, were almost drowned in the noise of the surf, but Brice heard them all the same. They were words that took him by the throat.

A big sea came running in, hurling itself against the cliff and rearing up in a great folding curve that licked its way up the granite wall and broke over the parapet. Brice and Maggie leant back on their heels but the spray caught them even so and they tilted their faces away from it, eyes closed while the stinging drops skittered and splashed over them.

The green and white wave curled back and sank, teeming at the foot of the cliff, and Brice and Maggie, standing together, their hands on the cold wet parapet, could feel the sea's mighty power pulsing vibrantly in the granite blocks. Brice turned and looked at Maggie's face; it was wet with spray, as though with tears, and he watched her as she wiped her cheeks with a corner of her knitted shawl; then he looked out to sea again.

'So,' he said, very carefully, 'if things were different and you were free, you would be willing to accept my love?'

'If things were different,' Maggie said, still in the same quiet voice, 'I would be in your arms by now.'

Another big sea came in and Brice watched it as though in a trance. Outwardly he was perfectly calm; his eyes were half-hidden under their lids and his face might have been carved in wood; and only by the quickening of his breath did he betray the tumult within as his heart leapt with the leaping wave.

The wave rose, higher and higher, climbing the wall with slow-seeming swiftness, and this time Brice and Maggie held their ground, letting the spray break over them, each glad of its cold sharp sting. They glanced at each other, blue eyes meeting grey, and then turned again into the wind; and so careful were they to keep their faces expressionless that nobody, seeing them there together, could have guessed what message had passed between them in that one quick, deep glance.

Brice felt that his lungs would burst and when, in a while, he spoke again, his voice was not quite under control.

'You chose wisely, didn't you, saying that here and now, in this public place where you are safe? Otherwise . . .'

'No,' Maggie said, firmly. 'There can never be any "otherwise." It must always be like this. And I didn't choose the time or the place. It was something that just happened to me. But always, in future, after today—'

'We must be as we were before. Do you think I don't know that? But what you've just said . . . you can't take it back . . . it's mine now till the day I die. But you don't need to worry, you know. When we meet, in the ordinary way, I shall keep my feelings to myself. I've had plenty of practice in the past. As for my uncle Gus, I know he has a down on me, but—'

'Brice, I must tell you something he said, only a few days ago, when I spoke to him about the boat. He was talking about dying – no, wait, let me finish – and he said he knew that when he was dead you and I were bound to marry.'

'He knows that you care for me, then?'

'He knew it before I did myself.'

'No wonder he hates me the way he does.'

'He doesn't hate you,' Maggie said. 'It's just that you're young and he's not. You can walk and he can't. And sometimes he thinks you wish him dead.'

'You don't think that?'

'Of course I don't. Neither does he, in his heart of hearts.'

Away in the town the church clock struck three.

'Brice, I must go. I really must. He'll be wondering what's become of me.'

'Maggie, wait,' Brice said. 'Maggie, I want you to understand – it's what I was trying to say just now – that I am not the sort of man . . . I mean, whatever I feel for you, and whatever I said about uncle Gus just now, I wouldn't ever do anything that would hurt his feelings in any way.'

Maggie smiled at him with her eyes.

'You don't have to tell me that. I know what sort of man you are.'

Drawing her shawl more closely about her, she turned and walked away from him, the wind now whirling behind her, sending her hurrying down the hill. Brice, resisting the impulse to watch her all the way down, leant further over the parapet and stared at the water seething below. The cold spray came up into his face and he tasted its salt tang on his lips.

'You haven't gone off with him, then?' Gus said as Maggie, coming in on a gust of wind, struggled to close and fasten the door.

'No, not yet!' she answered lightly. She hung her shawl up on its hook and faced him with a resolute smile.

'No, you wouldn't do that, would you, cos that'd mean losing all those things you married me on purpose to get?'

The extreme bitterness of these words drove the smile from Maggie's lips. She stood before him, silent and still, and he, seeing the look in her eyes and the way the colour drained from her cheeks, was suddenly stricken with angry shame.

'God! Why do I say such things?' he said in a voice that was wrung from him. 'And why do you always take it so meekly, without ever hitting back at me? I suppose it's because I'm a crippled old man and you can't help feeling sorry for me. But you shouldn't be so considerate and kind. You should damn well give as good as you get and let me have it hot and strong.'

'Well,' Maggie said, recovering, 'when I've thought of something, perhaps I shall.'

'Surely that isn't so difficult? There's plenty of things you could throw up at me that'd catch me admidships if you liked. You could scuttle me in no time at all.'

'Is it to be a sea-fight, then?'

'Damme! Why not? Tes what I deserve!'

Suddenly he waved his hand.

'For pity's sake sit down in that chair,' he said. 'You make me feel so small as a worm, standing over me like that.'

Obediently Maggie sat down, and they looked at each other across the hearth, the firelight glimmering in their eyes.

'Hadn't I better get the tea?'

'No, I want to talk to you.'

'Jim will be in presently.'

'Then I'd better get a move on with what I've got to say to you.'

For a little while longer, he looked at her. His mood of the past few days was quite gone. He could read a great deal in her face and because he knew her very well he could guess what had happened between her and Brice. It was only what he himself had foretold, after all, but now that it had come to pass and he saw the sadness of it in her eyes, he found he was able, once and for all, to put his own feelings aside and accept it without jealousy.

'I suppose you've sorted things out with Brice? Begged pardon for my bad behaviour and made peace with him on my behalf?'

'Well,' Maggie said, uncertainly.

'And I would say, by the look of you, that you got your own feelings for each other sorted out at the same time.'

Maggie, speechless, looked down at her hands.

'You don't need to feel guilty,' he said. 'It was bound to happen sooner or later and if it's happened today, well, I have only myself to blame. I drove you together, didn't I, by picking on Brice the way I did? And tes only where you belong after all. If anyone should feel guilty it's me. And I *do* feel guilty. That's just the trouble. Tes because my conscience is troubling me that I've been behaving the way I have.'

Maggie looked up.

'Why should your conscience be troubling you?'

'You know well enough what I mean. Tes because of what I've done to you. Such a mess I made of things when I tied you down all those years ago! I thought it was such a clever plan – to marry you and provide for you and learn Brice a lesson at the same time. I felt sure that you and him would come together in your own good time but I thought I'd be out of the way by then and that everything would go suant for you. But my clever plan went astray and here I am, still alive, nothing but a wretched hinderment, getting in the way of your happiness. But tesn't no good railing about it. We've got to schemey to put it right.'

There was a pause. He studied her.

'What I said to you just now, about you going off with

161

Brice . . . that was just a bit of spite but I'm not being spiteful now . . . I've thought about it oftentimes and I reckon that's what you ought to do.'

'Go off with Brice?'

'That's what I said.'

'You surely don't mean it?'

'I surely do. Look at me! – I'm as tough as old boots! I could live to be old as Methuselah and what chance of joy will you have left by the time you've seen me into my grave? But if you and Brice and young Jim were to go clean away from here – Guernsey would be a good place to go – you could start a new life together there and nobody would ever know but that you and Brice were man and wife and boy Jim your son by him. Your name's Mrs Tallack right enough so you wouldn't have to tell lies about that. Twould all be as simple as ABC. And as for my bit of property, I should see Frank Rogers about that and come to some arrangement whereby—'

But here Maggie broke in on him.

'Do you think I would do that to you?' she asked in a tone of sad reproach. 'Go off and leave you alone like that, after all you've done for me?'

'I thought if you knew you had my blessing, you would find it easy enough.'

'No, it only makes an impossible thing even more impossible.'

'You mean, if I was to beat you, you would leave me soon enough.'

'Perhaps,' she said, with a little smile, 'but it's no good your beginning now, because I should know it was just a trick.'

'Perhaps I should have spoken to Brice, not you.'

'He would only say the same. You've told me often that Brice would always do what's right, so how could he ever treat you like that? And how could he ever leave his mother?'

'You and Brice should think of yourselves. You're still young, the pair of you, and got your own lives to live, but Rachel and me are both grown old, and if you and Brice've got any sense, you'll leave the dead to bury the dead.'

'And what about Jim in all this? What would he say to such a plan, that he and I should go with Brice to some strange place, goodness knows where, and leave you here all by yourself? It's out of the question. You must see that. It's so much out of the question that I don't know how you can talk of it.'

'So you won't allow me to set you free?'

'No, never,' Maggie said. 'I am your lawful wedded wife and you will just have to put up with me!'

'I suppose, if I was to tell you the truth, I knew all along what your answer would be.'

'Of course you did,' she said, gently scoffing.

'I had to say it all the same and if you should ever change your mind—'

'I shall never change my mind.'

'H'mm,' Gus said, and was silent a while, still looking at her intently as he pursued his own thoughts. At last he came to a decision. 'Well, if you won't let me set you free, at least there's one thing I can do. – Give Brice the boat, as you asked me to.'

'But I ought never to have asked you that. I told Brice I'd suggested it and he said at once that I had done wrong.'

'No, you did right. Tes a good idea. Oh, I know I've said this and that, and been dragging my anchor about it all, but that was the devil at work in me. I've been wrestling with *him* for days but I've thrown him brave and fitty at last. Why should I hold on to the boat? *I* shall never sail her again. Tes just my selfishness, no more than that. Much better fit if I give it to Brice and that's what I intend to do. – For *your* sake, since it's what you want, and for boy Brice's sake, too, so that he knows I mean well by him in spite of the way I treat him sometimes.'

'You've made up your mind, then?'

'Yes. Fair and square. I'll send for Frank Rogers first thing tomorrow morning. But I don't know what boy Jim will say when he hears I'm giving the *Emmet* away.'

Jim, however, though surprised, showed nothing but pleasure on hearing the news and had only one question to ask.

'Uncle Brice will still take me into his crew just the same, won't he?'

'Of course he will!' Gus said. 'And if so be you should ever

163

fall out with him, why, I'll build you a new boat of your own! – A bigger and better boat, even, than the old *Emmet!*'

The next day, true to his word, Gus sent for Frank Rogers, who came in the early afternoon and drew up the deed of gift whereby that lugger known as the *Emmet*, registered PY 19, with all her gear and tackle and everything pertaining to her, was given up by the present owner, Edward Augustus Tallack, and became the personal property, without let or hindrance, of the donor's kinsman, namely nephew, Brice Henry John Tallack; 'this gift being made in a spirit of goodwill, affection, and esteem; signed in the presence of witnesses this day, the twelfth of April, in the Year of Our Lord 1880.'

Chapter 8

The weather had improved during the night; the wind had
gone round to the north, and although there was still plenty of
sea, the waves were no longer breaking; and all morning,
around the harbour, there was much bustle and noise as the
lugger crews made ready for going to sea with the afternoon
tide.

At half past two Brice and his crew were at the net-store
under the sail-loft, loading their bait-nets and baskets of line
onto a handbarrow, when Gus appeared in the cottage
doorway and called Brice inside.

Brice, with the events of the previous day very much in his
mind, entered the kitchen with mixed feelings, but, as he stood
before Gus and Maggie, not knowing what to expect, he had
little time to speculate, for the old man, without preamble, put
the deed into his hands and bade him read it.

As he read the deed of gift, Brice was not only surprised but
deeply moved, and when he looked at the old man he found it
difficult to speak.

'I don't really understand.'

'No doubt you think I'm off my head. Nothing but needling
yesterday and today I'm giving you the boat. You must put it
down to senility.'

'Uncle Gus—'

'Never mind about thanking me. It's more Maggie's doing
than mine. As you know, it was her idea, so she's the one you
have to thank.'

'I thank you both,' Brice said simply.

Maggie was standing nearby; he knew he would have to
look at her; and just for a moment he was afraid. What had
passed between them the day before was too disturbing, too

immense, and he felt he would give it away in a glance. Yet when he did look at her, her gaze was so steady, so serene, that the weakness he feared he would betray passed completely out of him and he felt instead a renewal of strength, warm, quiet, reassuring.

Still, there was constraint all the same, and he was relieved when his uncle Gus suggested calling in the crew, to hear the news and to celebrate it 'with a nip of something warm.'

The crew were called and came clumping in, in their great stiff leather sea-boots. On hearing the news about the boat, there was a murmur of approval among them, and when a bottle of rum appeared, together with a proper number of glasses, there was only a modicum of protest, delivered for the sake of form. Being staunch Methodists, they were teetotallers to a man, but, as Gus dryly observed, were always willing, with a little persuasion, to set their principles aside.

'Seeing how tes a special occasion . . .'

'And a celebration, you.'

'Don't want to be a wet blanket, do us, and spoil it all for everyone else?'

'Not too much for me, skipper. Just to the top of the glass, that's all.'

'I'd like to give the toast if I may,' said Billy Coit, raising his glass. 'To the old boat – and her new owner.'

The toast was echoed with a warmth that took Brice by surprise. Plainly the crew were pleased for him. And of course, although it hadn't been mentioned, they were pleased for themselves, too, since it meant that in future the *Emmet's* profits would be shared between six men instead of seven. The glasses were drained and put down. Gus leant forward and filled them again.

'So you're going out?'

'Yes,' Brice said. 'The whole fleet's going out tonight. We thought we'd try the Bara Breck.'

'Good place for pollack.'

'Yes, and hake.'

'Might even get the odd turbot there.' Gus cocked a bushy brow. 'I haven't had turbot for many a day.'

'Right. We'll see what we can do.'

Brice emptied his glass and set it down and the crew, catching his eye, did the same. Together they moved towards the door, each man nodding politely to Maggie, and young Reg Pascoe, staring at her, stumbled against a small stool. His father, Clem, apologized for him.

'Reg edn used to strong drink, you see, especially tip-top stuff like that.'

'Went down handsome!' Reg said with a grin.

'Straight into his feet,' said Billy Coit.

'He'll be all right when we get to sea.'

'Aw, that'll sober him up, sure nuff.'

Brice and his crew went back to their task of loading bait-nets and baskets of line onto the old handbarrow. The crew were all in good spirits; the rum ran merrily in their blood; they had an item of fresh news to pass on when they got to the quay; and in another few hours would be out at sea after fish for the first time in a whole week.

'This'll be a good trip for us, I seem,' said Martin Eddy, confidently. 'I can feel it in my bones.'

At three o'clock Brice went home to collect the big bag of provisions his mother had filled ready for him. He told her the news about the boat and gave her the deed of gift to read.

'Well!' she exclaimed, having read. 'To think that after all these years he's done something decent for you at last!' She laid the document on the table and put away her spectacles. 'And what about her? That wife of his? Does she know he's given you the boat?'

'Yes, it was Maggie's idea,' Brice said.

'Was it indeed?' Rachel said, and then, recovering from her surprise: 'Well, I suppose it's the least she could do, seeing she's robbed you of everything else.'

'Have you no charity in you at all? Do you still feel the same about her, even now, after all these years?'

Rachel looked at him long and hard.

'*You* still feel the same about her. It's just that your feelings are different from mine.'

'Yes, that's true, I love her,' Brice said.

'Does she know it?'

'Yes, she knows.'

'And does she care tuppence what you feel?'

'Yes, she cares more than I deserve.'

He slung his crowst bag over his shoulder, took up his oilskin smock and sou'wester, and left the house. Rachel followed him out through the yard; his tidings had given her food for thought; and at the gate she did her best to put her thoughts into words.

'If, as it seems, your uncle Gus is trying to make some amends for his meanness to you in the past, then I think perhaps it's only right that I should go down and call on him. In other words let me say, my son, that I am willing to do my own part in putting things right between us all.'

Brice looked at her with understanding. He knew what this speech must have cost her pride. And on an impulse of the moment he did a thing that was rare with him: he bent towards her and kissed her cheek. Then he went striding out of the gate.

When he arrived at the fish-quay he was hailed from all sides by the other skippers and their crews who had heard the news from Billy Coit. There was banter from some of them and especially from Ralph Ellis whose boat the *Bright Star* was berthed immediately next to the *Emmet*.

'So now you're owner as well as skipper? No wonder you look some pleased with yourself! But dunt that feel queer to be in a boat after sticking at home so long? Maybe you'd better follow us, else you might get lost in the bay!'

Brice merely flashed him a glance, jumped down into the *Emmet*, and stowed his gear away in the cuddy. He then went to help his crew, who were lashing the baskets of line to the bulwarks, for although there was only a slight swell in the bay, it would be a different matter 'outside.'

'We'll get it out off Burra Head,' Clem Pascoe observed to his son, 'and the motto on this boat is "never leave anything to chance."'

From all along the quayside now came the krik-krik of masts being stepped, the grunting of men as they strained at the falls, and the cheep-cheeping of blocks and pulleys as sails were run up and made secure. A flapping of canvas here and there; men's quiet voices talking, sometimes interspersed by a shout; and the first boats moved away from the quay, gliding towards the harbour mouth. No sweeps were needed today; they had all the wind they required; and first the *Speedwell*, then the *Swift*, followed by the *Sea Horse* and the *Minette*, passed out of the harbour into the bay.

The *Emmet* was the next boat out and Brice, at the helm, turning his head, saw Maggie and his uncle Gus and young Jim, just home from school, watching from the yard above the old quay. They waved to him and he waved back and his uncle Gus called out something that he failed to hear.

'He says to remember and bring him a turbot,' said Jacky Johns, who had sharp ears.

Behind the *Emmet* came the *Bright Star* and, the wind coming down hard upon them the instant they left the shelter of the harbour, they were soon beating swiftly across the bay, standing out on the first tack that would carry them past Struan Point. The *Bright Star* was keeping close – 'Too blamed close,' Clem Pascoe said – and Ralph Ellis, enjoying himself, wedged the tiller between his legs so that he could put up his hands and cup them about his mouth to shout.

'This'll take the creases out of your sails!' he roared, and then, as he bore away from them: 'I suppose you still know what a fish looks like? If not I'll draw you one on the slate!'

The *Emmet*'s crew, with fine dignity, swallowed these jibes and said nothing. And it happened quite soon that they had their revenge.

They were two hours south of Crockett Lighthouse, a distance of some fifteen miles, and the sun was going down dimly in a misty greyness that hid the sea-line. As it vanished from sight completely Brice gave orders to heave-to and here, with the early twilight settling about them, they shot their four drift nets for pilchards to use in baiting their lines.

As darkness grew they lit their lamps and all around them, mistily, other lights began to glimmer, showing the rest of the fleet strung out like a necklace of stars afloat on the sea. With the coming of darkness the wind had changed and now blew straight from the west. There was less tide now and the sea had settled to a slow swell.

Hauling took less than an hour and soon they were getting under way, beginning at once to cut up the pilchards and fasten the bits to the hooks on their line. Some of the fleet had already gone; most of the others were making sail; but a few boats still remained, having so far failed to get their bait, and the *Bright Star* was one of them. Brice, with a word to his crew and a touch of helm, altered course just enough to bring them within hailing distance of her and this was when they had their revenge.

'Not got your bait yet, *Bright Star?*' he asked.

'No, not a sniff of 'm!' Ralph called back. 'But no need to ask if you've got yours, I suppose?'

'Yes, first shot, no trouble at all. Ten or twelve stone. Just enough and no more.'

'Where did you shoot?' Ralph asked.

'We shot where the fish were!' Brice replied, and aboard the *Emmet* as she went on her way there were chuckles of satisfaction because the score had been evened out and because surely, with such a beginning, the night was bound to go well for them.

Four hours' sailing brought them to the Bara Breck where, already, the sea was dotted with boats from Carnock, Polzeale, and Porthcoe. This meant that the Polsinney fleet had to press on, further west, and it was almost midnight when the *Emmet* at last found a berth, well clear of all other boats, and shot her line before the tide, which was now running from west to east.

By this time there was fog coming up, blowing in swirls

before the wind, and the lights of the boats eastward of them were slowly dwindling and fading away.

'West wind, best wind, when fishing the Bara Breck, but why did it have to bring this fog?' Martin Eddy asked gloomily.

'Aw, you can't have it all ways,' Jacky Johns said, 'and there's fish down there, I'm sure of that.'

While they ate a bite of food and drank the hot tea Reg Pascoe had made they drew lots and settled the watch. It fell to the two Pascoes so Brice and the other three men made their way into the cuddy, stretched themselves out on their narrow bunks and, with the ease of long practice, fell asleep instantly, lulled by the motion of the boat rocking gently on the swell.

When they emerged, an hour later, they found that the fog had gathered and thickened. It pressed up into their faces in dense, blinding swirls and surged about them, impatiently, cold and wet and enveloping. The *Emmet* was completely enclosed, cut off from all other sight and sound of life except that every now and then there was a faint mew, mew, from the gulls that floated, unseen, on the sea around them. No other boats' lights were visible now. The fog had swallowed them utterly. Even their own masthead light could not be seen from below, and the big lantern on its spear amidships cast only the dimmest glow, in which the fog twisted and squirmed.

'Some old skew,' Clem remarked, as Brice and the others joined him. 'You won't have seen many worse than this.'

'No,' Brice agreed, 'it's as thick as cheese.'

'Thick as Grammer Opie's breath,' said Jacky Johns, close behind him. 'We shall need our magic specs on if we're to see the fish tonight.'

Dark shapes in the swirling fog, the crew came together around the lantern, shrugging themselves into their oilskins and strapping on their sou'westers. There was no time wasted that night and they were soon ready to begin their task of hauling in the three miles of line.

'Tedn no night for hanging about,' Billy Coit said to Brice.

'We shall have some old job of it, as it is, getting home in this old skew.'

'I'm hoping it will have cleared by then.'

'No harm in hoping, I suppose.'

But although the wind blew steadily, keeping the fog on the move, it still came pressing up in waves, closer and denser all the time. It was like flannel, Billy said, and wrapped them round, cold as a shroud, in a silence as of the grave. Somehow the boat felt very small, shut in as it was by the fog, and every sound the men made as they prepared for the night's main work was muted and muffled and made unreal by the fog's close density.

The noise of the hatches being removed, the squeak of the capstan as it wound in the warp, and the tramp, tramp of the men's feet as they trudged stolidly round and round, all had a dim, dead quietness as though falling on ears gone deaf. And when, as the first length of line came aboard, bringing the first few fish, and the waiting gulls rose from the sea and came floating pallidly out of the darkness, the cries that issued from their throats were small and thin, almost pathetic, as though they were nothing but the ghostly echoes of cries they had uttered in the past.

By now the tide had turned again, thus lifting the line from the bed of the sea and making their task that much easier. Some lengths of line came in without any fish on the hooks but if this caused disappointment at least it meant less work. At the end of two hours the whole line was in and they had, at a rough estimate, a hundred and ten stone of fish. It was mostly skate and ray, with some conger, pollack, and dogfish, and a small number of cod and ling. There were also three sizeable turbot and these were carefully put on one side.

'Could've done better, could've done worse,' Billy Coit said to Brice. 'But tedn a bad catch, I suppose, for your first catch as owner, eh? At least it came in without any hitch and you've got the old skipper's turbot all right. He can take his pick of three.'

'Yes, we haven't done badly, all things considered,' Brice agreed.

The baskets of line were stowed away, blood and fish-slime were swilled from the decks, and hatches were replaced over the holds. Reg had been sent to make tea and was taking a long time over it and now that the others had finished their tasks they were beginning to grow impatient.

'Drat the boy! Where's he to with that tea? I reckon he've fallen asleep down there.'

'Tell him if he don't hurry up, we shall go without'n!' said Jacky Johns.

In his own good time Reg came and the men, now gathered in the stern, ate their food and drank their tea. The fog was just as thick as ever and nothing much could be seen beyond a distance of ten feet. It would be a difficult journey home and although they talked cheerfully enough they were acutely aware of it. Seamen feared and hated fog; it preyed on their nerves; and Billy Coit spoke for all when he said:

'Give me a gale of wind any time. At least you can *see* what you're up against then.'

The crew, as they ate and drank and talked, kept glancing towards Brice, who had lit the lamp in the binnacle and was closely studying the compass. They were aware of the tension in him; could sense the deep concentration of thought as he took his bearing and worked out his course; and they knew that all his faculties were keyed up to the highest pitch as he faced the task of getting them home. He, as skipper, would take the helm; on him would lie the responsibility of guiding them through the fog; and they knew what a strain that put on a man.

But they had complete faith in him. He had brought them through fog many times and never once in thirteen years had he failed to make a perfect landfall. He was like his uncle Gus in this. There was a particular quality to be found in certain seamen, as though they had some special knowledge, implanted in their very bones, and although it was a difficult thing to define, it was always quite unmistakable. Gus Tallack in his prime had had it, and Brice Tallack had it too. The *Emmet*'s crew recognized it in him; acknowl-

173

edged it without question; and, to a man, put their faith in it.

Brice, having finished his deliberations, stood erect. He finished his food and drank his tea. Although keyed up, his senses alert, he was at the same time perfectly calm, with the calmness of self-confidence, and, finding that his crew were watching him, he said:

'I'm setting our course east by north. That way we don't run any risk of overshooting Crockett Light.'

'Two man watch?' Billy enquired.

'Yes, and eyes well skinned,' Brice said. 'There's a good hundred sail of boats out there.'

'For as much as I can see tonight, I might so soon keep my eyes tight shut.' Billy, coming to stand beside Brice, tapped the glass on the compass-case. 'Tes a blessing that needle can see in the fog. I'd say we owe more than a groat or two to the man who invented the North Pole.'

'Cousin of yours, wadn he?' Clem Pascoe said sarcastically.

'Ess, that's right, on my mother's side.'

The men, chuckling, began to move, handing their empty mugs to Reg and piling their crowst-bags into his arms so that he could take them below, and as they did so they teased him, telling him not to get lost in the fog.

'Think you can find the cuddy all right or shall us come with you to lead the way? Well, don't you fall asleep again, cos we'll want your help with heaving the mast. And remember, if you're gone too long—'

'Quiet! Listen! What's that?' Jacky Johns said suddenly, and turned his head, straining his ears to catch again whatever sound had come to him faintly out of the fog, over on their port bow.

All six men became very still, heads cocked identically, mouths fallen slightly ajar. Brice, standing with his hand on the tiller, listening for he knew not what, felt the cold, creeping sensation of hairs rising on the nape of his neck; but although he strained his ears to the utmost he could hear only the wind in the stays and the cheeping of the halyard blocks. And he saw that the others were just as perplexed.

174

'I can't hear nothing,' Billy Coit said, in a hollow whisper. He turned sharply towards Jacky Johns.

'Hush! Listen!' Jacky said. He put up an urgent, imperious hand.

Suddenly it was heard by them all: a loud swishing noise, getting louder and nearer, coming at them from out of the fog; growing so loud that it filled their ears. Brice felt his head would burst with it; burst with the knowledge of what it meant; for the noise was of a great sailing-ship cutting swiftly through the water. And with the knowledge he found his voice.

'Look out, she's coming straight for us!' he roared. 'For God's sake save yourselves if you can!'

But even as he shouted his warning the oncoming ship loomed out of the fog, her tall masts, crowded with canvas, towering greyly over them. The six men cowered away, instinct making them throw up their arms, as though the great ship could be warded off. Her prow passed clean over them and her bows caught the *Emmet* broadside on. There was a terrible splintering crash, a screeching of wood against wood, and, as the *Emmet* broke in two, the loud, angry, sibilant rush of the sea pouring in between the halves and spreading out to engulf her.

Brice, jarred in every bone, was sent hurtling through the air, and his right shoulder, close to the neck, struck the toppling mizzen mast. Then he was in the cold churning sea and the waters were closing over his head. The pain in his shoulder and neck almost robbed him of consciousness but the cold shock of the seawater, sucked in at nose and mouth, flashed its message of danger at the centre of his brain and he fought his way up to the surface, spewing out water and gulping in air.

The great ship had gone on its way and in the tumult of broken water caused by its passing a few of the *Emmet*'s timbers and spars tossed and bobbed and clashed together, amidst a strewn-out tangle of cordage, amongst which floated a mass of dead fish that brought the gulls swooping in, no longer quiet,

175

awed by the fog, but restored to their normal boldness, clamouring raucously in their greed.

The seething of the water gradually lessened, the sea flattened out and became smooth again, and a spar bumped gently against Brice's head. He got his left arm over it and, thus supported, trod water until he had managed to kick off his boots. Through the crying of the gulls he could hear the voices of his crew calling out to one another and as he paddled his way towards them he heard Reg Pascoe crying shrilly: 'Feyther! Oh, feyther! Are you there?' But he could not be quite sure whether he heard Clem answering.

A dark shape loomed out of the fog immediately in front of him and his heart gave a jolt as he saw that it was the *Emmet*'s punt, right way up, undamaged, and with two of his crew clinging to it, Martin Eddy and Billy Coit. He swam closer, let go of his spar, and reached up to grip the gunwale. He and Billy remained where they were, steadying their side of the punt while Martin splashed his way round and climbed in at the other side. He then gave them a helping hand, but as they clambered into the punt it canted over dangerously, shipping a fair amount of water and a few dead fish. Martin, splashing about on his knees, groped in search of the boat's dipper which, together with the rowlocks, was fastened with twine to one of the thwarts. He wrenched it free and got to work, bailing out water and fish.

Brice and Billy, peering into the fog, cupped their hands about their mouths and set up a long, loud halloo that scattered the rabble of squabbling gulls and sent them wheeling and crying overhead. There was an answering call from nearby and very slowly, out of the fog, came floating the punt's four oars, still lashed together in a bundle, and with Jacky Johns swimming beside them. They hauled him inboard, bleeding from a gash in his cheek, and then hauled in the oars. The rowlocks were slotted into place, the oars were untied and put into them, and the four men settled themselves on the thwarts. The two Pascoes were still missing but young Reg's voice, faint and despairing, could

176

be heard not far away and in a short while they were pulling towards it.

To their surprise they found that the two shattered halves of the *Emmet* were still floating, only partly submerged, a space of fifteen feet between them, but tethered together and borne up by a great tangle of nets and cordage and by the floating mizzen sail which, still attached to its splintered mast, lay out flat on the sea's surface. And in the midst of this terrible tangle, made worse by the fishing line floating in coils out of the baskets, they found Clem Pascoe and his son.

Clem was caught up in the coils of line and young Reg, with a knife in his hand, was desperately trying to cut him free; but in their frantic struggle together they had become more and more embroiled, the line coiling itself about them, the barbed hooks sticking in their clothes and their flesh; and all about them, as they struggled, the screaming gulls flapped and swooped, gorging themselves in a frenzy of greed on the dead fish floating everywhere. Reg, with sobs of fear and frustration, hit out at them with wide sweeps of his arm, for in their frenzy the ravening gulls took so little heed of the two men struggling in the water that they kept buffeting them with their wings.

Father and son were close to exhaustion, but strong hands now reached out to them, the tangle of line was cut away, and they were hauled safely into the punt. For a time Clem lay on the boards, his whole body shaken in spasms as he fetched up water from stomach and lungs, helped by Billy Coit who was squeezing his sides. Then, at last, it was over; Clem gave a protesting groan, humped himself over onto his back, and raised his head to look about him.

'Are we all here?' he asked weakly.

'Ess, one and all,' Billy assured him.

'I thought my last hour was come.'

'So it would've done, sure nuff, if it hadn't been for boy Reg.'

Clem, with an effort, struggled up and was helped to the seat in the stern. The other men resumed their places, unshipped the oars, and, with cautious strokes, because of the tangle, began pulling away from the wreck. It was scarcely a moment too soon, for the two halves of the *Emmet* were now sinking rapidly.

When they had got well away from danger, and well away from the noise of the gulls, they took a rest and leant on their oars, allowing themselves not only a breather but time to absorb what had happened to them. In silence they followed their own thoughts. Then Billy Coit spoke.

'To think that a great smart ship like that should come all the way from America just on purpose to run us down!'

'She've certainly made a good job of it!' Jacky Johns said bitterly. 'And where was her look-out, I'd like to know?'

'Think she'll come back and look for us?' Reg Pascoe asked.

'Not she! Oh dear me no! All these merchantmen think about is getting where they've got to get and God help those who get in their way. Anyway, if they did come back, they'd never find us in this fog.'

'Anyone see what she was called?'

'Don't talk so soft as you are, boy. Wadn no chance of seeing that.'

'She must've got some damage, surely, sheering clean through us like that.'

'Ess, I daresay, and serve her right.'

'Poor old *Emmet*,' Billy said. 'She was a good old boat to us. She didn't deserve to end that way.' He turned his head and spoke to Brice. 'Only yesterday she was given to you and now, this morning, she've been taken away. Tes some queer old mysterious job, the way things belong to be sometimes, and I don't understand it at all.'

'No more do I,' Brice said.

'The old skipper'll have something to say when he hears she've been all scat up like that.'

'My uncle's first concern will be to ask what shape her crew are in.'

'Well, you can tell him we're middling, then.'

'Ess, that's right,' said Jacky Johns. 'Twill take more than a barquentine to sink us old Polsinney boys!'

178

'I could do with a change of clothes, mind,' Billy Coit said wistfully.

'You can change with me and welcome,' said Clem Pascoe's voice from the stern.

'I'm sticking to mine,' Martin Eddy said, 'cos when the water inside'm gets warm, that'll keep me warm as well.'

'You're right there, Martin, sure nuff. Edn nothing like saltwater for keeping you warm, I believe.'

'Or for bringing you up in boils.'

'Or for drowning you,' Reg Pascoe said.

'You haven't been drowned yet, have you, boy?'

'No, just practising for it, that's all.'

Sitting hunched in the open boat, coldly blanketed by the fog, the six men, by joking together, defied the danger they were in and sought to keep their courage alive in a mixture of faith and obstinacy.

Underneath their oilskin smocks, their sodden clothes were icy cold upon flesh that cringed and shrank on the bone, and each man had to fight, with all the willpower at his command, to still the spasms that swept over him and brought teeth clicking together in rigor-clamped jaws. All of them had lost their sou'westers and all except Clem Pascoe had kicked their boots off in the sea. But at least they were still alive; at least they had the punt and the oars; and if they had been spared this much, surely they could hope for more? And so gradually, by degrees, and always with a touch of grim humour, they came to a discussion of their plight.

The *Emmet*, when they had shot their line, had been seven hours south west of Crockett Light and had made eight knots almost all the way. So now, in the little twelve foot punt, they were more than sixty miles from Burra Head, their nearest landfall; had no compass to guide them, nor any glimpse of the stars; and were on a westward going tide which would not turn for another two hours.

Their only present guide was the wind, which had blown all night from the west. But if it changed – and it probably would – they could, as Billy Coit said, row themselves to Kingdom

179

Come 'and be none the wiser in this skew'. But row they must, to keep themselves warm, and, being all of one accord, they brought the boat cautiously round till the oarsmen had the wind in their faces and Clem had it on the back of his neck. The boat rose and fell on the long-backed waves and the oars creaked and splashed in unison.

'Good practice, this, for the June regatta.'

'Ess, so long as we get there in time.'

'What are the chances,' Reg Pascoe asked, 'of coming up with one of the fleet?'

'What do you think they are?' Jacky Johns asked.

'Well,' Reg said, and gave it some thought, 'there's a brave lot of boats out here, counting the ones from Carnock and all.'

'Ess, and a brave lot of open sea, too.'

'Not much hope, then? Is that what you mean?'

'There's always hope, boy,' said Billy Coit.

They pulled for a time, then took a rest; pulled again and rested again; and when they rested they shouted together, sending a long hallooing call, hopefully, into the fog. But fog and darkness swallowed their shout and all that came back to their listening ears was the cold heave and surge of the sea.

'Nobody home, seemingly.'

'No, not even Sally Quaile.'

'I keep thinking about my crowst. I was saving the best to eat going home. Now they old gulls will've had it all.'

'There's a few fish down here, somewhere, floating about round my feet.'

'Ess, and we might be glad of them, some time before we're done.'

'Raw?' said Reg Pascoe in disgust.

'Aw, you're some faddy, boy!' Jacky Johns said.

They pulled again, two hundred strokes, and Brice counted them to himself. The pain in his shoulder and neck had grown intense and the upper part of his arm was swollen, filling the sleeve of his guernsey so that it pressed tight and hard on his flesh; and although he shared his oar with Reg Pascoe, the effort it cost him was such that the sweat poured from his forehead and dripped down into his eyes; and this time, when they stopped for a rest, he was glad to yield his place to Clem, who, perceiving the pain he was in, crept quietly from the stern and edged him off the thwart.

'You sure you're all right now?' Brice asked.

'Ess, fitty,' Clem said, 'but could as a quelkin, just about, and got to do something to warmy myself.'

Brice, now sitting in the stern, took off his oilsin smock and dipped his arm in its tight guernsey sleeve into the cold sea water, leaning over to plunge it in right up as far as the armpit. This brought him some relief, the coldness gradually quenching the fire that raged up and down his muscles; and when, in a while, the arm became numb, he withdrew it, dripping wet, and shrugged himself back into his smock.

The men began pulling again; the oars creaked hollowly; and the fog licked and curled about the small boat as though trying to devour it.

They had hoped, with the coming of dawn, that the fog would lift and clear away, but instead it persisted, thick as ever, so that even when daylight whitened the sky, the sun itself remained in recession, yielding no trace of its orbit to guide the watchers in the punt.

'The fleet'll be on their way home by now.'

'So are we on our way home. Tes just that we're more behinder than they.'

'Tes all very well saying that,' said Reg Pascoe despondently, 'but in this durned old blinding fog we don't even know for sure whether we're even going the right way.'

'No, that's perfectly true, my son. We can only hope for the best and maybe say a word of prayer.'

To some extent they lost count of time but when at last the fog did lift they saw by the height of the sun in the sky that it was well after ten o'clock. To their dismay they saw, too, that the wind had gone northerly and they watched as the fog drifted before it, rising to form a dusky bar that gradually fell away to the south.

As the pale daylight grew they searched the sea with hungry eyes; with gaze that ranged about swiftly at first, skimming

181

impatiently over the surface and all around the clearing skyline; but then more slowly, meticulously, searching the dark patches of sea as well as the light, watching every rise and fall, always hoping that out of some trough a sail would be revealed to them. But there was nothing. Not a sign. From one horizon to another they had this stretch of the sea to themselves. And those horizons were utterly bare. There was no slightest smudge to suggest a landfall.

'Silly, I know,' said Billy Coit, in a voice grown husky with tiredness and thirst, 'but when that old fog began to clear, I thoft to see Crockett just over there and Burra Head rising handsome behind it.'

'I was the same,' said Jacky Johns, 'only I thoft to see the *Ellereen* or maybe the old *Betty Stevens*, perhaps, cos they were the last two boats we passed before we got a berth of our own. But there, twas only a foolish dream and I did know it all along, cos the fleet'll be just about nearly home by now. Twas all a sort of mirage in my mind. Wishful thinking, as they say.'

The men's disappointment was bitter indeed; their screwed-up faces were grey with it and had a shrivelled, defeated look; but in their eyes as they scanned the sea there was at the same time a steely glint, showing keen minds at work, weighing up the odds against them. Tired men, chilled to the bone, out in a small open boat in the Channel, without food or water, unable even to tell how far they were from land: they knew only too well what peril they were in; and yet about each man's mouth there was a certain grim twist that seemed to say to the sea: 'You have not seen or heard the last of me yet!'

'Anyone like to guess where we are?'

'A pure way from home, I can tell you that.'

'I fancy the Bay of Biscay myself.'

'Why, have you got a cousin there as well?'

'Ess, that's right. Cousin Frog, he's called.'

'Jacky, you're nearest. – Give Billy a clip.'

'We're certainly too far south and west. We took a wrong turning somewhere back there.'

'That old wind played us false, going about like that,' Billy said. 'I knowed it would, sure as fate, but I can't forgive'n all the same, cos that've put another few miles between us and the breakfast we deserve.'

'Breakfast!' Reg Pascoe said hollowly, and looked with loathing at the dead fish lying in the scummy pool at his feet. 'We shall miss more than our breakfast, I seem, before we make harbour and home again.'

'Yes,' Brice said, still scanning the sea, 'we've got a long pull in front of us.'

But at least they now had the blessed daylight and could take a bearing from the sun, and this they now proceeded to do, debating the matter quietly and pooling the knowledge of many years. Together they then studied the waves, which, with the wind obliquely behind them, were just beginning to break a little, curling delicately at the crests. The tide was now running from west to east, which meant a strong drift southward, and to counter this they judged it best to set their course north east by east. And so, guided by the sun and the set of the sea, they brought the punt gently round and, at a word from Brice, began once again to straighten out.

While they were easing the boat round, one of the long, low-backed waves came at them in such a way that they shipped the top of it over their bows and as the water swirled round their feet, Brice reached for the dipper and bailed it out. He had to use his left hand, for his right arm had stiffened completely, all the way from shoulder to wrist.

'Can you manage all right, skipper?' Clem Pascoe asked.

Brice, sitting up again, made a wry face.

'This is all I'm good for,' he said.

'Well, we're bound to get a few more of those, so you won't lack employment, you may be sure. Anyway, tes *your* job to keep us clean on our proper course.'

'Keep a look-out for ships, boys,' Jacky Johns said hopefully. 'Any old sort, it don't matter which, so long as there's Christian men in them.'

They needed no telling; their eyes were skinned; but even if they spotted a ship, what were their chances, young Reg asked, of being seen in this small craft, sitting so low in the sea, without any sail sticking up from her?

'Chances, my son? Only God knows that. Tes up to us to have faith in him. But if the worst should come to the worst, well, our chaps'll be out again tonight and *they'll* be looking out for us. Trouble is, twill be dark then, and if we get another foggy night—'

'Seems to me,' Reg said, 'we'd better put our backs into it.'

As the sun rose in the clear sky the men lifted their faces to it, gratefully, this way and that, so that the faint warmth of its rays should play over their stiffened skin and penetrate their weary flesh. But gratefully though they lifted their faces, the sun's faint, teasing warmth only made them more keenly aware that their bodies were chilled through to the bone, and when they gazed out over the sea they felt its unending coldness and greyness flowing in their very veins.

Shivering, they bent to the oars.

Chapter 9

On the quay at Polsinney that Tuesday morning, the fish merchants and local jowsters had resigned themselves to a long wait, for the fog lay thick on the sea and at ten o'clock showed no sign of clearing. By half past ten it was shifting, however, and soon the greater part of the fleet could be seen, lying-to outside the bay, waiting until it should be safe enough to venture close inshore. By eleven o'clock the fog had quite gone, the April sun was shining thinly, and the first boats were drawing in to the quayside.

Gus, sitting out in the yard, watched them through his spyglass. *Speedwell. Trelawney. Ellereen. Cousin Jacky. Samphire. Sea Breeze.* These were the first boats to come in and each had its escort of hovering gulls, showing that the fishing had been good that night. He saw Bob Larch of the *Ellereen* throw a good-sized dogfish to Dicky Limpet on the quay and, watching Dicky's wild efforts to catch and keep hold of his slippery prize, he quietly joined in the laughter that floated across the harbour pool.

At half past eleven Maggie brought him a mug of cocoa. She stood looking across at the fish-quay, where the boats were now berthed two and three deep.

'Has the *Emmet* got a good catch?'

'The *Emmet* haven't come in yet.'

'Not come in?' Maggie said. She put up a hand to shield her eyes and looked out across the bay. 'It isn't like Brice to lag behind.'

'He's not the only one late in today. There are quite a few to come yet. The fog must've been pretty bad out there.'

Gus swung his spyglass round until he too was looking

across the bay. Four boats were rounding Struan Point. The spyglass dwelt on each in turn.

'Is the *Emmet* among them?' Maggie asked.

'No,' he said.

He put the spyglass into his lap, took the mug of cocoa from her, and blew on it with noisy breath.

'They seem to have had a good fishing last night. *Speedwell*'s got a pretty good catch. So have *Trelawney* and *Ellereen*. And I heard Watty Grenville shouting the odds that he'd got half a stone of turbot aboard.'

'Then there's a good chance that Brice will have got a turbot for you.'

'If he haven't,' Gus said, 'I shall have something to say to him!'

Maggie went back indoors, leaving Gus sipping his cocoa. But the instant he knew he was alone he put the mug on the bench beside him and took up his spyglass again. Two more boats had appeared off the headland, *Maid Molly* and *Little Hob*, and these were soon followed by three more, *Betty Stevens*, *Pintail* and *Swift*. Gus gave an anxious sigh and counted the boats in the harbour pool. All except the *Emmet* were accounted for. Once again he looked out to sea.

When next he picked up his mug of cocoa, it had gone quite cold. He emptied most of it onto the ground. And then, as he moved to set down the mug, he saw that Maggie had come to the door again and was standing quietly watching him.

'You're worried about them, aren't you?'

'Yes,' he said, 'tes time they were in.'

'You think they've missed their way in the fog? Gone aground somewhere, perhaps, like the *Samphire* did last year?'

'Any skipper can miss his way in bad fog but I've never known Brice to do it yet. Even the *Maid Molly* is in and if Sam Cox can make harbour any fool can!'

The *Maid Molly* had now come into the harbour and, there being no room at the quayside itself, she was berthing beside the *Shenandoah*. Gus, through his spyglass, was watching her, and he saw that her skipper and crew, instead of setting to work at once to unload their catch, were talking to the men on the other boats. They then crossed the *Shenandoah* and stepped ashore, and something in the way people gathered, coming from all over the quay, confirmed the old man's growing fears. He closed his spyglass with a click, thrust it down into the chair, and swung himself round to face Maggie.

'Wheel me down there, will you?' he said. 'Something's happened. Something's wrong.'

They were seen coming, of course, making their way round the harbour road, and as they turned onto the fish-quay, Sam Cox and his crew, with a number of other fishermen, came forward to meet them. Their faces showed that they had bad news. There was some constraint among them and all looked towards Sam Cox. Sam carried something in his arms, which he laid on the ground in front of Gus. It was one of the *Emmet*'s hatches. It bore the number PY 19.

Gus, in silence, looked up at Sam, and Sam, haltingly, told his tale. They, like the rest of the fleet, had been out fishing the Bara Breck. They had started for home at five o'clock and at half past five, still in thick fog, they had found themselves amongst the floating wreckage of what they judged to be a fair-sized lugger.

'There were broken timbers and spars and all sorts, bobbing about everywhere, and there were a few baskets, too, with the lines all trailing out of them, so we knowed twas a fishing-boat straight away. Then we got that hatch inboard and there was her number painted on it. That told us who she was. The old *Emmet*. PY 19.' Sam paused. Cleared his throat. 'Seems she was run down,' he said, 'and that must've been a pretty big ship, cos some of those timbers had been smashed right through.'

Gus and Maggie both stared at the hatch and its white-painted number, PY 19, but what they each saw, in their mind's eye, was the helpless lugger at sea in the fog and the six men caught up in that moment of horror as the ship came at them to smash and destroy.

Maggie still stood behind Gus's chair and he turned himself round to look at her. Pale with shock, she met his gaze and then, with eyes full of pain and pity, she looked towards a group of women standing nearby, at the edge of the crowd. These were the women whose menfolk made up the *Emmet*'s crew and they had already been told the news. Martin Eddy's young wife, scarcely more than eighteen and soon to give birth to her first child, stood with the tears streaming down her face, and the older women, no less stricken, were gathered about her protectively.

Gus began questioning Sam Cox.

'I take it you didn't find any bodies?'

'No. We'd have brought them home if we had.'

'What about the *Emmet*'s punt? Was that broken up along with the rest?'

'I don't know. Tes hard to say. Everything was so scat to bits—'

'Easy enough, I should've thought, to tell bits of lugger from bits of punt.'

'We didn't *see* no sign of the punt, neither whole nor in bits,' Sam said, 'but more than likely she was sunk.'

'What makes you say that?'

'On account of how everything looked.'

'Did you search around at all?'

'Ess, we did. Of course we did. But what with the fog being so bad, there wadn no chance of seeing much.'

'What time did you say that was?'

'Half after five, near enough.'

'Daylight, then.'

'Just about. But what with the fog being so bad—'

'If you had waited for the fog to clear, you'd have stood a better chance of seeing something.'

'Ess, we might've done, I suppose. – *If* there'd been anything to see. But we should have had some good long wait cos that didn't clear till well after ten and we'd got a catch of fish to get home.'

There was a silence after this and the *Maid Molly*'s crew looked uncomfortable. One of them, Amos Saundry by name, muttered something under his breath. Then Sam Cox spoke again.

'That was a nasty shock to us, finding the *Emmet* wrecked like that, and we all thought the best thing was to come on

188

home as fast as we could and let folk know what had happened to her.'

'No wonder bad news travels fast,' Gus said. 'Tes because people like you are always in such a hurry-all to spread it around. But if only you had waited a while you might've brought good news instead of bad.'

'What good news?'

'You might just have found the punt and maybe the crew alive in her.'

'I understand how you d'feel, Gus Tallack, but if you'd seen that wreckage for yourself, and the way those timbers were splintered and smashed, you wouldn't pin much faith on the punt coming out of it in one piece.'

'If you'd had a nephew on board of her, you'd pin your faith on *anything*.'

'Tedn fair to say that,' said Sam Cox, 'cos Brice was always a good friend to me and Jacky Johns was my brother-in-law.'

'Was? Was?' Gus exclaimed. 'You said you didn't find any bodies.'

'No, that's true, there wadn no sign—'

'Then how do you know they're not alive?'

Sam Cox shifted uncomfortably and his glance kept straying, in a meaningful way, towards the missing fishermen's wives who had drawn close and were listening.

'Seems to me you do wrong to raise poor people's hopes like that.'

'Don't worry about us,' Betsy Coit said to him. 'If there's any hope at all, we d'want to know about it. And the next thing we d'want to know is – what is there to be done about it?'

'Well, I reckon the first thing we should do,' said Tommy Bray of the *Ellereen*, 'is to send a message round to Polzeale for the lifeboat to go and search for them.'

'I've got a better idea than that,' said another voice from among the crowd, and Ralph Ellis of the *Bright Star* elbowed his way forward until he stood in front of Gus. 'Why waste time sending round to Polzeale when we can send a boat ourselves?'

'What boat had you got in mind?'

'The *Bright Star* of course.'

'You mean you're willing to go out and search?'

'That's what I mean, sure nuff, and I speak for my crew as well.'

'Why you more than anyone else?'

'First, cos the *Bright Star*'s a good fast boat. Second, because when we went out last night, we didn't manage to get our bait. We shot three times without a sniff and at midnight we decided to come back home. So we're all fresh men – we slept in our beds – and we haven't got any fish to unload.' There was a pause and then Ralph said: 'Besides, they're all old shipmates of mine, and I know they'd do the same for me.'

'How soon can you be ready to go?'

'Twenty minutes. No, say half an hour. We shall need to put plenty of food aboard—'

'Then we'd better get a move on, I seem.'

'We?' Ralph said.

'Yes, I'm coming with you,' Gus said.

News that the *Emmet* had been lost at sea was already spreading fast and as Maggie and Gus returned home they were watched by little groups of people who had gathered along the harbour road. One or two tried to question them but Gus gave only the briefest answers and ordered Maggie to wheel him on.

On entering the cottage kitchen, Gus went straight to the cupboard under the stairs and got out his old white oilskin smock and sou'wester, his old brown leather sea-boots, and two big hessian bags which he handed to Maggie. Into one bag, as instructed by him, she put all the food the larder offered, together with two bottles of rum; and into the other she put blankets and shawls and all Gus's spare warm clothes.

While they were thus occupied the door burst open and Jim came in. He had heard the news on his way home from school. He looked at Gus with anguished eyes.

'Do you really think they might be alive? Out there somewhere? In the punt?'

'I don't know, boy. I aim to find out.'

'You're going out in the *Bright Star*?'

'Yes.'

'Can I come with you?'

'No,' Gus said. 'You must stay at home and look after your mother. But there *is* something you can do.'

'What?' Jim asked.

'We haven't got nearly enough food and I want you to go to Mrs Beale's.'

Gus, busy with pencil and paper, wrote these brief words: '1 Whole Cheese. 4 Quartern Loaves. Butter for Loaves. Jar of Jam.' He gave the note to boy Jim and found him another hessian bag.

'Don't bring the things back here. Take them straight down to the quay. I want you to be as quick as you can, so don't let anyone hinder you.'

For an instant the boy hesitated. There were things he wanted badly to know. But then, with a nod, he turned and ran.

Gus was now ready to go. The two heavy bags lay close to his chair. He gave a little sign to Maggie and she lifted them into his lap where, already, his oilskins and boots were stowed together in a bulky bundle. She stepped back and stood looking at him.

'Gus, is it wise for you to go?'

'You want me to find Brice, don't you?'

'You're not really fit,' Maggie said. 'And you haven't been to sea for years. Leave it to the crew of the *Bright Star*.'

'Brice is my nephew. My own kith and kin. I *belong* to go out and look for him. And if he's out there, still alive, I swear by Almighty God I shall find him and bring him back to you. As to my being fit, I'm just about as strong as a horse! Tes just that my legs aren't much use to me and that won't matter much in a boat.'

'You're an obstinate man.'

'Yes. Maybe.'

'You *will* take care?'

'Be sure of that.'

'Very well. I'll wheel you down.'

When they returned to the fish-quay, they found that two or

three boats had moved, thus making room for the *Bright Star* at the farthest end of the quay, the best place for getting away. The mast had been stepped and the sails hoisted and Ralph Ellis and his crew were carrying casks of fresh water aboard, together with the blankets, clothes and provisions which Betsy Coit and the other *Emmet* men's wives were hurriedly bringing to the quayside. Ralph Ellis's wife was there, too, and so were the wives of some of his crew; and altogether such a crowd had gathered at the far end of the quay that Jim, arriving with his bag of provisions, had difficulty in getting through.

Just after one o'clock Pony Jenkin, the *Bright Star*'s first hand, lifted Gus from his wheelchair, carried him aboard in his arms, and put him to sit on a straw pallet placed on a coil of rope in the stern. In another few minutes the boat had cast off; there was a regular creak and splash as her great sweeps were brought into play; and, with the floodtide strong against her, she was moving slowly and cumbrously towards the narrow harbour mouth. Maggie lifted a hand to wave and Jim beside her did the same. Gus touched the peak of his cap in response, then turned his bearded face to the sea.

The watching crowd were almost silent, perhaps because many people there felt the boat's mission to be forlorn, but as it slowly drew away, Betsy Coit, at the quayside, called after it in a clear voice that carried across the harbour pool.

'The Lord bless you, *Bright Star*, and grant you find our men alive.'

And everywhere along the quay the voices of two or three hundred people, who had heard Betsy Coit's prayer, quietly said 'Amen'.

For a while longer the crowd remained, watching as the *Bright Star* moved from the harbour into the bay and stood out to sea. Then people began to disperse; the fishermen returned to their work of unloading their catches; a few jowsters, already supplied, drove away in their carts. But one fisherman, Matthew Crowle, came over to where Maggie was talking to Betsy Coit and the three other *Emmet* wives.

'Tedn only the *Bright Star* that'll be looking out for that punt,' he said. 'Tes all of us. The whole fleet. We'll be out at the Bara Breck again tonight and we shall be sailing well spread out so that if she's there we shall surely see her. Of course it'll be dark by the time we get there and if there's fog like there was last night we shan't see nothing at all. But tomorrow we shall wait till it clears – we're all agreed on that – and we shall be keeping a sharp look-out. The whole lot of us. One and all.'

He touched his cap and walked away and Maggie, absently watching him, found herself thinking of Rachel Tallack. She turned to speak to Betsy Coit.

'Has anyone seen Mrs Tallack? Has she been told what's happened?'

The four women eyed one another. None knew the answer. They shook their heads.

'I'd forgotten all about her,' Ann Pascoe said, 'and, wicked or not, tes only the truth.'

'Yes, so had I,' Maggie said, and was filled with shame. 'I'd better go and see her straight away.'

Jim, with Clem Pascoe's two younger sons, had gone aboard the *Maid Molly* and was talking to Sam Cox and his crew. Maggie went to tell him that she was going to Boskillyer and the boy looked at her with a frown.

'Shall I come with you, mother?'

'No, there's no need,' Maggie said. 'Go home when you're ready. I shan't be long.'

She pushed the empty wheelchair home and left it in the yard. She spoke briefly to Eugene Kiddy and walked up to Boskillyer Farm.

Rachel was in the kitchen, busy preparing the midday meal. She had seen the first boats coming in more than two hours before and, assuming that the *Emmet* had been among them, she expected Brice home at any moment.

When she opened the door to Maggie, her face at first was blank with surprise, but slowly it darkened with instinctive foreboding.

'Mrs Tallack, there's bad news,' Maggie said.

Rachel was silent, absorbing the words. Bad news meant only one thing; there was no need to ask the nature of it; only the details remained to be told. For a moment she stood with her hand resting on the door. Then, with a gesture, she stepped aside.

193

'I think you'd better come in,' she said.

On getting home from Boskillyer, Maggie revived the fire in the stove and put the mutton stew on to heat again. While she was laying the table Jim came in.

'Did you see Mrs Tallack?'

'Yes, and I'm very glad I did. She hadn't heard the news at all. It was a terrible shock to her.'

'Did you tell her uncle Gus had gone out in the *Bright Star* to look for the punt?'

'Yes.'

'Some of the folk out there seem to think he's wasting his time.'

'Did they say so?'

'Not straight out. But I heard Dicky Limpet and Skiff Annear talking about other boats that've been run down by ships. They said there'd been a good few of them, though never one from Polsinney before. They said they could think of five at least. And I heard Dicky Limpet say—' here Jim took a tremulous breath – 'that out of those five boats only two men were saved.'

Mother and son looked at each other.

'We must just have faith,' Maggie said, 'like your uncle Gus.'

Jim went off to wash his hands. He had carried fish home for old Horace Wearne. When he returned and came to the table he found his bowl filled with hot mutton stew. He sat down and stared at it numbly.

'I'm not hungry.'

'You must eat what you can.'

'Horace Wearne said if the punt *is* out there, there edn much chance of the *Bright Star* finding it today. Only by a miracle, and that's too much to expect, he said. So when it gets dark the *Bright Star* will heave-to for the night and start looking again in the morning.'

'Yes, and the fleet will be out there by then. They will be searching, too. Matthew Crowle told me that.'

'I wish there was something *we* could do.'

'Yes, so do I,' Maggie said.

Jim picked up his spoon; fished a piece of meat from his stew; blew on it; put it into his mouth. Maggie, too, began to eat, glancing up at the clock on the wall. The *Bright Star* had been gone an hour.

It was a typical April day that day, with the wind veering between north and west, bringing a skitter of rain now and then, short and sharp and rather cold. These showers came down from the moor, 'off the top of Teeterstone Hill' as folk in Polsinney always said; they darkened the slate roofs of the houses for a few minutes at a time; then blew away out to sea and were seen like dark patches of smockwork puckering the flat grey surface.

The fishing fleet left early that day and there were more people than usual gathered on the quay to watch. Maggie was among them, having been to Mrs Beale's for food to replenish the empty larder, and although it was only three o'clock, Jim was there, too, for the schoolmistress, Miss Trembath, finding the children restless, had closed the school early and sent them home.

'Cissie Birch kept crying,' Jim said. 'She said her grandfather was drowned and would only come back as a seagull.'

Cissie Birch was barely six. Her grandfather was Billy Coit.

'Do you think it's true,' Jim asked, 'that when seamen drown they come back as gulls?'

'I don't know,' Maggie said. 'It's what people say, but I don't know.'

Out in the bay the fishing fleet was standing boldly out to sea, each boat under full sail and 'keen as mustard to do ten knots' as one old retired fisherman said, leaning over the harbour rail.

'Handsome wind for them,' said another, 'and let's hope it d'hold as it is, cos they won't be hindered with fog, not while it do blow like this.'

The boats sped away over the sea, growing smaller all the time, and at last vanished beyond Struan Point. Maggie began walking home and Jim, without being asked, took her basket and carried it for her.

'Tis strange to think uncle Gus is at sea. I can't get over that at all.'

'Yes, it is strange,' Maggie said. 'And the house seems terribly empty, too, without him in it.'

'Mother, when you think of uncle Brice . . . out there, on the sea, I mean . . . do you see him dead or alive?'

Maggie hesitated. She had already told Jim that they must have faith. She could not possibly tell him that she was filled with dread for Brice; that, having lost three men to the sea, she had little room in her heart for hope; so, after thought, she told a lie.

'I see him in the punt, alive.'

'With Billy Coit and the rest of them?'

'Yes, I see them all,' she said.

'That's how I see them, too,' Jim said.

Jim could not bear to stay indoors. He had to be out and about the harbour. And Maggie, having given him his tea, did not attempt to keep him back.

It was no good expecting news that day because even if the *Bright Star* found the *Emmet*'s crew at once, say forty miles or so from home, she would not be back until well after dark. Jim was well aware of this but the harbour was the place to be all the same and he, with other boys of his age, was drawn more than ever to the company of those old retired fishermen who leant on the wall and looked out to sea.

Jim and Clem Pascoe's two younger sons could not have enough of the seamen's talk as they argued out the chances of the *Emmet*'s crew being found alive. And Jim persuaded William Nancarrow, now eighty-four and long retired, but once the most respected skipper all along that stretch of coast, to tell again the familiar tale of how, as a young man of twenty-six, he had been swept overboard in a gale, some twenty miles off Kibble Head.

'The old *Sea Owl* I was in at that time, and the crew soon turned back to look for me. But there was some old sea that night and Wally Davey said afterwards the only reason they found me was because I'd got white oilskins on. They'd never have seen me else he said, cos the night was just so black as a shaft, and of course I was too far gone to shout. But that's how twas in those days. — A lot of us always swore by white oilskins because we knowed they showed up in the dark.'

'My uncle Gus has got white oilskins. He've taken them with him in the *Bright Star*.'

'Ess, and he'll be glad of their warmth, out there on the sea tonight, even though tis April month and we've got a touch of spring in the air.'

Once Jim and the other boys climbed the cliff above Porthvole because from there they could see out as far as Burra Head and the wide stretch of open sea beyond. There was nothing to be gained from seeing thus far; it would not bring the *Bright Star* back any sooner; it was just something to do.

And yet, even so, the sight of a sail, out there abeam of Crockett Lighthouse, was enough to bring their hearts to their mouths. It was only an old hooker, making its slow way into Polzeale, and they told one another they had known *that* the instant she had hove into sight. And so they *had* known it, sure enough, for what else could she be? But they felt disappointed all the same.·

They made their way down to the harbour again; helped Dick Geach and Figgy Tregenza to unload lobsters from their gig; and were still loitering on the slip when the sun went down behind Mump Head and the harbourmaster came out of his cottage to light the lamp on the quay-head. Lights were showing in the houses, too; the boys knew they would have to go home; they separated and went their ways.

On his way home, thinking of his mother alone all these hours, Jim felt guilty and hastened his step, for his uncle Gus had told him that he was to take care of her. But his mother was not alone. She had Martha Cledra with her, her old friend from those days long ago when they had both worked in the fish cellars. Martha worked in the cellars still, in the summer seining season, but she was Martha Jenkin now and her

197

husband was the giant, Pony Jenkin, who was one of the crew of the *Bright Star*.

'I've been keeping your mother company over a nice cup of tea. Tes lonesome for us women, you know, when our menfolk are all away. And *you'll* be off yourself, I daresay, not many years from now, though it won't be in the *Emmet*, will it, now she's gone to the bottom of the sea?'

Jim did not know how to answer this but Martha, heaving herself from her chair, was already preparing to leave.

'I'd better get back to my childern, I suppose. They dunt much care for Granfer Dark. They'll be wanting a candle to go to bed.'

The door closed. Martha was gone. And Jim, shivering, drew near the fire, spreading his hands close to the flames. Evening and the fall of darkness had banished his bright optimism and touched him with fear. A cold, cruel fear that squeezed his heart.

'I suppose *she* thinks, like all the rest, that uncle Brice and his crew are drowned.'

'I don't know what she thinks,' Maggie said. 'I don't know what to think myself. All we can do is pray for them.'

'Even praying won't help,' he said, 'if they're already dead, will it?'

His voice broke and he bowed his head, and Maggie, with a little cry, drew him fiercely into her arms.

Maggie did not go to bed. She sat fully clothed in a chair by the fire, listening for footsteps in the yard and a knock at the door that would mean news of the *Bright Star*'s return. But the night passed without bringing news and towards morning she fell asleep.

She awoke to a loud noise of wind and knew at once it had changed direction by the way it blew down the chimney and flue, keeping the embers alive in the stove. She got up and poked at the ashes; put more wood on the fire; swung the kettle onto the hob. Dawn was a greyness at the window. It was nearly five o'clock.

Jim came downstairs, barefoot, in his nightshirt.

'Wind've gone sou'westerly. Tes getting up rough by the sound of it.'

'Did you manage to sleep?' Maggie asked.

'Yes, but I'm not going back to bed.'

'No. Well. You can fetch me some more coal. There'll be hot water soon for you to wash.'

Just after six Jim was on the quay. There were red streaks in the eastern sky and as the sun rose above Goonwelter it made a crimson splash on the sea, all around Black Pig Rock, and a red rippling path across the bay. There were quite a number of people about, some going to their work, some standing in groups on the wharf and the quay. Most of these were women and girls and, huddled against the wind as they were, their heads and shoulders rounded by shawls, they looked, Jim thought, like the grey seals that sometimes came ashore at Porthmell.

He hurried past them, awkward and shy, for he knew that they, like himself, were out watching for the *Bright Star*, and if they were to speak to him he would not know what to say. Martin Eddy's wife was one and he was afraid of seeing her tears. He walked out to the end of the jetty, stayed for an hour looking out to sea, and walked back again. There was no sign of the *Bright Star*. He went home and ate his breakfast.

'Do I have to go to school?'

'Yes,' Maggie said. She thought it best. 'You'll hear at once if there's any news.'

All morning the wind blew hard from the south west, bringing black ragged clouds up with it, but no rain.

'That won't come till the wind drops,' Isaac Kiddy said to Maggie, 'and there edn no sign of it dropping yet.'

Neither he nor Percy Tremearne were doing much work in the sail-loft that day. They kept coming out on the stairs, the better to see across the bay. Eugene, too, was on the watch, from the door of the barking-house, and once Maggie heard him say:

'I dunt like the sound of that wind. There's more than a mite of spite in it. Twill get a lot worse before tes finished.'

199

Maggie tried to keep herself busy. There were plenty of chores to do in the house. But she could not make herself concentrate and when she heard the sound of the tide beginning to slap at the sea wall immediately below the house, she abandoned all thought of work and, putting on her shawl as she went, hurried out to join the people waiting and watching all round the harbour. The wind was now blowing ferociously and on the fish-quay itself the watchers stood close in under the wall or sheltered behind the fish-merchants' carts. It was after ten o'clock. The fleet was expected imminently.

'They said they would stay out all day and help to look for the *Emmet*'s punt but with this gale blowing up—' William Nancarrow shook his head. 'They will have to think of themselves,' he said to Maggie, with simple directness, 'and that goes for the *Bright Star*, too.'

At eleven o'clock the first boats appeared, running swiftly before the gale, and William Nancarrow and Peter Perkin, watching them through their telescopes, called out their names to the waiting crowd: *Speedwell*; *Jenefer*; *Ellereen*; *Little Hob*; *Midge* and *Minette*; and these six were soon followed by others: *Starfish*; *Sea Breeze*; *Betty Stevens*; *Trelawney*; *Swift*; *John Cocking*; *Boy Dick*.

As the *Speedwell* came in beside the quay, closely followed by the *Jenefer*, their skippers and crews were besieged at once.

'Did you see the *Bright Star*?'

'No, not a sign, neither hide nor hair. But visibility was bad. There were black squalls on the Bara Breck. We didn't like the look of it so as soon as we'd hauled we ran for home.'

Prosper Geach looked around. His gaze came to rest on Betsy Coit and the rest of the *Emmet* wives.

'About the *Emmet*'s punt,' he said, and had to take a deep breath before he was able to go on. 'I hate to have to say it, midears, but if the *Bright Star* haven't found them by now, there edn no hope for them in this.' He glanced towards the black south west. 'Ralph Ellis will be on his way home by now. Else if he edn he ought to be cos there's worser weather to come yet.'

The women said nothing in reply. They were already watching the other boats drawing in beside the quay. But the question eagerly put to their crews brought the same answer again and again: No one had seen the *Bright Star*.

The first boats began to unload. Their catches were all fairly small and the merchants and jowsters were soon driving away. Three boats had no fish at all. Alarmed by the weather, they had cut away their lines.

Just before twelve o'clock Rachel Tallack drove onto the quay in the milk-float and Maggie went to speak to her.

'There's no sign of the *Bright Star* yet. Nor any news of her.'

'How many more boats to come?'

'Another fifteen,' Maggie said.

For a while Rachel waited and watched. The *Shenandoah* and the *Rose Allan*, the *Pintail*, the *Samphire*, the *Sea Horse*: these were coming in across the bay and their names were called out by William Nancarrow; but still the *Bright Star* did not come.

'I must get home,' Rachel said. 'I can't keep the pony standing here. I'll come down again later on.'

By twenty past twelve all the boats were in. People counted. There were thirty-one. Out in the bay there was nothing to be seen except the grey blur of the rising sea. The wind was blowing harder than ever. It had a loud whining note in it. And as Maggie walked home many people who lived along the harbour road were fastening the shutters across their windows.

On getting home she made up the fire and began preparing the midday meal. The little house shuddered and rocked, for the tide was well in on the foreshore now and, with the full force of the gale behind it, was pounding high against the sea wall. In her mind she heard Gus saying with relish, as he so often did in rough weather, 'Ho! We're fairly getting it now! We'd better put an anchor down!' But Gus was out on the sea in this gale and suddenly, seeing his empty wheelchair standing in the corner by the door, she was overcome with dread.

'Oh, Gus,' she whispered helplessly, 'I should never have let you go.'

In a little while Jim came in. He had been talking to the men on the quay.

'They say the gale is going to get worse. They're worried about the *Bright Star*.'

'Yes. I know.'

'She's a good sea-boat. She'll be all right. She *will* be all right. I *know* she will.'

'Yes, of course she will,' Maggie said.

She put a plateful of fried hog's pudding in front of him. Usually it was his favourite meal but today he looked at it with indifference.

'There's no school this afternoon. Miss Trembath spoke to the vicar and he said we were all excused.'

'Well, when we've had our dinner, then, we'll go down to the quay,' Maggie said.

She brought her own food to the table and sat down. Together they ate, mechanically, listening to the wind thumping in the chimney.

Although Polsinney, with its stout-built harbour, made a safe anchorage in most conditions, it lay directly open to the fierce south westerly gales that swept in clean past Burra Head with nothing whatever to break their force. And all through that afternoon the gale blew with increasing venom. Huge seas came rushing in, hurling themselves over the quay-heads and causing such waves in the harbour pool that the thirty-one luggers, moored strake to strake along the wharf, were often washed over with foam.

By three o'clock, the greater part of Polsinney was out watching for the *Bright Star*. All the fishermen were there, numbering nearly two hundred men, and so were most of their families. And in their midst were the two groups of wives, the *Bright Star* wives and the *Emmet* wives, standing on the same part of the quay, sheltering in the lee of the wall, yet never quite mingling together.

Rachel Tallack was also there, but kept herself aloof as always. She would not seek comfort from anyone nor, when Maggie spoke to her, had she any comfort to give.

'Men talk about the harvest of the sea but the sea always takes more than it gives,' she said with angry fatalism.

202

Jim, at the outer end of the fish-quay, climbed into one of the look-out gaps in the ten foot thick wall and looked down onto Porthvole beach, at the tide surging in over sand and rocks. When he put his head right out, past the shelter of the recess, he felt the full force of the wind cutting along the wall like a knife and when a big sea came in, rushing all along its base, the spray came up off the rocks and stung his face with the sharpness of gravel.

The strength of the wind took his breath away and the sharp spray hurt his eyes but he bore it all for a count of one hundred because of a superstitious feeling that by enduring these hardships he would bring the *Bright Star* in. At the end of the count he climbed down. There was still no sign of the *Bright Star*.

A handful of watchers stood on the cliff above the beach, blurred figures in the grey wind, leaning against it to keep their balance. Jim had an itch to be up there too; to see out, beyond and beyond; but he wanted to be everywhere at once and it seemed more important to stay on the quay. For one thing, his mother was there somewhere, and he felt he must not stray too far from her; for another, he wanted to be near the seamen, to hear what they had to say to one another; and anyway, he very much doubted if the watchers on the cliff could see past Burra Head today, for the sea beyond it was storm-dark.

He stood with his hands in his pockets, staring at the ground, and again began counting up to a hundred. If he did not look out to sea, the *Bright Star* would come, he told himself. And if he counted very slowly . . .

But supposing the *Bright Star* came without uncle Brice and the rest of the *Emmet*'s crew? His mind seemed to swing dangerously, refusing to fix itself on this thought; finding it impossible to understand how life could offer two such extreme alternatives: on the one hand a thing so miraculous; on the other a thing so unthinkable. Had he reached one hundred yet? He didn't know. He had lost count. He would just have to start again.

Restless, he turned and walked a few paces. Then back again, kicking the ground. An old man stopped him and spoke to him but the words were whipped away by the wind and before the old man had time to repeat them there was a stir among the crowd and a great throbbing cry went up from half a dozen throats at once:

'Here she comes!'

Jim spun round and stared out to sea. It took him a troubled moment or two before his eyes could focus again on that distant grey swirl of sea and wind so ferociously mixed together. But yes! *Yes!* There she was! The *Bright Star* was coming, sure enough, although scarcely more than a black speck out there in the turbulent greyness; a speck that appeared and disappeared, moment by moment, with the heave of the sea.

'Here she comes! Here she comes!'

The cry, taken up by all the watchers, became a roar like the roar of the wind. People hurried this way and that and some of them went to speak to those women whose menfolk made up the *Bright Star*'s crew. There were tears and a sort of hushed laughter among them. But there was awkward concern, too, because of that other group of women who stood in stillness and silence nearby, not yet knowing the fate of their own menfolk. Hoping. Praying. Yet fearing the worst.

Jim sought his mother among the crowd.

'Uncle Gus is coming! I knew he would!'

'Yes, I knew it, too!' she said, in a voice he had never heard before, and she caught hold of both his hands, squeezing them hard between her own.

But what of the *Bright Star*'s mission? That was the question in every mind; the question that now brought a hush on the crowd; drew all eyes seaward again.

Slowly the lugger was coming nearer, keeping well clear of Struan Point, one small jigger sail set on her foremast. But it was still impossible to see how many men were in her. William Nancarrow and Peter Perkin had their telescopes trained on the boat and a great many eyes were trained on *them*. Seven men had gone out, in search of six. How many were coming back?

The boat rose on a great running wave; seemed to hang there, eternally; then sank and vanished into the trough. A heart-stopping moment that lasted for ever and then she rose again to the sea, lifting, climbing, humouring the wave, balancing on it and riding it down.

'How many men?' people asked. 'William? Peter? Can you see?'

'I think I can see . . .' William Nancarrow said, and his deep voice had a quiver in it, 'I think I can see . . . nine men.'

'I make it ten,' Peter Perkin said.

The boat disappeared. Reappeared. William Nancarrow spoke again.

'I can see eleven . . . Wait . . . Twelve!'

'I can see thirteen!' Peter Perkin roared. 'Thirteen men! They've found them all! The *Emmet*'s crew – they're all alive!'

This time the roar from the crowd was louder even than sea and wind. The two groups of women most closely concerned moved together and became one, wives of the rescuers and the rescued all weeping and laughing together, touching one another with eloquent hands. And part of the crowd surged about them, jostling them, sharing their joy.

Maggie still had hold of one of Jim's hands. She was squeezing it to the very bone. She turned to him with radiant face and gave a little broken laugh.

'Oh, Jim, they're coming! They're all alive! Was there ever anything so wonderful?'

They looked out again at this miracle, the *Bright Star*, with her one brave sail, coming to them out of the storm. William Nancarrow and Peter Perkin were letting their telescopes pass among the crowd, but those with keen eyes could now count for themselves the figures, seen each as head and shoulders, sitting tight in the boat as she rose and fell.

'Thirteen men, sure nuff. No doubt of that. I can see them plain.'

'Thirteen men – that's unlucky,' a voice said behind Jim and he turned with hatred in his heart for the man, Skiff Annear, who could say such a thing at such a time.

For Jim knew, quite as well as anyone there, that the danger was by no means past. That in fact the worst was yet to come. The gale was blowing as hard as ever and huge seas were breaking on the harbour walls; and the *Bright Star* faced the one task more dreaded than any other: that of coming in on a lee shore, driven before a living gale.

Rachel Tallack knew the dangers too. That was why she did not rejoice but stepped aside and stood alone as the crowd thronged round the waiting wives. Someone came up to her. It was the vicar, Mr Rowe.

'Well, Mrs Tallack! Our brave men are coming and your son among them. We must thank God, all of us, for showing his goodness and mercy to them.'

'I shall only thank God,' Rachel said, 'when I've seen our brave men come safe ashore.'

Jim had moved away from his mother and was once again drawing close to William Nancarrow and the other seamen as, with the first excitement over, they talked in grave, quiet voices, all watching the boat as she came, all speculating on the helmsman's intention. It would be madness, the watchers agreed, for her to attempt to come in at the narrow harbour entrance, with such seas breaking there. Her best chance – indeed her only chance – would be to come in on Porthvole beach.

Even that would be fraught with danger because of the many sharp-ridged rocks, some now covered and hidden by the tide. It would take skilled seamanship to bring her in, avoiding those rocks, and to beach her successfully on the shelving sand, and although no one said it in so many words, there were serious doubts in many minds as to whether Ralph Ellis was seaman enough.

'He'll need to keep a cool head,' – not something Ralph was noted for – 'and he'll need the judgment of Solomon,' said William Nancarrow soberly. 'But I will say this for him – he's doing very well so far. He's riding those big seas like a cormorant riding a bit of a lop.'

William Nancarrow's telescope was now in the hands of Albert Grose and he was narrowly watching the boat.

'Ess, he's doing a brave handsome job, but tedn Ralph at the helm,' he said.

'Who is it, then? Brice Tallack, I suppose. Well, of course, that explains it, and thank God Ralph's got more sense than conceit, to hand over to the better man.'

'No, tedn Brice, neither, cos I can see him in the bows and seemingly he've hurt himself, cos his right arm is hanging down at his side.'

'Who is it, then?' Peter Perkin asked.

'Just a minute. She've gone again.'

The boat disappeared; reappeared; and Albert made a strange sound in his throat.

'God in heaven, tes Gus Tallack!'

'Are you sure?'

'Here, see for yourself.'

'Damme, you're right!' Peter Perkin exclaimed and he in turn passed the telescope on. 'Tes Gus Tallack at the helm or I'm a Dutchman and can't say fish!'

There was a ripple among the crowd as this fresh piece of intelligence was passed along and William Nancarrow, in his deep voice, said:

'Well, if anyone can bring her in safely, Gus Tallack is that man.'

Jim felt that his heart would burst. His uncle Gus was at the helm and was bringing the *Bright Star* in, which meant that twelve men, including Ralph Ellis, had chosen to put their trust in him. And soon Jim could see for himself the thick, squat figure in white oilskin smock, sitting hunched in the stern like a graven image, one arm lying along the tiller, bearded face stolidly set under the peak of his seaman's cap, and with eyes staring steadily straight ahead.

The *Bright Star* was coming nearer. She was almost abeam of Craa Point. Would she make for the harbour mouth? Or would she make for Porthvole? Which, from out there, seemed most perilous? The boat rose and fell; her nose seemed to point; and soon the helmsman's intention was plain.

'He's putting her in onto the beach!'

Most of the crowd turned at once and surged back along the quay, round past the coopers' huts on the wharf, and down the slipway onto the beach. For, however skilful the seamanship that was bringing the *Bright Star* in, she would nevertheless need help as she made her way into shoalwater and came cutting through the boiling surf. And already, at the water's edge, many of the younger fishermen were tying ropes round their waists, ready to act as the moment required. Women and children were also there, willing and eager to play their part, and William Nancarrow directed them all, bellowing to make himself heard above the great noise of wind and sea.

The tide now reached that part of the beach where shingle gave way to sand, and as the pounding waves receded, shingle and sand were sucked down together in an almighty rushing roar. Here, too, were the first of those rocks that made the beach dangerous at high tide.

Some of the flatter rocks were covered already with water deep enough to hide them while other, taller, more jagged rocks were only partially surrounded, and on these the great waves broke, sometimes rising in spirals of spume twenty or thirty feet high. As these waves sank down again, the water swirled around the rocks and flung itself out shallowly, further and further up the beach, to lick with a kind of angry snarl at the feet of the people gathered there.

The *Bright Star* was coming in fast, with plenty of way on her, and she would certainly need it to carry her safely past the rocks and up onto the shelving sand far enough to prevent her, steep-sided boat as she was, from toppling over and broaching-to.

'She's coming! She's coming!' William Nancarrow said. 'Stand by, boys! Any minute now!'

The lugger came in at a place nicely judged, midway between two reefs of rock, where the water shoaled innocently over clean shingle and sand. The men could be seen crouching in her, bracing themselves against the shock, alert for all the possible dangers that would threaten them as the boat grounded. Ralph Ellis crouched in the bows with a rope, one end of which was fastened to the stemhead, the rest coiled in his right hand, ready to fling to the men ashore.

On the boat came, a big wave running behind her, and as she was now well into the shallows, the wave broke completely over her, running full length from stern to stem like a moving escarpment of water which, as it spread and flattened out, seethed over her decks in a mass of white foam. Out of this welter of broken water Ralph Ellis stood up in the bows and the rope, uncoiling, went snaking shorewards. There was a scramble on the sand and the rope was seized by many hands.

But the weight of the sea swamping the boat had caused her to lose way and as the underwave receded, so the boat receded too, sucked back with the yielding shingle and sand. The men on the rope were dragged down the beach, some into the water itself, and before they could regain their footing, the boat, caught by a smashing cross-sea rebounding from the harbour wall, had tilted sharply over to starboard, flinging all thirteen men headlong into the boiling surf.

The hawsemen dug in their heels. More men had come to help them now. And before the boat could broach-to completely, she had been hauled far enough up the beach for her keel to cut a path in the sand, making a bed into which she sank, still tilting at an ungainly angle, but resting unharmed on her starboard bilge. The end of the rope was passed through a ringbolt in a rock above the high water mark and a number of men stayed there to maintain their pull on the boat as the tide came further in around her.

Meantime those men who had stood by with ropes round their waists were already going forward, breast-high into the surf, where thirteen of their brotherhood were fighting desperately for their lives.

Brice, tossed about in the turbulent waters, with only his left arm to help him, was thrown onto his left side against a partly submerged rock. He tried to grip it with his hand but the sea was too strong for him and a fresh wave tore him away. Feeling the rock under his feet, he kicked himself vigorously up from it and rose, head and shoulders, above the sea. It was only two or three seconds before another wave engulfed him, but in those brief seconds he had seen his uncle Gus's white oilskins in the water ten or twelve yards away.

Again his feet touched rock and again he kicked himself up from it, striking out towards his uncle who, having no power in his legs, was unable to swim. The sea, however, was too much for him; he was soon overwhelmed; but this time, when a fresh wave caught him, it took him and carried him up the beach, where three or four rescuers quickly reached him and hauled him to safety.

One by one, all thirteen men were pulled from the sea and carried up to the top of the beach, where there were plenty of helpers willing and able to minister to them. Dr Sam Carveth was there and to those who were tending Brice he said:

'He'll be all right, but he's got a dislocated shoulder. I'll come back to him when I've seen the rest.'

Maggie and Jim had got separated but both, from different parts of the beach, saw Gus taken from the sea and laid upon the dry sand well above high water mark.

By the time they reached the place, his rescuers had removed his smock and were giving him artificial respiration. He lay on his stomach on the sand and Matt Crowle, crouching astride him, was strenuously squeezing his sides. His bearded mouth was open and water was trickling out of it but in a while the trickling stopped and with a terrible heaving shudder Gus's lungs filled with air.

Matt Crowle and Scrouler Tonkin turned him over onto his back. Matt thrust a folded jacket underneath his shoulder-blades, so that his head lay well back, and Scrouler worked his arms up and down. Soon Gus gave another heave; his eyes flickered open; his lips moved.

Scrouler now made him more comfortable by removing the folded jacket and placing it under his head. Matt said something under his breath and the two men stood up. They turned towards Maggie, who stood nearby, and she came and dropped on her knees beside Gus, stifling a quick indrawn cry as she saw the deep wound in his temple, from which the blood ran streaming down, reddening his wet grey hair and beard.

'Gus, don't try to speak. Dr Sam is coming.'

If Gus heard, he did not obey. His dark gaze was on her. His lips moved again.

'Others?' he said. 'Are they all right?'

'Yes,' Maggie said, 'they're all safe now.'

'Boy Brice?' he asked.

'Yes,' Maggie said. 'You don't have to worry. He's alive and safe. I saw him myself just a moment ago—'

'I told you,' Gus said, in a hoarse whisper and gave a short, exhausted cough. 'I told you I'd bring him back to you.'

Somebody touched Maggie's shoulder. She rose and gave way to Dr Sam. But Dr Sam could do nothing for Gus, and Maggie knew it. She saw the dark eyes close, the wet bearded lips part slightly, and the shaggy grey head fall sideways as though he had turned to kiss the sand.

Jim, beside her, saw it too. His young face was white with the knowledge of death. She reached out to him with enfolding arms and he hid his grief against her breast.

Chapter 10

On a hot sunny morning in July, Maggie and Jim rode in the cart with Isaac Kiddy to Martin Laycock's boatyard, situated on 'the bank' up behind the fish-cellars. In the cart, neatly rolled, lay the new suit of sails that Isaac and Percy Tremearne had made for Brice's new boat which, caulked, tarred, and painted, stood on the stocks in the boatyard. When the cart drew up, Martin Laycock and two of his men came at once to help Isaac unload the sails, so well barked by Eugene that even now, after six days' drying, the cutch came off brown on the men's hands.

'Ess,' Isaac said, complacently, 'they've been barked to within an inch of their lives.'

As soon as the sails had been unloaded, Isaac drove off in the empty cart, leaving Maggie and Jim behind. Jim had brought her to see the boat and now, in a great state of excitement, he escorted her across the yard, between the piles of pitchpine planking, past the sawpit and sheds and a half-built gig, to where his uncle Brice's new lugger stood ready for launching the following day. It was the first time Maggie had seen the new boat and as she stood under the big black hull her gaze instinctively went to the bows and dwelt on the boat's name and number painted boldly and clearly in white: *Gus Tallack*, PY41.

Although she had known from the beginning what the boat's name was to be, the sight of it affected her and brought the quick tears to her eyes. Jim perceived this immediately and put his hand into hers.

'Don't be upset, mother. Don't be upset. Uncle Gus—' The boy cleared his throat. 'Uncle Gus would've been pleased at having the boat named after him. And such a brave handsome boat she is, too! Just you wait till you've seen all round!'

Maggie smiled at him through her tears. She gave his hand a warm, hard squeeze. And in a few minutes more he was persuading her to climb the ladder and board the boat so that she could inspect its marvels with the thoroughness they deserved.

Jim, of course, knew everything there was to know about the new boat. He had been in and out of the boatyard at every opportunity ever since the morning, early in May, when the elmwood keel had been laid on the stocks. The boat was modern. She was also big. And everything about her was of the best.

Jim showed his mother the roomy cabin, with its neat little lockers and bunks for six men and its cooking-stove fixed to the bulkhead. He showed her everything everywhere: fish-hold, net-hold, capstan, pumps; and he pointed out how beautifully finished everything was inboard: the decks and bulwarks all painted a dazzling white, with just the right amount of blue used to pick out the coamings, the cleats, and the chamfered edges on the stanchions.

At last Maggie was allowed to descend and Jim, preceding her down the ladder, watched over her anxiously lest, encumbered by her skirts, she should catch her foot and fall.

'Careful, now, on this next rung. – It's the one that's got a split in it. And watch out for your hands. – There's some lot of splinters in this old ladder, you.'

On the ground there were more things to see: the two stout masts, of Norwegian larch, and the hatches stacked in a neat pile, all varnished to perfection; the lugger's punt, fifteen feet long, painted white, with a blue gunwale; and the two shiny black anchors, each weighing forty-five pounds, delivered a few days before from the Carnock foundry.

These things, and many more, lay on one side in orderly fashion, all moveable gear and fitments having been taken off to lighten the boat ready for moving down to the slipway early next morning. As Jim was explaining this to his mother, the boatbuilders came and set down the sails. There were eight of them altogether: foresail, two mizzens, two jiggers, one jib, a mizzen topsail and a spinnaker; and now, as Martin Laycock said, every last bit of tackle and gear was assembled for carting down to the slipway.

'All excepting the ballast, of course, and that's already down there, loaded into hundredweight bags.'

'Yes, I know,' Jim said. 'I helped uncle Brice and the crew to shovel the shingle into the bags.'

'And shall you be here tomorrow morning to see us haul the lugger down?'

'Yes, I'll be here at six o'clock.'

'Honour bright?'

'Cross my heart!'

'And what about the launching, you? You won't be there for that, I suppose? You'll have something better to do than hang about all day just to see a new boat launched?'

'I *shall* be there,' Jim began and then, perceiving his mother's smile, realized that he was being teased. 'I shan't only see her launched,' he said. 'I shall be going out in her, on her first trials round the bay.'

On the wharf, as they walked home, Maggie and Jim met Brice, who had been to see the harbourmaster to discuss arrangements for the launching. – Always a Herculean task, with a boat of the *Gus Tallack*'s size, and one that required all available help.

'I hear you've been delivering the sails?'

'Yes. And Jim has been showing me the boat.'

'What do you think of her?' Brice asked.

'Oh,' Maggie said, and spread her hands, looking at him with a smile that said, What do women know of such things? 'She's very big. Very beautiful. And I know she's the finest boat in the world because Jim keeps telling me so.'

'Tes only the truth,' Jim declared.

'Gus always said that Laycock's yard built some of the best boats ever to sail out from this coast.'

'Certainly the *Emmet* was one of the best,' Brice said. 'She'd have sailed another thirty years if that barquentine hadn't done for her. And if the new boat turns out as good as the old—'

'She will do!' Jim said. 'Of course she will!'

'Then I shall be well pleased,' Brice said. He glanced up and around the sky. 'It'll be a fine day for the launch, I believe. A day pretty much like today, I would say, with the wind going nicely round with the sun.' He turned to face Maggie again. 'The crew are all down at Enery Trennery's, getting their hair cut,' he said. 'They mean to make a smart come-out of it tomorrow, be sure of that.'

'I'm glad the new boat will have the same crew.'

'Yes, so am I,' Brice said.

Since the loss of the *Emmet*, the crew had got work where they could, 'filling in' on other drifters that happened to be a man short, perhaps, but often obliged to go to Carnock and earn what they could on the quay there, helping to unload other men's fish.

Billy Coit and Clem Pascoe had in fact been offered permanent places on certain boats where they had filled in but, knowing that Brice was building a new boat with the insurance money from the *Emmet*, they had chosen to wait for the chance of crewing with him again. And they, like young Jim, had spent all their spare time at the boatyard, watching the *Gus Tallack* grow and sometimes giving a hand with the work.

'I reckon that's a good idea, naming her after the old skipper,' Billy Coit had said to Brice, 'cos he was a good old sort in his way, and I've got a funny old feeling that whenever we put to sea, he'll be watching over us, seeing we dunt come to no harm.'

As Maggie and Jim and Brice walked together along the wharf a number of people passed by and each had something to say to them, for everyone in Polsinney knew that the *Gus Tallack* was due to be launched the following day and, the launching of a new boat being always a great occasion, young and old alike looked forward to it with pleasure and interest.

'Handsome weather you'll have for it!' said old Horace Wearne, and Annie Tambling, touching Brice on the arm as she passed, said: 'There's my good luck on you, my son, but dunt say nothing back to me or that'll only send it away!'

Everyone had some special word and many, as they passed by, turned to look at Maggie and Brice with lively curiosity. In the three months that had passed since Gus's death, they had been closely observed, the subject of much speculation, and because they were well aware of it, they had throughout that time conducted themselves with great correctness.

Their feelings were in accord over this and had never needed to be put into words. They loved each other and in time they would marry; it would cause a good deal of talk and people would say they had known all along just how it would turn out; but there would be no undue haste for the more spiteful gossips to fasten on. Maggie was in mourning for Gus and it was no mere formal display; she mourned for him quite genuinely and knew that Brice did too; and much as they might long for each other, neither of them wanted marriage while Gus's death was still fresh in their minds.

That morning, early, Maggie had been in the churchyard, trimming the grass on Gus's grave. She liked to go there very early, before anyone else was about, and she liked to keep the green mound well trimmed because Gus had respected neatness and order above all other things. On the headstone, above his name, was carved, in the simplest fashion, a boat under sail. 'I am the Lord,' said the text, 'which maketh a way in the sea, and a path in the mighty waters.'

She had been to the grave many times but on that particular morning, as she knelt beside the mound, she had received a strong impression of Gus's presence close beside her. This feeling was with her still and although it filled her heart with sadness, it also brought a sense of peace and a sense, somehow, of being protected. She spoke about this now to Brice, as they reached the gate of the barking-yard, and he told her what Billy Coit had said about Gus watching over the new boat and keeping it safe from harm.

'Uncle Gus was a seaman and spent his last hours at sea. He was happy doing that. And I know even the way he died will have been more to his liking than dying slowly in his bed.

These things, and the way we remember him, are enough to bring peace to his soul, I think, don't you?'

'Yes,' Maggie said, quietly, 'his soul is at peace with itself, I'm sure.'

At three o'clock the next afternoon, watched by a huge crowd that thronged the fish-quay and the wharf, Maggie launched the *Gus Tallack* from Laycock's slipway at Porthvole.

The day, as promised, was fine and sunny, with a hot south easterly wind giving a sea that was deep blue and calm, with just a bit of a lop on it. The boat had been hauled down to the slip without any mishap just after six that morning and from then until midday men had swarmed all over her, crew and boatbuilders working together, rigging her out ready for sea.

At one o'clock, washed and shaved, and wearing their best dark serge suits, they had gathered again at *The Brittany Inn* for the special launching feast, where cold roast beef and pickles, followed by apple tart and cream, had been washed down by beer or cider or, in the case of the teetotallers, by Mrs Kemp's special lemonade.

At half past two, out on the slipway, the crewmen were joined by their families. Maggie and Jim were already there, with Rachel Tallack; Isaac Kiddy was there with his wife and son; and Percy Tremearne was there with his new sweetheart from St Owe. These, together with the boatbuilders and all the other stout-armed men standing by to help with the launching, almost filled the slipway; and everywhere about the harbour, wherever there was a piece of ground that commanded a view of the proceedings, the onlookers were thronged in their hundreds, the young girls in their summer frocks, some carrying parasols, making splashes of bright colour among the men in their sober blacks, under the red and green bunting fluttering gaily overhead.

The *Gus Tallack*, with her stern towards the sea, stood with her keel resting on rollers, well and truly chocked underneath and supported all along her sides by struts of timber firmly wedged under bilge-keels and strakes. Jim, gazing up at the boat, which was forty-four feet in length and weighed sixteen

217

tons, thought how immense she looked, standing here on the slipway, and yet how small such a boat could seem once she was out on the open sea. And he thought, too, with a tingle of pleasure, of the silver shilling which, earlier that day, watched by uncle Brice and the crew, he had placed underneath the foremast as a token to ensure the boat's good luck.

All around him on the slipway the launching party, in high spirits, were chatting with one another and with a few privileged persons, including the vicar, Mr Rowe, the Methodist minister, Mr Hoskins, and, representing the 'parliament' of old retired fishermen, the stalwart William Nancarrow. The boat was inspected, discussed, admired; compared with famous boats of the past; and made the subject of predictions concerning the speed she might achieve and how she would most likely behave in a lively seaway.

But Brice and his crew, though they chatted, had one eye on the time, and promptly at five minutes to three they boarded the boat, with young Jim and Martin Laycock. The ladder was taken away and the launching team, numbering thirty men, took up the stations assigned to them, each man watching Martin Laycock, directing proceedings from the boat's bows.

Now William Nancarrow, with conscious dignity, went to a small wooden table, set conveniently by, on which stood a bottle of French red wine and a glass. He filled the glass with wine and gave it to Maggie and she, somewhat flushed in the cheeks at being the centre of attention, turned and walked towards the boat. The whole crowd was utterly silent, watching her and listening, and for a brief interval the only sound heard on the slipway was the lapping and slapping of the water, a few yards from the lugger's stern.

Maggie raised her glass aloft, took a deep breath to steady herself, and spoke in a loud, ringing voice that carried clearly all round the harbour.

'I wish prosperity to this boat and name her the *Gus Tallack*, and I ask God's blessing on her and her crew.'

She drank some of the wine from the glass, then dashed the rest against the boat, and such was the splendid timing achieved by the launching team in removing chocks and struts that as the wine splashed against her bows the *Gus Tallack* began to move, slowly at first, with scarcely a sound, but very soon, as the rollers turned, picking up speed in a way that was almost frightening to behold.

A burst of clapping broke out among some of the onlookers but most were watching, hearts in mouths, for now the lugger was beginning to run, rolling and rumbling down the slipway with a noise like thunder. There were shouted instructions from Martin Laycock, a scraping of boots on the granite setts as men lay back on the check-ropes, and then, with a satisfying splash that brought the spray up over her stern, the *Gus Tallack* was afloat in two or three fathoms of water.

The crew, having cast off the check-ropes, waved their caps and gave a cheer, which was echoed and very quickly drowned by the cheer that went up from the watching crowd. Brice, at the helm, gave a salute, and as the lugger moved out on the ebb, the water deepening under her, he very slowly brought her round until her stem pointed seawards.

By now the crew were at work; there were a few quiet commands, a flapping of canvas, a cheeping of blocks; and Billy Coit, in charge of the tack, looked up at the two brown sails as though willing them to draw. And in another moment or two, as the boat cleared the lee of Scully Point and the hot wind came breathing down on them, bringing a scent of Goonwelter furze, the sails very gently and gracefully filled.

Jim, standing with Brice at the helm, watched as his mother, on the slipway, grew smaller and smaller still. He put up a hand to wave to her; a special wave, for her alone; and saw the flutter of her blue and white sleeve as she waved back to him. Brice also was watching her. He watched until, as the distance lengthened, her figure grew blurred and merged with the crowd. He turned his head and looked at Jim and Jim, as yet too full to speak, looked up at him with a smile of pure joy.

The boat now began picking up speed, making westward across the bay. Martin Laycock came aft to speak to Brice.

'Going handsome so far, edn she?'

'Yes, she's going like a bird.'

Rachel, with Maggie on the wharf, listening to the good

wishes, the congratulations, the compliments, had little to say in reply. She did not approve of the new boat. She had wanted Brice to give up the sea. But men, as she well knew, would do whatever they wanted to do, for it was their nature and couldn't be changed.

'That boy of yours will be the same. He will go to sea, sure as fate, and nothing you say will make him see sense. And he will spare no thought for the feelings of those he leaves behind.'

The well-wishers had moved away and Rachel and Maggie, alone together, began walking slowly along the wharf.

'Jim's got the sea in his blood. He's grown up within sight and sound of it. The pull of it is too strong for him. He could never resist it even if he wanted to.'

'It seems you accept it.'

'Yes. I do.'

'You are wise,' Rachel said. 'I suppose it's been bred in you.'

She herself had learnt acceptance rather late in life and only after much inner conflict. She was beginning to feel her age. Becoming resigned. Bowing to fate. But there were some compensations to make up for the sense of defeat. She accepted that Brice and Maggie would marry and even found satisfaction in it, for it meant that Gus Tallack's property would come back into the family even if, one day, Brice's children would have to share it with Maggie's illegitimate son.

All along the wharf, as Maggie and Rachel strolled along, there were little groups of people still watching the new boat performing her trials out in the bay.

'You launched her brave and fitty, midear,' Kate Cox said as Maggie passed, and old Thomas Lean called out: 'Proper job! Proper job! And a more handsome craft never put to sea.'

Maggie smiled; made some reply; and walked on at Rachel's side. The two were silent for a while. Then Rachel came to a halt.

'We're very different, you and me. I've lived in this place more than thirty-five years but I still feel myself a stranger here, and that's how people see me, I'm sure. But you are at home here. You seem to belong. It's as though you had lived here all your life.'

'Yes, that's how I feel,' Maggie said. 'Polsinney is my home in a way Porthgaran never was. I've been happy here. I've put down roots.'

'Yes, and the tree has borne fruit, in more ways than one,' Rachel said, with a touch of her old acerbity. And after a while she said briskly: 'Well, I must be getting home. *You* may stay here if you like, watching that boat go to and fro, but *I've* got things to do on the farm.'

'I would come and help you but I promised Jim I'd stay here and watch them come in,' Maggie said.

'You'll have a long wait, I can tell you that. They'll be sailing about for hours yet, if I know anything about it. Still, waiting is something you'll have to get used to, once you are married to Brice. And I daresay there is justice in that because God knows he has waited for *you* long enough.'

Rachel went off along the wharf, giving a perfunctory nod to the groups of people who made way for her. Maggie walked on to the quay, to join the watchers still gathered there, and fair-haired little Cissie Birch, leaving her grannie, Betsy Coit, came with a hop-skip-and-a-jump to take hold of Maggie's hand.

Out in the bay, off Volley Head, the *Gus Tallack*, under full sail, sped smartly before the wind, a few gulls flashing behind her, omen of good things to come.